The
Vanguard

ARNOLD BENNETT

By ARNOLD BENNETT

NOVELS

THE VANGUARD
THE WOMAN WHO STOLE EVERY-
    THING
LORD RAINGO
ELSIE AND THE CHILD
RICEYMAN STEPS
LILIAN
MR. PROHACK
THE ROLL-CALL
THE PRETTY LADY
THE LION'S SHARE
THESE TWAIN
CLAYHANGER
HILDA LESSWAYS
THE OLD WIVES' TALE
DENRY THE AUDACIOUS

THE OLD ADAM
HELEN WITH THE HIGH HAND
THE GATES OF WRATH
THE BOOK OF CARLOTTA
BURIED ALIVE
A GREAT MAN
LEONORA
WHOM GOD HATH JOINED
A MAN FROM THE NORTH
ANNA OF THE FIVE TOWNS
THE GLIMPSE
THE GRAND BABYLON HOTEL
HUGO
THE CITY OF PLEASURE
THE MATADOR OF THE FIVE
    TOWNS

POCKET PHILOSOPHIES

HOW TO MAKE THE BEST OF
    LIFE
SELF AND SELF-MANAGEMENT
MARRIED LIFE
FRIENDSHIP AND HAPPINESS
THE HUMAN MACHINE

HOW TO LIVE ON 24 HOURS A
    DAY
LITERARY TASTE
MENTAL EFFICIENCY
THE AUTHOR'S CRAFT

PLAYS

THE LOVE MATCH
BODY AND SOUL
SACRED AND PROFANE LOVE
JUDITH
THE TITLE
THE BRIGHT ISLAND

THE GREAT ADVENTURE
CUPID AND COMMONSENSE
WHAT THE PUBLIC WANTS
POLITE FARCES
THE HONEYMOON
DON JUAN DE MARANA

IN COLLABORATION WITH EDWARD KNOBLOCK

MILESTONES   LONDON LIFE

MISCELLANEOUS

OUR WOMEN
BOOKS AND PERSONS
PARIS NIGHTS

LIBERTY
THE TRUTH ABOUT AN AUTHOR
OVER THERE: WAR SCENES

THINGS THAT HAVE INTERESTED ME
THINGS THAT HAVE INTERESTED ME. *Second Series*
THINGS THAT HAVE INTERESTED ME. *Third Series*

NEW YORK: GEORGE H. DORAN COMPANY

THE
VANGUARD

A Fantasia by

ARNOLD BENNETT

THE LITERARY GUILD
OF AMERICA

NEW YORK   MCMXXVII

CONTENTS

The Vanguard

The Vanguard

CHAPTER I

THE SPLENDIDE

MR. SUTHERLAND rang the bell once, in his private sitting-room at the Hotel Splendide, and expected the prompt arrival of the waiter. Mr. Sutherland was a man of fifty, clean-shaven, spare, rather austere, with the responsible and slightly harassed demeanour which comes of having married young and remained married, and the thin lips and logical jaw which usually develop on the faces of men who have been called to the bar. Brown-grey hair that might soon, but not yet, be described as scanty. Pale blue eyes, whose glance denoted a certain mild self-complacency on the part of Mr. Sutherland. The reasons for the self-complacency were various and sound.

In the first place, Mr. Sutherland was a seventh child: to be which is always a mystical asset in life, and further, his parents had indicated his ordinal position in their family by christening him, not Septimus, which is banal, but Septimius, which is rare and distinguished. That extra "i" had virtue for Mr. Sutherland.

In the second place, Mr. Sutherland some thirty years earlier had stroked the Cambridge boat. Nobody, in giving an account of Mr. Sutherland to

9

people who were unacquainted with him, ever omitted to mention this fact, and only cynical or malign persons would mention also that he had not stroked Cambridge to victory.

The third reason for self-complacency was that Mr. Sutherland was, and knew himself to be, an organizer. He organized everything in his existence and when, as now, he was enjoying for a space the absence of his delicious, disorganizing wife and girls, and of a devoted, incompetent valet, he would organize with abandonment and utterly revel in his talent for organizing.

The apartment gave evidences of organization. Mr. Sutherland was leaving the city that evening by train. The receipted bill, much stamped, for his sojourn at the Splendide lay open on the centre table. His suitcase lay open on a side-table, with a couple of books all ready to slip into it. The suitcase was labelled with two labels, one adhesive, the other attached by string. In the bedroom lay Mr. Sutherland's flat American trunk, still open, lest Mr. Sutherland might have forgotten something. It could be snapped to in a second. Hanging over the raised lid of the trunk (which had three labels) was Mr. Sutherland's rug, conveniently folded, and on an adjacent chair were his hat, overcoat, and gloves. The spectacle of all this organized order gave pleasure to Mr. Sutherland.

The bell was not answered. Mr. Sutherland's organization, however, was not disconcerted by the delay. He always allowed a margin for the imperfections of mankind and the malice of heaven; and now he utilized this margin by systematically opening every drawer in the sitting-room, bedroom, and bathroom, and demonstrating to himself, for the second time, that he had forgotten nothing. Thereupon he shut the American trunk.

Still the bell was not answered. And now Mr. Sutherland began to have a new and dark idea about the organization of the Hotel Splendide, which organization he had hitherto admired without reserve. The Splendide was the best hotel in the city. There were four other leading and in every way first-class hotels—the Majestic, the Belvidere, the Royal Palace, and the Grand Miramar, and according to advertisement each of these four was also the best hotel in the city. The Splendide, however, had two advantages over its rivals—due to two discoveries made by its designers. The first discovery was that the visitor does not care to overhear everything that passes, by word or action, in the rooms adjoining his own, or even in the corridor; and the second was that the visitor finds little pleasure in the continual sounding of a bell—once for the waiter, twice for the chambermaid, and thrice for the valet—especially when the rung bell is situate, as it always is, just outside his bedroom door. Hence the designers of the Splendide had established double doors between adjoining rooms and between rooms and corridor, and had entirely done away with the sound of bells. When you pushed the button at the Splendide—the top one for the waiter, the middle one for the chambermaid, and the lower one for the valet—a white, a green, or a red light shone in the corridor above your door and kept on shining until the waiter, the chambermaid, or the valet (duly warned by a bell far, far out of hearing of the visitor) came and extinguished it. Thus, if you closed your double windows, you could live at the Splendide as in the isolated silence and select privacy of the grave, until you died from steam-heat and lack of ventilation.

It was all most ingenious, and Mr. Sutherland had loved it all. But now he perceived a psychological flaw in this organization. The visitor, having rung without getting a reply, could not be sure whether or not the apparatus was in order. Supposing the distant bell was for some reason not functioning! A terrible thought! Mr. Sutherland, after a further pause, opened the double doors into the corridor and looked forth. Yes, the white light, symbolic of his desire for the waiter, was burning over his door and burning brightly, steadily, patiently, waiting for the waiter. But had the bell rung? Mr. Sutherland could not and did not know. He did not even know where the bell was to be found. Silence and solitude in the long corridor! Dozens of doors, and only one of them illuminated, Mr. Sutherland's!

Septimius felt himself to be a victim, and yet somehow guilty; the white light seemed to accuse him of something. He was at a loss. He knew not what to do. His great gift for organizing had been rendered futile. He hesitated, most absurdly, to step out into the hostile wilderness of the corridor. At last he did step out, and it was as though he had gone over the top in battle. Then Mr. Sutherland saw a waiter in the distance, and stepped back into the ambush of the doorway and halted the waiter at the moment of passing the door. The waiter, startled out of his professional self-control, gave Septimius a look of murderous hatred. The glance covered perhaps the tenth of a second, and was instantaneously succeeded by the conventional acquiescent smile of his calling;

but Septimius had noted it, and was afraid in his heart, for the glance seemed to symbolize and lay bare the awful secret antagonism which divides the servers from the served—seed of revolutions. Septimius even feared for his life, for he was in a strange and sinister city, where lives were worth much less than in London, and some people might possibly find their advantage in the sudden death of Septimius . . . Pooh! Ridiculous!

"Please bring me the menu," Mr. Sutherland, speaking in English, addressed the waiter, whom he had never seen before. And he carefully spoke as one man to another, in order to indicate his belief in the dogma that all men are equal before heaven. "I shall dine here in my room. And when you serve the dinner let me have the bill with it—receipted. You understand. I'm leaving to-night."

The waiter smiled charmingly to indicate his belief in the dogma that the least wish of a visitor is a law to the waiter. He smiled, bowed, and departed. He had understood only two words, "menu" and "bill."

Mr. Sutherland felt reassured, though he had had a shock.

After a brief delay the waiter returned, without the menu, and made quite a long foreign speech to Mr. Sutherland, not a word of which did Mr. Sutherland comprehend. The black-coated fellow was one of those waiters, prevalent in the splendid hotels of distant and picturesque lands, who can speak no language but their own, and sometimes not even that. Ten key-words of English or French may suffice a waiter for the common affair of human nature's daily food, but in a crisis they quickly prove inadequate.

Mr. Sutherland saw that this was a crisis. He could

speak Sutherland-French, slowly, and he now did so. But the waiter's face was an amiable blank before the persuasions of Sutherland-French.

"Menu, menu, menu! Carte, carte, carte!" Mr. Sutherland repeated firmly and kindly, but foolishly.

The waiter shook his head. At last Mr. Sutherland in blank despair waved him from the room.

"Is it conceivable," thought Septimius, "that in a hotel with the pretentions of the Splendide, they should place you at the mercy of servants with whom it is impossible to communicate?" He saw that it was conceivable, and sighed.

There was only one thing to do—namely to adventure forth into the general publicity and promiscuity of the vast hotel. The necessity for so doing oppressed Mr. Sutherland strangely.

CHAPTER II

THE two principal public rooms of the Splendide were the lounge and the restaurant. They lay side by side, separated by a wall of glass, and they were both vast and both ultra- or super-gorgeous. Every square foot of their walls and ceilings was decorated with the last extreme of ornateness in either oils, fresco, mosaic, porphyry, gilt, or bronze. On the ceiling alone, of the lounge, were depicted, in various mediums, over seventy slim and beautiful young women in a high state of physical development and chiefly in the fashion of Eden, perilously tasting the dubious society of thirty or forty fauns and satyrs whose moral code seemed to illustrate the joyous effrontery of a past age and who had no preoccupations about rates, taxes, bad weather, or class-warfare. The colours of this ideal world were rich, fresh, and brilliant, for it was only in the previous year that the designers had finished spending two million lire in the creation of the Splendide: which was meant to respond, and indeed did respond, to the secret aspirations of the élite of Cincinnati, Leeds, Buenos Ayres, Philadelphia, Bath and Boston (Mass).

From the lounge, through the gilded crystal partition, could be seen the equally opulent restaurant, full of tables richly set with napery, cutlery, glass, and flowers, and perambulated by many restless waiters. And not one diner at any of the tables, though the hour was after half-past eight!

While the forlorn restaurant held waiters but no guests, the lounge held guests but no waiters. Twenty-three guests were congregated together in the middle of the huge parqueted floor upon which, on normal evenings, they were accustomed to dance. A small number for so large an hotel; but the season had scarcely started; moreover, the Splendide much depended for its customers upon the arrival and departure of Transatlantic and Transmediterranean steamers, and no important boat had arrived or departed now for several days. The present guests were chiefly not mere migrants but steady supporters of the hotel and the city, whose purpose was to stay, and see, and leave quantities of good money behind them. Of the twenty-three, fifteen were American, five English, and the rest of doubtful origin; seventeen were women and the rest men. Their anxious and perturbed demeanour was in dismal contrast with that of the gaudy, carefree inhabitants of the ceiling-kingdom overhead.

Alone among them a tall, dark, massive, romantic gentleman of forty years or so seemed to be enjoying life. He was fat, and it might have been said that the pores of his stretched skin, being open, exuded gaiety, and that gaiety escaped frothing from his lips. As, lightly, with little mincing steps of his small toes, he moved about gesticulating and chatting with an inner group of ladies, he had the air of being continuously animated by a private and particular zest of his own. His manner was easy and affable to the point of patronage, for he knew that he was adored.

Suddenly this gentleman noticed afar off, in one of the arched entrances to the great lounge, a solitary hesitant individual in a tweed suit.

"Ha!" exclaimed the gentleman of zest. "Ha!" he called out, more loudly, smiling as it were secretly to himself.

And all the company turned and gazed at the individual under the arch, inimically and yet with respect. His tweed suit, exhibited at such an hour in such a place as the lounge of the Splendide, of course offended the sense of propriety of every swallow-tail, dinner-jacket and evening frock on the floor. Also, the company beheld a man who, during the fortnight of his mysterious stay in the hotel, had systematically, by the blank repudiating look on his superior face, discouraged the advances of those visitors who liked to be sociable and who resented a repudiating look. The man indeed had not exchanged a word with a single soul in the hotel, servants excepted. Why was he in the hotel at all? He seemed never to indulge in any of the usual and proper sight-seeing excursions. Who was he? Nobody knew anything about him, beyond his name. What justification had he for being so stand offish? . . . Nevertheless the company had respect for the man, if only because he was so strictly loyal to the dying British tradition of keeping oneself to oneself. And further, the company somewhat pitied him for the shyness and diffidence which obviously were mingled with his amazing self-complacency.

The man thus criticized was Septimius, who had been to the managerial offices and found them deserted. The gaze of the crowd certainly incommoded him and made him wish for the gift of invisibility. Like most persons, however, Septimius had not one mind but quite a number of minds. And while in one of his minds he felt abashed, in another of his minds he was saying: "What an ignorant lot they are. They don't guess that I once stroked Cambridge. They don't guess that I was once called to the Bar. They haven't a suspicion in their silly heads that I am *the* Sutherland, Septimius Sutherland, who abandoned the Bar for finance and became something of a power in the City and richer and more important than anybody else in this hotel, I lay. Probably they've never heard of Septimius Sutherland. It hasn't occurred to them that I'm here on what's called 'big business'— indeed the biggest, and that I've been taking risks that would frighten the boldest of 'em. And won! And won! Well, it amuses me—their ignorance does. And it amuses me to look a bit bashful and awkward. What do I care, really? Fact is, I rather like being taken for a nobody by nobodies."

And still another of his minds held the thought: "I may be the great Septimius Sutherland, but I am also a perfect ass! It's a holy nuisance to be self-conscious like this."

He kept a tactical silence.

"You know what's happened of course?" the gentleman of zest proceeded.

"I do not," Mr. Sutherland replied, bland, amiable, and now rather less self-conscious under the bombarding stares. After all, he was not unaccustomed to handling shareholders of limited companies at annual meetings.

Because he did not care to talk across a great empty space of floor he unwillingly advanced towards the crowd in the centre of the lounge. The gentleman of zest went to meet him. Mr. Sutherland had on previous occasions taken this individual for a foreigner, but his English was impeccably that of Kensington.

"A strike in the kitchens!" explained the gentleman of zest, and his zest seemed to ooze forth from him. Apparently he saw in the situation a rich and juicy humour that he thought nobody else could see. He paused and looked humorously at the floor, as if sharing the joke with the parquetry. Then: "Or perhaps not a strike, because strikes are forbidden by law in this country. But at any rate an omission to work. Some trouble with the management. Plenty of cold food in the kitchens, but the waiters will not serve it. Sympathetic inaction no doubt. Hence we are all hungry with no prospect of a dinner. I am Count Veruda."

Septimius felt a great relief. He had been vaguely suspecting, upstairs, some kind of a machination against himself, a powerful man whom unprincipled opponents might find it convenient to put away. He now saw that the machination, if any, was directed against all the guests equally. Moreover, the performance of the incomprehensible floor-waiter upstairs stood explained. Septimius pleasantly savoured the situation.

"I see," said Septimius, almost at ease. "Where is the manager?"

"Ha!" said Count Veruda. "The manager has prudently disappeared."

"I see," Septimius repeated, quite at ease. "Now supposing we went into the kitchens and fetched this food for ourselves?" Already he had begun to scheme out the organization of such a raid.

"I am told by the maître d'hôtel, who is entirely on

our side, that that might cause really serious complications."

"I see," said Septimius, for the third time. "But there are restaurants in the city."

"Not a good one. And we could hardly go in a body to any one restaurant. We should burst it. And as for going separately, many single ladies would not care to venture on such a course—in a town like this." The Count smiled within and without, and his body seemed to vibrate with rich fun.

"There are other hotels."

"If we went to another hotel, the fact would be instantly known, and the kitchen staff there might adopt the same tactics as the kitchen staff here. Solidarity! Solidarity!" The Count had completed his case very happily.

Mr. Sutherland had frequently noticed the word "solidarity" in newspaper accounts of altercations between labour and capital, and now for the first time really understood its significance. He glanced around at the stricken faces of the well-dressed, well-fed, but hungry crowd. In every face he saw precisely what he was beginning to feel in his own heart, namely, the gradual, terrible, disturbed realization of the utter instability and insecurity of society. All had been well, and now all was ill. The members of the groups, and Septimius, had been nurtured in the beautiful, convenient theory that anything could be had by ringing bells and settling bills. They did naught for themselves, and could do naught for themselves, and were somehow proud of their helplessness. With them, to ask was to have, and to pay was the solution of all difficulties. And now they were hungry and thirsty; they were in the grip of the most powerful

of human passions, and no amount of bell-ringing and
bill-paying could procure their satisfaction. No wonder they were perturbed. The situation was horrible.
It seemed to announce blood in the streets and the
downfall of kingdoms and of the entire social order.

"But," said Count Veruda, triumphant in his
sense of the dramatic. "I have suggested a remedy.
My yacht, the *Vanguard*, has come into harbour this
afternoon. I invite everybody to dinner on board.
If I may say so, I think I can offer as good a dinner
as could be had in any hotel in the town, if not a
better . . . And the Bay of Naples! . . . By moonlight!"

This was the Count's grand climax.

"You are most hospitable," said Mr. Sutherland
blandly.

"Not at all," the Count deprecatingly protested,
without, however, any attempt to be convincing.
"But there are ladies who hesitate. Perhaps naturally!" The Count shared his polite amusement with
the parqueted floor. "I hope I may count on you,
Mr.——?"

"Sutherland."

"Mr. Sutherland, to give me your support."

"Count," called a masculine old lady imperiously,
at this important juncture.

Count Veruda left Mr. Sutherland and humorously shot backward to the old lady.

A dark, youngish and stylish woman thereupon
came up to Mr. Sutherland, who bowed to her smile.

"I don't think he's what we should call a real
Count," murmured the dark young woman, confi-
dentially, and with a certain assurance of manner.
"Count of the Holy Roman Empire, or something

like that. Official of the Papal Court. Probably when he's on duty he wears a uniform designed by Michael Angelo. He imagines he's a humorist, but he's funnier even than he thinks he is. However, even if he isn't a real Count, he has a real yacht, because I've seen it, and it's like a liner, and I don't see any reason why we shouldn't oblige him by eating his dinner. But of course, no unattached woman will go unless all the others go, too."

"Of course not," Mr. Sutherland concurred very calmly, though he was somewhat disturbed and over-set by the young woman's extraordinary directness of approach. He comprehended, however, that the strike had altered everything.

He definitely and immediately liked her. She was downright, humorous, and attractive, if not strikingly beautiful. She was young, but not too young; virginal, but not too virginal. She was not over-jewelled. The shingling of her hair fascinated him, and her tone flattered him. He found pleasure in her nearness to him. She was the finest creature in the lounge. "I might sit next to her at the dinner," he thought adventurously. He was the very pattern of propriety. He had a wife, and grown-up daughters; but in that moment he suddenly grew younger than his wife, younger, even, than his daughters; and his one regret was that he had to catch the midnight train. The cynic says that all women are alike; it would be still more true to say that all men are alike, and that no man is old until he is dead.

"Then you agree?" said she.

Septimius answered with due gravity.

"I agree. I think we might quite properly accept the Count's invitation. After all, he is very generous."

"He may be an adventurer," said the young woman.

"Quite."

Count Veruda returned to Mr. Sutherland.

"Well, Mr. Sutherland?"

"I am with you, Count," said Septimius gaily, in a loud voice that all might hear.

"Hurrah!" exclaimed the dark young woman under her breath.

The whole company signified approval, and the affair was decided. Mr. Sutherland's reputation in the hotel for keeping himself to himself, together with his unmistakable air of prudent respectability, had carried the waverers.

CHAPTER III

THE YACHT

THE large, low, oval dining-saloon of the yacht *Vanguard*, with a pale stained-glass ceiling faintly lighted from above. The pale, curved walls, diversified with mirrors and with panels of mythology in the Della Robbia style. The huge, oval table, glittering white, with crested earthenware and crystal and many flowers. Stewards in blue and gold, with white gloves, circling watchfully round and round with food for the famished and the dyspeptic. The chief steward, behind Count Veruda's chair, attentive, directive, imperative, monosyllabic: exercising dominion by glance and gesture. Between the ring of stewards and the edge of the table—the guests!

Now, as regards the guests, it would seem that the yacht's dining-room must have become a mortuary and a lunatic asylum; for many of them reiterated that they were tickled to death at being aboard the yacht, and the rest reiterated that they were crazy about being aboard the yacht. The truth rather was that they were crushed, morally, by the magnificence of the spectacle and the entertainment offered to them by Count Veruda. In vain did the more brazen ones try to pretend by an offhand demeanour that they had been familiar with such scenes from their youth up and were therefore quite unmoved; they failed every minute to maintain the pose. And if

24

suspicions had existed in the minds of some of them concerning the authenticity and solidity of the Count, those suspicions were now in a fair way to be destroyed.

The process of crushing had begun as soon as the invited horde crossed the street from the hotel portals to the landing steps. Two great mahogany launches were awaiting them at the steps, each manned by a blue-and-gold crew of four. There was plenty of room for everybody in the capacious bosoms of the launches. If these commodious craft were only the attendant launches, what must the yacht be? Persons whose notion of a yacht and yachting was a frail, wobbling bark, with a tin of sardines, a cottage loaf and tea out of a tin mug, were obliged at once, and radically, to revise that notion. The launches shot off like torpedoes, tandem, into the dark, mysterious, balmy bay. Up the invisible flank of Vesuvius ran a rope of fire—the electric lamps of the funicular railway. The shore-lights of Naples gradually spread out into two semicircles behind the foamy wash of the launches, and above these tiaras rose the lighted hills of the background of the city. A Neapolitan moon had poised itself aloft in the deep purple sky. Then the whiteness of the yacht *Vanguard* grew plainer, and larger and still larger! Commands! A shutting-off of engines! To the high side of the yacht clung an illuminated stair of mahogany, teak, and shining brass—broken mid-way by a flat space for the recuperation of the short-winded. At the top of the stair stood officers, who with dignified respect raised their caps in grave welcome to the exalted guests. And lo! the guests were fairly on board the main deck, which was lighted like Broadway or

Piccadilly Circus. No hitch! No hesitations! No delay! A set of gongs played a tune, and in three minutes or less the guests were at the table.

Of course the *Mauretania* or the *Majestic* was bigger; but for real style, from table-appointments to stewards, the *Vanguard* had every transatlantic liner well beaten: so much was admitted unanimously and handsomely by all Americans well experienced in marine travel.

But what crushed the spirit most effectively was not the style, nor the grandeur, nor the glitter, but simply the cost of it all. The *Vanguard* belonged to one man, not to a limited company with a capital of fifteen million pounds. The Americans had no qualms about the concentration of such a quantity of wealth in the hands of a single individual; for they knew and felt that just as every soldier of Napoleon had a field-marshal's baton in his knapsack, so every American citizen has a two-thousand-ton yacht in his capacious hip-pocket. But in the pockets of certain humble Britons were concealed misgivings as to whether all was for the best in the best of all possible worlds. These faint-hearted persons thought of the droves of unemployed in the streets and slums of their industrial towns; they even thought of the perspiring, rebellious kitchen-serfs of the Splendide desperately risking a livelihood to snatch perhaps an extra fourpence-halfpenny from the Splendide's managerial till; while Count Veruda, owner of the *Vanguard*, spent as much on petrol in a month as would have kept seven Neapolitan families for seven years. However, as sherry followed cocktails and champagne followed sherry and port followed champagne and Chartreuse followed port, these crude sociological qualms vanished away, together with the sense of being morally crushed. A golden mist spread in the saloon, and through it gleamed the bright truth that everything positively *was* for the best of the best of all possible worlds. As, of course, it is.

Meanwhile, Count Veruda, with the chief steward behind him, was modestly trying—and not without success—to look as though he were not the owner of the gorgeous *Vanguard* and a multi-millionaire. Indeed, he wore his wealth most unpompously; it was apparently naught to him.

Then a faint vibration made itself felt in the yacht, and particularly in every part of the dining-saloon. The vibration grew in strength. And straightway the more alert spirits in the company began preposterously to suspect that Count Veruda was not all that he seemed to be, that he was indeed a perfidious and cunning pirate, and that the yacht's engines were being made to revolve as the first action in a plot to abduct the entire body of guests and hold them to ransom for incredible amounts in some distant, inhospitable isle hitherto uncharted on Mediterranean maps.

Dismay sat on the faces of several. The dismay spread. Glasses were no longer raised. Gratitude vanished from the hearts of the entertained. The nervous imaginative could feel the heaving of the yacht at sea.

"That is the dynamos," said Count Veruda, silently laughing. "I expect we're using rather more electricity than usual, and the Chief Engineer wishes to be on the safe side."

How absurd those slanderous suspicions!

But a few of the wary and the timid were not quite

reassured. An old lady on Mr. Sutherland's left tremblingly murmured something in his ear. Mr. Sutherland, gently smiling, tranquillized her ridiculous fears with a word.

"The yacht cannot be moving," said he. "She must have had an anchor down, if not two, and in a comparatively small ship like this the anchor could not possibly have been raised without our hearing the noise of the chain." Still, the old lady was not quite at her ease, and spoke again. Mr. Sutherland forgave her tedious insistence because he knew what old ladies were, always had been, and always would be. And not old ladies only.

A white screen was at this point let down on the after wall of the dining-saloon; and Count Veruda unassumingly announced:

"I now propose, with your permission, to show you the new Valentino film. It has been seen in London, and I think, in Paris. But nowhere else."

The whirr of cinema apparatus seemed to put an end to the vibration caused by the dynamos. The dining-saloon suddenly became dark. The effect was highly disconcerting. The unrolling of the reel started.

"I hate films," said Mr. Sutherland quietly to the dark young lady who, in the hotel, had expressed doubt as to the authenticity of the Count's title; Mr. Sutherland had contrived that she should be on his right.

"So do I," the young woman replied.

Mr. Sutherland greatly dared.

"Shall we creep out and explore the yacht a bit?"

He trembled lest she should refuse the audacious suggestion.

"Let's," said she.

Mr. Sutherland thrilled in anticipation of joy in the exclusive possession of her companionship.

The darkness hid their furtive departure from the eye of the host. They passed through the lounge into which the dining-saloon opened, and so to the deck.

CHAPTER IV

ON DECK

THEY climbed up one story and leaned speculatively side by side against the rail of the main-deck. The boat-deck, with the bridge and the captain's quarters, was above them. The warm Neapolitan gloom, relieved now by only a lamp or so at the ends of the long deck, wrapped them softly round about. Not an officer, not a deck-hand to be seen. And nothing to be heard save the faint murmur of vibration ascending monotonously from the depths of the ship. A ship of mystery, enfolded in the magic influences of the universal enigma—and those banal idiots were all sweltering in a room downstairs, watching a film!

"I say," said Mr. Sutherland, "you might tell me your name?"

He was aware of agreeable sensations. She was elegant, she was intelligent. He had made some progress with her during dinner—and she with him.

"Harriet Perkins."

"Thank you."

"Do you mean to say you didn't know?"

"How should I? I never speak to anyone in hotels."

"And quite right too! If you do, you may find yourself glued to a bore for the rest of your stay before you know where you are. What's yours?"

30

"My what? Christian name?"

"Of course not," she laughed. "Your size in gloves."

"Septimius."

She turned a glance on him and clapped her hands.

"I've won five hundred pounds," she said.

"A bet?"

"Yes. But only with myself."

"Oh!"

"I always knew you were the man in the City. You are, aren't you? There couldn't be two Septimius Sutherlands, could there?"

"No. I am in the City."

"Everybody knows about you—except people who stay in hotels. How thrilling!"

He was flattered, and somewhat surprised.

"Then do you read about company meetings?" he asked.

"Yes," she said. "And I read prospectuses and things."

"Well, well!"

"I only read them for fun, like divorce reports. You like divorce reports, don't you?"

"Oh, of course!" he admitted bluntly.

What he especially liked in the composition of Harriet Perkins was that you could talk to her as to a man. In his simplicity he had not grasped, or he had forgotten, that the first care of every young woman of the world is to be talked to as a man. The desire to be talked to as a woman comes later. Long ago, what he had liked in the composition of the delicious, maddeningly feminine creature who afterwards became Mrs. Sutherland was that he could talk to her as to a man. And it had not yet occurred to him that

31

his daughters were constantly endeavouring to get themselves talked to as men by men.

"*Some* dinner!" said Miss Perkins reflectively.

"Yes," Septimius agreed. "And it was a rather wonderful effort in organization, that dinner was! Thirty people, I suppose."

"Twenty-three," Harriet casually corrected him.

"Oh!" Septimius was a little disturbed by his error of thirty per cent. in a computation. "Well, twenty-three, then. It would be reckoned a biggish dinner in any household, wouldn't it?"

"It certainly would!" Harriet eagerly assented.

"And considering that our friend the Count must have sprung it on his staff at a moment's notice! Why, I understand that at seven o'clock nothing was known of any trouble in the hotel kitchens. And there couldn't have been twenty minutes between our deciding to accept his invitation and our arrival on board, and when we got here everything was ready. I've always been interested in questions of organization, and I must say that to-night's affair is one of the finest examples of sheer, rapid organization I've yet come across."

"Have you ever had to organize a big dinner yourself?" Harriet suddenly demanded. She spoke cautiously, with respect, as though careful not to assume that he had not personally organized big dinners.

"I can't say I have."

"Because if you had," she proceeded, with less respect now, "you'd know for certain that a big dinner like to-night's simply cannot be improvised in twenty minutes. Why, the soup we had would take at least half a day to prepare."

"Would it!"

"It would." Dogmatically.

"Do you realize, my dear Miss Perkins, that it follows logically from such a statement—I don't dispute the statement for a moment—that the dinner was not improvised, that in fact it must have been all carefully prepared beforehand?"

"I realize it all right," Harriet answered quietly.

"She's no ordinary girl, and I knew she wasn't," said Mr. Sutherland to himself. And aloud: "Then how do you explain the matter?"

"I don't explain it," Miss Perkins dreamily murmured; then added with more liveliness: "The situation can't be explained till it's been explored. Suppose we explore the yacht a bit, shall we? Your idea, you know."

CHAPTER V

LUGGAGE

HER snub nose and her grey eyes seemed to challenge him to peril. He wondered fearfully what might happen to his sacred dignity if he was caught, with her, in the act of exploration. Pooh! Such challenges from female to male are always accepted, at whatever risk. They compel the male to rise gloriously above common sense.

Feeling more like a burglar than a knight, Mr. Sutherland followed her through a doorway, across the bottom of which was a thick slab of wood designed to keep out the intruding sea. Of course, as a knight, he ought to have gone first, but she had taken the lead, and he did not quite see how to wrest it from her. Now, they were in a sombre passage, and a beam of light shot slantingly up from below. An open steel gate; a hole in the solid floor; a glinting steel ladder with a thin steel handrail to it! The ladder seemed to extend downwards without end. Harriet lightly and rapidly engaged herself in the rungs of the ladder, and Mr. Sutherland still rash followed.

"Mind my fingers!" she warned him, for he was vertically above her on the ladder, and there was only one rung between his brown boots and her ringed hands.

"Oh!" exclaimed Mr. Sutherland in alarm, and paused for a moment.

They came to a little landing, and then to another steel ladder, apparently even longer than the first one. Harriet began the second descent. Mr. Sutherland thought of the bottom of the sea.

"Oh, how lovely!" he heard Harriet remark under him, with a voluptuous sigh of appreciation.

"This must be the engine-room," said Mr. Sutherland, as he joined her on the comparative security of a perforated steel floor.

"If it isn't the kitchen," Harriet smiled nicely, yet quizzically.

"Why did I make a banal remark like that? Naturally it's the engine-room!" thought Mr. Sutherland, disgusted with himself but somehow happy.

The great engine was fenced in by steel hedges, as if it were an untamed and dangerous leviathan. Wheeled parts of it were slowly revolving, and pistoned parts of it moving slowly up and down and to and fro. It was like an immense cat, playing idly with itself, keeping itself in condition by means of gentle and otherwise quite futile exercise. It made very little noise. There was no escaping steam, no jar of metal against metal, no sensation of active power. Various dials and clocks showed meaningless faces; the polished brass of their forms made bright yellow spots of light in the dusky steeliness of the huge chamber.

Suddenly they both saw something move under the perforated floor beneath them. It became very clear that they had not yet arrived at the bottom of the ship, much less the bottom of the sea. Mr. Sutherland started, and he hoped that Harriet had started also, but as to this he could not be sure. He obscurely descried the shape of a man below the floor—a djinn imprisoned in the very entrails of the *Vanguard*. This man, who was middle-aged, presently climbed up to a steel gate within a couple of feet of Harriet's short skirts, unfastened the gate with a click, stepped into the engine-room, and fastened the gate with another click—a click which seemed as final as a decree of fate. He was well dressed in blue and gold, and wore a peaked blue cap with a white cover over its crown. He politely raised the cap.

"We were just admiring your perfectly heavenly engines," said Miss Perkins, with an alluring, placatory sweetness of tone.

"Ay, miss!" the man agreed laconically. He did not smile; on the other hand, he did not frown. He was evidently a most respectable and superior man, incapable of being surprised, and well accustomed to holding an impartial attitude. He said no more.

"Is this the largest yacht in the world?" asked Mr. Sutherland.

"Nay!" the man answered. "But she's the largest motor yacht in the world."

"Ah! She's a motor yacht," said Mr. Sutherland. "The Count didn't tell us that." He glanced at Harriet as if for confirmation. "Then no stokers, or anything of the kind?"

"No stokers. No coaling. A few greasers."

"And her speed?"

"Fifteen. Sixteen-and-a-half if I put her to it."

"You are the engineer, I presume."

"Chief."

"I'm sure it's all very interesting," said Mr. Sutherland, after failing to think of a more brilliant remark.

The Chief then raised his cap again, and suddenly and at surprising speed climbed up the ladder which Count Veruda's two guests had just descended. He appeared to have no objection to leaving the pair alone with his heavenly wild leviathan.

"What a *nice* man!" Miss Perkins burst out. "I think he's adorable . . . The far-away look in his blue eyes!"

Mr. Sutherland was rather astonished at this verdict. He had not even noticed that the man's eyes were blue, and in the lined, grim features he had seen naught worthy to be called nice. Still, he was pleased, because the man who had thus taken Harriet's fancy was certainly older than himself, and certainly not more handsome. Hence his own middle-age and lack of physical witchery could be no bar to her approval. And he desired her approval more than anything.

At this juncture, Septimius became aware of two matters. The first, was that in his tweed travelling suit he felt far more at home and at ease here than he had felt either in the hotel lounge or in the yacht's dining-saloon. And the second, which was somehow exquisitely contradictory of the first, was that Harriet's evening frock made a better showing in the engine-room than in environments of the character for which it had been designed. The frail white and pale green thing, with the olive-coloured fringed shawl over it, had an extraordinary piquancy amid the stern, sinister, formidable steeliness now surrounding her: which piquancy excited Mr. Sutherland.

Important changes were occurring within Mr. Sutherland—changes perhaps as important as can occur within anybody. Miss Perkins had full, luscious lips, and eyes sparkling with romantic vitality. She had a good figure. She had a rich, low voice. She was rather tall. Her hands and feet were small, her ankles and wrists thin. She had perhaps other fascinating qualities which Mr. Sutherland could not determine. But beyond all such there was something else, something which Mr. Sutherland could not define: namely, the totality of Miss Perkins. It was not this or that item in a catalogue of charms which was working the changes in Mr. Sutherland's heart, it was the whole Miss Perkins herself who was the cause of them, and the result would no doubt have been the same if her eyes, voice, lips, feet, hands, ankles, wrists, had been quite otherwise than they were.

Mr. Sutherland knew by unshakable conviction that on earth no other woman existed to compare with Miss Perkins. She possessed a unique gift. She was romance itself. Mr. Sutherland wanted to work for her, to shower presents upon her, to make her smile and laugh, to protect her from the possibility of mishap, pain, discomfort, all unhappiness. He had little hope of being able to do so. He was so humbled by her that he could discern in himself no quality capable of pleasing her. He had the sense to understand that the changes occurring in his prim, sedate, unromantic, married, fatherly soul were terrible. But he gloried in their terribleness, while fearing it. He felt that he had just begun to live, and that, until that moment, he had never lived. He sympathized with, admired, and comprehended men who had ruined their careers for the sake of a woman—men such as General Boulanger and Charles Stewart Parnell, whom, hitherto, he had frigidly despised as weakling voluptuaries.

Yes, in one of his minds Mr. Sutherland was alarmed, and in another he was gloriously ecstatic. And the entire business was astounding in the highest degree, and most probably nothing comparable to it had ever come to pass in any floating engine-room before.

The engine continued lazily to revolve and slide its parts, as if dozing.

"And how come you to know about the organizing of big dinners?" Septimius inquired, with an effort towards archness.

"Oh!" answered Harriet vaguely. "Mother . . . The old days."

The single word "mother" reassured Mr. Sutherland. (Not that he would have admitted that in any point he needed reassurance concerning Harriet Perkins!) She came, then, of good family, family used to lavish hospitalities, solid family. They talked about organization, a subject which seemed to interest Harriet as much as it interested Septimius. Septimius always talked very well on this his favourite subject, and Harriet listened admirably and stimulatingly. They talked for ages and æons. Gone from Mr. Sutherland's mind was all thought of exploring the mysteries of the yacht! Gone also, apparently, from Harriet's mind! Mr. Sutherland saw that, despite her energy and initiative and independence, she was one of those delightful, acquiescent women . . . He had shown a wish to discuss organization, and she had charmingly concurred.

The middle-aged man, with the face that had so appealed to Harriet Perkins, came scurrying violently down the steel ladder from above, and he was followed by another and younger officer at similar speed. They both stood by. Two greasers also appeared. Mr. Sutherland and Miss Perkins, their talk thus brought to a sudden halt, both had the feeling that the moment was big with great events. They were not mistaken. A bell rang out loudly and imperatively within a yard or so of their ears. A steel arrow moved by itself on an indicator, and pointed to words which said "Stand by," though the officers were already standing by. The younger officer sprang towards a lever.

"Shall we go back to the deck?" Miss Perkins gently suggested.

"I think we ought to," he answered, with an outward calm at least equalling her own.

They hastened up the steel ladders; Miss Perkins again took the lead. But now the steel gate, which had been open when they went down, was shut, and also it was fastened. Mr. Sutherland shook it, and Miss Perkins shook it; and they both tried hard to manipulate the bolt; but the gate was obstinate.

"Caught!" exclaimed Mr. Sutherland, but soundlessly—in his heart. Nevertheless his faith in Harriet Perkins was not a bit diminished. They heard, far below, the renewed summons of the autocratic bell. Then there was some enlivening change in the character of the sound of the engine, and a moment later the whole ship began to throb and shake in earnest. Then a deck-hand appeared in the darkness of the corridor. He produced a key of some sort and unfastened the gate, and Mr. Sutherland and Miss Perkins had the freedom of the corridor. They emerged excitedly, like a couple of children, on to the main-deck. They saw, over the rail, a huge form rising on ropes out of the water. It was the starboard launch. It vanished above their heads, being swung in on to the boat-deck. Through the windows of a deck-house they saw the port launch similarly treated.

"The others have all gone back," said Septimius.

"Looks like it," said Harriet. "See the bedroom windows lighted in the hotel."

And in fact many windows were now gleaming in the façade of the Splendide across the water.

"We're left behind," said Septimius.

Harriet shrugged her shoulders.

"Why do I make these idiotic remarks?" Septimius asked himself. "Obviously we're left behind."

"We ought to have been warned," said Septimius.

"Oh!" murmured Harriet. "In the confusion . . . Two launches. . . . The people in one launch would think we were in the other."

"Quite! But those engineer fellows might have told us."

"None of their business," said Harriet.

"Still—But she's moving!" cried Septimius.

"I do believe she is," Harriet agreed.

"But we must have heard the anchor chains. We couldn't possibly not have heard them," Septimius protested.

"Perhaps she wasn't anchored at all," said Harriet. "Perhaps she was only moored to one of those buoy things that you see in harbours. Then she'd only have to slip a rope hawser or whatever they call it, and off she'd go."

Septimius, silent and corrected, remembered with shame the superiority of his tone in giving marine explanations to the old lady in the dining-saloon.

"But this is simply awful!" observed Harriet, though her tone seemed to be saying that it was the greatest lark conceivable.

"It is!" Septimius concurred. "We must get the yacht stopped instantly, and be put ashore—somehow." But in his tone there was no apparent eagerness for such a course of action.

Nevertheless, he led the way aft along the deck, Harriet following. A door stood ajar, showing the faintly lit interior of a cabin. Septimius paused—he knew not why—at the doorway and looked within. Harriet glanced over his shoulder. Lying on the floor of the cabin were a flat American trunk, a suitcase and a rug, which so remarkably resembled Septimius's trunk, suitcase and rug that he was moved to examine them. They were indeed his trunk and suitcase, duly labelled in his own City hand for London via Rome, Paris and Calais; and the rug was his rug. The presence of those three articles in the dim, rich cabin appeared absolutely magical to Septimius; but the magic of it was most sinister, and it illustrated the instability and insecurity of Society far more affrightingly than the strike at the Hotel Splendide. Mr. Sutherland saw that he must maintain his nerve, and he did maintain it. He said no word, and Harriet said no word either. But then Harriet, not being acquainted with the aspect of Septimius's luggage, perhaps had not his reasons for amazement.

"Somebody else can organize too!" thought Septimius generously.

The strange thing was that he was not furious with resentment against the mysterious and unspeakable Count Veruda. For the Count's machinations, whatever their aim, had at any rate secured to him for a time the enchanting society of Miss Perkins. This detail presented itself to Septimius as more important than anything else.

Returning to the rail, Septimius and Harriet saw very clearly the whitening wake of the yacht under the Neapolitan moon. The *Vanguard* was unquestionably gathering speed. She must be making for either Capri or the open Mediterranean. The notion of bringing to a standstill the mighty and resistless movement of the great vessel became preposterous to Septimius, and he gave it up. Besides, none of the crew seemed to be about. All the navigation was being conducted from the unseen boat-deck overhead.

"Miss Perkins, please!" called a respectful voice from somewhere: not the voice of Count Veruda.

Harriet started, and then without a word to Septimius walked off and disappeared round the after end of the deck-houses. Mr. Sutherland was alone.

CHAPTER VI

LYING DOWN

MR. SUTHERLAND walked about the deck; he made a complete circuit of the dark, deserted deck-houses, and met nobody save one deck-hand, who ignored him, and whom, from pride, he ignored, though he was hungering for information on a number of important points. He could not see the mast-head navigating lights because of the intervening upper-deck. But forward, he saw the green and the red glare of the starboard and port navigating-lights, and they seemed to throw a baneful illumination upon the vast, vibrating, silent organism of the moving yacht. Never had Mr. Sutherland been caged in an environment so uncanny and oppressive.

At last he was once more in front of the cabin tenanted by his self-transporting baggage. He carefully inspected it and found therein every device of comfort and luxury; beyond it was a bathroom of equal merit. By way of experiment he turned on a tap marked "Hot," and the water which cascaded therefrom was more than scalding enough to satisfy the most exacting apostle of efficiency. He stood still, meditative, and falsely pretended to himself that he was not hurt by Miss Perkins's inconsiderate and offhand departure. He thought, besides, of all that had so inexplicably happened to him; he gazed at his luggage. He then said, aloud:

LYING DOWN

"Shall I take this business lying down?"

Now Mr. Sutherland, like many persons commonly supposed to be without a sense of humour, was capable on occasion of being most queerly and disturbingly humorous. He answered his own question:

"Yes, I shall take it lying down. I'll go to bed."

And he rang the bell by the bedside. A knock followed, and the chief steward entered.

It seemed odd to Mr. Sutherland that the bell of an ordinary guest-cabin in so important a yacht should be answered by so stately and majestic an individual as the chief steward. Mr. Sutherland, who was still successfully maintaining his nerve, thus coldly addressed the chief steward:

"Apparently my things have not been laid out."

"Sorry, sir."

The chief steward proceeded, with a dignity comparable to Mr. Sutherland's own, to unfasten the suitcase and lay out all necessary matters for the night: while the guest began to undress.

"Can I have something to drink?" asked Mr. Sutherland.

"Certainly, sir."

"What can I have?"

"Anything you like, sir."

"Well, I will have a cup of weak camomile-tea; very weak, not more than one flower to the cup—if it's a breakfast cup."

Mr. Sutherland often took camomile before retiring. It was in France that he had learnt the digestive and sedative qualities of properly infused camomile. People, especially relatives, had tried to laugh him out of camomile; but they had failed. He was not a man to be frightened by the absurd associations of the word "camomile."

The chief steward, having departed, came back.

"Very sorry, sir. We have no camomile on board."

"No consequence. No consequence," said Mr. Sutherland blandly.

"Can I get you anything else, sir?"

Mr. Sutherland reflected.

"A tot of rum?" he suggested. Not that he had the least intention of drinking the rum, but the phrase "tot of rum" struck him as excellently marine and in keeping with the aquatic situation.

"Certainly, sir."

The chief steward disappeared and re-appeared.

"Very sorry indeed, sir. We have no rum on board."

"No consequence. No consequence," said Mr. Sutherland blandly. "I regret to have troubled you. Might take that eiderdown off the bed. I think I sha'n't need it."

The chief steward did as he was told, and went away humbled.

It was a proud moment for Mr. Sutherland; but a moment does not last very long. Mr. Sutherland reflected with grief that he had lost his berth in the train de luxe, the costly price of which was not under any circumstances returnable, and that all his appointments in London would be broken. And when, in his white pyjamas, he had sunk down on the soft bed and turned out the lights and lay listening to the faint straining sound of elaborate wood-work due to the quivering of the yacht as her twin propellers urged her through the placid moonlit waters of the Mediterranean—then, Mr. Sutherland's mood

changed quickly to one of utter dismay and apprehension. True, by the superb calm of his demeanour,
and by his magnificent inactivity, he would compel
his enemies and captors sooner or later to explain
themselves and thus to play the first revealing move
in the game about to begin. True, his brilliant tactics
must have astonished and perhaps momentarily
baffled them. But his predicament was none the
less monstrous, incredible, unthinkable. He could discover absolutely no clue to the absurd, nightmarish
enigma of it. The affair was too big to be a practical
joke. On the other hand, if the affair was serious, as it
positively must be, to what end had it been under-
taken? His common sense forbade him to believe
that he had fallen into the hands of bandits who
would hold him to ransom. Such adventures did not
happen to big financiers—save of course in the film
studios of California. Further, his knowledge of
character forbade him to believe that airy Count
Veruda had wits enough to conceive and execute the
enterprise of which he, Septimius, was the victim.
Hence Count Veruda could only be the agent of
mysterious and invisible brains as gigantically bold
as they were recklessly unscrupulous. Mr. Sutherland
had sufficient wisdom to be afraid. He was afraid of
the mere spirited grandeur of the plot in which he
found himself entangled. He had not spent twenty-
five years in the City without hearing rumours, and
indeed circumstantial stories, of strange, nefarious
deeds attempted and accomplished for the purposes
of what was called "big business." But he had never
heard of anything at all comparable to the present
prodigious matter. And he could think of none of his
own financial schemes which might be prejudiced by

the enforced absence of their author from London. As a fact, all his current schemes were completed, and the last one had been definitely completed that very morning in Naples.

Then there was the question of Miss Harriet Perkins. Was she among the conspirators? She unquestionably was. The people in authority knew that she was on board, and they knew her name; and she had answered quite calmly and obediently and shamelessly to her name. Without doubt she had been employed to keep him in the yacht while the rest of the company departed. With that aim she had inveigled him into the engine-room and by her wily arts had held him there. He had been her dupe. Men had been hoodwinked by their passions before, and he had been hoodwinked. That Harriet Perkins was a vampire was as clear as daylight to Mr. Sutherland. And yet Mr. Sutherland would not credit it. He would not because he simply could not. Harriet a vampire? Ridiculous! Harriet was the finest feminine creature he had ever seen, or would see, and she had not duped him. Still, she was plainly a vampire, an evil woman, and he was her dupe. So his thoughts ran round and monotonously round in his head, and never stopped, and therefore never reached any conclusion.

The oddest thing of all was that he did not care whether Harriet was a vampire and a villainess or not. She might be anything she chose, provided she was the unique Harriet. It was unnecessary for her to make excuses for herself. He could make all the excuses for her. She could not sin in his eyes. Such was his principal mind. But in another of his minds he perceived dispassionately what was going on in his principal mind, and he was afraid, he was terrified, by the wonders therein. His happiness in the thought of Harriet Perkins frightened him as much as his astounding physical predicament. Awe filled him, and he trembled. Sleep was impossible. . . . Then he woke up with a start, for sleep is never impossible. His ears had heard a scream followed by an outburst of apparently hysterical laughter or sobs. Harriet's scream! Harriet's laughter or sobs—perhaps the laughter or sobs of a girl overwrought by the presence of acute danger! Mr. Sutherland jumped up, switched on the light, sprang to his scarlet dressing-gown (for nothing would have induced him to appear on deck in pyjamas), and opened the cabin-door.

CHAPTER VII

THE MILLIONAIRE

Miss Harriet Perkins was invited by the gestures of a silent, timid, fair-haired young man to follow him down the stairs which led to the lower deck, where were the lounge and the dining-saloon earlier put at the disposal of the twenty-three guests from the Splendide.

The young man, whose austere dinner-jacket had no touch of the marine, switched on lights as he went forward and then extinguished them behind himself and Miss Perkins. For this purpose he had to pass and re-pass Miss Perkins several times; it was rather as if they were playing a game for position; she smiled at him and he smiled blushingly back. She knew he was admiring her; she liked him; she judged him to be honest. But she could not help thinking how odd it was that the yacht *Vanguard* should be so sparing of its electric light, unless indeed, it had a reason now for keeping as dark as possible.

Also she wondered that her hotel name should be known there, too. Then she decided that in this particular she was alarming herself unnecessarily. Various persons, including Mr. Sutherland, had addressed her as Miss Perkins in the hearing of various stewards. Nevertheless she was alarmed, because she had other reasons for alarm.

At the forward end of the lounge the young man murmured:

"His lordship desires the pleasure of a few minutes' conversation with you, madam."

It seemed strange to Harriet that a mere foreign Count should be referred to as "his lordship." For herself she determined to deal very faithfully with the foreign Count.

"Are you 'his lordship's' secretary?" she asked the young man.

"One of them," replied the youth, and revealed a further room, small, but of great richness. "Miss Perkins," he announced loudly and timidly. Harriet gave him a smile as he withdrew and shut the door behind her.

A cigar-smoking, carelessly-dressed gentleman of medium height, with a head of very considerable size, formidably glinting orbs, untidy greyish hair, and a welcoming, almost benevolent smile, sprang awkwardly out of an easy-chair much too large for him, and advanced to grasp Harriet's hand.

She had a shock; she wanted to gasp (but of course did not gasp) at the sight of this personage whom she at once recognized but had never before seen. The mystery of the *Vanguard* seemed suddenly in some parts to be illuminated and yet in others to be further darkened. She thought, severely shaken:

"I'm right up against it. I must have a policy." But no policy offered itself to her questing brain.

"Miss Perkins?" said the man, dashing away his cigar. "I believe ye *are* Miss Perkins, aren't ye?" He had a deep, strong, rough voice and a Midland accent. He showed none of the marks of the public school, the University, or the best clubs. If a gentleman, which had yet to be proved, he was one of nature's. . . . Not even a dinner-jacket!

"I am," said she, nervous and challenging. "But who are you? Perhaps I'm more at sea than you think."

The man laughed pleasantly at her simple wit.

"My name's Furber. Lord Furber."

This was Maidie's terrible, legendary husband. She rather liked him, while sympathizing with Maidie and resolving to stand up for Maidie with every resource at her disposal. She liked his eyes, with their occasional faint gleam of dangerous fun.

"Not the great engineer?" she exclaimed in a tone falsely tremulous, assuming both awe and fearful joy. It was as if she had said: "Dare I believe that I am actually in the presence of the prodigious Lord Furber?"

"Ye're flattering me. *Once* I reckon I was a bit of an engineer."

He affected to be insusceptible to flattery, but he was flattered. Harriet was confirmed in her belief that there exists on earth no man who cannot be flattered by an attractive woman. She felt his admiration descending upon her. Therefore she was at ease, and capable of concealing anything and everything except a delicious tendency towards impudence.

She went on:

"Newspaper proprietor, then, if engineer's too good for you! Capitalist! Millionaire! Yes, now I recognize you from your portrait—it's always appearing in your own newspapers, isn't it?"

His lordship laughed again, but not quite so naturally as before. She suspected that it might be perilous to affront him, but she had a certain taste for peril, and when his lordship asked her to sit down she sat down with gusto, with excited anticipation, with a full sense of the liveliness of life, and with a queer satisfaction that the door was shut and she had him all to herself.

And all the time her brain repeated monotonously: "Imagine *him* being on board! Imagine seeing *him* here!"

Lord Furber said:

"I'm sorry ye've got carried off like this from your hotel."

"And from my luggage too," Harriet put in.

"Yer luggage too," he concurred.

"I shouldn't have minded so much if they'd carried off my luggage with me. I might have rather liked being carried off if only I'd had my luggage."

"Oversight!"

"What was an oversight? Carrying me off, or forgetting my luggage?"

"I apologize," said Lord Furber, not answering her question.

"I should have thought it was Count Veruda's place to apologize. The yacht's his."

"Who told ye that?"

"He did."

"Well, I lent him the yacht for the evening. She isn't his and never was. I own her and I run her, and nobody else does. And she's more expensive than ten women."

Maidie had indeed mentioned a yacht, but very casually as being a matter in which she herself felt no personal interest; she had not even given its name.

"Then the Count is a liar," she said.

"Yes," Lord Furber admitted judicially. "Yes, I

reckon he is. But I'm bound to say he asked my permission first, and I gave it."

"Asked your permission?"

"Veruda's my secretary."

"One of them," corrected Harriet quickly, recalling what another secretary had said.

"One of 'em. But my favourite. I picked him up because of his picturesqueness. He amuses me. He keeps me interested."

"I always felt the Count was an adventurer. And yet he looks like a rich man."

"Not he! He looks like the popular notion of a rich man. *I* look like a rich man, and I am rich—very rich." Lord Furber laughed, as if to himself. "Now, Miss Perkins, what do you want me to do?"

"About what?"

"About yeself."

"Turn back at once and put me ashore where I started from."

"Certainly. Like a shot—if you insist. But listen now; wouldn't it meet the case if I wirelessed the Splendide to have yer luggage sent on by motor to the next port we call at?"

"Where's that?"

"Depends."

"On what?"

"Circumstances."

"And my hotel bill?"

"Oh! We could fix that."

"And my clothes in the meantime? I haven't a thing except what I'm in. And even you can't make it perpetual evening, Lord Furber."

"Yes, I can. We'll stay below. The curtains sha'n't even be opened. Breakfast by electric light. Lunch by electric light. Every meal by electric light till your luggage arrives. . . . Of course, I admit there's your reputation to think of. But that'll be all right. You needn't worry about that."

Miss Perkins hesitated, and then, as it seemed to her, jumped into a deep river.

"Lord Furber," said she. "Where in heaven's name do you come from?" The challenge in her tone frightened her for a moment. But she was getting a little used to Lord Furber, and after all, he was only a man like other men.

"The Five Towns."

"You would!" she exclaimed, striking wildly out into the very middle of the river. "And you've never really left them. And perhaps that's what's the matter with you. And what's more you're still in the nineteenth century. You can't have looked at the calendar lately, or you wouldn't talk in that antediluvian style. Do you suppose my reputation is going to suffer because you and your secretaries and things have bungled their organization? I don't need anybody to tell me not to worry about my reputation. 'My reputation to think of' indeed! Have you any ladies on board? Or women servants?"

Lord Furber smiled, unruffled.

"One woman. I can't travel without my chief steward—he's my butler on dry land—and he can't travel without his wife. So his wife's here." He sighed.

"Then I'll see her. She'll arrange things for me for the night. And the yacht shall go back at once, and when I've had my sleep out you shall land me yourself at Naples."

Lord Furber shook his head.

"Can't."

"But you said you would."

"Yes, but I can't. I was hoping ye'd oblige me by not insisting."

"But I do insist."

"I tell ye I can't do it."

"You mean you won't."

"Have it yer own way, then. I mean I won't." He gave a short laugh, loud but grim.

Harriet murmured:

"So now we know where we are." She threw up her head and answered his laugh with a laugh light and negligent. But she was feeling by this time the strength of the current of the river. All Maidie's accounts of her husband's peculiarities had not prepared her for so curt a refusal. She saw in the man's eyes some hard glint of the force which had made a Lord Furber out of a working engineer.

"Ask me anything else and I'll do it."

"Then send for Count Veruda. I feel as if I could talk to him for his own good."

"He isn't on board. He took his guests ashore and hasn't returned. . . . But you needn't be afraid," Lord Furber added kindly, protectively.

"I'm not."

"Are ye sure?"

"Yes, I'm sure. But *you're* afraid."

"I admit it," he indulged her. "Have a cigarette, will ye?"

"I don't smoke," said Harriet drily. "You're afraid because you're puzzled. It's my reasonableness that's puzzling you. If I'd made a scene you'd have felt safe. But now you can't make me out. I said we knew where we were. It isn't quite true. I know where I am, but you don't know where you are. I've got *that*

56

advantage. And I'll tell you another thing. Like all millionaires you're suspicious, and because I'm keeping calm you're suspecting all sorts of things about me."

"For instance?"

"You're suspecting I got myself left behind on your yacht on purpose."

"Well, I *was*," he said bluntly. "But I don't now."

"I do smoke—but only my own."

Miss Perkins opened her bag and took out a cigarette case. Lord Furber held a lighted match.

"I'll hold it, thanks," said Miss Perkins, and when she had lighted the cigarette she carefully dropped the match on the Persian carpet. Then she looked up at him as he stood almost over her. "You're so deliciously naïve, aren't you?"

"What do you mean?" Lord Furber spoke gruffly, and stepped back.

"Perhaps that's why I like you."

"What do you mean?" he repeated. "Tell me why you think I'm naïve."

"No. You might lose your temper. You haven't got much self-restraint, and I hate scenes. If I wanted a scene I should make it myself."

"I sha'n't lose my temper."

"I say you might."

"What do you know about my temper?"

"Anybody can see you've got a temper."

"Tell me why you think I'm naïve. Tell me." Harriet shook her head. "Hang it all!" he went on, and threw an ash-tray violently to the floor. "Must I go on my knees to you? Tell me."

"Sit down, then." Harriet laughed. "And don't jump up again." Lord Furber sat down. Harriet could feel her heart beating. "You're naïve because you think everybody has the same kind of motives as you have yourself. You've got Machiavelli written all over your face. You love plotting, and so you imagine that everybody is plotting something against you. And because you fancy you can detect scheming everywhere you think you understand human nature. You've never grown up. Perhaps that's a reason why you're rather adorable." She deliberately dropped some ash on the Persian carpet.

A pause.

"And what plotting d' ye accuse me of being up to now?"

"Well, the whole business of the dinner was obviously a plot. There was no improvisation in it at all. It was all completely thought out beforehand. And the brains that planned it certainly didn't leave two of the guests behind by accident. Mr. Sutherland and I must have been left behind on purpose. I'm not a millionaire, but I'm not a simpleton either."

"Miss Perkins," said Lord Furber. "Just listen. I sha'n't ask ye to believe me, because I know I can make ye believe me. No. Don't drop yer eyes. Look right at me."

Harriet, who in fact had lowered her gaze, raised it again.

"Well?"

"I didn't know ye from Eve until ye came into this room. I'd never heard of ye. I don't want anything from ye. If ye got left behind it was yer own fault. And you can understand that with two launches and twenty-three people, it would be easy enough for one or two to be left behind. I hear ye were seen in the engine-room with Mr. Sutherland. I suppose you and he are old friends."

"Lord Furber," said Miss Perkins. "Just listen to me. I sha'n't ask you to believe me, because I know you can't help believing me. Till this evening, I'd never spoken a word to Mr. Sutherland in my life. I know nothing at all about him except what everybody knows who reads the newspapers. He's naïve like you. But he's a nice old thing, and he fell in love with me at first sight. Oh yes, in love! I wanted to be kind to him, and I went down with him into the engine-room, and I stayed talking there with him simply because I saw he was enjoying it. But——" she stopped.

"But?" Lord Furber's eyes gleamed provocatively.

"But I know very well now your people only left me quietly in the engine-room because I was with Mr. Sutherland. You didn't want to disturb him, and you couldn't disturb me without disturbing him, and so I am to share Mr. Sutherland's dreadful fate." She laughed. "It was Mr. Sutherland you wanted to capture. Once you'd got him on board you'd have kept him here somehow whether he'd been in the engine-room or anywhere else. And to get him on board you gave a dinner to twenty-three persons, and I shouldn't be at all surprised if you even organized the hotel-strike. Nothing would surprise me. I haven't shown a great deal of surprise, but you must admit that I'm entitled to be astonished by what's happened to me since I was enticed into your two-thousand-ton yacht."

"And why d'ye settle on Mr. Sutherland as the victim of all this wonderful Machiavellianism? Don't answer if ye'd prefer not to."

"Of course, I shouldn't answer if I preferred not to. But I don't a bit mind answering. His luggage! That's why I settle on Mr. Sutherland. His luggage! We discovered it together in one of the cabins. I didn't know it was his till I saw the labels."

"He might have had it sent on board himself for anything you know."

Miss Perkins rose to her feet.

"Don't be so silly," she somewhat crudely advised Lord Furber. She was shaking. The cigarette shook in her hand.

"*What?*"

"I say don't be silly. And what are you going to do about it? Hit me? It's time somebody talked straight to you. You're a millionaire, and so everybody humours you and flatters you—and pulls you to pieces behind your back. I know you turn your home into a perfect hell with your childish tantrums."

"You know nothing about my home!" growled Lord Furber.

"I know a lot about your home. I can see your home in your face at this very moment. You're all alike, you self-made millionaires. Spoilt children, every one of you. You ought to be well smacked—and in the right place, too."

At this point Lord Furber, genuinely amazed and furious, overthrew a table. A siphon rebounded on the carpet but did not break.

"Hell's delight!" cried he.

"There you are! I told you you hadn't got any self-restraint. Naughty little thing! Do try to be a man and don't be silly with your absurd suggestions about Mr. Sutherland having sent his luggage on board himself. I never saw anybody more staggered than Mr. Sutherland was at the sight of that luggage. He didn't say one word. He didn't know that I'd read the labels. He just kept quiet. He's got a thousand times more self-restraint than you have, and I can tell you if you're up against him you've got your work cut out and no mistake. . . ."

Harriet dropped back into her chair. She thought: "I can't keep this up any longer. It's about time I felt faint. I believe I do feel faint." And to Lord Furber in a weak voice:

"Brandy."

The cigarette fell to the carpet and began to burn a neat hole in its pricelessness. Harriet sighed because, climbing up all wet the further bank of the river, she felt safe once more.

CHAPTER VIII

HER STORY

LORD FURBER instantly became one of nature's gentlemen. From the sideboard, which seemed to contain all liqueurs and spirits (except rum), each decanter secure in a round socket, he took some 1821 brandy, and in ten seconds was holding, almost with tenderness, the glass to Harriet's languid lips. She coughed. She sighed again, shut her eyes, and opened them.

"I'm saved," she breathed.

His lordship beheld her with equal respect, humour, and admiration. But she had terribly shocked the vanity of the autocrat in him and frightened the child in him. Not even Maidie his wife had ever, in the wildest moments of her red hair, handled him half as roughly as Harriet Perkins. Harriet had shown him to himself. He was too much of a realist to deny the truth of the picture she had drawn. He had always vaguely known, but never realized clearly, that he in fact was as she had painted him. He was too proud to sulk or to resent, and too proud to be ashamed. And in that moment he wanted more than anything to win her good opinion. He felt as though he was sitting for an examination. The ordeal occupied the whole of his brain; his millions were so useless in the test that they seemed to have been reduced to the equivalent of twopence. His sense of values was drastically altered. In sum, his emotions were unique, and such as he had never expected at the hands of destiny.

"Oh!" said Harriet. "I smell fire."

The fire of the cigarette was steadily boring its way through the Persian carpet.

"Oh, no!"

"I hope it isn't your lovely carpet."

They both looked calmly at the burning carpet.

"It's nothing," said Lord Furber. "These carpets are fire-proofed. Always have 'em like that on board, ye know."

Then he stamped on the red glow, and with dignity picked up the siphon and the overthrown table.

"Have you forgiven my remarks?" she asked coyly.

"I've forgotten," his lordship replied, and he had.

"You must excuse me nearly going off like that. But I'm not used to being spirited away in two-thousand-ton yachts and having to keep my end up against millionaires and barons and things."

"What *are* ye used to?" asked the baron eagerly, standing near her with his hands in his pockets. "Tell me what your line is. I'm very interested, and I'd like to know something about ye."

His interest was genuine, and violent. Indeed, he was coming to the conclusion previously reached by Mr. Sutherland—namely that there was none like Harriet Perkins in the whole world. He had been dazzled, and he rejoiced in the exceeding novelty.

"I'm nothing. And you can't tell something about nothing can you?"

"See if ye can't. Just try. And after ye've tried I'll tell ye something." His tone was very persuasive.

"About yourself?"

"No. About you. It'll be my turn. Ye've been telling me quite a lot about myself."

Harriet sat up.

"Have you ever been in a ladies' club?" she asked.

"No. I don't like clubs and clubs don't like me. Why?"

"If you'd been in a woman's club—London, I mean —you'd have seen in the dining-room at night a row of small tables and a solitary woman sitting at each table and horribly pretending to be jolly and self-sufficient. I'm one of those women. Younger than most of them, but in quite a short time I shall be older than most of them. I'm thirty, and I shall go on being thirty for years yet—only my face won't go on being thirty. It's a pleasant age while it lasts, and our business is to make it last as long as ever we can. I've no relatives, except distant ones—and the more distant they keep themselves the better I'm pleased. I've got just enough income to wear presentable frocks, but not enough to cover myself with jewels. I was never brought up to do anything: and I don't like bridge, golf, or tennis. I like dancing, but if you don't pursue bridge, golf, or tennis, it isn't easy to find partners for dancing. I get asked out—more often to lunch than to dinner—because I can be bright, if I haven't got a headache. In fact, I have a tongue in my head. You may have noticed it. Sometimes I'm not asked twice to the same house because absurd persons think I have rather too much tongue in my head. I can produce wonderful silences at lunch-tables by some quite simple remark. Strange isn't it?

"People wonder why I don't marry. So do I wonder. Because I can certainly arouse feeling in the male bosom. Only, the men I like don't seem to get as far

as a definite proposition—I expect they're frightened
of what I might say to them. And those who do get as
far as a definite proposition somehow always leave
me cold. And then that's that.

"When I'm sick of my flat in London and my club,
I go 'abroad'—as they call it, and wander from hotel
to hotel, and make heaps of acquaintances, mostly
female, and I don't care for any of them, and none of
them care for me. There are thousands and thousands
of us wanderers, particularly in Italy. When I'm sick
of 'abroad' I go back to London and begin to hope
for the best again. Yes, and then more 'abroad.' For
ever and ever Amen. I'm not physically repulsive;
and I've brains and brilliance—who'd deny it!—but
I'm a thoroughly unsatisfactory creature because I
don't *fit in*. And I'm growing worse every year. . . .
You asked me to tell you, and I've told you—I don't
know why. And it's heaven's own truth that I never
told anyone before."

Lord Furber ceased to be one of nature's gentlemen.

"There's only one thing the matter with you," he
said, suddenly fierce. "Ye're an idler before God. You
ought to work. Ye're taking from society everything
ye need, and giving nowt in return."

"And what about you?"

"That's a different question. Let's keep to the
point."

"How can I work? I was never taught to work. I
don't know how to work."

"Anybody can learn to work."

"I'm not strong. I have headaches and backaches."

"Aches be blowed, miss. Bad health never yet
stopped anybody from working that wanted to work.
Think of Herbert Spencer, and Mussolini here. Bad

health's always the last refuge of the female waster." The baron's eyes blazed, and his hands removed from his pockets, were gesticulating, and his feet restive.

"And there's another thing," Miss Perkins proceeded calmly. "Why should I take the bread out of other women's mouths? Lots of them need work and can't get it. I don't need work."

Lord Furber clinched his teeth together, and pulled a face, and seemed to dance about in fury.

"Great Scott!" he growled. "I thought those ideas were dead and buried and 'd begun to stink years ago. And here I have to stand and listen to 'em now! Of course ye need work. Work's just what ye do need. And if ye do honest work at a fair price ye won't be taking bread out of anybody's mouth. On the contrary, ye'll be putting it in. All work's to the good. Look at ye! Look at yeself. Other people are keeping ye, making yer clothes and cooking yer food and cleaning yer room and washing yer fal-lals and playing music for ye. And ye do nothing yeself except sit around and complain of headaches and backaches. How's that, Miss Perkins?"

Lord Furber felt quite happy.

"You're rather a brutal baron, aren't you?" Harriet fenced feebly.

"If I am, I'm taking lessons from you. I'm treating ye as an equal. Of course, if ye want me to treat ye like a doll again——"

"Again?"

"Yes, again. I said I'd tell ye something about yeself. Here it is. Ye were only pretending just now when ye nearly fainted. Ye'd got tired of fighting and ye wanted a rest. And so ye thought ye'd play up to

me with a touch of the doll business. D'ye suppose I
didn't see through it? Ye thought ye were deceiving
me, but I was deceiving you by pretending to be
deceived. What about it?"

"What made you think I was only pretending?"

"Yer colour. It never changed. When a woman
faints it's because the blood's leaving her head. So she
goes pale."

Miss Perkins laughed gaily.

"Five Towns again!" she said. "You're still in
them. Won't you ever get away? Haven't you ever
heard of rouge? I expect not."

Lord Furber turned his back, walked away, and returned. He was frowning. Then the frown vanished
and he gave a loud laugh and lifted his arms.

"Kamerad!"

"Still, I *was* pretending," said Harriet.

Lord Furber dropped his arms and stamped.

"Confound ye."

"Now, as you're so clever, tell me how to find work,
and I'll find it."

Lord Furber wrestled with a wild, foolish impulse,
and was thrown.

"Ye've found it."

"What d'you mean—I've found it?"

"Be my secretary."

There was a pause in which his lordship had a terrible fear that she would not refuse his offer.

"And take the bread out of Count Veruda's
mouth?" she smiled blandly.

"Yes. I couldn't stick the two of ye."

"You're very adventurous, baron."

"Well, perhaps I am."

"But I don't know shorthand or typewriting or

67

filing or book-keeping. I did once try to learn typing, but I was beaten off with great loss."

"I don't want a clerk. I've got scores of 'em. I want a secretary."

"What should I have to do?"

"I'm an idiot. I'm an idiot. And I canna help it," said Lord Furber to himself. And aloud: "Oh! All kinds of odd jobs. Ye'd be very useful to me. Ye're tempted?"

"Who wouldn't be."

"It's agreed then. Salary doesn't matter. Start to-morrow."

"How like you!" observed Miss Perkins. "Do you imagine I'd take any post without knowing quite a lot about my employer? It's employees who ought to ask for references, not employers."

"Just listen, then. I'll tell ye about yer employer."

CHAPTER IX

THE BARON'S DEFENCE

LORD FURBER stood and then sat down. He lighted a cigar and immediately threw it away. The Titan was nervous before Harriet. He felt that he was still sitting for an examination and must pass it, if possible, with honours.

He said to her:

"I'm a self-made man—don't be afraid, I'm not going to give details of the manufacture. Now there's always something amateurish about anything ye've made yeself. I know I'm amateurish, say rough-finished, in parts. That's enough about that. I began as a mechanical inventor, and from the first my inventions brought me in a lot of money. When I say a lot, I mean a lot. I wasn't out after money, never have been, but money overtook me and I couldn't escape it. Royalties on patents, ye know. I went on inventing until I was thirty-five, and then I dried up. I suppose I'd run through the vein. Happens sometimes. You do come to the ends of things. But money rolled in just the same. Even more. One day I found all of a sudden I was worth a million in gilt-edged stuff. That was nothing. To-day if I was reduced to a million again I lay I should think myself a pauper. Ye notice I don't tell ye how much I *am* worth. No reason why I shouldn't; but it's more effective not to.

69

If ye knew the figure ye wouldn't be half as impressed as ye are—no matter how big the figure was."

"Oh! Shouldn't I!" said Harriet, rising out of her chair and strolling about the room.

"No, ye wouldn't! And this piling-up business is still going on, and I can't stop it. Nothing can stop it. I don't mind telling ye that Henry VII paid all the expenses of governing England out of an income less than mine is. That'll give ye a notion. People call me one of the new Huns, because I'm so darned rich. Well, I can't help it. What could I do? I couldn't refuse my royalties or the interest on my investments. Silly! I couldn't burn the money. I've been asked why I don't use my money trying to regenerate society. Society's all wrong, but it can't be set right by chucking money about. Silly! It can only be set right by common sense, and common sense is a thing money can't buy. Same with charity. I do a bit of charity, because I'm afraid not to. But I hate it. I don't believe in it. It only does harm. Some of the New Huns spend their money on social schemes and charity because they're ashamed of being rich and they want to dope their consciences. I haven't a conscience, and if I had one it would be a perfectly clear conscience as far as my money's concerned. So what in hades am I to do? I try all I can not to let my money accumulate. This yacht's one of my efforts in that line. My wife does her best, too. No good." He shook his head. "Nobody can spend more than a certain amount, and nobody's wife can. You see the difficulty?"

"Quite."

"Then sit down. It's against nature for a woman to be trapesing about while a man's in an easy-chair as easy as this one. Sit down."

Miss Perkins obeyed.

"Please, may I speak?" she asked modestly

"I haven't quite finished," said Lord Furber.

"I only wanted to remind you that I'm not your secretary yet."

"No. And if ye keep on tapping your feet like that ye never will be."

Miss Perkins arose and resumed walking.

"Well," Lord Furber continued, with a sort of deep growling sigh, "as soon as I stopped inventing I began to be bored. Rather a lark to be raised to the Peerage, and waking up the House of Lords. But I got tired of that after a few months. I had to find something to do. If I'd kept on doing nothing, with all my energy, I should soon ha' been doing nothing in a lunatic asylum. Then I discovered I had judgment—and financial judgment. I found that out by looking into my investments myself, just for something to occupy myself with. I'd always left 'em to stockbrokers before. I soon found stockbrokers were listening to me, instead of me to them. So I took up finance. Great pity, because it made me richer than ever. But if a man has a faculty he must use it."

"Besides," said Harriet, "on the whole I suppose it's better to be too rich than too bored, isn't it?"

The baron gazed at her, frowning absently.

"Interested me for quite a time, finance did. But in the end I saw there was no real point to it. Ye see, it isn't creative, and doesn't get ye anywhere. Then I simply let my money stew in its own dividends. Then I thought of the press and bought a newspaper. Bought several. Before I knew where I was I'd grown into a press-lord. Imagined I should have power if I owned a few papers, and I expect it's power I'm after more than anything. Disappointing. Yes. A newspaper must pay. If it doesn't it's a toy. I hate toys. If it is to pay it must be read. But the public will only read what it wants to read. So the newspaper owner must keep his ear to the ground. It's like this. Ye find out what the public's thinking, and then ye tell 'em they must think just that, and they go on thinking just that, and ye say ye've influenced 'em—and call it power. There's nothing to it. It's not real. The world will roll on in its own way. Newspaper stunts are childish. Two o' my papers are now trying to get taxi-fares lowered in London. They may succeed. But lowering taxi-fares isn't much to sing about for a newspaper enterprise with twelve millions of capital, and charging advertisers £1,400 per insertion for a front page. No, young woman, the power of the press-lords isn't worth mentioning compared to the trouble they take and the money they make and the infernal worries they have with labour."

At this moment the bashful under-secretary, Tunnicliff, ventured timorously into the room and stood close to the door awaiting notice.

"Well, my lad?"

"If Mrs. Bumption could speak to your lordship for a moment. She says it's urgent."

"Where is she?"

"In the dining-saloon, my lord."

"All right."

Mr. Tunnicliff vanished.

"I've tried the stage," his lordship went on, very deliberately and gloomily. "A bit of a bottomless pit, that. And I never was fond of children. Nobody on the stage ever grows up. They'll spend five shillings on a telegram to tell you they haven't three halfpence to buy stamps with. They'll interview you about putting on a play that's a sure fortune, and they promise to come and read you the thing next day, and ye never hear of 'em again until ye read in the paper they've gone to New York to play an English gentleman in a French melodrama; and they don't come back for ten years. That's the stage."

He moved towards the door, thinking: "I'm doing this rather well. It's a good story. She's impressed." Then he stopped.

"There's racing. Scoundrels behind ye. Snobs in front of ye. If the jockey's to be trusted the horse isn't. Ye can have racing."

"But the cinema!" said Miss Perkins vivaciously. "Surely Providence allowed the cinema to be invented in order that a Lord Furber might exploit it."

"Young woman," the baron replied. "Yer tongue'll get ye into mischief one day."

"It has done already. I told you."

"And sooner than ye think for, too. I've tried the cinema. I could stand the film kings, and I could stand the film stars. It was the lady continuity-writers that drove me off. They all have flaxy hair and come from Nebraska. No! Ye couldn't give me the cinema. Well, I suppose I must go and get it over with Mrs. Bumption. She's the majestic consort of my chief steward. Hell's delight!" He yawned. "I'm more bored than the prince in the fairy-tale."

"Your case is serious," said Harriet.

"It's more serious than ye think, miss."

"It couldn't be, you poor dear!" said Harriet brightly.

The baron went out. But already he was looking forward to the moment when, having pitched Mrs.

Bumption overboard, he could return to Harriet. Not that he had any real hope of finding the courage to pitch Mrs. Bumption overboard.

It suddenly occurred to him that he had forgotten one point, and he went back to Harriet.

"I say. A bit ago ye had the impudence to suggest that I was like yeself, taking everything from society and giving nothing. What about my inventions?"

"My fault!" said Harriet. "Honestly, I'd never heard of them. Another grievance, I suppose."

Lord Furber slammed the door on her. And while talking to Mrs. Bumption he was thinking: "I know the wench'll end by being my secretary, and I don't want her to be my secretary. Might as well have a catherine wheel for a secretary. Could I safely pretend I was only joking when I offered her the job? I wonder if I have impressed her—passed my exam."

CHAPTER X

THE SNORE

"WELL," said Lord Furber, returning to the room after an absence of five minutes. "I've heard your story; ye've heard mine. My offer's still open, but it won't be open much longer."

Miss Perkins was seated.

"And what would my duties be?"

"Ye've asked me that once already."

"I suppose I should be expected to take part in conspiracies. Crimes with violence. And so on."

"Ye've got quite a crazy notion of me."

At that moment, for Harriet, Lord Furber had the wistful aspect of a child, conscious of having been naughty and trying without much hope of success to defend itself. He seemed absurd, touching, kissable, and pathetically unlike the legend of the London Titan. She was almost inclined to take his side against his wife, her old crony, Maidie, Lady Furber. "What he says is true," she thought. "He's bored—and so am I. That's why we're both restless, and why we're both going wrong."

"Still," she said judicially. "I've been the witness of one crime myself, and a victim of it, too. At any rate it would be a crime in England."

"The Sutherland business!" his lordship exclaimed in a fierce tone. "It wouldn't be a crime either in England or anywhere else. I didn't bring the fellow on

75

board. And I haven't kept him on board. If he chooses to stay after other folks go, that's his look-out. I couldn't be expected to hang about the Bay of Naples till he's ready to go ashore. People who deliberately flirt in engine-rooms of sea-going yachts have darned well got to accept the consequences. And I could say a lot more for meself. Supposing I accused you and Sutherland of being stowaways? What about that?"

He glanced at her with positive ferocity in his gleaming eyes, and then suddenly he was the erring child again.

"I don't care what you say," Harriet persisted. "You've abducted Mr. Sutherland, and well you know it."

"Now listen here, miss. Why can't women ever stick to the point? Are you going to take on the job I offer ye or aren't ye? Yes or no. There's no compulsion."

"It isn't true!" Harriet burst out in the most surprising manner.

"What isn't?"

"You! Me! This yacht! This night! Mr. Sutherland!" The fact was that she had suddenly awakened to the wonder of existence and could scarcely believe that she was not in a dream.

"It's all a bit of a lark, isn't it?" said Lord Furber in a lower voice, but brightening sympathetically.

"He understands," thought she. "And there are moments when he isn't bored—nor me, either." And aloud she said, benevolently: "I'll give my answer tomorrow morning—and not before."

He hesitated, as if undecided whether to smack her or to kneel at her feet.

"All right. Let's take a stroll on deck. It's devilish hot down here."

"Not hotter than I can stand," said Harriet.

"I was thinking of meself."

She rose, and impatiently he flung her wrap on her shoulders.

"You haven't told me about Mrs. Bumption," she said.

He grinned.

"Just had a rare fine example of Mrs. B. What d'ye think she wanted me for? It seems Mr. Sutherland has gone to bed in his cabin after ordering various drinks which they couldn't supply. She told Bumption that I ought to know about it as she hadn't received orders from me about Sutherland. Fact is, I never did give any orders about Sutherland, and it didn't occur to me that he'd go to bed. I was waiting for him to ask for me and kick up a row. Bumption, for once in a way, defied his wife. Swore he wouldn't disturb me for anything—after I'd said I wasn't to be disturbed. So she decided to disturb me herself. Said she didn't like strangers going to bed in this yacht without her getting instructions from me about them. Said she'd always supposed she was in charge of all domestic arrangements and if she wasn't she'd prefer to give notice and Bumption would give notice, too. I had to soothe her. Such is my life on board, miss. Don't ye think I need a lady-secretary?"

Miss Perkins laughed a long, quiet laugh, which died very slowly.

"So, Mr. Sutherland has gone to bed." The laugh was resuscitated.

"That's the news of the night."

"Without seeing me again! What a shame!"

"Not so much in love with ye as ye thought," said Lord Furber like lightning. There was malice in his tone. "Shaken ye up, his going to bed without consulting ye, miss!"

"And hasn't it shaken *you* up? He's a great man, Mr. Sutherland is, and I adore him. His going to bed is the most marvellous example of self-control I ever heard of. The poor man's abducted, and he just goes quietly off to bed, while you're waiting for him to come to you and make a row. Don't you wish you'd never got him on board? Aren't you afraid of him?"

"There's only two people in this yacht that I'm afraid of."

"Who are they?"

"Mrs. Bumption."

"And——"

"Come *along!* They say it's a grand night on deck."

Harriet Perkins followed the wistful, naughty child, who was now gloomy and now gay, who wanted her and didn't want her, and who was ready either to do her a violence or embrace her feet.

It was indeed a grand night. Moonshine on a smooth sea. Shore lights twinkling. The jagged shape of Capri on the port quarter. Astern the flank of huge Vesuvius no longer lighted by its electric string, rising dimly against the dark velvet sky. Vibration of twin propellers. Warm freshness of the Mediterranean evening, and yet not a breath of air—for the wind, the zephyr, was dead aft.

The pair walked side by side along the deck, past the long range of the deck-houses. The tramping of the navigating officers unseen on the bridge could be faintly heard.

THE SNORE

Suddenly came a new sound through the open window of a cabin. Mr. Sutherland's cabin. A steady, not unmusical snore. Mr. Sutherland's snore. Mr. Sutherland, like many persons considering themselves to be the martyrized victims of insomnia, had been mistaken as to his entire wakefulness. There was something at once grotesque, comic and formidable about the noise of that snore from the nose of Harriet's admirer. Harriet tried to master her sensations, failed, screamed, and finally yielded herself, not without hysteria, to something which she had thought would be laughter but which seemed, even to her own ears, most curiously to resemble sobbing.

CHAPTER XI

CHIVALRY

MR. SUTHERLAND, in his scarlet dressing-gown over white pyjamas, framed by an oblong of light in the doorway of the cabin, looked like the devil. He also felt like the devil (not being yet entirely awake). He saw the hand of some sinister male on Harriet's shoulder; for Lord Furber, fearing that Harriet, in reaction from the stress of the scene below, had lost control of her feminine nerves, had essayed to steady her by a firm masculine touch.

The spectacle presented itself to Mr. Sutherland in such a manner as to raise instincts which, unsuspected by himself, had descended to him through perhaps hundreds of years of ancestry. Mr. Sutherland was transported by the misunderstood spectacle back into the age of chivalry.

All of a sudden he became uplifted, wildly happy, reckless, in the overwhelming consciousness of a great mission in life. In the thousandth part of a second he recalled his athletic youth, and how he used to keep fit for rowing by daily bouts with the gloves against a hanging football or a fellow-oarsman. He jumped forward and, clenching his fists, hit Lord Furber violently under the point of the chin. Lord Furber, quite unprepared for the onset, was not employing his feet properly; he had the wrong stance, and he fell backwards; his head caught the end of a brass belaying pin which transfixed the yacht's rail, and the next moment he lay a crumpled, moveless object on the deck, in the full light from Mr. Sutherland's cabin.

"He loves me!" thought Harriet Perkins, triumphantly reassured. "He may have gone to bed and to sleep without asking my permission, but he loves me and he is magnificent." And she, too, was uplifted and wildly happy.

For a space both of them forgot Lord Furber.

"What was the fellow trying to do?" Septimius demanded, breathing rather hard.

"Nothing," said Harriet feebly.

"But you screamed and he had his hand on you!" Septimius drew his dressing-gown about him.

"I—I think he must have thought I was going to faint or something, and he wanted to soothe me."

"You're sure you aren't——"

"Quite, thanks. But I'm very much obliged to you all the same."

She was giving another brief sound between a laugh and a cry, but stopped herself.

"But—but," exclaimed Septimius, bending down a little and coldly gazing at his victim. "Surely this isn't Lord Furber? This can't be Lord Furber?"

"Yes, it is."

"What's *he* doing on board this yacht?"

"It's his yacht," Harriet answered. "Only that! It isn't Count Veruda's yacht at all. It's Lord Furber's!"

"All this seems to me somewhat unusual," observed Septimius placidly. The instincts of the primitive age were withdrawing again into his subconscious self, and he was ceasing to be a knightly defender of dames.

"Now for goodness' sake, please don't be calm," said Harriet sharply. "Something must be done. If you've killed him——!"

"If I've killed him, of course, there may be a certain amount of trouble," replied Septimius. He spoke grimly, not without a mild satisfaction. It occurred to him that his right arm had been actuated partly by an obscure, unrealized desire to revenge himself, upon anybody who chanced to be about, for having been abducted in the yacht.

The deck was silent. Not an officer, not a seaman in sight. Not a sound save the faint reverberation of footsteps on the bridge above. The woman's scream, the man's fall, had not been heard. The ends of the deck were dark. Only in the middle thereof was the sheet of light from Mr. Sutherland's cabin crudely displaying the stricken baron and a bending figure on either side of him. The faces of the two watchers were as pale as that of the victim.

"Anyway, I seem to have knocked him out for the time being. I'd no idea I could do it. But he's breathing."

"Are you sure?"

"Yes. Why did you scream?"

"It was your funny snoring."

"I never snore," Septimius protested frigidly.

"Don't you think you'd better do something, Mr. Sutherland?"

"Yes. But what am I to do? I haven't the least idea. He'll come round soon. Perhaps we'd better put him on my bed. Will you take his legs?"

In a moment, the body of Lord Furber was lying on

Mr. Sutherland's disordered bed. Neither Septimius nor Harriet noticed a faint trail of red spots on the deck and the floor of the cabin.

"You run and fetch someone," Mr. Sutherland suggested.

Harriet, herself a little breathless, disappeared to obey. Septimius looked inquiringly at the white, senseless countenance and inert hands. It seemed to him that now he was on the very edge of understanding why he and his luggage had been carried off in the yacht. The name of Count Veruda conveyed naught to him, but the name of Furber, a terrific adventurer in the City of finance, inspired him with all sorts of fearsome notions. Hearing quick footsteps on the deck, he shut and bolted the cabin door.

"One minute," he called out when Harriet tried and failed to open the door. "One moment, *if* you please."

He had taken off the red dressing-gown, and was summarily putting on a suit over the pyjamas. The fact was that he could not bear any longer to be seen in a dressing-gown. His self-consciousness was stronger than his humanity. The baron might expire from neglect, but Mr. Sutherland's modesty must be preserved from further outrage. He hastily tied a muffler round his neck and opened the door, praying that he did not look too much like a burglar or a worse criminal.

Bumption, the chief steward, stout and impassive, followed Miss Perkins into the cabin.

"Lord Furber has apparently had a fall and fainted," Mr. Sutherland blandly explained.

Bumption glanced at his master and instantly his fat cheek blanched. A spot of blood was showing on

83

the pillow to the left of the baron's head, and it was spreading, spreading. Bumption ran away. In a few moments Mrs. Bumption sourly appeared. Bumption stood in the doorway behind her. Mrs. Bumption weighed as much as any two other persons present. Her ageing features had for years past been fixed in a permanent expression of hostility to all mankind and all mundane phenomena, for owing to a slothful liver she flourished on grievances, which she would create faster than kind fate could destroy. Even Bumption's perverse passion for her was a grievance.

"What's this, miss? What *is* this, sir?" she asked.

"His lordship's had a fall. He fell on the back of his head. Cut himself on something." This from a laconic Septimius.

"His lordship must have fallen on his chin too," said Mrs. Bumption acidly.

The baron's chin showed an excrescence, which seemed magically to grow larger and darker every second. Mrs. Bumption, who had resource, took a spent match from the ash-tray by the bedside and with it tickled the baron's nostrils. The baron unclosed his eyes and beheld Mrs. Bumption's stupendous bust heaving above him.

"Good Lord!" he murmured faintly, and closed his eyes again.

CHAPTER XII

THE SKIPPER

"I'M THE captain of the ship," said Captain Joseph Slapser. "I hold a master-mariner's certificate. I am responsible, and what I say goes. And I don't care who it is. There's me and there's the crew, and all the rest is passengers. The owner is a passenger, and I put him down as a passenger in the ship's papers as I gave to the harbour-master at Naples. 'The Right Hon. Lord Furber' I put, and his lordship knows it. There isn't any such person as an owner in sea-law when a ship's at sea, and no such persons as owner's friends. There's me and the crew—and passengers."

"Quite," agreed Mr. Sutherland.

"It's something chronic," said Captain Joseph Slapser, complainingly.

The skipper was a grandly dressed, solid, ruddy figure with blue eyes, a firm chin, and a defiant expression which was designed to cover the fact that he was not what gentlemen call a gentleman. He came from the same class as his owner, and his owner was a gentleman while he himself mysteriously was not. He possessed ample knowledge, skill, and experience to navigate a ship through all the seas of the world, and yet he felt inferior to Mr. Sutherland.

He had been summoned to Mr. Sutherland's cabin by the chief steward, at the command of Mrs.

Bumption, and he was trying to take charge of a situation which he did not in the least understand. His remarks had followed upon the remarks of at least two people whose tongues had betrayed an imperfect appreciation of what sort of an almighty a captain is when you come down to brass tacks; people who had apparently failed to comprehend that a private yacht is merely a ship in the eyes of the Board of Trade.

The brilliantly lit cabin, with its sculptured woods, its engravings, and its furniture and upholstery, was thronged: three portly beings, and two slim ones—the latter Septimius and Harriet. Mrs. Bumption alone was not nervous. Mr. Bumption was but little nervous because, in the presence of his wife and mistress, he always felt eased of all responsibility. Mr. Sutherland was nervous and admirably concealed his nervousness. Harriet Perkins was rather agreeably nervous, and advertised the fact to the perspicacious by a too light demeanour. The most nervous of all was the Captain, and the least successful in hiding his nerves. The Captain would have preferred a gale and a lee-shore to the present quandary.

And on the bed lay the baron, his head bandaged, his chin glistening with Pond's Extract, his eyes closed, his face very pale, his hair awry, his suit disarranged, his collar and necktie unfastened: utterly inscrutable.

"I'm not a passenger," said Mrs. Bumption, glaring fearlessly at the Captain.

"I didn't say you were. You're crew . . . And I'm captain." The skipper glanced aside momentarily at the baron, who had an unfortunate habit of addressing him as "Joe" in the hearing of subordinates.

It was as if he were saying to the helpless baron:
"Put that in your pipe and smoke it; and give me the
sack afterwards if you like."

Suddenly the Captain sprang to the doorway, where
two men, a steward and a deck-hand, were strenuously eavesdropping.

"You get forrard," said the Captain to the deck-
hand, and to the steward: "You get aft. And hurry."

No need there of any explanations concerning his
precise status on board. They hurried, and their
obedient haste gave confidence to the Captain.

When he turned his face again towards the interior
of the cabin, Harriet Perkins was whispering to Mr.
Sutherland. In the circumstances, Captain Slapser
objected to any whispering, but he did not quite see
how his powers could prevent it.

"Don't you think this room ought to be cleared or
Lord Furber removed? The place is really too full for
an ill man. Couldn't you say something?" said Miss
Perkins to Mr. Sutherland, in a whisper which even
in that crisis was delicious to his ears.

Miss Perkins was steadily getting less nervous, for
she perceived that her rôle was that of observer only,
and her chief sensation was curiosity to see how her
two antagonistic heroes, the baron and Septimius,
would conduct themselves in the crisis. She felt as
though she were reading a serial story in which she
was a character to whom no harm could possibly
arrive.

Thus challenged, Mr. Sutherland was bound to
play the man, and in spite of danger, squarely con-
front the testy skipper.

"It seems to me," said he blandly to Captain
Slapser. "It seems to me that Lord Furber ought to

be removed to his own apartments. What do you say, Captain?"

"I say, better leave his lordship be," the Captain replied curtly. "We don't know how bad he is: and so long as he looks comfortable——"

Miss Perkins watched expectantly her placid hero.

"I'm a little surprised you've no doctor on board a yacht like this," said Septimius.

"You may be," the Captain retorted. "Nobody wants to stop you from being surprised, sir." The "sir" slipped from him unawares, from habit, and he regretted but could not recall it. "I've nothing to do with doctors. If an owner chooses to carry a doctor, that's all right. If he don't there's no call for any *visitors* to complain."

"Merely a remark, sir."

"Nor remark, sir. Some folks may wish before they're much older that we did have a doctor aboard. As I said, we don't know how bad his lordship is. You and this young lady say you saw him fall, but I never noticed his lordship was one for falling about all over the decks, even in a sea, which there isn't. If I'm asked my opinion by the police or a British Consul I should say he'd had an upper cut on the jaw before he fell. I don't mind telling you as I've seen a man drop in the ring from an upper cut and never speak again, though he *did* open one eye once. And it was at San Francisco that was, and I knew his widow."

"Very sad! Very sad!" murmured Mr. Sutherland. "I've never seen a prize-fight, but I've often boxed."

"And I'm not surprised to hear it," observed the Captain, his voice charged with sinister significance.

"You made a mistake there, Seppie," Harriet inwardly reflected.

"I said too much," thought Mr. Sutherland, and remarked aloud: "Then if his lordship isn't to be moved, I venture the opinion that this cabin ought to be cleared." He glanced at Harriet for approval of the moral courage which he was exercising at her behest.

She nodded to him. He was content.

"You're right," said Captain Slapser. "And I'll thank you to go first. And you too, miss," he added, to Harriet Perkins. "I don't know who you are, either of you. His lordship never said anything to me about you."

"No. Nor to me," said Mrs. Bumption severely. "At least, not till I asked him—about Mr. Sutherland, if that's the gentleman's name. And he didn't say much then."

"I'll thank you," the Captain proceeded, "to go at once to the purser's office, you and your lady friend, and tell him who you are and everything, so as he can enter you in the ship's papers. And I don't want any hanky-panky. The purser will have to see your passports."

"Certainly," said Septimius.

"My passport's at Naples in the Hotel Splendide," said Harriet.

"Well," said the Captain, "well, miss, you can tell that tale to the next British Consul we see. I shall ask him to come on board specially. No one's going ashore off this ship till I know where I am. And if I have to call in the Italian police, I shall call 'em in, and that's all there is to it. What! This young lady has a long interview with his lordship, and this Mr. Sutherland is supposed to be asleep in his cabin. And the next thing as happens is we find his lordship knocked senseless, and blood all over the place; and then I'm told he slipped and fell down!" Captain Slapser grunted—the grunt of a man who has no doubt at all of his capacity to put two and two together.

At this juncture Lord Furber opened both eyes, as if to suggest to the company that his presence in the cabin was being rather unduly ignored. The gesture drew general attention and caused excitement. Captain Slapser and Mrs. Bumption seemed at once to feel a certain loss of prestige at the awakening of supreme authority. Mr. Bumption stood by to give aid to the sufferer, and was made happy by a somewhat plaintive smile from his partner and tyrant. Harriet Perkins was uplifted. Mr. Sutherland saw hope, and glanced warningly at the Captain.

"Furber, my old friend," Mr. Sutherland murmured encouragingly to the sufferer, though he had never been more than an acquaintance of the powerful millionaire.

The words frightened Captain Slapser. They produced, however, no effect whatever on the baron. The baron continued to stare at the ceiling, seemingly quite oblivious of all other phenomena.

"Furber, my friend."

No response.

"Can I get you anything, my lord?" asked the portly Bumption, in a tone affectionate and devoted.

A pause, in which hearts almost ceased to beat in intense expectancy. The vibration of the propellers filled the cabin.

"Me feyther's dead—died yesterday," said Lord Furber, weakly, in a very marked Midland accent. But there was no other sign of delirium. The eyes closed again.

After a long time Mrs. Bumption, controlling a sob, muttered:

"They lose their memory—and they never get it back no more. There's funny things happen in the brain. That I do know . . . His lordship's father's been dead five and twenty years and more . . . Second childhood."

"You heard me," Captain Slapser addressed Septimius shortly

Septimius turned submissively towards the door of the cabin. In the unsearchable recesses of his soul he was alarmed for himself. And also the strangeness of existence terribly weighed him down. In an hour his past life, so sedate and regular, had receded so far from him that it seemed to be the life of another man. Even the scene in the engine-room was slipping beneath the horizon of experience.

A sudden blow! One dart of his fist! And the whole world had been changed. An hour ago a policeman was a benevolent official who held up a traffic-stopping hand in order to escort perambulators and nursemaids from pavement to pavement. An hour ago a prison was an enclosed place which ought to be inspected and reformed of its abuses. But what now was a policeman and what a prison? In vain he protested to himself that his apprehensions were ridiculously devoid of foundation. The most revolting things were constantly happening in courts of justice. Extradition! Imagine the humiliation of being the subject of extradition. Imagine his name streaming across the front page of Lord Furber's newspapers! Imagine himself being visited in a cell by his wife and daughters! Where would he look when they came? How could he carry it off?

He had given the blow, and he would be obliged to admit that he had given the blow. And why had he given it? Why had he, formerly a great master of self-control, yielded so swiftly to the madness of an impulse? The answer was plain: the magical effect upon him of the personality of Miss Harriet Perkins! Toils of a woman! The awful potentialities of fundamental instinct made him dizzy. And perhaps the worst was that he was not in those acutely anxious moments cutting a good figure in the sight of the woman. True, it was solely for the sake of the woman that he had so rashly tempted fate; but that could make no difference. At best the woman could only pity him; she could not respect him. And to be pitied, especially by her, was loathsome to his sensitive pride. Perhaps it was a desire to force her to admire him that led to his final remark to the Captain:

"Would you mind telling me what your sailing orders are?" he asked, in a voice superbly casual.

"My sailing orders are my affair," replied the Captain.

Mr. Sutherland, picking up a cap, went out, with a parting glance at Harriet to follow him.

The Captain said:

"You'll stop here for a bit, miss, if it's all the same to you." Evidently the Captain in his astuteness was determined that those two should not plot together on the way to the purser's office. "Mr. Bumption, show this gentleman where Mr. Antinope's room is."

Harriet Perkins, for her part, was not pitying Septimius Sutherland, and his effort to force her admiration was absurdly unnecessary. She was admiring him with all her heart—for his modesty, sangfroid, self-control, and his scrupulous respect for the authority of Captain Slapser. With the directness and the ruthless realism characteristic of a woman, and especially of a young woman, she regarded the Captain as a vain, preposterous, and bloated jack-in-office whom Septimius, had he chosen, might have morally smashed to pieces with about twenty quiet words. And she remembered every instant with pride that the whole trouble had arisen through Mr. Sutherland's mad passion for herself. She beatifically saw Harriet Perkins as the inspirer of grave men to romantic and terrible deeds. Yet she refused to credit that Mr. Sutherland's deed was terrible or might have disastrous consequences. But, if it was to have disastrous consequences, she was inclined to think that she would not care.

Her pity descended upon Lord Furber. This mighty legend of a man, whose marvellous success in life he had himself indirectly admitted to her to be after all nothing but a gigantic failure, seemed now to be almost intolerably pathetic. So much so, that if she had continued to look at him as he lay on the bed she might well have shed tears! He was like a child with a toy, and his toy was the earth, and he was tired of his toy and wanted a fresh one and couldn't find a fresh one. He was also strangely like herself. Yet she was his mother, and she had impulses both to chastise him and to pet him.

She gazed challengingly at the Captain, and walked out of the cabin to the deck. The Captain would have given much to prevent this disobedience to his commands, but at the moment could think of no method of doing so. He limited the expression of his feelings to a grunt. Hearing the grunt behind her,

Harriet turned back into the cabin and, smiling very agreeably, said to the Captain:

"Captain!"

"Miss?"

"You may grunt."

The permission to the Captain being gracefully accorded, she finally quitted the cabin.

The night was persistently exquisite in its balmy and moonlit freshness. The zephyr, now on the quarter, gently flirted with Harriet's cheek. The great yacht urged its solitary way through the calm water, masterless, without a purpose, at the mercy of a preposterous jack-in-office who was losing his head because there was no supreme authority to call him Joe and rule him. Harriet felt sorry even for the yacht. And sorriest of all, most disquieted, for herself.

"I've simply nothing to wear to-morrow morning!" she exclaimed tragically in her soul.

CHAPTER XIII

ON THE RAIL

HARRIET PERKINS, leaning over the rail, heard cautious footsteps on the after stairway leading to the boat-deck. There were four stairways of communication between the promenade deck and the boat-deck, two forward and two aft. She turned; the nearest stairway rose almost directly behind her. Mr. Septimius Sutherland was descending it; she recognized him in the gloom by his self-possessed (some would have said self-complacent), slightly perky carriage. As he was evidently trying to achieve noiselessness, she gave no greeting. Indeed, she resumed her original position at the rail and stared into the water.

Mr. Sutherland came silently to her side, and his left elbow on the rail touched her right elbow on the rail. The dark water slid swirling far under them, apparently at a tremendous speed, to form the wake of the vessel; its swift, smooth motion had a magnetic quality to hold human vision in a spell. No reason why eyes gazing at it should not gaze at it for ever and ever!

The girl heard a pleasant murmur in her ear:

"You should put on your wrap. The temperature is falling."

The olive-coloured wrap was wound round her arm. She thought teasingly, yet benevolently:

"'Temperature is falling'! How like him! Why

couldn't he say, 'It's getting a bit coldish'? Silly old dear!"

His elbow left hers, and the next moment the green wrap was unwound from her arm. She liked the untidiness of the muffler about his neck. It seemed to her to be much more romantic than a collar and tie. The cap helped the romance of the muffler. To reward his attentiveness she snuggled her shoulders into the cloak as he settled it around them.

"I understood the Bumption had marched you off to the purser," she murmured.

"So he had. But the Antinope was not in his right place, and the Bumption went off to look for him. So I decided I would look for him myself." The words of Mr. Sutherland were spoken so low as scarcely to be distinguishable, but Harriet caught them.

Mr. Sutherland continued:

"I thought I'd look for him in the cabin of the wireless operator." He emphasized the last two words, and glanced at her.

Harriet started.

"I see."

And she did see what Mr. Sutherland meant her to see. She saw also that her admiration for Mr. Sutherland's scrupulous respect for the authority of Captain Slapser had been premature. Mr. Sutherland's respect for the Captain's authority was an illusion, and now Harriet admitted that if it had not been an illusion it would have been ridiculous. Mr. Sutherland was living up to the reputation which she had made for him in her own mind.

"And did you see the wireless operator?"

"Yes. But he wouldn't do anything."

"What did you ask him to do?"

"Send a message—to Rome."

"And he wouldn't."

"Said he couldn't without the orders of either the skipper or his lordship."

"You told him Lord Furber was—ill."

"Oh! He knew about Lord Furber."

"Seems to me they're all banded together, against us," Harriet whispered.

"Yes."

"But what's the good of sending a message? What sort of a message should you have sent?"

"Well, I hadn't decided. I thought I'd find out first if a message could be sent at all. Then you and I'd have had a chat."

"D'you know where we're going to?"

"Genoa, I should imagine. By the moon we should be moving in a north-westerly direction. That lighthouse there behind ought to be on the island of Ischia. Hullo! Hullo!" These last words a little louder.

About a couple of hundred yards off, on the bow, a huge curved form rose out of the flat sea, and the moonlight glinted upon points of metal. It might have been some marine monster; but marine monsters do not usually carry a long gun on their backs.

"Submarine," said Mr. Sutherland casually. "Night manœuvres. Probably Italian. A near shave, that! If she'd come up under us . . . But she couldn't have done. They have instruments, you know. So it's all right."

He did not know that submarines had "instruments," but he thought that they should have, and the idea soothed the imagination and also gave him an air of being immensely informed.

The submarine produced an eerie and intimidating effect on the watchers. It ran level with the yacht for a time, showing no lights; then slackened speed, dropped astern, and disappeared into the depths.

"Pity we couldn't communicate with her," said Harriet.

"No use! What could we have done if we did communicate with her? Submarines don't carry a doctor."

"No. But what fun!"

"Ah!... Fun... Yes." There was a certain reserve in Mr. Sutherland's tone.

Harriet said:

"You don't really think there is anything seriously wrong with Lord Furber, do you? I mean, really." She had now turned herself into an ingenuous, trustful girl appealing with confidence to the fount of all wisdom. She was atoning for her levity, in a manner to bewitch.

"I hope not. I think not. I'm almost sure not. But you can't be *quite* sure. There might be some lesion of the brain—you never know."

"However, it's not a bit probable," said Harriet, determined to be optimistic.

"No. But it's a bit possible," said Septimius solemnly, determined to be realistic. He shed gloom around him. "Naturally I'm very sorry about it all. I oughtn't to have done it. I ought to have reflected." He vaguely knew that he was blaming himself in order that he might hear her take up his defence.

"I don't think you were to blame at all," said Harriet in a most serious, solacing whisper. "In fact, it was simply splendid of you. Simply splendid! And of course you didn't realize your own strength."

These words were surpassingly sweet to Septimius; and, further, Harriet found surpassing pleasure in offering them to Septimius.

"Well, to be frank," said he. "I did not realize my own strength."

"Strong men never do," said she.

They were both uplifted into a strange bliss. Mr. Sutherland's wife and adult daughters existed no more for him. He had again that grand sensation of recklessness—so intoxicating to a middle-aged gentleman with thin lips and fixed habits.

"Besides," said Harriet, "Lord Furber brought it on himself."

"Quite. If I hadn't been kept on board——"

"Tell me," Harriet spoke very confidentially and persuasively; "why did he keep you on board? I know why I was kept on board."

"Why?"

"Because they couldn't have warned me the launches were going off without warning you as well. But *you?* Why? You must have some idea."

"I haven't," said Septimius. "Honestly. And if you'll excuse me saying so, that's not the immediate point. To my mind the point is that something ought to be done about Lord Furber."

"Well, the only way to get anything done is to go and tell the Captain that he mustn't do it. He's in such a state of dithering conceit that he'll only take suggestions by contraries."

"How well you understand people!" murmured Mr. Sutherland. His tone seemed to imply: "And how wonderfully, how nicely, you've understood me."

"I think you ought to speak to the Captain," said Harriet. "I'll go with you if you like. If we insist on his making straight for Genoa as quick as he can, he'll be sure to put back to Naples; which would be the best thing. We know the English doctor at Naples—and all my frocks are there, too."

"Excellent!" agreed Septimius. "I fancy we can deal with the Captain—prick his balloon, eh?"

Septimius stood upright in his sudden decision, and simultaneously felt a touch in the small of his back. He swung round. Harriet swung round also. A tall man faced them. Felt slippers had enabled the fellow to come right up to them soundlessly.

"I'm the purser," said the man to Septimius. "Mr. Antinope my name is. Captain's sent me. I'll thank you to come along at once."

No "sir"! Neither the formulæ nor the accent of respect.

Septimius raised his hand, whereupon with great swiftness Mr. Antinope seized the wrist in a terrible, flesh-lacerating clutch.

"No more o' that," said Mr. Antinope briefly.

Septimius could not move.

Harriet laid a restraining finger on Mr. Sutherland's right arm.

"Don't hurt him," she appealed to Mr. Sutherland. "Remember you didn't realize your strength. We don't want more trouble."

"Very well," said Septimius. He was ashamed of his duplicity; but he had to say just those two words, and in just that tone of lofty forbearance. And to Mr. Antinope coldly: "I am quite ready to come along."

The frightful torturing vice which Mr. Antinope carried at the end of his arm loosed its grip.

CHAPTER XIV

ON THE FLOOR

WITHOUT the society of Septimius, Miss Harriet Perkins felt lorn and chilly. But she also felt more adventurous. In a moment she decided to do some prospecting.

The majestic, curving, double companion or stairway leading down from the promenade-deck to the main-deck was lit by one tiny blue electric star. Beyond it, in the lounge which separated the dining-saloon from the owner's state sitting-room, were no lights whatever. Harriet remembered the situation of the switches used by Mr. Tunnicliff, and used them, revealing the closed door of the state sitting-room. She opened the door, and beheld the scene of her exciting interview with Lord Furber brightly illuminated. Little Mr. Tunnicliff was seated solitary therein, examining a very large sea-chart. He jumped up, blushing. The chart sank on to the carpet, waving as it fell.

"All alone!" she said, smiling.

"Yes," said Mr. Tunnicliff, modestly.

She suspected that she had put him into a delicious confusion.

"I came down because I was beginning to feel the cold," said she. "Whose is that fur coat?" She pointed to a garment that lay on a sofa at the end of the room.

"Lord Furber's. It's always left there for him every evening in case he should want it."

Suddenly, perceiving a crushed cigarette-end on the carpet, Harriet knelt over it.

"Have you dropped something? Can I find it for you?"

Mr. Tunnicliff was kneeling by her side.

"No," she said. "I was only looking at the hole I burnt in the carpet to-night. Quite a good hole, isn't it? The carpet will never be the same again. But his lordship didn't seem to mind. In fact, he told me I hadn't burnt any hole. Very polite of him, wasn't it?"

"Yes, it was."

"But he always is polite, isn't he?"

Her eyes smiled. Mr. Tunnicliff's shining eyes smiled in response. He blushed again; but said naught. There he was, kneeling close by her, feeling very self-conscious, yet somehow content; but not daring to rise till she rose. They were like two domestic animals amicably and curiously surveying each other.

"How is Lord Furber now? Have you heard?" Harriet demanded.

"About the same. It seems he's quite conscious. At least he isn't unconscious. Only he doesn't hear anything, or at least he doesn't understand anything, and he can't speak."

"Dazed?"

"Yes."

"Very strange, isn't it?"

"Yes, it is." Mr. Tunnicliff coughed.

"What's that chart thing?"

Harriet padded along on her knees towards the

chart, and Mr. Tunnicliff did likewise. They pored together over the chart.

"You see, it's the environs of Naples," Mr. Tunnicliff explained. "The coast, that is, and the islands."

"What are all those funny figures in the sea?"

"They're the depths, in fathoms."

"Do you know which way we're going?"

"To Genoa. Genoa isn't on this chart, of course. I think the Captain didn't like the Precida channel to-night. He's gone outside all the islands. I don't know why."

This was Mr. Tunnicliff's first volunteered remark. The emission of it seemed to give him ease and a slight confidence in himself; it certainly increased his already considerable charm in the eyes of Miss Perkins.

"Poor boy!" she thought. "I mustn't be too nice to him. It would be cruelty to children. He ought to be in his cradle." Still, she did not get up from the floor.

"Where's Rome?" she asked; her finger wandered over the chart.

"Rome's not on this sheet, either. There aren't any more sheets down here."

"Oh! But I did so want to see Rome."

"There's an atlas here," Mr. Tunnicliff said. "If that would do."

She nodded.

"Shall we look at it?"

Now the atlas was the lowest of a pile of volumes on the floor, and Mr. Tunnicliff padded on his knees towards it, and Miss Perkins padded in his wake. It was a large and heavy atlas, clearly meant to be consulted on floors by students on their hands and knees. Mr. Tunnicliff found Southern Italy and then Rome, and he pointed to the mouth of the Tiber and to the town of Ostia, and said that Ostia was the ancient port for Rome.

"What a lot you know!" observed Harriet teasingly. "Why do you look at me like that?"

Their heads were adjacent.

"I was only thinking how nice it would be for me to kiss you," said Mr. Tunnicliff, astonishingly.

Harriet had to collect herself.

"You rude little boy!" she protested, but in a tone to indicate that in her opinion they had been playing together on the carpet of a nursery.

"Well," said Mr. Tunnicliff, jumping up in sudden resentment, his cheeks now a deep crimson. "If you want to know, I'm older than I look by a long chalk, and as for little, I'm quite the average height. You're tall—for a girl."

Harriet, twisting herself, sat on the floor and raised her glance to him; but he would not meet it.

"That makes it all the worse," said she. "If you're so fearfully old, you're old enough to know better."

"You asked me why I looked at you and I told you," he sulked, his full lower lip drooping. "If you hadn't asked me I shouldn't have said anything. And now I've said it, you don't like it—or at least you pretend you don't. That's a girl all over, that is. You're all the same." He was walking about, hands in pockets.

"And here I was thinking butter wouldn't melt in your mouth!" observed Harriet, leaning back and supporting herself on her arms stretched out behind. "I suppose you've got Spanish blood in your veins."

"I haven't. I'm just as English as you are."

"Perhaps Don Juan came once to England," said Harriet.

"I daresay you think you're very funny."

"I do. But not half as funny as you are." She laughed outright.

"Oh go to blazes!" Mr. Tunnicliff shockingly exclaimed.

"Mr. Tunnicliff," she said. "I don't mind pointing out what's the matter with you. You've no sense of humour."

"Possibly not," said he, dryly.

"And I wanted you to help me."

Mr. Tunnicliff's manner immediately changed. The drooping lips lifted and he smiled.

"Of course if I can *do* anything——"

"You can, you nice *man!* What's the name of the wireless operator here?"

"Tunnicliff."

"Same as yours."

"He's my cousin. As a matter of fact I got him his job."

"How heavenly you are! Have you a visiting card? If so, just write on it what I tell you, and give it to me. I expect your cousin would do simply anything for you?"

"I'm not so sure," said Mr. Tunnicliff searching his person for a card, which he found. "My cousin's a bit of a Tartar."

"All the better. Now just write this, will you? 'Please do what you can for the bearer, who is in distress.'"

"But are you?"

"Yes. Of course I'm in distress! Would I ask you to write a lie? Aren't we all in trouble, with poor Lord

Furber as he is? Where does he live, your Cossack cousin? Somewhere on the top deck, isn't it?"

"I'll go up with you, if you like."

"No. I shouldn't like. Your temper is too uncertain."

"Oh! All right, all right! Here!"

He vouchsafed the card. Harriet read on it: "The Honourable Luke John Tunnicliff."

"Ah!" she murmured. "Entertaining angels unawares, was I? And now will you officially lend me Lord Furber's fur coat? I'll bring it back, honest Injun."

She got up from the floor, and he obediently endued her into the rich, warm, and not heavy garment.

"How lovely it is!" she murmured, and looked at him. He was assuredly adorable. A baby, naturally, but his eyes honest and incandescent, and what delicate nostrils! As for height, their faces were on a level.

Then in a new tone, she said:

"I think on the whole you may kiss me if you want to."

Mr. Tunnicliff threw his head back.

"No thanks," he said stiffly. "I don't want to now." His face was darkly lowering again.

"Why?" Harriet showed some pique.

"I couldn't kiss any girl for the first time in cold blood," said Mr. Tunnicliff.

"Fish!" Harriet burst out. Then, controlling herself to a gentle irony. "A kiss is nothing."

"Is it!" the youth exclaimed savagely. "You wait —and you'll see."

"You ought to write your memoirs," said teasing Harriet, not so much to daunt Mr. Tunnicliff as to reassure herself by wit. For his kindled eyes were unexampled in her experience.

CHAPTER XV

WIRELESS

HARRIET tapped at the door of the eyric of the wireless operator on the navigating deck of the *Vanguard*. There was no answer. She knocked again. Still no answer. A proper maidenly feeling prevented her from entering without due permission, for she had heard or read somewhere that wireless operators at sea passed the whole of their lives in these mysterious shanties, sleeping and even eating in the same; and she hesitated before an indiscretion. Cousin Tunnicliff, the Tartar, might be asleep, or dead, or otherwise not in a seemly state to receive an unknown lady. As she waited, the inhospitable cabin took on a mysterious and sinister air. Her heart began to beat at the thought of what dread secrets the place might hold. At last she turned the knob and pushed open the door about an inch.

"Come in, d—n you," grunted an Oxford voice menacingly.

The greeting admirably suited Harriet. She said to herself:

"I think I can do something with a man who begins like that."

And she went into a very stuffy interior, preparing a smile for the taming of Tartars.

A young man in shirt sleeves, with a listening

apparatus which resembled a tiara and ear-ornaments clasped about his devoted head, was ensconced
in an arm-chair. His position was peculiar. He leaned
his back against one of the arms of the chair, and his
legs dangled freely over the other. In one hand he
held a ragged paper-bound book, and in the other a
glass of whiskey. From his thin-lipped mouth drooped
a cigarette.

"Good evening," said Harriet, throwing back the
plenteous folds of Lord Furber's fur overcoat.

"I'm sorry," said wireless-operator Tunnicliff,
without the least sign of confusion. He squirmed
himself gracefully out of the chair, dropped the book,
placed the glass very carefully on a table, and removed the cigarette from his mouth. He was tall and
handsome—a contrast to his cousin—and his nostrils
had a delicate curve. It was at once evident that he
was a member of the caste which confers a favour on
the world by condescending to be born.

"Is that your usual form of welcome, Mr. Tunnicliff?" Harriet asked brightly. And she exerted
charm, aware that the masculinity of the vast overcoat would increase rather than diminish her piquancy.

"I apologize. Please take a chair," said the operator coolly, if not coldly. At any rate, he was in full
possession of himself. "Important people," he explained, "important people don't knock. The rest are
a nuisance, and I treat them as such."

"But I'm very important. At least, I think I am,"
said Harriet, sitting down and arranging the coat as
artistically as possible.

"No doubt," the operator agreed calmly. "Do you
object to smoking?"

"Not at all."

"Excuse me," said the operator, searching for a jacket and putting it on in a corner. The flex joining his tiara to the aërial magic followed him as he moved to and fro.

Harriet glanced at the room. It seemed to be divided into a business or professional half and a domestic half. The latter comprised a bed and bedstead the lower part of which was a chest of drawers, a chair, a row of bottles, a rug, a pipe-rack, and (on the walls) two interesting prints cut from old numbers of *La Vie Parisienne*. Nothing was shipshape. Everything was untidy, and nearly everything was shabby. None of the drawers was quite shut, and from several of them portions of attire indecently protruded. The top corner of one of the prints had escaped from its pin and hung over triangularly. The place seemed to be defiantly protesting: "No, I am not pitiful or pathetic. This is the way my owner likes me to be, and those who don't care for it can do the other thing."

"Please look at this," said Harriet, handing the visiting card to an outstretched hand, nicotine-stained and aristocratic. "And my name is Harriet Perkins."

The operator perused the card, dropped it on the table, and resumed the glass of whiskey.

"You'll pardon me just finishing my supper," said he, in the tone not of a question but of a positive assertion, and emptied the glass.

"I adore your little house here," Harriet remarked, in the way of conversation. It was true; she did.

"Oh!"

"It seems so *natural*," said she.

"Yes?"

"And it's so *male*. Women's wigwams are so frightfully prim," Harriet added.

"Are they? Never seen one."

"Are you listening to anything just now?" she asked, indicating his ear-ornaments.

"No. There's nothing at the moment."

"You don't mind if I slip off this overcoat, do you? It's Lord Furber's. Such a warm night, isn't it?" She emerged from the overcoat, and, having shed it, shed also her wrap, and incidentally dropped her handbag. "I mustn't lose that," she said, picking it up. "It contains all my liquid resources. I always carry my traveller's-cheques about with me, and it's a good thing I do. I got left behind on the yacht, you know; sort of innocent stowaway, and if I hadn't had my traveller's-cheques just *think* how I should have been fixed—no clothes and no cheques—when I reached dry land again! I daresay you've heard how the yacht ran off with me."

"I did hear something. Now what's this 'distress' that Luke talks about?"

"It's this," Harriet answered, deploying all her resources to be ingratiating. "I haven't a rag except what you see. And I simply must have some clothes. I was wondering if you'd be so very, very kind as to send a wireless to Count Veruda at the Splendide at Naples asking him to meet the yacht at Ostia with my trunks, and to wireless a reply that he is coming. He could get a maid to pack. Most of the trunks are packed already—I was meaning to leave Naples the day after to-morrow, anyway. You see how tremendously important it is for me . . . Would you?"

She leaned forward with bright eyes and parted

lips, as if thirsting for the nectar of his affirmative response. Far from being a Tartar, he showed himself the quietest, coolest, most matter-of-fact thing imaginable.

"But the yacht isn't calling at Ostia," he said.

"No. Not as at present arranged," she said. "But of course it will call, when you receive the reply from Count Veruda."

"Well, perhaps she would," said the operator. "I should be sorry to contradict you. But it would depend on the wording of the reply."

"Oh! That could be fixed," said Harriet obscurely.

"You aren't the first person to-night to ask me to send off a message." The operator smiled.

"Really!" she exclaimed, as though the information was of immense interest. "And did you?"

"No. I couldn't oblige."

"But you'll oblige me, won't you?"

"I should love to," the operator replied, placidly, unexceptionably, ruthlessly polite. "But I can't. I have my orders. And they are to send nothing out except what I receive from Lord Furber or the Captain."

"But Lord Furber's ill. He's had an accident."

"So I believe," said the operator. "I'm sorry. Very sorry." He spoke with as much emotion as though he had heard the sad news that a great-aunt's favourite Pekinese had been suddenly struck down by ear-complaint.

"That leaves only the Captain. Well, we all know the Captain, and we know he wouldn't understand about the importance of a woman's clothes."

"Probably not. I'm very sorry."

"Do you mean you're sorry about Lord Furber's

illness or about the limitations of the Captain's understanding, or about your not being able to do me this small favour?"

"About everything," said the operator, nobly and with fortitude.

CHAPTER XVI

THE VAMP

HARRIET leaned back in her chair.

"Your orders are quite definite?"

"Quite."

"Well then, of course, you can't disobey them, even for a few minutes and to do a perfectly innocent job for a poor damsel in distress?" Harriet gave him a humorous, detached, easy, friendly smile.

"I can't." The operator spoke with equal detachment.

"Anyhow, there's no harm done, is there?"

"None."

"You'll think me very curious," said Harriet. "But do you wear those things on your ears all the time—for instance—in bed?"

"Not when I'm in bed," the operator replied. He went on as judicially as if he were describing the case of a third person: "You see, it's like this. A ship is not allowed to send wireless messages while she's in port. Our voyages are generally very short. A dozen or twenty hours at the most. Few yachtsmen care for a day and a night at sea, especially owners of big yachts. They use their yachts more as hotels than ships. So when we *do* happen to be at sea, I sit up most of the time, as a rule."

"And read?"

"Yes."

"What's that book you were reading? I'm always frightfully interested in other people's lives." Harriet became eager.

"That's the Tauchnitz volume of Swinburne selections."

"How amusing! And are you an 'Honourable' like your cousin, Luke John?"

"No. How could I be?"

"No. Of course you couldn't be unless both your fathers were peers. And it isn't often two brothers are peers, is it? How stupid of me! But you're the nephew of a peer."

"I'm sorry to say that I'm also the grandson of an earl—through my mother."

"And yet you're a wireless operator."

"Why not? I'm a product of the public school system. My family is poor on both sides. The male paupers of the aristocracy—pardon the word—are educated in such a way that they inevitably leave the university with one of two ideas in their heads. Either they mean to be engineers or to go into the City. There is nothing else. I could imagine few trades more ignoble than the City. Engineering provides at least some pleasant toys for an intelligent child. I specialized in wireless because of its mystery. And here I am. *Voilà!*"

"And Luke John got you the situation?"

"It just happened so." The operator shrugged his shoulders.

"I should have thought you would have hated to serve under the new rich."

"Quite the contrary. I rather enjoy studying the present specimen at close quarters. I'm told he's

marvellous. It's quite conceivable. Nothing is
inconceivable. I admit he has a certain barbaric force.
But he hasn't a notion how to live. He's unhappy
and he's bored. He doesn't know what he's alive
for."

"How true!" Harriet murmured with feeling.

"It's really touching to see how he loves to employ
people who are better bred than himself. There's
Luke and there's me. Not to mention the alleged
Count Veruda. And I am told that one of his shore
secretaries is the daughter of a dead Colonial Gov-
ernor or something of the kind. There may be others.
Yes, our present specimen is an extremely diverting
study. And the point is that he doesn't know it and I
do. I give him credit for wanting to stand well with
me. Also for a dim, savage suspicion that I simply
don't care a gooseberry for him. The fellow is not
without insight."

The operator made a little noise in his nose, apparently to signify a kindly sneer.

Harriet was now beginning to understand why the
other Mr. Tunnicliff had called his cousin a Tartar.
He was a Tartar in a deeper and more terrifying sense
than she could have previously imagined. But at the
same time he was proving himself to be a Tartar
such as she might utilize. She collected her faculties.
She had captured Mr. Sutherland, without an effort.
She had fascinated Lord Furber, without an effort. She
had captured Luke John Tunnicliff, without an
effort—though in a fit of childish temper the youth
had broken loose and was temporarily out of hand.
Surely she could capture the operator. Never had she
consciously used the gifts of heaven to gain any but
the most trifling social ends. She had always scorned

to do so. But she was determined to use them now for an end of importance, and she had the conviction that she would be successful.

She stood up, thrilled. In the rough masculinity of the cabin she felt herself to be endowed with irresistible feminine magic. All men (she had always heard) were alike, at bottom. They would all fall like ninepins before a certain form of attack.

"You're wonderful!" she exclaimed in a voice whose calmness was contradicted by her eyes and attitude. "I don't say it to flatter you." Her voice grew almost stern in its sincerity. "But you really *are* wonderful. Now be honest with me. Don't let's fence and be conventional. Don't *you* think you're rather wonderful?" Exquisitely she seemed to be entreating him for the precious truth.

"Yes, I do," said the operator, quite simply. "That is, by comparison."

"I should have despised you if you hadn't answered just like that," she said quietly and seriously, even harshly. "I should have been terribly disappointed. Good night!" she said with sudden finality.

She picked up the enormous fur overcoat, which now she seemed scarcely able to lift.

"Let me help you."

"I won't trouble to put it on, thanks."

"You'd better. I know this cabin is horribly close. You might easily take a chill. The tramontana is beginning to blow."

"Do you think so?"

"I know it is."

He helped her with the overcoat.

"Good night again," she said over her shoulder.

"Good night."

She had reached the door when she turned back.
"My bag."

The bag was on the floor again. The operator picked it up.

"Thanks so much."

At that instant, as she was accepting the valuable bag at his hands, the whole cabin gave a lurch, and Harriet stumbled.

"She's meeting it," observed the operator, steadying Harriet by a firm touch on the shoulder.

Harriet thought: "The tramontana is helping me." And she blessed the famous wind.

"May I sit down just for a moment?" she asked. "I'm not a very good sailor."

She told this fib with the most appalling convincingness, and unsteadily, with the operator's assistance, sat down.

"Could I have something to drink?" She smiled plaintively.

"There's only one glass."

"One will be enough." She smiled bravely.

"Whiskey."

"Anything."

She drank—and tried to read the operator's mood. He had offered her the sole glass with all the grace that would naturally be expected from an earl's grandson and a baron's nephew.

"I'm better."

"I'm so glad." The operator bent over her attentively.

She sighed with relief and said:

"Mr. Tunnicliff, can you give me a bit of paper and a pencil?"

When he had supplied her want, she wrote a few

words, using the volume of Swinburne as a support for the paper.

"Now Mr. Tunnicliff," she said, "I quite see that it would be wrong of me to urge you any more to send off any message that hasn't been authorized by the powers. And I wouldn't dream of urging you. But you've got no orders against *receiving* messages, have you?"

"Well, of course not, dear lady. I'm here to receive messages."

"Any messages?"

"Certainly There's no choice. I don't quite understand you."

"It's very simple," said Harriet. "Will you receive this message?"

She handed him the paper, upon which he read: "*Captain, Yacht Vanguard. You are requested to anchor at mouth of Tiber and await visit from officials. Benito Mussolini, Palazzo Chigi, Rome.*"

The operator, reading the shaky script, maintained a most meritorious impassivity.

"You wish me to write out this message and hand it to the skipper as though I had got it on the wireless?"

"Yes. Why not?" Harriet looked up at the man with an imploring, inviting smile—a smile surely irresistible.

The operator smiled to match. "Yes," thought Harriet, "he is extraordinarily handsome."

"It is you who are wonderful," he breathed, softly gazing at her. "I'm not flattering you."

She shook her head modestly, but her thought was: "So I am wonderful!" And she did not take her eyes off him. Her glance as it were melted into his.

The cabin gave another slight lurch. She put out a hand to steady herself. The operator held it.

"Of course," said he. "There's no order to prevent me from doing this."

"I've won!" thought Harriet.

"And what a lark!" the operator added.

"Yes, isn't it!" Harriet agreed. "But it's serious, too. You don't know how important it is that I should get off—I mean go ashore—as quickly as possible. I do beg you as a favour—I throw myself on your good nature—I——"

The operator squeezed her hand ever so delicately.

"A strange yacht," he seemed to be musing aloud, "where guests are forbidden to communicate with their friends ashore! . . . Come to look at it!"

"Just so!" Harriet concurred humbly.

"Had you already had this very brilliant idea when you came in to see me?" asked the operator. "Forgive my question. It's all so interesting."

"No! The idea came into my head just now."

Harriet spoke with pleased confidence. The tension of expectation was nearly over. Yes, she had captured the operator as she had captured others. The ancient wise saws of mankind about the power of woman and the weakness of wicked men were profoundly true in their estimate of human nature. She realized triumphantly that through this elegant and untidy youth she was mistress of the movements of the mighty yacht. And she laughed to herself as she waited for his formal surrender to her seductiveness.

CHAPTER XVII

THE MESSAGE

"But, dear lady," said the operator, and his voice was as winsome as Harriet's own, "you're acting rather dangerously, aren't you? I think it my duty to warn you before anything is done that can't be undone."

"How dangerously? Nobody will be able to prove that you haven't had the message. And if any trouble does arise we can always put down the message to some practical joker."

"But the Marconi offices keep records of all the messages they send out."

"I dare say they do. But what about a practical joker on some other ship? If you only knew it, you wireless operators, you've got the control of ships entirely in your hands. A secret league of wireless operators could disorganize the traffic of the whole world for their own ends."

"Quite. I agree. You have imagination. But I wasn't looking at it from my own angle at all. I'm thinking about the yacht. This is no ordinary sort of yacht. I don't mind telling you from my own knowledge that the *Vanguard* is a very peculiar sort of yacht. I could startle you if I chose. Only my lips are sealed—as they say. Anything might happen on this yacht. And remember that the owner has been assaulted and knocked senseless, and that his assailant is on board. If the Captain's instructions

were to go direct to Genoa, you may depend there was
an important reason for it. Your scheme might upset
something that really oughtn't to be upset. And
there's another point. This Mr. Sutherland, the
bruiser, has to be watched. At Ostia he might get
away in spite of the Captain. There's no police force
worth talking about at Ostia. The port of Genoa has
all the most modern developments of policing."

Harriet said easily:

"I'll take all the responsibility. After all, I'm Lord
Furber's secretary."

"You're what?" Astonishment in the tone!

Harriet thought:

"He's holding my hand rather a long time."

She said:

"His lordship's confidential secretary. At least, he
offered me the place only about an hour ago. I didn't
accept it instantly. But, since—since things happened I have accepted it, though of course he doesn't
know. So I *am* Lord Furber's secretary, and while
he's ill I'm entitled to act on his behalf, seeing that
I stand higher than your cousin." She thought she
saw in the operator's demeanour a clear indication
that he was considerably impressed.

The operator replied:

"Forgive me if I say that I doubt if you know
exactly what you want, and anyhow I don't think you
fully realize what you'll be doing if I carry out your
suggestion about this message. For instance, when we
reach the neighbourhood of Ostia, what shall you do
next?"

"I'll decide that when we get to Ostia, dear Mr.
Tunnicliff," Harriet murmured softly. "I admire
your caution. But I repeat, I'll take the responsi-

bility. All I ask just now is your help, and hope you won't refuse it." Her tone said: "I'm perfectly sure you won't refuse it—can't refuse it."

The operator smiled with a chivalry almost tender, and his next words were uttered in a low, enveloping voice that surpassed even the smile.

"Just let me say this," he began. His face approached Harriet's. He paused.

"When will he loose my hand?" thought Harriet. "Really he's going rather far."

She had a horrid fear that she had been carrying seductiveness to excess, with the possibility of very disagreeable consequences to herself. And she wondered what she would do if, as a response to her tactics, the naïve young man attempted to kiss her. In other words, having asked for trouble, she objected to receiving it.

"Just let me say this," the operator recommenced, even more sweetly and ingratiatingly than before. "This Mussolini scheme of yours is merely silly. You can't play about with two-thousand-ton yachts in such a fashion as that. You had a pleasant fancy, but you're letting it run away with you. It's the fancy of a schoolgirl." His hold of her hand tightened. "Still, I don't mind that. I always expect a woman to behave like a woman. Your fancy amuses me. But I'm much more amused at your simplicity. Believe me, you aren't cut out to be a vamp. Here for the last ten minutes you've been absurdly using your absurd feminine charm to get me to do something perfectly absurd that you know I oughtn't to do even if it wasn't absurd. You can't do it. I am just as insensible to fashionable women as I am to Napoleonic multi-millionaires. You leave me cold."

He pressed her arm anew, and continued to coo at her most gently:

"I don't know what you're after with your anchoring off Ostia, and I'm pretty sure you don't know either. What I do know is that you're a simpleton. You imagined you were serving me up on toast for yourself. Well you weren't, my dear young lady . . . Sea-sick indeed! Let me advise you to go and lie down."

During these remarks, his dulcet note and his tender admiring smile had not varied.

Harriet, magnetized for a space by amazement, snatched away her hand at last. More completely than ever did she comprehend the meaning of the word "Tartar" in Luke John Tunnicliff's dictionary.

When she got outside the cabin, and the door was shut behind her, she remained standing sometime to reflect upon her strange situation. A head-wind was blowing freshly; the moon was obscured by clouds, but of diffused light there was sufficient to show the fretted surface of the sea far below. The forms of the great launches and other boats hung suspended and stayed on either side of her. A lamp in the Captain's quarters cast a beam through his starboard windows. The moving and the stationary figures of officers on the high navigating bridge were faintly silhouetted against the dark sky. She could see the mast-head lights overhead. Turning to the left she noticed that a whole galaxy and procession of lights, a few coloured, was overhauling the yacht on the port beam; some liner shifted from the Atlantic to carry tourists on a Mediterranean pleasure-cruise; the huge and formidable affair, magically afloat and urgent in the night, passed the yacht as though she had been standing still and reduced her to a trifle on the ocean. On the starboard beam some distant shore-lights feebly twinkled. In a few minutes, the liner was a mile ahead and fast diminishing to a blur on the horizon.

All was romantic, nocturnal, scarcely believable. But for a mere hazard of existence Harriet would at that moment have been asleep in a hotel-bed amid circumstances completely prosaic. And here she was on a strange vessel, surrounded by people whom she had never before seen, and by inexplicable mysteries, and by perils against which she could not guard. An astounding adventure! A subject for epic poetry.

But she did not feel in the least poetical. She felt very angry with the wireless operator, and still angrier with herself. She had been baffled, humiliated, beaten: and she had invited her fate. What the wireless operator had said about her was odiously true. No! It was untrue and monstrous! Yes, it was too true! And so on. She was innocent! She was guilty! She was a queen of men. She was a silly, raw schoolgirl! And so on! She would have liked to cry! But she refused to cry, and instead stamped her foot on the vibrating, slightly heaving deck. She swore profoundly under her breath.

She was in two minds whether or not to go back into the cabin and give the operator a few choice specimens of the things she thought about him, when the cabin door opened behind her. She did not budge. She could see her own shadow thrown on the deck in front of her by the cabin-lamp, and the lengthening shadow of the operator himself.

She thought, unschooled by her experiences: "He's given in! I've won!"

"Miss Perkins."

"Well!"

"I've just received this message."

In the ray of the cabin-lamp the man held up to her with both hands a numbered form on which he had written the following words—words which she would have preferred, for the sake of her dignity, not to read but which she was somehow compelled to read:

"*Lord Furber, Yacht Vanguard. Kindly send launch with ship's papers into Ostia, and reply that you will do so. Farinacci, General Secretary Fascisti, Palazzo Chigi, Rome.*"

"Do you expect me to believe that you've really received that?" She laughed shrilly.

"No. I don't expect anything. I never expect anything from anybody. But I've received it."

A deckhand came up the after starboard companion.

"Did you ring, sir?"

"Oh no! The bell rang all by itself. Take this to the Captain."

"Yes, sir."

The operator returned to his cabin and shut the door.

Harriet knew that he had really received the message. It was the most remarkable and disturbing coincidence she had ever known. And she was frightened. As a sort of symbolic protection she drew Lord Furber's coat more tightly around her.

CHAPTER XVIII

MRS. BUMPTION AS NURSE

By THE instructions of Mrs. Bumption Lord Furber had been carried into his own sleeping cabin. It was much larger than the one from which he had been removed, and it had a special system of automatic ventilation, devised by Lord Furber himself. These facts, however, had not influenced Mrs. Bumption. She wanted his lordship to be withdrawn more completely from the world of the yacht, so that none might interfere with her nursing and management of him; hence the change. Mrs. Bumption had had no experience of nursing, and in any case could not have made an ideal nurse. But she was the only lady in the yacht with an official position, and therefore the sufferer was her prey.

Captain Slapser had said, in the other cabin, that what he said "went." But Mrs. Bumption really had a better title to the boast. The Captain was a blusterer; Mrs. Bumption was not. Mrs. Bumption's confidence in herself was complete. The Captain had consulted Bumption, who as his lordship's butler had a prestige far surpassing that of either the first officer or the mate—or even the chief engineer. Bumption, of course, had consulted Mrs. Bumption, and it was Mrs. Bumption who, through Bumption, had decided that the wireless message should be disregarded. Mrs. Bumption had never heard of Mussolini, much less of Farinacci; she scorned newspapers, politics, and all other masculine playthings. But she had learnt that Ostia was the port for Rome, and she was a strong low-church protestant. Rome was accordingly ruled out, as being a dangerous and improper place for any sensible Briton. Captain Slapser adopted her view because he misdoubted the merits of the anchorage at Ostia.

Accordingly, the yacht held her original course for Genoa and Mrs. Bumption reigned. She knew that she reigned, and everybody in the ship knew that she reigned. She had had no sleep and desired none. She sat in Lord Furber's own easy-chair and surveyed Lord Furber in his richly-ornamented bunk, and she smoothed out her white apron over her measureless hips, and drank a little of the brandy and milk which Lord Furber had refused to swallow, and she was pleasantly conscious of mastery.

Lord Furber's eyes were shut; he lay with one cheek on the pillow, so that the dressed wound at the back of his head might suffer no pressure, and his breathing was faint, though slow and regular. He had been undressed. His face was very pale, except the swollen chin, which in colour was somewhat variegated. Nothing had happened since the first great happening, and it seemed as if nothing would happen until Genoa and a doctor should be reached. Lord Furber's few audible remarks had been apparently quite senseless, and it was clear that he did not know who he was.

Mrs. Bumption could wait. Omnipotence can always wait. Deep night and a majestic silence dominated the cabin, lit by one blue-tinted lamp just over the telephone switch-board, by means of which Lord

Furber (when in his right mind) could, and did, communicate direct with every part of the ship. Lord Furber had always said that he would have the sleeping cabin isolated from all sound, and he had succeeded in achieving his ideal.

Mrs. Bumption thought she heard a movement of the outer of the two heavy doors which were part of the silential system of the cabin. She turned her head menacingly. She was not mistaken. The inner door slowly swung open, and Miss Harriet Perkins appeared, smiling, still swathed in the immense fur coat. Mrs. Bumption hated Harriet. She had no right reason for doing so; but she hated Harriet because Harriet was an interloper, an intruder, a pert minx, slim, youngish, stylish, and exercised charm over mankind.

Now at this moment Mrs. Bumption's solid body became strangely light, to such a degree that Mrs. Bumption had all she could do to prevent it from rising respectfully at Harriet's entry. She did, however, succeed by an intense effort of will in keeping it down in the chair. She just stared and glared fixedly at Harriet, and her hard eyes said:

"Saucebox, you know you've no business here, and for two pins I'd tear that coat off your impudent back."

"I've had a nice little nap in the lounge," Harriet remarked brightly. "I thought I'd just step in and see how his lordship was getting on."

"I'm looking after his lordship," Mrs. Bumption replied firmly and gloomily. "And what's more, this room's private."

"The devil it is!" Harriet retorted. "Considering that I'm his lordship's latest confidential secretary! . . . You're the stewardess, I think."

Her tone was very kindly.

Lord Furber stirred in his bunk. Mrs. Bumption, to cover her feelings, stood up massively and gazed at her patient. She could think of nothing effective to say to Harriet, and wisely said nothing, save with her bulging eyes. She thought to herself that Harriet was a mischievous liar, and yet she thought also that Harriet spoke the truth.

Harriet approached the bunk and took a glance at Lord Furber. His appearance was pathetic to her. She felt that in trying to vamp the wireless operator and in allowing herself ever so little a nap, she had been shamefully callous towards the victim of Mr. Sutherland's passion and power.

"Aren't you Lord Furber?" she asked, seeking to restore the victim's lost memory.

"Who the 'ell's he?" Lord Furber retorted. "Me a lord! Tell us another."

"Do you know where you are?" Harriet made a fresh start.

"I'm in some bloomin' hotel," was the answer. "But I've forgotten its name. Perhaps it's the Tiger. Yes, it's the Tiger. I've run off wi' that fat wench there. Us 's skedaddled together. Her's been making love to me. They're never too old for that, ye know."

Lord Furber raised his eyelids and beheld Mrs. Bumption with a long look grimly sorrowful.

"Wouldna' think it from the size of her, would ye?" he proceeded. "But she's been after me for years. Husband's a good 'un, too." He shut his eyes.

"Mrs. Bumption!" exclaimed Harriet.

Mrs. Bumption, always crimson of face, had put on a scarlet hue. Her mouth worked over her teeth and over the void spaces where teeth once had been. Her whole head trembled. Her hands clasped and unclasped.

"He's wandering," said she glumly, and then heavily swept, with her sense of outrage and the poor remains of her reputation, from the room, and Harriet was alone with Lord Furber.

CHAPTER XIX

RUPTURE

HARRIET first of all closed the doors, both of which Mrs. Bumption had left open, and then she came to the bunk side.

"So you haven't lost your memory," she said, with a glance, soft and quizzical, at the suffering baron.

"Artistic performance, wasn't it?" said he, sleepily, and not looking up at her.

"Crude, I should call it," said she.

"I say," he looked up sharply now. "What the dickens do ye mean by saying ye're my latest confidential secretary?"

"Why? You haven't engaged another one since me, have you?"

"I haven't engaged ye yet, Harriet."

He employed her Christian name quite nicely—with benevolence rather than with familiarity. So that she smiled at him.

"You offered me the post. I said I'd decide later, or something of the kind. Well, I've decided. The bargain is closed—except about salary—and so I now *am* your confidential secretary. Only of course, you must be confidential with me—otherwise I shall resign at once. Tell me why you did it?"

"Did what?"

"Pretend to lose your memory."

"Oh! Just for a change. When they first spoke to

me, after I come to, I was a bit dazed and I didn't answer. I saw at once they hadn't a notion what to do, without my orders. And all of a sudden it struck me I'd let 'em alone and see what sort of a mess they'd make of things if I left 'em to themselves. So I lost me memory, and it was such thundering fun I thought I'd keep it lost for a while. I've discovered one or two interesting things already. For instance— my skipper is a blatant ass when it comes to the point. I doubt if he'll be my skipper much longer."

"Well, it was very clever of you."

"Oh, I am clever. Ye'll soon find that out."

"Still, you're only a child. You made yourself a new toy, and you've been so interested playing with it that you've forgotten to be bored. Of course, it was easy to play with. You couldn't have pretended to be unconscious. Nobody could—I mean not to take anybody in. But anyone can pretend to have lost his memory. It's so simple."

"Yes. Only it wanted me to think of the scheme, Harriet. All the good things are simple—when they're done. It's all very well for ye to call it crude. . . ."

"I shall have to ask for three pounds a week extra if I'm expected to be always praising you, Lord Furber. And why should I praise you when you can do that so much better for yourself? I won't praise you. I'll never praise you again. I'm sorry now I even said you were clever."

The baron smiled contentedly.

"And ye can say what ye like," he proceeded. "It was artistic of me to go back to the old Five Towns accent. My God! How I lived in those days!" He was proud of his low origin.

"Oh! Very well then. Have it your own way.

You're the most brilliant man on board, or that ever lived, or ever could live. Will that satisfy you?"

"That's better. But I'll tell ye something else. Another reason why I pretended to lose my memory was that I couldn't settle on the spur of the moment what attitude I should take towards yer big City friend, Sutherland. I needed time to think it over."

"Oh! Mr. Sutherland won't mind what attitude you take towards him. He'll always keep calm."

"Mind! Him! Calm! Him! Was he keeping calm when he knocked me down without a word of warning? And why did he knock me down? That's what I've got to know. Why should he knock me down? It's a fortunate thing for him that I particularly want to keep on good terms with the fellow."

There was a faint trace of passionate feeling in the baron's voice as he uttered these last words; at the sound of which Harriet's brain began to work more eagerly and more intelligently than before.

"Then it's perhaps all to the good that he did knock you down."

"What the blazes do you mean?"

Lord Furber sat up as he savagely put the question. He looked pathetic and wistful to Harriet, probably because of his swollen chin and the dressing on the back of his disarrayed scalp. But his tone was not in the least pathetic. On the contrary it was rather frightening. Harriet enjoyed swinging between the two warring sensations which he produced in her.

She said:

"I mean he's a decent kind of a man, and I expect he feels he owes you some apology, and that'll make it easier for you to keep on good terms with him. If he hadn't knocked you down, he might have refused to discuss anything with you at all, because you'd deliberately plotted to make him a prisoner on your yacht."

"Yes," Lord Furber agreed thoughtfully. "That's an argument all right, that is. *You*'re brilliant too." Then he struck the pillow a dastardly, uncalled-for blow, and cried: "But *why* did he knock me down? Ye're a woman and ye can't understand the feelings of a man who's been knocked down."

"Yes I can," said Harriet. "A man who's been knocked down feels that he's been treated in a disgraceful and inexcusable manner, and his one idea is to behave in the same manner himself."

"Why did he knock me down?" the baron reiterated, and the pillow suffered a second time. He added quietly, in sudden change: "At least I suppose he knocked me down. I remember him rushing at me but nothing else."

"If you have any doubts as to what he did, dismiss them. He certainly did knock you down. And he knocked you down because he wasn't fully awake, and I'd screamed or shrieked, and he saw your hand on me and he imagined—well, he imagined I was in serious need of defence."

"Oh! I shouldn't have thought he was that sort of a fellow."

"Well, he just is."

"Then I forgive him. Curse him, I forgive him. But he owes me an apology. And he shall pay me."

"I'm sure he'll apologize."

"Apologize be d—d. What he ought to have is one over the costard himself . . . On my own decks too! . . . As if anybody 'ud believe his tale about my slipping and falling!"

A bell rang very modestly and discreetly in a corner of the room. Harriet started. It was as if a mouse had stirred in a corner of the room.

"What's that?" she asked, alert, and apprehensive in spite of herself.

"The telephone-bell. Ye wouldn't think it would wake me up if I'm asleep. But it does. That's the sort of sleeper I am."

Lord Furber, without moving his body, took down the receiver and listened. He listened for about half a minute or more.

"I thank ye," he murmured low into the telephone, and hung up the receiver again. Silence in the room.

"Who was it?" Harriet demanded as if by right.

Lord Furber made no reply.

"It's no use you pretending not to hear," said she, with sweet cajolery, as to a child. "If I'm your confidential secretary—and I *am*—you must be open with me. You must hide nothing from me. And above all you mustn't be ashamed of telling me *anything*."

"Aren't ye asking a lot?" said the baron, warningly firm.

"No confidential secretary that was worth anything would agree to work for you on any other terms."

"This is a new notion of secretaryship."

"And I'm a new sort of secretary."

"Well, it was the wireless operator, telephoning, as ye're so curious."

"I'm not curious at all. I'm only being a confidential secretary. In my private capacity do you suppose I care a pin what your Tunnicliff's been saying to you? I'm only inquiring for professional purposes. If I can't know more about you than anybody else in this yacht I'll resign at once." Harriet laughed, and undid the buttons of the fur coat, which she removed.

"Well, he told me there's an Italian submarine knocking about, and he thinks she's wirelessing like anything to somebody, but he can't make out what she's saying, because of the code she's using. That satisfy you?"

"Thanks so much," said Harriet, turning her agreeable, challenging face towards his from the glass by whose aid she was restoring her complexion with instruments taken from the handbag.

"That's not the first time to-night you've tried this dodge of taking off my fur coat and showing yerself as ye are."

"Ah! Who told you?"

"Wireless operator."

"He's a sneak then. Perhaps you'll be interested to know that he despises you."

"Now you're being a sneak yourself," the baron said.

Harriet snapped her fingers, and then snapped together the sides of the bag.

"He may despise me," said Lord Furber. "He's entitled to think for himself, even if he's entitled to nothing else. But he plays the game with me. Trust him for that. I 'phoned to ask him if he'd anything to report and he said he had, and he reported it. That was all."

"I expect he told you what I wanted him to do for me."

"He did."

"And what did you say?"

"I said he'd better receive a message from Farinacci telling the yacht to call at Ostia. Good thing Mrs. Bumption was out of the room or I couldn't have done it—not safely." The baron grinned.

Harriet openly displayed her astonishment.

"I might have guessed it," she breathed.

"But ye didn't. Didn't I say ye'd soon be finding out how clever I am?"

"And I suppose you told him as well to show me the message?"

"I did."

"Why do you want the yacht to call at Ostia? You aren't ill. You don't need a doctor. You were going to Genoa."

"I want the yacht to call at Ostia because you want her to call at Ostia."

"You're a dear!" Harriet exclaimed, approaching the bunk. "And d'you know *why* I want the yacht to call at Ostia?"

"Of course I do. Ye want to slip up to Rome to get some clothes. Ye can't wear my fur coat for ever. But I'll say this—it suits ye."

"You really *are* a dear! And I'm so sorry for you."

"Why?"

"Because I can see you've got a splitting head-ache, and you aren't saying anything about it."

"Yes, I have," said the baron. "And so you'd have if you'd been treated as I've been treated by your cursed City friend."

"I'll give you some aspirin, and then you must go to sleep." Harriet suddenly became a nurse.

"Mrs. Bumption wouldn't let me have any aspirin. Said it was dangerous for me."

"She would. She's the sort of woman who finds out what you want, and then finds a reason why you mustn't have it. Of course you must have aspirin. It will ease your poor head and send you off to sleep too."

"But Mrs. Bumption keeps the aspirin."

"Not all of it," said Harriet. "Because I've got some in my bag here. You don't suppose that I travel anywhere without the greatest drug in the world. It doesn't matter whether you've got nerves through flirting, or indigestion through cocktails, or whether you've been knocked down by a jealous rival, aspirin is the stuff to take, and you're going to take it. And if you like, I'll go out and tell Mrs. Bumption I've given you some."

"She'll give notice and leave. And then Bumption will leave." The baron made a humorous noise to imitate sobbing.

"She won't leave if I stay," said Harriet. "She'll never leave me alone in the field—of her own accord, I mean. Here now!" She had unscrewed the phial. "You'll want some water, won't you? You must sit up a tiny bit. Oh! What a funny millionaire and strong man you are! This yacht of yours is pitching, you know."

Harriet became more than a nurse; she became a mother to him. It was the mother that shook his pillow while he sat up; and the eyes gazing at him as he swallowed and drank were the eyes of a mother— sympathetic and sternly, sharply watchful, and superior and teasing. Her eyes were saying: "What a silly child to go and get itself knocked down!"

But the mother was shot through with the girl who had cast off the fur coat in order to display herself in an evening frock. The girl was rapidly permitting within herself an honest affection for Lord Furber.

She liked him now because of his broad, generously-accepting mind. A native impudence had led her to visit him, uninvited, in his own fur coat. He had shown not the least sign of resentment at her self-possessed effrontery. He had even found pleasure in the sight of her wearing his entirely unsuitable fur coat.

And, far more important, he had not resented her inexcusable attempt to cozen the wireless operator and change the destination of the yacht. He had seen the incident simply and benevolently, ignoring her naughtiness. She had wanted to go to Rome, and he would let her go to Rome. He had imaginatively understood the force of her tremendous desire for clothes, and had decreed that she should have clothes. There was no meanness in him. He might be a brute, but he was not a mean brute. Thinking of all that her intimate old friend, his wife, had related to her, she began to suspect that there might be two sides to the disturbing story of his domestic life—such as it was. She felt happy in the singular fact that she had been carried off in the yacht.

"What was that about a jealous rival?" Lord Furber murmured the question as he lay back on the smoothed pillow, conscious of the taste of aspirin in his mouth.

"Nothing," said Harriet. "Go to sleep. Dressing comfortable?"

He seemed to snigger, magnanimously. He was not a man to pick up and critically examine every chance, impulsive word that slipped out of a woman's mouth; not he. He would treat women as women. Yes, she would simply love being his confidential secretary.

He settled himself in the bunk, while she restored the phial of aspirin to her bag. She was happy in appreciating and in being appreciated.

There was a quiet knock at the door. Harriet answered it.

"Who was that?" Lord Furber asked, when she had shut the door again. He had not heard the voices.

"Mr. Sutherland."

"Oh! I thought he always went to bed and snored in times of crisis," remarked the baron.

"He's just going to bed. But he wanted to know first how you were getting on."

"Yes, I should say he did. It's to his interest to keep me alive. If I'd gone and died on him he'd have looked a bit soft, wouldn't he? . . . Manslaughter at the best. Nobody could say he was acting in self-defence."

"No." Harriet agreed, smiling, and anxious to soothe. "Well. Good night."

"I say!" the baron imperiously called her back. "Ye can do something for me now—at once. Ye know my secretaries have no hours. At least the only limit is twenty-four."

"Quite. I quite understand," said the new secretary eagerly.

"Well. Catch Sutherland before he goes to bed again."

"Yes. What about? What am I to say to him?"

"Spin him the yarn. Tell him the tale. Put him in a good temper about me. I want him to wake up well-disposed towards me to-morrow morning. Say I've treated ye throughout with the greatest respect, and never had any evil designs on ye. Say I didn't deserve to be knocked down."

"Oh! He knows that now."

"Anyhow, tell him I forgive him. No ill-will at all. Tell him I think very highly of him as a City financier. Tell him I knew nowt about his luggage being brought on board. I didn't, till it was too late. That was one of Veruda's bits of embroidery on the bare scheme. Very pretty and thoughtful of course, but we should ha' been better if we'd left it out. Wants a bit of explaining, that luggage does. Scheme was wild enough without it. Still——"

"But what's the point?"

"Point!" cried the baron, sitting straight up with one bound of his torso. "Point! I've got to get something out o' that chap. That's why he's here. I never wanted in all me born days to get anything out of anybody as much as I want to get something out of him. I'd sooner lose every penny of all my millions than I'd fail with Sutherland. I could always make more millions, but if I fail with Sutherland, millions of money won't be any use to me. Got it?"

"Yes," Harriet softly answered.

The baron's tone was so serious, so sincere, so passionate, so startlingly violent that Harriet knew at once that she was on the very edge of the mystery of the strange proceedings of the *Vanguard*. And she thrilled with a delighted expectancy. She foresaw hours of marvellous excitation. She was happier, perhaps, than she had ever been in her life.

"And I——" the baron's voice was raised again. She stopped him with a gesture.

"Will you please remember you've just had a dose of aspirin, and I want you to go to sleep. If you go on like this, how can you hope to go to sleep?"

"All right!" The baron was obedient to her counsel and lay back. "Run along and do as I tell ye." His voice was now tired.

"Just let me know first exactly what it is you want to get out of Mr. Sutherland," said Harriet, with an air of casualness.

"Have ye gone stark, staring mad?" the baron asked sleepily, with shut eyes.

"No. I'm only asking for information which of course I must have."

"Well, ye won't have it. Get away and carry out instructions." The baron still spoke sleepily, half-humorously.

"I'll get away," Harriet answered negligently, even superiorly. "But either you'll tell me what I ought to know, or I sha'n't carry out instructions. I absolutely refuse to be your confidential secretary if you won't be confidential with me."

"I sha'n't tell ye, and ye're nowt but an impudent wench."

"Very well. I resign my post."

Lord Furber sat tempestuously up again.

"Go to—the Five Towns!" he shouted.

She inquired, with exasperating calmness:

"Why the Five Towns?"

"Because they're worse than hell, Hull and Halifax! You're dismissed. On the spot."

CHAPTER XX

THE SNACK

SEPTIMIUS SUTHERLAND rose early, and his freshness matched the freshness of the morning. For although he had had a disturbed night, he had contrived to get quite a fair amount of sleep, sleep being one of his specialties. If he was proud of being a "blue" he was also proud of his Napoleonic skill in composing himself to slumber at nearly any suitable moment. He had slept well before knocking Lord Furber down, and, callously, he had slept well afterwards, even though his cabin was impregnated with the odour of the aseptic which had been employed upon Lord Furber's damaged head.

Further, being aboard a yacht, he had dressed for the part, as well as he could, in white flannels and shoes and the rich jacket which his University blue-ship entitled him to wear, together with a yachting cap offered to him by an eager junior steward.

The sun had lately risen upon a calmer Mediterranean, whose various shades harmonized with Septimius's jacket.

The decks of the *Vanguard* had already been swabbed down, and now many hands, in fatigue-overalls of yellow, were busy here and there polishing her endless brass. Not one of the hands seemed to be in the least preoccupied by the astonishing events of the night. Their day's programme was proceeding precisely as usual, and they were chatting quietly among themselves about the diurnal matters which constituted the main interest of their lives.

The scene mightily pleased Mr. Sutherland. He loved order, routine, tidiness, cleanliness; and it delighted him to think that whatever might happen on board, the regularity of the yacht's toilette could never be disturbed. Reflecting upon certain defects which he constantly noticed in the functioning of his own household, he wished that all house-mistresses could take a course of study in the house-keeping of a really smart yacht such as the *Vanguard*.

In short, Mr. Sutherland physically, morally and spiritually, was at his best, his most philosophic, his most sagacious. He strolled aft, on the drying promenade deck, along the mahogany façade of the deck-houses, and under cover of the boat-deck above. At the after extremity of the deck-houses the boat-deck overhung in a huge semicircle, beneath which was the stairway leading down from the promenade deck to the main-deck, with a considerable amount of sheltered space on either hand for lounge-chairs, occasional tables and flower-stands. Contemplatively he lit a cigarette, the heavenly, unequalled first cigarette of the day, and stared absently, as if absorbed in the manufacture of profound wisdom, at the white wake of the yacht. In fact, he was saying to himself:

"Why have I never had a yacht? Is not a yacht the most perfect, self-contained, self-sufficient organism in the world?"

Then his thin nose detected the wonderful smell of first-rate coffee, which reminded him that he was both thirsty and hungry. The smell came from the boat-deck above. Then he heard the faint murmur of voices—not the voices of deck hands nor even of officers, but a deep voice of civil authority and a woman's voice. Mr. Sutherland was tempted upwards, and he was also perturbed, though pleasantly perturbed. He was a little disappointed that others had left their beds before himself, and he felt bound to prove to those others that he too could get up early and spry after any sort of a wild night. He hesitated a moment, then quitted the shelter and braced his shaven cheeks to the tonic wind of morning, and began slowly to climb the companion leading to the top deck.

He paused, listening to some dialogue:

"Then ye aren't my confidential secretary any more?"

"No."

"Sure?"

"Of course I'm sure." (Rather sharply).

"Ye'll miss a lot o' fun."

"Perhaps I shall. But what I have said I have said."

"Yes. That's what I used to say myself once."

"I suppose you won't let me call at Rome now for clothes?"

"Well, don't ye go and suppose any such thing, Harriet. I said ye should have fal-lals from Rome, and ye shall. I arranged all that after ye left me last night. What's one secretary more or less to me?" A laugh.

"Oh! Hurrah! I won't be your secretary, but I don't mind helping you a bit if you want me to very much."

It occurred to Mr. Sutherland—and not too soon—

that eavesdropping was an improper pursuit for the righteous. Also he was aware within himself of an unpleasant spasm of jealousy. Those two above were extraordinarily friendly. And Miss Perkins's Christian name had been used in a tone of easy intimacy which was surely unusual after an acquaintance of scarcely twelve hours.

Deciding that he must survey the scene for himself, Mr. Sutherland proceeded up the stairs. He beheld two persons seated at a table behind the wireless cabin, from both sides of which gleaming white windscreens had been rigged. Lord Furber, with a patch on the back of his tousled head, was wearing a more joyous dressing-gown than Septimius had ever dreamed of. Miss Perkins was still enveloped in the baronial fur coat. On the table were a silver coffee-service, cups and saucers, rolls and butter, and a box of cigarettes.

Lord Furber jumped up at the splendid sight of Mr. Sutherland.

"Morning, Sutherland," said he. "Glad to see ye looking so well. I hope ye'll be glad to hear that I'm no worse for my fall last night."

"This fellow," said Septimius to himself, "may be a millionaire, but he is a gentleman—besides being a sound actor." And aloud: "I'm immensely relieved."

"I thought ye would be," said Lord Furber with a peculiar emphasis, and glanced at Harriet, who glanced at Septimius.

"Rayner!" his lordship cried out fiercely.

A steward appeared with the magical celerity of a conjuring trick.

"'Nother cup."

"Yes, my lord."

"And a chair."

"Yes, my lord."

"Now sit down and join us," Lord Furber urged, still standing. "Have my chair. Yes, have it. I insist." He walked about. "Coffee and rolls. Rolls fresh baked on board this morning. Don't be alarmed. This isn't breakfast. This is only a preliminary snack."

Lord Furber in his walk now met Mr. Sutherland and shook his hand.

"Chin a bit wanky. Can't think how I happened to fall on it. But it's better than it was."

Then the baron forced Septimius into the chair. From the assured mastery of his tone and gestures nobody could be in any doubt as to who was the leading authority on board the *Vanguard.*

"Morning—Harriet," said Mr. Sutherland boldly but calmly.

"Good morning—Seppie," replied Miss Perkins after an infinitesimal pause.

Two stewards appeared, one with a chair and the other with a cup and saucer. Lord Furber sat down. The trio had the air of being cronies of long standing. Cronies of any standing at all, however, they were not.

Lord Furber, as usual, was absorbed in himself; which no crony in the presence of other cronies ought to be. He was thinking of the adventure just begun and about to develop in a manner which might or might not succeed in saving him from a disastrous defeat, and which at the worst had mitigated and would still further mitigate the profound secret boredom of his splendid and opulent existence.

Harriet Perkins, absorbed as usual in herself, dwelt happily, triumphantly, on the presence of two very important men both of whom had yielded to the force and the attractiveness of her individuality. She had measured her power against the renowned millionaire, and had so far beaten him; while the magnate Septimius merely adored her and was her private property.

As for Septimius, absorbed as usual in himself, he reflected that his situation in the yacht on that lovely Mediterranean morning amid circumstances extremely ideal, was due solely to some mad, audacious, imaginative, unscrupulous and entirely incomprehensible scheme of Lord Furber's (renowned in the City for his inventive daring). He knew that he had been kidnapped, but he knew also that he could never prove it. And on the whole he rather liked the quandary in which destiny had involved him, especially as Miss Perkins was part of it. He did not admit that he was far gone in love with Miss Perkins. The dangerous word "love" was not in his dictionary. How could it be in the respectable, bowdlerised dictionary of a middle-aged gentleman satisfactorily married and the father of two quite adult daughters? He admitted only that his joy in the nearness of Miss Perkins was extreme, and different from any other sensation of his career as a male—and that if he had not chanced to obtain the sensation free of charge, he would have been ready to pay any price for it. True, he sniffed distant peril in the air—a pleasing peril, but still a peril. The peril was connected with Miss Perkins, not with Lord Furber. He blandly considered himself to be the equal of Lord Furber in any contest of duplicity and chicane which Lord

Furber might force upon him. And he was well aware that in the probably imminent affray he possessed a marked advantage in that whereas Lord Furber no doubt wanted something from him, he wanted nothing from Lord Furber.

He decided that the polite affray might as well begin at once.

"Furber," said he, at his blandest and most modestly amiable, "I really don't know how to apologize to you for my carelessness in getting myself left behind here like this. It looks as if I was forcing myself on your magnificent hospitality. And the worst of it is"—he gave a slight, half-humorous smile—"I'm enjoying it enormously. I ought to regret it, but somehow I can't."

"My dear fellow!" replied the occupant of the gorgeous dressing-gown, with rough geniality. "I'm the one that ought to apologize. I can't think how it happened. Infernal carelessness of one of my chaps, of course! The one bright spot in the muddle is that through some more muddling your luggage is here. But I suppose that was the hotel people. I hear ye were leaving Naples last night——"

"How did *you* hear that?"

"Don't know," murmured the baron, after slight hesitation. "I expect it was Count Veruda who told me, or told someone who told me . . . And as ye were leaving, the hotel concierge jumped to the conclusion that you were leaving in the yacht."

"Yes, no doubt that was it. He must have forgotten to give a glance at my luggage labels. However, it *was* my intention to leave Naples last night, and apparently I did leave Naples last night. And here I am."

"Well," said the baron. "I'm glad to have ye here, and very sorry indeed if I've put ye to any inconvenience."

"Not at all. I had three rather important appointments in town for to-morrow afternoon. At least they seemed important last night, but this morning, sailing along like this, nothing seems important—except what's going on in this really wonderful yacht of yours." Mr. Sutherland's glance met that of the baron for a moment. The baron glanced aside.

"I hope ye'll stay with me as long as ye can," said the baron.

"Oh! I will, thanks very much," answered Septimius with surprising enthusiasm. "If I might be allowed to make use of your wireless."

"Sure," said Lord Furber, and yelled "Rayner!" Rayner appeared.

"Send Mr. Tunnicliff to me."

"Yes, my lord."

"Yes," Harriet put in suddenly. "It's all very well for Mr. Sutherland. *He's* got his luggage. And don't we all know it!" She gazed as if enraptured at his fine raiment. "But poor me!"

"Yes!" laughed Lord Furber. "Poor Harriet hasn't a clout to her back, except my fur coat."

Mr. Sutherland had again a sense of disturbance. "Harriet." And the pair had exchanged a peculiar smile, as though they had come to some mysterious understanding in the night hours or at dawn. Mr. Sutherland did not like these phenomena at all. It immensely annoyed him that anybody at all (except of course himself) should have come to a mysterious understanding with the enchantress in the fur coat. And he hated that the fur coat she wore should belong to Lord Furber. If it had been his own fur coat he would have been happy. But then Mr. Sutherland never travelled with a fur coat. He saw that he ought to do so.

"My lord?"

The Honourable Luke John Tunnicliff had arrived on the boat-deck. Harriet offered him a delicious smile, which he received with a blush. Then Harriet looked defiantly at the baron, as if saying: "See how friendly we are, your secretary and your ex-confidential secretary."

"Tunnicliff," said Lord Furber. "Will you please tell your cousin that he is to send off any messages that Mr. Sutherland gives him." Mr. Tunnicliff gravely nodded.

"And what about me?" asked Harriet.

"And any of Miss Perkins's too—of course," Lord Furber added.

"Not that I shall have any to send off," said Harriet.

"And any of Miss Perkins's too," Lord Furber repeated.

Mr. Tunnicliff bowed again and departed.

"The wireless is yours," said Lord Furber, heartily generous, to Mr. Sutherland. "At any time."

"Oh, there's no hurry, thanks," Mr. Sutherland replied calmly. "A few hours more or less—what does it matter?"

Harriet, having lighted a cigarette, arose and leaned over the rail.

"The sea's rather yellow here, isn't it?" said she.

Mr. Sutherland arose and joined her.

"How very interesting!" said he. "All one's life one has heard of the yellow Tiber, and here it is. See!

We've passed the mouth already. That must be Civita Vecchia over there." He pointed.

"Then where's Ostia?"

"Oh! Ostia must be behind us."

"Behind us!" She turned. "Lord Furber, we've passed Ostia!" Her gaze was a reproach; it was a charge of bad faith.

"Rayner!" yelled the baron.

"My lord?"

"Ask the skipper to speak to me at once."

"Yes, my lord. Afraid he's turned in, my lord. He was on the bridge most of the night."

"Get him."

"Yes, my lord."

Lord Furber sprang up and walked about, muttering to himself and to the world at large. Having regard to the vocabulary which he was employing, Harriet turned sharply back to the rail, and glanced privately, with amusement, at Mr. Sutherland. Her wish to share her malicious amusement with him gave Mr. Sutherland much satisfaction and quite extinguished his jealousy. They both continued to examine the surface of the sea with exaggerated ease, as tactful guests always will when trouble is afoot between the owner and the captain.

Captain Slapser knew his owner and came hurrying aft with as much speed as dignity would allow. Mr. Sutherland noticed out of the tail of his eye that the supreme navigating authority was very summarily clothed.

"Joe!" cried the baron, before the Captain was quite near him.

The Captain, gloomy, resentful, and apprehensive, said naught to this most improper greeting.

Said the owner:

"I thought we were calling at Ostia."

"No, my lord," answered the Captain, with a demeanour of unconvincing surprise.

"But haven't you had an official message from Rome? I was told so."

"I did have a message. But there's nobody in Rome has the right to give orders to a British yacht—and flying the blue ensign too. My orders from you were Genoa."

Miss Perkins joyously nudged Mr. Sutherland in the side; which gave him still further satisfaction: he permitted himself roguishly to return the nudge. At the same moment he thought, frightened, of his middle-age and of his wife.

"Why didn't you ask me?" Lord Furber fiercely inquired.

"Your lordship was ill in bed. I did mention it to Mr. Bumption, my lord, and he thought——"

"You mean Mrs. Bumption thought," Lord Furber stopped him. Something on the surface of the Mediterranean attracted the baron's attention. With lightning quickness he said: "Look here! See that?"

A submarine was emerging from the depths.

"Yes, my lord."

"Well, what d'ye think of it, Joe? It's Italian navy, that is. What d'ye think it's here for?" He put a terrible, slow sweetness into his powerful voice. "Take my advice, Joe, and put back to Ostia as fast as ye can. And try not to tell me anything more about your friend Mrs. Bumption."

"Yes, my lord."

"And I say, Joe. We aren't on the course for Genoa

here. You don't hug the shore when you're going from Naples to Genoa. What's the meaning of it?"

"Well, my lord, I wasn't sure what you'd decide. So I kept her in a bit. I thought ye'd tell me."

"Well, I've told ye."

Captain Slapser, cowed and furious, went forrard to his bridge. Soon the yacht swerved as it were savagely to port.

The baron laughed aloud. His guests, reassured, answered the signal by turning round to him. The baron winked at them. The submarine was steaming northwest, ignoring the *Vanguard*.

"Well, what d'ye think of it?" asked the baron.

"We sha'n't say," said Harriet. "Shall we, Mr. Sutherland?"

"No, we sha'n't."

"Ye think I was a bit rough on the feller?"

"We sha'n't say."

"No, we sha'n't."

"Anyhow the submarine was a godsend," grinned the baron. "Hell's delight!"

And he laughed again and more loudly.

"Now, what are those?" asked Mr. Sutherland half an hour later, when the *Vanguard's* anchor chain was rattling down into ten fathoms about a mile and a half from the shore. He pointed to a procession of small motor boats which were heading for the yacht.

Lord Furber, without answering, disappeared.

CHAPTER XXI

CHIFFONS

THE motor-craft, as they approached the yacht, showed themselves to be nothing better than jackboats with engines in them, unkempt, shabby, nondescript launches such as abound in ports and are hired out for all kinds of occasional use; manned by dirty and untidy fellows who evidently had no feeling whatever for the smartness of the sea, and who no doubt regarded the spick and span condition of the great yacht and everything appertaining to it as the vagary of incomprehensible British madmen who paraded the ocean for fun. One of the boats, the leader, was less small than the others; indeed it proved to be quite large.

An increasing number of high, excited Latin voices rose across the water from the boats to the lofty upper deck of the yacht. The arrival of the procession seemed to stir the stodgy British phlegm of the yacht's crew. A couple of officers leaned peering and smiling from the starboard end of the bridge; and seamen and stewards lolled over the rail here and there and condescendingly grinned outright at the chattering, gesticulating persons in the boats. In each boat was a pile of cargo hidden beneath ragged sail-cloths. The noisy exhausts of the three primitive engines added to the din. The boats passed

along the starboard side of the yacht, skirted her
stern and bore up on the port side where a gangway
was dropped from the lower deck to meet them.
Cries, shouts, shrieks, bursts of laughter: the whole
amounting almost to hysteria; and growls from the
steersmen and engineers and from the deckhands
engaged in fending the frowsy boats off the *Vanguard's* virginal white paint. It was apparent that
there were quite a dozen women of various ages in
the boats, that in fact the majority of the passengers
were women with some pretensions to fashion, style,
and charm; some were beyond question lovely. The
curiosity of Harriet and Mr. Sutherland was keenly
aroused. But before direct communication could be
established between the yacht and the boats, Lord
Furber hurried back, the breakfast gong melodiously
sounded, and the baron somewhat forcibly led his
guests downstairs towards the dining-saloon. Septimius and Harriet would both have preferred to stay
where they were; they both thought that breakfast
proper was following much too closely on the snack;
but they could not protest; they could only furtively
glance at one another. After all it is the host who
settles the hours of meals in a yacht as in a house,
and guests are not supposed to be inquisitive about
what may be presumed to be the host's private
affairs. Septimius and Harriet submitted, and the
enormous cacophony was gradually lost to their
ears.

But when the doors of the dining-saloon were
opened at the end of the meal (which did not excite
in the guests the interest that so pretentious and
costly a repast deserved to excite—possibly because
of the strange absence of Bumption, the head

steward), the same cacophony, but perhaps still more strident, met the ears.

"Well," said Lord Furber at the doorway, "I reckon this is the best I can do for ye, Harriet."

He waved his hand, with an air of casual disdain, in the direction of the lounge, which was full of very vivacious women, with the Honourable Luke John in the midst, conducting as it were the orchestra of tongues. The Honourable Luke John made a sign and spoke in Italian and the hubbub was magically stilled, and the ladies at once put on that expression of timidity, defiance, and expectancy which is proper to the faces of the humble in the presence of the mighty, and to the faces of sellers in the presence of prospective purchasers.

Harriet gave a squeal quite Italian in intensity. Every couch and every chair in the big lounge was covered with all descriptions and varieties of feminine attire. There were day-frocks, evening-frocks, sports-dresses, jumpers, jackets, cloaks, shawls, wraps, stoles, furs, gloves, stockings, shoes, hats, slippers, negligés, matinées, and what not and what not; together with lingerie, from *chemises de nuit* to cami-knickers, displayed with an enchanting and truly Latin shamelessness. A profusion of stuffs! An astounding multiplicity of contrasted colours. The delicate essence of the salons of a dozen couturières, modistes, furriers, and shoemakers! Dazzling! Perilous! Intoxicating! Irresistible! The sack of Rome brought up to date! Harriet's mouth happened to be open after the squeal. It remained open. She tried to speak; and could not, so complete was her realization of the inadequacy of language.

Mr. Sutherland could not conceal his jealous

amaze. The baron could not conceal his pride in a unique achievement. The Honourable Luke John could not conceal his illusion that he alone had made all the clothes and was alone responsible for their presence in the lounge. The handmaidens could not conceal their glorious anticipations of vast profits to their employers and proportionate percentages to themselves. It was a scene entirely unprecedented in the history of yachting.

"How *did* you do it?" Harriet exclaimed weakly at last.

She had a wondrous sensation of happiness and exaltation. She felt as she might have felt after the finest champagne and plenty of it. Often, in the hotels of great capitals, she had caused her bedroom to be littered with tempting finery brought to her on approval by the sirens of the shops; she had known the felicity of damning the financial consequences in a debauch of buying. But this incredible maritime experience reduced all previous experiences of the kind to nothing, to less than nothing. She comprehended now that the baron really was a millionaire, a milliardaire, with a generosity of imagination worthy of his uncountable resources.

"Well," said the baron, "the fact is I wanted my fur coat for my own back. And I got busy with my correspondent in Rome and told him to get busy, and he's a man who knows what getting busy is. He must have been running around Rome pretty early this morning—the moment the shops opened in fact. It isn't twenty minutes from Rome to Ostia in a fast car; he had three or four cars waiting, and those launches waiting too. All they had to do then was to wait for the yacht to drop anchor. It was very simple.

Everything *is* very simple when the word is passed that money doesn't matter. And I never do let money matter."

"But I'm bound to let money matter," said Harriet. "I can't afford the hundredth part of these things."

"Ye needn't" replied the baron. "Ye won't get any bills."

"But I can't accept clothes from you, my friend. Surely you must see that."

"Why can't ye accept clothes from me? Of course ye can accept clothes from me, and by Jove ye will too! I want my fur coat back. It's all owing to me ye haven't got any clothes. Well, here's yer clothes. Choose 'em and be hanged to ye!"

The Honourable Tunnicliff looked at the carpet. Mr. Sutherland coughed. The sirens, though they understood little or naught of the conversation, began to tremble for their percentages.

Harriet divested herself of the fur coat and Lord Furber put it on over the splendour of his dressing-gown, and then took it off again.

"You are quite right," said she, laughing. "I was being absurdly conventional. Nobody ought to be conventional with a millionaire."

And she abandoned herself to the orgy of fashion, and the sirens began to coo round about her.

CHAPTER XXII

THE QUEEN

THE chief actress, with a couple of the sirens, was hidden behind the doors of Lord Furber's private state-room, which adjoined the lounge and which was being used as a *salon d'essayage*.

Expectation in the lounge! The sirens there were either mute or whispering low to one another. One or two were busy displaying to better advantage the creations under their charge. The Honourable Tunnicliff kept an interpreter's eye upon them; for the moment they were his flock. They were all self-conscious, and little Mr. Tunnicliff himself was self-conscious, owing to the strong presence of the baron and Mr. Sutherland. And these two also were self-conscious, owing to the presence of the sirens so tittering, posing, and provocative. The baron would have given half a million not to be self-conscious, but he could not achieve the natural, and the louder he talked to Septimius, and the more peremptory he was in putting absurd questions to Mr. Tunnicliff for translation into Italian to the sirens, the further he receded from naturalness.

Both the magnates were restless; and they were bored, and inclined to place women lower than ever in the scale of reasonable beings. Already, before her disappearance, Harriet had dissipated an immense amount of time in darting about from one attraction to another like a butterfly in a meadow, glancing at everything and properly examining nothing. Apparently the brilliance and variety of the exhibition had deprived her of the power of concentration, of the sense of order, and of the maturity of her years; she had gone back again to the unreflecting, giggling gaiety of early girlhood. Even Mr. Sutherland had begun to suspect that her more solid qualities were perhaps inferior to her dazzling charm and to think that if impossibly she were his wife he might venture to offer her a few mild hints about deportment. She would still have been hovering in the lounge between shoes, furs, petticoats, sports-coats and shawls if Lord Furber had not picked up an evening dress at random and told her abruptly to retire and get into it without further delay. The dress happened to be green. "Here! You like green!" he had said, and had thrown the dress at her. "Don't run off till you have seen me in it," she had warned the magnates. Not that they would anyhow have run off, either of them. They might be bored and impatient, but they were as anxious as even Mr. Tunnicliff to see the show, and their legs would have refused to carry them out of the lounge.

Lord Furber lit a cigarette. Mr. Sutherland would not smoke. Lord Furber finished the cigarette. Lord Furber threw the cigarette-end into a copper bowl of flowers. And still the doors of the state-room did not open.

"Good God!" he cried. "At this rate we shall be lying at anchor here for a week."

"They always take twice as long as you'd think anybody could take," said Septimius mildly. "They lose the sense of time. This is the sort of thing that makes cynics say that all women are alike." But he uttered these cynical sentences with benevolence and charity.

Then the doors parted, and Harriet, stepping forward in green, was disclosed to the company. And though she was instantly the mark of every gaze, she showed not the least trace of self-consciousness. The two sirens behind her seemed to be saying to the three men: "Acknowledge that this spectacle is marvellous. Acknowledge that this moment is supreme." And Harriet, with proud lifted chin, seemed to be saying: "I am here to be admired. Admire me. I was never more alive and enchanting than I am now. The sensations which I can inspire in you are the justification of my whole existence. And if you are not thrilled and delighted you are blocks of stone and wood, and worthy to be spurned and kicked into the sea."

The males, however, responded in a manner more than sufficiently satisfactory to save them from being kicked into the sea. Lord Furber clapped his hands. Mr. Sutherland said "Ah!" with as much fervour as though he had eaten a perfect strawberry. The Honourable Tunnicliff blushed.

And there were murmurs of approbation from sirens who were nevertheless hinting to one another criticisms of the work of a rival house. All memory of boredom and impatience was blotted out, as one sunny morning will blot out the memory of a week's rain.

"Well?" the queen on her throne demanded.

"Have it!" the baron replied.

The two attendant sirens smiled happily. The other sirens eagerly prepared to take other con-

fections into the privacy of the state-room. But the
queen on her throne would not yet budge; she desired
more worship.

"You don't say a great deal," said she. No reply.
"Have you ever been to a dressmaker's in all your
lives?" she demanded.

"Not me!" answered Lord Furber forcibly.

"Yes. Once," answered Mr. Sutherland.

"What do *you* think of it, Mr. Tunnicliff?"

Mr. Tunnicliff blushed once more, aware that the
minx was mischievously placing him in a difficult
position; he was an employee and had no right to any
opinion, even his own. He was further aware that the
question had aroused against his guiltless self the
sudden jealousy of both the magnates.

"I'm no judge," he said. "But I like it very much."

"Nobody here's any judge—I mean any of you
men," Harriet retorted. (Imagine her classing the
Honourable nonentity with the magnates! Conceive
the minx not knowing that private secretaries are
not men while on duty. But she was certainly making
mischief with intentional malice. She enjoyed setting
the men at loggerheads, and here for her there was
no difference between a secretary and his employer.
They all equally had to be subjugated.)

"And you, Mr. Sutherland?" she continued. "You
admit you did once go into a dressmaker's. So you
ought to be a judge." She laughed.

"I think it's most becoming," said Mr. Sutherland
primly.

Not a word did Harriet address to Lord Furber, the
sole authentic begetter of the lovely finery she wore
and of all the other finery in the littered apartment!
Lord Furber knew that she was only teasing him; he

knew that she was paying him out for his refusal to be
confidential with her; he knew what women were.
Yet he allowed himself to be mortified by the minx;
for was he not accustomed to everlasting adulation,
deference, and all thinly-hidden servilities?

He thought:

"Am I going to stand this?"

Well, he had no alternative but to stand this. His
millions could not protect him from the humiliation.
And he chafed, lighting a fresh cigarette—and eating
it too in his annoyance.

"By the way," Harriet asked, turning to her
attendants. "Whose model is this?"

One of them understood enough English to reply:

"It is a Laller, signorina."

"Oh!" Harriet murmured.

The house of Laller was not among the ten greatest Paris houses; but it seemed to the expert and the
initiated likely soon to reach that tremendous dis-
tinction. The curious thing about the house of Laller
was that it had originated in London, and the Paris
house was theoretically but an offshoot of the London
house. Harriet had never before tried on a Laller
creation.

"Shouldn't have thought Laller could do anything half as fine as that!" Lord Furber most sur-
prisingly exclaimed.

Harriet was quite startled by the sudden savage
disdain in his tone, and by his swift challenging
glance at Septimius.

"And why wouldn't you have thought so?" Mr.
Sutherland returned, blandly, but grimly too.

Something obscure and disturbing had happened
between the magnates. Harriet could not solve the

riddle of their mutually defiant demeanour. Lord Furber had said that he had never been to a dressmaker's; Mr. Sutherland had said that he had been to a dressmaker's once only. And yet they were glaring at one another over the name of Laller—a name which could mean nothing whatever to six-nines men in a million! She returned to the state-room, thoughtful.

CHAPTER XXIII

JEALOUSY

WHEN, after another very considerable interval, Miss Harriet Perkins emerged once again from his lordship's state-sitting-room into the lounge, she wore a yachting costume of blue and white, with a trifle of a hat, and white and blue shoes, to correspond. It was not an authentic yachting costume; but Lord Furber had given special wireless orders to his agent that a yachting costume should be included in the display, and this specimen of attire was the best imitation of a British or French yachting costume that could be got together in half an hour in Rome, Rome not being in the least a yachting city as, for instance, Stockholm, Amsterdam and Copenhagen are.

And it was a pretty good imitation. The dressmakers of Rome, like the dressmakers of Buenos Ayres, Rio, and New York, visit Paris once or twice a year, and they take back with them every time the newest spirit of Paris together with copies of the newest secret trade periodicals.

The attire was delicious upon Harriet. Few would have noticed that a button needed shifting and a sleeve adjusting, and nobody except Harriet herself was aware that the shoes were too small for her feet. The second couple of sirens, though cognizant of the faults, were extremely enthusiastic about the total effect. They saw the costume, as did Harriet, not as it actually was, but as it should, could, and would be after an hour's corrective work on it. And Harriet shared their enthusiasm.

Yet the apparition from the state-room was received in the lounge with melancholy and indifference.

Harriet was no longer a queen. She was no longer exercising the supreme social function of her sex, nor demonstrating that she had a right to be alive and to be spoilt and flattered and gifted with costly gifts. She was merely someone who was trying on new clothes. All the waiting sirens showed by their weary demeanour that they were sick of the sight of clothes and would not care if they never saw another woman's frock again. Even the couple attendant on Harriet for this particular *essayage* shed their enthusiasm in a moment, while Harriet felt sadly that clothes do not after all amount to much in the mysterious equation of life. Indeed Harriet wilted and seemed to shrivel, as one who has suddenly lost friendships or prestige. She felt humiliated and resentful. The eyes of everybody seemed to be asking the eyes of everybody else: "What's the use of going on with this silly game any more?"

The explanation was that neither Lord Furber nor Mr. Sutherland happened to be in the lounge. They had deserted and left the garments in the lounge without a decent excuse. So also the Honourable Luke. The Honourable Luke, however, returned himself to the lounge after a brief interval. But his importance in the scheme of things was insufficient to produce any noticeable improvement in the lackadaisical attitude of the sirens.

"Where is Lord Furber?" Harriet asked sharply.

"In the dining-saloon, madam."

"And Mr. Sutherland?" Still more sharply.

"I think he's up in the wireless cabin, madam. Can I do anything?"

"No, thanks."

Harriet was now angry. She went out of the lounge on to the deck.

The Honourable Luke's glance, following her, said: "Well, anyhow, empress, you did offer to kiss me and I declined. So it's no use you attempting to come the cinema star over me."

She ran up to the wireless cabin, the door of which was ajar. Mr. Sutherland was within, but alone.

"What are you doing here?" she asked impetuously.

"Oh!" ejaculated Septimius, admiring, wonderstruck, at the spectacle of her in the yachting costume.

Now, Harriet had by this time actually forgotten that she was wearing the yachting costume. But Septimius's monosyllable and the liquid gaze of his blue eyes reminded her of the fact, restored her sense of sovereignty, renewed the lost conviction that she had a mission to perform in life, and determined her to be ruthless in the exercise of power. And did all these things in the fraction of a second.

"I said, what are you doing here?" she repeated more harshly than before.

"I'm going to get off some wireless messages," Septimius apologetically replied.

"Why just now? You know I wanted you to see these frocks?"

"And I do see one of them!" said Septimius with an impressive bland fervour.

"Yes. And I suppose you expect me to run after you with my frocks."

"The truth is," said Septimius, very placatory and yet dignified. "Our friend suggested that I should do my wirelessing immediately. Difficult to ignore such a suggestion from one's host, you know, dear lady. Especially when one's host is in a—er—certain mood."

"When I last saw you I thought you two were on the edge of having a quarrel."

"Not at all. I have never quarrelled with anyone in my life."

"What do *you* know about Lallers?"

"Nothing."

"Nothing?"

"Well, nothing except the name, and the last balance-sheet. You see it's a limited company, and you know that part of my professional business is to keep an eye on limited companies. Nothing else."

"I don't believe you," said Harriet, deviating somewhat from maidenly politeness. "You're hiding something from me. And what's this about wirelessing? You can't wireless yourself. Where's the operator?"

"I don't know. Furber said he would be here. And he isn't here. I fear the organization of this yacht is not all that it might be."

"The organization of that dressmakers' display was not too bad," said Harriet. "But perhaps you think you could have done it better."

"Not at all."

"And you said last night that the dinner was not so badly organized either."

"True. But, did you notice the breakfast just now? The eggs, for instance! The service! And the service in my cabin really leaves a lot to be desired. It was so last night, and it's the same again this morning."

"Mrs. Bumption is at the bottom of all this," said Harriet, suddenly meditative, after a pause.

"I beg your pardon, sir," said Tunnicliff the operator, appearing in the doorway. But he spoke in a tone which signified: "You ought to beg mine." His nostrils were superbly disdainful.

"Lord Furber kindly told me that I might get some messages off with your assistance," Mr. Sutherland said.

"Won't they do a bit later, Sep? I want you downstairs now." Harriet murmured. And, her demeanour magically altering, she presented Septimius with an exquisite smile so effective that his very spine melted like a candle in the warmth of the tropic sun.

"Certainly," said Septimius with eagerness.

Harriet looked through the wireless operator as though he had been transparent, and in triumph led away her captive, who completely ignored the wireless operator.

But when the captor and the captive reached the lounge together, the former loosed her hold of the latter, and with no word of excuse to him whisked into the dining-saloon and banged the doors after her. And there was Lord Furber seated solitary at the vast oval table. The baron was staring gloomily, even glumly, at the polished surface of the table. He looked up at the invading Harriet, and then looked down again, taking no further notice of the yachting costume.

"This," said Harriet, dropping on to a chair exactly opposite the baron. "This will not do."

No reply.

She repeated:

"This will not do."

No reply. Harriet proceeded:

"And to think that you are the great Lord Furber! This is the millionaire and the engineering genius and the grand general Titan and panjandrum sitting here in front of me. Not to mention my host." She spoke cheerfully, gaily, with the superior smile of a cat addressing a worm. "You put yourself to a tremendous lot of trouble, and expense—though I don't count that, with you—to get enough fal-lals, as you call them, to fit out a whole beauty chorus. It isn't as if I wanted them. I didn't. I was frightfully happy in your fur coat. I was only having them to please you. And you only took the fur coat from me because you knew I simply loved wearing it. You bring all these poor little Italian creatures here, and you make me try on, and as soon as I've tried on one dress you run off and I have to look for you everywhere! And not only that—you tell Mr. Sutherland to make himself scarce, too. I wonder you didn't clear out the little Tunnicliff as well, while you were about it. Who do you think I was trying those clothes on for? Myself? Did you imagine I'm one of the doll-women you're so fond of? You thought you'd impress me and everybody else by your display, and your power, and your will, and all the Aladdin-lamp business and so on. You only did it for that. And then after you've seen only one dress on me——"

"Ye're repeating yeself," said Lord Furber to the table.

Miss Perkins rode over him imperturbably.

"And why did you do it? Because you were vexed. Because you were jealous. Because I hadn't asked *you* if you liked the dress. Well, I did it on purpose, just to see how you'd behave, if you want to know. And see how you have behaved! I've told you before you're spoilt and impossible. And so you are. You think because you are a millionaire and a personage you are entitled to behave as you choose and nobody must say anything on pain of being frowned at by the great panjandrum. And you choose to behave like a silly boy!"

Said Lord Furber:

"Every man is a boy."

"Oh! Is he!"

"And every girl is a woman," Lord Furber added.

"An epigram no doubt. But listen to me, my only millionaire. You can't put it over. You simply can not put it over."

"Is that all—for the moment?" Lord Furber inquired. "If it is, I'll just tell ye a couple o' things. The first is I'm not fond of doll-women. That was a downright lie, and ye knew when ye'd said it it was a thumper. And the second is I came in here, partly because I was sick of waiting for ye, but much more because Mrs. Bumption wants to see me on urgent business—she sent me word. I'm expecting her in here every moment. How's that, miss?"

Harriet shook her head.

"Were you hurt and jealous or weren't you?"

"Yes. I was. But that was only because I knew ye'd be so d—d disappointed if I wasn't. Ye wanted me to be jealous. And ye wanted Sutherland to be jealous. And young Tunnicliff, too, I bet. Ye're a woman. I'm a boy. I like that dress. How's that?"

CHAPTER XXIV

THE PILLAR

THROUGH the service door Mrs. Bumption entered the dining-saloon, and beheld a baron who seemed to be humorously defying and spurning a youngish woman who in turn was humorously spurning and defying the baron.

Mrs. Bumption had arrived with a definite aim, and she did not mean to be hindered in her purpose by the presence of any other woman whatsoever. She walked towards the end of the table like a magnificent pillar—a pillar of society and its proper conventions. Her eyes glared. Her thin, straight nose twitched. Her lips were locked together. Her stout arms were crossed upon the broad surface of the apron which covered the major and more interesting shires of her bodily kingdom. She came slowly to a standstill; at last she was definitely motionless in a massive equilibrium. And now she so imposed upon the baron and Harriet that in the mighty disturbance of her mere advent, expected and duly heralded though it was, they forgot completely the friction of their private politics in waiting for her thunder. She had put the magnate and the unillustrious globe-trotting, hotel-haunting spinster on a level.

"I wish to give notice my lord," said Mrs. Bumption, with majesty.

"Sorry to hear this, Mrs. Bumption," said the baron. "But why? What's amiss?"

"There's nothing amiss, as you may say, my lord," the pillar replied. "But the words as your lordship remarked about me this morning, or should I say, in the night while your lordship was in bed, cannot be stood."

"Remarks!" exclaimed the baron. "What remarks?"

"Well, my lord, your lordship gave out as it were that I'd been in the 'abit of running after your lordship. And this 'ere young lady was present to hear—not that I'd asked her to come in—though I was in charge of your lordship."

"But, did I really say any such thing?" The baron put this question direct to Harriet.

"I'm afraid you did," Harriet answered solemnly. "But of course your mind was wandering at the time. In fact Mrs. Bumption said herself you were wandering."

"His lordship may have been wandering like in his mind," said Mrs. Bumption, "and I hope and trust you was, my lord. But they do say there's no smoke without fire, and my character's my character."

She spoke seriously as a woman profoundly convinced of her power over the romantic sex. She was not obese; she was not fifty; she was not ugly; she was not exasperatingly carping—she was the girl who for twenty years and more had held Mr. Bumption fast and fast by the tremendous attraction of her femininity.

She went on:

"And as I'm here I'll say I don't hold with this yachting. I've known yachting lead young people astray, and I don't hold with it and there's a lot of things in this yacht as I don't like, if your lordship will excuse me."

Her titanic frame immobile, she shifted her eyes from side to side, glancing first at the baron and then at the girl, and so to and fro several times: like a statue with movable painted orbs set in a carven face.

Lord Furber and Harriet had the same thought: namely, that here was a social situation which Lord Furber ought somehow to be able to deal with in a manner at once dignified and triumphant. Mrs. Bumption was nobody at all—the wife of a butler. Lord Furber was a high figure in the world; and he had arrived at the state of being a high figure in the world by reason of his brains. Mrs. Bumption had no brains worth mentioning. In every way she was mediocre or worse than mediocre. Moreover she was dependent, whereas Lord Furber was just about as independent as any human being could be. Again, Lord Furber was accustomed to handling, for his own profit, many different kinds of people, while Mrs. Bumption had had but little occasion for diplomacy, and indeed disdained it. All the material and intellectual and social advantages were on one side; all the disadvantages on the other.

Yet Lord Furber could think of no effective method of engaging Mrs. Bumption in battle and defeating her. Harriet being present, he wanted to shine, and he could not shine. Mrs. Bumption outglared his diminished ray. And Harriet was there to witness his affliction and his humiliation. He was a great man; he knew that he was great and that he had earned his greatness; but the great man was being exposed and thrown down, and Harriet was there to see. Already she, Harriet, had severely criticized him, and he had not answered her. Mrs. Bumption's arrival had prevented him from answering Harriet.

Like a tiger enticed into a cage, he felt that fate was unkind to him. Rage began to rise in perilous, intoxicating vapour out of the depths of his mind. He was on the brink of doing something violent and silly, when Mrs. Bumption, stately, deliberate, implacable, turned round in the similitude now not of a pillar but of a ship going about, and left the dining-saloon by the door through which she had originally entered.

Surcease of hostilities! Lord Furber's dignity and reputation for brilliant manœuvring, if not definitely saved, was at any rate reprieved. The baron laughed, loud and uncouth, and waited to counter whatever Harriet might say. Harriet said nothing. Lord Furber could not bear the silence.

"That means I've lost Bumption," said he at length, deciding that he would stand best with Harriet by squarely facing the facts.

"What of it?" said Harriet. "Bumption is only a habit."

Dash the chit! How clever she was! She had defined the relation in a word. He forgot that he had himself previously given her the word. He privately admitted, as he had admitted before, that a habit was just what Bumption was. But he would not admit it to her.

He said gravely and grandly:

"Bumption is my butler and he is devoted. Ye can't do without a devoted butler. What would happen to the house?"

"What *has* happened to the house?" Harriet demanded quickly.

"What d'ye mean?"

"Is your house open?"

"Yes."

"Anybody living there?"

"My wife."

"Doesn't she have to manage without Bumption?"

"Bumption always goes with *me*."

"And be hanged to your house, I suppose, so long as you aren't in it! That's just like you, that is! It seems quite natural to you, of course, to be the only person whose convenience has to be consulted. It would. You've lost Bumption for your wife as well as for yourself. Your wife doesn't matter. Any butler ought to be good enough for her. And now she'll have all the worry of getting a new butler who'll suit you, and all because you think it's funny to behave like a child. Why did you go out of your way to insult Mrs. Bumption this morning? Because it amused you and you thought you were perfectly entitled to do it, because you're so rich."

"Harriet, ye're repeating yeself. I've told ye once."

He smiled easily at the impudent girl. She looked delicious in the yachting costume (which his brains and his volition had procured for her). She had barely enough to live on. She had not denied that she could do nothing in the world. She possessed wit, but no practical faculties. And there she was behaving towards him as though she held in her frail hands all the cards of life. The spectacle of her was comic—far too comic to be taken seriously.

"What are you?" Harriet said venomously. "You're only a bladder—and Mrs. Bumption has pricked you."

Suddenly the baron lost his temper, and broke into

vituperation, employing the vocabulary of his Five Towns picturesque youth. He had positively meant not to lose his temper, but now that he had in fact lost it, he enjoyed the sensation—as always. Harriet stood up in exasperating, gentle glee.

"Ah!" she said. "I knew I could make you lose your temper."

From that moment the baron passed beyond mere enjoyment into something more emotional, sublime, and, to Harriet, ludicrous. Her glee became a dance. It would be rash to say that the baron would have laid hands on her, but that the table was between them cannot be denied. He shouted his uncontrolled fury. . . .

The door opened and Mr. Sutherland entered.

CHAPTER XXV

LALLERS

DESERTED in the lounge by Harriet, Septimius had returned to the wireless cabin and sent off his messages; and, incidentally, en route had encountered both Captain Slapser and Mr. Antinope, the tall purser, both of whom had treated him with an extreme and uneasy deference which delightfully contrasted with their demeanour towards him in the night. He had come back to the lounge only to discover that Miss Perkins was still in the dining-saloon. Therefore he had gone unasked into the dining-saloon, partly from impatience at further waiting, partly because he thought that Harriet, having forcibly brought him from the wireless cabin, should not have abandoned him for a private interview with Lord Furber, partly because he liked to spend as much time with her as possible, partly because the interview between Harriet and Lord Furber had developed on such lines that a lot of it could be heard in the scandalized lounge, and some moderating influence must clearly be needed, and partly because he feared (or rather hoped) that Harriet might be in danger (real danger this time) from which he could rescue her.

When he beheld the altercating pair on either side of the dining-table, his mind sub-divided itself into an unusually large number of minds. One of them adored Harriet; another regretted that she should have lowered herself to the level of a mere shindy; another remembered that he was a boxer and had once stroked the Cambridge boat; another remembered that he was a husband and father and quite fifty; another regretted that Lord Furber's behaviour should match so ill the splendour and loveliness and classic grace of this room and of the whole yacht (imagine a man quarrelling, and like a navvy, while environed by those exquisite Della Robbian panels of mythological subjects!), and another keenly desired to repeat the precious night's performance of felling Lord Furber with a single blow.

Harriet raised her hand.

"Sep!" she warned Mr. Sutherland. "Not again! Once was enough. I must ask you to respect his wounds." She vaguely indicated the baron's amorphous chin and plastered head.

"My dear Harriet!" Septimius blandly exclaimed. (How attractive and amusing she was, and how friendly and intimate they were together, with their tossing to and fro of Christian names!) "My dear Harriet!" he repeated. "I really don't know what you mean. I heard you arguing, and the topic seemed to be one in which I might usefully join. If I'm wrong I'll go out again."

Lord Furber's mouth had remained wide open, as as though the arrival of Septimius had put a petrifying spell upon him. With an effort he broke the spell, roared with laughter, and sat down.

"Take a chair, Sutherland," he said genially, and roared afresh with laughter.

And he glanced at Harriet, as it were wistfully, boyish, appealing, and yet roguish.

Harriet warmed to him instantly. As an individuality he was apt to be extremely inconvenient, but he had an art to attract affection. She thought of the wireless operator's remark: "He doesn't know what he's alive for." And indeed he didn't. And the same dictum applied equally well to herself. Harriet did not know what Harriet was alive for either. All that he did, and all that she did, was but an expression of the desire to escape from the boredom of an undirected existence.

She suspected that her friend Maidie, his wife, did not entirely comprehend the baron's psychology, and that she, Harriet, did.

"I am a cat!" she reflected transiently.

It was possible to laugh at him for his ridiculously excessive riches and the inevitable consequences thereof; but he was a great man and a generous. What a magnificent gesture to send for all those marvellous frocks and finery! At that very moment was she not looking most satisfactorily chic as a result of the gesture? And who but him could have devised and executed such a gesture?

"The worst o' me," said the baron, "is that— Sutherland, didn't I ask ye to sit down?—is that when I argue I get carried away. I reckon there's summat of the poet in me." He smiled.

"Of course," said Mr. Sutherland, seating himself. "*I* knew you were merely arguing. But all those Latins in there"—he pointed towards the lounge— "had begun to think it wasn't an argument you were busy with. So I thought I'd warn you against being misunderstood."

"Both of us?" asked Harriet.

"Yes. Both of you," said Mr. Sutherland. "And what really *was* the topic?"

"The argument was just finished when you came in," said the baron. "She won."

"In that case, Furber," said Mr. Sutherland. "May I take this opportunity of asking you a favour?"

"If it's anything I can do, I'll do it, and at once," replied the baron.

"I'm speaking for both Miss Perkins and myself."

"Oh!" said the baron in a tone slightly changed. He looked about the room, which was apparently full of every imaginable thing except the thing he wanted at that moment. "Got a cigarette, Sutherland? I never carry cigarettes, and I never carry money."

"Why don't you?" asked Harriet, who was wondering what could be the favour which Seppie was about to implore on her behalf as well as his own. She was very impatient for information on this point, but she could not resist an occasion to twit the boy of fifty in the dressing-gown opposite to her.

"Oh!" the baron answered negligently, grandly. "I don't know."

"Yes, you do," said Harriet. "You know perfectly well. It's because you once read somewhere that some great king never carried money, and so you decided *you* wouldn't. Makes people talk. 'He's so rich, and yet he never has a penny in his pocket.' And you said to yourself you'd go one better—with cigarettes."

Mr. Sutherland had opened his cigarette-case, which was empty.

"Got a cigarette, Harriet?" the baron demanded grimly, ignoring her dissertation upon his motives.

"I have some cigarettes," she said. "But they're in my bag, and my bag's in your room."

"Conf—" muttered the baron, and rose to ring a bell.

"Don't ring," Harriet enjoined him.

"Why not?"

"Be a man for once in a way, and do without a cigarette. Show Mr. Sutherland what you're really made of. I'm speaking for both him and myself."

The baron wavered and then resumed his seat.

"I should think pretty nearly everything's happened in this yacht except murder; and that'll be happening soon," he muttered, half to himself, and made a face at Harriet. "Well, Sutherland, what is it you want?"

"I should like to know, if it's quite convenient," said Sutherland, "why Miss Perkins and myself have been abducted in this yacht of yours." He used the gentlest, calmest, most christian tone. And he amiably smiled.

"Abducted?"

"Abducted. I don't want to seem curious or impatient. I've sent off my messages to London—they are to be relayed from Milan—and I'm in no sort of hurry to leave, and I don't think Miss Perkins is in a hurry either. Your yacht makes an excellent hotel. You are very hospitable, and your society is very pleasantly exciting. But just by way of interesting information I *should* just like to know why I'm here."

There was a pause.

"But ye came to dinner, and ye stayed the night. That's all," said Lord Furber with what appeared to be an utterly candid laugh.

"I'm afraid I don't make myself clear," Mr. Sutherland went on. "You say 'that's all'! But is it all? Why am I here? I hoped you'd understand that now at last we're *talking*."

Lord Furber tattoed faintly on the table.

"Out with it, my beautiful lord!" said Harriet. "Or he'll bash your head right in this time."

"Well," said Lord Furber deliberately. "I'll tell ye. I see no reason why I shouldn't." He went on more loudly and staccato. "I want to buy Lallers."

Mr. Sutherland raised his eyebrows.

"You mean Lallers Limited."

"I do. At your own price."

"But I don't own Lallers. I haven't got a single share in Lallers."

"Nor a debenture?"

"Nor a debenture. But what does a man like you want with an affair like Lallers? A hundred thousand pounds ought to cover the lot of it. Millions should be more in your line."

"I'll give ye two hundred thousand then," said Lord Furber.

"But don't I tell you I've no holding in it at all?"

"Look here," said Lord Furber, facing Mr. Sutherland. "Ye say we're *talking*. I'll give ye a quarter of a million. I want Lallers, and ye needn't keep on saying ye've got no holding in it. Perhaps ye haven't. But ye've got a rare pull over them that have. Ye must have an option. If you're ready to sell, Lallers will be sold."

"That may or may not be so. But assuming that it were so, you may believe me that I shouldn't be ready to sell."

"Ye mean it?"

"I certainly do."

"Then be d—d to ye."

"Quite!" said Mr. Sutherland with undiminished blandness. "And so you had me in your yacht in order to buy Lallers, lock, stock, and barrel!"

"Yes," Lord Furber agreed, "I kidnapped ye just for that and nowt else."

"Well, it's all very interesting," Mr. Sutherland commented, and having exchanged a mild and utterly uncompromising stare for Lord Furber's defiant and semi-murderous glance, he rose and abruptly left the room.

Harriet was impressed and a little frightened, in spite of herself. Deeps, chasms, had somehow opened at her feet. Men might be boys, but they were rather terrifying at times. Her charming yachting costume had lost the whole of its importance in the scheme of things. Still, she had one consolation. Both her admirers, of whose admiration she was very proud, had acquitted themselves well. They had kept her respect —and something more. The pity was that just at the moment they were not fighting for her.

"But I'll have Lallers," the baron formidably growled. "I've got to have Lallers!"

To hear him his life might have depended on having Lallers.

Harriet was perfectly nonplussed.

Then through the service-door Bumption entered.

CHAPTER XXVI

A GREAT WOMAN

"Oh, I beg pardon, my lord." Having made this appeal, Bumption turned away again, as if to leave the room.

"What is it, Bumption?" The baron stopped his butler with an encouraging tone.

"I was only——" The man hesitated.

Miss Perkins was struck by the contrast between his grand, assured demeanour as chief priest of the banquet on the previous evening and the apologetic, nervous, almost human air which now characterized him. Physically he was massive, like most of the personnel of the *Vanguard* (Mr. Antinope the purser being an exception as to girth); and his style could be massive also when occasion needed, but at the moment his style was no more massive than that of a leaf blown about by the wind. Miss Perkins noticed further that the baron's mien and voice had altered at the sight of the faithful servitor; the baron undoubtedly liked the idea and conception of a faithful servitor, because it symbolized for him all that his early years had not contained; the baron became suddenly benevolent.

"Ye can talk," said the baron. "Miss Perkins won't mind. Miss Perkins has been on board in an official capacity." He put a faint emphasis on the words "has been," and gave Harriet a surreptitious glance, which she richly returned.

"I only wished to apologize for the way the breakfast was served this morning, my lord."

"Quite!" said his lordship. "Don't let that trouble you. The ship's been upset a bit. Thirteens, eh?"

"Thirteens, my lord? I don't follow your lordship."

"Sixes and sevens."

Mr. Bumption produced a dutiful smile, which played fitfully over his obvious pain. The smile vanished, his hands moved a little uncertainly over the front of his impressive blue-and-gold uniform.

"I don't hardly know how to tell your lordship—I mean—I——"

"That's all right, Bumption. Ye needn't tell me. I know what ye've got for me—notice to leave. That's it. Isn't it?"

"Well, my lord, it's like this. The wife——"

He paused once more. In referring to Mrs. Bumption he usually said "the wife," as though there were, and could be, no other wife on earth worthy of the name of wife; or, if you chose to interpret the phrase differently, as though he possessed many wives, of whom this one was the principal or favourite.

The baron again helped him.

"She's leaving. She's just told me."

"Yes, my lord. I've explained to her it must have been all a misunderstanding. But your lordship knows how they are, even the best of 'em."

"Oh, I do!"

"I said I was sure your lordship must have been delirious at the time."

"I was. I was. I couldn't have been anything else."

"May I say how glad I am to see your lordship so much better?"

"Thank ye, Bumption. I'm sorry I've put ye into

such an awkward position. I'm very sorry. Ye're sure it can't be mended?"

"I think not, my lord. And that's not all of it, either. The Captain don't seem to hit it off very well with Daisy." Daisy was Mrs. Bumption. "Not that that matters so much. Still he don't. He told her she was 'crew' last night, and she didn't like it. I explained that to her as well, but somehow she can't swallow it."

"And so she's leaving."

"To-day, my lord. She says if she's 'crew' she need only give twenty-four hours' notice, and she'll leave now and ask Mr. Antinope to take a day off her wages in lieu of notice. I regret it, my lord, but you see how I'm placed."

"It's all as plain as a pikestaff, Bumption. But, tell me how yer Mrs. Bumption means to leave. She's at sea, and she can't leave except in one of the yacht's boats, and supposing I won't let her use one of the yacht's boats? What then? Will she swim ashore? Has she thought of that?"

Mr. Bumption faintly smiled—a smile which disclosed a certain humorous pride in Mrs. Bumption's resourcefulness.

"Oh! She's fixed all that, my lord. She's been packing her things this morning and mine, too. And in another five minutes she'll be in one of them Italian launches that are waiting alongside. Not that she thinks your lordship would keep her aboard unwilling. No! But she says she won't be beholden to anybody. She always was very independent, my lord. If your lordship remembers, I told your lordship she was when you engaged her for the yacht. Of course, if she'd been in service in Belgrave Square your lordship would

have known. But me having a little place in Chesham
Mews and going home to her every evening, your
lordship couldn't be expected to know, and that was
why I took the liberty of warning your lordship beforehand, if your lordship will excuse me."

"Bumption," said the baron. "Be honest. Ye gave
her a very good character——"

"And so she has it, my lord."

"Ye said she'd been in service as housekeeper at the
Marquis of Amberley's, and she'd been to sea in the
Marquis's schooner, and she'd come to me if I really
wanted her. But the only reason I engaged her was
that you wouldn't leave her behind."

"No more I would, my lord. How could I? I never
have left her, and she's never left me. We've always
been what they call inseparable."

"Yes," said the baron, leaning on his elbow and
looking up at Bumption. "It's a wonderful story. But
don't ye think ye ought to give her a bit of a holiday
from her husband? Pleasant change for her?"

"She isn't one for holidays, my lord. I have suggested it, once or twice. For her sake. But she isn't
having any."

"Try her again. Tell her I'll pay all her holiday
expenses."

Bumption shook his grieved head.

"And supposing she did go off alone, which she
won't, we couldn't manage aboard without her. I
couldn't face it, my lord. She sees to everything—I
mean in my department."

"And not only in yours, I should say," the baron
put in.

"No, my lord," said Bumption firmly. "She never
interferes with the navigating; I'll say that for her."

"Well, it's a lot to say, Bumption."

"It may be, my lord. But I'll say it. And your lordship can ask anybody aboard. No, my lord. I really couldn't manage without her. And what's more I like a woman under me. There's so many things about my job that they understand better than any man could. Laundry work, for instance. And mending. And I don't know what all. And even if I could manage, I couldn't leave the poor little thing to go home from here all alone. It's a two-days' journey, and all customs and frontiers and changing trains! I couldn't bear the thought of it, my lord. I've always looked after her hand and foot."

"But she needn't go, Bumption. I'm not asking her to go. She's going of her own accord."

"Yes, my lord. But she's going."

"And you're going?"

"And I'm going, my lord. And very, very sorry I am. I know how inconvenient it'll be for your lordship. And I don't expect your lordship to take me on again at Belgrave Square. Much as I shall miss it. And I don't know as I expect your lordship to give me a character. But I shouldn't be easy in my conscience if I didn't go. At once."

"Then yer wife does realize that she's making things just a bit rough for me?"

"Oh, she does, my lord!"

"Well, that's something. Has she happened to say what she thinks I ought to do in the circumstances?"

"Yes, my lord. She's one that thinks of everything. It's her opinion that your lordship's best plan would be to leave the yacht and go and stay in a hotel in Rome or somewhere handy until you can get a new chief steward and housekeeper over from England."

Lord Furber stood up.

"Bumption," said he solemnly. "Your wife is a great woman. You're right about her. There's nobody like her. You go to Mr. Antinope and tell him I say he's to pay her her full wages and twenty pounds in addition. I should like to show my admiration of your poor little Daisy. And I hope she won't refuse the money. You tell her I'm sorry I said anything in my dreams to upset her, and tell her I'll see her d—d before I leave my own yacht. You tell her I'll see her d—d first. Be sure to say d—d."

"Yes, my lord."

"And I shall take you back at Belgrave Square because I understand the position. Yes, by G—d! I understand it. That'll do. Ye can have one of my launches if ye want it."

CHAPTER XXVII

THE ANKLE

"By the way," asked Harriet, when Bumption had thankfully left the room. "What is your Christian name?"

"Ralph," said Lord Furber.

"Well, Ralph, you behaved very well that time, if you don't mind my telling you. You were both a philosopher and a philanthropist for at least five minutes—I'm beginning to admire you."

Harriet spoke with faint enthusiasm. She tried not to be patronizing and the baron tried not to be patronized. Neither succeeded fully, but both were pleased with their efforts.

"Ye'd better put that in writing," said the baron.

Said Harriet:

"And I must tell you something else. He's the nicest man in the yacht, and I love him."

"Who?"

"Bumption, of course! I'd no idea."

"Ah!" said the baron. "He's always at his best with me. And I'm at my best with him. That fellow likes me, and I like him—as much as I hate his wife. More. I don't really hate her. I admire her, because she's the only one around here that doesn't care a damn for me. See me coaxing her sometimes, and her not having any! If you ask me, the explanation is that she's jealous of him being fond of me, and me

192

being fond of him. She's the devil, but she's a great woman and don't ye make any mistake, Harriet Perkins. She's got him under her foot, and I'm sorry for him. No, I'm not. I envy him, because he has a grand passion. He knows what he wants. I don't know what I want, and you don't know what you want, Harriet Perkins. That's where he's got the pull over us."

"I think I admire you more and more," said Harriet.

They looked at one another and kept silence for a moment.

"Well," said the baron. "I've lost him. Oh yes! I've lost him."

"And it was your own fault—now wasn't it?" said Harriet persuasively.

"No," growled the baron. "She always meant to go and she always meant him to go, too. And if she hadn't found one excuse she'd have found another. And no money could ha' bought her. That's where she knew she had me. Well, I did the best I could. Couldn't have gone further, could I?"

"Naturally you could."

"How?"

"Didn't I say I wouldn't be your secretary, but I'd help you if you needed it? And you didn't ask me, and yet you say you couldn't have gone further!"

"Ye couldn't have helped me, wench."

"Supposing you'd ask me to be housekeeper here instead of Mrs. Bumption; I'm a very good housekeeper—at least, I used to be at home. And I'm never sea-sick. I could have worked with Bumption. Who couldn't? Mrs. B. could have lived on board like a lady in her own part of the yacht. And I should have had some work to live for. I haven't any aprons here, but you could have wirelessed to Rome for a selection of aprons and had them sent down in three motor-cars, according to your usual practice with fal-lals."

"She'd never have agreed."

"Yes, she would."

"How d'ye know?"

"Because she'd have loved to stand by and see me make a mess of her job. Not that I should have made a mess of it. She'd have glared at me and never said a word. But what things she'd have said to Bumption every night! What a time she'd have had! So don't tell me she wouldn't have agreed, Ralph. If you do, you might as well admit that you don't understand women. And I *should* like you to understand women. It would be such a nice change for you, and you'd be the first man that ever did."

She smiled. He smiled. . . . They looked at one another again, silently, and grew into brother and sister, and the sister was the elder of the two.

"I wonder!" the baron murmured, almost humbly, as he reflected upon the possibilities of sister's ingenious scheme.

Harriet could see in his eyes the resurrected hope of retaining the precious Bumption; and it was a sweet spectacle to her, and she was proud of herself.

"I'd like to see ye housekeeping," the baron said appreciatively.

"I'm sure you would; and, you know, you wouldn't have to be confidential with me."

The baron jumped up and rang the bell. A steward, an ordinary, nameless steward, responded.

"That bell was for Bumption," said his lordship curtly. "Ye know that."

"Bumption is busy at the moment, my lord," the steward apologetically explained.

"Get him," said his lordship, laconic and intimidating.

"Yes, my lord."

"Harriet," said the baron. "Perhaps nobody's ever told ye before, but ye're the goods."

She laughed, happily.

"But," the baron added. "I lay ye a hundred to one Mrs. B. won't give in."

Bumption entered in an obvious state of flurry.

"Bumption, listen to me——"

"Excuse me, my lord. Daisy's slipped and sprained her ankle getting into one of them greasy Italian launches. I asked her to wait for me, but she said she wasn't taking any chances and she'd wait for me in the launch. Now she can't stand, and she says her ankle's hurting her dreadful, and Mr. Antinope's giving her brandy to stop her from fainting, and what's to be done I don't know, swelp me bob—I ask your lordship's pardon."

Mr. Bumption was really excited and Lord Furber had never seen him excited before.

"She'll have to be brought back on board, Bumption," said Lord Furber, "whether she likes it or not. And I hope this'll be a lesson to both of ye."

"Yes, my lord," Bumption agreed, hasting to the door. "But how is she to come back on board? She'll never get up the steps of that gangway. And nobody could get her up. Seventeen stone, she is."

"Well, she can't go ashore with a sprained ankle."

"No, my lord." Bumption was now disappearing through the door.

"Hi! Bumption!"

"No, my lord," the man's voice sounded faintly from outside the room. . . . He had gone. Nothing, not even the sharp summons of his worshipped master, could keep him.

"Harriet, my girl," said Lord Furber, laughing with deep gusto. "Heaven's been watching over us. Ye shall be my housekeeper. There's nothing to stop it now."

The doors of the dining-saloon opened suddenly, and Mr. Sutherland burst in. Mr. Sutherland was really excited, and neither the baron nor Harriet Perkins had ever seen him excited before.

"I say," he exclaimed. "Mrs. Bumption's fallen into one of those launches and broken her leg."

"Yes," said Harriet. "And she's dead."

"Dead! Who?"

"Queen Anne, Seppie."

CHAPTER XXVIII

THE HORSE—BOX

ONLY the deepest students of human nature and of human relations are not astonished at the high percentage of people in any given population who can find leisure to witness any event that is really unusual and interesting. In the busiest industrial city, supposed to be inhabited exclusively by incessant toilers, fifty persons will immediately appear from nowhere to watch a dog-fight, five hundred to stare at a fire, and five thousand to see a wedding procession of the exalted. The news spreads, none knows how, and no physical obstacles will prevent a congregation.

Thus at Ostia that morning, the *Vanguard* was anchored fifteen cables' length from shore; no messages seemed to go from the yacht to the port, and yet very quickly, very magically, the yacht was surrounded by a ring of small boats of every description carrying sightseers of every description.

And on board the yacht a similar phenomenon existed. The ship's company consisted of about eighty immortal souls, and about seventy-seven of them were excitedly peering from one post or another over the side of the yacht. Discipline had temporarily vanished; the conspicuous presence of the owner in his remarkable dressing-gown, and with his patched cranium, had not sufficed to preserve discipline. As a fact the owner was as excited and undisciplined as anybody else, and more than some.

Four cooks in their caps, whitely imitating the head-dresses of Russian priests, leaned on the rail of the main-deck, and they were flanked on either side by stewards and deckhands. Below, gazing from various apertures, were visible the grimy faces of greasers. The chief engineer and two of his important aids surveyed the scene from the bows on the main-deck. And the bright-coloured sirens were all around them chattering. Lord Furber and Septimius Sutherland were on the boat-deck. The wireless operator had perched himself on the roof of the wireless cabin. And above all, on the bridge, were the skipper, the first-officer and a mate. The first-officer was directing the operation upon which the universal curiosity was centred.

So great was the concourse on the port side of the *Vanguard*, that she would have been justified in showing a distinct list to port.

And be it remembered that many of these steadfast beholders, on account of the night voyage, had been out of bed and sleepless all night. Yet they felt no fatigue.

Only Miss Perkins and the Honourable Luke John Tunnicliff were absent from the muster.

The manner of the fascinating operation thus observed had been the subject of anxious discussion, and some heated argument, among the experts. The Captain himself had been torn from his cabin (where he was engaged in looking through the ship's papers preparatory to a scrutiny by the emissaries of Farinacci, for Lord Furber had not yet told him that he had been hoaxed in that matter—in order to give an unwilling opinion as to the proper mechanical procedure. In the result a couple of long booms had been lashed to the floor of the bridge, with their joint extremities sticking out far beyond the topsides. At the said extremities had been rigged a stout double tackle (used for the main halliards when the yacht happened to be assisting motor-power with sail-power). Through this tackle ran a tremendous rope, which in more normal circumstances was the sheet. Attached to one end of this rope was a kind of horse box which the ship's carpenter had hammered together, and the other end was in the horny hands of four seamen and two stewards.

The seamen and the stewards hauled: the horse-box (carpeted with cushions) rose from the deck and was fended off with boathooks until it swung clear of the rail and over the sea, or rather over the largest of the sirens' launches.

"Hold on!" cried Lord Furber loudly, usurping the authority of the first-officer. "Where's Mr. Tunnicliff? Where is Mr. Tunnicliff?"

Everyone looked round for Mr. Tunnicliff; and in the nick of time Mr. Tunnicliff appeared carrying the film-camera without which his lordship would have regarded the inventory of no yacht as complete. The horse-box was slowly revolving in mid-air from the four cords which fastened it to the sheet.

"Shoot it as it goes down!" ordered the baron, being acquainted with the vocabulary of the film-studios.

Mr. Tunnicliff adjusted the camera on its stand.

"Lower away!" cried the first-officer, resuming command, and Mr. Tunnicliff (whose secretarial duties were manifold) duly shot the horse-box as it disappeared downwards.

Heads and trunks were projected still further outwards over the rails, so that eyes could watch every detail of the descent.

The horse-box settled gently into the bottom of the large Italian launch. Mr. Bumption with a terrific effort raised Daisy till she could stand on her sole sound leg, and manœuvre her massive frame until she could subside on to the cushions. So established, she set her teeth and clung to the sides of the horse-box, and the ascent began. How else could she have been salved? She could not walk up the gangway steps; she could not hop up; nor could she have been carried up without serious risk of a plunge into the Mediterranean. Moreover, she would allow no one but her husband to lay hands upon her. The entire launch itself might have been hauled up on davits, but it could only have been swung in on the top deck, and the top deck was not Mrs. Bumption's final destination, to reach which from the top deck she would have had to descend impossible stairs.

She might more conveniently have been hauled up on one of the falls of the davits of the yacht's port launch. But this method she had strenuously declined, stating that it was notorious that in times of need davit-tackle invariably fouled—as a rule with fatal consequences.

"Tunnicliff!" cried the baron, and then corrected himself. "No. You're busy. Rayner! Rayner! Where's Miss Perkins? Go and find her wherever she is and ask her to be good enough to come up here at once." He turned to the bridge: "Hold on there! Don't haul yet."

Rayner, hiding as well as he could his disgust at

being thus forced to run the risk of missing the culmination of the show, ran off.

Soon afterwards, Harriet appeared on the top deck. She wore a white apron over her new yachting costume, and the apron was ample enough to have asphyxiated two yachting costumes.

"Miss Vamp!" a voice hailed her from the roof of the wireless cabin as she passed. Involuntary she turned her head. "Ha! You recognized yourself then, dear lady. Didn't I tell you this was no ordinary sort of a yacht? Look!"

The wireless operator seemed to be in the very highest spirits.

"Thank you," said Harriet pleasantly.

She looked, but saw nothing save a perpendicular rope. She passed on, forward along the deck.

Septimius came to meet her, as she stopped near the film-camera.

"You look ravishing in that apron. Ravishing!" said Septimius. "We've been waiting for you." His eyes shone. Apparently he was in an ecstasy at the sight of her.

"My shoes hurt dreadfully," said she, with maidenly calmness. They did.

The Honourable Luke glanced aside at her from his camera. His eyes outshone the eyes of Septimius. Never had she met such a gaze. It thrilled and frightened her. She recalled his words on the previous night in the owner's state-sitting-room. "You wait and you'll see."

She thought:

"The wireless operator is dangerous, but Luke is more dangerous. He's more dangerous even than Ralph."

She saw Lord Furber beckoning to her, and she obeyed the gesture, Septimius following.

"I'm studying my new job, Ralph," she murmured. "I can't stop long. I'm very busy."

Near by, the four deckhands and two stewards were hauling on the halliard. They stopped.

"Go on! Higher!" said the baron to them in a low voice. Bumption had appeared, panting, to greet his enchantress from above.

"She's level with the main-deck, my lord," said one of the deckhands.

"Higher, I tell you!" enjoined his lordship impatiently. The gang hauled again.

"Tunnicliff!" called the baron, and the Honourable Luke started once more to turn the handle of the camera.

Lord Furber gazed with young rapture at Miss Perkins, who thought how agreeable and stimulating it was to be the only woman among all these vitalized males.

"Look!" said Lord Furber to her.

The horse-box was rising clear of the rail of the navigating deck, and therein reclined Mrs. Bumption, revolving as the horse-box revolved, with one foot unshod and the ankle thereof bandaged. She could be plainly seen through the open ends of the box. Her face was stern and yet composed. Her knuckles showed white as she clenched her hands on the sides of the box. She went higher. She revolved more quickly. She dominated the yacht and all on board. The film-camera made its rapid click-click-click. Mrs. Bumption ceased to rise, for the horse-box was nearly touching the topmost block of the tackle.

Harriet perceived that she was not the only woman

among all those vitalized males. A greater than she glared mountainously down upon her.

"I wouldn't sell this film for ten thousand pounds," said Lord Furber to Harriet. "Look at her. She's a great woman. She was beaten, but now she's beating me, beating all of us. Nothing can beat her."

"*Viva! viva! viva!*" came from the sirens with their shrill voices. The signal was too tempting to be ignored. The British crew cheered loudly in response. Some of them imagined that they were taking their revenge on the yacht's formidable housekeeper. More *vivas* ascended from the launches beneath.

"Lower away!" muttered the baron, glutted with spectacular satisfaction, and Mrs. Bumption, still twisting very slowly, began to sink towards the level of the main-deck.

"We're nobodies," said Lord Furber in Harriet's ear. "She knows what she wants, and she'll have it. That's where she's got us."

"Pardon me," said Harriet. "I wanted a job, and I have it."

"Pooh!" said Lord Furber. "Ye're only a parasite on a parasite."

"No," said Harriet. "I have a job and I shall do it. Au revoir." She left her employer.

"That's my apron, if *you* please," called Mrs. Bumption as she sank.

Laughter! General laughter! The cheering and the *vivas* ceased. Mr. Bumption had disappeared. A few minutes later news came to the upper deck that Mrs. Bumption, the horse-box having been swung in on the main-deck, had hopped to a cabin there, in the arms of her husband.

CHAPTER XXIX

THE FILM

LORD FURBER and his bland guest, Mr. Septimius Sutherland, sat down to lunch in the dining-saloon which earlier had been the scene of dramatic encounters.

Reaction follows the greatest events, and reaction had followed the raising of Mrs. Bumption from the Italian launch into the bosom of the yacht. Reaction affected the atmosphere of the lunch itself, despite the benevolent cheerfulness of the chief steward (or rather the chief priest), Bumption.

And the sense of reaction was intensified by the absence from the meal of Miss Harriet Perkins. Harriet had sent word that, being extraordinarily busy upon her new duties, and indeed absorbed by them, she had no time for the frivolities of eating and of masculine society. The convert is always fanatical, and Harriet had just been converted from idleness to industry. Without being aware of the fact, she was determined that her industry should disturb the world as much as possible.

Her industry had certainly disturbed the sirens of the frocks. Harriet would have no more truck with them. She decided on the first green dress and on the yachting costume, and on a quite appreciable amount of lingerie, and would listen to no further arguments. Was she not a working maritime housekeeper? In pity, Septimius bought a frock or two, which he hoped might both suit and please his delicious absent wife. (The transaction was perhaps intended to soothe his conscience in the matter of the warmth of his regard for Harriet.) Then Lord Furber, hearing of the business, plunged into the lounge and bought twenty-three frocks in addition to many oddments of attire.

The sirens were going away happy; but they were stopped at the very gangway by order of Harriet. Harriet the housekeeper had caused a meal to be prepared for them. As a perfect housekeeper she naturally thought of everything. That meal the sirens had to eat, and did eat, with twittering enthusiasm.

And let no owner or guest imagine that her attention to the repast of the sirens might prejudice the lunch of the mighty in the dining-saloon! Quite the contrary. The character and plenteousness of the lunch had occasioned some friction between the new housekeeper and the chef. The new broom swept clean, and in so doing was inspiring the usual opposition and sinful sulkiness.

Hence the lunch, triumphant gastronomically, did not prove to be very successful as a social gathering. And yet both Lord Furber and Mr. Sutherland had apparently forgotten the small unpleasantness which had arisen out of the former's strange attempt to gain control of the house of Laller.

It was not until the arrival of the coffee and the final disappearance of a beaming Bumption that reaction was overcome. The baron's eye happened to catch the rolled-up cinema-screen which was suspended above the service door. The sight put an idea into his head, and he rang for the Honourable

Luke, who came with a demeanour which indicated recent excitement not wholly recovered from.

"Tunnicliff," said the baron. "What about that film you took this morning? I suppose it ought to be a pretty good one. Good light and everything, eh?"

"So far as I can judge," answered Tunnicliff carefully.

"Well, you'd better get it to Rome this afternoon—take it yeself or send someone—and have it developed. Venables could fix the thing for ye. Ye know his address. 19 Piazza di Spagna."

"Yes. Only——"

"Only what?"

"Miss Perkins has got it."

"What d'ye mean, Miss Perkins has got it?"

"She asked me to explain the camera to her, and take it to pieces and so on. And she was very interested in the spool particularly, and she took it away."

"Well, go and ask her to return it, will ye?"

"I have asked her, but she won't."

"D'ye mean she refused?"

"Yes," said the Honourable Luke, somewhat curtly: he was thinking of her rudeness to him and of his rudeness to her: the glint in her eye, and the heat which he felt on his own cheek, and her tone and his tone, and the bright language they both employed in the brief altercation—from which, indeed, he had just emerged.

Lord Furber said, in soft accents which surprised his hearers:

"Oh, all right. It doesn't matter. I hope I didn't disturb yer lunch."

When the Honourable Luke had departed, the baron rang for Bumption.

"Bumption," said he, "I wish ye'd ask Miss Perkins if she can oblige Mr. Sutherland and me by coming in here for a moment, at once."

"Yes, my lord."

And in due course Harriet came in—through the service-door. She was wearing neither the yachting costume nor the apron, but a black frock which seemingly she had obtained from the sirens before their departure—a frock as simple as it was obviously costly, ornamented with a girdle and a bunch of keys.

"And now?" she demanded formally, and perhaps a little defiantly.

"Sit down, won't you?" Lord Furber suggested.

"No, thanks. I'm very busy. Have you any orders?"

"We only wanted to compliment ye on the lunch," said Lord Furber. "It was the best lunch I've ever had in this yacht."

"Glad you liked it."

"We did indeed, Harriet," said Mr. Sutherland.

"I suppose ye've nobbled the chef," said Lord Furber.

"No," said Harriet, vaguely. "Anything else?"

Lord Furber shook his head and smiled appreciatively. Harriet moved away.

"I say, Harriet," he called to her as she was reaching the door. "The film we took this morning. I hear ye've taken charge of it." And he laughed.

"I did," said she. "You can't possibly have a film like that developed, much less shown, even privately."

Lord Furber's face altered.

"Why not?"

"Well, it's not nice. Mrs. Bumption would hate it."

"She won't see it."

"She'll hear of it. And think of Bumption. He'd be terribly hurt."

"Not he! He knew it was being taken—saw it being taken, part of it. And I've never known him more cheerful than he was at lunch."

"Of course he was. But can't you guess why? He was cheerful because he knew I'd thrown the film into the sea. I'm the housekeeper."

"I don't see the connection," said Lord Furber very drily and ominously.

"Don't you? Well, it's like this. I'm the housekeeper. I'm following as well as I can in Mrs. Bumption's steps. I model myself on her. And I said to myself, 'If she had that roll of film in her hand what would Mrs. Bumption do?' I said 'She'd throw it into the sea.' And so I threw it into the sea." She opened the door. "And," she added simply, "you ought to be glad I did. And you *will* be."

"Say, Harriet," the baron cried. "It's wonderful how servants stick together against their masters, isn't it?"

Harriet looked into the room again.

"Are you keeping your temper?" she asked.

"Ay, lass!" said the baron, jovially. He was indeed.

"Well, then I've two things to tell you. You see these keys," she flourished the keys of office. "When I'm wearing them my name isn't Harriet—it's Perkins."

"And what else, Perkins?"

"I was sorry to have to humiliate you in front of your guest. But I see you're persisting in that bad habit of yours of interviewing servants when you aren't alone with them. I hope this will be a lesson to you."

She left.

"Well," said the baron, passing a hand over his brow, "I had a near shave then."

"Of?"

"Losing my temper. I shall be getting over-righteous if I succeed every time like that. . . . See here, my friend, this yacht's no place for us."

"In any case," answered Septimius, unmoved by what he had witnessed. "I must be leaving you. You wanted to see me about Lallers. You've seen me, and that little business is over. So I'll go as soon as it's convenient. I expect I can hire a car at Ostia. You've been exceedingly hospitable." He finished on an enigmatic tone.

Lord Furber burst out expansively, amiably, persuasively:

"My dear fellow. Ye can't desert me like this. I tell ye ye can't do it. You said a bit ago—this morning, that ye weren't in a hurry."

"I'm not," replied Septimius. "I got my business over at Naples three days sooner than I expected, and I've cancelled my appointments, as you know. But I don't quite see anything to stay for."

"Anything to stay for! And we aren't a dozen miles from Rome! We'll run up there together and make a night of it. If we clear out for a while, it'll give these people a chance to think a bit, especially if we don't tell 'em how soon we're coming back to 'em again."

"I'm quite willing," said Septimius, with the utmost calmness and gentleness.

"Good for ye!" the baron cried in sudden glee.

He rang the bell with considerable emphasis.

"And only last night I was thinking to myself how acquiescent she was! Good God!"

"I beg your pardon?"

"Nothing! Nowt!"

The hundred horse-power launch was ordered forthwith.

The entire yacht seemed to spring into life.

Suitcases had to be packed. Rugs and wraps provided. And everything in the twinkling of an eye. Amid the uproar the baron and Septimius placidly paced the deck.

"But I must change," said Septimius suddenly. "I can't go to Rome in these clothes."

"Why not? Change in Rome."

"But I shall be cold in the car."

"Car. There is no car. The launch will do thirty knots. We'll enter Rome by water, my lad, and wake up the Tiber. New sensations for you! New sensations!"

CHAPTER XXX

THE COLISEUM

"So THIS is the Eternal City!" said Lord Furber thoughtfully, as the launch passed the gasworks.

He stood up. Over the stern of the great mahogany craft the blue ensign of the British Naval Reserve stuck out with the stiffness of a board in the high wind caused by the craft's swiftness. Grimy workmen at the grimy gasworks, which was wreathed with fluffs of steam and smoke, gazed astonished at the speed of the launch. And indeed, the launch had aroused astonishment all the way up the yellow and feature-less Tiber from the moment when a pilot-skiff, hailing it for a job, had been nearly capsized in its heedless wash. Lord Furber wanted no pilot, nor did he pay the least attention to the damage done to the banks of the sacred river by the big twin waves which the launch threw up on either side. He had soon come to the conclusion (correct) that the Tiber presented no interest whatever to the voyager beyond certain me-chanical fishing nets actuated by the force of the current.

In another minute the launch was within the City; Rome had begun; the Dome of St. Peter's glinted afar off in the afternoon light.

"There's a quay here, my lord," said the steersman, as they shot under the first bridge, the Palatine. "Shall we tie up?"

"Not on your life, my son," the baron replied. "You go right ahead. Ye'll see the tower of St. Angelo soon—you can't miss it, it's the biggest tower you ever saw—after that go under two bridges, and then I'll tell ye where to stop."

"I thought you'd never been to Rome," said Mr. Sutherland.

"No more I have. But I've been meaning to go for a long time now, and so I've picked up a bit about it. When ye enter Rome by water it's obvious ye must tie up at the Ripetta; where they tied up a couple o' thousand years ago. Slow her down a bit," he added to the steersman, who was the officer in charge. "There's something to see here."

The launch subdued itself to the pace of a fast-trotting horse. Bridges, trams, domes, an island, trees, tenement houses, palaces, churches, palaces, fishermen.

"Hold on!" cried the baron. "Here. This must be it. That's the Cavour Bridge ahead, isn't it, Sutherland?"

"I don't know," said Sutherland.

"Well it is, because it must be."

In a moment one of the crew was ashore with a mooring rope in his hand, and in another half-minute the man was the centre of a crowd.

"Dump that baggage here," ordered the baron, springing ashore himself, and he called into the crowd, as a sportsman shoots "into the brown," the magic word, the word which in all the languages of the world is the same: "Taxi."

Then towards the launch:

"You can go back to the yacht now."

The launch cast off, buzzed loudly, made a sharp

curve into midstream. and slipped at full speed down the current. It had vanished under the Umberto Bridge before the deliberate Septimius Sutherland had fully realized what was happening to him. Septimius, as is the fate of a rich man whose duty it is to satisfy the curiosity and the demand for novelty of three idle ladies, had several times entered Rome, but never in this manner.

"You haven't told them where we're staying," he said.

"And why should I? It's none o' their business. Where *shall* we stay?"

"Oh!" said Septimius, "I suppose there's only the Paradiso."

"I suppose so," Lord Furber agreed.

Thus in a word did the two plutocrats eradicate and destroy a hundred hotels in Rome, leaving but one intact on its foundations.

By this time, four Roman citizens, by their united efforts, were carrying, unbidden, two light suitcases, and a fifth was urging the visitors to follow the suitcases. A taxi appeared.

"Paradiso!" cried Lord Furber to the driver, and paid out five five-lire notes, according to demand.

"Sha'n't you call to see your agent on the way?" asked Septimius.

"Why should I?" the baron retorted. "What do we want an agent for?"

"I thought he might save you some trouble."

"I'll save all the trouble myself," said the baron.

At the majestic Paradiso, the tourists were informed that the hotel was practically full.

"I'm Lord Furber," said Lord Furber. "I've just come here from my yacht at Ostia."

"In that case, my lord. . . ."

Within a minute and a half the management of the full Paradiso had manufactured a perfectly unoccupied suite consisting of a sitting-room, two bedrooms and two bathrooms and placed it at the disposal of the British aristocracy.

"How much?" the baron inquired, after inspection of the accommodation.

"Twelve hundred lire, my lord."

"A day?"

"Yes, my lord."

"Grand!" said his lordship.

"Say," he questioned the head waiter in the restaurant of the Paradiso during dinner. "Is there any moon to-night worth talking about?"

The omniscience of the head waiter received a shock, for the man had not seen the moon for several years. Also the idiomatic quality of his lordship's question was rather puzzling to him. The head waiter had spent the evenings and nights of a quarter of a century past either in the Paradiso or in hotels exactly like the Paradiso, and his private opinion was doubtless that no moon was worth talking about.

"I—I will inquire, my lord."

"Yes, do," Septimius cut in. "Ask in the office. They're bound to have the latest information there!"

The head waiter did not ask at the office, his situation being too exalted for such an act; but he sent somebody else to inquire at the office, and in the meantime he favoured with his presence and knowledge other tables in the crowded room. He had a great and succulent piece of information for the other tables: namely, that Lord Furber, the famous English millionaire, was staying in the Paradiso. Before he had finished his round, the entire restaurant had been made aware that Lord Furber was patronizing the Paradiso, and of the precise geographical position of his lordship's table. The identity of Septimius Sutherland evoked little curiosity; for the Paradiso public the first and last pertinent point about Septimius was that he was the one who was *not* Lord Furber.

"The moon was full two days since," said the head waiter, hastening back to his lordship's table and bearing, as it were, the precious information on a silver dish with both hands.

"Ah! And is it a clear night?"

"Quite clear," said the head waiter, on the chance that he might be accurately representing the heavens hidden from mortal eye by the splendid window-curtains of the Paradiso dining-room. (Chance favoured him; the night was in fact quite clear.)

"Anything to do in Rome this evening?" Lord Furber demanded. The head waiter bristled at a question so nearly bordering on an insult to Rome, his Rome. He catalogued the opera, eight other theatres, and some sixteen cinemas, besides a music-hall, and a nocturnal ceremonial in one of the churches.

"Septimius," said the baron, "it seems to me that the Coliseum by moonlight is the stuff for to-night. I'm an innocent abroad in Rome, but I'll lay my shirt the two greatest things here are the Coliseum and St. Peter's. What do you say? Coliseum by moonshine?"

"I say it," was the calm reply.

The pair were becoming more and more intimate. They were positively enjoying one another's society. As for Septimius, he now understood why his wilful friend, in the automobile of which they had at once hired the exclusive services, had during the afternoon steadily resisted the chauffeur's keen and natural desire to display to them the Coliseum and St. Peter's. His friend had been saving these choice morsels for the future.

"Good organization that!" thought Septimius approvingly.

They immediately departed from the Paradiso, that supreme illustration of modernness, and in ten minutes, in less than ten minutes, they stood facing the supreme illustration of the wicked ancient world; and one of the desires of the chauffeur had been appeased.

Lord Furber, standing close to the façade of the Coliseum, gazed upwards at its tremendous height, story upon story rising into the illuminated skies.

"Yes!" he murmured to himself. "Yes!"

The two grandees were like flies at the foot of a precipice. The automobile, near by, was like the microscopic carriages to which in old days seaside entertainers used to harness performing fleas.

Lord Furber examined minutely the fitting of the vast blocks of travertine of which the exterior was constructed.

"That's true enough," said he. "They did put it up too quick. Jerry-built! Jerry-built! No mistake! But it's lasted."

Then he hurried across the darkness of the immense ground-floor arcade into the interior. The moon, though it had not yet topped the curve of the vast wall, was shining brilliantly according to prediction through multitudinous arches, displaying the grass-grown arena with its mysterious pits and sub-terranean chambers, the gigantic granite stairways climbing here and there and ending in nothing, and the jagged silhouette of the stone summits. In the distances tiny human figures could be descried darkly moving. Desolation, majestic and unconquerable!

"Yes," said Lord Furber, not to anyone in particular. "The Wembley Stadium's bigger, but this place has Wembley beat. This is the sort of thing I can understand." There was awe in his deep, rich voice. "How many gladiators were killed here in the first three months after it was opened, Sep? D'ye remember? I know five thousand lions and tigers were done in, but I can't remember the number of men. Fancy them having an inauguration that went on every day for three months!"

Septimius said he didn't know. With a hurrah the baron ran off like a rabbit, and up a moss-grown stairway. He was stopped by a barrier and had to return, stumbling. "You'd better be careful," Septimius warned him. "You'll be breaking your leg before you know where you are."

The baron ignored him and ran off again: the eager child had been reborn in him. Septimius, who had the precious faculty of always reconciling himself to facts, saw that he had been cast that night for the rôle of kettle to a dog's tail, and hurried after his host. He was convinced that the child could not find a way upwards, but luck favoured the child in the maze of arcades, slopes, tunnels, and stairs. Within five minutes the richest newspaper-proprietor in Europe was perched a hundred feet above earth, his legs dangling over a wall, a Roman arch for a frame above his head, and a full view of the measureless oval of the interior in front. Septimius joined him, but instead of sitting on the wall, leaned against it. Both were puffing, not too hard considering their middle-age.

Septimius began to share the childhood of the baron. He was excited, happy, proud. He felt glad that his wife was not there to ask distracting, silly questions and complain of the cold or the danger. On the other hand, he had a vague notion that the scene was somehow incomplete without Harriet. He turned up the collar of his overcoat. The baron unloosed his overcoat.

"And this is less than half of what it was," said Lord Furber. "When ye think that lords and bishops and things, carted away pieces of this place for three hundred years and built half the palaces and churches of Rome with 'em! And this is what's left. . . ! By G—d, Sutherland! We're nobodies! What a crew they were! Fifty thousand free seats! Talk about bribing the people! Well, they knew how to do it. *We* bribe 'em with promises. This is what they bribed 'em with. Makes ye think, what!"

"Here, my friend," said the placid Septimius— seventh olive branch, and bearer of a Roman name— "Have a cigarette. And button up that overcoat."

Lord Furber absently took a cigarette and lighted it from Mr. Sutherland's in the chill air, but he would not button his overcoat. But Septimius, cigarette between teeth, drew the sides of the overcoat together and buttoned them and then turned up the collar. It was a firm, friendly act, quickly and neatly done. Lord Furber was touched. The intimacy of the pair was continuing to develop.

They smoked. And the ascent of the moon gradually lightened a strip of grass on the western side of the arena, and the strip became broader and broader. One half of the great, gaunt interior was dark, the other illuminated in every detail. Not a sound. No rats, bats, mice, mosquitoes, nor winging night-moths. Then the faint, thin accents of an American voice, the human forms moving pigmy-like across the waste.

"Say, Sep! What are you after?" It was the baron, reflective, who put the question.

"What am I after?"

"In life?"

"A quiet life."

They smoked.

"And you—what are you after?"

The baron threw away the end of his cigarette, and the red-glowing particle wavered downwards and was lost to view beneath.

"Hanged if I know!" A sigh. A long pause. "All I *do* know is, I'm out to win—everything."

"Well, you've won everything, my friend."

"Not with you," said the baron.

"Surely you didn't expect to win there!" said Septimius. "You didn't start right."

"Sep," the baron took him up. "Now let me tell ye. I know I didn't start right. Let me tell ye. But I thought I might—I only heard day before yesterday that you were in Naples. I heard ye were soon leaving for London, but I didn't know for certain ye meant to leave that night. I wanted to see ye. And I wanted to see ye before ye got to London. It might have been too late for me after ye'd got to London. If I had asked ye to come aboard in the ordinary way, ye might have refused. And I *had* to see ye. Of course if I hadn't heard ye were in Naples I shouldn't ha' bothered. But seeing I did know, I had to bother. Besides it was great sport—I mean all that arranging of the dinner and so on. Great sport. Chicane, Sutherland! Chicane! Perhaps that's what I'm after in life. Well, it was a biggish thing in conspiracies—I knew it. . . . And then when I'd got ye on board, ye know, ye did play into my hands. No need for me to keep ye on board in spite of yeself, though I'd fixed that, too. Ye stayed of yer own accord. All I had to do was to hurry the rest of 'em ashore. If yer luggage hadn't come, and if I hadn't stayed talking so long with that Harriet of ours, and if ye hadn't gone to bed and snored—(Sep, ye put me out of my stride when ye went to bed; nobody else on earth would ha' done it) —and if I hadn't had my hand on Harriet's shoulder, it might all ha' been a bit different to what it was. . . . I'll say this, Sep, ye took it grandly. And so did I —I mean that knocking down business. But ye beat me, and there's no two ways about it. Then I was a trifle shirty with Harriet—she'd upset me—when I happened to mention Lallers to ye this morning. Yes, I didn't begin right. I owe ye an apology; and here it is. And I won't say anything about the black eye I owe ye for knocking me down.''

There was something so persuasive and appealing in the baron's rather disconnected account of his performance that Mr. Sutherland's heart was touched. Could this piece of naïve youthfulness, with legs dangling over a wall on the upper works of the moonlit Coliseum, be the hard and formidable individual who had made a huge fortune by invention and was doubling and trebling it by masterly combinations in the City? Mr. Sutherland was so affected that the said performance appeared to him now to be perfectly natural and such as no reasonable being could decently resent. But then Mr. Sutherland, after all as canny as most, began to reflect:

"Why did this master of chicane offer me a hundred per cent. more for Lallers than I'd said it was worth? What does he want with Lallers, anyway? What lies beneath all this wonderful exhibition?" And he told his heart that it must cease to soften.

Then the baron gazed at him with a boyish, candid smile, and Mr. Sutherland perceived that his heart was not completely under control. He thought:

"If this fellow with his Coliseum by moonlight asks me now to let him buy Lallers as a favour, just because he wants it and won't be happy till he gets it, I shall give in to him. I shall make him a present of Lallers, I know I shall."

And he almost trembled as the baron opened his mouth to speak again.

But at that moment a voice at some little distance behind them among the dark masonry called out, with a twang like a banjo:

"Say, you guys! Can you give me a line on this ruin? Is it the Baths of Diocletian or the Baths of Caracalla? I only made Rome this afternoon and I kind of wandered out from my hotel to-night without my wife, and had a drink, and I've lost myself."

Lord Furber coarsely and unfeelingly burst into loud laughter.

"Don't fall off the wall, my friend," murmured Mr. Sutherland placidly.

To himself, Mr. Sutherland said:

"I am saved."

And indeed the stranger had unwittingly brought down the curtain on the scene.

CHAPTER XXXI

THE DOME

MR. SEPTIMIUS SUTHERLAND had a disturbed night in the splendid accommodation so generously provided for him by his intimate friend Lord Furber in the Paradiso Hotel. He thought a great deal about Harriet Perkins. He disliked being so far away from her. He wished that she could have joined the excursion—of course properly chaperoned. On the other hand, he considered that it was just as well she had not joined the excursion. He wondered whether a man as notoriously prudent as himself would not best show his prudence by bolting off at once to the safety of London and his very domestic hearth. But he could not bear to go, because he could not bear the prospect of not returning to the yacht and Harriet.

Again, he wondered whether, as the safest measure of precaution, he ought not to telegraph to Mrs. Sutherland to come to Rome, bringing with her their daughters; he knew they would come like birds, and like tame birds settle on his shoulders. His anxieties as to his own behaviour would then be at an end. But no! He could not bear that prospect either. How terrible would it be if Lord Furber, fascinated by Rome, kept the yacht dallying at Ostia and invited the whole Sutherland family for a cruise! Lord Furber would be quite capable of the act, and capable, further, of manœuvring his new housekeeper into comic

222

and impossible positions for the mystification of the Sutherland ladies. And Harriet herself would be quite capable of casually addressing him in the presence of his family as "Sep"!

What was the sinister and delicious power over him of the piquant Harriet? Why had absence from her increased her power? If he dozed off he was sure to dream of Harriet arrayed in one of the multitudinous dresses which Lord Furber had lavished upon her in his crude, millionairish way. Mr. Sutherland also passed long stretches of the night in reflecting upon his relations with Lord Furber. He ought to have detested Lord Furber. But he did not. He ought to have cursed their intimacy. But he did not. He constantly felt that sensation of having had a narrow escape in the Coliseum. And he foresaw that he might easily soon find himself in new danger. Lord Furber had mentioned the Coliseum and St. Peter's. He, Septimius, had come scatheless out of the Coliseum. If they went to St. Peter's, would he come scatheless out of St. Peter's? In the night Lord Furber's cleverness, his chicane, seemed to grow more and more diabolic and irresistible. Why was the fiend so set on buying Lallers? . . . Something dark at the bottom of all that! If in the morning Lord Furber suggested a visit to St. Peter's, what ought Septimius to do?

However, when morning tardily arrived, Septimius rediscovered his self-confidence. His brain had the hard and glittering brilliancy which comes of insomnia and fatigue. What precisely had he been fearing in the night? His fears had been absurd. Lord Furber could not force him to do anything that he wished not to do. The sun shone in at the bedroom window and completed Mr. Sutherland's restoration to sanity. He dressed himself unaided, and at nine-thirty precisely, the hour of the breakfast rendezvous, he appeared in the private sitting-room. Five seconds later, through the opposite door, Lord Furber also appeared, all fresh and diabolic.

"How did ye sleep, Sep?" said the baron cheerily.

"Fine," answered Mr. Sutherland.

Why this lie?

"So did I," said the baron. "And I don't often. It must be a great place for sleep, Rome must." Septimius knew that Lord Furber really had slept well.

"What d'ye think of the valet here?" Lord Furber demanded.

"Never saw him."

"Ye didn't! Well, Bumption has made me nearly helpless. I can shave myself, but I can't wipe my own razor. The dago here cut himself wiping it. Look at my only clean collar."

The baron pointed gaily to a blood spot on his only clean collar. He was enjoying the simple life. His eyes were full of laughter, innuendo, charming menace, chicane. His voice was rich with subtle significances.

"Hm!" murmured Mr. Sutherland, non-committal.

"Well now," said the baron, after the breakfast was brought in and they had begun to eat. "What d'ye say, Seppie? Shall we drive back to the yacht, or shall we see something else first?"

"Better see something else," said Mr. Sutherland, "as this is your first visit to Rome." He had meant to say "Go back to the yacht," but he could not. The baron was strangely putting words into his mouth.

"What?"

"St. Peter's, do you think?"

Madman! Ass! He might just as well have said the

Pantheon, the Forum, the Cloaca Maxima, or the Borghese Villa. But he had to say "St. Peter's."

"All right, if ye like," said Lord Furber, just as though he was politely yielding to a whim of his beloved crony's.

In the still, warm air they walked to St. Peter's— arm in arm. Mr. Sutherland in spite of himself enjoyed the pressure of the baron's arm. It seemed to him that the friendly intimacy of two boys of fifty or so was rather beautiful. On a thousand points the baron sought information from his crony, and listened to the replies with admirable respect. But no sooner were they actually within St. Peter's, having beaten off ten or a dozen guides, than the baron's demeanour changed, and St. Peter's became his, and not Mr. Sutherland's. He loosed Sep's arm, and, gazing around at the overwhelming yet austere interior upon which ten million pounds had been spent in three centuries, remarked:

"I like this place. It's a good answer to the Coliseum. Nothing dogmatic about it. It's as impartial as a railway station. Haven't you got the feeling that if we went down some steps somewhere we should come to the trains of the Pennsylvania Railroad— say the Chicago Limited?"

A bell rang. From some distant chapel they heard the sound of singing. They walked on for a few minutes over the marble floor and stared at the marble walls and the immense mosaic pictures, and stood under the dome; and Lord Furber raised his sparkling eyes to the skyey roof of the dome.

"Well," said the baron. "He could do it. He came across with the goods, no mistake."

"Who?"

"Michael Angelo. See here, Sep. I reckon we've got to climb up to the top of that contraption."

"Yes," answered Mr. Sutherland, weakly acquiescent. "You certainly ought to see the view."

In fancy he saw himself in the gallery at the summit of the dome, four hundred feet above Rome, in the compelling society of Lord Furber; and he said to his heart that he was undone. Why had he not replied that the view was not worth the trouble of the climb? They returned to the portico and bought tickets, for which Mr. Sutherland paid.

"A lift!" cried the baron with glee. "A lift in St. Peter's! I wouldn't have missed it for anything . . . I say," he said to the liftman, a rosy, fat man who seemed delighted to have company, "what would Clement the Sixth have said to this lift of yours?"

The liftman smiled uncomprehendingly, and Lord Furber, who for this trip had handsomely broken his rule against carrying money, made a present of ten lire to the official.

They ascended a chequered shaft, and the liftman bowed them out with zealous cordiality, and they were on the vast roof of St. Peter's, which is also the roof of Rome—a hill-town in itself, this roof. Little domes, shops, dwellings, girls selling picture-post cards, workmen, palisades, railings, roads, colossal statues. All Rome and the history of Rome beneath them. The Mediterranean on one side. The Appenines on the other. The rolling Campagna, on which here and there cities gleamed. The Tiber. The gasworks. And the wind blowing freshly across the plateau of the roof. In the streets far under was calm; but here half a gale. They turned. Michael Angelo's dome rose from the plateau apparently as high as when seen from the streets. And beyond the dome, in the clouds, the cupola, and beyond the cupola the ball!

"Come on!" said Lord Furber, and started off almost at a run towards the beckoning dome.

Mr. Sutherland followed as he had followed in the Coliseum, the kettle rattling after the dog. He knew that he was now in another and a morally dangerous world. He trembled lest he should be going to defeat; but he could not hold back. They reached the dome and climbed stairways and passed through a tunnel and entered a gallery, and they leaned forward dizzily, and the interior of St. Peter's was beneath their feet, with tourists walking like dolls on the marble floor. And all around curved thousands of square yards of littering mosaic, every inch finished with the minuteness of a jewel.

"I give in," exclaimed Lord Furber.

Mr. Sutherland breathed relief. He thought that the baron would go no higher. But the baron was simply acknowledging in Michael Angelo a superior. They hurried out again, and broached another and a darker stairway, and at every turn an official saluted them, and in proportion as they rose higher the salutations of the officials grew more welcoming at the sight of these rare visitants from earth.

They passed through another tunnel, and had another view of the interior: and now the tourists had dwindled to beetles crawling over the marble floors. And then they engaged themselves in ladder-like twisting stairs that wormed their way between the inner and the outer domes; and breaths shortened and puffs quickened from *adagio* to *allegro*, and cheeks reddened. Higher, higher. The world well lost and sunken away. Higher, higher, and higher!

An official at the top of a staircase scarcely a foot wide seemed to be standing on Mars itself. He beamed at the adventurers who had arrived to mitigate by their earthly presence the tedium of his withdrawn and solitary existence. His smile rested lovingly upon them. They paused. He pointed reluctantly to a door. They passed. They were magically in the open. A gale, a great wind, smote their pink faces. They clutched at their hats. They were in the exposed gallery of the cupola, and the roof of St. Peter's lay thrice as far below them as the city lay below the roof.

"Yes," thought Septimius. "It is all over with me."

CHAPTER XXXII

INTERRUPTION

"THIS gives ye a better notion of Rome than any ye would get down there," said Lord Furber.

They had skirted round the gallery to the east face of it where an absolute calm seemed to obtain. They sat, side by side, in a niche in the sunshine. They had taken breath. Their cheeks were still pink, and their hearts still a trifle overworking at the great engineering job of circulating the blood. But they tingled with the unfamiliar sensation of perfect health, and suddenly comprehended the perilous foolishness and futility of all drug-taking. Further, they were as proud as boys, because they were two boys who had said they would climb the dome of St. Peter's, and had climbed it.

Much of the city lay directly in front of them, a criss-cross of streets dotted with a thousand towers. Two human beings like ants were traversing the vast Piazza exactly in front of them. They moved slowly, scarcely perceptibly, crawling.

"Ye see those two fellows crossing the Piazza?" said Lord Furber. "Look, they're just at the fountain on the left! That's you and me, Sep. I mean there isn't *that* much of difference between them and us. Nobodies. Insects. And they don't know it. And we only know it because we're up here. I feel like Jehovah laughing in his beard at Ralph Furber and

S. Sutherland down there. . . . Sep! Have ye got all ye want?"

A curious, benevolent, familiar, boyish tone, as though the baron was saying also: "I hope ye have. I want ye to have had all ye want."

"I should think so," Septimius replied placidly.

"I reckon ye have." The baron added, unable to bear the idea that Septimius had done fundamentally better in life than he himself had: "So have I, I suppose. But what does it all matter, anyhow? This perch is doing me good. Clears yer brain. Gives ye a sense of proportion. That's what it does. Eh, Sep?"

"Yes," Septimius agreed. "Yes."

"For two days past, I don't mind telling ye, I've been wanting summat. Terribly. I wanted it last night. Now I don't want it. No, I *don't* want it."

"Oh," said Mr. Sutherland blandly. "What was that?"

"Nothing. Only that Laller business. It got on my nerves. Funny thing, I was beginning to be a bit superstitious about it! Did *I* know there were any Laller frocks in that stuff that I had sent down to the yacht? Not me. And when Harriet said 'Laller' it gave me a regular turn. And yet I could have sworn there wasn't one iota of superstition in me. Upon my soul, I thought I was the only man in the world who wasn't superstitious." He laughed. "I can see now clear enough from up here. I thought it meant I was bound to get hold of Lallers. Fact! I was so sure of getting it I didn't care what tone I used to ye, Sep. Harriet had vexed me, and I let it out on ye. I never wanted anything as much as I wanted Lallers. And for very good reason. But it's all altered now. Now I don't want Lallers. I don't care who has

Lallers. But by G—d I wanted it yesterday and last night! I thought last night if I didn't get it I shouldn't ever be able to go home again and hold my blooming head up. I thought I should be humiliated for ever and ever. Comic, ain't it?"

"Very," said Mr. Sutherland calmly. He was relieved. He saw how wrong and entirely silly he had been to imagine that it was going to be all over with him when he reached the cupola. Lord Furber had abandoned his prey.

"Of course," the baron continued. "I know why ye wouldn't sell me Lallers. At least I think I know. Ye're going in for a combine of some sort, and Lallers'll be part of it." Mr. Sutherland at these words had a slight recurrence of apprehension. Was the millionaire trimming round?

"You aren't so far out," Mr. Sutherland candidly admitted . . . "It'll be a two-million affair."

"Well," said the baron, "yesterday, if I'd known that for sure, I'd have suggested ye let me take the whole affair off yer hands, and I'd find all the capital, and take all the risks, and give yer a hundred thousand for yeself. That's what I'd ha' been ready to do yesterday, or even this morning before we came up here," Lord Furber spoke sadly and courageously. He did not even glance at Septimius, but fixed his eyes in philosophical meditation upon the town of Tivoli glistening in the hills a dozen or more miles off. "And *you* don't want Lallers either, Sep," he added nicely. "Not really!"

"Well," said Septimius, not to be behindhand in true wisdom. "If you look at it like that, I don't. Everything's only an idea. I admit it."

He felt the stirring of an absurd impulse to relinquish Lallers and the entire scheme to his crony. It seemed to him that if he did so he would be rising superior to his crony. And beyond that, and purer than that, was an obscure motive of mere benevolence. What a gesture to say: "Lallers is yours, my friend"!

Then he stiffened suddenly. How clever the fellow had been to guess at the existence of a scheme for a combine! Yes, he was too clever. He was a necromancer; that was what he was. He was a fellow to beware of. Why should Septimius make him a present of anything at all? Besides, the fellow didn't want Lallers any more.

Lord Furber had been wearing his Homburg hat at the back of his head, so as to hide the white patch over the wound. He now tipped the hat forward over his brow, and deliberately felt his chin.

"My chin still look queer?" he inquired.

"No. Nobody would notice it who didn't know about it."

"It doesn't hurt nearly so much this morning . . . Of course," he went on dreamily, "I know I've been spoilt. I'm far too rich to escape being spoiled. If I want anything I'm always convinced I positively *ought* to have it. And when any one stops me from having it I think I've got a genuine grievance against them. Funny, isn't it?" He smiled, half wistfully. "I *should* ha' liked Lallers. I won't deceive myself. I *should* ha' liked to get it."

Then he gazed at Mr. Sutherland as if desiring to share with Mr. Sutherland the rich joke of a multimillionaire's complicated psychology.

Mr. Sutherland was at last overcome. He knew he was about to behave like a grandiose fool, and that later he would regret his action. But the wish to hear himself, seated there in the skies on the top of St. Peter's, utter the wonderful words: "See here, old man. Lallers is yours,"—this wish was terrific in him. He could no more resist it.

"See here, old man," he started.

He was just plunging over the precipice when somebody walked round and faced them. And not an inebriated American! Harriet Perkins herself! Mr. Sutherland felt—and with awe—that some divinity was shaping his rough-hewn ends.

Harriet wore the yachting costume, hat and all, but with a different pair of shoes. And she was as bright as the morning.

"Now you needn't look so startled, you two. I'm not startled to see you here. Why should you be startled to see me here? Everything is simplicity itself. I had to come to Rome on professional business. I knew you'd be staying at the Paradiso. It's one of the very worst hotels in Rome, but it's the place where all your sort of people go, and so, of course, you couldn't be seen anywhere else. So I went to inquire for you at the Paradiso. You'd gone out, but the giant at the door told us he'd heard you tell your chauffeur to go to St. Peter's. I felt sure you couldn't possibly come to St. Peter's without making the ascent of this Matterhorn of a dome. At least, I knew that Ralph couldn't, and that Seppie would be forced to follow him—much against his will. I wanted to see you on urgent business, and here I am. I should have caught you at the hotel, but I absolutely had to get a larger pair of shoes to match this costume . . . Ralph, you must have wirelessed very good instructions to the dressmakers about my figure, but you went rather wrong on the size of my feet. They're larger than you imagined."

Not a trace of breathlessness in her: after climbing half a thousand stairs the girl was as fresh as though she had never left earth! This seemed wonderful to Mr. Sutherland who was still conscious that his heart was working under pressure. As he stood up and shook hands he was particularly conscious also of an unreasonable pleasure at the sight of her, and he definitely decided that he could neither leave Rome nor send for his wife and family to join him in Rome. He felt both happy and wicked: a sensation than which there is perhaps no finer in human life.

"I think I'll sit where you are, if I may," said Harriet persuasively to the baron, who rose, took her hand, and pressed her into the seat.

"And what's yer business?" asked the baron. "Why have yer deserted yer post as housekeeper of my yacht?"

"Ah!" exclaimed Harriet, with a teasing piquancy. "Wouldn't you like to know!" She examined the baron's face, and concluded that his mind was far away on some matter of which she knew nothing. "But you must listen as if you were interested," she added. "Not that you won't be interested. You will."

CHAPTER XXXIII

THE PRESS

"I CAME up in the launch," said Harriet.

"Not the flyer?" the baron demanded.

"The flyer. Why not? I'd a lot of important house-keeping to do."

"The caterer does all the buying—except the big things that the purser does. And he knows the whole job. I reckon he's marketed in pretty nearly every big port in Europe."

"But Rome isn't a port," said Harriet. "And even if it was, your caterer wouldn't know how to market in it. I've seen yacht caterers at their deadly work in Southampton and Torquay. They go into shops like sheep to the sacrifice. The tradesmen can sniff them half a mile off. No! But I brought the caterer with me, as well as the purser with his purse. Mr. Antinope informed me that he'd never known a yacht have a woman-housekeeper before. What fun he is—and doesn't guess it! They're waiting for me. I haven't begun to shop yet. But when I've finished with those two sometime this afternoon, they'll be worth a great deal more to you than they used to be. It's fortunate for you that my mother put me through a stiff course of housekeeping when I was young. Also, among other things, I speak Italian—and not like an Englishwoman either."

Lord Furber curtly asked:

"And have yer climbed up here just to sing yer own praises and show off yer frock? Or is there anything else?" He had ceased to be an insect crossing the Piazza of St. Peter's, and was once more a full-sized millionaire.

"Plenty else," Harriet replied. "What I've told you is only the overture. I've sent a doctor down to the yacht by car."

"Anybody ill?"

"Depends what you call 'ill.' Mrs. Bumption's ankle was about a yard in circumference this morning. She didn't sleep all night. And Bumption didn't sleep. Bumption forsees himself a widower, and Mrs. Bumption is terrorizing the stewards, so that I thought I'd better wait on her myself. I told her if she wasn't quiet I should pour some water over her face. She would not lie quiet. I got the water all ready in a jug, and held it over her . . . And she was quiet. We now understand each other. She is an old dear. Nobody's ever handled her before."

The baron laughed.

"Harriet," said he, "I can see ye're destined to make some good man unhappy for life. But it isn't going to be me—I promise ye that. What else have ye for me?"

"Bravo, Harriet," said Mr. Sutherland, blandly and daringly.

"Oh! I've hardly begun yet. Mr. Robbington came on board at seven o'clock this morning in a great state."

"Who's Mr. Robbington?"

"Don't you know? You ought to. He's the Rome correspondent of your paper, the *Courier*."

"Of course he is. Well, I can't be expected to remember the names of all the foreign correspondents of my newspapers, can I? What was he after? He wasn't supposed to know that I was anywhere near Rome. Nobody was supposed to know. Smart fellow, Robbington! Smarter than I thought."

"He didn't know you were near Rome. At least he didn't know last night when he was telephoning his message to the *Courier*. He only found out after the message had gone."

"What message?"

"About a strange English yacht being at Ostia, and sensational things going on on the yacht. Women being entrapped from launches and swung on board against their will like cattle. And all that kind of thing. He'd got wind of it. He knew it all except the name of the yacht—and that seems to have gone wrong on the Italian telephone."

"Who told ye?"

"He told me himself. He saw the Captain first. He didn't say much to the Captain. The Captain sent him to me—everybody seems to come to me. He was very confiding to me, Mr. Robbington was. An artless young man—quite the journalist. He rushed back to Rome in his car, and I daresay he's now trying to find your lordship."

Lord Furber walked to and fro in the gallery of the cupola.

"What *was* there in the darned message? D'ye know?"

"Oh yes. He showed me a copy of it, and then forgot to take it away with him. Here it is." Miss Harriet Perkins opened her bag and produced a paper.

Lord Furber read (to himself):

"Ostia, which is the port of Rome, was to-day thrown into feverish excitement by the doings of a mysterious large and luxurious yacht flying the Blue ensign of the British Naval Reserve, which dropped anchor there this morning. A considerable number of beautiful and handsomely dressed young Italian women came down in a procession of motor-cars from Rome at an early hour to meet the yacht, and were taken on board from launches. A little later one of these ladies, apparently not satisfied with what was going on, escaped back into a launch. She refused to return, and was ultimately forcibly taken and strapped into a box, which was hoisted on board, the lady still courageously struggling. It is impossible to obtain further particulars yet; but the local authorities have been informed of the affair and doubtless more will be heard of it within the next twenty-four hours."

Lord Furber put the paper in his pocket. Then he took it out again and showed it to Mr. Sutherland.

Said Harriet:

"You can imagine that on the front page of your lovely *Courier*, and the sort of headlines it will have, can't you? Well, this is the brand of news you instruct all your men to look out for, all over the world, I expect; and now at last you've got some results."

Mr. Sutherland and Harriet regarded one another cautiously.

"When did the fellow find out the name of the yacht?" demanded Lord Furber.

"About midnight," she said. "Long after his message had gone."

"Oh well. We can let it die. Nobody ever remembers these things for more than a day," said Lord Furber grimly.

"I don't think it'll die as quickly as all that," said Harriet maliciously. "It was the correspondent of one of your rivals, the *Evening Telegraph*, that told Mr. Robbington, and a message with full particulars will appear in the *Evening Telegraph* this afternoon, he says. What fun for Fleet Street! Your large and luxurious yacht will be the talk of all England by to-morrow morning. No wonder Mr. Robbington rushed down to Ostia to see you. He was in a very peculiar condition. I gave him some breakfast."

CHAPTER XXXIV

THE PRESSMAN

THE facial expressions of Lord Furber became so multitudinous and fearsome, the glitter of his eyes so formidable, and the movements of his legs so antic, that Harriet Perkins walked away, disappearing round the curve of the gallery. Mr. Sutherland followed her.

"It *is* a bit of a blow for him," said Harriet, smiling. "Do you think it's safe to leave him?"

"If you ask me," said Septimius, "it's a great deal safer to leave him than to stay with him."

"Not with you there!" said Harriet. "Seppie! Never shall I forget you knocking him down! That was the most wonderful thing that ever happened to me or ever will."

Septimius unsuccessfully tried to hide his satisfaction at this statement so deliciously made by the bewitching creature, and to hide also his consciousness of the facts that he was a seventh child, had stroked the Cambridge boat, and had conducted himself heroically in dramatic circumstances on the yacht.

He said blandly:

"Anyhow, I don't think he'll do anything very serious without an audience."

"That's the cruellest remark I ever heard. Your fist may be a man's, but your tongue is a woman's, Seppie."

Mr. Sutherland smiled mysteriously to himself.

"But I like him," he added. "He's the cleverest man in my experience—and—you're the cleverest woman, Harriet."

At this moment the high wind carried off Mr. Sutherland's hat, which, being somewhat of the shape and lightness of a parachute, sailed away clear of the dome, sank slowly and vanished, seemingly determined to examine for itself the privacies of the Vatican gardens.

"No importance," said Mr. Sutherland blandly. "It isn't mine. I took somebody else's from the Paradiso this morning." The wind made waves on his sparse, short hair, as on a field of young corn.

Then a man came puffing out into the gallery through the orifice which led to the five hundred stairs. A very fair, youngish person, with a short, fair beard and a nervous demeanour. You would guess at once, from the beard and the demeanour, that he belonged to the British colony of a foreign city.

"Oh! Mr. Robbington!" Miss Perkins greeted him. "Then you called at the Paradiso, and they gave you the message I left for you in case you did call!"

"Thank you, I did. The janissary at the concierge's counter failed you not. Of course he knew me."

"Yes," said Harriet. "He told me he knew you. This is Mr. Septimius Sutherland. Seppie, Mr. Robbington, Rome correspondent of the *London Courier*."

Septimius and the journalist bowed to each other, and Mr. Robbington's bow was the courtlier. Mr. Robbington also had the advantage of being able to raise his hat in token of polite deference.

"One of the hatless brigade," said he, with such a

charming and humorous smile that nobody could have been offended by it. "Lest I should be misunderstood," he continued, "I ought to tell you that an average of seven hats are lost in this gallery every day of windy weather. Then Lord Furber is not here after all?"

Harriet explained that the baron was round the other side of the circular gallery.

"I'll go to him. I feel quite ready for him," Mr. Robbington concluded.

And he went.

"You'd better come too," Harriet murmured to Mr. Sutherland. "You might be needed." She laughed.

The baron was staring over the parapet. He had not quite ceased laughing at the spectacle of the voyage of Mr. Sutherland's hat. He turned sharply at the sound of Mr. Robbington's footsteps, and frowned, because Mr. Robbington, whom he did not know and had never seen, evidently had the intention of addressing him, and the baron hated to be addressed by strangers.

"Have I the honour of speaking to Lord Furber?" Mr. Robbington ceremoniously inquired, again bowing and raising his hat.

"Ye have."

"My name is Robbington, and though personally unknown to your lordship I am the Rome correspondent of the *London Courier*. An unfortunate thing has happened, and I have come to inform you. I was quite disturbed about it up to a couple of hours ago, but now I am strangely calm. The truth is that it has occurred to me that if I am to be hung I may as well be hung for a sheep as for a lamb."

The baron pierced every portion of Mr. Robbington's body with darts from his homicidal eyes.

Mr. Sutherland and Miss Perkins had gone round the curve the opposite way from Mr. Robbington; they had gone round quietly. Lord Furber, facing Mr. Robbington, did not see them; neither did he hear them; moreover they half hid themselves in a niche, like Sir Toby Belch and his companion hiding to watch Malvolio.

"I know what's happened," said Lord Furber.

"Miss Perkins told you?"

"What the devil has it got to do with you who told me?"

"Just so," said Mr. Robbington, with surprising imperturbability. "Nothing to do with me. Still, it must have been Miss Perkins. I'm sure she told you much more concisely than I should have done. I'm apt to be a little long-winded, especially when I'm excited. Well Lord Furber, the first thing I want to say is that I resign my post on the staff of your esteemed, sensational rag, or, more properly, newspaper. Nobody shall ever be able to say that I was dismissed. I am also preventing you from doing something which in calmer moments you might regret."

He drew down the corners of his lips, sardonically.

"I cannot imagine why I ever took on the job," he continued. "The money, though it doesn't amount to wealth, is useful, but you can pay too high a price for money. My new-found leisure will enable me to get on with my handbook to Rome, which, perhaps I may be allowed to mention incidentally, is conceived on an entirely new plan; and also with my translation of Dante, which will bring in less money than prestige. I have reason to believe that my translation of the great mediæval poet is better than Carey's. Not that that is saying much. I have always thought that Carey has been grossly overpraised. However, possibly you will say that all this is beside the point. I will only add that, being not entirely bereft of the milk of human kindness, I feel a certain sympathetic sorrow for your lordship in the predicament in which providence, through my unwitting agency, has placed your lordship."

Mr. Robbington then drew breath, still amiably, yet sardonically smiling at the speechless baron—and waited.

"Why don't ye verify yer facts?" the baron at length asked, in a voice terribly calm and quiet.

"Yes," said Mr. Robbington. "I was expecting that question. But supposing I had stopped to verify my facts, and supposing some other paper had got hold of the same incomplete facts that I got hold of, my editor would have been wanting to know by cable what the deuce I meant by not getting in first, and what the deuce I thought I was in Rome for. Perhaps you don't know the side of the *Courier* editor that I know. I'm not stating my position very clearly, but your lordship has brains enough to catch my drift. And I should like to ask what the deuce your lordship means by coming to Rome without letting me know. I am the finest guide in the world to Rome. I could have put you wise on lots of things. Here you are, for instance, wasting your time on this hackneyed panorama, while I should have taken you to see Hadrian's villa—a private country house—it would give you millionaires something to think about. You think you understand luxury, whereas you simply haven't begun to understand luxury. In the matter of luxury you are about eighteen hundred years behind the times."

"Ye shall show it me, young man."

"Oh no, I sha'n't. I'm no longer at your beck and call. And I'll tell you another thing, since we're talking. You make a fuss about verifying facts. But the *Courier* doesn't want its facts verified. It never prints facts, save by accident. I except the racing tips, which I admit are rather remarkable. Have you ever considered how humiliating it must be for a man of my tastes and ambitions to work for a sheet like the *Courier?* No, you haven't. Of course you haven't. I have the honour to wish your lordship good-day."

Lord Furber stuck his hands into his pockets and approached Mr. Robbington, who involuntarily stepped backwards.

"Say," said he. "Say, my friend. Do ye live in Rome for choice?"

"No," answered the journalist. "I live in Rome because it's cheap, and because I just happen to be in Rome and haven't the enterprise to leave it."

"Where should ye live if ye could choose?"

"What a foolish question! London naturally! There's no other place."

"Well," said the baron. "Ye're the best highbrow and brow-beater I've struck yet. I'll give ye a job in London—editor of the literary page of the *Evening Mercury.* Thousand a year. Start at once."

"Thanks," said Mr. Robbington, with a most expansive smile. "I'll take it. I think I could help you there. You might write and confirm. Good-day."

He turned away and then came back.

"If there's anything I can do," he suggested in a

relenting and benevolent voice, "to clear up this
Vanguard mess, I'll be glad to do it."

"We'll just let that alone and sit tight," said Lord
Furber.

"I think you're very wise," said Mr. Robbington.
"Let time do its healing work, my lord."

And he departed.

CHAPTER XXXV

THE WATCH

LORD FURBER was in many respects rather old-fashioned. In the matter of watches, for instance, he adhered to the ancient chain or cable principle, as opposed to the new bracelet principle. When he wanted to know the time he drew his watch from the depths of his waistcoat pocket by hauling in a chain or cable whose other end lay in the opposite pocket of his waistcoat. He held that bracelets were proper for women only, and moreover he did not care to have to twist his forearm and crick his elbow-joint in order to look at his watch.

The baron's umbilical region was crossed by an exceedingly thin gold chain, at one end of which was the thinnest gold watch ever constructed and at the other end a flat gold pencil.

Now immediately upon the departure of the newly-appointed editor of the literary page of the *Evening Mercury,* Lord Furber snatched at the middle of the chain and dragged out both watch and pencil. His fingers slipped down the chain in the direction of the pencil, and the next instant the watch was whizzing with incredible velocity round and round in thin air and forming the circumference of a circle of which the centre was the pencil and the radius was the watch-chain. His features were contorted as if in anguish, his teeth set, his head sunk, his shoulders lifted, and all the muscles of his right arm strenuously taut, in the effort to get the very maximum of speed out of the revolving watch. And the watch made a hissing sound as it whizzed in its orbit.

Such, on this occasion, was Lord Furber's method of relieving his feelings after a period of undue and unaccustomed strain. The watch, in fact, was suffering in place of Mr. Robbington. Suddenly the chain parted at its jointure with the pencil, and the watch, like a shot from a howitzer, described a marvellously beautiful parabola in the air, the chain rushing after it as the tail rushes after a comet. The watch and chain travelled an immense distance ere they disappeared somewhere beyond the back of the dome of St. Peter's.

Lord Furber, as soon as he had recovered from his astonishment at the celestial spectacle, dashed the pencil furiously down on the ground and attempted to stamp it with both feet into utter shapelessness and uselessness. However, his feet being inaccurately aimed, and the pencil very small, the pencil escaped destruction. Whereupon the baron with extraordinary calmness stooped and picked up the pencil and put it back into his pocket and seemed to pretend that nothing had happened. The crisis was passed. The baron's reason was restored. The baron had conquered himself. He breathed and smiled softly as a babe.

"Come out o' that. Come out of it," the baron said, agreeably inviting, "I knew all the time ye were there spying on me."

And Harriet and Mr. Sutherland came out of it.

"I say, Sep," said the baron. "He was a bit like

yeself. He attacked me before I was ready for him."
Septimius only smiled, for he could think of nothing
to say in answer to this allusion to the prize-fighting
episode.

"And he was a bit like you as well, Harriet," said
the baron. "He was all for bullying me and teaching
me how to live." And Harriet also smiled.

"But," said the baron, "he was ready enough to
take my money. They always are."

"I don't know that I am," Septimius put in
blandly.

The baron stared at him darkly.

"But why did you throw the watch away, Ralph?"
Harriet quizzed.

"I didn't throw it away. It's a hunter, and I sent it
to track down Mr. Sutherland's hat."

"Well," said Harriet. "You kept your temper very
wonderfully. And we congratulate you. You're making progress, Ralph."

"Now listen here," said the baron. "I don't want
any sauce. And I warn ye I'm still dangerous. I *did*
keep me temper. But I only kept it because I thought
I'd disappoint ye. And it might ha' been better for ye
in the end if I hadn't kept it."

"Don't boast, Ralph," said Harriet. "We're proud
of you—at least I am; Sep doesn't know you as well
as I know you. But you can't frighten us any more.
We can see now you're a Christian after all. Be good,
and tell us like a man how you do intend to get out
of that hole that Mr. Robbington has put you in."

Lord Furber said:

"There is no hole. So I'm not in it. I'm not going
to do anything at all. I told yer already. The thing'll
be forgotten in three days, and I shall get square with

the *Evening Telegraph* pretty soon; you may bet I shall. I sha'n't laugh it down. I shall live it down. Anyhow it's a good joke, and if the joke's on me it's still a good joke."

At this point a man in wide knickerbockers with green tabs at the tops of his patterned woollen stockings, appeared round the curve. He was the first stranger to visit the cupola since the baron and his friends had taken possession of it, for the hour was still early. The man stared around, murmuring half-audibly in a pleased tone: "The Woolworth has this beat." Mr. Sutherland made a sign to the baron. The visitor was he who had disturbed their colloquy in the Coliseum on the previous evening. Lord Furber went up to the stranger.

"No," said Lord Furber to him. "This isn't the golf course. It's the dome of St. Peter's."

The stranger regarded the baron uncertainly, and then, no doubt concluding that lunatics might be unsuitable company at a great height, hurried away.

"I told ye I was dangerous," said Lord Furber to his friends. "But if that chap had had his deserts he wouldn't ha' got off so cheaply."

"I don't quite understand why you should go and behave like that to people you don't know," said Harriet correctively.

"I do know him," said the baron. "We both know him, don't we, Sutherland?" He related, in somewhat exaggerated terms, the incident of the Coliseum, and continued in a louder and an excited tone: "That chap cost me a 'deal' last night. I'd just got Sutherland into the right mood for closing the 'deal.' He was just ready to give way to me against all his instincts. I'd put the evil eye on him. And then this half-tipsy

ANGEL FIRE

WITHDRAWN

ANGEL
FIRE

l. a. weatherly

CANDLEWICK PRESS

Copyright © 2011 by L. A. Weatherly

First U.S. edition 2012

Library of Congress Cataloging-in-Publication Data is available.

Library of Congress Catalog Card Number pending

ISBN 978-0-7636-5679-9

11 12 13 14 15 16 BVG 10 9 8 7 6 5 4 3 2 1

Printed in Berryville, VA, U.S.A.

This book was typeset in Rialto DFPiccolo.

Candlewick Press
99 Dover Street
Somerville, Massachusetts 02144

visit us at www.candlewick.com

To the memory of my mother,
Billie Cruce Seligman

Mom, I wish you could have read this book.

PROLOGUE

IT TOOK THE WOMAN A LONG TIME to leave her house.

Across the street, Seb stood propped against a run-down grocery store, hidden in the dawn shadows as he watched the woman's front door. His high-cheekboned face had light stubble on its jaw; his lean body was simultaneously as relaxed and alert as a cat's. He was sure this was the right place. It looked exactly like what he'd seen: a golden-yellow house on the main street with a paneled wooden door and a small wrought-iron balcony filled with flowering plants—a jumble of red and yellow. With his hands in his jeans pockets, Seb counted the front door's panels: ten. Then he counted the flowerpots: seventeen.

Come on, chiquita, you're going to be late for work, he thought.

The door opened at last, and a small, round woman wearing a business suit came out. She delved fussily into her handbag for keys; when she finally found them, she locked the door behind her, then teetered to her car on plump feet that looked pinched in their high-heeled shoes. By the time she reached the car, she'd somehow lost her keys in her handbag again and had to stand on the sidewalk searching for almost a minute, shaking her head in irritation. Seb held back a smile. Yes, this was all very like her.

The moment the woman's car disappeared around the corner, Seb grabbed a battered knapsack that sat at his feet and slung it over his shoulder. He'd already checked out how to get to the back of the house; now he took a quick second to send his other self flying, making sure the way was clear. It was. He crossed the road, strolling through the early-morning silence. A tall wooden fence bordered the house on one side; Seb jumped to grasp the top of it and vaulted over easily. The back of the house was just like he'd seen, too — a tidy concrete courtyard, again filled lushly with potted plants. A faded deck chair stood folded near the sliding patio door.

The window with the broken lock that had been worrying the woman was up on the second floor. It took only seconds for Seb to scale the trellis and slide it open. He dropped silently into her bedroom — pale green, lots of ruffles. There was a smell of perfume, as if dousing herself had been the last thing she'd done before leaving.

And now she'd be gone for hours. Her job was so far away that she didn't have time to come home for lunch; it had been one of many niggling concerns on her mind the day before. The woman's thoughts had been like leaves in a whirlwind: none weighty in themselves, but the overall effect had left Seb with a headache from trying to focus on them. Psychic readings weren't always an easy way to pick up a few pesos, especially when all he wanted was to get them over with quickly, so he could buy something to eat and get back to the only thing that mattered to him. Even so, he hoped what he'd told the woman had helped. She definitely needed to relax more — though he was glad she hadn't decided to start doing it today.

Leaving the scented bedroom, Seb started searching, his steps echoing on the tiled floors. Though he rarely broke into houses anymore, there'd been a time when he'd done it all too often, with much worse motives than now. Gently, he pushed open doors, peered into rooms. His face creased into a frown. She would *have* one, wouldn't she? He hadn't seen for sure; he'd just assumed. Then on the ground floor, he found it: a computer sitting on a desk in the corner.

Perfect. Seb swung himself into the chair and hit the *on* button. The local school had computers the public could use, but it was closed today. And he hadn't been able to get a bed at the hostel for the last few nights, where he might have borrowed someone's laptop. He entered a few words into the search engine, typing slowly. A list of options came up; he found the one he was looking for and selected it.

Diaz Orphanage, read the website's home page: *A haven for children.* Seb's lip curled. He'd seen many orphanages over the years. Few could be described as havens. But he'd only found out about this one yesterday, and he needed to check it out. Who knew? It might turn out to be the place where he'd finally find what he was looking for. His heart beat faster at the thought, though he was only all too aware by now how unlikely it was. He took a piece of paper from the woman's desk and carefully wrote down the address, tucking it in his knapsack; the orphanage was around a hundred miles to the east, in the foothills of the Sierra Madre.

Then, on impulse, he brought up a map of Mexico, gazing at its familiar shape and mentally tracing the lines he'd traveled up and down it for years now. He'd started in Mexico City and since then had rarely spent more than a few weeks in one place. Currently he was in Presora, not far from Hermosillo, with its white beaches and throngs of tourists. Presora was quieter, though — a smaller town that had still taken him days to search, checking out every person he passed on the street, entering every building he could, sending his other self into the ones he couldn't.

There'd been nothing. Nothing at all. It wasn't really surprising — in his whole life, Seb had never seen even a hint of what he hoped so much to find. But he had to keep trying. It was all he could do.

Enough of this; he'd gotten what he came for. He turned off the computer and stood up, swinging his bag over his shoulder — and then his glance fell on the woman's bookcase, and he was lost. He drifted over to it, crouching onto his haunches as he gazed hungrily. A lot of the paperbacks looked as if they hadn't even been opened, and for a heartbeat Seb was tempted — he'd almost finished his current book and didn't know when he'd next find a used bookstore to trade it for another one. He touched the cover of a thick historical novel. It would keep him going for a week.

But no. He hadn't broken in here to steal, even if in the past he wouldn't have thought twice. With a sigh, Seb straightened up.

As he started for the stairs, he saw a hallway beside the kitchen, with a shower room visible. He hesitated, then went and looked inside. The white-tiled room was almost bare: just a hand towel and a bar of dusty-looking soap, as if the shower in here was rarely used. Which was probably true — the woman lived alone; the pristine pink bathroom he'd seen upstairs was the one with all her potions and powders in it. A mischievous smile began to tug at Seb's face. OK, *this* he couldn't resist — he hadn't been able to get really clean in days. His clothes were cleaner than he was; it had been easier to find a Laundromat in this town than a bed at the hostel.

He entered the small room, locking the door behind him. There was a tube of shower gel in his knapsack; he dug it out, then stripped off and took a long shower, relishing both the hot water and the privacy. Even after so many years, it still felt as if he could never take either for granted. His body was firm and toned; as the water washed over him, scars he barely noticed anymore gleamed from his wet skin — some white with age, others newer,

5

puckering redly. He hated not feeling clean almost more than anything; it felt wonderful to wash away the grime of the last few days.

Afterward, Seb dried off as best he could with the hand towel and glanced in the mirror, slicking his wet hair back. It curled when he wore it too short, irritating him, and so he kept it slightly long, shoved away from his face. A loose curl or two always fell over his forehead anyway, just to torment him.

His jeans and T-shirt clung to him when he got dressed again, but the heat of the day would soon finish drying him off. He glanced around the shower room to make sure he'd left it the way he'd found it; then he jogged back up the stairs, eager to get going toward the Sierra Madre and the address in his knapsack. In the frilly green bedroom, he paused at the window, glancing around him.

"*Gracias,*" he murmured to the absent woman with a smile and then nimbly swung himself out.

Hitchhiking to the orphanage took a while; hitching sometimes did. Toward evening, a trucker was giving Seb a lift the final stretch of the way, talking nonstop about his girlfriend. Smoking a cigarette the man had given him, Seb sat leaning back against the vinyl seat of the cab with one sneakered foot resting on the dash, only half listening as he savored the familiar taste. He didn't often have the money these days to waste on cigarettes.

"And so I told her, *chiquita,* I'm not having this — I told you twice already. You have to *listen* to me when I talk to you. Take in what I'm actually saying, you know what I mean?" The trucker glanced at Seb for confirmation. He had a broad face, with heavy eyebrows.

"Yeah, you're right, man," said Seb, blowing out a stream of smoke. "Good for you." He'd far rather be reading than listening to this crap; unfortunately there was a sort of etiquette involved with hitchhiking. Making conversation was the price of the ride.

"But she never listens to me, does she? No, off in her own world, that one. Hopeless. Beautiful, but . . ." The man went on, talking and talking.

Seb watched him idly, noting the angry red lines that had appeared in his aura, like lightning flashes. When he'd first gotten into the cab, he'd shifted the colors of his own aura so that they matched the trucker's blue and yellow hues. He knew the man wouldn't be able to see them or tell; it was just a habit left over from childhood, when blending his aura in with those around him had made him feel safer. More hidden.

But the more Seb listened to this jerk, the more he really didn't want to share his aura. He shifted back to his natural colors as he got an image of the man standing in a kitchen shouting; a dark-haired woman looking frightened. Not exactly a surprise. The trucker didn't feel like he'd be a danger to Seb, though; he seemed strictly the type to bully those who were weaker. Seb knew he'd probably have sensed it if he had anything to worry about — and there was always the switchblade he carried in his pocket in case there was trouble. You didn't travel alone in Mexico without a weapon unless you were terminally stupid.

"Now, take you for instance," the truck driver went on. "How old are you — seventeen, eighteen?"

"Seventeen," said Seb, blowing out another stream of smoke. He'd be eighteen in less than a month; he didn't bother volunteering that.

"Yeah, and I bet you don't have any trouble getting the girls, do you?" The man gave a guffawing laugh; his aura chuckled along with him, flickering orange. "You look like a rock star, with that face and stubble — like all the girls would have you up on their wall. But take my advice, *amigo*: never let them . . ."

Mentally rolling his eyes, Seb tuned out, wishing he could snap on the radio at least. People often commented on his looks, but looks couldn't get him the one thing he wanted.

"So where are you from?" asked the man finally, stubbing out his cigarette in the overflowing ashtray. "Sonora? Sinaloa?"

"El DF," said Seb. The Distrito Federal, Mexico City. It was almost dark now; the traffic heading toward them was a series of lights swooping out of the gloom. "My mother was from Sonora."

"Thought so," said the man, glancing at him again. "French, I bet. Or Italian."

Seb couldn't resist. "Italian," he said, keeping a straight face. "Venice, originally. My great-grandfather

8

was a gondolier — then he immigrated here and there weren't any canals, so he became a *ranchero*."

The truck driver's eyes widened. "Really?"

"Yeah, sure," said Seb, leaning forward to tap the ash off his cigarette. "Over ten thousand head of cattle. But I think his heart was always with the canals, you know?" He could have gone on in this vein for some time, except the guy was such an idiot that it was too easy to be much fun.

The truck driver went back to the endless subject of his girlfriend, outlining her many failings and the ways in which she was going to have to improve. A few more flashes of the woman being bullied came to Seb as the trucker droned on, so that by the time they reached Seb's destination and pulled over to the side of the road, he could have happily choked the guy. Instead, he filched the pack of cigarettes and lighter from the truck driver's pocket as they shook hands. He hadn't picked a pocket since he was a kid on the Mexico City streets, but it gave him a certain satisfaction — though really he should let the *cabrón* keep smoking, since it was bad for your health.

As the truck pulled away, Seb gave himself a quick shake, freeing himself of the unpleasant energy like a dog shaking itself dry. He was almost in the Sierra Madre now, standing on a hill in the gathering dark with the shadowy hulk of mountains rising up from the horizon. He focused briefly to make sure there weren't any angels nearby, then sent his other self searching. As he soared, he found the orphanage easily; it was about half a mile down the road, a sprawling building with a barren-looking playground. He pulled on a sweater from his knapsack and started walking, letting his other self keep flying as he did. The feeling of stretching his wings was nice; it had been a few days since he'd flown any distance.

Thinking of what he'd told the truck driver, Seb smiled slightly as he walked. Actually, where his mother had been from was almost the only thing Seb knew about her — she was dead now; the last time he'd seen her was when he was five years old. From the few memories he had, he knew that he looked a lot like her. Light chestnut-brown hair with a curl to it, high cheekbones and hazel eyes, a mouth that women sometimes called beautiful, which made him inwardly roll his eyes even more. It was a distinctly northern face; Sonora was a state where European immigrants had mixed for generations. On the streets, *gringo* tourists were always assuming Seb was one of them and asking for directions in English — clueless to the fact that millions of Mexicans didn't look like the ones in Westerns on TV.

As for his father, who knew? But Seb knew he couldn't have been unattractive. None of them were.

As he crested the hill, the orphanage came into view, and he stood staring down at it for a moment, his grip tight on the strap of his knapsack. Now that he was here, he was almost afraid to look — the continuous hope, and then the inevitable letdown, was becoming so much harder to bear. Yet he had to go through with it. The last hour of his life stuck listening to that *cabrón* in the truck would have been completely wasted if he didn't do what he'd come for. And besides, this might be the place. This really might be the place where he would finally find her.

Despite himself, Seb felt a stab of anticipation so sharp it was almost painful—the hope that he couldn't ever totally quench. He left the road and lay down flat in the grass on his stomach, with the orphanage in view below. Concentrating solely on his other self, he closed his eyes.

He glided down the valley toward the shabby building, his wide wings glinting in the dusk. With barely a ripple, he passed through a wall of the orphanage and flew inside. As usual, his muscles tensed to be entering one of these places. Unwanted, the memory of the room came, with its total darkness that had pressed down on his five-year-old self like a weight. But the room had turned out to be a blessing in disguise—because it was there that he'd first realized what he really was. It was practically the only thing that had kept him from going insane in that place.

No one saw Seb's other self as he flew noiselessly from room to room. He saw immediately that this orphanage was one of the few that weren't too bad. It was clean, if depressingly bare. And the auras of the children and teenagers looked healthy enough, once he found them, all sitting in a dining room eating their dinners with the staff—they showed signs of boredom rather than abuse. Circling overhead, Seb scanned their life energies, noting all the colors. A dull blue, a flicker of lively pink, a gentle green. None had even a hint of silver, but that didn't necessarily mean anything; he'd been shifting his own aura since he was a child. As he focused on each one, he opened his senses, inspecting the feel of the energy — *listening* almost, his whole being craned with anticipation as he touched each person's aura with his own. They were all completely human.

He checked again, just to make sure, but his heart had gone out of it. Then he forced himself to explore the other rooms, though he knew already that he wouldn't find anyone else in them, and he didn't.

She wasn't here, either.

The disappointment tightened his throat as if someone was standing on it. Opening his eyes, Seb brought his other self out of the orphanage and lay motionless, still gazing down at the stark building below.

She. He snorted slightly. He didn't even know if there *were* any others of his kind, much less what sex they might be. Yet somehow he'd always known it was a girl around his own age who he was looking for. He could feel her so strongly. Even though he had no idea of her name or what she looked like, he knew *her.* For as long as he could remember, Seb had had a sense of the girl's spirit; who she was. He thought he could almost hear her laugh sometimes, catch glimpses of her smile. Not being able to actually see her, or touch her, was a constant ache inside of him.

Roughly, Seb pushed his hair back with both hands. Why wasn't he used to the disappointment of not finding her by now? How many cities had he searched? How many orphanages and schools, how many miles spent walking how many streets? Suddenly he felt tired—so tired. This latest failure felt like the last straw.

It's never going to happen, thought Seb. *I've only imagined her all these years, because I wanted so much for it to be true.*

Rolling over onto his back, he watched his angel self as it soared in the night sky, snowy wings outspread. For once the sensation of flight didn't soothe him. He'd been searching for his half-angel girl for so long—first for years on the streets of Mexico City after he'd run away from the orphanage, checking out every aura he passed. Then when he was eleven, he'd been thrown into a young offenders' facility, he'd broken out at thirteen and soon after had started his quest in earnest, traveling up and down the country, searching every town, every city and village. Everywhere, for almost five years now, without encountering a single other aura like his own. Without once catching even a hint of her energy, except in his thoughts.

Above, Seb felt a cool wind whispering past his wings; the evening was quiet and peaceful. *Enough,* he told himself. The thought seemed to float into his mind of its own accord, but the moment it did, he knew that it was true.

He couldn't do this anymore, couldn't take the never-ending disappointment. If he'd never seen another of his kind in all these years, in a country as populated as Mexico, then it was time he finally faced the truth—there were no others. No half-angel girl was going to miraculously appear to ease his loneliness, no matter how strongly he thought he sensed her. She didn't exist. She'd only been a figment of his imagination all this time, a beautiful phantom. By some bitter joke of nature, he was alone — the only one of his kind — and it was time to just accept that and try to get on with the rest of his life, whatever that might bring.

The decision felt right. It also felt like something had just been ripped out of his chest, leaving a jagged hole that would never be filled. Seb lay on the soft grass and watched his angel self fly, so effortlessly agile against the stars. And he knew that what he'd been thinking wasn't quite true — as long as he had this other part of himself, he would never be completely alone.

It only felt that way.

CHAPTER ONE

THE SCISSORS WERE COLD against my neck.

I stood with my eyes shut in the bathroom of our motel room, trying not to notice how much I hated the sound of each metallic snip and the odd, awful feeling of lightness that was slowly spreading its way across my head. Even though I knew how much we needed to do this—of course I did; it had been my idea in the first place—that didn't mean I had to enjoy it. Alex wasn't enjoying it much, either. In fact, he probably hated it even more than I did. But when I'd brought up the idea earlier that afternoon, he admitted he'd been thinking the same thing—and now the scissors didn't hesitate as he worked them. If I hadn't suggested this, he would have.

It was weird, though . . . both of us so eager to do something that neither of us actually wanted.

I heard Alex put the scissors down on the bathroom counter. "OK, I think I'm done." He sounded uncertain. Dreading what I was about to see, I opened my eyes and stared at myself in the mirror.

My once-long hair was now short. Very short. I don't even know how to describe it. Sort of a pixie cut, maybe, if the pixies had gone berserk with the scissors. And more than that, it was no longer blond — it was a deep red-gold that made me think of autumn and bonfires. I'd thought it might go better with my skin tone than brown, but now . . . I swallowed. In the mirror, my green eyes were wide and unsure.

I looked nothing like myself.

Alex was staring, too. "Wow," he said. "That . . . makes a big difference."

I wanted to blurt out, *You still think I'm beautiful, right?* I bit the words back. Still being beautiful was not the point — not that I'd ever really thought I was, anyway; it was Alex who thought that. But the main thing now was just staying alive. In the bedroom, I could still hear the newscast that had been going nonstop ever since we'd turned on the TV: "*Police are searching urgently for the pair for questioning. . . . Again, if you see them, do not approach them yourself; call our special hotline. . . . They are assumed to be armed and dangerous. . . .*"

I knew without looking that they were showing my sophomore school photo again — and that it was probably on every Church of Angels website in the world by now. So to be honest, changing my most noticeable feature hadn't exactly been a tough decision. At least no one knew what Alex looked like. There was a police sketch, but it was laughably wrong: the security guard who'd been at the cathedral had remembered him as being about ten years older and fifty pounds heavier than he really was, bulging with muscles like a football player.

I couldn't take my eyes off the girl in the mirror. It was like a stranger had stolen my face. I reached for the red eyebrow pencil I'd asked Alex to buy and traced it over my eyebrows. The effect was much more dramatic than I would have thought. Before, I barely even noticed my eyebrows when I looked at myself. Now they seemed to jump right out at me.

This was me now.

Feeling oddly shaken, I put down the pencil and ran my fingers through what was left of my hair. Half of it spiked up; the other half flopped down. Someone, somewhere, might pay good money for a haircut like this — like the type of runway model who'd wear a garbage-bag dress held together with safety pins, maybe.

"I'm glad you don't want to be a hairdresser," I said to Alex. "Because I don't think your work is very mainstream."

He smiled and touched the back of my neck; it felt weirdly vulnerable to have the skin there so exposed. "No one will recognize you — that's what's important," he said. "Christ, I almost wouldn't recognize you."

"Oh," I said. I didn't mean to sound quite so forlorn, but the thought of Alex not recognizing me was just . . . wrong.

He caught my look and wrapped his arms around me from behind, drawing me close against his chest. The top of my head came up just past his chin. "Hey," he said, his eyes meeting mine in the mirror. "We'll both get used to it. And you're still gorgeous; you know that, right? It's just different — that's all."

I let out a breath, relieved he hadn't stopped thinking that. Maybe it was petty, with everything else that was happening in the world — but so much had changed already, without changing how Alex viewed me, too. I wanted that to stay the same forever.

"Thanks," I said.

He propped his chin on top of my head, looking amused. "Well, it's sort of a no-brainer. You'd be gorgeous if you shaved *all* your hair off."

I laughed. "Let's not test that one, OK? I think this is radical enough for one day." I rested back against his chest, taking in his tousled dark hair and blue-gray eyes in the mirror. *Gorgeous* was actually the word I'd use to describe Alex, not me. It still gave me a tingle like Christmas morning sometimes to realize this boy I was so much in love with felt the same way about me.

Meanwhile, my hair had not stopped being very short. Or very red. I kept getting mini jolts of surprise every time I saw myself, as if my mind hadn't caught up to what had happened yet.

18

"I wish there were some kind of dye we could use on your aura, too," said Alex after a pause.

I nodded, rubbing his toned forearms. "I know. We'll just have to be really careful."

My aura—the energy force that surrounds every living thing—is silver and lavender; a distinct mix of angel and human. Any angel who spotted it would know instantly who I was: the only half angel in the world, the one who'd tried to destroy them all. It was a risk that couldn't be avoided, though, unless we planned to go live in a cave somewhere.

"Anyway, hopefully now people won't be trying to shoot me quite as often," I said.

"That's the idea," he agreed. "Because, you know . . . I kind of want you to stick around for a while." His eyes flickered with memory, and I knew what he was thinking without trying, because I was thinking about the same thing. The worst day of both our lives: the day before, when he'd held me in his arms and thought I had died. My arms tightened over his. The truth was I *had* died. If Alex hadn't been there to bring me back, I wouldn't be here now.

"That's what I have in mind," I said softly. The crystal teardrop pendant he'd given me sparkled in the light. "Sticking around with you for a very, very long while."

"Deal," said Alex.

His head lowered in the mirror, and I shivered as his warm lips brushed my neck. Then he glanced up, listening, as a new voice came from the TV: a woman caller with a southern twang to her voice. "She must be sick — that's all. But just because she's mentally ill doesn't mean she's not dangerous. Why, you can tell from that photo — there's just a deranged look in her eyes. . . ."

Actually, my eyes looked more worried than anything else just then. Alex and I went back into the bedroom, where the two news commentators on the screen were nodding gravely, agreeing that yes, I must be deranged to have attempted an "act of terrorism" against the Church of Angels — which was what the media was calling my attempt to seal the gate between the angels' world and our own.

I sank onto the bed. The Church claimed I'd been trying to set off a bomb in the cathedral, that I hated the angels so much I'd planned to blow the whole place up, regardless of the thousands of worshippers there to witness the arrival of the Second Wave. Me, a fanatical bomber. It would have been funny if Alex and I weren't in so much danger.

An image of the cathedral in Denver from the day before appeared: its broad white dome and massive columns; its parking lot, choked with cars and people. And its high silver doors, standing open as countless angels streamed out. I'd seen the footage several times now; I still couldn't take my eyes off it. I watched in morbid fascination as the angels' wings flashed gold in the sunset, pouring out from the cathedral in an endless river of light and grace. In their ethereal form, angels weren't normally visible except to the humans they were feeding from, but they'd made an exception as the Second Wave invaded our world. They'd wanted to hear people's cheers, Nate had told us. The cattle, cheering their slaughterers.

The Second Wave and I were the big news of the day. Everyone on the planet seemed to be debating what this meant: whether the angel footage had been faked, what it meant for our world if it hadn't been. The news program showed the same clips over and over, with the headline ANGELIC ARRIVAL scrolling past at the bottom of the screen. Then when they got tired of that, they took more phone calls from all across the country: people who'd seen the angels arriving, people who wished they'd seen the angels arriving, people who thought they'd seen *me*, people who wished they could see me so they could give me "what I deserve."

I sat watching tensely, still hardly able to believe that just six weeks ago, my life had been relatively normal — or at least as normal as possible, when you're a teenage girl who's psychic and likes to fix cars. And then I'd done a reading for Beth Hartley, a girl in my high school back in Pawtucket, New York. I'd seen her joining the Church, becoming sick and listless, I'd tried to stop her but hadn't been able to — and, in the meantime, an angel named Paschar had foreseen that I was the one who'd destroy them all.

I sighed as I watched the angels flying across the screen. God, I wished he'd been right. I thought of my mother, lost in her dreams, her mind forever destroyed by what Raziel — I hated calling the angel my *father*; he didn't deserve the word—had done to her. She wasn't the only one. Millions of people had been hurt just as badly by the angels. Millions more were probably being hurt by them right this second, while all the callers on TV exulted about angelic love.

Angelic love. The words left a bitter taste when you knew that the angels were here to feed off human energy, as if our world were their own private fish farm. And thanks to something called angel burn, they were seen as creatures of beauty and kindness, even as their victims' life energy crumpled under their touch. The result might be a mental illness like my mother had, or MS or cancer or almost any other debilitating disease you could name. Because when an angel feeds from you, there are only two certainties: one, you'll be damaged forever in some terrible, irrevocable way . . . and two, you'll worship the angels until the day you die.

I glanced at Alex, taking in the firm lines of his face, the dark eyelashes that framed his eyes, the mouth that begged to have my finger on it, tracing its outline. By the time Alex was barely sixteen, his entire family had been destroyed by angels. Now dozens more of his friends had been killed by them besides.

The black AK tattoo on his left bicep didn't stand for *Alex Kylar*; it stood for *Angel Killer.*

Alex was the only AK left. The only person in the world who knew how to fight them. The thought of anything happening to him was like razors slicing my heart, but our plan to recruit and train new AKs wouldn't exactly keep us out of the line of fire. Part of me really did want us to go live in a cave — or up on a Tibetan mountaintop or out in the middle of a swamp somewhere — *anyplace* that was remote and safe, so we could just be together without worrying, forever.

But we didn't have a choice, and we both knew it. No matter how we felt about each other, we had to do something about what was happening.

I leaned against Alex; he put his arm around me and drew me close. His jaw had tensed — the special number to call if you'd seen me was flashing on the screen again. "God, I'm tempted to just stay here for a few more days," he muttered. "No one would expect you to be holed up so close to Denver. We should wait until things have calmed down a little, so that —"

"Alex, wait," I broke in. Urgency had swept me; suddenly I felt sick with tension. *The front desk,* I thought.

I could see it in my mind: the slightly battered counter where Alex and I had checked in the night before, both of us so tired we were reeling. It had been covered by a sheet of glass, with a motel map on display under it. There'd been an old-fashioned bell, too, the kind with a little button on top for guests to ring for attention. The inane details beat through my head, feeling dark and ominous. I had to go there. Now.

Concern came over Alex's face. "Willow? What is it?"

"I just need to go check something," I said faintly.

I saw him start to protest at the thought of me leaving the motel room; then he realized what I meant. "Yeah, OK," he said. "Be careful."

I nodded. And taking a deep breath, I went within, reaching for my angel.

She was there, waiting — a radiant winged version of myself; the halo-less angel who was part of me. Her wings were folded gracefully behind her back, and I saw that her hair was short now, too, framing her serene face. My shoulders relaxed a little. Just being near her was a caress.

With a mental flick, I shifted my consciousness to hers and lifted out of my human form. My angel wings stretched wide; I passed through the motel roof with a shimmer, soaring out into the Colorado late-afternoon sky. *Flying.* Even at a time like this, it gave me a stir of pleasure. I was still getting to know my angel self; for most of my life, I hadn't even known she was there.

The chill of November stroked my wings as I flew to the reception building. Another brief ripple as I glided through the wall, and then I saw the clerk from the night before, talking on the phone with one elbow propped on the front desk. He was staring at a TV that was on in the corner of the lobby.

On the screen, my school photo smiled back at him.

"Well, I couldn't say for certain, but — yeah, I'm pretty damn sure," he said. "They got in about ten last night, looking dead to the world; then this morning they asked the manager to have the room for another night. They're still in there now. Been there all day, as far as I know."

Fear clutched my throat. At least he didn't realize Alex had left for a while, to go buy the hair dye and scissors. I swooped down and landed; under my ethereal feet, the carpet felt strange, insubstantial. Back in the motel room, my human form still sat on the bed with Alex's fingers linked tightly through mine.

"They're supposed to come down and pay for the extra night soon. You want I should hold them for you? . . . Oh, OK. . . . Yeah, I see. . . ."

Behind the desk, another clerk stood waiting with wide eyes. When the man hung up the phone, she said, "Well?"

"She said not to go near them; they're sending someone right out. There's a squad car coming now — it's just a few blocks away." He shook his head. "Man, wouldn't it be wild if it was them? Dangerous fugitives, holed up in a sleepy little place like Trinidad —"

I didn't hear the rest; I was already speeding back to our room in a flurry of wings. I found my human self again; merged. My eyes flew open. "The desk clerk from last night — he's recognized us," I burst out. "The police are on their way."

Alex swore as he lunged off the bed. "OK, we've got to get out of here now." He undid his jeans to strap on his holster and pistol under his waistband; when they were securely hidden, he ducked into the bathroom and grabbed the eye pencil and hair dye stuff, shoving it all in the shopping bag it had come in, along with the long strands of my hair that had fallen to the floor. He swiped

25

a motel washcloth over all the surfaces, removing any sign of the dye, and stuffed that in the bag, too.

Trying to stay calm, I fumbled for the black pumps that were the only shoes I had now. Then I heard what was being said on TV and glanced up. My hands slowed and stilled.

"A dramatic new development has just been released from law enforcement officials in Pawtucket, New York. This was the scene last night on Nesbit Street, at the former home of suspected terrorist Willow Fields. . . ."

Aunt Jo's house appeared on the screen. I heard a ragged gasp, then realized it had come from me. I sat frozen, my mind unable to process what I was seeing.

The house where I had lived since I was nine years old was in flames.

There was no doubt, even with the trembling footage that looked like someone had taken it with their cell phone — it was Aunt Jo's run-down Victorian home, crackling and crumbling to the ground. Even the garden ornaments in the front yard were ablaze. I could just make out one of the gnomes, standing enveloped in flames like a weird fire spirit.

The picture changed to blackened ruins, with firefighters picking through them. The entire second story of the house was gone, with only dark, skeletal fingers sticking up here and there. I stared at a smudged piece of lavender wall. My bedroom.

"The cause is unknown, though local police suspect vigilantes from the Church of Angels might be behind the blaze. Early

reports indicate there were no survivors. The bodies of two women have been found in the ruins, thought to be Miranda and Joanna Fields, the mother and aunt of Willow Fields. . . ."

On the TV screen, two body bags on stretchers were being carried out from the house's charred remains.

Chapter Two

I STARTED TO SHAKE as the world thudded in my ears. On the screen, one of the firefighters slipped on the rubble; I stared wordlessly as the too-human-looking bag shifted on the stretcher.

"Willow!" Alex was crouching in front of me, his voice almost harsh as he gripped my shoulders. "I'm sorry, but if we don't get the hell out of here, it'll be us next. Come *on!*"

Somehow I managed to nod. I couldn't breathe; my entire body felt crushed by the weight of what I'd just seen. Mom. *Mom.* I got up and took the small photo of myself with the willow tree from where I'd placed it on the bedside table, shoving it numbly in my jeans pocket. It was all I had left from my old life now. With the TV still going, Alex edged the door open, peering out. "It's clear," he whispered, half turning and holding out his hand to me. "Don't look like we're in a hurry. But be ready to run."

No *survivors, no survivors.* The words beat through my skull as we walked to the parking lot, holding hands. The only people in sight were a couple unloading their things from a car; neither of them looked at us. As we reached the motorcycle, Alex handed me the helmet and shoved the plastic bag in the storage compartment. My fingers felt thick and clumsy as I worked the helmet's straps.

A police car was just coming down the street as we roared off in the other direction. I hardly noticed. I clung tight to Alex; over and over, I kept seeing the two body bags. Had Mom come out of her dream world before it happened? Had she known what was going on? Oh, please, no. The thought of her being scared and trapped, unable to get away, hurt so much I thought it might kill me. I huddled against Alex's back as the cold mountain air rushed past, keeping my eyes closed and trying not to throw up.

I'm not sure how much time passed; it could have been minutes or hours. But sometime later, once we'd crossed the state line into New Mexico, Alex turned off the highway and into a small town. When we came to a gas station, he pulled in and parked the bike out of sight behind it. My legs felt stiff and unreal as I climbed off, as if I were a zombie that had just crawled from the grave.

Alex's face was tight with sympathy as he put his arm around my shoulders. "Come on, we've got to talk," he said. He steered me into the restroom.

Talk. The word seemed alien; I found myself turning it over for different possible meanings. I stood hugging myself as he locked the door behind us. Somewhere deep within, I could feel the tears waiting like a tidal wave. If I gave into them, they'd sweep me away and drown me.

Alex's hair was ruffled from the wind as he turned to me; his hands gripped mine, feeling warm and strong. "Willow, listen," he said urgently. "The more I think about it, the more this doesn't make sense. I mean, yeah, the Church of Angels might want your mother dead, but why would they target your aunt, too? Everyone in Pawtucket knew that the two of you didn't get along, right?"

I shook my head, too shell-shocked to get where he was going with this. He was right, though. It was a small town, and Aunt Jo wasn't the type to keep her complaints to herself. Everybody had known how put-upon she felt having to support the two of us, even with the money I sometimes brought in with my psychic readings.

"Plus, your aunt believed what the Church said about you running off with a secret boyfriend, so why have her killed?" Alex went on. "It helps their story if she's around. And if the target was your mother, it would make more sense to just stick her in a home somewhere and then quietly get rid of her. You don't do away with someone by burning their house down — there are just too many ways it could go wrong."

A headache spiked my temples; I could hardly take in the meaning of his words. "Alex, what are you saying?"

He hesitated, his hands still holding mine. Finally he

said, "This may sound weird, but can you try to sense your mother?"

The realization thundered through me. "You—you don't think they're really dead."

I could see the conflict in his eyes: his reluctance to get my hopes up versus whatever he was thinking. "I don't know," he said. "But this doesn't feel right. The house burning down that way just seems too convenient. Almost like something you'd do for show."

I swallowed hard, barely daring to hope. "It could have been a—an unruly mob, though. People do burn places down sometimes. And people die because of it."

"Yeah, they do. Look, I could be totally wrong. But—just try it, OK? See if you can sense them."

I almost didn't want to try, didn't want to believe even this small amount, only to be disappointed. I took a deep, shuddering breath, attempting to clear my mind enough to focus.

Mom.

I envisioned her soft blond hair, so like my own natural shade; her green eyes that used to sparkle with recognition when they saw me. Her scent, which wasn't shampoo or body lotion but a mixture of both, plus something else that was just her, my mother—a smell that when I was little I wanted to curl up in. Even later, when she'd stopped responding to anyone at all, I'd still sit close to her sometimes as she sat lost in her dreams, breathing in that scent and wishing for things to be different.

It didn't take long for Mom to be firmly in my head;

she was never far from my thoughts. I stretched my mind out, drifting, searching. Was she out there anywhere? Please?

Endless minutes went past. I stood against the cool porcelain sink with my eyes closed, trying not to force things despite the thudding of my heart, the tiny agony of hope that had sprung up within me. *Don't push. Just relax . . . drift. . . . Mom, are you there?*

Nothing. Darkness. My throat tightened as the hope flickered and died.

And then somewhere in the emptiness, I thought I caught something — the faintest hint of a presence. I reached out, exploring it cautiously, and in a rush, a wild jumble of sensation swept over me — Mom's smell, her voice, her *essence.*

She was content. She was safe.

"Alex, she's alive — she's OK!" I cried. "I can feel her!" I flung myself at him, hugging him hard; he caught me up, laughing, and lifted me briefly off the floor. At first I thought I was laughing, too, but then I realized that the tears had come after all — that now, when everything was all right, something in me had snapped like a frayed rubber band, and I was crying as if I'd never be able to stop.

Alex's arms tightened around me. "It's OK," he whispered, his lips moving in my hair as he rocked me. "Shhh, babe, it's all right. Everything's OK. . . ." I tried to answer but couldn't. I'd thought she was dead. Oh, God, I had really thought my mother was dead. Distantly, I felt Alex pick me up and sink to the cracked tiled floor, his arms still firm around me. He didn't say anything else, just held me close and let me cry, stroking my back and occasionally kissing the top of my head.

Finally something resembling calm started to return. I pulled away, swiping at my damp cheeks. "How did you know?" I asked shakily. "How?"

He brushed a strand of hair from my temple. I could see the depth of his relief. "I didn't — I just really, really hoped I was right. Is your aunt Jo OK, too?"

Shame scorched me like a flamethrower; I'd forgotten all about her. But when I checked, she was fine. Actually, better than fine — she seemed happier than I'd ever sensed her. I let out a breath. Aunt Jo and I had lived in the same creaky, full-of-clutter house for years without becoming close — in fact, there'd been times when I hated her — but knowing she was all right made me go limp all over again.

I felt battered as we stood up, as if I'd been pummeled by a hundred fists. I reached into a cubicle for some toilet paper to mop my face. "So, was the fire just a cover, then? Someone must really want the world to believe that Mom and Aunt Jo are dead."

Alex nodded, resting a firm-looking shoulder against the wall. "I think it might have been the CIA."

I looked up from wiping my eyes. "You mean Sophie?"

"Yeah, maybe. Nate told you that another department was sheltering Project Angel now that it's been infiltrated.

She could have gotten their help to set the fire and get your mother and aunt out of there — keep them both safe, so the angels can't use them to get to you."

I fell silent as I threw the damp tissue away in the overflowing trash can. Project Angel was the covert CIA department Alex had worked for; after it had been taken over by the angels, Sophie and Nate had been its only two agents left. Now Nate — a renegade angel who'd tried to help humanity — was dead, and though I assumed Sophie was still alive, I had no idea where. She'd left me at the Church of Angels cathedral with no way to contact her, believing I was going to die just like Nate.

And yeah, maybe I'd agreed to that plan, but it was still kind of hard for me to like Sophie after that. But if Alex was right and she'd really taken Mom into protection, then she was officially my new favorite person.

A chilling thought came. "Wait a minute — since Mom and Aunt Jo are OK, who was in the body bags?"

Alex shrugged. "Two women of about the right age? It wouldn't be hard for the CIA to find a couple of unclaimed bodies; the morgues in New York City must be full of them."

In a flash I saw again the body bag on the stretcher, slipping as the firefighter stumbled. Oh, my God. Who had been in it?

"Or maybe the bags had living people in them, to make them look right for the cameras," added Alex. "It depends on who was at the scene; whether they were CIA or not."

"I like that version better," I said softly.

"OK. We'll go with that one, then." He wrapped his arms around me, and I closed my eyes, just drinking in his solid warmth. There were no words for what I felt for Alex, for how grateful I was that even with everything that had happened, we still had each other.

Finally I cleared my throat, fingering the damp patch on the collar of his T-shirt. "I got you all wet."

"Don't worry — I'm waterproof." He squeezed my hand. "Come on, we'd better get going. We've still got all of New Mexico to get across."

"No, wait," I said. "There's something I want to do first." And rising up on my tiptoes, I twined my arms around his neck and pressed close against him, kissing him deeply.

I felt his heartbeat leap against mine and caught my breath as his hands slipped into the back pockets of my jeans, pulling me closer still. The soft-rough heat of his mouth, the feel of his hair as I stroked my fingers through it. . . . I wanted this to never end. But finally, softly, we drew apart.

"Wow," murmured Alex. He nuzzled at my neck. "What was that for?"

"Well, (a) because I wanted to, and (b) . . ." I stopped. "And (b), to say thank you. I don't know if it would even have occurred to me to search psychically for Mom after what I saw on TV. I would have spent the rest of my life just . . . thinking she was gone." My chest clenched; I couldn't say any more.

Alex rested his hand on my cheek. His eyes looked darker than usual — a stormy gray that melted me. "We're a team," he said quietly. "Always, remember?" Then he grinned. "Hey, do I get to say 'You're welcome' now?"

I gave a casual shrug as my pulse skipped. "You know, I think you should. It's good to be polite."

He put his arms around me. "Polite's my middle name."

"I thought it was James."

"Yeah, 'Polite James.' My parents had weird taste in names." He lowered his head to mine again, then both of us jumped as the doorknob rattled.

"Hey," came a man's voice. "Is anyone in there?"

I stifled my laughter against Alex's chest. "Be out in a minute," he called.

"What's he going to think when we both come out?" I whispered.

"Well, the truth, obviously. Two wild teenagers, making out in a bathroom." He gave me a quick kiss, and we pulled apart.

I went over to the sink and hastily splashed cool water on my face. In the mirror, my short hair was like an explosion from the wind and the crying. And it still looked very red. I held back a sigh as I tried to smooth it down, wishing I'd asked Alex to buy a hairbrush.

"You know what? I think that color makes your eyes look greener," said Alex suddenly.

I looked up in surprise. "Really?"

He nodded, studying me. "It really does. They look

a lot more . . . vivid now, or something." He touched a spiky lock of my hair, his finger stroking gently through it. "You look beautiful, Willow."

He meant it; I could tell. I smiled. "So, you think you can get used to me as a redhead?"

"Hmm, tough call. Yeah, I think I can deal with it." Alex dropped a kiss on my nose, then closed his eyes. I felt the slight shift as he lifted his consciousness up through his chakra points until it was hovering somewhere over his crown.

"OK, it's clear of angels at least," he said after a second. "What about you? Do you sense anything?"

I'd already been checking, relaxing my mind and imagining the gas station forecourt. No particular feelings came. "I think we're all right."

We left the bathroom holding hands. My cheeks were burning.

"Sorry," said Alex to the man waiting outside. He didn't sound sorry; I could tell he was trying not to laugh. The man shook his head and didn't answer, just disappeared inside and banged the door.

"He thinks I'm a floozy," I said as we started back to the bike. It was almost dark now; the town's streetlamps were casting soft pools of light up and down the main road. Happiness that Mom was alive was still pulsing through me, making my steps feel light and springy.

"Definitely," said Alex. "But he thinks I'm lucky." He started to say something else and stopped, looking across the street.

Following his gaze, I saw a small shopping strip with a Goodwill store on the corner. The lights were on, and I could tell that Alex was thinking of going in, if it was safe. Neither of us had any clothes, apart from what we had on—or hardly anything else, for that matter.

I let my thoughts drift toward the store, scanning it. "It's OK," I said. "It feels almost empty."

He nodded, eyes narrowed in thought. "Maybe we should risk it," he said. "If they have some secondhand camping gear, we could avoid motels until we find some-place safe in Mexico to hole up. And we could maybe get another helmet, so that both our faces are hidden."

"Oh," I said.

Alex glanced down at me. "What?"

"Nothing. I just thought you were thinking about clothes."

His dark eyebrows arched in amusement as we continued to the bike. "We're on the run, and you think I'm worrying about clothes?"

"Alex, I've worn this same outfit for three days now; it's getting *foul*. And, you know—as long as we're in there, anyway . . ."

"This is a girl thing, isn't it?"

"It's possibly a girl thing," I admitted.

The Goodwill store was huge, but it was so near clos-ing time that we were the only ones in there. The old woman behind the counter was reading a romance novel; she didn't even look up as we came in. We both got some clothes, and Alex found another helmet for the bike. Plus a pile of camping stuff, including sleeping bags and a two-person tent. Then as we were carrying our things to the checkout counter, I saw them: an almost-new pair of grape-juice-purple Converse sneakers, just my size.

"Alex, look, look!" I darted over and tried them on; they fit perfectly. And they were only four dollars. "OK, these are definitely mine." I put back the pair of old Reeboks I'd been going to buy.

Alex grinned. "Hey, excellent." Then he took in my face and started to laugh. "Is this another girl thing? I've never seen someone look so happy over a pair of shoes before."

He was right; I couldn't stop smiling. Maybe it was stupid, but it felt like I'd gotten back a little piece of myself that I'd lost.

We'd parked around the side of the building, in the shadows. When we got back to the bike, Alex pulled off the blue T-shirt he'd been wearing for the past few days and reached for the bag with our clothes. Warmth stirred through me as I watched the muscles of his chest and arms move. We'd been together for over a month, but it felt like longer — I couldn't imagine my life without Alex now.

"It's not really fair, you know," I said, leaning against the bike. "I can't just start changing my clothes out here the way you can."

The AK tattoo on Alex's bicep flexed as he pulled a long-sleeved white thermal shirt over his head; he put on a faded red plaid shirt over it, leaving it hanging open. He raised an eyebrow at me as he rolled up the sleeves a few turns. "Go for it. I don't mind."

I laughed. "No, I bet you don't. Nice try." I put our clothes bag in the motorcycle's storage compartment, shoving it down so the lid would close. "How much money do we have left?" I asked. Everything had been really cheap, but we'd still spent almost a hundred dollars.

Alex squatted down to fasten the tent under the rear of the seat. "Let's just say I'm really glad we don't have to spend money on motels anymore."

I bit my lip. That bad. Part of the reason we were going to Mexico—apart from practically the entire United States being on the lookout for us now—was that it was cheaper. "We should try to save money on food, too," I said as Alex strapped the sleeping bags to the bike. "If we go to grocery stores instead of fast-food places from now on, we can—" I broke off, breathing in sharply.

A flock of gleaming white angels had just glided out from over the top of the strip mall—fifteen or twenty of them. They flew across the street from us at an angle, their great wings stroking the air.

Seeing my face, Alex rose hastily; I sensed his energy shifting. His expression hardened as he spotted the angels. "Get back," he said, not taking his eyes off them. We pressed against the side of the building, Alex shielding me with his body, trying to hide my aura with his own. He drew his gun out from under his waistband. I heard a faint click as he took the safety off.

The angels continued on their way without noticing

us, achingly glorious against the mundane buildings. I stared at them from under Alex's arm, my emotions in a tumult. That deadly beauty was half me. I wasn't a predator like they were, but half of me was angel all the same. As the flock grew more distant, they winked in and out of the streetlights like stars, finally fading from view.

I felt Alex check out the area around us, and then relax. "It's OK; it's clear now."

We stepped out of the shadows and glanced at each other. My legs felt like cotton. If the angels had seen us, we'd be dead right now. Especially me, after what I'd done — and if they still thought I was the one who could destroy them all. I knew Alex was thinking the same thing, but neither of us said it.

"That was a really large flock," I said at last.

"Yeah. I've never seen one that size before." He put his gun away, showing a ribbon of toned, flat stomach. "I guess they're from the Second Wave — maybe heading down to Albuquerque to live."

I swallowed. It was already starting, then. The Second Wave of angels, settling into our world alongside the First Wave. Silently, Alex crouched to finish strapping our stuff to the bike; when he straightened up, he wrapped his arms around me for a long moment, holding me close. "Are you ready?" he asked.

I nodded; suddenly I could hardly wait to get away from this place. "Yeah. Let's go."

We drove for hours, heading south on minor roads, stopping only once to grab food from a tiny convenience store in the hills north of Alamogordo. The land turned to desert, vast and empty, with the stars shimmering overhead. Once, as we skirted a town, I saw another angel in flight, its pure-white figure clear against the night sky. As I watched, it wheeled sharply on one wing and plummeted, deadly as an arrow. I turned my head away as we sped on, hating what I knew was happening at that very moment.

We started climbing back into mountains; the cold wind whipped at my face and arms. I shivered, pressing against Alex's back, and was glad when he finally pulled off the road. It felt late, after midnight.

"I thought New Mexico was supposed to be hot," I said as we got off the bike. He'd taken us down a dirt road that led deep into the woods; we were at the bottom of a narrow canyon. Moonlight cast a faint, silvery light — I could see my breath in the air.

"Not up here," said Alex as he unstrapped the tent. This was his home state, and he seemed to know it inside and out. I fumbled coldly in the storage compartment for the sweater I'd bought, then pulled it on over the one I was already wearing — and remembered how Alex hadn't even needed a map back in September, when he'd guided us over a hundred miles of New Mexico back roads.

"But we're not too far from the border now, and then it'll be desert again," he went on. He tossed the rolled-up tent onto the frosty ground and started undoing the sleeping bags. "I just thought we could get a couple of hours' sleep up here where it's hidden, then cross before dawn when there's a little more light—I don't remember exactly where the crossing place is; I might miss it in the dark."

Needless to say, we weren't going into Mexico by the legal way. I pushed aside my apprehension over what the next few hours might bring and helped Alex put up the tent.

"I've never gone camping before," I commented as I unwound a guy rope.

Alex was wrestling one of the tent pegs into the hard ground; he glanced at me in amazement, his face looking sculpted in the moonlight. "Never? Really?"

"No, Mom never took me, and Aunt Jo . . ." I shrugged. I had told Alex what Aunt Jo was like; I didn't have to explain.

He smiled, knowing what I meant. "Well, we're sort of roughing it," he said, moving on to the next rope. "You can get, like, fridges and stoves and stuff, but that's never really seemed like camping to me."

"Not that any of that would fit on the bike, anyway," I added.

Alex shook his head, making a tsking noise. "What, so you wouldn't carry a fridge on your lap if we got one? That's a serious lack of dedication."

"Yeah, I know. Sorry."

Crawling inside, we got the sleeping bags zipped together. The ground felt freezing through the nylon floor of the tent. "I don't need a fridge, but a *heater* would be nice," I said. My teeth were practically chattering.

Alex grabbed our things from the bike and brought them inside; then he fastened the tent closed, securing us in. "Come here, I'll keep you warm."

He drew me to him, and we snuggled together in the softness of the sleeping bags. We were both fully dressed, apart from having kicked our shoes off — it was way too cold to contemplate taking anything off.

"Promise me it's warmer in Mexico," I said, nestling against him. Slowly, I was starting to feel less like an ice cube — and even better, safe, at least for the moment.

"I promise," murmured Alex. He was lying on his back with his arms around me; one hand had slipped under my T-shirt and was lazily stroking my spine. I could sense how tired he was, now that we'd finally stopped moving. So was I. It felt like a million years had passed since I'd crouched in the Church of Angels cathedral in Denver, trying to stop the Second Wave from arriving. And it hadn't even been two days.

"Alex?" I whispered.

"Hmm?"

"What are going to do when we get to Mexico? Do you have any idea where we're going?" I knew he'd been to Mexico dozens of times; from the sound of it, he and the other AKs had crossed the border often.

His hand trailing up and down my spine stopped. For a minute I thought he'd fallen asleep; then his voice spoke in the darkness. "I thought we'd go to the Sierra Madre," he said. "There should be someplace safe there where we can hole up and start trying to recruit other AKs."

As he said the words, I got a flash of his thoughts: a dense, wild mountain range, full of plummeting canyons and almost unpassable roads. You could hide up there for years and never be found. It was the best possible place to do what we needed to do and still keep me safe; he was sure of it. Even so, I caught a sense of cold dread running beneath the images.

"Alex? What's wrong?"

"Nothing," he said.

I hesitated, wondering whether to push it. "No, there is. I mean, if you don't want to tell me, it's all right, but I can feel it."

There was a long pause; outside the tent, the wind stirred through the bare bones of the trees. Finally Alex gave a soft laugh. "OK, I'm still getting used to this psychic girlfriend thing," he said. "I'm fine. I just—" He sighed. And suddenly I knew, the thought dropping into my head as if it were my own.

"You're worried about being in charge," I said in surprise. I rose up, trying to see his face in the darkness. "That's it, isn't it?"

The dread flickered again like the tongue of a snake, then faded as if he was making a conscious effort to control it. "It's nothing," he said gruffly. "I just saw enough about what it's like to be a leader when my dad was in charge. I'd rather work on my own or as part of a team under someone I trust. But, you know—" His chest

45

shifted under me as he shrugged. "That's not the way it is; we've got to train new AKs, and I'm the only one who knows how. So I'll deal with it."

It didn't really feel like he was telling me everything, but I let it go — he obviously didn't want to talk about it. And even though I was psychic, I'd never thought it was OK to go probing around if someone didn't want me to. I closed Alex's thoughts away from mine, so that I wouldn't pick up anything by mistake. We were so close that this happened more and more now when I wasn't even thinking about it.

"You'll be great," I murmured. I kissed his smooth neck. "And I'll help all I can. Psychic consultant, remember?"

I could almost hear his smile. "Don't forget mechanic. If the Shadow's anything like the Mustang . . ."

The Honda Shadow parked outside our tent was over twenty years old; I knew Alex was suspicious of it. "Hey, you leave the Mustang alone," I said. "It was a complete classic. And Shadows aren't bad either, you know — for a cheap bike, they're pretty classic themselves."

"Why did I know you were going to say that?" The sleeping bags gave a soft rustle as he rolled toward me. It felt much warmer in the tent now; almost cozy.

"I don't know. Maybe because . . ." My voice trailed off. Alex had taken my hand and was kissing my fingers, one by one. His lips seemed electric, zinging at my nerve endings as if I were an exposed wire. I felt myself go weak as he bit gently at my little finger; then his warm mouth slid down to my palm, pressing against it, and I shivered.

"Let's stop talking for a while, OK?" he whispered.

That night I had a dream.

I was standing at the top of a high tower, gazing out at what looked like the largest city in the world. It was endless, like something out of a science-fiction film. Low mountains crouched on the horizon; in every direction, the city crept over them and kept right on going, fading into hazy infinity. Somehow I knew it was in Mexico and that it was where Alex and I were meant to be. My heart tightened with urgency as I stared at the sea of buildings. We had to come here. We *had* to.

In the middle of the city lay a broad stone space: an immense square with a cathedral at one end and a long, official-looking building stretching down another. There was a stage set up near the cathedral, and rock music playing — it thumped through me as thousands danced. Dozens of angels glided over the square, too, like hawks hunting over a field. I took a panicked step backward. They'd see my aura; they'd know what I was —

The world whirled and shifted; the crowd scene disappeared. Now twelve angels hovered over the city, brighter than any I'd ever seen — like twelve blazing suns that poured light over the concrete buildings below. An ancient, ruthless power connected the twelve; I shuddered as I felt it. The angels started to glow even brighter still, burning at my eyes until I had to duck my head away. As I did, they vanished in an explosion that was sensation rather than sound — a shock wave that howled past, knocking me off my feet.

Seamlessly, I was in my angel form, flying from the tower as the screams of a million angels tore through me. But my wings were too heavy. I couldn't stay aloft; I was falling — I had to hold on tighter, fly harder —

I landed with a bump. Silence, so still and perfect, like cut glass. I was in a park, in my human form again. Soft green grass, palm trees mixed with poplars and cypress. The twelve angels were gone . . . but I wasn't alone.

A boy stood watching me. He was a little older than me, about the same height as Alex, with lightly curling brown hair. A glinting of stubble; high cheekbones and strong features — a beautiful face that I knew had been through great pain, yet it held such humor and tenderness that it twisted my heart.

We stared at each other. I had no idea who the boy was, but the thought of ever being without him filled me with despair. The unexpected feeling robbed the breath from my throat, so that at first I couldn't speak.

"Who are you?" I whispered at last.

In answer the boy stretched out his hand. "Come, *querida*," he said softly.

His eyes were urging me to say yes, and part of me wanted to link my fingers through his so badly that it hurt. *No, I'm in love with Alex,* I thought. And then: *But, oh, my God, to not be with you — how could I possibly bear it?*

◆ ◆ ◆

I woke up with a start. It was still nighttime; I was in the tent, safe in the sleeping bag with Alex asleep beside me. What had all *that* been about? Heart thudding, I pressed against Alex's bare chest. He shifted in his sleep and pulled me closer, and I hugged him hard, feeling almost guilty. Even in a dream, how could I have ever felt that way about someone else?

Especially now. My cheeks heated slightly; I smiled to myself as Alex's breath stirred my hair. We'd been taking things slowly since we first got together, and earlier tonight . . . well, basically we'd both been kicking ourselves that Alex hadn't made another purchase along with the hair dye and scissors at the drugstore. We'd managed to hold back, though, and meanwhile it had still been just—incredible, and wonderful. I kissed his shoulder, feeling the warm weight of his bare leg looped over mine.

OK, *forget the part about the boy,* I told myself. *That was just the dream disintegrating into weirdness.* But the rest of it . . . I frowned as I went over the images: the endless city, its huge square pulsing with music and people. Then the twelve fiery angels exploding—the heaviness of my wings, the millions of angels screaming. Remembering, urgency tugged at me even stronger than before, along with a cold dread that coiled in my stomach.

The dream was a premonition—I was sure of it. Wherever this city was, Alex and I had to go there.

CHAPTER THREE

THE ANGEL RAZIEL drifted in and out of consciousness, memory mixing with the now.

He was lying in bed in his chambers; the covers were soft. Sometimes there was the hum of the central heating as it came on, then the faint click as it went off again. Over and over, Raziel saw the assassin: the dark-haired youth who stood pointing a gun at him, with his arm around the half-angel abomination. The girl's face was pale, her green eyes wide.

The knowledge that he was the thing's father had rocked him. But there was no doubt. He'd felt the unmistakable echo of his own energy as their angel selves had fought — plus she looked almost exactly like Miranda, the young music student he'd once enjoyed. Thankfully, she bore no resemblance to him. Seeing the assassin again, Raziel groaned aloud. Next time he would move faster. Next time he would tear the energy forces from them both and watch them crumple into lifeless heaps on the ground—

"Hush, hush," whispered a voice. A young human woman was there. She stroked his arm, and even in his current state, Raziel found this irritating and wished she would stop. More voices: "Is he coming out of it yet?" "No, I don't think so. I don't know what to do for him; they're so different from us. . . ."

The assassin's finger pulling the trigger. The searing wrench as the bullet hit his halo. His wings going into flapping, helpless spasms; his body shuddering, closing down in protest—and the *anger* that had seethed through him as he collapsed to the floor and the world turned black. The Second Wave was arriving, and instead of being there to greet them and show off his status in this world, he'd been brought down by the very assassin whose life he'd so stupidly spared for his own purposes. He'd thought he'd been so clever, using Kylar to kill the angelic traitors, letting him think he was following standard orders from the CIA. Who'd have guessed that the young assassin would have such a mind of his own?

It was a mistake Raziel would soon rectify. Oh, yes, he'd relish every second of it. But it was the girl who incensed him the most—the girl who caused his fists to clench beneath the covers. He'd been told she was dead, and instead she'd had the gall to actually try to stop the Second Wave from arriving.

"Shhh," soothed the woman's voice. A cool, damp cloth brushed across his forehead. If the girl had succeeded, it would have meant death for them all, Paschar's vision fulfilled. And even though she'd failed, Raziel still burned with humiliation — the entire angel community knew that Willow Fields was the half angel he'd been trying to find for weeks. They'd know exactly what she'd been attempting to do in the cathedral, would know he'd been deceived and nearly bested. It was this that made him long to kill his daughter slowly, listening to her screams. And she felt so *close* now — so infuriatingly close. Raziel's head turned restlessly on the pillow. He could sense her energy, even though she was hundreds of miles away, in a sleeping bag with the assassin. The knowledge felt fuzzy; he wasn't sure how he knew it. Why, why, hadn't he managed to kill them both when he had the chance?

"Can't we at least make him more comfortable?" pleaded the woman. "He seems so distressed."

"Let's try this — it's very mild, but it might help."

A pinprick of pain in his arm. It did nothing, of course; angels were unaffected by either stimulants or sedatives. Raziel found himself drifting deeper anyway, exhausted by his own thoughts. As he did, other knowledge came to him . . . the most unwelcome knowledge he could have imagined.

Though individuals, angels were also all linked as if by an invisible web; when one died, they each felt it. Now, with the arrival of the Second Wave, the angelic energy in this world had more than doubled, humming with new life. And at its heart there pulsed a purposeful presence that Raziel recognized all too well.

In his long life, he'd only rarely felt fear, but he felt something akin to it now—a jolt of shock and wariness so great that for a moment he almost surfaced back into consciousness. No one had told him this. It was inconceivable that none of the other angels in this world had known, but the information had not been shared with him. The fact held ominous implications. He hadn't expected this to happen for several more years at least; he'd thought the Council would wait until the last Wave to make their move, holding reign in the angels' old world for as long as possible.

But no, they were here—and it could not bode well for him.

The Twelve had arrived.

"Manhunt for Terrorist Suspects Continues," read the headline.

They'd stopped at a small twenty-four-hour gas station near the Mexican border; dawn was still an hour away. As he glanced over the story, Alex was relieved by its lack of details— not to mention the photo of Willow with her long blond hair spilling past her shoulders, reassuring him again just how different she looked now. The picture of Raziel was an old one, he noticed. He felt a grim satisfaction, knowing the angel was probably still incapacitated from the bullet that had nicked his halo. Alex would have far preferred to have killed the bastard, but knocking him out for as long as possible would do for second best.

"Pump three," he told the guy behind the counter. He put down two Styrofoam cups of coffee, too.

Willow was waiting beside the motorcycle as he went back outside, her short red-gold hair spiking in the breeze. She had on faded secondhand jeans that she'd bought the day before, and a tight, pale-blue top with long sleeves that looked great on her. Behind her, the night sky was starting to lighten, the stars fading to the east. Alex smiled, his blood warming as he remembered the silky feel of her in his arms the night before. It had taken a serious effort to get going that morning; all he'd wanted to do was stay in the tent with Willow for a while — like, the rest of his life.

As he walked up, she stood gazing off into the distance, frowning as if she was thinking about something. She seemed to shake it away when she saw him. "Thanks," she said, taking one of the coffees. "And here, you take this. I hate even holding it." With a quick look around the empty forecourt, she covertly handed him the pistol.

Alex never felt good about giving Willow the gun. Handing a loaded weapon to someone who'd never shot one before and was nervous of them anyway wasn't really the best plan in the world. But it was a million times better than her *not* having a weapon if any trouble happened. He tucked the gun away in his holster, keeping his back to the camera that he knew would be perched on the gas station's roof.

"I need to teach you how to use this," he said, thinking aloud.

He saw her start to protest. Then she looked away and took a sip of coffee, her green eyes troubled. "Yeah, OK," she said finally.

Alex's eyebrows flew up. "Really? I thought you'd hate the idea."

"I do," said Willow. "But I can't not do something just because I don't like it. I don't have that luxury anymore." She gave a small shrug. "I mean, all I have to do is look in the mirror to see how much things have changed. And I can't depend on you to protect me all the time."

"You protect me, too," Alex pointed out. The memory of Willow's angel flying above him, shielding him while putting herself in mortal danger, flashed into his mind. It had been the moment that he'd first realized he was in love with her, though he'd been too much of an idiot to admit it to himself. He gulped down his coffee and tossed the empty cup into a trash can.

"OK," he said. "You ready to become an illegal alien?"

Willow shook her head with a smile and threw away her own empty cup. "This is the ultimate bad-boy date, isn't it? Breaking into a different country."

"Hey, it makes a change from hot-wiring cars together."

"Been there, done that. . . . Alex, seriously, are you sure no one's going to shoot us?"

"Don't worry—if anyone's around, we won't cross," he said. Border guards weren't exactly his number-one concern just then, but he still had no intention of taking any risks.

They sped down the highway again; the southern New Mexico desert stretched out around them, silvery in the predawn. A ghostly-looking coyote loped alongside the motorcycle for a few seconds, as if they were running a race, then veered off on errands of its own. To Alex's relief, he found the dirt road easily, leading off from the highway a few miles farther on. He took it, leaning into the turn and feeling Willow's hands tighten on his waist as she shifted her weight behind him.

The border wall came into view. In some places this was a concrete barricade with razor coils glinting at its top; here it was just a tired-looking barbed-wire fence separating the two countries as if they were neighboring ranchers. The fence went across a dried-out riverbed; where it came up one of the banks, it gave up for a few feet, collapsing onto the ground with its posts sagging.

There was no one around; it was still almost dark. Alex trundled the bike to a stop, and Willow helped him maneuver it over the slant in the riverbed, into Mexico. "I thought the wall would be more . . . wall-like," she said.

"It is, in some places," said Alex. "But in others, it's just like this. And look." He nodded at a rusty metal sign. It said, You must enter the U.S. by a designated entry point. This is not a designated entry point. If you enter by this route, you are committing a felony.

Willow stared. "But—it probably cost more to make the sign than it would have to repair the fence. It's almost like they *want* people to sneak in."

"They do," said Alex. Pebbles skittered down as they

got the bike up over the edge of the bank. "Or at least the angels who live around here do. Illegal immigrants mean fresh energy supplies, without them having to go looking." He remembered when Juan had first showed them this route—and how he and his big brother, Jake, had encountered a border guard here once, smiling with angel burn and talking about how important it was to do the angels' work.

Kara had been with them that time, too—an exotically beautiful AK with nerves of steel; both he and Jake had had crushes on her back then. "Idiot," she'd said as they'd driven away, shifting gears with a tight, angry motion. Sitting in the back of the Jeep, Alex had taken in her profile. And despite the easy banter the AKs usually shared, in that instant he could think of nothing at all to say to Kara—but had instinctively understood the mix of fury and sorrow that made her mad at the guard, as if getting angel burn were his own fault.

Now Willow looked slightly queasy at the thought of the predatory border angels. "Oh," she said. He saw her throat move. "That's—that's really . . ."

"I know," said Alex, understanding exactly how she felt. Unfortunately, there were plenty of angels in Mexico, too, and had been even before the Invasion. There was hardly anyplace on earth now that he thought he could take Willow where she'd be really safe.

But he'd do his best—or die trying.

Nearby, he could just see the rough dirt track he remembered, heading off to the east. "OK, that connects up with the highway eventually," he said, climbing back onto the bike. "Or at least it used to." He hoped it hadn't been washed out; struggling the Shadow over miles of trackless desert would definitely not be his idea of fun.

Willow started to put on her helmet but hesitated, playing with its straps. "Alex, are there any really big cities in Mexico? I mean — *really* big?"

He looked at her in surprise, taking in the worried lines that had appeared on her forehead. "Yeah, Mexico City. It's one of the largest cities in the world. Why?"

She didn't reply immediately. "I'll tell you later," she said at last. "But maybe we could find a place to stop soon, where we can talk."

Apprehension tickled his spine. Whatever this was about, he didn't much like the sound of it already — but hanging around a few feet from the border wasn't the place for a long discussion. "Yeah, OK," he said reluctantly, and pulled on his own helmet.

The dirt road seemed to last forever, but as the sun came up, they finally turned south onto Highway 45. This part of Mexico looked almost identical to the New Mexico landscape they'd just left behind: hard, dry ground scattered with juniper bushes and cactuses, with rugged-looking mountains rising in the distance. Alex grimaced as they passed a billboard: the familiar image of an angel with wings and arms outspread. LA IGLESIA DE LOS ÁNGELES, it read.

Dusty pickup trucks passed by, driven by men with dark hair and white straw cowboy hats. Though no one gave Willow a second glance in her helmet, Alex knew he wouldn't be able to relax until they were holed up in the Sierra Madre, as far away from the Church of Angels as possible. It was a lot more remote up there in what they called the *monte*: the wild.

And then he could start trying to recruit people and training them.

The dread Willow had sensed the night before touched him again with its clammy fingers. *Get a grip*, he thought, irritated with himself. *You have to do it; you're the only one left.* If he didn't get some other AKs trained — didn't somehow get a camp set up and then, he hoped, other camps, too, until they had a network of them, up and down the continent — then humanity could just kiss itself good-bye in a few years.

Even so, Alex's hands tightened on the Shadow's handlebars as the wind rushed past. It wasn't that he didn't want to fight the angels — God, apart from being with Willow, it was the only thing he *did* want. He'd willingly give his life; he'd do it a dozen times over if it meant defeating the angels in this world. He just didn't want to be responsible for the lives of a whole team, too. His brother's death shuddered through his mind. Yeah, he'd already shown how great he was at covering someone's back, hadn't he? And if one of his decisions killed someone —

Alex pushed the thought away, hoping that Willow wasn't picking up on any of this crap. There wasn't anyone else who could be in charge, so he'd deal with it. End of story.

The sun beat down on them as it rose higher, chasing the clouds away until the sky was an almost painful blue. He drove until about ten o'clock that morning, wanting to get a few hours between them and the border before stopping. Finally, near the outskirts of Chihuahua, he saw a roadside taco stand and pulled over. He killed the engine and did a quick scan. Good — no angels nearby.

"What do you think? Is it all right to stop here?" he said to Willow as they got off the bike.

Her short hair was ruffled as she took off her helmet; she smoothed it absently, gazing around her. "I think so," she said. "There's *something* here, but . . ." She trailed off with a frown.

Alex kept quiet, letting her concentrate. While she did, he leaned against the bike, smiling slightly as he took in her slim figure, her face with its delicately pointed chin and wide eyes. God, she was so beautiful. He still wasn't sure how he'd gotten lucky enough to be with Willow, but he was thankful for it every day of his life. The years he'd spent alone before he met her seemed like a black-and-white film to him now, a time devoid of color.

"I think we're OK," Willow said finally, sounding more certain. The day had grown warmer, and she pulled off her long-sleeved shirt; under it she wore a green camisole top. She put the shirt away in the Shadow's storage compartment. "Anyway, *señor*, we're supposed to be saving money on food, remember? What are we doing at a taco stand?"

"It's OK; these places are really cheap," he said as they

started toward the stand. Back when he'd had even less money than he did now—it had never occurred to Alex's father that perhaps his sons should receive a salary like the other AKs—he and Jake had used to live off these roadside stands every time they came here.

TACOS, QUESADILLAS, MULITAS, TORTAS, said the weathered sign. Willow gave it a quizzical glance. "Hmm, Toto, I don't think we're in Kansas anymore. You choose for me, OK?"

He got them each a Coke and a few tacos with *carnitas*: chopped roast pork. "And don't worry—I told her you want extra chilies on yours," he said to Willow, keeping a straight face. They were actually for him; he loved spicy food.

She gave him a look. "Dude, if there are *any* chilies on mine, you're going to be wearing them."

Alex paid with dollars—most places down here accepted U.S. bills, though he knew he'd need to change their dwindling funds into pesos at some point. A worn picnic table stood to one side; they carried their food over. For a few minutes, they ate the Mexican tacos, with their soft cornmeal wraps, in companionable silence, a light breeze stirring the dusty ground.

Finally Willow sighed and put down her last taco. "So, I guess we need to talk."

The remains of their food went uneaten as she related her dream. Alex listened intently, his skin prickling as she described the twelve bright angels and the sound that was like a million of the creatures screaming.

"It was all so vivid—and there was such an incredible sense of urgency," Willow finished. Her face was tight with worry. "Only I don't even know for sure where this place is."

"Mexico City," he said absently, still thinking of the images from her dream. He'd been there twice, on hunting trips with Juan and a few of the others.

"Definitely? You're positive?"

Alex shrugged. "No other place is that big. And that square you described has got to be the Zócalo—it's one of the largest city squares in the world." He rubbed his forehead, where a dull ache was beginning to pound.

Willow started to say something but stopped, touching his arm. "Are you OK? You look really pale."

"Yeah, I'm fine." He dropped his hand. "Listen, if what you're leading up to is that you think we need to go there—"

"We *do* need to go there," she broke in anxiously. "The Sierra Madre isn't where we're supposed to be; Mexico City is—I'm sure of it. Only I don't know what's going to happen once we're there. The dream didn't feel very . . . cheerful, exactly."

Great. He let out a breath. "Willow . . ."

"Alex, listen to me. It wasn't just a dream; it was a premonition. We have to go."

His voice hardened. "You do know that Mexico City is literally about the last place on the planet I'd ever want to take you, right? The Church of Angels is huge there—and the city was full of angels even *before* the Invasion.

Any angel that saw your aura would know exactly who you are. We're in enough danger just sitting here, but at least we can do a scan first. In a city that size? No way."

"I know." Willow was still touching his arm; her fingers felt warm against his skin. "But how often do angels scan auras when they're in their human bodies? Don't they usually wait until they're in their angel form, about to feed?"

"The ones I've tracked usually do," he admitted.

"And you've tracked hundreds," she pointed out. "So it must be pretty typical. If an angel saw my aura when it was about to feed on someone, then we'd probably see it, too. We'd have a good chance of getting it."

When it came to Willow's safety, *probably* and *good chance* were not his favorite words. Looking down, Alex took her hand, playing with her fingers. "How strongly do you feel we need to go there?" he asked at last.

"Really strongly," she said without hesitating. "The sound of all those angels screaming . . ." She trailed off. Slowly, she said, "Alex, it feels like something's going to happen in Mexico City that could cause the angels serious harm. Only we have to be there for it to take place. We have to be."

Alex fell silent. Willow's premonitions had never steered them wrong so far, and if what she'd dreamed was even partly accurate, then she was right—they had to go. And even apart from her dream, he knew it would be a lot easier to recruit people in a city rather than up in the *monte*. If he were on his own, then Mexico City would have been exactly the place he'd be heading. Plus there were the rogues, angels who believed that their kind didn't have the right to destroy humanity. Nate had explained that they did something called marshaling—implanting a tiny bit of resistance in a human's aura to make it unpalatable to angels. There were bound to be some rogues in Mexico City; if he could somehow hook up with them, it might be just what was needed to swing the balance in an almost-hopeless fight.

Alex massaged his forehead as the headache jabbed at him again. Yeah, going to Mexico City was all really logical . . . except that he'd already nearly lost her once.

Willow sat taking in the movement of his fingers on his brow. She didn't comment this time, though he saw the concern in her eyes. "Alex, we have to go," she said instead. "We really do."

"All right," he said finally. He managed a smile. "I mean, if you've got a psychic girlfriend, then I guess you'd better listen to her, right?"

She reached across and gripped his hand; he knew she was only all too aware of how much he dreaded anything happening to her. "OK," she said softly. She started to pick up her taco again and then stopped, narrowing her gaze. "Wait a minute. So, does that mean you wouldn't listen to me if I *weren't* psychic?"

She looked so cute that he almost grinned despite his apprehension. He raised an eyebrow at her. "Is that a trick question? Of course I wouldn't—you're a girl."

Willow's mouth pursed as her green eyes flashed with sudden merriment. She started laughing. "Oh, you are in so much trouble for that."

"I am?"

"Definitely." She propped herself up on her elbows and kissed him, stretching across the picnic table. Alex cupped his hand around the smooth skin at the back of her neck, holding her in place for a moment and savoring the feel of her lips on his.

"Is that really your idea of being in trouble?" he said when they drew apart. "Because I don't think you've grasped the whole punishment/deterrent thing. See, you're supposed to make me not want to do it again."

Willow was laughing, wiping her mouth with the back of her hand. "I'm the one who doesn't want to do it again. Your lips are all spicy from those chilies —" Suddenly her face slackened in alarm. "Alex, the bike!" she cried.

He leaped up from the bench without asking for details. A pickup truck had pulled in front of the taco stand while they'd been talking, blocking the motorcycle from view. As Alex hurtled around the side of it, he saw a stocky guy with black hair crouched beside the Shadow, untying the tent. On the ground beside him sat a bulging knapsack and both sleeping bags.

"What the hell are you doing?" shouted Alex in Spanish. "Get away from my bike!"

Leaving the camping stuff, the guy grabbed the knapsack and ran, his heels kicking up dust. The jimmied-open storage compartment gaped emptily. Alex swore and took off after him, pounding across the dry soil. The guy was as fast as he was, though; he wove around Dumpsters and abandoned cars like a rabbit and finally veered off to the right, scrambling over a high concrete wall. Alex started to follow but stopped, acutely aware that he'd left Willow by herself, when anyone from the Church might stop by the stand and see her. Still cursing the thief, he turned and jogged back to the bike. Jesus, how was that for luck? They'd lost their stuff twice in one week now.

Willow was waiting beside the Shadow, looking anxious; the taco stand woman stood beside her, chattering in worried Spanish that Alex knew Willow didn't understand. "He stole your things!" the woman cried as Alex approached. "I'm so sorry—I didn't see him until you shouted. Is there anything I can do?"

"No, but thank you, *señora*," replied Alex. If they'd been in America, he knew she'd have probably already called the police. Thankfully, running to law enforcement didn't usually occur to people here—which was good, since the Mexican police were as much in the angels' pockets as the police back home were.

Willow's face was tight with distress as the woman returned to her stand. "God, I'm sorry—I *knew* there was something! I was focusing so strongly on the Church of Angels, but I could tell it wasn't that, and I guess I sort of disregarded it—"

"Hey, come on, it's not *your* fault," he said, squeezing her shoulder. He squatted beside the bike, shaking his head as he examined the forced-open lock. The thief must have worked fast; he obviously knew what he was doing.

"Well, at least he didn't get much," he said as he stood up. "And I've still got my wallet. We can always buy more clothes; the marketplaces in Mexico City are really cheap."

Willow nodded as she hugged her elbows. "Yeah," she said finally. And then it hit him. Her photo. The one of her as a child, standing beneath a willow tree and tipping up her head in delight at its trailing leaves. It had been taken by her mother; it was all Willow had left of her now. And it had been in the storage compartment, in the pocket of her other pair of jeans.

He swore, his fists clenching as he glanced back toward the wall the guy had disappeared over. The thought of the slimy creep stealing Willow's photo — tearing it apart to see if there was money in the frame, then throwing it away in the garbage somewhere . . .

"Alex, it's OK," said Willow, touching his arm. "It's — it's only a photo. You couldn't catch him now, anyway. And besides, we shouldn't draw attention to ourselves — just let it go."

He let out a breath, hating himself. "I almost had him. . . ."

"It's OK," Willow repeated. "It really is." She stepped forward and hugged his waist. As he held her close, Alex knew he was never going to forgive himself for this, even if Willow already had.

"I love you — you know that?" she said.

He tried to smile. "Why, because I let that jerk steal your photo?"

Willow looked up; her eyes were like a forest washed with rain. He could see the happiness in them as she regarded him. "No, actually it's because you're everything I ever wanted."

"I love you, too," he said softly, kissing her. Then he sighed. "Anyway, you're right—I won't catch him now. We better get going."

He reattached the camping gear. Just as they started to climb back onto the bike, the woman hurried out from behind her stand again with a paper-wrapped package. The rich aroma of roast pork rose up from it.

"Please, take these for later," she said in Spanish. "It's the least I can do."

"*Gracias, señora.*" Alex put the food in the damaged storage compartment, grateful to have it. They could save some money on dinner now.

"*Gracias,*" echoed Willow fervently. "*Muchas, muchas gracias.*"

A few minutes later, they were speeding down the highway once more, leaving Chihuahua in a haze of heat behind them. The houses they passed were small and dusty, in various pastel shades with black water tanks perched on top of each one. Alex gazed beyond the homes to the rugged shape of the Sierra Madre, looming off to the southwest. And with all his heart, he wished that Willow had never had her dream. He'd have had a decent shot at keeping her safe up there in that wilderness. Mexico City was going to be anybody's guess.

But they'd made their choice now. As they roared down the desert highway, he reached for Willow's hand at his waist and twined his fingers through hers.

CHAPTER FOUR

"WILL I FIND TRUE LOVE?" asked the woman. She was in her mid-twenties, pretty, with a serious, earnest face.

They were sitting in a corner of the Chihuahua marketplace. Seb considered how to answer as he pretended to inspect her palm — though the information he was getting had nothing to do with the woman's life line and everything to do with her aura, the feel of her energy, sudden flashes of knowledge.

"There's a man in your life — his name's Carlos," he said. He wasn't usually good on names, but he was sure this one was right; he was sensing it so strongly. "You've been hoping he'll propose to you. *Señorita*, I don't see this happening."

Her expression fell. "But . . . he told me just last night to give him a little more time."

Seb was getting it clearly now. Not only did Carlos have two other girlfriends—he was also married already. The woman had no idea; she'd believed everything the *cabrón* had told her. It was hardly uncommon—a lot of men didn't seem to know the meaning of the word *faith-ful*, unless they were talking about what their wives and girlfriends better be to them—but Seb had given too many readings over the years to stomach that attitude. He knew only too well by now what it did to women, how it made them feel.

"Carlos's life is complicated," he said, managing to hide his irritation at the man. "I'm sorry, *señorita*, but he isn't in a position to propose to you. I'm afraid he never will be."

He wasn't usually this blunt, but he could tell that on some level the woman already knew it was hopeless; it was why she'd stopped to get a reading from him. Now she winced and ducked her head. "I've been praying so hard to the angels that things will work out," she said in a whisper. "I thought— I thought so many more of them arriving might be a sign they'd heard me."

"The angels are very kind," said Seb diplomatically. He could see that the woman's energy field was undamaged; she was just one of the ones who loved the angels any-way. There were plenty of them, and now that the angels' numbers had increased by so many, he supposed there'd soon be plenty more. "But I can hear them now," he went on, "and they're saying to me that you shouldn't wait for Carlos."

The woman's eyes widened. OK, he was making this part up—but he had to give her *something*, or else she wouldn't make the break. "They want you to get on with your life," he said firmly. "To be happy. You haven't been happy in a long time, *señorita*."

By the time the woman left, her expression was thoughtful; Seb could sense the hope that had taken root in her. He leaned back against a palm tree, savoring the mental silence. A few hours of readings had left him drained. He wasn't really sure why he put so much into them for only fifty pesos. When he'd made the decision to quit thieving, readings had simply been a way to keep from starving—and back then, he hadn't worked at it; he'd just cobbled together quick fortunes from whatever he saw. Somehow, as the years had passed, he'd started caring a lot more.

Thinking of the angels' arrival, Seb sighed. When he'd glimpsed some of the TV footage in a café two days before, he'd wondered for a heart-pounding moment if the presence of so many more angels might lead him to his half-angel girl after all. But he couldn't see how it might—and so for him, the world hadn't changed, despite how much happiness the angels' arrival might have brought everyone else. The realization had depressed him; he'd avoided looking at the footage after that.

Seb scraped his hand roughly across his stubble—enough of this. As he got to his feet, a female voice called his name. Turning, he saw two girls a year or two older than he was heading toward him, both with bright

American smiles and bouncing ponytails. "Hey, remember us?" said the redhead in English as they reached him.

"How could I forget?" Seb swung his knapsack over his shoulder. Lucy and someone else. Amanda, that was it. They were part of a group of American students staying at the same hostel that he was; Seb had sat up with a few of them the night before, drinking and talking. The girls' Spanish wasn't nearly as fluent as they thought, so that he'd found it easier to speak to them in English, which he'd picked up from giving readings to American tourists over the years. He spoke a little French, too — was good at languages almost without trying. He knew being psychic helped.

"So, are you finished with 'work'?" asked Lucy, the redhead, giving him a flirtatious smile as she made quote marks in the air. They'd thought it was hilarious that he gave psychic readings. He wouldn't have bothered telling them, except that one of their group had seen him here in the marketplace the day before. "Because if you are," she went on, "maybe you could show us the sights."

He hesitated. Both girls were pretty and fun to be with, but all he really felt like doing was going back to the hostel and reading his book — maybe sitting outside with a cigarette. But Lucy was already laughing, pulling at his arm. "We're not taking no for an answer. Besides, you promised last night."

"I don't remember this," he said, smiling despite himself.

"Well, you *practically* did. Come on, give us the grand

tour of *el mercado* — we want to see a typical Mexican marketplace."

He gave in. Why not? It wasn't as if he had anything else to do with his time, now that he was no longer searching. The thought brought a wince of pain; he pushed it away.

"All right," he said. He raked his hair back; he could feel the curls hanging over his forehead, annoying him. "The first thing, I think, is that we go find something to eat."

"Ooh, good idea," said Amanda. She had dark hair and eyebrows that were too perfect for nature. "Lead the way."

The bright chaos of the marketplace enveloped them: vendors shouting their bargains, the smell of spicy, cooking food, crowds of shoppers. Seb had been in Chihuahua for almost two weeks now. After his decision at the orphanage, he'd hitched a ride with the first truck he'd seen to wherever it was going, but had somehow felt compelled to get off here — so strongly that he'd almost shouted at the truck driver to stop. It didn't make much sense to him now; the town was as dusty and shabby as he remembered. Still, he supposed it was as good a place as any to figure out what to do with the rest of his life.

The problem was, he had no idea — all he knew was that ever since he'd arrived in Chihuahua, he'd had a feeling there was something he was supposed to be doing. It was a constant irritation, like a bee buzzing at his head.

They got tacos and wandered around the stalls. Lucy

kept close to him as they walked, frequently touching his arm as she and Amanda chattered about the Copper Canyon train trip that their group was taking the next morning, to see the plunging canyons of the Sierra Madre. They were excited about experiencing the "real Mexico," which amused Seb. The Copper Canyon tour — so safe and so geared for American tourists — was not remotely like the real Mexico he knew

"You'll have a good time" was all he said. "Make sure you don't fall out the window — it's a long way down."

"Hey, maybe you could come with us!" Lucy gave a little skip to get ahead of him, walking backward. She was wearing tight jeans and a halter top that showed off her creamy skin. "Why don't you? I'm sure we can get you a ticket. We'd have a great time!"

Amanda rolled her eyes. "Um, hello — we had to book those tickets months ago, remember? There's no way we can get him one."

"It's OK; I've seen it," said Seb. He crumpled up the wax paper that his taco had come in and pitched it into a garbage can. He was dryly aware that even as he was talking to the girls, part of him was scanning every aura he passed. Yes, he'd certainly given up searching — didn't even think about it anymore.

Lucy gave a little pout. "Oh. Well, will you still be here in a few days? Doing your *psychic readings?*" She bantered the words, making it clear that she didn't believe in that stuff for a second.

"Maybe — I haven't decided yet." Or decided what to

do with the gaping years ahead of him, either. Not wanting to think about it, he said, "Who knows? Maybe I'll give it all up and become a violinist."

"A violinist?" Amanda nudged him. "No way, you look like you're strictly an electric-guitar man. I keep expecting you to whip out your ax and start doing 'Stairway to Heaven.'"

Seb held back a smile. He could never resist an opening like this. "No, my father's a classical violinist," he said seriously. "I guess it's just in the blood, you know?"

She blinked. "Really?"

"Yes, I was raised on that stuff. My mother's an opera singer. She plays, too. Piano. She says it helps her relax, so she likes to take it on tour with her—it's so difficult getting it on flights. Because it always has to be *her* piano; no other one will do."

Amanda's brown eyes had gone wide. "Wow—are you serious?"

"No, he's not serious," Lucy said, laughing. "Get your brain in gear, Amanda."

The dark-haired girl gave an embarrassed groan. "OK, you got me, Seb. So what do your parents do really?"

"Really? They run a circus training school."

Lucy snickered. "You're not going to get anything out of him. Don't you remember from last night? Seb's the original man of mystery." She squeezed his arm, giving him an arch smile. "I bet your parents are really Mr. and Mrs. Ordinary of Boring, Mexico."

He laughed out loud at that — if only she knew. "Yes, I think maybe you're right," he said.

Leaning close, Lucy traced the long, thin scar on his forearm, from a knife fight when he was younger. He caught a whiff of her shampoo; it smelled like oranges. "Let me guess — a sword fight with pirates, right?"

"Just a cat scratch. It was a big cat, though." Even without the sultry pink lights shifting through her aura, Seb was very aware that Lucy was coming onto him. As she touched his arm, he knew without trying that she was wondering what it would be like to kiss him, planning how she could get him on his own at the hostel later.

From habit, he started to pull gently away — and then stopped. For the last year or so, the sense of his half-angel girl had grown so strong that Seb had stopped having even flings with human girls; it had felt like he was betraying her. But she wasn't real; she never had been — he had to get that through his head. Since giving up his search, he'd been even lonelier than usual, achingly aware that he was the only one of his kind. This girl didn't want a *relationship* with him, so why not? She obviously liked him — and it had been so, so long.

As if in response, he caught the sense of his half-angel girl again, like a whiff of perfume floating past. Seb's jaw tightened. Why wouldn't she just leave him in peace, instead of taunting him with what he could never have?

He didn't pull away. After a moment he felt Lucy's hand slide down his arm and find his. "Maybe you can give me a psychic reading later," she said softly, under cover of the sound of a mariachi band that had just started up.

Seb took in the clear invitation in her eyes. No human girl could ever give him the true companionship he craved; he knew that. This, right here, was the most he could ever have — and he'd take it, because he wasn't saint enough to spend the rest of his life alone, never even feeling the warmth of someone's touch.

Fighting the wistfulness he felt, he pushed the beautiful phantom out of his mind and let his fingers close around Lucy's. "Are you sure?" he said. "I'll find out all your secrets."

"Promise?" She smiled and flipped her ponytail back. She said something else, but he didn't hear what it was; in a sudden flash, a blinding white figure had come into view overhead. There was an angel cruising over the crowded stalls. Its wings burned in the late-afternoon sunlight as it glided, gazing down at the shoppers.

Reflexively, Seb shifted his aura to the drabbest colors he could think of, making it look stunted, unappetizing. He'd fought an angel only once before; he had no desire to ever do it again. "Come on, let's go this way," he said, pulling at Lucy's hand. Amanda was lagging behind, looking at jewelry; he took her arm, too. "Come, there's a stall over here I want to show you."

"Hey!" Amanda protested as he dragged her off. "I was going to buy that."

"No, don't bother," he said. "This stand's better — I promise."

Glancing over his shoulder, he saw the angel select its victim and land, so dazzling with radiance that the marketplace seemed to fade away. The man stared at the being in wonder as it reached toward him. Smiling gently, it rested its gleaming hands in his aura and began to feed.

Seb led the girls to another jewelry stand. While they stood laughing, trying on rings, he found his gaze drawn back to the angel as it finally flew away in a piercing shudder of light. Though he no longer wanted to be pure angel himself, he couldn't completely hold back his old longing for their strength and power, which had seemed so desperately appealing to him at thirteen. When it came to the creatures' feeding, he had never quite decided what he felt about it. The angels hurt people, and he wished they didn't — but they also made them genuinely happy. From the readings he'd given to people with angel burn, he knew this happiness was real, even if their health was damaged. When humans hurt other humans, there was no happiness at all — just pain and misery. At least the angels gave something back. Then Seb sighed as he wondered how the man was damaged now. The issue wasn't an easy one; he'd never resolved it in his mind.

The girls were trying on necklaces now, admiring themselves in a small mirror.

"I like the turquoise one," said Amanda, her dark hair beside Lucy's red.

"Really?" Lucy cocked her head to one side as she inspected herself. "I can't decide; I like the shell one, too. Wait — are there matching earrings?"

Seb drifted to the next stall. It sold a mishmash of things: clothes, cell phones, used paperbacks and CDs. He took his cigarettes from his knapsack and lit one as he started looking over the books, arranged spine-up in long, battered rows. He'd first started reading for pleasure in the measly library of the orphanage, while checking out every book they had to try to find out about others like him. There'd been nothing, of course, but he'd stumbled across a story about a boy and a horse and been hooked ever since.

Now he found a popular science title that he hadn't read and propped an elbow on a shelf to his side as he flipped to its opening page. Soon he was immersed.

"I've got some stuff to sell," said a voice. "You buy clothes and things, right?"

Seb didn't look up, distantly aware that the stall owner was going through a pile of goods with someone, the two of them haggling over prices. "Man, you've got to be kidding. This shirt alone is worth fifty pesos—"

Deciding that he'd get the book, Seb took a final puff of his cigarette and ground it out. As he glanced over, he saw that the speaker was a stocky guy a few years older than himself, holding up a girl's light-blue shirt with long sleeves. Seb frowned. The sense that he was meant to be doing something tickled over him again, more strongly than ever. A price was finally agreed; the stall owner put the shirt to one side.

For some reason, Seb couldn't stop himself—he

reached for the shirt. As his fingers touched the thin cloth, he breathed in a quick, stunned breath.

Familiar. How could it feel so familiar?

Lucy came dancing up, her eyes alight. "Look — aren't I pretty?" Squeezing his arm, she shook her head at him, showing off her new earrings. Then she glanced down at the shirt and her eyebrows rose knowingly. "Ooh, what's that? Are you buying me a present?"

"I — uh, no," Seb said faintly, hardly noticing she was there. He was still gripping the shirt; he wasn't sure he'd ever be able to let go of it. He watched as the owner examined a pair of girl's jeans. The man pulled a small framed photo out of the pocket and squinted at it.

"Pretty girl. I can sell the frame; the photo's no good to me. Do you want it back?"

The stocky guy glanced at it. "Nah. How much for the frame?"

Seb's throat went dry. Without taking his left hand off the shirt, he said, "Wait — can I see that?" and plucked the framed photo from the owner's hand.

The picture was of a little girl with long blond hair, peering up through the trailing fronds of a willow tree. For a moment Seb almost couldn't breathe as he looked at her smiling face; it felt like he'd been punched in the stomach.

Lucy stood staring at him. At the other end of the stall, Amanda had appeared, flipping through the CDs. "Hey, what's wrong?" said Lucy. "I didn't catch all of that."

"I'll take this," said Seb hoarsely to the owner. "And the shirt—how much do you want for them?"

The man gave a bemused shrug. "A hundred pesos for both? It's a nice little frame."

Seb dug the money out of his pocket and shoved it at him. He put the shirt and photo into his bag, then zipped it tightly as if to protect them. "Where'd you get these?" he asked the stocky guy. His voice was shaking. "Who's the girl, do you know?"

The man looked shifty suddenly. "No one in particular. Why are you so interested?"

"Because I *need to find the girl*," Seb said with gritted teeth, each word low and distinct. "Did you steal this stuff? Where from—just tell me!"

"Hey, I'm no thief! No, it was just on the side of the road. Like someone had lost it all."

He was lying—his aura had turned a devious mustard yellow. Seb's muscles were trembling; he knew he was this close to lunging at the guy and attacking him. He stepped closer. "Don't lie to me, man. I'm asking you one more time—where'd you get it?"

"Seb!" cried Lucy, tugging at his arm. "God, cool it. What's going on?" He shook her off, not taking his eyes from the thief. The man swallowed, a nervous expression on his face now.

"Look, I don't want any trouble," put in the stall owner. "You boys got a problem, take it somewhere else."

"Tell me," said Seb in a low voice, ignoring him. And he knew that his tone was the same as from the dark time when he was thirteen. He'd enjoyed fighting then; he didn't now, but he'd have no hesitation about doing it.

He could sense the guy realizing this, coming to a decision. "You won't find them," he said finally. "It was hours ago—they're gone now, OK? They were *gringos*; they'd only stopped to get some food. And that's all I'm telling you."

It was the truth. Seb let out a breath. Amanda was standing beside Lucy now, both of them gaping at him as if he'd gone insane. Maybe he had. "Sorry," he muttered to Lucy, taking a step backward. His pulse was throbbing in his ears. "I've got to go."

"Go? You mean back to the hostel?"

"No—no, I've got to go." And before she could answer, he turned and took off at a run through the marketplace, leaving her startled face behind him in a blur. He had to get someplace private, had to look at this stuff again. He must be going crazy; this couldn't possibly be true—

The hostel would be full of people. Veering east, he pounded down the streets and into the Plaza de Armas with its small, pattering fountain; its mix of palm trees and spruce; the white stone cathedral that looked almost pink in the sunset. There was a bandstand across from it—an elegant wrought-iron structure from a different age. Seb saw that it was empty and took its four steps at a single leap. Breathing hard, he pulled the photo from his knapsack and then hesitated, clutching it tightly, the image hidden as the small frame dug into his palm. It couldn't be true. He had just wished for it so often that he'd finally gone insane. He was going to open his hand and it would just be a human girl. That was all—just a human girl.

Swallowing, Seb finally dared to unclench his hand and look down. He stared. Without realizing it, he sank to the worn wooden floor, still holding the photo.

From the time of his earliest memories, he'd been able to see auras—the angry, crackling red of his mother's boyfriend's energy as he beat Seb; the soggy blue of his mother's as she'd put him in the orphanage, crying that it was Seb's fault for not getting along with the man. His own aura, whenever he brought it into view, was the only one he'd ever encountered that was mostly silver, with forest-green lights shifting through it. The difference had bothered Seb deeply—he'd been convinced that his aura's strangeness had been the reason for the beatings. That had been the start of his lifelong habit of shifting his aura's colors, of learning how to blend in. He hadn't known then that it was pointless around humans—that nobody except him could see the bright shapes of energy anyway.

But he didn't just see auras when he met people face to face; he could see them in photos, too. And now—Seb gazed down at the framed photo in his hand, and it was as if the whole world had stopped breathing. It was true. He hadn't been mistaken. The little girl peering up through the willow branches had an aura like his own: silver with lavender lights.

Another half angel.

It was her.

Seb's heart thundered in his chest. Jesus God, he had to find her. Where was she, though? Who was she? "They," the guy had said, so she was traveling with someone. He'd seemed certain that they wouldn't still be in Chihuahua, but—

Seb closed his eyes and sent his other self soaring, even though he usually kept his angel self hidden in cities—the violent encounter with the angel years ago had taught him that. Right now he didn't care. Lifting up through the bandstand's roof, he spread his shining wings and glided over the city, scanning its roads, its parks, the highway that stretched through town.

There was nothing, of course. Nothing.

His angel rushed back to him. Seb opened his eyes and stared unseeingly at one of the ornate iron posts. The possibility that he might have finally come so close to finding his half-angel girl, only to have *missed* her, made him sick with dread.

His gaze fell on the knapsack near his feet. Suddenly he remembered the girl's shirt—the feeling of familiarity that had swept over him in the marketplace. He pulled it out; the material felt soft against his fingers. With a steadying breath, Seb closed his eyes again.

It washed over him all at once. The sense of an energy so similar to his own was dizzying, and Seb's hands turned to fists that grasped the thin material like a lifeline. His phantom half-angel girl, whom he'd spent so many years of his life trying to find — she was real; she had worn this shirt. He could feel her so strongly, her spirit whispering through the fabric. Everything about her that he'd been in love with for so long — her kindness, her strength, her humor — it was all here, and more. Seb's pulse was battering at his veins.

When he could finally focus again, he realized that she was about his own age, and that she'd been worried about a dream. Pictures started appearing in Seb's mind; he frowned in surprise at the familiar streets. El DF. She had dreamed of Mexico City, and of angels, and a sense of urgency that pulled at her like the tide. They had to go there, she and her human boyfriend — they had no choice. The details from the dream swirled over him; he could feel the girl's fear, her anxiousness.

The final image jolted him with shock. A boy in her dream stood watching her in a park. He held out his hand, called her *querida*. Seb could feel how much the girl wanted to go to him — the longing that came over her as their eyes met.

And the boy was him.

As the dream faded Seb lowered the shirt, his mind reeling. She had dreamed of him — she'd longed for him just as he'd always longed for her. For a minute he couldn't help it, and still clutching the shirt, he slumped against the side of the bandstand, burying his head in his arms as he struggled against tears. Oh, God, it was true — it was really true. She was real; he wasn't alone.

The cathedral bells began to ring through the evening,

tolling six o'clock. As the last note died from the air, Seb rose shakily to his feet. If the two of them were following the girl's dream, then they were on their way to Mexico City. It didn't matter how much he hated El DF; he had to get down there now, this second, so that he could find this girl, if he had to search every square inch of the place to do it.

Folding the shirt, Seb tucked it into his bag, his fingers leaving it reluctantly. The photo he studied for a moment, drinking in the girl's delicately pointed features, her smile and green eyes. He shook his head in wonder as he touched the upturned face. So this was what she looked like; he'd yearned to know for most of his life. So beautiful, even as a child. Was she with her human boyfriend for the same reason he'd been tempted by Lucy — just because the loneliness had become too much, and there was no one else? Maybe this girl had always felt alone, too, the same as he had.

Seb tucked the photo in the pocket of his jeans, wanting to keep it close. There were more than twenty million people in Mexico City, but he'd find her somehow. They had to meet, had to be together. The certainty of it was like a heartbeat drumming through him. No other option was possible — it was meant to be.

She had dreamed of him.

CHAPTER FIVE

THE FIRST THING I NOTICED about Mexico City was the traffic. It was endless, chaotic: cars, taxis, other motorcycles. Horns blaring, red lights being run, hardly any attention paid to the painted street lines, except to see how blatantly they could be ignored. When the traffic stopped for even a second, shouting sellers appeared in the street, striding past with cigarettes and candy. I kept my hands on Alex's waist as he wove us deftly in and out of it all, swerving and putting on the brakes as people tried to blindside us.

The second thing that hit me was the smell — a dizzying cocktail of exhaust fumes, spices from food vendors, and dust from construction projects. And then the noise: jackhammers, rock music, brakes squealing. I couldn't stop staring, taking everything in. As Alex and I made our way toward the center of the city, I saw businesses everywhere—

crumbling walls covered with painted advertising, corrugated metal doors that were swung open to reveal dingy restaurants and car-parts stores. Medieval buildings jostled for space beside modern glass structures and Art Deco ones from the thirties; others were abandoned, ridden with graffiti. I blinked as I noticed something else: a lot of the buildings seemed slightly tilted, as if you were viewing them after a drunken night out. The whole place looked like the aftermath of a giant party.

Then there were the angels, of course.

I spotted the first one soon after we entered the city, gliding over a neighborhood a few streets away. As we got farther in, I kept seeing others circling here and there, at times plummeting downward in flashes of light. I even saw one feeding on a littered sidewalk as we passed by, not ten feet away. My scalp went cold; I couldn't take my eyes off it. The old man being fed from stood smiling dazedly as his aura collapsed; the angel towered over him, its halo burning brighter and brighter. It was surreal, the way people on the sidewalk were just shoving past the man — how no one could see what was so painfully obvious to me.

The light turned red, and we came to a stop. Alex glanced over his shoulder, pushing his visor up. "We should start thinking about where we're going. Any ideas?"

I swallowed. Not even Alex could see what I saw, unless he shifted his consciousness up through his chakra points. Feeling very alone suddenly, I looked away from the feeding angel, thankful that the thing was too distracted to notice me. "No, no ideas," I said.

Then as the traffic started up again, I thought of something. I raised my voice over the noise. "Wait — can we go to that square, the one I dreamed about?"

"Yeah, I guess," Alex called back after a pause. I knew he was thinking about the hunting angels I'd seen in my dream and wasn't crazy about the idea — but he didn't argue.

It was nearing sunset, the sky spectacular with the pollution: wild streaks of red and pink that swirled across the gray dusk like oil on water. I'd have known the city was seething with angels even if I couldn't see them — on practically every street corner, silver-and-blue Church of Angels signs were painted on the sides of buildings like giant billboards. And lots of people were visibly sick. As Alex stopped for another light, I watched a young woman pause on the sidewalk, gripping a streetlight for support. It could have been a coincidence, of course. She could have just had a dizzy spell or something. But I doubted it. And if it was this bad here *now*, what was it going to be like in a few more weeks, now that the Second Wave had arrived? I bit my lip, hating the thought.

Slowly, I saw a massive stone cathedral loom into view, heaving into sight over the other buildings. It had two ornate bell towers; they stood to either side of a central dome, where a golden angel perched on one foot, lifting a garland toward the sky.

I felt Alex's muscles tense; when we stopped for another light, he whipped toward me again. "I don't *believe it* — that angel's the most famous statue in Mexico

City! It's always been on top of a column on the Paseo de la Reforma, and now suddenly it's up there on the Catedral Metropolitana."

"The what?"

"The Metropolitan Cathedral," he said. His jaw was tight. "It's the oldest cathedral in the Americas — it's been here for, like, four hundred years. And I've got a really bad feeling it's a Church of Angels cathedral now. It must have happened just recently."

"Oh," I said weakly. That . . . didn't seem like a good sign.

"Anyway, it's on the Zócalo; we're almost there. And guess what?" Alex added, nodding at a brightly colored poster on a streetlamp. "That sign says there's a Love the Angels concert going on in the square tonight."

My eyes met Alex's. I knew we were both remembering the dancing crowd in my dream. A terrible sense of inevitability came over me — déjà vu times a hundred. Just like when I'd realized that I had to go to the Church of Angels in Schenectady, to try to help Beth. The comparison wasn't comforting, when the entire congregation had tried to kill me and I'd only barely escaped.

"So," said Alex finally. He faced forward again, lifting his voice as the traffic started to move. "I guess we should go check it out." I could tell he was thinking about his gun, and how many cartridges he had left.

I cleared my throat. "Yeah," I called back. "I guess we should."

A convertible filled with people wearing angel wings

passed by, honking. We turned onto the same road they did, leading to one of the streets that bordered the Zócalo. I stared as the square came into view, taken aback by how accurate my dream had been. The Zócalo was *huge*, with people streaming by the thousands into its broad expanse.

And just like I'd dreamed, a stage bathed in flood-lights had been set up at the cathedral end of the square. There were lots of food stands, and vendors who moved through the crowd selling angel wings, holding them up in feathery white clusters like giant dandelion heads.

It didn't look as if you were supposed to park beside the Zócalo, but people were doing it anyway. Alex pulled over, too, angling the Shadow alongside a car. We got off the bike. We were in front of the long, official-looking building from my dream; the cathedral rose up to our right. I stiffened as I took off my helmet — there were three angels gliding over the square.

Alex checked his pistol, concealing it between his body and the parked car. I felt him shifting through his chakra points, so that when he turned around again, his gaze found the angels as easily as I had. "OK," he said, regard-ing them grimly. "Any idea what we should do next? Was there anything else in your dream?"

The only thing in my dream I hadn't told him about was the strange boy and my reaction to him — it had just seemed too weird to mention. I shook my head, watching the angels as they hunted. I knew if Alex were here on his own, he'd be slipping into the crowd to kill all three if he could, before they started feeding.

"Don't let me hold you back," I said, looking up at him. "I'm serious."

He let out a breath; I could see the conflict in his blue-gray eyes. Still studying the square, he put his arm around me. "No, I'm not going to leave you on your own with angels around."

"Alex, it's OK. I can take care of myself."

"Your angel self can," he agreed. "But until you learn how to shoot, your human self is so vulnerable, it gives me nightmares. Willow, all it would take would be two angels ganging up on you, and they'd rip your life force away."

I opened my mouth, then closed it again. OK, I didn't exactly have an answer for that.

Alex squeezed my hand, then glanced at the roof of the parked car behind us. "Come on. Let's sit up here where we can keep an eye on things. See why your psychic powers brought us here."

He vaulted nimbly onto the car's hood and then the roof, leaning over to help me up. Plenty of people around us were doing the same, though presumably in their case the cars in question were their own. Some had even brought coolers full of beer and food, as if the concert were a giant Fourth of July picnic. The night was mild. Mexico City was high in the mountains; according to Alex, the weather here was like a perpetual springtime.

Trying to ignore the angels, I stared out at the square, with its buildings that looked so completely unlike anything in the United States. Especially the cathedral. It was actually *two* cathedrals: the massive main one with its tiered bell towers and angel-topped dome, and then another, smaller, one just beside it, with ornate stonework framing a broad wooden door.

"The tabernacle," said Alex, following my gaze. "It was built at a later date — I'm not sure why."

I nodded slowly, taking it all in: the ancient-looking stone, the cars, the vibrant crowd. There was a real buzz in the air — and not only here; I'd been noticing it ever since we got into the city. It tickled at my senses like something tangible.

"Mexico City is just amazing," I said, sitting cross-legged on the metal roof. We hadn't had a chance to buy other clothes yet, and I was wearing Alex's red plaid shirt over my camisole. "I've never seen anything like it."

Alex shrugged; I knew he wasn't much of a city person at heart. "Yeah, it's like New York on a caffeine jag. Jake loved it when we were here on hunts — he used to drag me out clubbing every night we could sneak out."

The momentary sadness crossed his face that always came whenever he mentioned his brother. I pressed against him, slipping my arm around his waist, and he managed a smile. "Anyway, the angels love it here, too — something about the energy really draws them." His eyes went again to the cathedral with its golden angel, and he shook his head. "They must have a complete stranglehold here now."

By the time a band called Los Ángeles Amigos came

on — four guys wearing angel wings and a girl singer with a slightly crooked halo — the square was packed with people, and there were over two dozen real angels gliding around overhead. It was ironic, I guess: as rock music celebrating the angels beat through the night, the angels themselves dipped and turned, taking their time as they chose which human to feed from. Occasionally one dove, disappearing into the dancing crowd. On the next car, the people on the roof had their arms around each other, singing along with the music. Alex and I watched in silence, holding hands.

Finally the band stopped; a woman in a short red dress stepped onstage and grabbed the mic. She shouted something about *los ángeles*, her voice booming out through the speakers.

"*¡Sí!*" roared the crowd.

"Let me guess," I said to Alex, leaning close so he'd hear. "'*Do you love the angels?*'"

He nodded. "Yep — got it in one."

The woman called out something else. "*Are you happy they're with us?*" Alex translated, his lips a warm tickle against my ear as the crowd screamed "*¡sí! ¡sí!*"

The woman crouched down on her high heels, shouting a third time as she flung one arm up. Noise thundered through the night; the crowd went berserk, screaming and jumping up and down.

Alex started to speak and broke off, straightening abruptly. I caught my breath as I saw it, too. One of the angels had dodged to the left, its great wings slicing through the air. The angel paused, hovering as it seemed to look around it. With a sudden flurry, it darted aside again.

And then on the far side of the square, another angel vanished in a petal pattern of radiance, like a firework going off over the crowd. Pieces of light drifted to the ground.

I stared dumbly as they twinkled in the floodlights. I could hardly get the words out. "Is — is there anything else that can cause that?"

When Alex spoke, his voice sounded rough. "No," he said. "No, there isn't. Somebody just shot an angel."

We glanced at each other. I felt the tense excitement pulsing through him; it matched my own. There was another AK out there in the crowd — someone else who knew how to fight the angels. More than one in fact, because back toward the stage, two angels were flying toward the one who had first dodged — and suddenly one of *them* lunged to the side, too, as if avoiding a bullet. At the same moment, the first angel jerked away again with a bright shimmer.

"At least three AKs," murmured Alex. The muscles in his forearms looked taut. "Christ, there's a whole team of them out there."

"*Can* there be?" I asked in a daze. "I thought you were the only one!"

"I don't know. . . . Maybe the CIA set up another group down here without telling us, or maybe someone else figured out how to fight them——" Alex broke off, tapping the car roof as he watched the scene. "Jesus, why are you letting them go on the offensive?" he muttered to the unseen AKs. "They know you're there; just *shoot* them already!"

As he spoke, one of the three angels twisted nimbly to the side, wings glinting. I went cold as it hit me: the AKs *were* shooting at the angels. They were shooting at them almost nonstop.

But they were missing.

I knew from Alex that everyone missed sometimes; an angel's halo wasn't an easy target, especially when they were in motion. You had to be accurate a lot more often than you weren't, though. If you missed too many times, then what was going on right now happened: the angels realized you were there and moved in for the kill.

Distantly, I saw another angel burst into nothingness at the opposite end of the square but couldn't take my eyes off the disaster that was unfolding here, near the stage. The three angels glided in a hunting pack, and now I could tell they'd spotted their attackers below: there was a sudden decisiveness to their moves, a deadly certainty in the way they banked as one and started plunging downward.

The AKs obviously saw it, too. There was a flurry of motion in the crowd, a small group shoving their way through the throng, panic giving them strength. "Get away. *Hurry*," I whispered, my hands clenched. The group burst out of the other side of the square, then went racing away down a busy road. They turned into what looked like an alleyway; the three angels headed after them, gliding with an ominous lack of haste.

Alex swore as he jumped off the car. "The *idiots*—why are they going for an enclosed space, where they can get backed against a wall? They're all about to be killed." He yanked on his helmet.

I'd already slid off the car behind him and was grabbing my own helmet. "Can we get through the crowd?" I asked, raising my voice over the sound of the next band that had just come on. Hundreds of pedestrians were milling around in the street, dancing to the music. Lots of them had on angel wings, feathery and surreal in the half-light.

"We've got to," said Alex shortly. We straddled the bike, and he revved it; at the sound of the engine, the people nearby gave way. He nudged the Shadow through as fast as he could, honking the horn. Finally we reached the main road and he opened up the accelerator with a roar. As we sped south, I could just see the flock of three, heading away over the buildings. Alex did, too; he took off after them, weaving in and out of traffic. They vanished from view, and he took an abrupt turn and then another, sending us hurtling around corners.

The angels were nowhere in sight.

Suddenly I could *feel* which way we should go, throbbing through me with absolute conviction. "That way!" I shouted in Alex's ear, pointing to a turning off to the right. He took it, and soon we were barreling down a long road that was mostly shabby-looking businesses. Behind a faded pink stucco house, the tips of the angels' wings flashed in and out of view.

Alex screeched to a halt. In the sudden silence, we could hear shouts. Bars covered the house's windows; a wrought-iron gate stood open, showing the drive. No lights—the place almost seemed abandoned, except for a white van in the driveway.

I felt Alex's energy lift again, scanning quickly.

"All three of them are back there," he muttered, flinging his helmet off.

I looked at the house . . . and the moment froze. My scalp prickled as the darkness of the barred windows reeled me in like a black hole. Something was going to happen here—something that would make both of us deeply unhappy.

I shook the idea away; it had to just be nerves or something. But the coldness remained, and as the frightened shouts rang through the night, they almost seemed to be coming from inside my own head, dreading whatever was to come.

Willow stood motionless, staring up at the house with wide eyes. "Come on!" said Alex. He grabbed her hand, and she seemed to return to herself with a start. They raced down the driveway as the shouts grew louder.

"Get away from me!" yelled someone. The words were in English; the voice sounded American. The faint thud of silenced gunfire came from nearby.

The drive ended. Alex pressed against the side of the house, deftly screwing on his own pistol's silencer before peering around the back.

A chaos of scrambling bodies, and three angels swooping about like giant moths to a flame. There were five AKs — two girls and three guys — all shouting and waving their guns around. The angels were toying with them, Alex saw grimly — laughing as they feinted toward their opponents and then away again, biding their time before ripping their life forces away.

They were in a concrete courtyard; there was a back door with a light on over it, casting a circle of luminance like a bizarre stage set. A muscular blond guy stood in the spotlight's center, grasping a gun with both hands and swinging it wildly.

"Come on, *cabrona!*" he screamed at a female angel. "Come and get me!" His accent was pure Texan.

Alex saw the angel decide it had had enough of playing; it went high and then dove at the guy, screeching. Alex tracked the creature as it moved, aiming for the pure, bright blue at the center of the halo. Even through his sudden concentration, he was shaking his head. Tex was flailing about so frantically, he'd be lucky not to blow one of his friends away.

"Oh, God, one's about to get that girl," gasped Willow. With a smooth shimmer, her angel form appeared overhead.

"Willow, no," he started. "Seriously, stay back —"

But her angel was already flying toward the cement wall that bordered the courtyard. Wings outspread, she swooped over a dark-haired girl with a sharp face, protecting her. The attacking angel drew back with a surprised hiss; the girl flinched and gaped upward.

"I can't just let it kill her!" said the human Willow crouched at his side. "I'll be OK," Alex gritted his teeth and tried not to worry. Willow's life force was in her human body, not her angel one — but neither of them knew what might happen if her angel self got injured.

The diving angel was still corkscrewing down, wings flashing. Alex aimed again and fired; the creature seemed to sense him, dodging aside at the last second. He shot again, anticipating the move this time, and it erupted into a million pieces of light. Tex gave a yelp as the shock wave blew him backward, off his feet.

One down, two to go. Alex glanced at the girl cowering by the wall. Above, Willow's angel darted from side to side as she held off the attacking female, which was beating its wings fiercely, trying to get past her. Willow's angel was smaller than average — only barely larger than her human form — but incredibly nimble in the air, like a kestrel.

"You!" Alex heard the female angel hiss. "Half-human thing —"

The remaining angel had been about to dive again; overhearing, it twisted in midair, looking for Willow's human form. Alex lifted his gun as it spotted her in the drive. It came at them in a rush of light; Alex shot, and the creature veered away sharply . . . and then it soared off and disappeared over the back wall.

Remembering the dozens of angels in the square, Alex's pulse quickened. Oh, Christ, the thing had gone to get them — in minutes they'd have an angel army coming down on their heads, all of them intent on killing Willow.

He broke from the shadows, pounding across the courtyard where Willow's angel still kept the female at bay. No one seemed to have realized he was there; he saw a rush of startled faces as he lunged at the wall, scaled it quickly, and dropped to the ground. He ran down an alleyway, bursting out onto another street. The angel was flying fast, heading away from him.

"Hey!" yelled Alex, his legs pummeling the pavement. "Hey!"

The creature whirled in surprise as he shot. Rage creased its glorious face, and it came at him, swooping down like a giant bird of prey. It was faster than he'd expected. Alex dove to the ground as the angel screeched overhead, its fingers reaching for his life force. He rolled and was up on one knee in seconds, wishing for his rifle; it handled ten times better in situations like this. The thought flashed past. He took aim as the angel roared toward him again in a fury of light and beauty, taking care not to look into its eyes, to keep his gaze only on the halo —

He shot.

Leaving the remnants of the angel floating gently behind him, Alex tore back up the alleyway. The whole episode had only taken a minute or two; as he dropped back into the courtyard, he saw Willow's angel still battling the larger female. Their wings blurred as they fenced and parried, and he could tell now that it was Willow's vulnerable human form the angel was trying to reach. A couple of the people stood watching with open mouths; the others dashed back and forth, trying to take aim. Tex was just struggling dazedly to his feet.

Alex jogged a few paces into the courtyard as he tracked the angel, getting her halo in his sights. "I'm on it!" he shouted to Willow. Immediately, her angel twisted away, plunging back toward her human form. The creature started to follow and then wavered, turning toward Alex as she sensed a trap.

It was all the time he needed. The muffled sound of his silenced bullet thudded around them, and the last angel vanished into a fountain of light.

Alex let out a breath as he put his pistol away. He looked toward the drive and saw Willow rising to her feet in the shadows. Their eyes met. She seemed shaken but gave him a small smile. She was OK; it was over. Alex felt himself relax a notch as he smiled back, and for a moment there was only the two of them. At a slight move ment to his left, he glanced over, his gaze leaving Willow reluctantly — and his blood froze.

Tex was aiming his gun right at her.

"No!" Alex hurtled forward, tackling him just as the pistol went off. They crashed to the ground together, the gun skittering across the pavement.

"What the hell are you doing?" he shouted. "She's on our side!"

The guy writhed under him like a fish out of water, struggling to get free. "Let me up!" he yelled. "She's not human — her aura is angelic —"

"She's on our side!" shouted Alex again. Tex's fists were flailing; Alex held him down, ducking to avoid being hit. "Jesus, will you *listen* to me —?"

Tex bucked upward, half getting away as he scrambled on all fours for his gun. Alex threw himself after him, grabbing him around the waist. The guy twisted and swung, his fist connecting hard with Alex's cheekbone. The world went red; Alex slammed him back to the ground. He drew his pistol and shoved it in the guy's face. The struggling stopped as Tex stared at it.

"Do. Not. Move," Alex gritted out.

Slowly, he rose to his feet, still holding his pistol on Tex. His cheek was throbbing; he hardly noticed. The others stood nearby, staring, not moving a muscle. "All of you — guns on the ground," he ordered without looking at them. Silence. "*Now!*" he barked.

They must have heard something in his tone that convinced them. There was a brief hesitation, then the clatter of weapons being dropped on concrete.

"Willow, are you OK?" called Alex, not taking his eyes off the muscular blond guy. He held an arm out in her direction and felt infinite relief as she appeared at his side, slipping under his arm.

"I'm fine," she whispered. "Alex, I'm fine; he didn't hit me."

Thank God. "Get behind me," he muttered, squeezing her shoulders briefly. Tex's gun was just beside his foot; as Willow moved behind him, Alex kicked it away, sending it spinning into the shadows.

"She's not human!" insisted Tex from the ground, his drawling voice fierce. "She's one of them. You must be on their side, too—"

"Yeah, that's why I just shot three angels and why she was holding one off until I could get to it," snapped Alex. He glanced at the others. Four of them, all looking shaken. "What do you think?" he demanded of the girl with the sharp face. "You're the one whose life she just saved. Do you want to take a shot at her, too?"

There was a slight shuffling as they all looked at each other. "Her aura . . . and there was the angel, with her face . . ." stammered the girl.

"That's so great that you know how to see angels," said Alex coldly. "You might want to work on your interpretations a little. Her angel didn't have a halo, or didn't you notice?" With his pistol, he motioned for Tex to get up, sending him to stand with the others. "Now, listen to me: she's on our side. Anyone who doesn't believe me, you'd better go for your gun and shoot me now—because I'll kill the next person who tries to hurt her."

His words hung in the air. Nobody moved. In the sudden silence, the drone of traffic could be heard, along with the fluttering of moths as they battered against the naked lightbulb over the doorway.

"Good, I'm glad that's settled," said Alex finally.

He took in the tense group, wondering who they were—all the voices he'd heard so far were American. They stood staring back at him. Apart from Tex and the sharp-faced girl, there was a short guy with wiry rust-colored hair who looked frozen in place; a curvy brown-haired girl, features tight with worry; a black guy who met his gaze sullenly, arms folded across his chest.

"So who are you all, anyway?" asked Alex. "You're sure as hell not Angel Killers."

Tex bristled. "We sure as hell *are*."

"Yeah? So that's why you managed to kill, like, none of them, right?"

Tex's muscles swelled as he glared at Alex, like a quarterback in a barroom brawl. Before the Texan could respond, the brown-haired girl cleared her throat. "We— we were angel spotters," she offered. "Back in the U.S."

Alex's forehead creased. "What, you mean for Project Angel?"

She nodded. She had an earnest face and blue eyes, her hair drawn back in a ponytail. "Until just a few months ago. And then—" The girl Willow had saved nudged her, giving her a piercing look; she flushed and fell silent.

Angel spotters. Alex nodded slowly. Yeah, that made sense. The angel spotters had worked for the CIA, too, the same as he had—their role had been to locate angels and send texts to the AKs with their locations. They were trained to see angels, but wouldn't have much of a clue about the rest of it.

He scanned the group again. "So what happened? How did you find each other? I thought you guys had to work in isolation, too, just like —" He broke off as he felt Willow stiffen behind him.

At the same moment, a low female voice came from the drive: "You want to explain why you're holding a gun on my group, hotshot? And it better be good, or I'll blow your freaking head off."

Alex whirled in place, ready to shoot. Instead he just stared.

The dark-skinned girl who stood holding a gun on him was beautiful, and almost as tall as he was, with high, chiseled cheekbones and close-cropped black hair. Her brown eyes widened abruptly as they regarded each other. She wore tan jeans and a sleeveless T-shirt; he could see the slim, hard muscles of her mocha-colored arms, as if she spent half an hour every day doing chin-ups.

On her left bicep was a black AK tattoo in gothic lettering.

Time had come to a stop. "Kara," whispered Alex.

The girl opened her mouth; closed it again. "Jake?" she got out. Her voice sounded ragged.

"No," he said. "No, I'm —"

"Alex," she finished for him. "Oh, my God, Alex!" The next thing he knew, she had catapulted herself into his arms, and they were hugging tightly. "I don't believe it!" Kara gasped, sounding close to tears. "It's really you. You're alive; you're OK. . . ."

"I thought you were dead," he said against her neck. *Kara*. His throat felt too small for speech. "I thought everyone was dead, except for me."

She pulled back and touched his face; her slender hand felt firm and strong. "Look at you," she said, her eyes shining. "You look so much like Jake! You're all grown up—"

Suddenly they were both laughing. "Yeah, all grown up, just like you," he teased, putting away his gun. Kara was only four years older than him, but when he'd been a lovestruck fourteen-year-old, it had seemed more like four decades.

The tension in the courtyard had faded; the AKs stood watching in bemusement. Willow stepped forward. He could see her joy for him that one of his old friends had made it—though the slight tension around her mouth reminded him of when she'd met Cully, back in New Mexico. She'd been worried then that all the AKs would hate her because of what she was.

"Willow, this is Kara Mendez," he told her. "We were at the camp together."

"Hi," said Willow, holding out her hand to Kara. She looked almost waif-like in the plaid shirt, her green eyes dominating her face. "I'm Willow Fields."

Kara's eyebrows flew up; she shook the extended hand cautiously. "Willow Fields—as in the terrorist who's all over the news."

Willow shrugged and gave a thin smile. "Yeah, some-thing like that. I was trying to stop the Second Wave from coming."

"And she ain't human," put in Tex sullenly. "Check out her aura, Kara; it's *weird*. Plus there was this angel with her face, and—"

"Shut up, Sam." From the way Kara said it, it was a phrase that got used often. But her expression turned wary as she glanced at Alex. "You want to explain what he's talking about?"

Alex started to answer; Willow touched his arm, stop-ping him. Lifting her chin slightly, she said in a steady voice, "He's talking about the fact that I'm half angel."

Kara took a sharp breath between her teeth; the others recoiled in shock, staring at Willow. "Whoa," murmured the wiry-haired guy, taking a step backward. Tex—Sam, apparently—had a mix of validation and stunned horror on his broad face.

"Half *angel?*" sputtered Kara finally. "That's supposed to be impossible!"

"I know," said Willow evenly. "But it's true. My father—" she stopped, a tautness crossing her features. "My father was an angel," she finished. "I never knew him, though. I never knew anything about any of this until just recently."

Alex knew that Kara's reaction was probably milder than his own had been when he'd found out about Willow's parentage, but he still hated it. She was staring at Willow as if she were some kind of unthinkable lab experiment.

"Willow and I are together." He put his arm around Willow's shoulders and drew her against his side. "She almost died in Denver, trying to stop the Second Wave."

Kara didn't move, but he had the impression she'd just been rocked to the core, that she was even more shocked at this than at the revelation of what Willow was. "Together," she repeated in a monotone, her chocolate-brown eyes narrowing. "Let me get this straight: you're telling me that you've got a half-angel girlfriend."

"Yeah," said Alex. "That's right." Their gazes collided; he saw the thrust of Kara's chin and suddenly remembered how stubborn she could be. She and Cully had once had a standoff for hours over a game of poker — the two of them bickering until late into the night, with Kara demanding that Cully take it outside with her. It had been funny at the time; he and Jake had taken bets on who would cave first.

It hadn't been Kara.

Willow cleared her throat. "Look, I don't want to cause any trouble or anything."

"You're not," said Alex, not taking his eyes off Kara. "Is she, Kara?"

Kara didn't answer at first; Alex couldn't tell what she was thinking. With deliberate movements, she put her gun away, tucking it into the holster under her jeans waistband.

"So," she said coolly. "I guess we should go inside, huh? Seems like we've all got a lot to talk about."

It took Alex a second to get what she meant. He glanced up at the dark house beside them. "Inside — what, *here?* This is your base?" He turned and stared at the other AKs in disbelief. "You mean, you actually led them back *here.* To your base."

Kara looked sharply at Sam. "Led who back? Was there trouble?"

Alex couldn't help it; he laughed out loud. "Yeah. Let's go inside," he said. "You're right: there's a lot to talk about."

Chapter six

KARA TOOK THEM through the back door and switched on the light. There were cardboard boxes stacked against the wall, and scuffed floor tiles with a blue-and-white floral pattern. A decorative niche that looked as if it should have a vase in it instead held a flashlight and someone's change.

"What is this place?" asked Alex. He was carrying their camping stuff and helmets from the bike; they didn't have much else.

"Welcome to AK Central." Kara led the way into a small kitchen. The other AKs stood hanging back in the hallway, watching Willow with distrustful expressions. Sam especially was keeping an eye on her every move, as if she were about to sprout a halo and swoop at him, screeching, to feed. Alex dropped their stuff in a corner and put his hand on Willow's back, stroking lightly between her shoulder blades. The small smile she gave him didn't touch her eyes.

Kara introduced them all. Sam he already knew better than he wanted to. The sharp-featured girl was Liz; she had long black hair and a pale goth look. She kept casting appalled sidelong glances at Willow — apparently saving her life wasn't enough to earn her trust. Trish, the freckled brown-haired girl, didn't seem any less appalled; she also appeared anxious at the tension, gazing worriedly at the others.

"Hi," they each muttered. After a beat, Brendan, the short one with wiry hair, stepped forward to awkwardly shake Alex's hand. With an apprehensive glance at Willow, he stepped hastily back again.

The black guy was Wesley, whose arched eyebrows and hooded eyes made him look a little like a young Will Smith. He shifted his feet, glowering. "Are you going to need us for this, Kara?"

"No, I don't think so," said Kara. "Why don't you guys go into the TV room or the firing range or something, so the three of us can talk?"

"You sure?" drawled Sam. He narrowed his blue eyes at Willow in a calculating way. "You might need some backup."

Alex snorted. With an effort, he refrained from pointing out that backup worked a lot better when the person backing you up actually knew how to shoot a gun.

"Yes, Sam, I am sure. Go on, now. I'll tell you guys whatever you need to know later."

After the AKs had drifted away, Kara put some water on to boil. She started getting mugs out of a cabinet, then hesitated as she looked at Willow. "Do you — do you eat and drink like we do, or —?"

A cold anger tightened Alex's muscles. "Kara, for Chrissake —"

"Well, I don't know!" she snapped back. "How am I supposed to know what a half angel does or doesn't do?"

"Come on! Do you think I'd even be *with* her if she was like them?"

Kara started to say something else and stopped; a flush tinged her cheeks. Not answering, she banged the cabinet door shut, opened another one, and took out a jar of instant coffee. She thumped it onto the counter.

Willow looked away and hugged her chest; the plaid shirt billowed loosely about her thighs. "Yes, I eat and drink like you do," she said in a soft voice. "But I don't want anything."

Alex put his arm around her; he could feel the tautness of her shoulders. Kara poured boiling water into the mugs and added splashes of milk. "Two sugars, right?" she said without looking at him.

He glanced up in surprise as his throat tightened. It was how Jake had taken his coffee. "No, uh — just milk."

He saw Kara realize her mistake; a pained wince crossed her face. There must have been a hundred times on hunts when they'd stopped at a 7-Eleven and Kara had walked back out to the Jeep balancing coffees for everyone — teasing Jake about the sugar and saying he couldn't take his java like a man. Now Alex knew she was seeing the same thing he was: his brother's grin as he said, *What you're really saying is I'm sweet enough already, right?* The flirting between Jake and Kara had never come to anything, though if Alex knew his brother, it hadn't been for lack of trying.

Kara handed him a mug without speaking; they sat down at a battered wooden table that dominated half the room. "You sure you don't want anything?" she said to Willow, her voice stiff.

"Maybe some water," said Willow. "I can get it," she added as Kara started to stand up.

Alex and Kara sat in silence as Willow found glasses in a cabinet and filled one from the bottle of water that sat on the counter. Kara was very pointedly not looking at Willow; she sat drinking her coffee, drumming her fingers on the worn wood. Her nails were short but shapely, painted bright pink. Memory stirred Alex as he noticed. Those incongruous feminine touches of Kara's had given him some sleepless nights when he was fourteen or fifteen; he'd speculated endlessly on whether she might wear lacy lingerie, too. Kara probably would have decked him if she'd known. No, not *probably*.

Willow sat down, slipping into the chair next to him and avoiding his eyes. Under the table, Alex rubbed her thigh reassuringly, wishing they were alone; he hated how tense she seemed. She let out a breath and darted a grateful glance at him.

"So, what is this place?" he asked Kara again. "How

did you hook up with the angel spotters, anyway? And how did you manage not to get killed? Cully said—"

Kara's brown eyes turned large. "You've seen Cully?"

"Yeah, just over a month ago." Alex glanced down, playing with the handle of his coffee mug. "He's got angel burn, Kara." Even now, he hated thinking about it. Once Alex's father, Martin, had started losing grip with reality, Cully had taken over as lead of the AK training camp, the place in the remote New Mexico desert where both Alex and Jake had been raised. And he'd done it so tactfully and unobtrusively that Alex's dad hadn't even noticed to take offense. Cully had been a father to him in everything but name.

He described the encounter — how Cully was staying alone at the old camp now and had tried to kill Willow because the angels told him to. The news brought a hard line to Kara's mouth, but then her manner turned thoughtful as she took in the pink scar on Willow's arm where Cully's bullet had struck her.

"So the angels want you dead, huh?" she said.

Willow grimaced slightly. "Yeah, you could say that."

"It's what the terrorist manhunt is about," said Alex. He drained the rest of his coffee in a quick gulp. "They think she has the power to destroy them."

Kara sat watching Willow; even when she was relaxed, Alex could see the muscles in her slender arms. "And? Do you?"

"No one's told me how yet, if I do," said Willow. Her spiky red-gold hair cut across her cheek as she looked down, tapping at her water glass. "Unfortunately, being a half angel doesn't come with an instruction manual."

"No, I guess not," said Kara. "But my guys saw *something* about you that freaked them out."

"My angel self," said Willow. "I have a . . . dual nature, I guess you'd call it. My angel form can appear at the same time as my human one. They're both me, though. My angel self doesn't have a halo; it doesn't — feed or anything."

Alex could tell how bizarre Kara was finding this. "Ohh-kay," she said. "So, you want to show me?"

Willow gave her a level look. "No, not really."

Kara's gaze narrowed for a second, then she shrugged. "Fair enough. But how is it that . . . ? I mean, I thought angels couldn't breed."

"I don't know," said Willow. "I'm the only one; it's a mystery to them, too." She offered a tight smile. "I'm just a fluke, I guess."

Briefly, Alex explained how he and Willow had first met, how Willow had almost died trying to stop the Second Wave from arriving. He didn't tell the final part of the story — how he'd held Willow's body in his arms and somehow willed her back to life. It still made his stomach clench to think how close he'd come to losing her.

When he'd finished, Kara tipped her chair back as she studied Willow carefully, her dark eyebrows drawn together. "I guess you really are on our side, then," she said finally.

Willow lifted a shoulder. "I don't think my AK

boyfriend would want to have much to do with me if I wasn't, do you?" Kara didn't answer. Willow went on, enunciating each word quietly but clearly: "My father destroyed my mother's mind. She would have been normal if it wasn't for him; instead she barely knows who I am. Of course I'm on your side — I *hate* what the angels are doing here."

Her hand was clenched on the table; Alex covered it with his own.

"OK. Got it," said Kara after a pause. Then she frowned, and her chair legs slowly came down to touch the floor. "Wait a minute — what are you two doing down here, anyway? How did you find us?"

"Willow had a dream that we should come here," said Alex. "She's psychic; she knew something was going to happen in the Zócalo."

Kara didn't move. "Psychic," she said at last, and Alex knew exactly what she was thinking: psychic skills were an angelic trait.

"Yes, I've always been psychic," said Willow. "Even before I knew . . ." She shrugged her slender shoulders, looking tired suddenly. "Even before I knew," she finished.

Alex circled her palm with his thumb. "Are you going to answer some of *our* questions now?" he asked Kara. "If the interrogation's over with, that is."

Kara rolled her eyes at the word *interrogation*. She pushed her chair back and got up. "All right, let's just get settled first. You guys hungry? Liz likes to cook; we've got some leftover spaghetti I could heat up."

"Yeah, starving," said Alex. He let go of Willow's hand and swiped his palm across his face; his cheek throbbed where Sam had punched him. It felt as if he'd been awake for days.

"Liz?" asked Willow as she pulled a knee to her chest.

"The one with dark hair," Kara reminded her, opening the fridge and taking out a covered casserole dish.

"Oh, yeah, her. The one whose life Willow saved," said Alex pointedly, and took a dark enjoyment at the startled look on Kara's face. "Man, Kara, that group of yours needs some serious training," he went on. "What did you even have them out on a hunt for? Are you trying to get rid of them or something?"

Kara rested her hands on the counter; closing her eyes, she hung her head for a second, shaking it. "OK. I've got to hear all about this, and I don't like the sound of it one little bit . . . but let me answer your questions first, and then we'll get to it."

She slid the casserole dish into a microwave and punched a few buttons; a low humming noise started. "So, I guess the first thing you should know is — this place isn't mine; it was Juan's originally. He bought it for us to use."

"Juan? Is he alive, too?" Alex sat up straight, heart thumping. Juan Escobido had been one of the best AKs at the camp — he'd often been the team lead on hunts, especially after the accident that had cost Cully his leg. If he was still alive, it was some of the best news Alex had heard in months.

"No," said Kara heavily, leaning against the counter. The fluorescent light overhead cast the exotic lines of her face into sharp relief. "He was the one who brought us all down here; that white van in the drive is his. But he was killed the day after we finished fixing this place up. He didn't even have a chance to start training the team."

Alex went still. He could feel Willow's eyes on him, gentle with sympathy.

Kara's voice turned rough. "And the way it happened was just—stupid. The two of us had gone out to get some supplies, and we forgot to scan. An angel linked minds with Juan to feed. He managed to break away enough to try to shoot it . . . but it tore his life force away."

Alex didn't speak. "I called an ambulance, but I already knew he was gone," Kara went on. "And you know the worst part? I had to pretend I didn't even know him, that he was just some man I'd found collapsed on the sidewalk. Thankfully, I managed to get his gun, and he never carried ID. . . ." She trailed off. "I got the angel," she added after a moment. "But it was sort of too late by then."

Unfortunately, Alex could picture it all too well; Jake's death had happened because he himself had forgotten to scan. Christ, it was so easy to do, sometimes—so stupidly, criminally easy. Willow squeezed his hand, obviously aware of what he was thinking.

"So, how did he get you all down here?" he asked finally.

The microwave went off; Kara took the spaghetti

out and started piling portions onto plates. "Well, when Project Angel first got taken over, the angels started getting rid of all the AKs and angel spotters — you already know that. They sent one of their lackeys out after us; I guess none of them wanted to get near us themselves. And when it came to Juan's turn — well, let's just say that now there's one less lackey in the world."

"Good," said Alex shortly. Willow sat without speaking, listening intently.

Kara handed them each a plate, then opened a drawer and fished out forks and knives. Putting them on the table with a soft clatter, she sat down again. "Afterward, Juan searched the guy's car and found his phone — and there was a document on it that had the names and contact numbers of everyone who hadn't been killed yet. Me and those five in there." She nodded toward the rest of the house. "We were all next on the list. Juan managed to get to us first and brought us all down here."

"Why Mexico City?" asked Alex. He wasn't that hungry anymore but knew he should eat; he took a bite of spaghetti. "Juan wasn't from here, was he? I thought he was from Durango."

Kara nodded. "He was. We're here because of an e-mail that Juan found on the phone. Alex, something big is going to be happening here soon. And we have to be here for it — we have to be ready."

Willow shot Alex a quick look. "What's happening?" she asked Kara. Her tone was full of dread; he knew she was thinking of her dream.

"I better start from the beginning," said Kara. "Juan didn't keep the phone after he got the information from it, but he wrote the e-mail down—wait, I'll show you." She got up and left the room, her tall, slim form moving almost silently.

Willow let out a breath, then her face creased in concern as she studied him. "Your poor cheek," she murmured, touching it tenderly. "Does it really hurt?"

"It's OK," said Alex, his mind half on what Kara had been saying. "I just wish I'd punched him back when I had the chance." Then he glanced at Willow, taking in her face. "Are you all right, though? Being here?"

He wouldn't really call the slight curving of her lips a smile. "I'm fine."

Alex fell silent, not knowing what to say. He knew how hard this must be for her—coming into a strange situation where all anyone saw was her half-angel self and no one trusted her as far as they could throw her. When she was probably the most trustworthy person on the planet. "Listen, they'll get used to you, if we stay," he said. "Kara's a really good person; she just—"

"I know," she broke in. "Alex, it's all right. I can't expect them to just—take it in stride, I guess."

She looked so beautiful, sitting there in his faded plaid shirt. He slid his hand around the back of her neck and leaned forward, kissing her. Her lips were warm and soft; he felt her tension melt as she responded.

They both sensed rather than heard Kara standing there. Alex drew back, not taking his eyes from Willow's.

He smiled at her again; her own smile looked a little more relaxed this time.

"So, here it is," said Kara. Her mouth was tight as she sat down; Alex didn't know if it was the document in her hand or what she'd just walked in on. Both probably.

She pushed a sheet of paper across the table. "The Church of Angels e-mail address this was sent to belongs to the priest at the Metropolitan Cathedral," she said. "You might have seen that it's a Church of Angels cathedral now. And you know the tabernacle, right beside it? It's all been redone into office space for the Church. The priest is the head honcho there — and believe me, he's as devout as they come."

Alex angled the page toward himself, sharing it with Willow; a pang hit him at Juan's familiar looping handwriting. He started to read:

Yes, I can verify that arrangements are under way for the Seraphic Council's planned visit to Mexico City. They have several vital orders of business there; one is to select an angelic head for the Church in Mexico. As we discussed, the utmost security during their stay is vital — the general populace is not to know of their presence. However, rest assured that Church officials will of course be allowed to pay homage to them, as will a few chosen members of the public. We shall discuss this when we speak next. Meanwhile, please send a précis of all security arrangements. Remember, the Council's safety is vital for all angelkind.

"Seraphic Council?" murmured Willow. Her hair tickled his cheek as she leaned close to read. "Didn't Nate mention that to us?"

"Yeah, but I'd never heard of it before." Alex rubbed his jaw as he frowned down at the page. "We knew all about their habits at the camp — nothing about their politics." It was interesting news that this Council, whatever it was, planned to appoint an angelic Church head for Mexico — Alex had always had the impression that Raziel, who was head of the Church in the United States, had simply grabbed power for himself. So did that mean this Seraphic Council was above Willow's father, in the angelic scheme of things?

But more than that, Alex found himself staring at the phrase "the Council's safety is vital for all angelkind." Kara reached across and tapped the words. "That's the reason we came here," she said. "It sounded like if we did away with this Council, then maybe it would be a real strike against the angels — only we didn't know that for sure, or when they were arriving, or even where exactly."

"Past tense," noticed Alex, straightening up to look at her. "You do now?"

"Some of it," said Kara. "When we first got here, the cathedral had just reopened, and I went there a lot, pretending to be a devotee. I, ah — well, I've managed to get kind of friendly with the priest's main assistant, a guy named Luis."

Alex held back a smile; he had no trouble reading between the lines. Obviously, Luis was not supposed to be talking to random devotees about this stuff — and just as obviously, Kara had the poor guy so enamored that he couldn't help himself.

She propped her forearms on the table. "First of all — this thing is huge. Much bigger than we'd even imagined." She took a breath. "The reason the higher-ups at the Church are so concerned about the security risk is because the Seraphic Council is like the angels' heartbeat. They're called the Twelve, and their energy is the original angel energy — they're what's known as the First Formed. And the angels can't live without them. *Literally* can't live without them. If the Council of Twelve dies —"

"They all die," finished Willow. Her face was pale as she looked at Alex. "My dream — the twelve angels vanishing, the sound of millions of them screaming . . . it all fits."

"Jesus," murmured Alex, sinking back against his chair. His heart started pounding as his eyes locked on Willow's. They had a second chance to destroy them. They actually had a second chance. If they managed to get rid of the Council, then eventually humanity would start to recover; the world would be safe. His family flashed through his head. Willow's mother. They had to succeed this time, so that what had happened to the people they loved would never occur again.

"Do you have any other details?" he asked Kara finally.

"According to Luis, they'll arrive in early January and then stay for three weeks at the Nikko Hotel," said Kara. "It's the most exclusive hotel in the city — the whole top floor is reserved for them. Security's going to be tight, but there's a reception planned for the last day they're here — and the Council will be holding private audiences then, so that selected people can worship them in their angel forms. I'm trying to convince Luis that I should be on that list with a few of my friends." She gave a hard smile. "Because I'm so *devout*, don'cha know?"

Alex nodded. This reception definitely sounded like the best time to do it, with the Council members in their angel forms, their vulnerable halos on display.

"And I'm hoping we can pull it off with as little damage to us as possible — I don't really want this to be a suicide mission." Kara rested her chin on her palm, her face tense with worry. "But everything depends on the team being able to take out the Council — because this is probably the only chance we'll ever get at them. If we fail . . ." She shrugged. "Well, I doubt that they'll let us get away to try again later."

"I think you're right — this is our only chance," said Willow in a steady voice. She told Kara about her dream; Alex watched Kara go still.

"So it's sort of . . . fated for you two to be here," she said.

"Looks that way," said Alex, playing with his fork. His mind was ticking over everything Kara had said. Depending on this Luis guy to get the team into the reception sounded a little too flimsy for comfort. Even if everything went according to plan, the hardest part was going to be escaping after the Council was killed, once everyone realized what had happened. There were almost certainly going to be casualties.

He rapped the fork against the table and put aside the logistic difficulties for the moment. "OK, so this reception is about eleven weeks away. If you need your team trained for then, what are you doing sending them out on hunts *now*, before they're ready? Are you trying to get them killed, or what?" He explained what had happened at the Zócalo; as he'd already surmised, Kara had been the lone AK who'd actually been hitting the angels, at the other end of the square.

"Sounds like they all stayed together," said Kara morosely. "Damn it — I *told* them to fan out."

"You shouldn't have sent them out there in the first place! God, you should have seen them out back just now, when those three angels were attacking — it was complete chaos. What did you think you were doing, anyway?"

Her dark eyes flashed. "What I've been *doing* is being in charge the best way I know how ever since Juan died, OK?" she said in a voice of steel. "Which was pretty horrific to deal with, in case you're wondering. And they seemed like they could handle it! They'd all been getting the bull's-eye over ninety percent; they're already experts at scanning; they —"

Alex let out a disbelieving laugh. "Come *on*, Kara, you know how different it is shooting angels for real, instead of just hitting targets! I remember Dad telling you that often enough, anyway."

"Yeah, well, I'm not your dad! And it wasn't exactly

my *plan* to have Juan die before we even got started, so that I had to be in charge of training this bunch—" Kara broke off suddenly. Exhaling, she rubbed her hand across her face; there was a silence. "Oh, hell, I messed up, OK?" she said, her voice weary. "They'd been doing target practice for what seemed like forever, and I'd just found out about the Council, and this being our only chance—and I guess I sort of freaked. I thought it might be good practice for them or something—like we couldn't just *sit* here with all this going on; we had to get out and do something. . . ."

Alex sighed—he understood this kind of frustration all too well. "Yeah, I know. Don't beat yourself up over it." He looked down at his plate again and took a disinterested bite. "No one could have been like Juan, anyway. He was one of the best leads I ever worked under."

Kara leaned back in her seat, crossing her ankle over her knee. She gave him a long, appraising look. "I bet *you* could be like Juan," she said. "Maybe even better."

Alex's muscles stiffened; he could see Willow watching him and knew she was thinking the same thing as Kara. His voice came out sharper than intended. "No way. You're in charge, Kara. I'll help however I can, but I'm not going to come in here and take over your team."

"What about if I begged and pleaded?" she said dryly. "Alex, seriously; I'm barely holding it together here. Give me an angel to shoot and I'm fine—but this?" She shook her head. "Even when you were a kid, you were a great AK. I bet you'd be fantastic at all the strategy stuff and the training—it's just in your blood; you've been around it your whole life. God, I remember you taught *me* the best way to go for a halo, and you were only around fourteen!"

Willow touched his arm; he could see the worry on her face, but her voice was steady. "You'd be great. I know it isn't really something you want, but you'd be so, so good at it."

"You've got to do it," said Kara. "You have *got* to. Or else we don't even stand a chance against the Council."

So here it was, the thing he'd dreaded so much—as inevitable as the coldness of ice. Alex's bruised cheek gave a throb. Somehow he'd known this would happen, from the moment he first saw Sam flailing around with the gun, screaming at the angel to come and get him. There was no escaping it, even though he wanted to refuse this more than anything he'd ever faced—because it wasn't just a team's safety he'd be responsible for now; it was all of humanity's.

"If I'm lead, then the first priority is to get floor plans for the hotel," he said finally. "I also need more specific security information. A lot more specific: every detail you can find out—how many guards, exactly what's happening at this reception, everything. And as soon as the team is ready, we'll have to start taking them out on safe hunts—the safest we can manage, so they can get some real-life practice. I don't want any of them dying if I can help it." His mouth twisted. "Not even that jerk-off Texan."

"You got it, Chief," said Kara softly.

Chief. Alex managed not to grimace. "Are you OK with this?" he said to Willow.

Her face had a resigned look, as if she, too, found this inevitable. At the same time, apprehension flickered deep within her green eyes, and he knew again how worried she was. "Of course," she said. "This is what we have to be doing."

"So, I guess I'll tell the team tonight," said Kara.

Alex started to eat again; the food had lost all its flavor. "Tomorrow," he said. "Let me get some rest first, OK?"

Kara nodded. And though he was exhausted, Alex didn't know whether that was the real reason he wanted to put the announcement off, or whether he just wanted a few more hours' reprieve before he had to take this on. He glanced at Willow, wishing again that they were alone. He wanted to find out how she really felt about staying here, given the welcome she'd received.

Willow stood up, squeezing his arm as if she knew what he was thinking. "Is there a bathroom I could use?" she asked Kara.

Kara turned, pointing with a slender brown arm. "Yeah — just go through that door and it's upstairs, second door on the left."

After Willow had disappeared, Kara said, "So. She does that, too."

Alex didn't look up from his meal. "Yeah, gosh, just like a real human being. Do you think you could you stop being such an idiot about this? As a special favor to me?" He shoveled another bite of spaghetti into his mouth.

"She's very pretty," said Kara after a pause.

"I know."

"So . . . can I ask you a personal question?"

He looked up sharply; her beautiful face was bland. "Yeah, you can ask," he said. "I might not answer, if it's none of your business."

She tapped her pink nails on the table. "Well, I'm guessing you two are—intimate. Am I right?"

Alex held back a snorting laugh and took another bite of spaghetti. If Kara thought he was going to discuss his sex life with her, she was insane.

"OK, fine, don't tell me," she said. "But what I'm getting at is—aren't you worried about angel burn?"

He let out a groan and dropped his fork. Kara went on before he could say anything. "I mean, all right, she's not on the side of the angels; I get that. But that doesn't mean being close to her won't hurt you. I'm not saying she'd do it on purpose, but—"

Alex ground the words out. "Listen carefully and I'll say it again—she is not like them. She doesn't feed. So how could she give me angel burn?"

Kara shrugged, her expression arch. "I don't know. Who the hell knows anything about a half angel? She doesn't even know, so how can you?"

"Yeah, well, thanks for your concern," he said, picking up his fork again. "I feel fine."

"Good," she said. "Glad to hear it." She picked up the sheet of paper from Juan and turned it over thoughtfully in her hands. "'Course, you don't always know these things, do you? Some of these cancers can take a real long time to start showing themselves—"

He glared at her, would have happily smashed the plate of spaghetti in her face. "Kara, I'm serious—*shut the hell up.*"

A strained silence fell. "Hey," she said eventually, touching his shoulder. "Don't be mad at me, Al. I mean, just put yourself in my shoes—I really hope that if I came strutting in here with some half-angel boyfriend, you'd start asking a few questions."

He managed a smile at her old nickname for him and knew that she was right. If he were in her place, he'd be saying the exact same things. He shook his head. "Kara, Willow is—she's the kindest, most unselfish person I've ever known. She'd die before she hurt me or anyone else."

Kara lifted a hand. "OK," she said, and he knew she was holding back from repeating that Willow might not be doing it on purpose. "Just keep it in mind, all right? That's all I'm asking." She changed the subject adroitly. "You know, I really cannot get over how much you look like Jake now—you've actually grown into those shoulders of yours. What a difference a couple of years make, huh?"

He was glad to feel the tension between them ease. "Yeah, but you still look the same," he said, scanning her face. Kara was half black and half Mexican; the mix had resulted in stark, dramatic features and a graceful neck—extremely short hair looked amazing on her; it always had.

She smiled and pretended to preen. "Thanks. When you get to my age, you kind of like hearing that." Her face grew more serious again. She examined her nails; he saw the same expression in her eyes as when she'd made the mistake over the coffee. "So . . . do you still think about him as much as I do?"

Alex looked down at his plate; the words wouldn't come. He felt Kara reach over and squeeze his wrist. "Sorry," she said. "Stupid question."

"Every day," he said finally. "I miss him every day."

They both straightened as Willow came back into the kitchen; he could tell that she'd picked up on the mood. She stood with her arms crossed over her chest and awkwardly attempted a smile. "Hey, I'm sorry to be boring, but . . . I'm actually getting pretty tired," she said. "I might just go on to bed."

"Me, too," said Alex, stretching. Then he remembered. "Kara, can we borrow some clothes from you guys? Some thieving asshole stole all our stuff up in Chihuahua."

"Yeah, we can fix you up, no problem," said Kara. She started clearing the plates away; Willow moved to help. "So, Willow, we've got an extra bed in the girls' dorm that you're welcome to. And, Alex, you can take Juan's old room if you want; it's right by the guys' dorm—it's pretty small; it's got a single bed in it—" She stopped, looking flustered as she glanced from Alex to Willow. "Oh, wait. I guess maybe you . . ."

"We'll both take Juan's old room," said Alex. He saw Kara start to say something and then stop, her lips narrowing. "What?" he said sharply. "Everyone knows that Willow and I are together; I'm not going to start hiding it."

"No, it's not that," said Kara. She scraped the remains of the spaghetti into the trash. "It's just—well, Juan thought it was better if people didn't couple up too obviously. For the team, I mean. He sort of laid down some ground rules when we first got here, and that was one of them. But look, you're in charge now; you do what you want."

He started to say, *Good, I will,* and then hesitated as he remembered—his father had had that rule, too. It wasn't that Martin had cared who was seeing whom—illicit meetings in the broom closet had been fine, as far as he was concerned—but he'd said it made the team feel like more of a unit if it was always team first, couples second. And when you were in a combat situation, that could be vital.

"Alex, it's fine—I'll go into the dorm," said Willow, rinsing their forks and knives off without looking at him.

He could just imagine what it would be like for her in there, with the other girls hating her. Then he got a closer look at her strained expression, and his eyebrows came together in concern. "Could you leave us alone for a second?" he said to Kara.

She put the rinsed-off dishes onto a drying rack. "Sure, I'll just go and find some clothes for you both. Back in ten."

Alex leaned against the counter by the sink and gently

pulled Willow to him, looping his arms around her waist. "You heard what Kara was saying before, didn't you?"

She gave a reluctant nod. "Just the last part of it, as I was coming down the stairs, but . . . yeah, enough to get the idea," she admitted.

"OK, so you know it's a complete fantasy, right? You do *not* cause angel burn. Not to me or anybody else."

Looking down, Willow fingered the crystal pendant he'd given her; it gleamed in the light. "Kara's right, though: you don't know that for sure." Her voice was unsteady. "How can you? No one really knows anything about half angels. I mean, I don't *think* I've ever hurt anyone, but you and I are so close, and maybe —"

"Wil-low. Come on. Babe, please listen to me —" He lifted her chin with his hand; her eyes were bright with tears. "Of course you're not hurting me," he said. "Do I look unhealthy to you? I'm fine."

"But just because someone looks healthy doesn't always mean they are. And what about that headache you got in Chihuahua? The night before, we almost —" She stopped, flushing slightly. "I mean — we came so close, remember?"

With a sudden grin, he said, "Oh, hey, yeah. Now that you mention it, I do seem to recall that." He bent his head down and kissed her, felt her start to respond and then pull away.

"Alex, I'm serious! What if that had something to do with —?"

"Shhh," he murmured, kissing her again. His hands

were on her hips; gliding them upward, he could feel the slim cello-dip of her waist. "Listen to me. You don't have a halo. You don't feed. The only way you could hurt me would be to stop touching me. That would hurt. A lot. This feels . . . really good, actually." The kiss deepened, their mouths moving together. He felt her give in to it, pressing close against him and twining her arms around his neck. He stroked his hands up her spine, relishing her warmth. The thought of sleeping separately from her was agonizing.

When they drew apart, Willow rested her head against his chest; he dropped his cheek onto it, caressing her back through the softness of the plaid shirt. "Promise me you'll tell me if you ever even suspect I'm hurting you," she said after a pause. "I mean, if you even have a *cough* that you don't think you should have, you've got to tell me, all right?"

He started to make a joke, and then Willow glanced up; her expression was gravely serious. "I promise," he said, touching her face. God, he could kill Kara for putting this idea in her head. "But, Willow, it's not going to happen. You're not hurting me. It was just a headache — everyone on the planet gets them sometimes."

She hesitated, her eyes searching his. "I really hope you're right."

"I am," he said. He stroked her cheek with his thumb. "I promise you. I'm completely fine."

Willow let out a breath. "OK," she said at last, nodding. "Maybe I overreacted." She reached up and covered his hand with hers. "I'll believe you until I have a reason not to. How's that?"

"Much better," he said. He drew her back to him again. Lowering his head, he whispered in her hair, "So now that we've got that settled . . . maybe we should think about finishing what we started the other night."

She looked quickly up at him; her cheeks reddened a little, but she was smiling. "Oh, I'm definitely thinking about it—believe me." She traced a finger over his chest. "But next time, someone needs to be a little more prepared."

Alex nuzzled at her neck. "I bought some on the drive down today," he murmured against her smooth skin.

"You did?"

"Mm-hmm." He nibbled at her ear, felt her shiver.

"Oh," she said faintly. "That makes it . . . really, really suck that I'm going to sleep in the girls' dorm while we're here."

He pulled away. "You are?"

Willow sighed. "I think I'd better. Don't you, honestly? I mean, I don't want to cause problems or anything, and it sounds like it's sort of the established thing."

He grimaced. "It doesn't have to be. I mean, I'm the lead now. . . . I could always just order you to sleep in the same bed as me."

"Oh, that's romantic."

Alex half laughed, half groaned, dropping his head onto her shoulder. He felt her stroke his hair. "Yeah, you're right," he said finally. "Dad had the same rule. He didn't care what people did, but . . ." He raised his head and smiled ruefully. "Maybe we could find a broom closet somewhere."

"It's amazing; this conversation just keeps on getting more and more romantic."

"So . . . that's a no to the broom closet, then."

"It is a definite, emphatic no to the broom closet."

Alex smiled. "You know I'm only kidding, don't you?" He found her hand and linked his fingers tightly through hers. "Willow, when it happens, I want it to be just — incredible for you. For both of us. Totally perfect."

"I know," she said, her eyes soft. "We'll find a way soon. Let's get used to being here first, OK? Then we can start sneaking around and checking out broom closets." She sighed. "I'm really going to miss sleeping with you, though," she said, running her hand up his arm. "I mean, just — talking to you. Being held by you."

Alex could hear Kara returning with their clothes. "Yeah, I know," he said, giving her another quick kiss. "Me, too."

And he thought wryly that that was probably one of the biggest understatements of his life.

CHAPTER SEVEN

"RAZIEL!" The female voice was low, urgent. A hand lightly slapped his cheek and then the other one. "You *must* wake up. Hurry—we don't have much time!"

The touch was angelic; the voice wasn't any that he'd been hearing since lying here in bed——and how long had that been? A day? A week? With terrible, sudden clarity, what he'd sensed while passed out came roaring back, and Raziel's eyes flew open. When he saw who was at his bedside, he struggled upright, his head still swimming.

"Charmeine," he said.

She was sitting on the side of his bed wearing gray pants and a black angora sweater that bared one shoulder, her long white-blond hair falling in a shining stream. Raziel regarded her, pleasure mixing with sharp suspicion. He and Charmeine had had a thing once and were now friends of a sort, though Charmeine was too much like him for comfort sometimes. They'd kept sporadically in touch these last two years, but he hadn't known that she'd planned to come across with the Second Wave. Given the Council's sudden appearance as well, it wasn't particularly reassuring to find her here now, perched on his bed.

"I know what you're thinking, but you're wrong—I promise you can trust me." Charmeine took his hand, and he felt her opening herself to him, showing her sincerity. Which was nice but meant little. It was standard procedure to let someone in and show them exactly what you wanted them to see.

"The Twelve are here, Raziel. And—"

"I know," he broke in bitterly, pulling his hand away. He still felt dizzy. "And only three or four years ahead of schedule. Fancy that. Why? Did someone tip them off?" Like many angels, Raziel had unconsciously taken on characteristics from some of his human energy donors; the English accent had been with him for years.

"No, I mean they're *here*," said Charmeine levelly. "Downstairs. In the cathedral. They sent me to summon you."

Raziel knew he'd been unable to hide his shock; he felt it leap within him like a flame. "They're *summoning me*—in my own cathedral?" he said finally.

"Yes," said Charmeine. "And yes, they're here in the first place because they were tipped off. I don't know by whom, but they know everything you've been up to—they have for months. They've been making plans."

Apprehension tightened his muscles. "What plans?"

She shook her head. "You'll find out soon enough, I'm afraid."

Typical Charmeine: to dangle information and then not supply it. Raziel scowled but didn't bother to go searching. Angels had had thousands of years to perfect the art of psychic maneuvering; Charmeine's defenses were as skilled as his own. "And what do *you* have to do with all of this?" he demanded. "What do you mean, they sent you?"

"I was, shall we say, strongly encouraged to come across with the Second Wave and serve them," said Charmeine. "They've decided that only family can be trusted. Even a black sheep like me."

Charmeine was one of the "First Family" — an angel who had been formed soon after the Twelve. She wasn't as close to them in lineage as some — more of a distant cousin than anything else. But her basic ethereal makeup was still more similar to the Twelve than other angels', which in theory meant they'd find it easier to have psychic control over her. Hence their sudden yearning to have their "family" around them, no doubt.

"So they've bound you," summed up Raziel. "You're one of their psychic lackeys now, and they know everything you do."

Charmeine shrugged; her exposed shoulder was slim and pale. "They think so. I think they'd be surprised how strong my defenses are. The familial energy works both ways, you know — I have layers they haven't even discovered yet."

Raziel regarded her; if true, it was interesting news. "And how long do you think you can keep *that* up?"

"Long enough, I hope."

Her tone was lightly casual, but he knew Charmeine had never said anything truly casual in her life — like most angels, she thrived on innuendo and subtext. Raziel shoved back the covers and got out of bed. He was wearing a pair of silken pajamas that he rarely bothered with; obviously one of his human attendants had put them on him.

"Delightfully mysterious as always, I see," he said. "Fine. I've got to take a shower and change."

"Don't be too long," cautioned Charmeine, glancing at the door. "They expect you down there shortly."

"I'll be as long as I like," he snapped. "This is *my* cathedral — they don't give the orders around here."

Despite his bravado, he still found himself hurrying as he bathed, which enraged him. Below it all, there was that same almost-fear he'd felt while passed out. He hadn't expected the Council to find out the true extent of his power in this world yet. Ever since the First Wave, their knowledge of what was happening here had been somewhat sketchy; only a few First Wavers had the ability to communicate with them across the dimensions. And as time had passed, loyalties had shifted. It hadn't taken long for these angels to feel more in tune with Raziel and others who were connoisseurs of this world than with the old guard back home — or to see the enticing possibilities for the power they could all share here.

Because what no one could have foreseen was the Church of Angels: the fastest-growing religion in history. Though founded by humans, the angels had been quick to take advantage of the Church — particularly Raziel, who'd always chafed at the Twelve's automatic reign as the First Formed. You could either spend eternity jockeying for position as one of their lackeys or try to carve out a niche for yourself elsewhere. The angels' mass presence in this new world had given Raziel the opportunity he'd been craving for millennia; it hadn't taken him long to wrest control of the Church and rise to its head.

With Raziel at its helm, the Church of Angels had become the most influential church in the world. Angels were now so firmly fixed in society's consciousness that people who'd never even encountered one were embracing their predators wholeheartedly. In Mexico City, the historic Catedral Metropolitana had recently been remade as a Church of Angels cathedral — an astounding coup, made all the more so by the relative lack of press attention; it was just seen as a natural course of events. Raziel planned to take over the running of this new cathedral himself in due course, dividing his time between the United States and Mexico. In London, there was talk of Saint Paul's being similarly redone; in Paris, Notre Dame.

So far, talk was all it was — the angelic presence wasn't as great in Europe yet — but Raziel had little doubt that in the wake of the Second Wave, these plans would go ahead. By then, he'd be in charge of most of the Americas and could set himself up in the role of a pope, with ruling angels under him. Once the Council had finally settled in this world and seen what was going on, it would have meant all-out war for them to try to wrest control back from him — and by then he'd have more than enough allies to take them on.

For now, the Church stood on the brink: it was poised to take over the world, and those angels who were on Raziel's side could help him do it. And so any reports back to the Council had always carefully downplayed the importance of the Church of Angels and Raziel's growing power base.

Or at least that's what he had thought.

As he turned off the shower, it hit him suddenly: Mexico City. The half angel was there — and she, too, was aware of the Council. The knowledge was as fleeting as a soap bubble, gone as quickly as it had arrived. Raziel was left frowning, water dripping in his eyes as he wondered whether he was going insane. *Forget the half angel*, he thought. He could still hardly bear to use the word *daughter*. He had more important things to think about right now.

When he emerged, Charmeine had moved to the sitting room. After putting on a pair of casually expensive gray pants, Raziel went in and found her curled up, catlike, in his favorite armchair. He knew they'd made a striking pair, once — her with her delicate moonlight beauty and him with his crisp black hair and poet's features. If he were the sentimental type, this might have caused him to view her with less suspicion. Fortunately, he wasn't.

"So what are you up to?" he demanded, buttoning a midnight-blue shirt. "Why are you tipping me off that there's trouble?"

Charmeine looked amused. "Old times' sake?" she suggested.

"How wonderfully altruistic of you," replied Raziel, tucking his shirt in. "Please remember that this is me you're talking to, and how very, very well I know you. What's your game?"

"No game," said Charmeine. Her beautiful gamine face was impossible to read. She rose and came over to him, lazily circling one of his shirt buttons with a fingernail. "I just have a feeling you're going to need a friend in this world soon — that's all. And I think our mutual needs could work together very well."

Raziel's expression didn't change as he looked down at her. "Does the Council know about you and me?" he asked sharply.

Her hand wandered up to the nape of his neck, playing with his hair. "Of course; they delved my mind and found everything I wanted them to see," she said. "And so they know I hate you very, very much and would do anything to get back at you."

Raziel started to say something else, then stopped as they both felt it — a harsh tugging at their minds, as if they were a pair of fish being reeled in by invisible fishermen. "Showtime," murmured Charmeine, dropping her hand.

"By the way, your cathedral is about to be used for something pretty disagreeable. Necessary, I suppose, but . . . disagreeable."

The riddles were doubly annoying when the place under discussion was his own territory. Without answering, Raziel shifted to his angel form and flew from the room, gliding silently through the walls. Charmeine followed with a bright shimmer of wings. As they soared out into the main space of the cathedral, with its high, arching dome, Raziel saw the Twelve gathered in their human forms below, near the white-winged pulpit. And what fun: they'd brought an audience with them — there were at least fifty angels seated in the pews nearby.

Raziel's ethereal eyes narrowed as he saw the results of the half angel's attempt to destroy the gate: the buckled floorboards, the missing ceiling panels, the metal scaffolding that stood in place. Fury seared through him again that she'd even attempted this — and that the damaged fruits were now on gruesome display for the Council and their sycophants to view. *Mexico City. She's there,* he thought again. And though he shoved the knowledge away for now, he dearly hoped it was true. Knowing the creature's whereabouts would mean he was only a few steps away from having her and her assassin boyfriend destroyed.

He touched down in front of the Council and changed back to his human form; Charmeine followed suit. The Twelve looked nothing alike, yet there was a commonality among them all the same — a similar bland expression, perhaps, or a certain way they all held themselves. Six males and six females who'd been leading the angels' affairs for millennia, since long before anyone could remember. From what Raziel had heard, most of them loathed one another heartily, though they were far too entwined, both psychically and politically, to ever separate now.

"Welcome to my cathedral," said Raziel, inclining his dark head.

He managed to keep the irony from his voice, but knew they'd pick up on it psychically; he wasn't especially bothering to hide it. "Thank you," said Isda, who was often the spokeswoman for the Twelve. "It's a pleasure to be here." She was tall and statuesque; her gray eyes rested on Raziel with no visible emotion. "Shall we get the unpleasantness out of the way first?"

"By all means," said Raziel smoothly, trying to bury his faint throb of alarm — what unpleasantness were they talking about precisely? And now he saw that in addition to the expected hangers-on in the audience, all the First Wavers who'd been in psychic contact with the Council were here, too. He could sense their anxiety; the expectation had been that Raziel would be firmly ensconced in power by the time their betrayal was found out.

"Good. You and Charmeine may take a seat," said Isda, nodding at a nearby pew.

Being given permission to sit in his own cathedral

grated; Raziel did so in moody silence. Charmeine perched beside him, looking straight ahead.

Isda and the rest of the Twelve stood in a row, their backs to the pews. The tall stained-glass windows in front of them glimmered in the sun; it was here, exactly, where the Second Wave had arrived mere days ago. "Now, please," called Isda in her low voice.

The stadium doors to the side opened, and a long line of almost a hundred angels was led in — all in their human forms, with their hands cuffed behind them. Raziel sat up straight, his pulse quickening in surprise as he recognized the remainder of the traitors: the angels that he'd been using Kylar, the assassin, to do away with. Though a diverse group, the traitors all believed that angels didn't have the right to use humans for their own purposes and were committed to helping humanity, even if it meant the extinction of their own kind. Raziel had gotten their names by chance over a year ago, from a rogue who'd been captured and had then turned in the others to save himself. Raziel had had him killed anyway, of course, but it had been a very useful meeting all the same.

The nature of the "unpleasantness" was now only too clear. The Council had been aware of the rogues' identities from the start; it had seemed politic to pass the information along. And they'd obviously realized that only a rogue — in this case, Nate — could have helped the half angel with her near-disastrous attack on the gate. As a result, the traitors had escalated themselves out of being a matter that could be taken care of quietly into one that merited a public statement. The Council would have drawn the rogues to them easily enough; one of the most annoying things about the Twelve was how their psychic call tugged on you, like it or not.

Gazing at the traitors, Raziel wondered why they stayed imprisoned in their chained human forms — and then realized uneasily that the Council had something to do with that, too. In a subtle undercurrent that he'd missed before, he could feel them working together to exert some kind of mental hold on the captured angels, preventing them from shifting.

The traitors stood motionless before the Council, awaiting their fate. The cathedral had fallen utterly silent; beside him, Charmeine sat unmoving. The Twelve didn't speak, but a heavy energy was gathering in the cathedral, crackling with power. Gradually, Raziel sensed their mental hold on the prisoners reverse itself, so that now it forced them into their more vulnerable divine forms. Knowing what it meant, they were resisting with everything they had — faces contorting, muscles straining. Raziel squirmed slightly. He didn't mind watching the traitors' deaths, but the Council's display of power was . . . unsettling.

A dark-haired angel named Elijah was the first to succumb. His angel form appeared in a rush, its winged figure darting upward as he tried to escape through the ceiling. A quick mental feint from the Council, and Elijah shuddered to a halt midair, wings flapping feebly like a pinned insect on a card. His halo began glowing, brighter

149

and brighter—too bright—it was throbbing, trembling under pressure—and then it exploded into silent fragments. Elijah's scream echoed through the cavernous building as he was torn to pieces . . . and then there was silence again as the remnants of his ethereal self drifted toward the ground.

Raziel winced—as Elijah died, it felt as if a small piece of himself had been torn away. The energy was even stronger now, pulsing through the cathedral like a heartbeat. With an anguished cry, several others lost the battle and erupted into their divine forms. The Council showed no strain in dealing with all of them at once. As the prisoners' halo-hearts burst one after the other, the remainder followed in a helpless torrent, taking to the air amid the shining shards that were now falling like snow. Screams echoed; angelic bodies writhed. Raziel gritted his teeth as the pain of death after death clawed at him. Beside him, Charmeine's face was emotionless but pale.

When the last executed angel had faded from view, the Council shifted and lifted upward. Their wings moved slowly as they hovered, turning to face their audience. Raziel just managed not to shield his eyes. The divine bodies of the First Formed were painfully bright, their features impossible to make out as they burned blue-white before them. A thought came like psychic thunder, twelve voices speaking at once: *This is how we deal with traitors. We are sure you all understand.*

Raziel swallowed, his throat suddenly dry. It was typical

of the Council: using a necessary execution such as this one as a helpful little *aide-mémoire*. He didn't have to look behind him to know how sick the expressions were of the First Wavers who had been on his side.

The Council stayed aloft for almost a minute, silently making their point. Finally they touched down again and rippled back to their human forms. Though they didn't look at Raziel, he abruptly felt singled out, as pinned to his seat as the rogue angels had been in the air. Still speaking psychically, the many-toned voice that was both one and twelve rumbled through him:

Raziel, may we see you alone, please?

The meeting was short and to the point.

Half an hour later, Raziel sat alone in one of the downstairs conference rooms, staring at the gleaming wooden table; the tasteful decorations; the silver water pitcher that had an arched, graceful angel as the handle. He had done all of this; he had made it all happen — and apparently, if he was very, very good and did exactly as he was told, he might be allowed to keep it for a little while.

Or not.

Impotent anger clenched his fists. No. They weren't going to get away with this — not after all his hard work, not after all he'd done in this world and still planned to do. He wouldn't allow it. He *would not*.

"Raziel?" Charmeine had appeared; she stood in the doorway.

151

"Shouldn't you be off doing lackey things?" he said bitingly. He shoved his chair back and began striding for the door.

She shut it with a gentle click and leaned against it. "If anyone goes checking psychically, that's exactly what they'll see," she said. "For your information, I'm currently going through your e-mail account upstairs, while the Twelve talk to some of your First Wave chums."

He snorted. "Aren't you noble? As if that's not exactly what you *were* just doing."

Charmeine gave a mild shrug. "It helps to have visual details in mind when you're creating psychic decoys. And let me guess," she went on. "They've told you about their plan to recognize only those angels in power who they've appointed themselves."

"Good guess," snapped Raziel. "And those they *don't* recognize will be traitors and dealt with accordingly." He swore and ran a hand through his hair. "Why couldn't this have happened a few years from now? I'd have had enough of a power base by then to take them on, to con-strain them in some way —" He stopped, aware that he was saying far too much.

He could feel Charmeine's sincerity again, her anger at the Council. "I really am on your side, Raz," she said softly. "You can trust me."

He half sat against the table, tapping his thigh as he tried to think. Just as Charmeine had said, the Council had apparently known about his schemes for months. They'd informed him that plans were already in place for them to make a state visit to Mexico City soon, where they'd appoint an angel of their choosing to be head of the new cathedral there. Then, once they returned, they'd decide his fate. The implication was clear: he should spend the time in the interim mulling over his wrongs and deciding whether or not he wanted to be their poodle for the rest of eternity.

He glanced at Charmeine, wondering if it was she who'd betrayed him. She'd known enough about his plans here and could have guessed the details he hadn't told her. But it could also have been almost any of the First Wavers — several had become increasingly greedy in their demands of late. He supposed he should have dealt with them more diplomatically, played them along until he could get rid of them. But who would have thought they'd go crying to the Council?

"So what now?" asked Charmeine. "Are you going to toe the line?"

Enough of these games. Raziel rose in a quick motion; he gripped her head in his hands and kissed her harshly, shoving her up against the wall. *Open to me,* he thought. Her arms twined around his neck as she responded. Using the connection their history gave them, he delved deep, deeper into her mind, probing her roughly. He could feel her slight tremor as she allowed him in, opening up layer after layer to him until there were no more to be explored.

Finally Raziel raised his head, frowning down at her. Her black sweater was askew on her bare shoulder; her white-blond hair still lay sleek and perfect. He'd only seen that in return for her help, she wanted to share power with him in this new world. He'd have expected nothing else.

"Well?" Charmeine was a touch paler than usual, but her voice was steady.

"All right," he said, letting go of her. "Maybe it wasn't you — and maybe you're actually sincere, for a change."

"Of course I am," she said intensely. "I hate them as much as you do; I always have. So will you answer my question now?" She rested against the wall without adjusting her sweater; he could see the firm upper swell of one breast.

Raziel's lip curled. "No, I'm not going to toe the line," he replied. He sat on the table again and shoved at the water pitcher, sending it sliding across the dark, shining wood. "I'll play their game for now — but that's all."

"That's what I thought," said Charmeine with quiet satisfaction. She traced her finger along the doorjamb, watching its movement musingly. "They're overconfident, you know. You really did delve me completely, but they only think they have. It hasn't even crossed their mind that the oh-so-sacred family energy might not be enough of a connection for them to get everything. And meanwhile, I've picked up a few things myself."

Raziel studied her. "Such as?"

"Such as I don't think it's ever seriously occurred to them that someone might want to take them out." Her eyes met his; she smiled. "They're a little concerned about the security risk from non-devout humans — we've been hearing stories about Angel Killers, and now there's been that episode with the half angel and the gate. But other *angels* wanting to destroy them, given the possible consequences to us all? They'd never even suspect it." She shrugged. "Still, the way I see it, this is a fresh new world, and we need a fresh new start. And we can never have that as long as the Council is around."

Raziel had been thinking the same thing. To hear it put into words, and to feel the passion behind them psychically, gave him a stirring of dark excitement that was like a rich red wine.

If the First Formed died, all angels would die: it had been drummed into them since the beginning of time. And much as Raziel hated to concede it, in their home world this was almost certainly true. But things were different here — the ether in this world was thinner; it was why angels had to feed from humans instead of the ether itself. The truth was that no one really knew what would happen if the Twelve were killed here, rather than at home.

The dominant view was that the exact same result would occur: without the First Formed energy, all angels would die. Yet there were other possibilities, too. The most enticing of them was that if the Council members were killed here, then only the Council members would perish. Hardly anyone believed this — seeing the Council as indispensable to their existence was second nature to most angels — but Raziel had by now spent so much time in this world that it seemed a real possibility to him.

Angels were still linked here, but not as strongly as back home; the thin ether made their bond weaker, too. If the assassination of the rogues had happened in their own world, he knew he'd still be reeling from the pain of it; not here. As far as he could tell, the Council members' deaths shouldn't necessarily mean the deaths of them all.

As other likely outcomes flickered past, Raziel shrugged mentally. None of them concerned him very much. Even the risk to the human world seemed a chance worth taking, when the single constant in every scenario was the death of the Council. And he himself would most likely be executed soon enough anyway, for he had no intention of succumbing to their rule. So if the risk paid off, it would pay off big—and if it didn't, he most likely wouldn't be around to catch the blame.

"You do know what you're saying, I suppose," he said finally, regarding Charmeine as she stood against the door.

"Yes, I know." Charmeine's eyes were alive with challenge. "Are you a gambling man, Raz?"

The question was how.

Late that night, Raziel sat at his desk in a black silk dressing gown, catching up on his e-mails while he considered the problem. Several messages included links to news stories; he'd learned almost the moment he'd switched on his computer that the half angel's mother and aunt had been killed in an arson attack. Good—it saved him the trouble of doing away with his damaged ex-lover himself. For of course Miranda couldn't have been allowed to stay alive, now that he knew her identity and that he was the thing's father. The possibility that his secret might get out was sickening.

Around him, the wooden-paneled room was sedately opulent—a plush gray carpet, antique books and furniture, and in the daytime a soaring view of the Rocky Mountains. In his bedroom nearby slept Jenny, the devout who'd sat by his bedside while he was unconscious. When she'd returned with the other ejected humans after the Council's departure earlier—crying and throwing herself worriedly into his arms—Raziel had been gratified to discover just how attractive she was. Not to mention how delectable her energy tasted, after days of not being able to feed at all. Once alone with her, he'd plunged his hands deeply into her energy's turquoise lights and drunk and drunk, leaving her swaying on her feet but wide eyed with wonder. Her body was no less delectable as it turned out, made even more so by the fact that the Council had made its disapproval about this sort of thing clear in their meeting. Raziel felt much more himself again now; more able to deal with the problem at hand.

But there was no easy solution. Though the Twelve could be killed like other angels, their powers of psychic control over their brethren were far stronger than he'd suspected—as the mass execution today had illustrated so well. An angelic army, even assuming he could raise one, would fare no better than the traitors. No, what was needed were more . . . conventional means.

Mexico City.

Remembering the strange glimmer that had come as he showered earlier, Raziel frowned. And now he recalled that the moment in the shower hadn't been the first time. He'd had a sense of the girl while he was lying unconscious, too — had known then that she and Kylar were in a tent together, near the Mexican border. What was going on?

Clicking a few buttons, he brought up the Church of Angels' website. It still showed the girl's image on its home page: blond and smiling, her green eyes sparkling with suppressed laughter. His daughter. Picturing Jenny lying asleep in his bed, Raziel snorted. If he thought for a second that such a perverse fluke as Willow Fields could ever be repeated, he'd volunteer himself for death-by-Council immediately. No, the anomaly had clearly been something to do with Miranda rather than himself, though finding out exactly what it had been was impossible now.

What he *could* find out, though, was how he knew where Willow was. He relaxed back against his leather chair, then closed his eyes and went searching, allowing any knowledge to come as it would. Images of the moments in the cathedral before the Second Wave had arrived began drifting past. The long line of acolytes from all around the country, kneeling in homage. A girl's screams. Willow's startled face when she realized her disguise had been seen through; her mad dash to the gate, with her angel self flying overhead. Himself, blocking her angel from its task and feeling the disconcertingly familiar energy as their wings and auras had touched.

In fact . . . he could still sense her energy inside of

him, even now. It was as if Willow had left a small part of herself behind, like pollen brushed from a flower.

Raziel went very still as he considered what this might mean. Then he took a breath and journeyed more deeply within. The room, the chair, the hum of the computer all faded to nothing. Soon he'd found the spark of his daughter's energy: a silver-and-lavender glow. Grimacing at the unnatural half-angel feel, Raziel prodded it carefully with his thoughts. It responded and grew, lengthening into a rich, pulsing stream of information that led to a similar spark of his own energy, now residing inside Willow.

She was lying in a bed in Mexico City—she and Kylar had found other Angel Killers. The thought that had come to Raziel in the shower was correct: She knew about the Council. She and the others thought that to kill the Twelve would kill all angels but didn't seem aware of the other possibilities—had no clue that it could backfire horribly, so far as they were concerned.

Unconsciously, Raziel swiveled his chair from side to side as he took everything in: how Juan had stumbled on the information, the help of Luis, all their plans and schemes. A slow smile grew across his face. He'd never have believed it, but he actually had reason to be thankful that he'd spawned an offspring like some animal of the lower orders—because the family tie between them had now resulted in a psychic link, set in motion by their inadvertent exchange of energies in the cathedral. And Willow was completely unaware of it.

Though he had everything he needed for now, Raziel

somehow found himself lingering. Willow's energy was unmistakably half him — he'd have known she was his daughter even if she looked nothing like Miranda. *Strange,* he thought with a frown, letting the feel of it wash over him. It wasn't quite as unpleasant as he'd initially thought.

Willow's angel was stirring — the girl had sensed the rushing energy between them, though she had no idea what it was. Quickly but thoroughly, Raziel hid the spark of his energy that dwelled within Willow, disguising it so that it was as similar to her own essence as possible. He was finished and gone long before Willow knew what was happening.

As Raziel opened his eyes again, he was sure the girl would never suspect their psychic connection; he could carry out any further explorations with no risk of detection. Willow's own spark within him didn't worry him, either — if she hadn't gotten anything from him yet, she was unlikely to. Raziel sensed strongly that his greater psychic experience gave him the advantage. His daughter's skills were impressive, but sadly for her, they were hardly on par with someone who'd been refining them for millennia.

Seeing that his computer had switched to the Church of Angels screen saver, he tapped his mouse and brought back Willow's photo.

Maybe Paschar was right after all, he mused, steepling his fingers. Paschar, an angel who'd been killed by Kylar almost two months ago, had had a vision that Willow could destroy all angelkind. A half angel who might have the ability to annihilate them all: Raziel couldn't hold back a grin. Yes, that sounded like a fair contender for someone to take out the Council.

The first thing, of course, was to tone down the man-hunt against the two of them. Ironically, keeping Willow safe needed to be his top priority now. He'd make a few phone calls tomorrow — get the media to gradually back off. After a few weeks of not being bombarded with her image, the general public would forget; they had the attention span of a squirrel. The other angels wouldn't be nearly so easy to divert, but at least with the human portion of the Church pacified, Willow stood a chance of not being killed by a lynch mob.

The Angel Killers' plot was unlikely to succeed without some help, though. Fortunately, he'd be happy to provide a bit of fatherly assistance from behind the scenes. Soon Charmeine would be traveling down to Mexico City for a brief preliminary trip with some of the other Council lackeys. It would be child's play for her to meet this Luis person and give things an angelic helping hand. And in due course, once Willow and her boyfriend and their little team of assassins had fulfilled their purpose and done away with the Council for him, he'd have them all put to a slow, lingering death.

Assuming anyone was still alive at that point, of course.

CHAPTER EIGHT

THE GIRLS' DORM was a large room on the second floor. Cool terra-cotta tiles lay underfoot; there was a tall, arched window and four single beds. Though I was so tired that it felt like I'd been wrung out like a dishrag, I lay awake for hours that first night in my borrowed pajamas. Curled tight on my side, I tried to tell myself that somehow we were actually going to defeat the Council, and everything would be OK — that the premonition of sorrow that had hit me in front of the house hadn't meant anything at all.

Or the feeling of dread in my dream, either.

It wasn't easy to convince myself, when the hunting pack over the Zócalo had been exactly like what I'd foreseen. Recalling the rest of my dream — the strange boy in the park — I frowned into the darkness, a worried flutter passing through me. If what had happened in the Zócalo was true . . . I shook my head, irritated at myself.

There was just no way. The idea that I could ever care for another boy the way I did for Alex was insane.

Forget the dream, I decided. Not all of it was accurate; that was completely obvious — and reality was more than enough for the time being anyway, with Kara and the others all half afraid of me, watching my every move. *They'll get over it once they figure out I'm basically as human as they are,* I thought. I stared at the window, where a streetlight shone through the thin curtains. *It'll just take time.*

Remembering the atmosphere in the dorm when Kara had brought me in, I sighed. *OK, maybe a whole lot of time.* Liz and Trish looked nothing alike but could have been twins, the way they'd stood watching me side by side with their arms folded protectively over themselves. Liz's expression had been cold, her black hair half hanging over her face. Trish had looked scared and anxious, biting her lip — the look didn't really go with her freckles and cheerful snub nose.

"So, she's staying?" said Liz.

"Seems that way," replied Kara shortly. She was putting fresh sheets on the one empty bed; it was in the corner, slightly away from the others. I don't think anyone was too upset about that, including me.

I moved to help her. "Yeah, we're staying," I said over my shoulder to Liz, and caught her whispering something to Trish — who looked almost ready to cry when she saw me watching; she waved her hand at Liz in a frantic shushing motion.

I straightened up from the bed. "Look, I know this

must be really weird, but—" I stopped. They'd both frozen, as if a chair had suddenly started speaking. Great. Instead of alarming them further, I turned away and picked up the pajamas of Trish's that Kara had given me: blue with white polka dots.

"Is there a shower I could use?" I asked Kara. There hadn't been one in the bathroom she'd directed me to earlier, and I was dying to get rid of the grime from traveling all day on the Shadow.

"Yeah, but only one, unfortunately," said Kara, finishing with the bed. I was trying not to stare at her the way Liz and Trish were staring at me—the sculpted lines of her face were so exotically gorgeous. "The boys usually get it at night; we take ours in the morning," she went on without looking at me. "But if you wanted to go ahead, since it's your first night . . ."

"No, that's all right. I'll wait," I said with an inner sigh. I started to go get changed in the bathroom—the last thing I felt like doing was getting undressed with Liz and Trish scrutinizing my every move—and then I stopped. If I did that, they'd be imagining God knows what about me; that I had angel wings sprouting out of my shoulder blades or something. So I set my jaw and got changed right there, keeping my back to them and feeling their eyes burning holes in my skin.

"I, um . . . don't need those back, or anything," Trish blurted out as I pulled the spaghetti-strapped pajama top over my head.

"Thanks," I said, as if I didn't know exactly why she didn't want them anymore. And as everyone else started to get ready for bed, too, the silence in the dorm had felt like a heavy, smothering blanket.

Lying awake now, I was starting to seriously regret insisting that Alex and I didn't sleep in the same bed here. I could be with him this very moment, nestled in his arms and talking through the day's events. And then later — my cheeks tinged as I stared up at the high, old-fashioned ceiling; I counted its cracks in the glow of the streetlight to take my mind off the fact my heart was suddenly beating faster. Yes, good call on not sharing Alex's bed, Willow. Thumbs-up.

Then I stiffened.

I could hardly even describe what I'd just felt — it was like a sort of *rushing past*, as if I were standing beside a river and could sense the intensity of its current, ready to knock me off my feet. But it wasn't beside me: it was inside of me, so powerful that it felt like I'd get swept away if I even dipped a toe in.

The feeling lasted only seconds; then it faded. My forehead creased as I closed my eyes and went deep within, searching. Nothing. I looked again to be sure, carefully exploring every corner of my mind. The weird energy was gone, if it had really been there in the first place — there was no sign of it. I shook my head at myself. OK, psychic glitch time.

Then I became uneasily aware of my angel. Usually

she waited inside me to be sought out, but now all at once she was just *there* in my mind, watching me with her wings opening and closing.

I stared back at her, wondering what was going on. Ever since we'd bonded, her presence had always brought such a sense of love, of comfort. Now it seemed different. Edgy. My angel's shining face was my own, but my scalp chilled as I realized: there were different thoughts from mine behind her eyes. Thoughts I couldn't read.

That sense of rushing power, like something had been awakened.

Shaken, I withdrew and lay huddled under the covers, listening to the sounds of the others sleeping and the faint noise of traffic. I'd never been conscious of my angel having her own thoughts before; she'd always simply been me. What had just happened? And what would have occurred if I'd shifted my consciousness to hers — this radiant twin who suddenly felt like a stranger?

The idea brought a shiver of apprehension, and I hated it. I'd only barely gotten used to having this other part of me, and now suddenly it seemed so . . . alien. I let out a breath. Had I really just been thinking about how human I was? The irony wasn't funny, somehow.

It took me a long time to fall asleep. And even when I did, I could still sense my angel, restless inside of me.

"OK, today I want to see what each of you can do," said Alex.

We were standing in the firing range — a long room

on the ground floor that looked as if several walls had been knocked down to form it. There were arched windows down here, too—and though I hadn't noticed when we'd arrived, they'd been boarded up from the inside. No wonder the place had seemed abandoned. Kara had told me that morning that Juan had bought it free and clear, plus all of their equipment. Apparently being a CIA-sponsored AK paid a lot, which wasn't really news, given Alex's Porsche when I'd first met him. And like Alex, Juan had squirreled away part of his money in cash, though clearly on a far greater scale.

"So we've got enough to keep us going for a while," Kara had said as she got dressed that morning, and I tried not to gape at her perfect body. She was so sleek and toned; she actually had a tiny six-pack. And an AK tattoo on her left bicep, just like Alex's. A strange feeling stirred through me at the sight of its gothic letters; I'd always associated that tattoo only with Alex.

She caught me studying her and stiffened, snapping a T-shirt over her head. "What?"

"Nothing," I said. "Sorry. You just—look like you're in really good shape—that's all. I guess I'm not, that much." It was true. I'd always been thin without trying, but I used to get C's and D's in PE, because my best friend Nina and I would just sit and talk half the time. Sadness pierced me at the thought of Nina. God, what must she think of me now?

"Huh," said Kara, her brown eyes narrowing as if she didn't quite believe I hadn't been up to something. "Well.

We'll get you into shape," she said grudgingly.

"So what's *she* going to be doing?" asked Sam as we all stood in the firing range.

"Excuse me?" said Alex coldly. He was wearing faded jeans and a black T-shirt he'd borrowed from someone. I'd never seen him wearing black before; it made his dark hair look a shade lighter, his eyes almost bright blue.

"Her. Your half-angel girlfriend," repeated Sam in his Texas drawl, folding his arms over his muscular chest. His short blond hair was spiky with gel. "I'm assuming she's going to be part of the team, right?"

The news that Alex was taking over as lead had been met with a mix of wariness and something like relief. Everyone obviously respected Kara, and admired her for stepping in after Juan died — but no one argued that she should stay in charge now that Alex was here. Remembering the apprehension I'd picked up from him that night in the tent, I watched him closely now, trying to send him good vibes. He didn't seem to need them. No matter what he might have been feeling inside, there was no hint he was even nervous as he stood facing the group.

"OK, I want to get a few things straight with all of you," he said, and though his voice was calm, I could tell how irritated he was. "*She* has a name. It's Willow. And yes, she is going to be part of the team. This is her fight, too. She cares as much about defeating the angels as any of you."

I tried to smile as everyone glanced sideways at me. I could feel the suspicion in the room, as if a snake had just slithered through it.

"If you're accepting me as lead, then you're also accepting Willow," Alex went on. "Because I'd trust her with my life. So I do not, repeat, *do not* want to hear any crap from anyone about her. Yes, she's half angel; no, she is not going to harm you in any way. And that is seriously the last time I ever want to have this conversation. Is that understood?"

Mumbled *yeses*. Sam looked like he was about to say something else, then thought better of it. My cheeks were in flames. I understood why Alex had had to do this, but part of me wanted the floor to splinter open and drop me into the core of the earth.

"Good," said Alex finally. "Let's get started. Kara, can you get everyone going with some target practice? Willow doesn't know how to shoot yet; I need to give her some basic training."

Oh. I'd forgotten that I'd promised to learn how to shoot. But even with my lifelong dislike of guns, it was still ten times better than just standing there while everyone avoided looking at me. Alex took me to the back of the firing range where there was a table, to show me how to load a magazine.

"You're doing great," I whispered to him. "Seriously."

He made a face as he looked down at the pistol he was holding. "Yeah . . . I guess we'll see how it goes." He pulled the magazine out with a *click* and discharged the cartridges, then started pressing them back in again in a smooth, rapid motion. "OK, look, this is really easy — all you do is push them down, one on top of the other."

I hesitated, wondering what was bothering him. I knew he must be even more worried about the situation with the Council than I was, when he was the one responsible for training everyone. But this felt like something else.

He glanced at me; a slight smile appeared. "You know, you sort of have to watch what I'm doing if you're going to learn this. Here, I'll do it again."

This time I took in the steady rhythm of his thumb as he pressed the cartridges in. "Like a PEZ dispenser," I said. All around us were the faint thuds of silenced bullets. They weren't loud, but they were *intense*; you could feel the whole room vibrating with them.

"Yeah, exactly." Alex took the cartridges out again and handed me the empty magazine. "And listen, I'm sorry about just now, with the group," he added in an undertone. "Hope I didn't embarrass you."

"It's OK," I said, thinking how strange it was for us to be standing this far apart. I'd gotten so used to touching Alex whenever I wanted — it seemed as natural to me as breathing. I knew he felt the same. Earlier that morning, he'd pulled me into one of the storerooms as I'd come out of the shower room wearing a borrowed bathrobe; he'd stroked my damp hair back with both hands, kissing me deeply, the two of us pressed up against the wall in the shadows.

"I missed you last night," he'd whispered between kisses.

"Me, too . . . me, too," I'd murmured. His arms had

felt so safe around me, as if the weird sensations of the night before would never have happened if I hadn't been sleeping away from him. As if they weren't important at all anymore.

I swallowed as I looked down at the magazine, struggling to push a cartridge in. I'd been trying not to focus on it, but that sense of my angel being restless was still there. I was so conscious of her as a separate presence that she almost felt loose inside of me; I was reminded of Peter Pan trying to sew his shadow back on. God, I hated this — not knowing what was going on with my own body.

"Hey. What's up?" asked Alex.

I shoved my worries down as far as they'd go and slammed a door on them. There was no way I was telling Alex this; it was too not-human for me to even want to think about it. "Nothing. I'm fine."

He rested a hip against the table, watching me carefully. "Those girls haven't been giving you a hard time, have they?"

"No. Well, a little. Nothing major." I maneuvered another cartridge into the magazine. It wasn't nearly as easy as it looked. You had to angle the cartridge in just right and hold down the one below it at the same time. "How did you do this so fast, anyway?"

He glanced down at my hands. "Practice. Plus it's easier if you hold the bottom of the magazine against yourself, to steady it — remember how I propped it against my stomach? What do you mean, 'nothing major'?"

Holding the magazine against myself did make it

easier, and the cartridges started to go in with a steady rhythm. I shook my head — Liz and Trish staring at me while I put on my jammies was really the least of my worries. "Seriously, Alex, it's OK. I've got to make my own way with them, you know? It's no good if my boyfriend, the lead AK, gets all involved every time someone looks at me funny."

I could tell he understood, even if he didn't like it much. "Yeah, all right," he said finally. "But listen, I have to make sure that everything's running smoothly with the team. So if it gets to the point where it might affect that, then I need to know, OK?"

"Deal," I said in a soft voice. His eyes were so warm, so concerned. The rhythm of the cartridges slowed as I took in the familiar strong lines of his face and the raw-looking bruise on his cheek where Sam had hit him. My gaze lingered on the bruise. I wanted to stroke it better, feather light kisses all over it. In fact, I just wanted to kiss him, period, so much that it hurt.

He grinned suddenly, and my heart turned over. "Oh man, don't look at me like that, or we're going to cause a scandal in the AK house."

And for a minute I felt better, just standing near him and seeing his smile. "Look at you like what?" I finished loading the magazine and put it down on the table.

"Yeah, you know *exactly* like what. Like you're thinking about the broom closet — that's what." Unobtrusively, he put his hand over mine on the table, stroking my index finger lightly. We smiled at each other; then he glanced over his shoulder and the smile faded. His expression turned preoccupied, intent. "I'd better get over there, see how they're each doing. Do you want to practice this for a while? I'll be back soon to start teaching you how to shoot."

He showed me how to empty the magazine and then went over to the others. My gaze followed him without meaning to, drinking in the firm set of his shoulders under the T-shirt, his rumpled dark hair. The sense of confidence that shone through without him even being aware of it, just in the way he walked — so easy and relaxed.

And then I saw something that I really didn't know what to think about.

Kara was looking at him in the same way.

As the days passed, things settled into a routine.

I learned how to shoot. Started target practice with the others. Watched the news a lot like everyone else, to see what was going on in the world now. And we all tried to avoid bumping into each other like peas in a can. There weren't that many of us in the house, but it always felt crowded — apart from the dorms, there was only the firing range, the kitchen, the TV room, and a couple of storage rooms, which were so full of boxes, you could hardly get into them, anyway. There was also a tiny gym in the basement, with a few exercise machines and free weights. Everyone worked out. I did, too, since I was going stir-crazy — Alex didn't want me outside on my own until he was satisfied I could defend myself. He wasn't just being protective of his girlfriend; the same thing was true for the other AKs, apart from Kara.

Other AKs. It was strange to realize that's what I was now.

Alex hadn't been satisfied at all with the way the first target practice went. Afterward he'd told the group they were way too static—great at shooting if nothing was moving, but unfortunately angels had this funny habit of not just standing there motionless with bullets coming at them. He rigged up targets that swung wildly from the ceiling and made them start practicing with those instead. In no time, the wall behind the targets was peppered with bullet holes, as if the room had been through a war.

"Man, this sucks," complained Sam a few days later, red-faced with frustration as he missed again. The target swung about on its chain: a manic, mocking pendulum. "It's all we've been doing for days! When are we gonna get out there and hunt some angels for real, so we can get ready for the Council?"

"When you're over ninety percent on the moving targets," said Alex shortly. He took Sam's pistol and aimed at the still-bouncing target; he shot once, twice, a third time. Bull's-eye each time. Silence fell over the group as they watched.

"That's what I want," said Alex. He handed Sam's gun back. "Until you can do that, you're not getting anywhere near an angel again—period. You're no good to me unless you can actually hit them."

No one said anything as he put them back to work, but it was as if a ripple of determination had passed through the group, as if they all suddenly got it. He kept everyone practicing for hours each day; when they weren't doing that, he made sure they were working out, keeping in shape. He discussed strategy with the team, too, drilling it into them — like, what to do when you're under direct attack, so you don't lead the angels straight back to your doorstep.

He was an excellent teacher — patient and good at explaining things — but I could tell he never forgot that in just over ten weeks, he had to have everyone trained for what might be humanity's only real chance against the angels. Though he never even hinted to the others that he had reservations about being in charge, I knew how heavily the responsibility weighed on him. It showed in his face, his eyes, making him look so much older than eighteen that it wrung my heart. And while I'd never met his father, as I watched Alex explaining diagrams at the kitchen table with everyone crowded around him, I somehow knew he was his dad all over again.

The TV showed that the world had changed already. Before, it was possible to go a day or two without hearing a reference to the angels. Not anymore. Almost every time you changed the channel, you got a talk show where los ángeles were being discussed, or a documentary about true-life angelic stories, or a music video with everyone bopping around in angel wings. We got CNN and a few other American channels on cable, and it was exactly the same in the United States. There were new TV shows galore: Who's the Angel?, Angelic Paths, Angels 1-2-3. They all looked sort of cheesy and rapidly thrown together but were obviously meeting a huge demand; everyone wanted to drown themselves in images of their predators. On the news, random street shots always showed people wearing angel wings: a new fad meaning you'd seen an angel. The camera often caught someone gazing dreamily into the distance, too, basking in the glow of a beautiful creature only they could see.

With all that, it wasn't surprising that the problem of overcrowded hospitals was getting worse. I remembered the documentary I'd seen back in Tennessee: the beds lining the hospital corridors; the teenage girl with exhausted, angel-burnt eyes. That was only a couple of months ago, and now those images seemed practically upbeat. In both the United States and Mexico, people were literally dying on hospital floors. You sometimes couldn't even get an ambulance now or find a hospital that could take you in. Protests were springing up all over, with people demanding that the government do something. Here in Mexico City, things were even worse, because renovating the cathedral into a Church of Angels had been paid for with taxpayers' money. Most people were all for it, but a group calling themselves the Crusaders for People's Rights were furious that the funds hadn't been used for medical care. Protests here were turning into sizzling confrontations, with the "Crusaders" and the "Faithful" screaming at each other on a regular basis.

We saw Raziel once on TV, too.

He was in his human form, walking through the Denver cathedral — apparently pointing out the damage, though the commentary was in Spanish. I sat stiffly on the battered sofa, unable to take my eyes away — and was so, so glad that nobody except Alex knew this was my father.

"That jerk," muttered Kara. Often she was out with Luis in the evenings, trying to get information, but she was home for a change — perched cross-legged in the armchair, painting her toenails. "You know, I hate all the angels, but that one is really something else. I want to throw stuff at the screen whenever I see him."

"Yeah, you're not the only one," said Alex, beside me on the sofa. He discreetly took my hand, squeezing it as the camera panned around the cathedral. There was scaffolding up, and dozens of workers were busy repairing the buckled floor and collapsed section of ceiling. I stared at the spot where I'd crouched only weeks before, my muscles clenching as I remembered what it had felt like to die.

Raziel appeared again. Jet-black hair; a refined, sensitive face. And long, slender hands that had buried themselves deep in my mother's energy field when she was only a twenty-year-old music student at NYU. As he spoke, Spanish subtitles scrolled across the bottom of the screen. "Yes, repairs are almost finished now," he said. "We're looking forward to getting back to business as usual and putting all of this behind us."

"And you, sir, you claim you're an angel yourself?"

Raziel gave a small, wise smile directly at the camera. An almost-dimple appeared in one cheek; his eyebrows arched good-humoredly. "It's not a claim; it's the simple truth. My kind are now living among you, to bring hope in these troubled times."

Hatred twisted in my stomach. He sure hadn't brought hope to my mother.

"Can we expect many differences, now that more angels have arrived?" asked the reporter. "Will the Church of Angels be making any changes?"

Raziel's benign expression vanished as his brown eyes narrowed — all at once I was looking again at the same deadly angel Alex and I had confronted in the cathedral. "No," he said. "There will be no changes to the Church." His smile returned, almost as pleasant as before, though I could see the calculation under it. "No changes at all," he repeated deliberately. "That is my promise."

I held back a shudder. For a weird second, it had felt as if he were looking right at *me*, as if he could actually see me through the screen somehow. As usual now, that slight sense of my angel shifting within me was there, and I tried to push it away, suddenly sickly aware of how *not* human I was — with this thing inside me and Raziel for a dad. Oh, God, I'd thought all of this was something I'd gotten used to. It so wasn't.

At least the manhunt for us seemed to have calmed down, though our pictures still flashed on the screen occasionally. I stared at my photo whenever it appeared, wondering who that blond girl with the bright smile was. Kara always teased Alex about the terrible drawing that made him look like an aging football player — and whenever he managed to unwind a little, he teased her, too, with stories from their life back at the camp. I could see the real affection between them, but it seemed so totally brother-sister on both sides that I thought I must have been insane to have imagined how soft and shining Kara's eyes had become as she watched Alex that first training day.

Except I didn't really think I was.

After what Alex had told them, none of the AKs gave me a hard time — but none of them spoke to me much, either. And this was not exactly a quiet group. They were always talking, arguing, bantering. Brendan was from Portland, Oregon, and like a terrier, all wiry hair and hyper energy. The only thing he and Sam agreed on was the need to rid the world of angels; they'd bicker about politics for hours, with Brendan clawing at his head and practically shrieking with frustration — "Man, how can you *think* that? Are you even listening to how ignorant you sound?"

Eventually Trish would step in and try to defuse things in her gentle way. Everyone liked her so much that Brendan might subside for a while, grumbling, and then Sam would make another drawling comment and they'd be off again. Liz was just as bad, dropping biting little remarks into the conversation and goading things along.

She was also the self-designated cook, which was

something I loved to do, too — but when I'd suggested that maybe we could take turns, she'd stiffened as if I planned to sprinkle poison in the food. So I dropped it. It wasn't worth it. Even with the others, "prickly" seemed to be Liz's default setting, though she and Trish got along really well. Once I walked into the girls' dorm to find them talking earnestly together. "I don't think you should blame yourself," Trish was saying. "Everyone's family has issues."

Then they saw me and clammed up. Liz scowled, lifting her chin; as always, Trish looked alarmed and slightly tense to have me around. "Sorry to interrupt," I said. Neither answered, and I held back a sigh as I got my shampoo and towel and left the dorm. The ironic thing is I think Trish and I could have been friends — she was so *nice*; there was no other word for her. But it was obvious how wary she was of me and how much she hated the strain I'd brought to the group.

Wesley was the only quiet one, always hunched over his laptop, more given to sullen grunts than talking. At first I thought he hated everyone, then I realized he was just excruciatingly shy. Though there was something else there, too — once I got a sense of sorrow from him so strong I almost said something. The *keep away* expression on his face told me to forget it. Mostly he avoided me, the same as everyone else, while I tried to ignore the fact that I was being avoided. As if there weren't this huge unspoken *thing* about me that made everyone stiffen if I accidentally stood too close.

I mentally gave myself a shake whenever I caught

myself thinking like that. I hated feeling this way; it was totally unlike me to be self-pitying. But I was just . . . really lonely. I missed Alex, even though we were in the same house together. There wasn't anyplace we could truly be alone here. The dorms and the kitchen always had people going in and out; the firing range and the exercise room were pretty un-ideal. The TV room always had someone in it — such as Brendan, who had insomnia and was usually surfing the Internet on his own laptop at three in the morning.

Though Alex's tiny bedroom should have been a haven, it wasn't much of one, because it was right off the boys' dorm. As in you had to pass directly through the dorm to get to it. When any of the guys were out there, we could hear their murmurs of conversation — so obviously we could be heard as well. And somehow Alex being the lead meant we couldn't just tell them to get out; it would have felt like he was getting special privileges or something.

So we could kiss, we could touch . . . but we couldn't let ourselves get too carried away. I was so aware of the box Alex had bought on our way down to Mexico City, still sitting in his bag unopened. He was, too — understatement — but neither of us mentioned it. Like me, I knew how much Alex wanted it to be perfect for us when it happened — not feeling tense because someone might hear or having to sneak down to the sweaty-smelling exercise room.

Anyway, that was bad enough, but not being able to

talk the way we used to was even worse. Alex had noticed how things were for me, though. "I'm sorry," he said in a low voice when we'd been there for over a week. "I know you're not very happy here."

We were closeted away in his bedroom for a few minutes before dinner; distantly, I could hear the TV going. "I'm fine," I whispered back. "Don't worry about me; this is what we have to be doing. And besides . . . you don't exactly seem happy, either." I traced the dark curve of his eyebrow. Obviously *being happy* wasn't the point, not when what we were doing was so crucial to the world. Neither of us would have chosen to be anywhere else, even if we could. But still, it made me sad when I realized that whole days had gone past since the last time I'd seen Alex really smile — that gorgeous, easy grin that melted my heart.

"I do worry about you," he said, ignoring what I'd said about his own happiness. "Willow, listen, if we manage to do this — if we actually defeat them — it'll be so different for you and me then. I promise —"

He broke off as we heard someone enter the dorm, moving around and getting changed. After that we fell silent, just letting the feel of our lips together do the talking for us.

Most of our conversations were like that now — snatched sentences; a quick touching of base with no time for details. I missed sleeping in the same bed as Alex. I missed it so acutely that I just lay awake aching for him sometimes, longing to slip through the dark house and go to him. I hadn't really known before just how much we *talked* as we lay in bed together, or how precious those soft conversations in the dark were to me.

And I thought if I could only lie curled up in his arms again and know that we were alone — really alone, the way we used to be — then maybe I'd be able to tell him how scared I was.

I hadn't contacted my angel since that first night, but I could *feel* her there, all the time. As the days had passed, her restless shifting had intensified into what seemed like a longing to break free. I became so self-conscious, trying to get through my days without letting on that this was happening. Without really letting on to myself, even. But it felt like everyone knew, anyway — because sometimes the nape of my neck would start prickling, as if they were all staring. Occasionally someone would be there when I checked; more often I'd find myself looking at an empty space. And meanwhile I could sense my angel, straining against me. What frightened me the most was that it was starting to take an effort to hold her back, like struggling to hang on to a tugging kite.

My life in Pawtucket was like something that had happened on another planet: Willow Fields, who, OK, was maybe sort of strange because of fixing cars and being psychic, but who had a pretty boring, ordinary life, actually. And who definitely didn't feel like a stranger inside her own body. I could hardly believe now that such a time had really existed, when I'd just felt . . . normal.

Human.

CHAPTER NINE

THE PARADE took Seb by surprise.

It had been just over two weeks now since he'd hitch-hiked down to El DF, and he'd spent every moment of daylight looking for the girl in the photo; he only vaguely knew what day of the week it was anymore. But now as he walked back to his hostel near the *centro*, he saw that it must be Revolution Day. A mariachi band was play-ing, with its warbling singers and the jaunty sound of guitars and horns, and there was a parade passing by — schoolchildren dressed as soldiers: the boys in sombreros and bullet belts, with eyebrow-pencil mustaches; the girls in long, bright skirts and snowy-white blouses, their hair in braids. Behind them was a group of older girls in green T-shirts, dancing and waving Mexican flags.

With his knapsack over his shoulder — there was no way he'd leave it in the hostel during the day — Seb edged through the crowd lining the sidewalk. A few angel wings brushed him as he passed. Everywhere he went now, people were wearing them. The mood of the crowd was exuberant, their auras practically bouncing against him; even those that were stunted with angel damage shimmered with excitement.

It was the same city he'd always known and yet completely different. The angels were everywhere — he'd noticed it even though he was spending most of his time wandering around Bosque de Chapultepec, searching for the same configuration of trees that had been in the girl's dream. It was turning out to be a heartbreaking task; Chapultepec was one of the largest city parks in the world. But in the meantime, hardly an hour went by when Seb didn't see a few angels cruising overhead, like white eagles on the hunt. Each time he passed the Zócalo, there were several swooping over it as well; others fed right on the sidewalk. Curiosity had taken him briefly inside the converted cathedral — he couldn't believe what had happened to the place — and here, too, angels had been hunting. He was so used to keeping his aura dim and unappealing that he did it almost without thinking.

"Hospitals for all!" shouted a voice. "We need more beds, more doctors!" Glancing over his shoulder as he crossed the street — darting between the girl dancers and a burro pulling a flower-laden cart — Seb saw a large group approaching carrying signs: EL DF IS DYING FOR MORE DOCTORS and ANGELS DON'T NEED MONEY — THE SICK DO!

Immediately, the mood of the crowd changed, the auras around him practically crackling with emotion. A woman sitting in a wheelchair yelled, "The angels would help you if you had faith!" Her cheeks looked sunken, her eyes fervent. Several voices called out in agreement, booing the group marching past.

Seb was glad to leave it all behind and reach the street that his hostel was on. Though even here, it looked like they were getting ready for some kind of dance later: a stage was being set up, and green, white, and red bunting hung from all the wrought-iron balconies above. The hostel's outer walls, once tan, were now smudged gray with pollution. Seb knew he'd been lucky to get a bed. Like every other hostel in the city, the place was packed with Church of Angels followers from around the world, here to see the newly converted cathedral. He passed a few of them now on the way to his dorm — a trio of pretty French girls in angel wings whom he'd encountered a few times in the lounge in the evenings.

"*Bonsoir*, Seb," said one of them, Céline, with a flirtatious smile as they passed. "*Ça va toi?*" He summoned up a smile as he returned the greeting, trying not to notice how sick her aura looked. Being around people who'd been hurt by the angels depressed him; he tried to avoid it.

Thankfully, his dorm was empty. Seb stretched out on his bed and lay staring upward. His birthday had come the week before, making him eighteen now; he hadn't even realized it until the next day. All he could think of was the half-angel girl — she was so close now that he could almost feel her, yet in a way she seemed farther away than ever. To know that she was probably right here, in this very city—only a few miles away from him at most—but to have no idea *where* exactly, was agony.

The framed photo was a small, solid rectangle in his jeans pocket. He didn't need to take it out to bring back the girl's image; he knew it by heart now. The sense of her spirit was with him already, just as it had been for so many years—and since touching her shirt, with its whispers of her energy, this sense felt even stronger: a line drawing brought richly to life with color. Seb shoved his hair back as he regarded the dingy plaster ceiling. God, he was in love with a girl he'd never even spoken to. But he *knew* her, inside and out.

Could she sense him as strongly? Had she always been in love with a shadow, too?

Outside, music had started up. With a restless sigh, Seb swung his feet off the bed and went to the ancient French windows; he swung them open with a creak and stepped out onto the small wrought-iron balcony. On the street below, couples were beginning to dance; paper lanterns cast a festive light. Seb stood against the railing, looking down.

During the day he was single-minded. Mostly he searched Bosque de Chapultepec, but he went to other parks, too—always scanning, never letting himself believe for a second that he wouldn't find her. It was these other, quieter times when doubt swamped him, leaving him cold. What if he'd gotten the girl's dream wrong? What if the park they'd seemed to be in wasn't in El DF at all, but somewhere else? She was American; it could be someplace in her own country — thousands of miles of it, with probably millions of parks. He'd most likely never find her at all, if that was the case. And to know that she really existed, that she wasn't a dream, but to never be able to locate her . . . Seb swallowed. No. He wouldn't believe that. He couldn't.

The door opened behind him. "Oh, hey, Seb," said a voice.

Mike, one of the Americans staying in the dorm — and one of the few people at the hostel undamaged by the angels. "Hi," said Seb from the balcony. Mike joined him; he was nineteen, with floppy brown hair and a friendly smile.

"So what's this all about, anyway?" he asked, resting his forearms on the railing as he took in the dancing. "Is it like the Fourth of July back home?"

Shoving his thoughts away with an effort, Seb tried to remember what he'd heard about the American holiday. "What's the Fourth of July? You have fireworks then, yes?"

In that way Americans sometimes had, Mike looked surprised that Seb didn't know — though *he* had no idea what Revolution Day was. "It's when we got our independence from England," he explained. "You know — the Boston Tea Party, Paul Revere. And yeah, lots of fireworks."

Seb nodded, remembering now. "It's sort of like that," he said. "It celebrates the day we started fighting to get rid of the *dictador* Porfirio Díaz."

"You got rid of a dictator? Cool," said Mike cheerfully. "And anyway, any excuse for a party, right?"

This made Seb laugh in spite of himself. "Yes, if you're Mexican. We like parties."

"Man, you're not the only ones. You should come to America sometime. Folks love to party there."

Seb knew he might have to someday, if his search in El DF proved fruitless. Except how could he ever leave, when the rest of the girl's dream had so obviously taken place here? Her light-blue shirt was still folded neatly in his knapsack, but he resisted the urge to bring it out again; its images were becoming fainter each time he touched the soft fabric, diluting the girl's energy with his own.

The evening softened into darkness, the lanterns glowing as the jubilant sound of guitars and trumpets soared around them. Mike had brought some cold beers into the room; he offered one to Seb, and they stood drinking them, gazing down at the swirling dancers.

"So I'm planning on going to Tepito tomorrow," said Mike, leaning against the wall and stretching his legs out. "Can't find anything about it in the guidebook, but it's north of here, isn't it?"

Seb was smoking a cigarette as he thought about the park again — wondering if he should focus more on its woodsy third section instead of the more popular first and second ones. At Mike's words, he blew out a quick breath of smoke and glanced at him, startled. "What? Why?"

"To see it, man. I want to see all of this place."

"No," said Seb flatly. "Don't go there."

Mike blinked. "Why not? It's just a market, right?"

"It's the worst *barrio* in the city," said Seb. "A gringo with a camera and cell phone who barely speaks Spanish? They'd think Christmas had come early this year. You'd be robbed in minutes, or worse." It was where he was from. The dark streets of Tepito, with their rustling plastic roofs from vendors' stalls, were as familiar to him as the various scars on his body — and living there had been just as enjoyable as getting them.

The American looked skeptical. "It can't really be *that* bad, can it?"

"Yes," said Seb. "Trust me — stay away. Go do all the tourist things in your guidebook. They don't put Tepito in there for a reason." He smiled, took another puff of his cigarette. "The paddle boats in Chapultepec Park are very nice."

Mike made a face; he opened his mouth to say something else and then glanced at the dancing below. "Hey, look at that." He laughed, propping his forearms on the railing again as he looked down. "The little scamp."

Crushing out his cigarette, Seb followed his gaze and saw a street child slipping through the crowd that stood watching the dancers — a girl of seven or so, with tousled dark hair. Seen from above, her hand motion was clear as she dipped it into a man's jacket pocket and then out again, quickly tucking whatever she'd found under her shirt. Seb smiled slightly, remembering all too well the feel of it — the quick flex of the fingers, the grasp and pull, all the while making sure you didn't touch the sides of the pocket.

Mike went back to talking about Tepito; Seb's eyes stayed on the girl, watching as she maneuvered through the crowd. Too thin, and so young, with big brown eyes and a dirty face. He knew she probably lived in one of the abandoned buildings not far from the *centro*, or maybe down in the sewers. It was a tough life—God, such a tough life, with so many dangers to it. Even now, years later, he was amazed sometimes that he'd made it out alive.

It had still been better than that place they'd put him in.

"Well, what about the Lagunilla Market?" Mike was asking. "Is that one all right to go to?"

"Yes, it's not too bad," said Seb distantly. "Just stay in the streets near Francisco Bocanegra and Comonfort; it's safer at that end."

"OK, thanks." Mike smiled. "Hey, maybe I'll ask those three French girls to come with me, if I can drag them away from the cathedral. You want to come, too? I think that one, Céline, has a thing for you."

Seb started to answer but broke off as he caught sight of an angel gliding overhead. He shifted his aura to dull grays and brought it as close to his body as he could, so that it appeared shrunken. On the balcony beside him, Mike's aura looked far too healthy. He found himself edging closer, attempting to hide it a little. The angel cruised silently past, almost level with them. Seb tried to look as if he couldn't see it, but its radiance burned itself into his skull anyway — the proud, fierce face; the powerful wings that seemed to glow blue-white, every feather outlined.

"'Cause I heard her talking with her friends yesterday," Mike went on. "And if my high-school French wasn't failing me, she was saying that she thinks you're really hot. Wondering if you're a devout or not." He grinned. "My advice? Just pretend that you are, man. Tell her how much you lo-ove the angels."

Seb was barely listening to him. Below, the angel had chosen its victim, landing in a flurry of wings on the festive street.

It was the street girl.

Seb went very still, staring. He'd never seen an angel choose a child to feed from before. The girl was gazing up at the angel with a look of awestruck joy on her face; her energy was pale blue. It wavered like a soap bubble, looking young and vulnerable.

"Seb?" He felt Mike shove his arm with a laugh. "You awake over there? God, I wish I had so many gorgeous girls drooling over me that I could take it in stride." He stroked his jaw with a musing expression. "Maybe it's the stubble. I could always stop shaving. . . ."

"Thanks, but I can't — I've got some things to do tomorrow." Seb heard his voice say the words. Somehow it sounded normal. Below, the angel was advancing on the girl, smiling, stretching out its shining hands toward her. With no conscious thought, Seb switched his awareness to his angel self and flew out in a rush, swooping down so quickly that the lanterns and the dancers were a blur.

He hovered in front of the girl, spreading his wings wide. The angel drew back with a flapping hiss. It was a male, and its gaze widened abruptly when it saw that Seb had no halo. "You — how —?"

"Not this one," said Seb. He had never spoken in his angel form before, but his voice came out with no hesitation, low and hard. Inside, he was screaming at himself. *What are you doing? For the first time in your life, you're so close to finding her — and you're risking it for this?*

"Another one!" snarled the angel. "Half-human mutant — you shouldn't even exist!" It came at him in a fury of brightness; Seb fought it back, beating at it with his wings. He sensed that it was scanning in great sweeps of thought, searching for the feel of his energy to find his human form. He could disguise his aura's look but not its feel; it would be on him in seconds.

A brief, frenzied attack, and then Seb darted away and whirled to face the girl. Her eyes were huge, full of wonder. They stared right through him. His spirits sank; he had meant to tell her to run, but she couldn't see or hear him — only her predator, whose mind was linked with hers. Behind him, he heard the angel cry out in triumph; it had found his human self. Unless Seb managed to destroy the creature, it would simply kill him and feed off the girl anyway.

No, he thought, staring at her small, grimy face. Many things had happened in his life that he couldn't stop — but he would stop this.

On the balcony above, Mike had lifted an eyebrow. "Really? What are you doing that's better than hanging out with three French girls who think you're hot? 'Cause this I have *got* to hear."

Without answering, Seb straightened quickly, shoving his beer at Mike; he took off at a run just as he saw the angel come swarming up toward him. He flung himself out of the dorm and barreled down the hallway; raced down the stairs. As he burst out the front door, he knew that mere seconds had passed. The angel was now nowhere in sight as it searched for him, gliding through the upper floor of the hostel.

And in doing so, it had, for the moment at least, broken its connection with the girl.

Seb came to a skidding halt in front of her, crouched down so he could look her in the eyes. She still seemed dazed — there was a happy smile playing at her lips as she stared after the angel. He gripped her thin shoulders and shook them fiercely. "Run, *niña!* Don't ask questions — just go — go!"

He gave her a shove; the girl gasped and seemed to come back to herself. With a frightened, startled look, she took off at a run, vanishing into the crowd.

Seb's own angel was hovering overhead, looking out for when the creature reappeared. His human self rose slowly as he stared at the hostel. It was too late for him to try to get away; it knew he was here and would stop at nothing to find him now — and besides, his knapsack was still upstairs with the girl's shirt inside. He couldn't leave it. Distantly, he was aware of Mike up on the balcony, gaping down at him, of the rollicking music and the dancers still twirling past.

The angel came soaring out of the building. It saw him standing on the street below almost immediately, its beautiful face creasing in fury. Seb's angel form darted in front of it, and the creature roared and charged at him in the air, burning with light.

The two battled fiercely in the street over the dance, flapping and struggling with each other; Seb felt the sizzle of the angel's energy where their wings touched. The halo — he had to get to it; it was the way he'd defeated the only other angel he'd ever fought. But the creature's great wings kept him at bay as they writhed together in the air — the angel trying to get to Seb's human form, with its vulnerable life force, Seb straining to reach that gleaming, pulsing circle.

"Hey, what's going on? Are you OK?" Mike had come out and was on the street beside him now, holding both bottles of beer. "Dude, you look like you're seeing ghosts or something."

Seb shook his head, unable to take his eyes off the invisible battle above. His angel self was fast and strong, but he could feel that he was tiring. The angel snarled at him as they collided again, shoving at him with its wings.

"I'm fine," he said with an effort. "Mike, go inside. Don't stay out here."

Mike laughed uncertainly. "What — is this another

dangerous place like Tepito? Yeah, we've got all these scary grannies and granddads dancing past — don't know what they might do."

Seb started to speak but knew with a chill that it was too late — the angel had seen Mike standing with him. He saw its eyes narrow; it plunged at the angel Seb with an even greater ferocity. *No!* Seb's angel managed to hold it off, his wings flashing in the light of the lanterns. Then the angel darted; Seb lunged, but it wrenched away, soaring straight at Mike — not bonding with him, just attacking for all it was worth.

Seb grasped the thing's plan instantly, knew it was a trap — but he couldn't let Mike be hurt when he'd only been trying to see if Seb was OK. His angel self put on a burst of speed, whipping in front of Mike to protect him just as he'd protected the girl. He stretched out his wings as the angel came at him in a frenzy of radiance. Mike kept talking, oblivious of the drama being played out only feet away.

In his human form, Seb's heart was thumping. He put his hand in the back pocket of his jeans, and his fingers closed around his switchblade.

As he'd known it would, the angel went for him while his angel self was still shielding Mike. Seb didn't let himself think. Dodging sideways to avoid its outstretched hands, he flicked out the blade to his knife and went for the halo before the angel could strike him with its wing. The blade glowed white as it sliced through; for an agonized second, his arm felt like it was on fire. Then the sound of the angel's screams — an explosion of light that knocked him off his feet.

It was gone.

Seb lay where he was on the sidewalk, breathing hard as the remnants of the creature glittered gently over the dance. He brought his angel back to himself, relishing the feel of it safe inside of him. He had done it. He had actually done it. The half-angel girl flashed in his mind, and the realization that he was still alive and still had a chance to find her was like diving into a clear mountain pool.

"Uh . . . Seb?" Mike was squatting beside him. "Tell me that was some kind of Mexican folk dance, right? And that you didn't *really* just start leaping around with a switchblade for no reason at all."

Seb smiled. With an effort, he sat up. He was still holding the switchblade; he flicked the knife away and stuck it back in his pocket. Then he took his beer from Mike, pulling at it in a long sip. "Folk dance," he said as the singers warbled into the night around them, guitars strumming. "It was definitely a folk dance."

Mike shook his head. Settling cross-legged next to Seb on the sidewalk, he said, "You Mexicans are weird."

"But you like us."

"Yeah. Guess I'm weird, too."

Seb sat gazing at the dancers, watching the bobbing colors of their auras as they spun past . . . and knew that sometime soon, he was going to have to think about what he'd done.

He'd always told himself that at least the angels gave something back to humans with their touch — but if he really believed this made a difference, then why did he try to protect every human he ever met from them? Why had he just risked his life for the *niñita*, when for the first time in eighteen years, he might be close to finding the only thing he'd ever wanted? If he'd let the thing feed from her, then the street girl would have been happy forever, no matter how she might have been damaged. Yet at least she had a choice now. Perhaps she could pull herself out of the streets and be safe and well — find a happiness that was grittier, more real, than anything an angel's touch could give her. Seb shook his head in amazement as he realized: if he had it to do over, he'd do the same thing again.

"Nice night," said Mike, tapping his hand on his thigh in time to the music. "The street dancing and the lanterns. Nice."

"Yes, it is," agreed Seb. He didn't really understand himself, but he supposed it didn't matter. He reached into his pocket and touched the brass frame of the photo, stroking his finger across its smooth warmth. And he knew that his half-angel girl *would* understand this, probably a lot better than he did. He could feel her compassion for what had just happened, for both the street girl and himself; see the warmth in her green eyes. He let out a breath, drinking in the sense of her that felt so close now. He needed her; he always had. Somehow he knew that she needed him, too.

I *will find you*, he thought. It was a promise to them both.

But for now, it was enough to just be watching the dancers, basking in their happiness.

Chapter Ten

"OK, THE RECEPTION'S going to be in here," said Kara, pointing. We were sitting around the kitchen table with mugs of coffee, looking at Brendan's laptop— he'd found floor plans for the hotel on the Internet. "There's a private party with just the Church of Angels officials first, then we lowly peons will be allowed in."

Alex and I had been at the house for over two weeks, and it was starting to feel like a plan was coming together. Luis, after being hesitant to tell Kara too much, was now a lot more forthcoming. Not only had he started opening up about security details, but he'd also given Kara invitations that would get her and her "friends" into the reception for a private audience. It was a huge relief—if the word *relief* can be applied to something that fills you with utter dread.

"So we'll be entering by the hotel front door at three o'clock," said Alex, lightly touching the screen. "We'll go in with the other guests . . . then up the elevator to the main function room." He glanced down at the printed schedule Kara had gotten from Luis. "Do we know yet where the private audiences are being held?"

Kara shook her close-cropped head. "But it's got to be one of the rooms on the same floor, right? Maybe that one?" She pointed to a meeting room down the hallway.

As they kept talking, my eyebrows drew together . . . because I wasn't picking up anything at all from the floor plans. I don't always from images, but given the circumstances I would have expected *something* — some glimmer of emotion. But it was like the plans were just empty pixels on a screen, instead of a map showing the most urgent operation in the world.

"The reception's not black-tie, is it?" asked Liz, chewing her fingernail. Most of her nails were bitten to the quick. "'Cause we can't exactly hide guns under formal dresses."

"Oh, God, I hadn't even thought of that," murmured Trish, her freckled face worried.

"Thankfully, no," said Kara. "Luis said the people representing Mexico City — that includes us — can just wear their normal outfits. Maybe something a little dressier, like you'd go to church in."

I kept looking at the floor plans, trying to feel something — anything — about them. Finally I shrugged it away. Maybe I was just nervous.

"Do you think the angels there will be scanning people's auras?" I asked Alex.

"Some are bound to be, because they'll be feeding." He glanced at me, and I could see the thought in his eyes — that the angels might recognize my aura before the team was ready to make a move. He wasn't really sorry about it. I knew he'd give anything if I wasn't involved in the attack, if I stayed away someplace where I could be safe.

"Don't even say it," I said quickly. "I'm going." The thought of waiting here at the house while they all left — of not knowing what was happening, if they were going to live or die — no, there was just no way. "Alex, I *have* to," I said before he could answer. "What about Paschar's vision, that I'm the one who can destroy them?" I sensed a wave of doubt from the others and knew no one took that very seriously — since I so clearly *hadn't* been the one to destroy them the last time I'd tried.

Alex sighed and pushed his hair back. I could see how tired he was — how heavily all this was weighing on him. "Maybe," he said. His blue-gray eyes caught mine, asking me to wait until we were alone to discuss it. Reluctantly, I nodded.

Across from me, Wesley sat examining the map in his usual dour silence. With Sam sprawled beside him, it was like an illustration showing "closed book/open book." "OK," drawled Sam, squinting at the screen. "Are the Council like ordinary angels when it comes to killing them? Or are they different, or what?"

Kara shook her head. "I don't know, but they must

be *able* to be killed, or their safety wouldn't be such an issue. Apparently they do feed, so I'm guessing it's their halo that's vulnerable, like other angels. Who knows if there's anything extra we have to worry about, though." She rolled her eyes. "I'm glad Luis is finally opening up," she added dryly. "There's really a limit to how many security questions I can slip in between *Oh, you're so wonderful* and *Ooh, do that again.*"

My cheeks tinged. Kara was so matter-of-fact about her relationship with Luis. Well, not a *relationship*, I guess, though he clearly thought it was. I studied her covertly, wondering again if I'd only imagined the way I'd seen her gazing at Alex that day. I couldn't get that soft-eyed look of hers out of my mind; I just had a feeling about it. Not that I was worried exactly — every time Alex touched me, I could sense how deeply in love with me he was — but it didn't make me feel all that great, either. Kara was so utterly, gorgeously human.

Brendan rapped a light drumbeat on the table as a thought seemed to come to him — even when he was sitting quietly, he wasn't quiet. "Hey, wait! Couldn't Willow help?"

I glanced at him in surprise. "I — sorry, help with what? I was off in my own world, I guess."

Thinking freaky half-angel thoughts, said the faces of almost everyone around me.

Brendan seemed alarmed to be talking to me directly — the most we'd ever said was a mumbled *hi* when we'd almost walked into each other in the hallway once. He cleared his throat, fidgeting with his teaspoon. "Um—help find out if there's anything we need to know about killing the Council," he said. "You're supposed to be psychic, right? So, maybe you could get a vision about them or something."

The room went quiet. "Could she do that?" Kara asked Alex.

"You'd better ask Willow," he answered tersely, still studying the printed sheet. He got very short with anyone who ignored me.

"It doesn't really work that way," I said before Kara had to say anything. "I mean, yeah, sometimes I get flashes of things, but mostly for me to get anything specific, I need to be touching someone. Like, holding their hand." No one said anything. Feeling awkward, I traced the design on my coffee mug. "I, um . . . used to do psychic readings a lot, back home. People at my high school would come to me and ask for them."

"You went to high school?" Liz blurted out. Her pale cheeks reddened when I looked at her. "I mean, that sounds so normal."

Normal. I tried not to think about the fact that even as I spoke, I was aware of my angel, shifting around inside of me. "Sure, I went to school," I said. "I didn't know anything about any of this until a couple of months ago—as far as I knew, I was just like you."

"Whoa," murmured Sam, staring at me. "Half angels going to high school, and we don't even *know* about it? That's . . . freaky."

I saw Alex give him a considering look and decide not to say anything. I shrugged. "I think it's half angel, singular, actually — as far as anyone knows, I'm the only one."

For the first time, the thought gave me a very strange feeling. It hadn't really struck me before how inherently lonely this was — being the only one of my kind in the entire world. I went on quickly, before I could think too deeply about it. "Anyway, I didn't go as often as I should have — my friend Nina and I used to skip a lot and just go clothes shopping. I'm into vintage stuff, so there's this store in Schenectady we'd go to . . ." I trailed off, wondering why I was telling them this.

Open mouths around the table now. I could almost hear the same thought from everyone: *You had a friend?* Followed hard on its heels by the girls with, *Wait — you're into clothes shopping?*

From the look on Sam's face, half angels going shopping was seriously his idea of conversational hell. "Yeah," he said. "So anyway, can we get back to this psychic thing? Couldn't she — Willow — go into the cathedral and start holding people's hands?"

I managed not to roll my eyes at his quick save. "It might look pretty suspicious," I pointed out. "I usually have to focus for a few minutes; it's not like a lightning flash the second I touch someone."

"But you said you get feelings sometimes," Kara commented, studying me carefully. "So if you did go into the cathedral, you might pick up something useful."

Alex sat reading the sheet with his head propped on

his hand, rubbing his forehead. "I'm not sending Willow in there; her aura's too distinctive. Any angel that saw it would know exactly who she is — all they'd have to do is sound the alarm, and there'd be a riot. Every Church member in the world wants her dead."

"Yeah, but we could *scan* first, right?" Brendan's voice quickened with excitement, just like when he was arguing politics with Sam. "Make sure there aren't any angels around."

Kara nodded. "Sure, and then you and I could go in with her, Alex, and make sure she's covered."

I was about to say it sounded good to me — and it really did; I'd been painfully aware that so far I was probably the least-contributing member of the team — but Alex glanced up and spoke first, his voice impatient. "You said angels cruise in and out of that place all the time, Kara. What good would scanning do?"

I hesitated. "But, Alex, if I did get something, we'd know a lot better how to plan. I wouldn't be in there *that* long; I'd probably know in five minutes if I could get something."

He gave me a look. "It's not just the angels. Your picture's been on every Church of Angels website in the world, remember? Someone could recognize you."

"Not with my hair like this." I touched the short red-gold strands.

He snorted. "Oh, yeah, like that's a master disguise no one could see through."

"But if you and Kara were covering me, then —"

"Do you even know what 'covering someone' means?" Alex asked coldly. "This isn't a movie. Do you really want us to have to start shooting at a screaming mob to get you out of there if something goes wrong?"

Where had this argument come from? "No, of course I don't *want* that," I said. Everyone had gone quiet, watching us. Trish's eyes were wide; her coffee mug paused in mid-motion. "But, Alex, you know I can usually sense if a place is going to be a danger to me. I mean, OK, it's not foolproof, but—"

"Willow." He lashed my name at me like a whip. "I said *no*, all right? Drop it."

It felt like he had slapped me. In the sudden roaring silence, Alex tossed the sheet down and shoved his chair back. He left the room without a word.

My cheeks were on fire; at first I was too shocked to move. There was a long pause. Finally Kara lifted a perfectly shaped eyebrow. "Well. I see that his temper hasn't improved any. I'll go talk to him." She started to get up.

"No!" The word burst out of me. "No—I'll do it."

She regarded me, her expression almost amused. "You sure? I've got a lot of experience dealing with Kylar boys when they get like this. It's kind of an acquired skill."

I hadn't really been certain what I thought of Kara up until then, even with the look I'd seen her give Alex— but now it was becoming clearer to me. I didn't like her very much. "I've acquired it, thanks," I said, getting up from my chair. "I'll go."

The silence in the kitchen erupted into words as I

went down the hallway. I let the buzz fade away behind me, not trying to decipher what was being said. I could guess easily enough.

I knew Alex had to be in his bedroom. But when I got there, his door was shut, and I paused as I stood in the faintly sweaty-smelling mess of the boys' dorm. His door was never shut, unless he was asleep or I was in there with him. Despite what I'd said to Kara, this was all new territory to me; Alex and I hardly ever argued. Then I remembered the way he'd snapped at me, and grimaced. We had to have this out.

I knocked. "Can I come in? We need to talk."

There was a pause. "Yeah," he said.

I opened the door, gathering my thoughts for what I wanted to say. It left me the second I saw him. Alex was sitting on the side of his bed with his shoulders slumped, elbows on his thighs as he massaged his temples with both thumbs. His eyes were closed.

Hurriedly, I shut the door and sat next to him. "Are you OK?"

"Yeah." His voice was distant, his fingers on his forehead white with tension.

I touched his arm and pain jolted through me, so sharp and furious it made me gasp. "Oh, God, you're not! Your head—"

"It's just a headache. I'm fine."

It didn't seem *fine* at all. I stood up, my words rushing together: "I'll go get you some Advil—there's some in the girls' dorm—"

Without looking up, Alex reached for one of my hands and squeezed it hard. "No. Just . . . stay with me. Please."

I bit my lip, not knowing what to do. I sank back down beside him, and we sat in silence, Alex still rubbing his temples. Finally he let out a breath and dropped his hands. He was pale, with tiny beads of sweat on his forehead. He gave me a rueful look. "Hey, you."

"Hey," I echoed. I could feel how tense he was, the pain that was still thudding through him.

He put his arm around me. "Sorry," he said against my hair. "I was a jerk. I shouldn't have—" He broke off with a wince, gripping his forehead again.

"Alex, I'm going for the Advil now—"

His arm tightened, holding me in place. "It's OK. It wouldn't help." After a pause, he sighed and dropped his hand from his head; shifting position on the bed, he lay back against his pillows, looking drained. "Shit. I thought I was over these."

"Over what?" I propped myself up next to him, gently stroking his forehead.

"That feels really nice," he murmured, closing his eyes again. I moved farther up the bed, leaning against the wall, I rested his head on my lap and kept stroking it, soothing the pain away. His breathing slowed, grew more relaxed.

"Over what?" I repeated softly.

"Migraines," he said. "I got them after my dad died and after Jake died. They went away for a while; I haven't had one in over a year. This one just — completely blind-sided me."

"You never told me," I said.

"No. It seemed pretty pathetic."

My heart twisted. I didn't think I'd even be able to keep my sanity if I'd been through everything Alex had — almost everyone he loved in the world dying. Migraines just seemed *normal*, not pathetic.

Then my mouth went dry. My hand stopped on his forehead. "Alex, you don't think —"

"What?" he said, opening his eyes. Seeing the look on my face, understanding came over his features. "Willow, no — don't even think it. It's got nothing to do with you; I started getting them years ago."

I swallowed. Just that morning, Alex and I had managed half an hour alone here in his room together; we'd almost been able to forget anyone else was around. "But to get one *now*, when you haven't had one for over a year . . ."

"Yeah, that might have a little more to do with being responsible for this mission, and everyone's lives. Not making out with my girlfriend." He reached for my hand. "Willow, you're not hurting me. I promise. It's just this stupid thing that happens sometimes —" He cringed again and went silent. His slight stubble looked inky black against the sudden pallor of his face.

"It's not gone yet?" Fear was curling through me.

"No, it won't be gone for hours." He gave my hand a tug, tried to smile. "Hey. That was nice, what you were doing before."

I started stroking his head again, trying hard to believe that this was really just a coincidence. After a few minutes, Alex turned his head on my lap and kissed my wrist. "I'm sorry I spoke to you that way before," he murmured. "Really. I was way out of line."

His eyes were so beautiful: stormy skies reflected in the blue sea. My fears started to fade, looking into them. *You're panicking*, I told myself. *He's gotten migraines in the past, and he's stressed out of his mind right now. He's right. It's got nothing to do with you.*

I ran my fingers through his dark hair. "I wasn't trying to argue with you in front of everyone," I said softly. "It's just that we've always decided things together."

"I know," he said. "We still do — I need you, Willow. But this time it's different. I don't want you going anywhere near the cathedral unless we don't have a choice; it's too dangerous."

I hated pressing the point when he was in so much pain, but I had to say it: "Even if we could find out more information about the Council? So that we know for sure what to expect?"

He shook his head. "How likely is that, though? I've never known you to get anything specific just from being inside a place. The most I've ever seen you get is feelings."

"I know, but there could still be a chance, even if it's a tiny one. Alex, if it weren't me — if it were someone else on the team who was half angel —"

"I'd be saying the same thing," he broke in. "Seriously, this isn't about me being in love with you. It's just too risky, for not enough return. That place is full of angels—if they saw that you were here in the city, it could jeopardize everything."

I sighed—when he put it like that, I could see his point. After a pause, I bent over and kissed his mouth upside down; he tilted his chin up to make it linger. Our lips left each other slowly. "OK," I said. "You're the boss."

"Yeah, I must have been really bad in a past life or something." He smiled, his eyes still in pain. Reaching up, he touched a strand of my hair. "Don't leave, OK?"

"Shhh. I'm not going anywhere." I kept stroking his forehead, trailing my fingers across it. His muscular shoulders gradually relaxed, his eyes closing again. His breathing slowed, became more regular.

I could hear the TV on in the other room, the sound of voices. None of it mattered to me. I stayed there until long after Alex had fallen asleep—gently caressing the brow of the boy I loved, trying to keep his pain at bay.

The other AKs kept improving at their moving targets, until Alex started doing combat variations with them, making them run across the room, drop into a roll, then shoot—that kind of thing. Their averages plummeted again, but I saw that this time it didn't take long for their scores to start climbing back up. They were getting there. Sam was the best shot by far; he'd obviously taken Alex's demonstration with his pistol that day as a personal challenge. At first Wesley had been as awkward with guns as he was around people, but now he wasn't far behind Sam, and Trish was pretty much level with him — she seemed to aim and shoot in a single motion, hardly even thinking. I don't know why that surprised me, except Trish was so nice that you didn't tend to think of her and guns in the same sentence. Brendan and Liz weren't doing badly, either — they were both consistent enough to be dependable at least.

Unlike me. Though I'd gotten pretty good at shooting a stationary target, I still hadn't reached ninety percent; I couldn't get over the habit of flinching every time I pulled the trigger. I really didn't think I was ever going to get used to this — the cold weight of the weapon, the acrid smell of gunpowder.

Standing in the target range with the muted thumps of gunfire around me, I braced myself for the kick of the pistol as I aimed — and that strange prickling feeling nagged at the nape of my neck again. I knew no one would be there, but I still had to glance and check. Only the wall of the firing range looked back. I let out a breath, wishing I could get over feeling so self-conscious in this place.

As target practice continued, part of me wondered why I was even bothering to learn how to shoot now, apart from my personal safety. When Alex and I had talked some more about the Council attack, he'd convinced me that it wasn't a good idea for me to go — that the threat of my aura attracting attention and putting the team in even more danger in that situation was too great.

I hated it, *hated* it. This was my fight, too. I couldn't stand the thought of staying behind while Alex and the others risked their lives, of not being there to do whatever I could to help them. But I knew he was right. No one had any idea what Paschar's vision meant, including me . . . and meanwhile, my aura was like a big neon arrow pointing right at me. This was the only chance we were going to get. My personal feelings about not being included couldn't even come into it.

I sighed and squeezed the trigger, felt the report jump through me. A hole appeared just at the edge of the bull's-eye.

"Hey, that's a lot better," said Alex, pausing to watch. He glanced at me; his mouth creased in sympathetic amusement. "You still totally hate this, don't you?"

"Me? No, I was born to be a gun moll." I set my jaw as I started to aim again.

He reached over and corrected my hold on the gun slightly, his fingers warm on mine. "You make a really cute one, you know that?" he said in an undertone. "All you need is one of those thirties gangster suits."

"Ho, ho."

I saw the kiss he wanted to give me in his eyes. Then he was gone again, heading toward Brendan. I held back a smile as I looked after him, wishing as usual that we'd had longer to talk.

Returning to my target, I squared my shoulders . . . and somewhere inside of me my angel gave a flutter, darkly restless. In an awful way, I'd sort of gotten used to this by now; only half thinking about it, I pushed her aside in my mind.

Only this time it didn't work.

My angel broke free in a shining rush, soaring out of me. With a startled gasp, I stood gaping up at her as she hovered. I *couldn't feel what she was feeling anymore.* Oh, my God, what was happening? Who *was* this creature with my face? Belatedly, I tore my gaze away, my heart thudding. I couldn't let anyone see me staring upward — couldn't let anyone figure out what was going on.

Before my angel could do anything, I quickly switched my consciousness to hers. All at once I was the one hovering overhead, looking down at the foreshortened Willow below, still aiming the gun as if nothing was wrong. My angel knew what I was about to do; there was a sudden mental frenzy as she fought against me. Gritting my teeth, I ignored her and swooped back into my human body. A flapping struggle; almost a scream of frustration as my angel tried to wrest free — but for now at least I was stronger, and I shoved her away inside of me.

The whole thing had taken only seconds. I took a few breaths, making sure I really had control. I could sense her frustration now, and that weird looseness again . . . but my angel had gone silent. Shakily, I put the safety on the gun and rested it on the floor. Alex glanced over, and I tried to smile.

"Bathroom," I mouthed, and he nodded.

Upstairs, I splashed water on my face. My eyes in the mirror looked large and frightened, my face pale. OK.

This was not good. This was really, really not good. I had to tell Alex, only what could he do? He wouldn't know what was going on any more than I did. But I couldn't keep this from him any longer, no matter how much I didn't want to face it myself; it had gotten way too serious. The possibility that I really *could* be responsible for his migraine — and that it might be a symptom of something far worse — came to me again, chilling my blood. Suddenly it seemed only too likely. I wanted so much to believe it wasn't true, that my touch wasn't hurting him — but how could I *know*, when I had this thing inside me that I didn't even understand anymore?

I caught sight of my crystal pendant in the mirror and went very still. I heard Alex's voice saying, *Your angel is you; she's a part of you. And that means she's . . . everything I love.*

Alex had always believed — always — that my angel wasn't something separate from me, that she was just another aspect of myself. What was he going to think when he found out that wasn't true? That she had separate thoughts from mine; that I couldn't even *control* her anymore?

My hands were ice. I slumped weakly against the sink, imagining the look that would be on his face when he found out. Oh, God, he'd defended me to the whole team, telling them that they could trust me, and now — I swallowed. The thought that his beautiful eyes might look at me with dread, or suspicion, made me feel sick. I knew how much he loved me, but the angels had killed his whole family. He'd devoted his entire life to fighting them. Could he really still feel the same about me when he found out my angel self had a mind of its own? I had to tell him; I knew I didn't have a choice.

But how?

CHAPTER ELEVEN

JENNY, NOW RAZIEL'S new assistant, sat cross-legged on the other side of the desk looking radiant with happiness — if a bit tired and drained. "Would you like to arrange a meeting with him, sir?" she asked.

Tapping a pen, Raziel glanced over the e-mail print-out in question. The town of Silver Trail was a few dozen miles up in the Rockies; the weather might be foul this time of year. Still, the proposed idea was intriguing.

"What do *you* think?" he asked, smiling at Jenny. Her almost-demure business suit hugged her figure. He couldn't imagine now why he'd wasted so much time with a male assistant whose energy he didn't even find appealing; he must have been insane.

She flushed, eyes shining. "I think it's a wonderful idea. It could make such a difference in so many people's lives."

Indeed it could; Raziel already had thoughts about how he could put his own spin on the scheme. "I think you're right," he said, handing the e-mail back to her. "Go ahead and arrange the meeting."

Once Jenny had departed, Raziel's momentary good mood faded. Scheduling meetings as if nothing had happened was all very well, but meanwhile he was going mad with nerves.

There will be no changes to the Church. No changes at all. That is my promise.

Raziel's face darkened as he recalled the TV interview. It had been big news for a few days, with his image smiling out at him from all the major papers. Not very clever, he supposed. But when the question had been posed, he'd been standing in the same place in the cathedral where the Council had demanded to see him in private, as if he were a naughty schoolboy called onto the carpet. Anger had bristled through him as he remembered, and with the reporter's microphone thrust in his face, the words had come of their own accord. Saying them had given him deep satisfaction at the time, but now he wished he'd been more circumspect. Though the Council probably hadn't had much doubt that he had no intention of toeing the line, they'd have none at all after this.

The Twelve had shown no reaction to his statement. Yet.

The knowledge that they were deliberately keeping quiet to let him do exactly what he was now doing — writhe uncomfortably, wondering how they'd respond —

made Raziel's teeth clench. The time for their demise couldn't come quickly enough for him now, in more ways than one. But if his own death was caused by the Council perishing, at least he'd have the pleasure of knowing he'd taken them out with him.

The plan was now securely in place — even though Charmeine had learned something that made its probable outcome less uncertain than before, and not in an especially reassuring way.

After her brief trip to Mexico City, Charmeine had managed a day away from the Twelve and spent it here at the cathedral with him, in his private quarters. He'd given orders to Jenny that he wasn't to be disturbed — he'd had a feeling that things would resume between him and Charmeine and was correct, as it turned out. Enjoyable but utterly calculated on both their parts, it had cemented their alliance even further, making it easier to read each other's thoughts.

"So I found Luis without any trouble," she'd said later on. Raziel had already gleaned some of this from her mind — flashes of an earnest-looking young man with brown eyes and thick black hair — but still listened with interest as she described the encounter. "He's pretty smitten with this Kara person. It didn't take much to get him to trust her."

"No, just a nice, lingering feed from his aura," said Raziel with a smirk. They were on the plush leather sofa; Charmeine had her long legs draped over his lap.

"Well, obviously. Several times, in fact, just to make

sure he got the message." She stifled a yawn. She had on Raziel's black silk dressing gown; her pale hair spilled down it in stark contrast. "Sorry. I have to keep myself shielded all the time around the Twelve, without them realizing — it's pretty tiring."

"You're holding out against them, though." Raziel's voice had sharpened.

"Yes, don't worry. I'm fine; it's all right." Charmeine rolled her eyes, nudging his thigh with a slender foot. "As if I thought for a second that my welfare is what's concerning you."

He hadn't bothered to deny it; she'd have felt the same. Just because he could, he slid his hand up her leg and let his thoughts go wandering through hers, relishing the sense of all doors opening to him — it had a thrill of its own. Naturally, his own mental doors weren't all open to her, though she'd think they were. He'd constructed an elaborate false memory detailing how he'd anonymously gotten into contact with the Angel Killers and gained their trust — the last thing he wanted was for anyone, including Charmeine, to realize he had a link with the half angel. A good false memory had the same vivid sensory details as the real thing; Raziel was quite proud of the level of attention he'd put into this one. Charmeine could have done something similar, of course, but he didn't think she had. He could sense her loathing of the Council seeping through her almost every thought; there was no way she could fake that. Hiding it was just about possible, though not easy. It wasn't surprising she was tired.

For a moment Raziel thought he felt a flutter of resistance. He gave Charmeine a sharp look. She lay against the sofa cushions with her eyes closed as he explored, her face untroubled. The faint feeling was gone just as quickly. Probing further, Raziel decided it hadn't been hiding anything in particular.

Then his hand froze on her leg as he came across something. *What?* He checked again; he hadn't been mistaken. He stared at Charmeine wordlessly.

"I was wondering when you'd find that," she said without opening her eyes. "They told us a few days ago; it's why we're spending three weeks in Mexico City. I always thought it was sort of a long time just to appoint a church head."

Raziel shook his head, still half lost in the images he was getting. "*What* do they think they'll accomplish by such a thing? They must be insane!"

Charmeine sat up as she glanced at him, her expression ironic. "Let's just say they're very eager for angels to remain angels. They think being in this world is turning us all into base gluttons who indulge ourselves for pleasure instead of necessity. They don't want us mixing with humans too much, except when we absolutely have to."

It was hardly news. Raziel thought of the Twelve's meeting with him in the conference room below and snorted. Drumming his fingers on the sofa, he considered the implications of what he'd just seen. Though the two dimensions had split off from each other eons ago, the human and angel worlds had once been one and the same — and this meant that the Twelve, as First Formed, had links to this world's energy. On its own, the fact didn't worry him overmuch. The possible cost to the human world after the Twelve's deaths had always seemed a low risk to him — it was the angels' link to one another that was the main issue.

But now there was this mad plan of theirs: to use their connection with the world's energy to bond with it and calm down places that felt "buzzy" to angels, so that angels around the world would be more inclined to resist their baser urges. How noble of them. And how . . . interesting, in terms of what consequences their deaths might now bring.

With a silken rustle, Charmeine swung her feet off his lap and sat close beside him. "You haven't changed your mind, have you? Because I certainly haven't, even if it does make things more of a gamble."

Raziel had given her a withering look. "Are they going to back off and recognize my leadership here? What's that? The answer's no? Then no, I haven't changed my mind, either."

Now, alone in his office, Raziel knew he'd increased their gamble even further by his impetuous statement to the press. Just to reassure himself that all was still well, he reached for the connection with Willow. He checked it often to keep abreast on the AKs' progress, though had to admit that he also found the girl oddly intriguing in a way. Not to mention how surprised he'd been by her angel's anxiety ever since he'd first entered her mind. On some deep level, Willow was obviously aware that there was something amiss. While his daughter's distress didn't concern Raziel enough to try to soothe things for her, he did find it interesting. Her psychic skills were stronger than he'd thought.

Before he could get very far, his cell phone rang, jolting him back to his office. With a glance at the screen, he saw Charmeine's name. She didn't often get a chance to ring with updates; he snapped the phone open. "Yes? What is it?"

"Something's up," she said tightly.

Raziel cringed; he'd been waiting for this. "Let me guess — they saw my TV interview."

"Raz, the *whole world* saw your interview. Yes, of course they did, and they're more annoyed than you can imagine. But no, that's not what I meant. Something else has happened —" Charmeine broke off; he could feel her tension as she listened to something. "I have to go," she said abruptly. "I'll call you back when I can."

"Wait! What's going on? What —?"

She was gone. Raziel swore, knowing he'd get nothing from her psychically now, other than whatever front she was putting on for the Twelve. He shoved his chair away and stood up, propping his hands on the windowsill as he glared out at the mountains. In the distance a heavy rain was falling, obscuring the peaks in dense clouds and heading his way.

✦ ✦ ✦

"I'm going to take the team on a practice hunt tomorrow," said Alex.

Kara was sprawled sideways on the battered armchair. She turned her head to look at him. "Are they ready?"

The two of them were in the TV room; the others were scattered around the house. Willow was helping Liz in the kitchen — Liz had thawed toward her enough to let her chop lettuce for a salad, or something. Alex didn't hear them talking much but supposed it was a start.

He shrugged. "As ready as they can get for now, without angel holographs to help train them. They've got to get some real-life experience." He felt his lips move into a small, wintry smile. "Can you imagine what my dad would say? Taking a team on a hunt before they've had at least a year of training?"

Kara had on sweatpants and a tight, cropped T-shirt, showing the sleek muscles of her arms and stomach. She smiled, too. "Vividly. It's different times, though, Al. I'm sure this is the right thing."

He made a face, hoping she was right. His mind was already ticking over the details of the hunt, how best to manage it. Bosque de Chapultepec, the large, leafy park off the Pasco de la Reforma, seemed the best bet to him — parts of it were kind of remote and quiet during the week. If the team came across any feeding angels, they'd have space to maneuver and little chance of being seen. The important thing was keeping them all as safe as possible.

A news story had come on: another confrontation between the Crusaders and the Faithful. Alex gazed at the

225

screen, only distantly taking in the shouting, angry faces. He'd known being in charge of a team would take over his life; what he hadn't anticipated was how much he'd care about all of them, even the ones he didn't particularly like.

It didn't matter. Training them, being responsible for their lives — it just got under your skin; you got to know them in a way that transcended personal feeling. Sam, who Alex could cheerfully clout a dozen times a day, had still impressed him by buckling down these last few weeks and turning into a damn good shot. Liz was really OK, despite being so prickly sometimes — he'd seen how hard she'd worked to gain her shooting skills, how harsh she was on herself when she didn't get it right. Brendan's incessant talking grated, but Alex knew he'd miss him if he were gone. And Trish, with her freckled face and blue eyes, was like the glue that held them all together: smoothing quarrels, making sure everyone was getting along, so that the others gravitated toward her like a den mother.

Not to mention Wesley. Alex had sort of discounted him at first, not having time to delve into whatever the guy's sullen deal was, as long as his training was coming along all right. Then one night he'd heard a noise in the firing range and gone to check — and there had been Wesley, at two o'clock in the morning, shooting targets on his own.

"Hey, aren't I working you hard enough?" Alex had joked.

A flush had stained Wesley's dark cheeks. He'd hastily put the gun back in the weapons cabinet, while behind him the target still bounced on its chain. "Couldn't sleep," he muttered.

Suddenly the truth had hit Alex. "Wait a minute — you do this a lot, don't you? That's why your score's been improving lately."

Willow had told him that Wesley was shy; Alex hadn't really believed it until now — a scowl was coming over his face, but underneath it he just looked mortified. "Look, I've got to get it, OK? I'm not keeping anyone awake."

"I didn't say you were." Alex leaned his shoulder against the wall. "But staying up all night won't help; you need to get a good night's sleep."

Christ, he sounded like his dad. Mentally rolling his eyes at himself, Alex had started to say something else — and stopped as Wesley exclaimed, "You don't understand! I've got to get it. It's my only chance to get back at the angels. I can't —" He broke off. The flush crept down to his neck, he crossed his arms over his chest and looked away.

Alex had slowly come away from the wall. "Angel burn?" he guessed.

Wesley swallowed. "My, um . . . my whole family. My mom was . . . was CIA; that's how I . . ." He trailed off.

Painful understanding had stirred through Alex, realizing how much they had in common. "I never knew that," he'd said at last.

Wesley was already looking sorry that he'd mentioned it. "Yeah, well, don't tell anyone, OK? I don't want to *talk* about it; I just want to *get* it."

"You are getting it," Alex had said quietly. "You're doing really well. Look, no more practicing this time of night, all right? Take an extra hour first thing in the morning if you want; no one will ask you any questions. But I need you in top form — and that includes getting enough sleep."

The target slowly swung to a complete stop; around them the house felt heavy with silence. Finally Wesley had nodded. "Yeah, OK."

There hadn't been any big dramatic change in Wesley after that; he was still closed off and didn't talk much. But as Alex stared at the TV, he realized that he felt like he knew the guy now. He knew all of them, just from watching them grow, change, get better — and he'd make sure they stayed safe through this, no matter what it took.

"Is Willow going on the hunt?" asked Kara.

Alex glanced at her; she sat curled up in the armchair with her forearm draped across its back. "I don't know," he admitted.

Though Willow didn't think so, she was doing great for someone who'd never touched a gun before — but she wasn't up to fighting angels yet. Leaving aside his fears for her safety, Alex knew that her angel self was incredibly useful in combat. Yet if an angel saw what she was and got away . . . He winced, seeing again the battle in the courtyard and the angel speeding off down the street.

"I don't know," he repeated, massaging his temple idly. Not a migraine this time, just a headache that had been grumbling at him for hours.

Kara glanced down at her bright-red fingernails, turning them this way and that. "Can I ask you something?"

He gave her a wary look, holding back a dry smile. "If this is about my sex life again . . ."

"No, not that. It's just—well, I've been wondering why you haven't used her angel to help train them."

Alex shrugged. "It doesn't have a halo. And I don't know what would happen if someone got excited and shot at it—whether that would hurt Willow or not."

"But that could happen on a hunt, too," Kara pointed out.

"Yeah, it could," he agreed. It was another reason why he wasn't convinced about taking Willow: the possibility of Sam or someone getting all adrenaline-rushed and trigger-happy with her angel in flight.

"If you want my advice, I don't think she should go," said Kara after a pause. "I mean, I know you've made it clear to everyone that she's part of the team, but—"

"But she's not, really," finished Alex sharply.

"I'm not saying it's her fault," said Kara. "It's just . . . well, the others still don't really trust her."

Alex felt a ripple of annoyance. "Then it's about time they got over it. Besides, they trust her a lot more than they did."

Kara sounded like she was choosing her words carefully. "They've gotten sort of used to having her in the house; it's not quite the same thing. Look, I just don't think taking her along on the first hunt would be great for morale when everyone's going to be nervous enough as it is. And she's not that competent with a gun yet anyway. There are more minuses than pluses—that's all."

Her tone was so reasonable that it made Alex's teeth grit together. "OK, I think you've convinced me," he said finally.

"You're not going to take her?"

"No, I am," said Alex. "Because she *is* part of the team, and you and the others need to start seeing her that way. She already can't take part in the Council attack or go into the cathedral. But there's not too much danger on a hunt like this, where we're all out in the open and can maneuver. There's no way I'm going to tell her she can't come."

Kara nodded, obviously unconvinced. "OK. Your call." She fell silent, gazing at the TV as a commercial came on. When the news started again, she said, "You really love her, don't you?"

He glanced over, taken aback by the wistful note in her voice. "Yeah, I do," he said. "More than anything."

Kara's mouth twisted; she looked down at her nails again. "I can tell. It's nice, you know? Once I thought that maybe Jake and I . . ." She trailed off.

Alex sat up a little, staring at her—and then realized he wasn't that surprised. She and Jake had always been close, though he knew his brother had given up hoping anything would ever happen; Jake had told him once how he'd made a play for Kara and been completely shot down.

Suddenly Alex felt as wistful as Kara had just sounded. God, Jake had been crazy about Kara, way beyond Alex's own adolescent crush on her. Getting together with her would have made him so incredibly happy.

"So . . . why didn't you?" he asked.

Kara sighed, propping her chin on her hand. "Oh, I don't know. He still had some growing up to do. Mostly, I think I just didn't want to mess up our friendship. But life's too short; you've got to go for it—what happened to Jake taught me that." She ran a finger along the arm of the chair. Then she said in a low voice, "Speaking of going for it . . . you're a lot like him, you know. I mean, a lot like how I hoped he'd turn out to be."

Alex's gaze flew to hers. Her brown eyes were serious, unwavering. Christ, this couldn't actually be what it sounded like, could it? He cleared his throat, half sure she was going to burst out laughing. "Look, um . . . Kara—"

Her hand went up, stopping him. "It's OK. I know you're in love with Willow. I'm just sayin'—that's all." She unfolded herself from the chair and came over to him; kissed his forehead with lips that were warm and gentle. "Don't worry: I won't say it again. I don't want to complicate things for you. You're a good guy, Al, the best. And if things are ever different . . ." She shrugged, gave a small smile. "Well, who knows?"

As she left the room, Alex stared after her, swamped in confusion. *Kara?* If this had happened a few years ago— no, a few *months* ago—he wouldn't have been able to say yes fast enough. Now it meant nothing to him, other than to somehow make him feel guilty, even though all he'd done was sit there. Thinking of his crush-ridden younger self, Alex had a fleeting moment of wishing he could have had this conversation with Kara back then, imagining what that would have been like.

OK, now he really *did* feel guilty. Mentally cursing Kara, he went and found Willow in the kitchen. She was squeezing a lemon into a bowl; Liz stood doing something with a tray of chicken breasts. He stood against the doorway, watching unseen for a moment — taking in Willow's slim curves in her jeans and tight T-shirt; the short red-gold hair that showed the graceful lines of her neck.

"You should try it some night," she was saying. "The tarragon adds a really nice flavor."

"Yeah, maybe —" Liz broke off as she noticed Alex standing there; Willow looked up, too.

"Hi," she said softly.

"Hi," he said, smiling at her. She had a tiny smudge of flour on her nose. "Can I talk to you for a second?"

She hesitated, then nodded. "Sure." She wiped her hands on a paper towel. "Back in a minute," she said to Liz.

He led her into one of the storage rooms and shut the door; the room was shadowy, crammed with boxes. "You might be longer than a minute," he murmured, lowering his head to hers. He felt her tense and drew back in surprise. "What's wrong?"

She started to say something and stopped. "Nothing. I just — think I'm getting a cold. I've been feeling sort of strange ever since target practice. You probably don't want to get too close."

Her voice sounded strained. He tipped her chin up with his hand. "Hey. You're not still worried about my migraine, are you? That was days ago."

Willow flinched. "Maybe a little." She took a breath, hugging herself. "Alex, I sort of . . . I mean, there's something . . ."

"What?" For an awful moment he thought she was going to say that she'd overheard Kara. Then he saw the expression in her eyes, and fear clutched him. "Willow, what's wrong? What is it?"

A burst of voices from the hallway: Sam and Brendan, arguing about some computer game. Willow bit her lip and glanced toward the door. Finally she shook her head. "It's nothing," she repeated. "Sorry. I — I guess I'm still just getting used to being here."

Unconvinced, Alex took her hands in his, studying her face. "But I thought it was getting better for you. I mean, you and Liz were just in there sharing cooking tips. I'm expecting you to teach Sam how to fix engines next."

Willow gave a short laugh. "Yes, dream on. It's not that much better, really — I think Liz has finally decided that I'm not going to use the pepper mill to grind glass into everyone's food at least. I don't know. Ignore me. I'm just feeling kind of strange today."

He didn't understand what was going on; all he knew was he hated seeing her so upset. He put his arms around her, and she buried her face hard against his neck. "I love you," she said in a muffled voice. "I mean — I really love you. You know that, don't you?"

Fear was now laced with complete bewilderment; this was so unlike her. Gently, he took her by the upper arms and forced her to look at him. "Babe, you're scaring me. If there's something going on, you've got to tell me what it is."

"I know," she said in a small voice. Again, she started to say something and then stopped, her eyes anxiously searching his own, her elfin face so lovely that it nearly broke his heart. The moment spun out around them; then Willow sighed and looked down, playing with the edge of his T-shirt.

"I'm just feeling worried about how everything is going, that's all," she said dully. "I mean — what's going to happen, if we'll manage to defeat the Council or not."

Alex watched her. "You're sure that's all it is?"

She let out a shaky breath. "Isn't that enough?"

He snorted. "Yeah," he said. "Yeah, that's enough." He sighed and leaned against a stack of boxes, rubbing his forehead. "Listen, I'll be telling everyone later tonight . . . but we're going on our first hunt tomorrow."

Willow went motionless. "We are? You mean, me too?"

"Yeah, all of us," he said. "I've got to get them some real-life practice, or they won't stand a chance when the time comes." Then he saw the worried tightness of her features. "Hey, you're OK with this, right? I mean, I'd sort of rather that you stayed here, actually, but I thought . . ."

"I'm fine with it," she said after a pause. "Well, nervous. But fine."

"Don't worry, I won't let anything happen to anyone," said Alex. God, he hoped that was true. He pushed it away; the hunt was the last thing he wanted to think about when he actually had a few minutes alone with Willow for a change.

He bent his head to hers again. He felt her hesitate, start to draw away — and then give in to the kiss in a rush. Alex's pulse leaped as she pressed against him. Gently slipping his hand under her shirt, he caressed the silky smoothness of her skin, the soft warmth of her. For a few endless minutes, it was only the two of them in the entire world.

Willow pulled away with an abruptness that startled him. "I — sorry, I'm still getting this cold, remember?"

"I don't care," he murmured as he reached for her again. "Germs are good."

"No, really. I don't want you to catch it." She stepped away, her cheeks flushed as she adjusted her shirt, not meeting his gaze. Alex's eyebrows drew together. He was just about to ask if something was wrong again when she gave him a quick, apologetic smile. "I'll see you at dinner, OK? Love you."

Before he could respond, she'd kissed him on the cheek and slipped out the door, shutting it softly behind her.

Chapter Twelve

THEY TOOK THE METRO to Chapultepec. In years past, Alex knew they might have been the only foreigners on the train; now, with the city so full of tourists to see the newly redone cathedral, their group hardly even merited a second glance.

Only Trish and Liz got seats on the crowded car. Alex stood with the others, holding on to a metal bar attached to the ceiling. Willow was next to him; as the train lurched, she stumbled slightly and he put his arm around her, steadying her. He could feel her tension. They were all tense. Hanging on to another bar, Sam stood tapping his thigh with his free hand; nearby, Wesley looked more sullen and closed off than ever. Brendan was chattering away about not much at all, his voice high and nervous. Alex started to tell him to cool it, then Kara gave Brendan a look that did the job for him. She'd kept her word since their conversation the day before, to Alex's relief—in fact, was acting so completely sisterlike now that he almost wondered if he'd imagined it.

They got off at Constituyentes; the entrance to the park stood nearby. Chapultepec was basically a giant forest and held everything you could think of—even a castle and an amusement park—but here it was quiet. Alex could see paths, trees, smooth manicured grass. As they crossed the road and stepped into the park's grounds, a hush seemed to fall, leaving the noise of the city behind.

From Willow's silence, Alex knew there weren't any angels in sight yet. As he'd counted on, there weren't many people, either, on a weekday afternoon—though he hoped there were enough to attract some angels. The irony of *hoping* for an attack brought a grim smile. Closing his eyes, he lifted his consciousness through his chakra points and felt the others doing the same.

"OK, we're going to split into two teams," he said. "Kara, you lead Wesley, Liz, and Brendan; I'll take Sam, Trish, and Willow. Keep out of sight if you can, but keep an eye on the main paths; that's where the action will probably be."

Kara nodded. "How long?" she asked, glancing at her cell phone. Alex had one, too; he'd bought it at one of the outdoor markets that morning. He'd also grabbed some more clothes for himself and Willow while he was at it; he knew how sick she was of wearing borrowed stuff.

"An hour, then we meet back here," he said, checking the time. He returned the phone to the pocket of his blue hooded sweatshirt. "Call me if there's any trouble. And happy hunting, guys — keep safe." He spoke the familiar words without thinking — it was what Cully had often said to them before a hunt and then later on, Juan.

And now him.

From Kara's expression, he knew she was thinking the same thing. "Will do," she said, and the four of them headed off through the trees.

"Come on, we'll go this way," said Alex to his own group. He led them down another path. "Start scanning, everyone. Tell me what you can sense." He'd already found angel energy about a quarter of a mile away — wanted to see how long it took the others. Angel spotters were supposed to be good, but he didn't know what their training had been like; the CIA had recruited them all.

A moment of concentration. "That way," said Sam and Trish almost in unison, motioning down the path. "Not too far," added Trish with an earnest glance at him. "And more than one, I think."

"Yeah, I got that, too," said Alex. "OK, let's start cutting through the trees." He looked at Willow as they made their way up a slight rise, wondering if she was all right. She was walking silently, staring down at her purple sneakers. She'd been quiet all day.

As if feeling his gaze, Willow looked up as the other two pulled ahead. To his alarm, he saw that her eyes were miserable, almost frightened. "Alex, listen, I — I can't take part in the hunt," she blurted out. "I know this is really bad timing, and I'm so, so sorry — I should have told you this yesterday — but —"

"There!" exclaimed Sam from ahead. "Oh, hell, it's a whole goddamn *feeding party!*"

Alex's head jerked up. Whatever Willow had been about to say was forgotten as he saw Sam sprinting off with Trish following after, both pulling out their guns as they ran. Oh, Christ, didn't they know any better, after all the hours he'd spent drilling strategy into them?

"Sam!" he called as loudly as he dared. "Trish, wait!" Trish stopped in her tracks, looking sheepishly back over her shoulder; Sam went on, barreling through the trees like a guerrilla warrior.

Alex pounded after him. Catching up, he grabbed Sam's muscular arm, yanking him to a halt. "Stop," he hissed. "Are you completely insane? You don't just go racing in — you have to scope things out!"

He could see the angels for himself now, a hundred yards away down a small hill where the walking path curved past. Sam was right, it was a feeding party: four angels clustered around four people. Their four touching wings made a shining flower shape, their halos bright and pulsing as they fed.

"We have to hurry!" Sam cried, jerking away from him. "Those people are being hurt, right this second —"

"Get down," said Alex, not taking his eyes off the angels. Sam didn't move. "Get *down*," he repeated in a snarl, shoving hard on the Texan's broad shoulder.

Sullenly, Sam lay on the ground beside him, both of them flat on their stomachs. Trish joined them and did likewise, her usually neat ponytail rumpled. Her face paled as she regarded the scene.

"OK, look," said Alex. "I know it's not easy to watch this, but they're already feeding—we can't save these people. The best we can do is wait for a clear shot."

"But we gotta shoot *now!*" Sam's voice rose. Trish glanced at him worriedly. "We can't just let them—"

"Lower your voice," said Alex, his own voice a knife that cut Sam's protestations short. "Look at how they're standing; their halos are too close to those people's heads. We could blow someone's brains out."

"Yeah, well maybe that's not such a bad thing! They've got angel burn now; what good is—?"

Alex swore as one of the angels looked up. For a brief burning second, its eyes met his—and he knew that it knew. He tore his gaze away and reached for his gun. "Well, you've got your wish; they've seen us. Nice going, hotshot. Stay in position, both of you. Shoot when you can, and *don't* look into their eyes—"

There was no time for further instructions; the angels were jetting toward them in a frenzy of light. One banked and soared high, ready to plummet; Alex ignored it for now and went for the angel in front. The sun dazzled off its halo, momentarily blinding him, then it flashed back into view and he fired. As the creature exploded into fragments, he felt the familiar rush of energy from angel fallout howl past.

Panicked shooting was going on beside him; a hasty scrambling in the grass. "Whoa!" shouted Sam, flipping onto his side as one of the creatures dove — its female face fierce and beautiful as it strained to grab his life force. Alex rolled onto his back and sat up in a single motion, tracking the angel as it wheeled on one wing, ready to return.

Beside him he heard Trish's gun go off, saw a bright explosion out of the corner of his eye. *Yes! Good one!* he thought as he fired. The female angel darted sideways, its wings cutting against the sky. Alex fired once more and got it this time — and as he twisted to track the fourth and last angel, Sam's gun went off again.

Silence. Light, falling toward the ground.

"We — we did it," said Trish, sounding stunned. "We really did it!"

Alex turned to Sam, giving him a long, level look. The Texan's gaze faltered; his face turned red as he put his gun away. "Don't you *ever* do that again," said Alex in a low voice. "If any of us had died, it would have been because you'd drawn their attention to us."

Sam swallowed. "Yeah, but —"

"Shut it, I don't want any excuses from you. You do *not* go running off before you know what you're getting into, and you do *not* keep talking loudly when I've told you to keep quiet. Do you understand me?"

"I'm sorry," said Trish in a tiny voice. "I went running off, too."

"You were OK," said Alex, still watching Sam. "At least you stopped when I told you to."

"I — I guess I acted pretty stupid," said Sam finally, looking sick. "I got excited — I wasn't thinking." His eyes rose to Alex's. "I'm sorry. It won't happen again."

"No, it won't," said Alex. "Because if it does, you're off this team for good."

Sam nodded, his lips white. "I understand."

"OK, then," said Alex as they got up. "Aside from that . . . you can both be pretty proud of yourselves." He gave Trish a quick one-armed hug; clapped Sam on the shoulder. "Listen, that was seriously *not* shabby — it's hard when they've seen you. Good work; I mean it."

Trish looked like the adrenaline was still pulsing through her; she managed a shaky smile. Sam winced and ran a hand over his short blond hair. "Yeah, but I — I completely choked at first — goddamn, I could hardly even shoot straight —"

A long-ago day in an Albuquerque park came back to Alex, and his throat tightened as he remembered Cully: *Weren't you listening to me? It's tough when they see you. You did good. You did good.*

"You did good," said Alex quietly. And he meant it. Though their first kills hadn't exactly gone smoothly, he was acutely aware they could have gone a hell of a lot worse, too. And he still had over seven weeks left to train them. With luck, it should just about be enough time.

Below, the angels' victims seemed to have come back to themselves and were walking away down the path, talking in low, ecstatic voices about *los ángeles*. One girl looked barely sixteen, with long black hair that gleamed

in the sunshine. As the group rounded the bend, she staggered and took the arm of the woman next to her.

Trish sighed. "So I guess this is the hard part, isn't it?
When you don't get to them in time."

"Yeah," said Alex. He put his gun away. "But when
you do manage to save them — it makes everything worth
it, believe me. And now that those four are dead, at least
they can't hurt anyone else."

"Hey, where's Willow?" said Sam suddenly.

Alex went cold as her frightened, unhappy face came
back in a rush. Oh, Christ, what had she been about to
tell him? Had something happened? He took off up the
hill at a run, burst onto its leafy crest with Sam and Trish
close behind. Dread thudded at his veins; he couldn't see
her anywhere.

"Willow!" he called, cupping his hands around his
mouth. "Willow, where are you?"

"Wait — is that her?" Trish gasped.

"Oh, *shit*," said Sam at the same moment. He stood
gaping upward.

Alex spun toward where Trish was pointing. And
stared. A girl who looked like Willow was far away down
the path, running toward the eastern gate to the park.
She was holding hands with a guy who had curly-looking
brown hair.

Dimly, he became aware that Sam was tugging at his
arm. "Alex! Look *up*."

Alex managed to tear his gaze from Willow and the
strange boy . . . and saw that high above them both flew a

long, shining stream of angels, a hundred strong, searing through the sky.

As Alex ran off after the others, I started to follow him, fumbling for my gun. The movement felt so unnatural, as if I'd morphed into a heroine in a cheesy action flick. I didn't dare let my angel out to help in the fight — I had no idea what she might do anymore — but I still had to be there with them, doing whatever I could. Then a thought came, like a drench of Arctic water. I stopped short as Alex's blue sweatshirt and dark hair disappeared through the trees.

What was I even thinking? I couldn't get anywhere near the angels. Before I'd bonded with my angel, she'd emerged without fail whenever others attacked, shielding me with her gleaming wings. What if she came out again now, and I couldn't control her? What if she did something that ended up with someone being hurt?

As if in response, my angel gave a vicious twist inside me, struggling to break free. *No!* I fought her with everything I had, somehow shoved her back with a mental wrench. I stood shaking, clutching my head and breathing hard. Oh, God, was this what the rest of my life was going to be like? I'd go insane. What *was* this — why was it happening to me?

I sank to the ground, pressing against a tree and burying my head in my arms. I could sense rather than hear the sound of gunfire not far away. I'd never felt so helpless in my life. I reached out with my thoughts, searching for

Alex — needing to feel him. His energy was there, strong and comforting, and I latched on to it, holding him tight even if he didn't know I was doing it. *Be safe. Please be safe. And please don't hate me when I tell you that my angel is a stranger to me after all . . . that she's not part of the girl you're in love with like we both thought she was. . . .*

Slow, hesitant footsteps were approaching. My head jerked up.

A few feet away stood a boy in faded jeans and a long-sleeved gray T-shirt, staring at me.

He was about Alex's height and build, with soft looking brown hair that had a curl to it — but there was nothing remotely feminine about him. Solid shoulders, a firm jaw with a light coat of stubble, high cheekbones. The boy's eyes were wide and fixed on mine. As I realized who it was, my thoughts stuttered to a halt.

The boy from my dream.

He closed the distance between us and dropped to his knees in front of me, letting the battered knapsack he'd been carrying fall to the ground. His throat moved as he swallowed. He looked down at my arms; reached out and touched them — I could feel him trembling as he stroked his way down their length, as if to reassure himself that I was real. When his hands came to mine, he gripped them tight; his were rough and warm. He said something in Spanish.

"I —" Why wasn't I pulling away? But it was as if he'd cast a spell over me. "I don't speak Spanish," I got out. "No *hablo español*." Then I did start to pull away — but suddenly the energy from him swept over me and I caught my breath in shock, unable to move. It felt so familiar, right down to the very core of me, like nothing I'd ever known before.

The boy looked up. His eyes were hazel — warm brown, with green radiating out from his pupils. "Yes, I'm sorry — I knew that; I forgot." His voice was distant, as if he wasn't thinking about what he was saying. He shook his head, staring at me as a wondering smile grew across his face.

"It's really you," he whispered. "I can't believe I found you." Letting go of one of my hands, he touched my cheek. The sun hit his face, turning the stubble on his jaw golden.

I jerked away from him, my heart beating hard. "Who *are* you?"

He started to respond, but then broke off as we both saw it: a flock of at least a hundred angels flying east across the park in a long, shifting stream that glinted in the light. At their very center was a small group that shone more fervently than the others — angels so bright I could barely look at them.

As I realized why that seemed so familiar, my pulse skipped. All the elements of my dream were suddenly crashing together at once, so that I hardly knew what was real and what wasn't. First the boy and now the twelve angels — I could count them, twisting and shining against the sky. My mind felt like it had stalled, trying to take everything in. What were they doing here *now?* They weren't due in Mexico City for five more weeks!

I stood up, gaping; the boy had risen to his feet, too. "The Council," I whispered. "Oh, my God, it's the Council from my dream. We have to follow them; we have to see where they go. Alex!" I shouted over my shoulder. "Alex, hurry! The Council's arriving!"

At the mention of my dream, the boy gave me a quick look and grabbed his bag up from the ground. "Come on— we have to be fast," he said.

"Alex!" I called again but knew he hadn't heard. A small part of my mind was still with him, and I could feel that he was OK; that he was pleased. They'd won against the angels, then— and hadn't seen this larger group yet, with the Council gleaming at its center.

"Come!" urged the boy, grasping my hand and peering upward.

"Wait— let go of me! I have to tell my—"

"There isn't time!" The boy started to run, pulling me along with him; I gave up and started running, too. He was right— there wasn't time. And more than that . . . more than that, I somehow just couldn't say no to him.

We pounded through the trees and onto the footpath— the boy's hand gripping mine, his long legs pumping rhythmically. The angels flitted in and out of view; he steered us sharply down one path, then another. We raced past sidewalk vendors, plunged down some steps and skirted a pond. Ducks took off with a startled flapping.

I wanted to tell him to slow down; instead I gritted my teeth and went faster. The boy half turned and put his arm around my shoulders, helping me along for a few paces.

"Hurry, *querida!*"

The endearment from my dream stunned me, even as we ran—and suddenly I realized that he'd seen the angels as easily as I had, without lifting his consciousness through his chakra points. Who *was* this boy?

The angels were farther ahead now but still in sight, glinting in the sky. The boy jogged to a stop at a bridge flanked by a pair of black lions on pedestals; he was barely even breathing hard. Ahead, I could see a set of park gates.

We stood side by side, staring. Beyond the park, a solitary tower was in clear view, soaring high over the trees—a half-cylinder of green glass that angled off at the top, reflecting a half-moon shape at the clouds. The angels veered up to this slanted peak, darting about it like moths around a flame, spiraling so brightly that the tower looked on fire.

Dimly, I was aware that the boy had put his arm around me again, drawing me close against him. It didn't seem strange for some reason. "What's happening?" I gasped. "Is that the Nikko Hotel?"

He shook his head, as unable to tear his gaze away as I was. "No—it's El Torre Mayor, the big tower. It's for business." A woman pushing a stroller strode past, oblivious. Overhead, the angels had started disappearing into the building. The twelve brightest ones were the first to vanish, gliding into the glass half-moon. The others followed gradually, until finally the last angel winked from view with a glimmer of wings.

"I've never seen anything like this before," murmured the boy, his hand gently rubbing my arm. "There were so many of them — and those twelve in the middle were so bright. . . ."

"It's the angels' Council," I said, still staring at the glass half-moon.

"Council?" The boy looked down at me with a frown. "You mean their government?"

I nodded. "I had a dream about them. Twelve angels and . . ." I trailed off. The boy had gone very still at the mention of my dream, his gaze locked on mine, and I knew he wasn't thinking about the Council anymore. Suddenly I noticed that I was standing pressed against him, with my head almost on his chest. God, what was I doing?

I jerked away, flustered. "Look, who are you, anyway? Because this is just — extremely weird."

Without taking his eyes from me, the boy propped himself against the base of one of the statues. There was a look of lean strength to him, with shoulders as firm as Alex's under his long-sleeved T-shirt.

"My name is Seb."

"Seb?"

"Sebastián," he amended. His eyes held such incredulous happiness, drinking me in as if he'd never be able to look away. "Sebastián Carrera. And you?"

For some reason it hadn't occurred to me that he wouldn't know my name already; he seemed so familiar with me. "Willow Fields," I said.

"Willow," he echoed. In his accent the word was a soft sigh: *Wee-low*. He smiled, seeming almost shy suddenly. "That's a tree, isn't it?"

The expression on Seb's face was the same one from my dream, and looking at him now, I saw how accurate my dream image had been: the lightly curling brown hair, the strong features and perfect mouth. The stubble that defined his jaw, making him even more attractive than he already was. God, what did it *mean*, that he was actually real?

I crossed my arms over my chest, feeling uncomfortable for more reasons than I could define. "Yeah. It's a tree."

"It's a pretty name." Seb's gaze lingered on my hair. "It's changed," he said after a pause. "You were blond before."

"How did you . . . ?" I trailed off, swallowed. "I dyed it."

He grinned suddenly, shaking his head. "I can't believe this; I can't believe I'm really standing here talking to you. Willow — you are so, so beautiful." As if he couldn't help himself, he reached for my face again, tracing a soft line down my cheek with the back of his finger.

I yanked away, hating the way my pulse had fluttered at his touch. "Stop *doing* that. Look, what's going on? You said that you found me — what did you mean? Why were you looking for me?"

His hazel eyes widened; I could see that I'd stunned him for some reason. "You don't know," he said, almost to himself. "But how can you not know? You've got to see —" He stopped, studying me up and down. "Wait — why aren't you changing?"

"Changing? Into what?" I took a cautious step backward, wondering why I was still standing here talking to this guy. And Alex. What in the world was Alex going to think? As far as he knew, I'd disappeared without a word. I had to get back; he wouldn't even know how to find me.

"Your —" Seb gestured impatiently at himself, sketching a quick circle around his body. "I don't know the word in English. Your energy. Your *self*."

"Aura?"

"Yes, aura. You shouldn't show your true aura out in the open this way — the angels might see you."

Time slowed as I remembered how he'd seen the angels, too. The truth hit me like a blow, so that all that existed was the two of us, standing on the bridge. Focusing on Seb, I brought his aura into view. It was pale green with darker green lights.

"Show me," I whispered.

He understood what I meant without my having to explain. A smooth rippling — and his aura changed. Silver with forest-green lights gleaming through it. In a dream,

251

I put my hand out, running it through the gently shifting colors as if I could catch them, watching as they played on my fingers. Seb stood very still. I felt him shiver and realized that he could feel this, just as if I was stroking his skin.

I lowered my hand, but couldn't stop staring at the beautiful silvery lights. My eyes were full of tears — the words almost wouldn't come.

"You're half angel," I said. "I thought — I thought I was the only one in the world."

Seb let out a breath that was almost a sob. "*Yes. Yes. Me, too . . . me, too.*" He tried to say something else; couldn't seem to get out the words. He reached for my hand again, squeezing it hard.

I stood with his fingers gripping mine as we stared at each other. I *should pull away*, I thought . . . but instead I was holding on to him tightly, too. I could sense his energy again, and now it all made sense. It felt so warm and familiar because for the first time ever, I was touching one of my own kind. The sensation of like touching like was indescribable — something I knew now that every human being on the planet took for granted. But to have never experienced this at all, and then to suddenly *find* it, after seventeen years . . . Oh, God, it was like sinking into a warm bath and not knowing where my skin ended and the water began.

Seb's eyes were so full of wonder that he looked almost frightened, and I knew he was feeling exactly the same thing. Other knowledge came, too: snapshots from his life, swirling through my head. The orphanage he'd been abandoned in, life on the streets, a young offenders' place that was so horrific I found myself wincing in pity. More than that, I got a sense of *him*. His inner strength. The teasing sense of humor he'd somehow hung on to, the charm that hid the utter loneliness he felt sometimes. He'd known he was half angel since he was a small child — had felt alone for most of his life. He'd searched for so many years. So many.

And underneath everything, steady as a heartbeat, was an emotion so intense it took my breath away.

No, I have to be wrong about that, I thought in confusion. He couldn't feel that way about me — it didn't make any sense. We'd only just met each other.

"How did you find me?" I asked finally.

Seb looked down at our hands together; his fingers tightened. "You dreamed about me," he said huskily. I stiffened. Oh, my God, how did he know that? "You dreamed we were in a park in El DF, so I came here," he went on. "I've been coming to Chapultepec for weeks, trying to find you."

"But —"

"I've got your shirt, your picture. I saw it was you, and I —" His hazel eyes rose again, and my chest clenched at the expression in them, so that other questions suddenly seemed meaningless. He swallowed; in slow motion, he reached out and touched my hair as if it were something fragile and precious. "Willow, I've been looking for you for so long. I can't tell you how I felt when I saw your picture for the first time—what it meant to me. I—"

The sound of running footsteps came from the path behind us. "Willow!" called Alex's voice, and all at once I was hotly aware that I was standing there holding a stranger's hand, staring into his eyes. I pulled away from Seb as Alex came jogging up, but I knew that he'd seen.

Alex stopped in front of us, dark hair ruffled from the run as he looked at me in bewilderment. His glance at Seb was tinged with suspicion. "Willow, what's going on? Who is this guy? I saw you running off with him, and I thought—are you OK?"

"I'm fine," I said, touching his arm. The pure human energy rushed through me; it took me a second to adjust, and then it was only Alex again, warm and familiar. "I'm fine," I repeated. I started to try to explain, then remembered in a rush. "Alex, the Council's arrived! They were part of that flock that was just overhead!"

His jaw dropped. "The Council? Are you sure? They're not supposed to be here for another five weeks!"

"Yeah, it was definitely them—twelve shining angels, just like in my dream. They flew into the top of that tower." I pointed, shading my eyes from the sun.

"The Torre Mayor," muttered Alex, staring upward. "What the hell are they doing *there*, instead of the Nikko?"

"The plans have changed, I guess." Feeble, useless words. "Or maybe they're going to the hotel later?"

Alex let out a strained breath, still gazing up at the gleaming pinnacle. "God, let's hope so. We don't know *anything* about that place—no floor plans, nothing. My team's not even fully trained yet." He shoved his hands through his hair; I could feel how shaken he was.

There was a pause, and then he looked down at me, and back at Seb again. Confusion crossed his features. Slowly, he said, "OK, so . . . who is this guy, anyway? Why were you —?" He stopped.

Holding hands with him. My cheeks flushed. Seb stood leaning against the statue's base, listening. I could sense how disappointed he was that we'd been interrupted — and in a daze, it hit me how easily I could read him already. I'd never felt such a strong instant connection to anyone in my life before.

"Alex, this is Seb. He —" I broke off. "Seb, is it OK if I tell him?"

"Tell me what?" Alex's dark eyebrows had drawn together. "Willow, what's going on?"

I glanced at Seb; he gave a resigned shrug. "He's half angel," I said.

Alex couldn't have seemed more stunned if I'd smashed him over the head with a mallet "He's what?" He looked sharply back at Seb; there was a rapid shift as his consciousness rose through his chakra points. "His aura's green, not silver. But his energy feels . . ." His eyes widened. "Christ, you really are one. What's the deal with your aura?"

As clearly as if I were thinking it myself, I knew how much Seb disliked Alex knowing this; the fact that he could change his aura was something he'd always kept secret. You wouldn't have guessed it from his body language, though. He looked like the definition of *casual* as he stood there against the statue.

"You can see auras," he said. "Most humans can't."

Most humans. The words gave me a start — Seb didn't see himself as human. And I still did, for some reason, even though I so clearly wasn't.

"I've been trained," said Alex shortly. "Answer the question."

Seb flicked a glance over him; you didn't have to be psychic to see he didn't like being ordered around. "It isn't smart, with angels around," he said at last. "So I changed it."

"Wait — you can change your aura?" repeated Alex, his eyes narrowing. "Like, at will?"

Seb's forehead creased; Alex said something in rapid Spanish, and he nodded. "Yes, at will." A small, sardonic smile. "Your Spanish is very good, *amigo*."

Alex gave him a look at the word *amigo*, and I knew he was still thinking of Seb holding my hand. "Yeah, thanks," he said. "So are there lots of half angels, or —"

"No," said Seb and I together. "No," I went on, clearing my throat. "Seb — he's never seen another one. He's spent most of his life looking."

I could see Seb realizing the depth of what I'd gotten from his hand. *Did he get anything from mine?* I wondered suddenly. Did Seb know me just as well as I knew him now? At the feel of his steady gaze on me, my face warmed; I couldn't meet his eyes. God, what was wrong with me?

Alex had fallen silent. I could almost see him turning all this over in his head. "Another half angel," he murmured. "Jesus." Watching Seb carefully, he rested against the railing of the bridge with his arms folded over his chest. The sleeves of his blue sweatshirt were pushed up, showing the toned muscles of his forearms.

"How did you find her?" he asked finally.

"Someone stole your things in Chihuahua," said Seb, speaking to me rather than Alex. "Some clothes and a picture. I bought them at the marketplace, and when I touched them, I could see . . . everything."

I have your shirt, your picture. It all became clear. Seb had seen my dream from my shirt — the last time I'd worn it, I'd been worrying for hours about what the dream might mean.

"And after that?" asked Alex after a pause. "How did you know where we'd gone?"

Seb glanced at me. My heart sank as I remembered: I hadn't told Alex about the strange boy in my dream; it had just seemed too surreal. But even though how I'd felt in the dream had been ridiculous, what would Alex think when he heard about it now — when the strange boy had been holding my hand, touching my hair?

To my relief, all Seb said was, "She was thinking that you needed to come to El DF — I touched her shirt, and I felt it. So I came, too."

"El DF is a big place," pointed out Alex dryly.

"Yes, I get feelings, sometimes. I got a feeling today, that I should come to Bosque de Chapultepec." Seb smiled;

there wasn't much humor in it. "Any more questions?"

Still leaning against the railing, Alex gave a soft snort. "Oh, sorry — am I being too nosy?" The traffic droned past below as he crossed his ankles, keeping his gaze on Seb. "I get like that when I find some guy hanging on to my girlfriend. Weird, huh?"

Seb arched an eyebrow. Neither moved as they regarded each other.

"Alex, it wasn't like that, honestly!" I said. From somewhere outside of myself, I was shaking my head in amazement that these two gorgeous boys seemed to be having some kind of standoff over me. From *inside* of myself, it felt awful. "It was just — this moment of realizing that we're both half angels, that's all."

Still watching Seb, Alex started to say something else, then stopped. He blew out a breath and shook his head. Glancing at me, he held an arm out; we hugged tightly. I could sense Seb's dismay as he watched, and I actually felt *guilty* for a second. It was insane; I'd only known him for about half an hour. Angrily, I tried to shove this weird hyper-awareness of Seb's feelings out of my mind.

Alex's arms were warm around me. "I'm sorry," I murmured against his neck. "I know it must have looked —"

He kissed me, halting my words. "Hey, come on; you know I trust you," he whispered.

Somehow I knew he wasn't including Seb in that sentiment. Not that I could really blame him. Then I thought of something, and I peered around us. "Wait, where are Sam and Trish?"

"They're going to meet us back home with Kara and her group," said Alex. "Sam really wanted to come with me, though — he thought I might be beating up who-ever this guy was." From his expression as he glanced back at Seb, he didn't think it was the worst idea he'd ever heard. There was more, though; I could tell he was turn-ing something over in his mind.

"So," he said finally, keeping his arm around my shoulders. "What now?"

Seb looked a question at him.

"See, I've got this really bad feeling that we're not going to get rid of you," said Alex. "Call me crazy, but I don't think you're planning on heading back up to Chihuahua now that you've met another half angel."

Seb's gaze went to me . . . and all at once I knew that no power on earth would make him leave. Now that he'd finally found me, he'd die before he ever let himself be sep-arated from me again. And to my alarm, what I felt wasn't far off from that. It made me shaky to admit it, but it was true — something primal that I couldn't even control. Seb might be the only other half angel I'd ever encounter. There was no way I wanted him to go back to Chihuahua.

"No, I'm not going anywhere," said Seb. "Not unless you want me to," he added to me.

I was so conscious of Alex standing beside me, of what he might be feeling about all this. "No, I don't want you to go," I admitted softly.

Alex glanced down at me in surprise. I tried to tell him with my eyes that this had nothing to do with him and me, and everything to do with needing to know another of my kind. To my relief, I saw understanding cross his face. He didn't look happy, exactly, but I could see that he got it.

"You were holding his hand," he said after a pause. "What did you get? Can he be trusted?"

Remembering what I'd seen, the question almost made me laugh. Seb had been a thief for years; he'd picked more pockets and stolen more cameras and purses than he could count. But I *did* trust him, I realized. I'd trust him with — anything.

"Yeah, he can be trusted," I said.

Alex seemed to make up his mind. "OK, look," he said to Seb. "If you came back with us, could you teach Willow how to do that aura thing?"

Seb's eyebrows shot up. "You don't know how?" he said to me.

I shook my head, shocked that Alex was even suggesting this — though on second thought, it made perfect sense. My half-angel aura put me in danger every time I went outside; I knew how much he worried about it. "I'm not usually that aware of auras," I told Seb. "I mean, I can see other people's if I try, but I've never seen my own unless I was in my angel form. Trying to change it never occurred to me — I wouldn't even know where to start."

Seb's hazel eyes were concerned. "Yes, I'll teach you. It's much safer."

I nodded, my emotions so mixed I could hardly make

sense of them. Part of me was still stunned that Seb was even *real*, much less that he was coming back to the house with us.

There was no sign now of Alex's own mixed emotions about Seb, though I knew he must still have them. "Good," he said, sounding like he was talking to any member of the team. "And you know what we do, right?"

Seb bent down to pick up his bag. "No. What do you do?"

"We're Angel Killers," said Alex. "AKs. Those angels you saw"—he nodded at the Torre Mayor—"if we can get rid of them, we can destroy all the angels in the world. That's our goal."

It was as if he'd knocked the breath out of Seb. He stood up slowly, staring. "You — this is a joke," he said. "You're going to kill all the angels? Really?"

"No joke," said Alex. "There's a group of us; that's what we're trying to do. If you come back with us, then you help us fight them; that's the deal. All right?"

Seb gazed up at the tower. From nowhere, I got an image of a young girl with big eyes and a grimy face. Seb would have come with us no matter what it was we did; I knew that—but something about this young girl in his thoughts made his shoulders straighten a little.

"Yes, all right," he said. "I'll help you fight."

We started heading back through the park, Seb walking on the other side of me from Alex. I could tell how much he still wanted to be talking to me, but he stayed quiet, his steps long and loping. Alex took my hand, weaving his fingers through mine and letting Seb go a few paces ahead of us.

"So what happened?" he asked in an undertone.

I explained as best I could, from Seb first finding me to Alex finding us. Uncomfortably, I was aware of how much I was having to leave out—such as Seb putting his arm around me and me not even minding at first, because it had felt so natural.

"Alex, are you really sure you're OK with this?" I finished. "I mean—Seb doesn't have to come back to the house with us." Though I knew if he didn't, I'd be counting the seconds until I saw him again. There was so much I was aching to ask him, so much I needed to find out.

Alex glanced at Seb. I caught a hint of resigned dislike, then it faded as he seemed to push his own feelings aside. "Yeah, I'm sure," he said quietly. "If he can teach you how to change your aura, so you can be safe . . . that's all that matters, Willow."

I hesitated, not totally convinced—but before I could say anything else, Alex looked down at me again. "Hey, what were you going to tell me, before Sam and Trish ran off? You seemed so worried—I almost had a heart attack, when we got back and you weren't there."

My angel. I swallowed hard. Ahead of us, Seb was standing against a tree, waiting for us to catch up. *Seb, please, please have some answers for me,* I thought. *I really need for you to.*

"Nothing," I said to Alex. "Sorry, I was just having a freak-out moment about the hunt. I mean, the thought of actually having to shoot something." I forced a smile. "I wasn't born to be a gun moll after all, I guess."

He searched my eyes; I felt both guilt and relief when he believed me. "Yeah, I know how much you hate it," he said, squeezing my hand. "Just promise me you'll try to shoot if an angel's ever coming at you, all right?"

"Promise," I said. More than that, I was promising myself that if Seb didn't have answers for me, I'd tell Alex about all of this immediately.

We caught up with Seb; he peeled himself off the tree and joined us again. When we reached the Metro station, my glance went to him as we headed down the concrete stairs. He was jogging slightly with his curly head down, knapsack bouncing on one shoulder. He looked so normal — so totally human. God, I could see why the team still felt wary of me; to look at Seb, there was no hint he wasn't completely human. And in his case, even his aura blended in with everyone else's.

His aura. As we jostled our way to the ticket machines, it suddenly struck me exactly what it would mean if I could learn to disguise my own. I knew it wasn't what Alex had had in mind when he'd asked Seb to teach me — it hadn't even occurred to him; he just wanted me to be safe. But if I somehow managed to get my angel self under control — and if my aura looked human, so that I blended in with the rest of the AKs . . . I stared at the ticket machines, feeling almost dizzy.

I could take part in the Council attack.

CHAPTER THIRTEEN

ALEX WASN'T SURE which caused a bigger ruckus back at AK house — the news that the Council had arrived five weeks early and were at the Torre Mayor, or that there was another half angel in the world, and, hey, here he was in their house with them. He explained everything to the team the best he could; it still felt like he'd set off a bomb. Soon after, Kara cornered him in the kitchen.

"*Another half angel?*" she demanded, hands on her slim hips. "Perfect, that's just what we need right now. Who is this guy? Can we even trust him?"

Alex was making himself a mug of instant coffee; he made another one for her without asking — she was as addicted to caffeine as he was. "I don't think I can trust him as far as I can throw him," he admitted. "The guy's got serious designs on Willow. But I think the team can trust him, yeah. And if he can teach her this aura thing, it'll be worth it."

Kara stood against the counter beside him as she sipped her coffee. She rolled her eyes. "You know, that's so reasonable, it makes my head hurt."

Alex touched his forehead, where — speaking of hurting heads — another headache was starting to throb. "Reasonable — right. I'm just trying to talk myself out of taking a swing at the guy next time I see him. If you'd seen the way he was looking at her . . ." Or for that matter, the way Willow had been looking at Seb, with her green eyes so full of wonder. Annoyed with himself, Alex pushed the image away and took a gulp of coffee. "Anyway, even if I threatened the guy at gunpoint, he's not going to just go away — he's spent his entire life looking for another half angel. So I might as well keep him close, where I can keep an eye on him."

"Keep your friends close and your enemies closer," Kara murmured. She shook her head. "God, this is just unreal. And if there are two of them, then there must be more, don't you think? They can't possibly be the only ones — or can they?"

The thought of Willow and Seb being the only two of their kind brought a small chill; it sounded like Noah's Ark and creatures going two by two. "No way, there have to be more," said Alex. "It must be pretty rare, though, when the angels themselves think Willow is the only one."

"And somehow the two of them found each other," mused Kara. Alex gave her a dirty look, and she shrugged. "Sorry. But it is sort of . . . poetic."

"Yeah, how'd you guess? I feel so much like writing a sonnet right now."

"OK, OK. I *said* sorry." Kara sighed and ran a hand over her close-cropped hair. "Anyway, I'd better go and meet Luis — see if I can find out what's going on with the Council."

Alex nodded. "Be careful."

"Always am." She went to the kitchen table, where her leather bag lay, and pulled out her gun; she briefly checked its cartridges before tucking the weapon back into hiding. "All right, see you later," she said, hooking the bag over her shoulder. "I'll text you in a while to check in."

Once Kara was gone, Alex stood where he was for a few minutes, worry over the Council throbbing at his skull. Jesus, he'd thought he had almost two months left to train everyone — but if the Twelve were following their original plan, they'd only be in Mexico City three weeks. *Three weeks.* And he still had a team that went running off without thinking.

He closed his eyes, squeezing his temples with one hand. *Don't panic,* he told himself. *It's not as long as you thought you had, but you can do it. You can get them ready in time. And maybe Willow got it wrong, and it wasn't the Council after all.*

That last one seemed like way too much to hope for. Alex let out a breath. Anyway, no point in worrying about this just yet—he'd have to wait and see what Kara came back with.

The only other half angel in the world.

He frowned as he looked down, swirling the coffee in his mug. It couldn't really be true, could it? And if it was, then, Christ—what were the odds of Seb being around Willow's age, and just happening to stumble on her things in a marketplace? Or getting a "feeling" that he should go to Chapultepec, on the only day of Willow's life that she'd ever been there?

Remembering what Kara had said about the two of them finding each other, a prickle ran up Alex's spine.

He drained his coffee, irritated that he was even thinking this way. There was no such thing as fate; Seb was obviously as psychic as Willow was, that was all. And had been determined to find another half angel. Once he had, learning that she had a boyfriend must have ruined the guy's day—because although Alex was certain that for Willow, the moment when he'd found them staring at each other really had just been about meeting another half angel, he severely doubted that the same was true for Seb. No guy looked at a girl the way Seb had been with only species solidarity in mind.

And now he was here in their house . . . and would be alone with Willow all the time, teaching her how to change her aura.

Alex put down his empty mug, a little harder than intended, and went to find them. He eventually discovered Willow and Seb up on the second floor, where a small balcony overlooked the concrete courtyard. Seb stood lounging in the doorway with his hands in his jeans pockets; Willow was on the balcony itself, leaning against its metal railing. They'd obviously been deep in conversation, but Willow broke off with a smile when she saw him.

"Hey, you," she said, resting a hand on his chest and craning up on her tiptoes to kiss him. Alex saw how carefully blank Seb's face went, and knew more than ever that he'd been right. *Yeah, take that, angel boy*, he thought before he could help it.

Willow sank back to her feet. "I'd better go see if Liz wants help with dinner," she said. "We'll talk later, OK, Seb?"

"Yes, I'd like that," he said softly. He watched her go, his eyes lingering on her petite form.

Alex propped himself against the metal railing where Willow had just stood. "OK, let's get something straight," he said in Spanish. "If you think I don't know you're after my girlfriend, you're crazy. And if you try to put any sleazy moves on her while you're here, you're going to wish you hadn't."

Seb's knapsack was at his feet. He took out a pack of cigarettes, tapped out the last one, and lit it. Settling back against the doorjamb, he gave Alex a considering, faintly humorous look. "Sleazy moves?" he repeated. "Don't worry, I don't do sleazy moves."

"Let me rephrase," said Alex coldly. "Any moves. Just keep your hands off her."

Seb was silent as he blew a stream of smoke toward the

sky. "This isn't really any of your business, you know," he said finally. "Whatever happens between Willow and me is up to her. Not you."

Alex gave a short laugh. "Not my business? Think again — this is my girlfriend we're talking about. And I want to make sure that *you* know it's up to her."

"Well, you can put your mind at ease, then." Seb's voice was mild, but had a thread of steel weaving through it. "Because I don't pressure girls, and I don't make moves where they're not wanted. If Willow only wants to be friends, that's all we'll be."

Alex nodded slowly, watching him. "OK," he said at last. "But if you do *anything* to hurt Willow — if you make her uncomfortable in any way while you're here — I will seriously make you regret it."

Seb took another puff of his cigarette. "Be my guest. Look, I really don't want to discuss this with you. But I'd die before I did anything to hurt Willow — or before I let anyone else hurt her, either. End of conversation, OK?"

Watching Seb as he smoked, Alex wondered despite himself what it would be like to finally find another of your own kind, after searching for so many years. He knew that if he were Seb, he wouldn't be prepared to just walk away from Willow, either. The realization didn't exactly make him warm to the guy.

"No, not quite end of conversation." He shifted on the railing, his arms folded over his chest. "How long have you known you're half angel?"

Seb's eyebrows rose. "Is that any of your business?"

"You're training my girlfriend how to disguise her aura? Yeah, it's my business."

The look on Seb's face wasn't amused, exactly, but it was heading in that direction. "You're big on the girlfriend thing, aren't you?" he observed. "She's not your property, you know."

The comment brought Alex up short; irritatingly, he knew Seb was right and that Willow would say the same thing if she'd heard him. "No, she's not," he said. "But as the leader of the team, I need you to answer my question."

Seb stretched across to the railing to tap ash off his cigarette. "You know, I'm trying my best to think of the possible relevance here. . . . Fine, whatever. I've known I was half angel since I was five."

"So, that's what — around thirteen years?"

"Yeah, I just turned eighteen."

"OK. You've known for thirteen years. Willow has known for about three months. When she first found out—" He broke off, remembering Willow's despair, her struggle to deal with all of this. "It was really hard for her," he said at last. "What I'm getting at is — I think she probably needs you, OK? She needs someone who can help her with all this."

Seb fell silent, his hazel eyes thoughtful as he smoked. "I understand," he said. "I'll do whatever I can."

For some reason the two-by-two thing flickered into Alex's head again; he shoved it away with a mental grimace. "I want you to start training her tomorrow," he said. "The sooner she can learn to hide her aura, the better."

"I agree; it's no good that she doesn't know how." Seb studied him. "Seriously, man, how do you even sleep at night, knowing she's so exposed all the time?"

"She's not *that* exposed—I'd die before I ever let anything hurt her, either," said Alex dryly. "But yeah, it's not easy, sometimes."

"I believe you," said Seb. "Because I won't be sleeping well now, myself, until she learns." His cigarette was almost gone by then; he took a final puff, seeming to savor it.

It was childish, but Alex couldn't resist: "Oh, and she hates cigarette smoke, by the way."

The look Seb shot him was now definitely amused. Breathing out a last plume of smoke, he twisted the butt out on the metal railing. "You know what? I had a feeling she did. Good thing I just quit, isn't it?"

Alex could tell he was serious. "So, that would be because you're not after her in the slightest."

Seb shrugged as he propped himself back against the doorjamb. "It would be because I've just found the girl I've been looking for my entire life, and she hates cigarette smoke. It's not exactly a complicated decision."

The girl I've been looking for my entire life. Alex resisted the urge to throw Seb off the balcony and see if he could fly. "Here's a tip: You might as well keep smoking. Have four packs a day; knock yourself out. Nothing's going to happen between you and Willow. Or don't you actually know that?"

Seb was standing with his hands in his jeans pockets; a

breeze ruffled one of his loose curls. "Yeah, that must be the only reason I want to stick around — because I think she's going to fall into my arms tomorrow. You know what? You're right. Now that I've met another half angel, why don't I just leave again? Willow won't care. Neither will I."

Alex had a feeling that Willow *would* care — a lot, actually. God, why had he even suggested letting this guy stay? But he knew why, and it was still the most important thing, bar none.

"Don't go anywhere until you teach her how to change her aura," he said. "After that — I'll help you pack. Anyway, back to business. Have the guys helped you figure out where you're sleeping?"

Seb looked unsurprised at the change of subject. "Yeah, they said they could put a camp bed in the dorm for me. It looks pretty crowded in there already, though. Plus I don't think anyone likes the idea very much, you know?"

Alex didn't like the idea, either; Willow was self-conscious enough already about being in his room, without him wanting Seb out there in the dorm, too. "You can take one of the storage rooms," he said. "It'll be pretty cramped, but if we pile some boxes up, we could probably just about squeeze a camp bed in."

"Sounds good. I'd like that better, anyway," said Seb. And apparently with that, he considered the conversation closed. He snagged his knapsack from the floor, then swung it over his shoulder.

Seeing Seb's knapsack reminded Alex of something.

"Hey, have you still got Willow's picture?" he asked. "The one of her when she was a little girl? Because I think she'd really like it back, you know. It means a lot to her."

Seb regarded him; suddenly his eyes were almost impish with humor. "Don't worry — I'll keep it safe and give it back to her soon. But for now —" He shrugged, smiled. "Hey, you've got the girl; I've got the picture. That's fair, right?"

As Seb walked off, Alex was tempted to haul him back by the strap of his battered knapsack and take out Willow's picture himself. Thinking about what he'd told Kara, he knew that it was true — the team could trust Seb; Willow's psychic insights were never wrong about that kind of thing.

Whether he'd ever like the guy was a totally different matter.

I helped Liz with dinner that night, though things had gone pretty stiff between us. Not that we'd ever become bosom buddies, but we'd at least started talking a tiny bit when we cooked together. Now her mouth was a thin line as she made the salad, and I knew it was because of Seb. When we'd first gotten back to the house, Alex had explained to everyone what had happened, his tone as matter-of-fact as if this kind of thing occurred every day. Even so, the team had been . . . surprised to have another half angel suddenly appear. To put it mildly. That plus the Council arriving early had put everyone seriously on edge.

I set the table in silence. My own thoughts were still

way too confused to try to alleviate whatever was going on in Liz's head.

We both looked up as the door opened and Kara rushed into the kitchen. "Where's Alex?" she said, yanking off her jacket. Without waiting for an answer, she called out toward the boys' dorm, "Alex! Alex, we've got to talk!"

"What's going on *now*?" asked Liz, wide eyed.

"Luis is gone," said Kara tightly. She paced the kitchen. "Totally gone; no sign of him. I went to his apartment, and it's just abandoned, like —" Alex came in, and she whirled toward him. "Alex! Luis is —"

"I heard," he said.

The others started arriving behind him as Kara explained. "He was visiting his family this weekend, but he was supposed to be home by now; I already had a date with him tonight," she said, her words tumbling over themselves. "But there wasn't any answer, so I let myself in, and . . . he's just gone. I mean, his bag's there, so he got home all right, but it's still unpacked. There was a half-eaten sandwich on the table, and a cold cup of coffee. . . ." She trailed off.

I bit my lip and glanced at Alex; he was standing behind one of the kitchen chairs, leaning on its back with both arms. "You didn't try to call him, did you?" he asked sharply.

Kara shook her head. "No, and I didn't touch anything in his apartment, either — just got out of there as fast as I could." She took a deep breath. "Plus the Council's not staying at the Nikko Hotel — I headed over there and couldn't feel any sign of them. So then I went to the Torre Mayor, but to get past the lobby, you have to have a pass for the card reader. I don't know if the angels are still there or not—they're really high up if they are; I couldn't tell."

There was a long pause as we all took this in. "So. Looks like the Church must have gotten wind of your boyfriend giving out security information," said Alex finally.

"Less of the boyfriend, please . . . but yeah." Kara looked more shaken than I'd ever seen her.

"OK, this is not good. This is officially really, really not good," muttered Brendan, clutching at his head.

For a change, Sam didn't argue with him. Neither did anyone else. Wesley stood glowering even more than usual; Trish and Liz looked as pale and stricken as I felt. At least Kara had never given Luis any information about us—though I felt guilty even thinking that, just then.

"So . . . I guess the same invitations for the party won't be any good now," said Trish faintly.

"No way," said Alex. I could hear the strain in his voice, though I doubted anyone else could. "Basically, we don't have a plan anymore—we're back to square one."

"Wait—what does that mean?" demanded Wesley. He hardly ever spoke with more than a few people around; now his fists were clenched at his sides. "Are you saying the attack can't go ahead? Because there is no way that—"

"Of course I'm not saying that," Alex cut in in a low voice. "This is the only chance we're going to have at the

Council. We'll find a way to get to them, no matter what."

My mouth went dry, but I knew he was right. Everyone glanced at one another. Three weeks — that was all we had now.

"Don't worry, we'll find out what's going on." Kara's voice was matter-of-fact again, back in control. "What do you want me to do? Should I go over to the cathedral tomorrow, see if I can get any information? Any change to the Council's visit was sure to have been organized by someone in the office there — they've been coordinating everything."

Alex nodded, looking deep in thought. "Yeah, good idea — we need anything you can get. Won't they recognize you, though?"

"No, I don't think so. I usually met Luis at his place. He didn't have my cell number or anything." She attempted a smile. "I was a woman of mystery."

I watched Alex's eyes scan over her. "Can you get hold of a wig or something, just in case? If the angels have him, they'll see you in his memories. And you're pretty distinctive."

Another time, I knew Kara would have bantered with Alex over this; now she just nodded. "I'll get one tomorrow. See what I can do with some makeup, too."

"Good," said Alex. "And I'll do some checking around myself. Plus keep training these guys — maybe take them on another practice hunt."

Sam was shaking his head. "Yeah, but what about —?"

He broke off as Seb came into the kitchen, looking

like he'd just taken a shower—his chestnut curls were damp, shoved away from his face as if he'd raked his fingers through them. When I saw him, something in me tightened . . . because I realized that the whole time we'd been talking, part of me had been thinking about Seb, wondering where he was.

Silence choked the room. Seb obviously noticed and knew it was because of him. His eyes found mine, and he smiled slightly. Despite my discomfort, I gave him a small one back; I knew exactly how he must be feeling. The team's stony faces were bringing back some not-so-pleasant sensations of déjà vu. Clearly I *had* made a little progress with them, even if I hadn't been all that aware of it—because now that Seb was here, this was something else that was back to square one.

Alex sighed. "Hey, Seb," he said, and I wanted to hug him just for managing to sound normal. "We were talking about something that's come up; I'll fill you in after dinner. You finding everything all right?"

Seb's eyebrows rose at "something that's come up," but he didn't comment. "Yes, fine, thanks."

As we all started sitting down to eat, Seb took the seat next to me—the place where Alex always sat. Obviously he didn't know that, but I could see everyone glancing at Alex, to see what he would do. As if there was some sort of competition going on.

My face went hot, and I cleared my throat. "Um, Seb, that's—"

"It's OK," said Alex briefly. He took the seat to my

other side, the one where Trish usually went, and Trish squeezed in next to Wesley, where I'd put an extra chair. I saw Seb get what had happened then; he looked like he was holding back a smile despite himself.

Hardly anyone spoke. The clinks of knives and forks against plates sounded deafening. My own awkwardness around Seb wasn't helping much, either, to be honest . . . and I was feeling a lot of it.

When Seb and I had been talking on the balcony earlier, there'd been so much to say that we'd just kind of skirted around the edges of it all, with the unspoken understanding that as soon as we could, we'd be sitting down for a long talk. I wanted that desperately. There was so much I needed to know: to ask if what I'd been experiencing with my angel was normal, to find out more about his life, to compare a thousand and one experiences and see if things had been the same for him.

But as we'd been talking, I'd also been scalp-tinglingly *aware* of Seb, even standing several feet away from me. It wasn't because of how attractive he was — and he really was gorgeous; you'd have to be unconscious not to notice — it was just . . . him. His energy, so like my own. The memory of our hands together, of how that had felt. It had been a huge relief when Alex had shown up and I could make my escape.

You don't even know him, I told myself.

Except that wasn't true. I did know Seb. Maybe not all the details of his life yet, but the kind of person he was, yes. And now I could feel him sitting beside me. Not only his physical presence, but his energy. We were close enough that our two auras were touching, and though I never really noticed this with Alex unless I concentrated, with Seb it was like I'd just gained an extra sense — one that tingled through me like electricity. His aura was so alive, so buoyant. I could feel it drifting through my own, just the way mine was drifting through his. Intermingling. Exploring.

My cheeks heated. Abruptly, I tried to bring my aura back to myself, but we couldn't avoid each other — we were sitting too close. I felt Seb notice, and try and fail to pull his own aura completely away. Now there was a sense of gentle, teasing apology where his aura mingled with mine, and I gritted my teeth. Wonderful. I was inadvertently playing aura-footsie with him.

And meanwhile, the silence had not become any less deafening.

"OK, come on, everyone, this is stupid," said Alex finally. "He's a member of the team. We can trust him. Just . . . act normal, all right? Please, for the love of God, before my brain starts to bleed."

For a moment no one spoke. "So, Willow," said Kara finally, a resigned look on her face, "maybe you could tell us more about what you saw today, when the Council arrived."

Relieved, I started to answer — but before I could, Sam jumped in. "No, wait," he growled, tossing his fork down with a clatter. "Alex, I want to know just how it is you're so sure we can trust this guy. At least with Willow, we all saw her angel defending Liz. Who is he, anyway? He's just appeared out of nowhere, and now he's on the team?"

Seb glanced at him. "I'm Sebastián Carrera," he said, cutting a piece of his pork chop. "I'm not from nowhere; I'm from right here, Mexico City. And if I say I'll help you fight, I'll help you fight."

"Willow's read his hand," added Alex as Sam opened his mouth to respond. "We can trust him."

"Got it," said Sam, giving me a look that wasn't massively friendly. "So I guess that's why she was holding hands with him when they went running off together this afternoon, right? 'Cause she was busy giving him a reading?"

My face went bright red as everyone stared. "Oh, *that* sounds nice and cozy," muttered Liz. Trish winced down at her plate, obviously hating the tension.

On either side of me, I felt both Alex and Seb bristle. "That was my fault," said Seb in a voice that was calm but had a challenge under it. "I grabbed her hand to help her run when we saw the angels. We had to go fast, you know?"

Sam snorted. "Yeah, you sure did go fast," he said to me. "You were in an awful hurry to go tearin' off with this guy, weren't you? Guess we must not have heard you when you tried to tell *us* what was going on."

"I *did* try!" I said, stung. "I shouted Alex's name, but—"

"Stop—you don't have to explain," broke in Alex, reaching for my hand. He enfolded it in his. "Drop it, Sam. Willow's already told us what happened."

Sam opened his mouth.

"*Drop* it," repeated Alex.

Silence fell again. I'm not sure whether the quality of it was any better than the last one. More crackling with tension around the edges, maybe.

"Well," said Brendan finally. "Acting normal was fun."

I could still feel Seb's aura mingling with mine; he was concerned for me, wanted to soothe me. On my other side, Alex's hand felt so warm, so safe. I held on to it tight. I longed to be someplace alone with him—really alone, the way we used to be. Things had been so simple when it was just the two of us, with no one else around. Nothing felt very simple at all anymore.

After a pause, Alex squeezed my hand and released it. His voice as he addressed the team was steady. "Look, guys, we're coming up to crunch time on the Council—if they're sticking to the same plan, they're only going to be here a few weeks. So we don't have time for this. Seb's here—that's it. Either you trust my judgment on this one, or you don't. You decide."

"We trust you," said Kara quietly. "Don't we, everyone?"

Mumbled *yes*es, nods. Sam's face was stormy, but he didn't say anything. Trish glanced at him, her gentle eyes anxious.

"Sam?" said Alex, watching him, too.

The Texan let out a long breath. "Yeah, OK," he muttered, pushing his blond hair back.

"Good." To my surprise, Alex stretched across me, offering his hand to Seb. "There, they've accepted you. Lucky you."

Seb's smile was ironic as he reached across me, too. "Yes, I'm very honored."

And as he shook Alex's hand, I knew two things. One, the team still wasn't happy about this, despite their trust of Alex. And two, somewhere deep down where I didn't want to think about it . . . was the terrible feeling that being caught between these two boys might be my fate for a long time to come.

CHAPTER FOURTEEN

THE EXERCISE ROOM was small—just a corner of the basement, really, with some free weights, a couple of treadmills, and a weight machine. It smelled of mustiness and sweat. When some of the guys got going on the treadmills—Alex and Sam, especially—the sweat would be literally flying. I saw Seb glance at the floor; it was cement and not all that clean, I guess. It was also the only place where we could sit.

"We could go to my room," he suggested.

Seb's "room" was tiny; it would be both of us on his camp bed. The thought was way too intimate, especially after the aura-mingling of the night before. I felt my cheeks warm.

"No, in here is better," I said. "We've got more space. Wait, though." I ran up the stairs, grabbed the cushions from the sofa in the TV room, and carried them back down.

"Here," I said as we spread them out. "This'll be fine."

Above us, I could hear target practice going on with a vengeance. Kara was at the cathedral, as she and Alex had discussed, seeing what she could find out. And meanwhile, everyone was comforting themselves by getting as good with their weapons as they possibly could.

The night before, Alex and I had managed to talk on our own a little, while the others were all getting ready for bed or watching TV. As I'd stood against the closed door of the other storeroom, I'd been very aware of how strongly Seb was still in my thoughts. Even though I knew it was just because he was another half angel, it made me feel guilty anyway.

"It's been a strange day, hasn't it?" I'd said, clearing my throat.

"Yeah, understatement," Alex had agreed. I could feel the tension in his muscles, though we weren't touching. "God—a half angel and the Council, both in the same afternoon."

I tried to smile. "Hey, have you got something against half angels?"

I saw him wince as he realized what he'd said; he shook his head at himself. "Not this one," he said, taking my hand and drawing me to him. "I like this one a lot, actually." He looped his arms around my neck, dropping his head to mine. "Look, I really am glad he's here," he said finally. "I just want you to be safe, Willow."

And all I'd wanted to do was hold him as tight as I could. I'd hesitated, still worried about angel burn.

Sometimes, like when I'd kissed him earlier, I thought I must be going insane to even be thinking about it; other times, the fear was an ocean of ice inside of me. Then Alex had pulled me gently to his chest, and I'd given into it. We stood against the wall holding each other for a long time, while the rest of the world faded away. Nothing else seemed to matter, apart from being in Alex's arms.

Now, sitting in the basement exercise room with Seb, I was desperate to get some answers about what had been happening with my angel. Perversely, she seemed to have calmed down a little since I'd met him, but I was still so aware of her, there inside me — so conscious that I didn't know what she might do.

Seb and I settled ourselves on the large square sofa cushions, sitting a few feet from each other. He was wearing faded jeans again and a blue T-shirt that had a swirling white logo in Spanish. The words looked slightly crumbled, like they'd ridden through the wash too many times.

"What does your shirt say?" I asked.

He glanced down at himself as if he couldn't remember. "It's for Cinco de Mayo — when we threw the French out of Mexico."

"The French were in Mexico?"

"A long time ago." Seb shrugged. "I bought it at a marketplace."

I nodded, realizing how very little I knew about this country. It wasn't exactly something that was covered at school, which was sort of strange when you thought about it — Mexico was so close.

Then, still gazing at Seb, I noticed something that was different. "Hey, you shaved," I said. He looked less like a rock star today, more like an actor playing the sexy new boy at school.

He touched his jaw, looking embarrassed. "Yes — I guess it's been a while."

"I think I liked you better before," I said, studying him, and then wished I had said *anything* except that — I was just making conversation, but his hazel eyes looked delighted suddenly. He grinned as my cheeks flushed.

"I'll never shave again," he said.

I was aware that my face was on fire. "Seb, look — you know Alex and I are together, right? I mean — I like you, but —"

"Yes, I know that," he said quietly. "It's all right." I had the sense of some deeper emotion being buried; then Seb smiled and ran a hand over his jaw again. "But, you know — if you think not shaving would *help* . . ."

To say I wasn't used to boys making their interest in me so obvious — even in a humorous way — would be the understatement of the century. I wasn't even used to boys *having* any interest in me, much less ones who looked like Seb. Back in Pawtucket, I had always been Queen Weird, the outcast of the school. I opened my mouth and then closed it again, trying to think of what to say.

Seb saw my discomfort, and the teasing look in his eyes vanished. "Willow, I'm only joking," he said. "I mean—yes, I would like to be more than friends; I'm not joking about that. But I know you're in love with Alex. If friendship is all you want, that's OK. It really is."

I shifted on the cushion. My cheeks were still warm, especially remembering what I thought I'd sensed in him the day before—the depth of his feelings toward me. Thankfully, I couldn't pick up on any sign of that now, though admittedly I didn't go looking very hard. If by some insane chance I'd been right, I seriously didn't want to know.

"Are you sure you're all right with that?" I said finally.

"Yes," said Seb. The corner of his mouth lifted. "My whole life, I've been looking for another half angel. Believe me, I don't want to leave now, just because you haven't realized yet you can't resist me."

My eyebrows flew up. "Yet?"

"That was a joke, too," he said hastily. "I mean— well, no, I do hope you'll realize that someday, but—" Half laughing, he broke off and put his hand over his face, shaking his head. "Ay, caramba, I'm not doing very well, am I?"

Somehow I was smiling, too. Seb dropped his hand. "OK, let me start over," he said. "Willow, just to be here with you—to be your friend—that's enough. I promise."

"You're really sure?" I asked, scanning his face. "Even if friends is all we'll ever be?"

Seb's hazel eyes were steady, without even a hint of teasing. "Yes, I'm very sure," he said. "I'll be your brother. How's that?"

He meant it. I let out a breath, relieved that he understood—and even more relieved he still wanted to stay. "A brother sounds . . . really, really good, actually."

"You've got one, then," he said. "For life, if you want."

"Thanks," I said softly. And even though we'd only just met, I knew I probably *did* want that—already I felt such a connection to Seb. Even more, I knew that I needed his help. Feeling shaky, I pushed my hair back; suddenly my words were coming out in a rush. "Seb, I've got so much I want to ask you about. I've been so worried—"

Seb had been sort of half lying on his pillow; now he sat up, immediately concerned. "Worried?"

"More like terrified," I admitted. "Your angel. Can you feel him inside of you? I mean—present, but *separate* from you. Not thinking your thoughts. Like he has a mind of his own?"

He frowned, watching me. "Not for a long time," he said. "But when I was younger, I felt that."

I shifted to the edge of my sofa cushion. "What happened when you were younger?"

Seb's body language was casual: one wrist on his knee; the other hand resting on the cushion, propping him up. But there was a swirl of emotion from him—and all at once I knew I was the only person in the world who he'd ever tell this to. "Maybe you saw some of this when we touched yesterday," he said. "When I was eleven, I was arrested for stealing."

"Yeah, I did," I admitted. "And that place they put you . . ." I trailed off.

"Here in Mexico, they're called *reformatorios*." Looking down, Seb added, "They used to say to us that we should be so thankful to be there — because now we could be made into better people."

Better people. Remembering what I'd glimpsed of the young offenders' place — running water for only two hours a day, vicious beatings, being strapped to the bed at night — my throat tightened. Irony wasn't the word.

Seb ran a fingernail along a thread of his jeans. "I saw a lot of things happen there," he said finally. "Things much worse than stealing a wallet, I think." He smiled again; there was a hard edge to it this time. "I saw a boy try to escape, and they caught him — they tied him to a tree and left him there for days. No food or water. None of us were allowed to help him."

I picked up a sudden image of this and desperately wished I hadn't. Oh, God, the boy's eyes. His face. I could hardly get the words out. "What — what happened to him?"

Seb gave a small I *don't know* motion with his hand. "After a week, he was gone. We didn't see him anymore after that."

"But — is that even legal? How can they be allowed to do that? Couldn't you have told the police when you got out?" My voice had gone high-pitched with horror.

Seb's eyebrows shot up in surprise — and with something almost like pity, that I'd think this might be a solution. "No one would care," he said. "We were thieves and runaways — street boys, with no families."

I hugged my knees tight, feeling shaken. Above us, I could still hear the others practicing in the target range. The exercise machines around us looked weirdly ordinary, as if they belonged to a completely different life from the one Seb had been through. I supposed they did.

"How did you get out?" I asked after a pause.

He shrugged. "There was a loose piece of metal on my bed. I got it off, and sharpened it against the wall when no one was watching. It took months, but finally it was sharp enough. I threatened a guard with it, and I got out. Then I ran as fast as I could," he added, his mouth twisting. "I ran so fast I could have been in the Olympics."

I stared at him, amazed that he'd somehow held on to his sanity enough that he could joke about this, even a little bit. I *threatened a guard*. The words didn't surprise me, yet I knew what a fundamentally good person Seb was—a gentle one, even. Thinking about my own life when I was eleven, I mentally shook my head at the contrast. Even with all my problems, I'd had it so, so lucky, and I'd never even known.

"Did you hurt the guard?" I asked.

"No, he was a coward," said Seb. And I think I probably looked very determined. Like I wasn't going to take no for an answer." Faint amusement crossed his face as he remembered.

"Would you have hurt him?"

The amusement faded. As his eyes met mine, I knew Seb wasn't going to lie to me—that he never would. "Yes," he said quietly. "I would have done anything to get out of there. And I hated humans back then. For what they did to each other—what they had done to me."

My eyes went to a small scar on his arm, just where the sleeve of his T-shirt ended: a deep, dimpled hole, white against his tanned skin. About the size and shape of a cigarette burn. My heart chilled. Oh, God, had they done that to him there?

Seb noticed me looking and glanced down at the scar himself. "No—this was from my mother's boyfriend, when I was small." He lightly fingered the scar. "My mother didn't have very good taste in men."

There was no real bitterness to his tone, though I sensed how much he hated the boyfriend. Fleetingly, I wondered about his angel father, but now didn't seem the time to ask. I swallowed. "Seb . . ." I couldn't finish the sentence; there were no words.

He saw my face, and instant regret came over his, that he had upset me. He reached out and put his hand over mine, gripping it gently. "Querida, it's all right," he said. "No one has hurt me in years."

I hated it that anyone had ever hurt him at all. I squeezed his hand back and then drew away, wishing my traitor pulse hadn't skipped at his touch. "Hey, you're supposed to be my brother," I said, trying to joke. "Brothers don't hold their sisters' hands or call them querida."

Seb smiled, his hazel eyes starting to dance. "Yes, they do," he said. "This happens all the time."

"Well, I guess things are different in Mexico, then," I said. "Because in America, no way. And I'm an American."

"But you're in Mexico now," he pointed out.

"Right. And you're saying that here boys hold hands with their sisters and call them *sweetheart*."

"Oh, yes. We're very friendly, we Mexicans."

I laughed then; I couldn't help it. Seb grinned. I could sense his pleasure to see me smiling again, and something stirred deep inside me, a feeling I didn't really want to analyze. I just knew I was very glad that Seb was in my life now. Aside from anything else, it felt wonderful to have a friend again — apart from Alex, I'd felt like such an outcast these last few weeks.

"So what about your angel?" I asked.

A few soft-looking brown curls were hanging over Seb's forehead; he shoved them back impatiently. "After I escaped the *reformatorio*, I went back on the streets. And for three or four months . . ." He shook his head. "I wasn't a person you'd want to know. I hated humans; I wanted to hurt them. All I wanted was to be pure angel, so nothing could hurt me. I got into fights all the time — I almost dared people to look at me wrong, so I could jump them. I smashed windows, I burned cars, I stole. . . ." He fell silent, his eyes troubled. "Not a good time," he finished finally.

And all I could think was . . . before he went to be *made into a better person* at that place, the worst he'd ever done was pick pockets.

"Anyway, my angel didn't like it," said Seb. "Before, I never really felt him inside me. He was always just — me. There when I needed him, but me."

"Yes!" I burst out. "Yes — that's exactly what it was like at first."

Seb nodded. "But then my angel saw I was going to die young if I kept on the way I was. So he was always" — he frowned in thought, then reached over and pushed lightly at my arm a few times — "like this, inside of me, day and night."

"Nudging," I said. "Yes. Yes, me too!" I was sitting straight up now; it felt like electricity was coursing through the room. "But, Seb, what does that *mean*? Does it mean they're separate from us? That they're *not* us?"

He was shaking his head before I'd finished speaking. "No, they're us. Definitely us. I think it's like — sometimes you have two thoughts at the same time, you know? You might be thinking, I *should do this thing*, and at the same time you're thinking, *I'm hungry*, or, *I don't like this person* — deep down but both at the same time. Do you see what I mean?"

I understood exactly. "So — sometimes our angels have their own thoughts? Or they don't agree with us about something, but they're still just a part of us — like having mixed feelings about something?"

"Yes, I think so," said Seb. "That's how it is for me." He was sitting with one knee up, his arms looped loosely around it.

I told him about my angel breaking free during target practice, and he looked like he was trying not to laugh — though in a friendly way that made my tension ease. "I

293

think your angel must want you to notice her very badly," he said mildly. "What's she nudging you about?"

I tried to think. "I don't know. This started a few weeks ago, when I felt this sort of . . . rush of energy." I told Seb what had happened—about the mental river that had trickled to nothing, how I hadn't found anything when I'd gone searching. It was such a relief to finally be talking to someone about all of this that the words tripped over themselves.

Seb listened carefully, his eyebrows drawing together. "I don't know what that was," he said when I'd finished. "I've never felt anything like that before."

"Oh." I looked down at the yellow sofa cushion. The disappointment wasn't easy to bear. I'd been hoping he'd say, Oh, that. Yes, that happens all the time.

"But, querida"—he caught himself with a grin—"Willow, whatever it was, your angel feels different about it from how you feel. You need to listen to her, that's all."

I let out a breath. "She's felt so separate from me lately," I admitted. "Scary. I've thought—I don't know what I thought. I guess that whatever it was had . . . set her off somehow, so that she can't be trusted now."

I could see that not trusting his angel had never even occurred to Seb. "She's part of you," he said simply. "She'd never do anything to hurt you. She might feel separate and nudging at you sometimes, when you don't listen to her—but hurt you, no. Never."

He made it sound like my angel was pure intuition, or

a conscience, or something—which actually made a lot more sense than whatever dire things I'd been freaking myself out over. The relief was so enormous that I almost went limp—but I still had no idea what my angel wanted me to listen to her about. With a flash of guilt, I knew I hadn't given her much of a chance to explain. The second that she'd seemed separate from me, I'd just shoved her away and built a wall around her. No wonder she'd felt restless.

"Give me a minute," I said to Seb.

I closed my eyes and went deep within myself, reaching tentatively for my angel. She was there in a burst of light, like sunshine on crystal—my own face gazing back at me, wings glimmering. We gazed at each other. The only movement was the soft shifting of her hair, as if a slight breeze was blowing.

I'm sorry, I thought, mentally stretching my hand out to her. *Can you tell me what's wrong?*

We touched with a gentle glow of energies. My muscles relaxed as the oneness between us rushed back— our thoughts swirling together, merging again. Forgiveness, understanding. But she'd been so, so frustrated; so desperate to get me to listen to her. The dark power of the energy stream had alarmed her greatly. And now she had a feeling something was wrong. She didn't know what; she'd looked, found nothing—but it was a constant worry she couldn't get rid of.

Frowning, I carefully searched my mind again,

exploring every corner. There was nothing there that shouldn't be — genuinely, truly, nothing. *I really think it's OK*, I said to her.

She didn't respond; I could feel she wasn't convinced. Leaving her for the moment, I explained to Seb what had happened. "I don't know what to think," I finished. "She seems really positive, but I just can't feel it."

Seb's expression turned thoughtful. "No, I don't know, either." Sitting up cross-legged, he held his hands out to me. "Yes? Maybe I can sense something."

I hesitated, looking at his hands.

"I'll be very brotherly," he assured me. His eyes were teasing again, but they were also concerned — I knew how much he wanted to help.

"All right," I said finally.

Moving my cushion closer to him, I put my hands in his. That same jolt of energy, of like touching like. His hands were warm and firm, and so reassuring as they held mine, as if just his touch could make things better. I closed my eyes, keenly aware of our two auras mingling again, too, and wishing I could shut all this out. Especially the part about how good it felt — how right. I shoved the thought away almost before it formed, hating myself for even having it.

Seb's hands tightened in mine; I could sense his concentration. I tried to just drift and not think about much at all. I kept picking up snippets from him anyway, such as the fact that he'd given up smoking recently — his unconscious desire for a cigarette was coming through loud and clear. Some of what I picked up made me smile, like the stories he made up when anyone asked about his past. I didn't think he'd ever given a straight answer in his life. An opera-singing mother who took her piano with her everywhere?

And yet with me, he'd been so unhesitatingly honest.

Finally Seb let go of me, and I opened my eyes again. We were still sitting close, our faces only a foot or so apart, and I saw that his eyes had flecks of pure gold in the green. I moved hastily back, scooting my cushion several inches away.

Seb pretended not to have noticed. "I can tell how worried your angel has been," he said, leaning back on one hand. "I didn't feel anything wrong, though. Something's been bothering her, yes, but I can't see what."

I could sense my angel's puzzlement as she checked again for herself, and then realized what Seb had said was true: she couldn't feel what had been bothering her anymore, either — it was as if it had simply vanished. Or maybe it had never been there in the first place. She hesitated for a long moment within me, her wings gently stirring. I could still feel her confusion, though it was fading now to relief. Maybe she'd been mistaken, she thought at last. Because everything seemed all right now — really all right.

She was nowhere near as relieved as I was. I let out a breath. Oh, thank God, things might actually go back to normal for me now — or at least as "normal" as being a half angel could ever be. "It's OK," I said to Seb. "She thinks maybe it's all right now. Thank you — thank you so much."

"I didn't do anything," he said. "But that's good. If she's happy, there's no problem."

I crossed my legs, pulling them up to my chest. "So, I wonder what the energy was that I felt. It's not something that's ever happened to you?"

"No, never. Maybe it was just — ah, I can't think of the word." Seb tapped his brow and said something in Spanish, looking frustrated.

I smiled slightly, watching him. "Do you want me to go get Alex to translate?"

At the suggestion of bringing my boyfriend down here, Seb gave me a comically incredulous look from under his hand — like, *Are you kidding?* "No, we can't take Alex away when he's teaching the others," he said in a voice so serious that I almost believed him for a second. "It would be very selfish of us. I'd feel so guilty."

"Oh. Well, we wouldn't want that."

"No. The guilt, it would keep me awake at night." Seb straightened up. "The word I'm trying to think of — it's like when something happens only once, then never again. If it happens, you're so surprised. You know? What's the word?"

"A fluke?"

"¡Sí!" His smile was like sunshine bursting through the clouds. "Maybe it was just a fluke. Just a strange thing that happened. Or I don't know — maybe it was a *girl half-angel thing*."

Somehow *a girl half-angel thing* made me think of Alex's migraines and the other worry of these last few days. My hands clenched in my lap as I cleared my throat. The words didn't want to come out. "Listen, what about — what about hurting other people?" I asked. "Us, I mean."

Seb's eyebrows came together. "I don't think I understand."

"Do we . . . ?" I took a deep breath. "Do we cause angel burn to people when we touch them?"

Surprise spread over his face. "You mean hurt them, like the angels do? No, I don't think so. I've touched a lot of people — holding their hand, giving them readings — and I think I'd have seen."

"I know; I've given a lot of readings, too," I said. "But what I've been worried about is whether it might be different for us. The angels only have to touch someone's aura for a few seconds, but maybe with us it's a matter of how close we get to someone physically. I mean . . . close like when you're in a relationship." My face was a forest fire. I hoped he got what I meant, because I really didn't want to be any more explicit.

"Oh." Seb rubbed the back of his neck. Yes, he'd gotten it. "No, I've never noticed that."

Suddenly I knew that he'd had a lot more opportunities to notice it than I had, and felt my face blaze even hotter. "I'm sorry. I'm not trying to pry—"

He dropped his hand. "You're not prying," he said, though he still looked a little embarrassed. "I'll tell you anything you want to know."

I tried to push my own embarrassment aside and think where to start with all this. Or how to even word it. "Well—did you ever notice any of your girlfriends getting sick? Or damaged, like from the angels?"

"No, never," he said. "I would never have touched any girl in my life if I'd thought I was hurting her."

"And have there . . . been a lot?"

He grimaced, scraping a hand through his hair. "Not *that* many, but—well, more than I like to tell you," he admitted. I could sense he wished the answer were different. "Not for a long time, though," he added.

"Why not?" The words came out without thinking. Seb was so good-looking, with his hazel eyes and lean, toned lines—it was hard to imagine he couldn't have any girl he wanted.

He hesitated as he regarded me; again I caught that feeling of something deep being buried. "I don't know," he said finally. "Always being with the wrong girl . . . I guess it made me feel lonelier than being by myself after a while."

A pang went through me. Alex was the only boy I'd ever been involved with, but it still seemed like Seb and I had something in common. I'd been lonely for so much of my life, too.

"I get that," I said softly. "I really do."

His smile was rueful. "I wish I'd figured it out sooner" was all he said.

I was aware of what a personal conversation this was, when before yesterday we'd never even met — but it didn't feel that strange, somehow. And if Seb had had a lot of experience with girls, and he'd *never* noticed anything like what I was talking about . . .

Seb was still studying me. "This is about you and Alex, isn't it?" he said suddenly. "You're worried about him; I can feel it."

"He got a migraine a few days ago," I confessed. "And he's been getting headaches a lot. I've been so scared that it's because of me, that I've been hurting him just by being with him."

Seb had closed his eyes, shaking his head at himself. He half laughed. "Ay, *caramba*. I gave the wrong answer, didn't I? Can I change it? Yes, we cause terrible harm to humans. You should break up with Alex right now, so that you don't hurt him. Do you want me to go upstairs with you and help you tell him? As your brother, I would be very happy to do this."

"Seb!" I almost laughed, though I still wasn't totally convinced that I didn't have anything to worry about. "So . . . you're really sure?" I asked. "You never noticed any of your girlfriends getting migraines or headaches, or anything like that?"

His expression turned gentle. "Yes, I'm sure. Willow, we're half human — why would our energy hurt them?"

He touched my hand again briefly, his fingers comforting on mine. "Please don't worry anymore, *querida*. It's all right, I'm certain of it."

Relief. Soaring, total relief. "Oh, thank God," I whispered. "I've been so scared these last few days that I've been hurting him, and hating myself for not saying anything. I've felt like such an awful person—"

"You?" Seb gave a sudden grin. "No, you couldn't be awful if you tried. You're much too sweet for that."

"*Sweet?*" I made a face, laughing despite myself. "I am not."

"Oh, yes. I've seen this about you from the start. You like to help people; you care about them a great deal. You're very—" Seb stopped, regarding me for a long moment. "Special," he finished finally.

I winced at the look in his eyes. "Seb—"

"I'm saying this only as a brother," he added firmly. "Brothers are allowed to say these things sometimes."

I couldn't help smiling, even though I was shaking my head at him. I wasn't hurting Alex—I really wasn't. It felt like a million sunrises inside of me. "So, you didn't finish telling me what happened with your angel," I said after a pause. "Did he keep nudging at you until you listened to him?"

Before Seb could answer, I heard the basement door open. "Hey," called Alex's voice down the stairs. "We're about to go out."

I scrambled up from my cushion and went up the stairs to him. He'd been checking his gun and was tucking it back into his holster. "Another hunt?" I asked, watching apprehensively.

Alex nodded. He had on his white thermal shirt with the red plaid shirt hanging open over it, and just looked so — gorgeous. "Yeah, I thought I'd take them out again — maybe to a different park this time, so the angels can't start to predict what we're doing."

I rested back against the wall, half-conscious of Seb sitting just below. "Be careful," I said in a low voice. "Please."

Alex smiled and touched my face. "I'll be fine; don't worry. I've been doing this for years. They've just got to get some more practice, that's all." A cloud crossed his features, and I knew he was thinking about the Council, hoping Kara could find out what was happening — otherwise it wouldn't even matter how much practice the AKs got. "Anyway, how's it going?" he asked, nodding toward the basement stairs.

"Really well," I said. "I mean, we haven't started the aura work yet, but — Alex, he's helping me a lot." I stopped, realizing that I couldn't say much without going into a long explanation; I hadn't told Alex about how worried I was in the first place.

"Good," he said. "I'm glad." And I knew he really was, though it was clear that Seb still wasn't his favorite person. He smiled and brushed a strand of my hair back. "Got to make sure the guy earns his keep at least."

Earned his keep. Was I even earning mine? I tried to smile back, but suddenly it wasn't easy.

"What?" said Alex.

"Nothing. It's just — here I am, hanging out in the house with Seb, while you and the others are going on another hunt, maybe risking your lives —"

"Stop," he broke in. He reached for my hand and gripped it reassuringly. "What you're doing here is just as important — I mean it." He hesitated, looking down at our linked fingers. "But Willow, listen — now that the Council's here in the city, I think maybe it's better if —"

"I know," I said. "Don't worry, I'd already decided. I'm not coming on any more hunts until I've learned how to change my aura." Though the thought of sitting at home while the others put themselves in danger grated at me, I couldn't justify the threat posed by my half-angel energy — not when I knew it was possible to change it.

Alex nodded, looking conflicted. I could feel his relief that I wouldn't be going out with them for the time being, but at the same time it bothered him that the team hadn't really accepted me yet, and we both knew this wouldn't help. Just then we heard the sound of the others congregating in the kitchen.

"Better go," he said. Leaning forward, he kissed me, and I linked my arms around his neck, relishing the warmth of his lips on mine. It felt like it had been years, not days, since I'd been able to kiss him without worrying; I had a burst of relieved pleasure that was almost giddy. Now that I knew everything was OK, all I wanted was to be alone with Alex — really alone, for as long as possible.

"See you later," he said when we drew apart. The

look in his blue-gray eyes melted me. He kissed my nose. "Love you."

"Love you, too." I stood against the wall, watching as he walked back through the firing range and disappeared into the kitchen. The sound of voices, the door opening and closing. My happiness faded and I sighed, hoping they were going to be OK. It felt so strange, Alex going someplace without me — this was almost the only time it had happened since we'd first met.

He'll be fine, I told myself. *If anyone knows what he's doing, it's Alex.*

Behind me I heard Seb get up and move to the bottom of the stairs. "They've gone out?"

"Yeah, they've gone on a hunt." I jogged down the stairs, brushing past Seb as he stood there, and started gathering up the cushions from the floor. "So I guess we can go upstairs to the TV room, where it's comfier."

Seb took the cushions from me, tucking them easily under his arms. "Yes, that sounds better."

Upstairs, we put the cushions back on the sofa and then went into the kitchen to get some Cokes. There was always plenty of stuff like that in the house — half the supplies in the boxes upstairs were things like canned food and drinks; the other half was ammo and combat gear. It was like Juan had been preparing for a siege.

I handed Seb a Coke and then kept the fridge door open a second, peering in. "Do you want anything to eat?"

He made a face as he popped the Coke open. "The food here is very . . . American," he said.

I glanced at him over the fridge door. "What? Like what?"

Seb shrugged. "Cheetos, Doritos, stuff like that," he said, leaning against the counter. I saw the muscles of his chest flex under his T-shirt and looked quickly back into the fridge again. *What is wrong with you?* I demanded of myself, irritated. *You're in love with Alex — why are you even noticing Seb?*

"Doritos are sort of like Mexican food, though, aren't they?" My voice sounded thankfully normal.

Seb laughed and picked up a bag from the counter. "Willow — they're *orange*," he said, holding them up. "And the Cheetos are also orange. They're both bright, bright orange." He shuddered. He had a point, actually.

I laughed, too, and felt my tension ease. "OK, I admit the nacho cheese Doritos probably aren't very Mexican," I said, still scanning the fridge. There wasn't much in there — the guys all ate like horses, so we didn't have leftovers very often. "I meant the plain ones that you eat with salsa."

"Maybe a little," Seb conceded, tossing the bag back onto the counter.

I closed the fridge door and grabbed a bag of chocolate-chip cookies from the counter behind him. "Here — *everyone* likes chocolate-chip cookies," I said, handing them to him. "Including Mexicans. And there's no orange in them."

He grinned. "You promise?"

"Sí, I promise."

306

In the TV room, I sat on the sofa. Part of me was hoping Seb would take the armchair, but he sat beside me. Not *right* beside me, but I was very conscious of him there, just a few feet away. Trying to ignore it, I kicked off my shoes and settled back in the corner of the sofa.

Seb bent over to take his sneakers off, too, and I saw another scar on his tanned forearm: a thin white slash this time, like from a knife blade. Time seemed to slow as I stared at it, thinking of everything Seb had told me — hating for his sake everything he'd been through.

"I wish we'd known each other when we were children," I blurted out. Immediately, I was embarrassed that I'd said it, but it was true. I wanted to go back in time somehow and just — be there for him, so that he knew he wasn't the only one of his kind.

A few loose brown curls fell over Seb's forehead as he looked up at me. He didn't seem surprised, just sort of wistful. "Yes, I wish so, too," he said softly. "All my life, I've wished that." He gave a regretful smile. "But I think it would be better if I was with you as a boy, in your home in the mountains. Not for you to be where I was."

And for a second, all I wanted to do was hug him. I looked away and crossed my arms over my chest, ignoring the treacherous voice that was whispering, *Friends can hug.*

"So, you were telling me about what happened with your angel," I said, hoping that Seb wasn't picking up on any of this. God, this must be what it was like for Alex, having a psychic girlfriend.

If Seb sensed my confusion, he didn't let on. "Yes. My

angel saved me, I think." He settled himself in the opposite corner of the sofa, stretching his legs out and crossing them at the ankles. The sofa was long enough so that his large boy feet in their clean white socks weren't touching me.

I sat cross-legged as I faced him. "He saved you?"

Seb nodded. Resting an elbow on the arm of the sofa, he took a gulp of his Coke and then stretched over to put it on the coffee table. "I was in a bad fight, and I think I must have had—" He frowned and touched his head. "¿*Concusión?* How do you say it?"

"Concussion?"

"Yes." He shrugged. "I was an idiot; I'd fight with anyone. And so I fought with someone twice my size, and he got me down and kicked me in the head. Once, twice— I don't know how many times. When I woke up, I was bleeding; I didn't know where I was. I lay there for a long time and thought I was going to die. I didn't really care, but I was furious that a human had done this to me."

The house felt so still around us. I could see it all clearly—the angry young half angel who'd been so badly hurt, in every way. Seb's expression was thoughtful; his body relaxed. I could tell that he had understanding for his thirteen-year-old self but no real connection to him anymore.

"Then my angel came to me," he went on. "He wasn't happy, because I'd been acting so stupid that I'd almost gotten killed. He helped me up—"

"Wait—he *helped you up?*" I stared. "Can they do that? Touch you, I mean, so that you feel them?"

"It only happened that one time," said Seb. "I don't know. I think he—" He broke off, frowning, and finally sighed in frustration. "No. I can't say what I mean in English."

"Wait, I think I know," I said slowly, remembering how the angels of the Second Wave had wanted to be seen by the masses when they first arrived, even though angels can't usually be seen except by those they're feeding from. "You mean he—changed his frequency somehow. Slowed himself down so that he was closer to the human plane and could touch you."

Seb lightly slapped the sofa arm. "Yes! That's exactly what I was thinking. You read my mind."

"Yeah, I guess we're both sort of good at that," I said, playing with the ring pull of my Coke. As we smiled at each other, warmth curled through me.

"So, my angel helped me up, and . . ." Seb paused as he remembered. "He showed me what might happen if I didn't change. Like, pictures in my head, you know? He showed me I would die—that someone would knife me in a fight or maybe shoot me when I stole from them. But what would really kill me would be the anger. It was eating me up inside."

"You mean you saw your own future? I've never been able to do that!"

"No, I can't, either. This was just a warning." Seb fell

quiet, his eyes still in that other time. He took another sip of his Coke and put it back on the table. "And so I looked at these pictures of how I might die, and then I knew — the only thing I wanted was to find another of my kind. It's all I've ever wanted, my whole life. When I was a young boy on the streets, I was always looking; but after I escaped from the *reformatorio*, I hated the world so much that I forgot. So then I thought, to hell with humans; I don't care about them enough even to be angry at them anymore — I'm going to find someone like me, no matter what."

I hugged a faded throw pillow, imagining it all. I knew what came next from his hand — the years of searching, up and down the country. "I'm glad you found me," I said after a pause. "Seb, I really am — I'm so glad. I've been lonely, too."

"I know," he said softly, studying my face like he was memorizing every detail. "I feel as if — I've known you forever. The whole time I was searching, I always knew how much we need each other."

He was so right that tears came to my eyes. I couldn't help myself this time, and I sat up, clearing my throat. "Seb, can I —? I mean, don't take this the wrong way or anything, but —"

Understanding came over his face; he sat up too, swinging his legs forward. "Come," he said in a quiet voice. "A brother can hug his sister, yes?" He held his arm out to me.

I wiped my eyes. "Yeah, he can. And — I'd really like that."

I shifted toward him on the sofa, and we hugged tightly for a minute. It felt so good just to hold each other — like something I'd been missing my whole life. Seb's arms around me were strong; he smelled of soap and a sort of clean woodsy scent. I closed my eyes and pressed against him, feeling his heart beating against mine, the gentle shiver of our auras as they mingled. Seb let out a breath and dropped his head to my shoulder. "Willow . . . I can't tell you how I feel, to find you after so long," he whispered. "I'd stopped looking. I told myself, *You'll never find this girl; she doesn't exist.*"

I pulled away. "'This girl'? But —"

He hesitated; I noticed again the gold flecks in his hazel eyes. "I always knew it was you I was looking for," he said finally. "I always felt so strongly there was only one other half angel: a girl my own age. Then I saw your picture, and your dream — and I knew I was right."

My dream. Feeling flustered, I looked down at the sofa, at our legs almost touching each other. I didn't even know how to explain my dream to myself, much less to Seb. Had I been reaching out to him in some way, without realizing I was doing it? I didn't know — the only thing I was sure of was that somehow we were meant to be in each other's lives.

"Why didn't you tell Alex about my dream?" I asked suddenly.

Seb looked surprised at the question. "It felt too private. Like something that's just for us."

Unfortunately, he was right. I let out a shaky breath.

If Seb's feeling had been right, too, and it really was *me* he'd been looking for all this time . . . then what did that mean? When I was in love with someone else?

"But there must be other half angels," I said after a pause. "We can't really be the only two in existence, can we?"

"I've never seen another one," said Seb with a shrug. "Never."

For a fleeting second, I wondered if Raziel had ever been to Mexico, but I knew it didn't matter if he had been. Because I was positive that Seb wasn't my half brother or even related to me in any way — there was no familial sense to him at all, the way I used to notice with Mom and Aunt Jo. No, Seb and I were just what we seemed — a half-angel boy and girl who had no connection to each other, beyond whatever force had somehow drawn us together.

I could tell Seb knew it, too.

Neither of us spoke. I stared at Seb, taking in his high cheekbones, the beautiful shape of his mouth — and I thought, *My God, what if we really are the only two half angels in the entire world?* My dream flew back to me again — the way he'd held out his hand to me, called me *querida* — and how all I'd wanted was to be with him, how just the thought of being apart from him, ever, had filled me with despair. And Seb *knew* I had dreamed this.

His eyes were very steady on mine. Remembering what I thought I'd sensed from him the day before, my cheeks caught fire. My dream couldn't mean what it seemed; that was all there was to it — so if Seb thought he and I were destined to be soul mates or something, he was wrong. No matter what kind of connection the two of us had, it was still Alex I was in love with — Alex who I wanted to be with for the rest of my life.

I moved away from Seb and snagged the bag of cookies from the table, busying myself with opening it. The plastic made a comforting crackling noise that filled up the silence. "You know, my dream wasn't — I don't think it meant anything," I blurted out. "Or it did, but just that you and I are really close — really good friends. Because that's all it can mean."

"Willow, it's OK," said Seb quietly.

Embarrassment wasn't the word; I could hardly even meet his eyes. I cleared my throat. "Listen . . . maybe we should start doing the aura work. All we've done so far is talk."

Seb got the hint that I really wanted the subject to change — like, yesterday. He nodded. "Yes, you're right," he said. "But first I think I should try one of these — see if there's any orange in it." Stretching across, he reached for the bag and helped himself to a few cookies.

He bit into one. There was a pause.

"Well?" I said finally.

"Maybe it's all right," he said with an über-casual shrug. "I'll have to try again to make sure." He took another bite, chewing slowly. "Hmm. No, it's hard to tell."

My embarrassment faded a little. "Yeah, you big phony," I said. "You just won't admit you like them."

He raised a chestnut-brown eyebrow at me. "You need

313

to be careful, you know," he said mildly. He gave me a warning glance as he licked a crumb from his finger. "I saw from your hand that you're very ticklish."

"Oh, now *that* is just completely unfair. I didn't get any of your weaknesses."

Seb looked smug. "Maybe you'll find out someday." And as he popped the rest of the cookie in his mouth, I felt my tension melt like ice cream in the sun. It was what he'd been trying to do, I realized — make me see it was all right, that he wasn't going to pressure me, not ever. No matter what else he might hope for, Seb was my friend. He'd told me that before, and he really meant it.

"Thanks," I said before I could stop myself.

He didn't ask what for, though I knew he knew — just *tsked* and shook his head. "I don't think you'll thank me when you see what a tough teacher I am."

"Are you?" I said with a smile.

"Oh, yes. Very strict." Seb sat up, brushing his hands off. "OK — let's get started."

That night I lay in bed in the darkness, listening to the soft sounds of sleep around me. Even with the worry about the Council, I felt happier than I'd been in a long time. I could trust my angel again; it was just me inside of me after all. And even better, earlier that night Alex and I had slipped away to his room for half an hour, and the world had fallen away into nothingness. I let out a shivering breath, hugging myself under the covers, and wished I were with him right now, that I could sleep wrapped up in his arms all night. But meanwhile, just having been close to him for a little while, without the gut-wrenching anxiety that had been chewing me up inside . . . well, it wasn't enough, but it was still pretty amazing.

As I rolled over onto my side, my gaze fell on the small framed photo of myself when I was a little girl, peering up through the feathery leaves of the willow tree. I gently touched its frame. After I'd had a few fruitless hours of working with my aura that afternoon, Seb had finally stood up from the sofa and stretched.

"Come on, you need to take a break," he'd said.

"Come on where?" I asked, getting to my feet. It was a relief to stop for a little while; I hadn't really expected this to be so hard.

"There's something I need to give you."

I'd glanced at him in surprise — and then I understood. "Is this what I'm thinking?" I asked as we left the room.

His face was a picture of puzzled innocence. "How could I know what you're thinking? Do you think I'm psychic, or something?"

"Yes, very funny."

Seb's storeroom bedroom was large, but filled with boxes; his camp bed took up the only empty space, so that he had to crawl over it to grab his knapsack. There was a ragged sound as he unzipped it, and then he stood up and handed me my shirt and photo. His fingers seemed a little reluctant to leave them, but he smiled. "Here, these are yours."

My eyes went straight to the photo of myself and the willow tree. I'd been so sure I'd never see it again. "Thank you," I said softly. Then I gave a small laugh, clutching its frame. "You know, it's so funny—this photo keeps getting stolen and then finding its way back to me somehow."

Seb didn't say anything, but I could feel his emotion—the photo had been how he'd known he wasn't the only one of his kind after all. Looking down at my seven-year-old self, I was so glad that fate, or whatever, had led him to that Chihuahua marketplace that day.

"Thank you," I said again, and tucked it in my jeans pocket. Then I glanced down at the shirt in my hand and thought of something. "Wait—you paid for these things, right? So I need to pay you back."

Seb's expression turned gravely serious. "Well, they were very expensive, you know," he said, stroking his chin. "But I'm sure we can work something out. What do you call it—a payment plan? Perhaps if we make an agreement, for how much you'll pay me back each month—but no, we need to think about interest, too—"

He broke off with a grin as I started laughing. "OK, OK," I said. "Why don't I just say, 'Thank you very much'?"

"You have said that," he said, his eyes warm. "And you're very welcome."

CHAPTER FIFTEEN

SILVER TRAIL, COLORADO, was a small mining town high in the Rockies. The place had had its heyday once, complete with several brothels and saloons — now, its silver depleted, it was home mostly to artists and people who wanted to get away from it all. There were also, Raziel believed, several llama farms, though thankfully he hadn't encountered one. The field he was currently examining appeared to have had cows in it at some point, though. He stepped carefully as they walked, surreptitiously checking the bottoms of his shoes at times.

"See, we could have the school here — and maybe a library or something nearby," said the man, motioning around them. He was named Fred Fletcher, and his round face was flushed with sincerity.

Raziel had almost canceled this meeting but decided it might take his mind off the news about the Council that he'd gleaned from Willow's thoughts two days before—with not a single word from Charmeine meanwhile. Not to mention that there was another half angel in the world; he'd barely even begun to get his head around the implications of *that*. The boy's energy as experienced by Willow hadn't rung any particular bells for him, though he'd dearly love to know who the father was—it could be a useful little piece of blackmail if he ever found out.

Raziel took out his phone again as Fred continued to talk. Nothing from Charmeine. Obviously this was what she'd tried to tell him—that the Council was in Mexico City weeks ahead of schedule, at a totally different place from what had been planned. He could sense that she was still alive at least, so presumably their alliance hadn't been discovered. But what was going on?

"So that was my idea, Mr. Raziel, sir," Fred finished up finally. "Because you see, as wonderful as it is for people to pledge themselves to the Church and live there, not everyone can do that. Lots of us are just as devout but have families, y'see."

"Yes, naturally," said Raziel absently. He linked his hands behind his back, scanning the frosty fields that sparkled in the late-afternoon sunlight, with the Rockies a dusky purple rising up behind them. Forcing himself to focus, he saw that Jenny was right. It wasn't a bad idea at all. Camp Angel: a community where entire families could live in honor of the angels, with schools, a church, a library devoted to angelic works—everything.

"We could have them all across the country," he said, thinking out loud.

Fred's face lit up. "Really? You like my idea that much, sir?"

"It has definite potential," allowed Raziel. Since the dramatic Second Wave TV footage, the demand for all things angel was exploding. A gated community where families could purchase homes and enroll their children in schools devoted to the angels would take off like wildfire.

And as he'd thought before, the idea would allow for another possibility, one he'd been mulling over for some time — something that, if the Council knew about it, he was sure would cement whatever plans they might now have in place for him. It didn't exactly go along with their vision of angels not giving into their baser urges.

"Yes, I'd like to go ahead," he decided. "I'll be in touch soon to discuss the building work." Though everything was now cast into uncertainty, Raziel still held out hope that soon there wouldn't be a Council to worry about. Meanwhile, in the same spirit of reckless defiance that had caused him to say too much on TV, he refused to put his various schemes on hold.

Fred seemed almost incoherent with gratitude and excitement; he stammered his thanks nonstop as they made their way back across the fields. "Think nothing of it," said Raziel, shaking his hand when they reached his black BMW. "You have the angels' gratitude."

One of the angels' gratitude, anyway. Grimly, Raziel checked his phone again as he got into his car.

For distraction on the drive back to Denver, he found himself exploring the psychic link with Willow once more. When both she and Seb, the half-angel boy, had gone looking for the spark of Raziel's energy — even if they hadn't known that's what they were looking for — he'd cloaked it even further, putting so many shields and disguises in place that even a pure angel would have struggled to find it. Now Willow's angel self seemed puzzled by her former fears, and Raziel was free to wander about the girl's mind without causing even the least misgiving. Willow's own spark of energy within him remained unsuspected by her, which was fortunate: if she ever stumbled on the risks to humanity that destroying the Council now posed, the Angel Killers would never go ahead with the attack.

Willow was currently talking to Seb, trying to learn how to disguise her aura's colors. It had been news to Raziel that this was even possible. The boy seemed unusually gifted with auras — though who knew what "usual" might be when it came to half angels.

Steering his way down the mountain roads, a considering almost-smile came over Raziel's face as he listened to Willow's thoughts and feelings. At first he'd told himself he was only delving to find out what was going on with the Angel Killers, but now he had to admit that his daughter's mental processes had become strangely addictive to him — like one of those reality TV shows that humans loved so much. He'd never have guessed that any progeny of his could be so *nice*. The idea was as alien as having a daughter at all. Raziel had spent days looking for some kind of edge to Willow — the angle from which she operated. There was none, unless it was her love for Kylar or her desire to help others.

Yet she was no doormat — the girl had a steely strength that Raziel was sure came from him. Miranda had been beautiful, but a limp dishrag of a woman. In short, Willow was a worthy adversary, which irrationally pleased him. If he had to have something as base as a daughter, he at least wanted her to have some wits about her before he put her to death.

Even so, Raziel was deeply thankful that no one suspected he was the father. His mind went back to the day he'd first woken up, and his meeting with the Council in the cathedral conference room: their expressionless faces that never seemed to smile or frown. They'd brought up the half angel, of course — it had been almost the first thing they'd thrown at him.

"We Twelve have tried to find her psychically but can't; her energy is once removed from ours." Isda's gray eyes had been as impassive as when she'd called for the traitors to be brought out. "How was she able to get into the cathedral and then escape again, Raziel? Exactly what kind of security do you have here?"

Raziel had gritted his teeth but kept his tone mild as he explained about his traitorous human assistant. He could feel the Twelve's minds craning toward one another; undercurrents of thought swirled about the room that he couldn't catch.

That's not good enough, said someone. The words weren't

spoken aloud; the meeting had apparently shifted to the psychic level, which was always a bad sign. If Raziel hadn't already had psychic defenses in place, he would have slammed them down at that moment, like a castle portcullis.

The voice became several voices, all communicating with him at once. *This kind of sloppy work isn't acceptable, Raziel. The girl should have been destroyed weeks ago. Who's the father? How was this even able to happen?*

Raziel had managed to keep the surface of his thoughts concerned, wanting to help. Far below, his mind was ticking away. "I have no idea," he replied. "The girl's existence is a complete mystery — believe me, I'm as concerned as you are."

"We're relieved to hear you share our concerns," said Isda's voice. Isda herself was leaning silently back in her seat, giving away nothing. Other mental voices chimed in as she continued: "Because as you know, we have never approved of angel-human relationships. It's unacceptable for angels to demean themselves in this manner."

"Yes, I'm aware you believe that," said Raziel smoothly. "But as newcomers to this world, you have to understand it's quite an ingrained thing by now — traditional, if you like."

There was a further cooling of the room's atmosphere. *You've spent far too long here, if you think that makes it in any way acceptable,* chided the many voices in his head. *We are angels; we do not cavort with pigs in the dirt.* He could feel a few of them beginning to tendril about, searching for anything interesting, and he put up a few extra defenses, retreating deep to the recesses of his mind.

Moderation is the key, Raziel, continued the mental chorus. Every face in the room was stony; he was uneasily reminded of the dozens of angels exploding in midair. *You'd better remember that if you want to keep your position here.*

Now anger touched him again as he pulled into the cathedral parking lot; how dare they have sat there and threatened him in his own cathedral? Striding back into his office, Raziel felt a smug satisfaction at the sight of Jenny, remembering that their liaison had begun the same evening the Council had left. After several weeks, she was almost as lovely as ever — though she looked more tired these days, and had developed a nagging cough. Raziel shrugged as he sat down at his desk. Perhaps it might be time for a new assistant soon. If so, there'd be no limit of enthusiastic volunteers.

Still no word from Charmeine. With another restless glance at his phone, Raziel tossed it to one side and brought up his e-mails.

His forehead furrowed at one of the title lines: *Some Information You Ought to Know.* As he scanned the e-mail, his eyebrows shot up. Now, this was interesting: it was from the security guard who'd been stationed at the cathedral's back door when the Second Wave arrived. Raziel regarded the words on the screen thoughtfully.

> The day of the attack, she was one of the ones who brought in Willow Fields. I'm sure it was her this morning, even though her hair was different. She

showed me a badge and started questioning me
about that terrorist guy who came running in. She
sure seemed anxious to find him. She gave me a card
and said to get in touch day or night if I thought of
where he might have gone. I haven't told the police
yet. I just feel better going to an angel with this
information.

The phone did a vibrating dance on his desk.
Charmeine. Raziel lunged forward and snatched it up.
"What's going on?" he demanded.

"I'm fine, thank you for asking," said Charmeine's
voice, sounding weary. "I'm in Mexico City. I don't know
if you've heard about it from your contacts, but the
Council came here early, with hardly any warning."

Raziel didn't correct her assumption that his com-
munications with the Angel Killers went both ways. "I've
known for two days!" he snapped. "I've been going mad,
waiting to hear from you — what happened?"

"Our darling little Luis — that's what. He let slip to a
woman in the office how curious his girlfriend was about
the Council, and that he'd promised to get her and some
friends in for a private audience."

Raziel groaned aloud; remembering the earnest face
he'd seen in Charmeine's thoughts, he could just picture
it. The warning not to tell anyone about Kara must have
worn off in the time that had passed since Charmeine's
encounter with him. Or else the lad had been so dizzy
from angel burn he'd forgotten he wasn't supposed to talk.

"Anyway, the woman told the priest, who went straight to the Council," went on Charmeine. "Apparently there'd always been a contingency plan in place. They switched to it just to be on the safe side."

"The Twelve didn't get hold of Luis, did they?" asked Raziel warily.

"No, they didn't. Do you think I'd still be around talking to you if they had? He'd gone to visit his family for the weekend; by the time they figured it out, I'd whisked him away."

Raziel's muscles sagged with relief. If Luis had been turned over to the Council, they'd have seen what had happened in seconds. "So what did you do with him?"

She snorted. "What do you think? I wasn't going to keep him as a pet."

He nodded to himself; Charmeine might be maddening at times, but she never balked at necessities. Something about her tone worried him, though. "Are you all right?" he asked abruptly.

Charmeine sighed. "Yes, I suppose. It's just—this isn't easy, Raz. They delve me almost every day, to make sure I'm still compliant. It's draining, having to keep them psychically at bay and act like nothing's wrong. But I'll keep holding out—don't worry. It's only for a few more weeks."

"Do I have a few more weeks?" he asked bluntly. "Or are they going to call me down there and execute me anyway?"

There was a pause. "I don't know," said Charmeine

finally. "They're planning some kind of response to your interview soon, but I'm not sure exactly what. I do know they'd prefer to take care of you in your own cathedral; they feel it's only fitting. If you lay low, you might be OK for now."

Raziel nodded, grimly hoping she was right. Before the Council had a chance to come for him personally, the tables would have turned.

"And anyway, they're pretty preoccupied with their own plans at the moment," added Charmeine.

Raziel's chair squeaked as he leaned back with a frown, remembering the images he'd seen in her mind. "They're still going ahead with that?"

She gave a short laugh. "Have you been to Mexico City lately? The angels here aren't exactly an advertisement for behaving with decorum. The Twelve are more concerned about our 'baser instincts' than ever. They're going to link with the energy here first, calming it down, then spread out to all the other places in the world where they think things are out of control."

Raziel's gaze narrowed at a painting on the wall. If the Twelve's energies were linked with those of Mexico City, and then the Twelve were destroyed . . . he gave a mental shrug. All right, so the Mexican capital would definitely take some damage; it could even be leveled. As for the world's other angelic "hot spots," who knew? The kind of long-range energy work the Council was planning wouldn't be instantaneous; maybe it wouldn't have had time to fully take effect. Thankfully, at the rate humans bred, the angels' food supply being curtailed wasn't really an issue either way.

He could almost hear Charmeine coming to the same conclusions, sense her identical mental shrug. "Anyway, we've got to get the new information to your little band of thugs," she said. "And it can't be someone that close to the Council again; I only barely got to Luis in time. Should I just give it to them myself?"

"They can see auras," pointed out Raziel.

"So? I'll pretend to be a rogue. They were all pally with Nate, right? I'll just put on my sanctimonious, holier-than-thou face."

Raziel clicked a silver pen open and shut as he considered it. Though the entire angel community knew of the rogues' mass execution, the Angel Killers did not—and he knew from Willow's thoughts that Kylar had once had hopes of joining forces with them. But remembering how the young assassin had refused to simply obey orders and kill Willow when he'd been told to, the idea made him uneasy nonetheless.

"No," he decided. "Kylar's too questioning if he's suspicious—the last thing we need is him poking around in things. We need to find a way to get him the information so he can trust it." Recalling the e-mail he'd been reading, he brought it up on the screen again. A calculating smile grew across his face.

"I might have an idea," he said. "Leave it to me."

"Not too long," cautioned Charmeine; he could hear her tension. "It makes me nervous, not even having a plan in place. I'll call you as soon as I can get away again."

After they hung up, Raziel wrote several e-mails; a few were from anonymous accounts. Finally he hit SEND on the last one, pleased with himself. A week or two was all it would take; he was sure of it. There was no way she'd be able to resist the lure he'd just cast. Once in Mexico City, she'd be the perfect liaison between themselves and Kylar, even if she thought her role there was completely different — and far less expendable, once she'd served her purpose.

For a few delicious minutes, Raziel allowed himself to daydream about what it would be like if his gamble paid off and the assassinations meant only the deaths of the Twelve. On the whole, angels were conservative beings. Once they got over the shock of the Council being gone, he didn't think he'd encounter a serious challenge to his leadership — just lots of angels asking for positions in his new reign. The thought was immensely satisfying. He had so many plans for this world.

The newest, Camp Angel, was particularly exciting.

Raziel had long wished there was a way angels could savor the energy of all humans, not just the ones who'd reached some semblance of maturity. The energy of childhood was so particularly delicious, though of course it wasn't really the done thing: to feed on too many children would soon spell the angels' own destruction. But with families encased behind gated communities, he

could keep track of exactly who was being fed from—
and so with careful management, angels would be able to
indulge their tastes regardless of their victims' ages.

Like a veal farm, thought Raziel. And remembering
the Council's admonition to him about the importance of
moderation, he laughed out loud.

Chapter Sixteen

ALL KARA WAS ABLE to glean from eavesdropping at the cathedral was that, yes, the Twelve were here for three weeks, but everything about their stay was top secret; hardly anyone in the church offices knew more than that. So after some research on the Internet, Alex had made an appointment at an insurance company on the Torre Mayor's fifty-fourth floor — one floor from the top.

He'd taken the Metro, then walked. The Torre Mayor was the tallest building in Mexico and looked it, soaring up over its surroundings. Approaching from the Paseo de la Reforma, Alex saw that the half-cylinder of green glass was only the front of the building — its back was a tan rectangular slab. The entrance — a graceful arch several stories high — mirrored the half-moon shape at the building's top; gray columns marched across it.

Going in, Alex had found himself in a lobby with a slanting glass ceiling. Like Kara had said, there were scanners in place; employees passing through briefly touched their passes to them. "Richard Singer," said Alex to a receptionist at a glass-topped desk. "I've got an appointment with Prima Life."

No flicker of suspicion; the woman made a phone call to verify, then pushed a clipboard at him to sign in. Alex took the temporary pass she gave him and went through the scanners. As he did, he noted the several cameras that were tucked away in various corners, watching his every move.

Going online, the team had found out quite a few things about the Torre Mayor: apart from being extremely secure, it was the most earthquake-resistant building in the world—it could withstand up to a level *nine* on the Richter scale. There'd been no floor plans to be found, though, not anywhere online. But while it wasn't mentioned on the Torre Mayor's website, they'd found a reference on someone's blog that said its top floor—right under that slanted half-moon—housed high-security VIP suites and meeting rooms.

In the elevator there'd been another camera and an attendant who asked him what floor he wanted. "Fifty-five," said Alex, just to see what would happen.

The man's eyebrows had knitted together as he checked Alex's pass. "Sorry, *señor*—you need a special card for that."

Alex pretended confusion, taking out the piece of paper where he'd scribbled down the details of the meeting.

"Sorry, I meant fifty-four," he said. As the elevator hummed upward, he observed a keyhole beside the button for the highest floor. OK, so what would happen if the team overpowered the attendant and got the key? But, remembering what they'd found out so far, he knew: computers ran everything here; the security staff would just stop the elevator.

The elevator reached his floor and he got off. To avoid raising suspicions any further, he actually kept the appointment — talking to an agent for half an hour about his insurance needs (he had many, apparently), while mentally scanning the floor above.

Angels, all right — more than he could count. And some of their energy was stronger than anything he'd ever encountered, hitting him like a physical slap.

On his way out, Alex had asked where the restroom was and then went wandering, keeping an innocent, slightly distracted look on his face. In a distant corner, he'd found the door for the stairwell and started to push it open. A woman coming out of another office stopped him, flashing an apologetic smile. "No, no, *señor* — don't go out this way. You can't get back into any of the floors without a code."

Alex had the heavy fire door half open by then; glancing at the outside of it, he saw it had a digital keypad for a lock. "Sorry, wrong door," he said, smiling like a clueless *gringo* and letting it swing shut again. "Could you tell me where the restroom is, *señora?*"

✦ ✦ ✦

Now, standing in the firing range with the team clustered around the table, Alex explained what had happened as he spread out the two blueprints he'd managed to get hold of. One showed the Torre Mayor's top floor — which unfortunately was depicted as an almost-empty area; the VIP suites and meeting rooms seemed to have been added at a later date.

"The Council's definitely still up there," said Alex, tapping the plans.

"I thought so," said Willow softly, her red-gold spikes framing her face as she took in the blueprints. She and Seb stood next to each other. Alex tried to squelch his slight irritation; though Seb had only been here two full days, he already stuck to Willow like glue.

The others shifted as Willow spoke, glancing warily at the pair of them. Alex knew that some of the team thought the two half angels must have known each other before somehow. It bothered him, but he didn't know how to combat it. He couldn't *order* them to trust Willow and Seb.

"That top floor feels . . . dangerous," Willow added. She looked up at Seb, who nodded.

"It feels like a place where something will happen," he said in his quiet voice. Frowning slightly, he touched the symbol for the service elevator, and then slid his finger across to the same icon on the other blueprint, which detailed the ground floor. "Here, too, I think." He circled the service elevator with his fingertip.

Despite his dislike of Seb, Alex was glad to get the

confirmation. The building's service elevator was accessed from the loading bays, where deliveries were made. He'd already earmarked that route as the team's most likely way in: if there was a weak spot in the building's security, he was pretty sure it would be there.

Liz brushed a strand of dark hair from her pale face. "How'd you get the blueprints, anyway? Aren't they classified now, with the Council staying there?"

Alex was studying the delivery entrance that led to the bays; he felt itchy with impatience to go check it out in person. "Town hall—I told them I was a design student, interested in how the building mirrors that half-moon shape. And yeah, they're supposed to be, but the clerk thought it must have been a mistake." It had been a stroke of luck, though Alex knew he wouldn't like to be the clerk once the error was found out.

"Well, I found out something today, too," said Kara. He glanced up; he could see her excitement. "I followed a couple of the church secretaries at lunchtime and got a table next to them at the café. The ceremony's still going ahead on the last afternoon of the Council's stay here, on the nineteenth. They were both hoping they'd get to go."

Alex felt his shoulders slump. Relief—that had been the one piece of information they couldn't do without. "OK, excellent," he said. "So that's still the best time for us to break in and make our move, since we know they'll be in their angel forms during the private audiences."

"And you definitely don't think we can just get invited to the party again?" ventured Trish.

Alex had been racking his brains for days trying to think of a way. "I don't see how, without someone on the inside helping us. No one's even supposed to know that the Council's here." He massaged his eyes; he'd hardly slept these last few nights.

The team fell silent, digesting this. Glancing at Willow, Alex saw the sympathetic support in her gaze. It felt as if she'd reached over and squeezed his hand. She understood, if no one else did, how worried he was about all of this. Fleetingly, he wondered how the hell his father had managed it—being in charge on his own, with no one to confide in.

"So we need all the information we can get our hands on," he concluded. "Whether the same schedule for the reception is still being followed, floor plans for the VIP level, where exactly the private audiences are going to take place, any security details we can find out—anything."

Kara nodded. "The only people who'll know all that will be the church officials. The priest, maybe one or two others."

"Could Willow get it psychically?" suggested Brendan. Alex bit back the automatic Ask her yourself. It wasn't needed; Brendan caught himself. "I mean . . . could you?" he asked Willow awkwardly. "If we found out who had the information, then you'd just have to hold their hand, right?"

Willow's forehead creased. "Maybe, but like I said before, it's not instantaneous. Getting that level of specific detail would take me a while. I mean, a few minutes of really concentrating, at least."

"Yes, for me, too." Seb stroked his stubbled jaw. "And even then, you don't always get what you're looking for."

"Don't you?" Willow's voice held mild surprise.

"I don't, no," he clarified, glancing down at her. "I get many images, but only what's on their minds. And sometimes not very specific. I hardly ever get names, things like that."

Alex could see how interested both Seb and Willow were by the fact that their psychic skills seemed to vary. He knew that if nobody else was around, they'd spend the next hour discussing it in great detail.

Meanwhile, Kara had made a face at "not very specific." "Alex, what do you think? Is it worth a try?"

He brought his attention back to the plan as he considered. In the wake of the security breach, he'd bet money that only the priest knew all the details they needed — and the man would be enough in the angels' confidence to know that Willow Fields the terrorist was psychic and worked by holding people's hands. Trying to maneuver the guy into a scenario where either Willow or Seb could grasp his hand and concentrate for several minutes was far too likely to raise suspicions; all the church higher-ups would be on red alert now for anything strange.

"No, we can't risk them figuring out what we're up to," he said finally. He glanced at Seb, knowing it was a long shot even as he asked. "Could you sense anything if you went into the cathedral? Willow can't go in there with all the angels around, but you'd be OK if you changed your aura."

Seb's eyebrows shot up. "You mean get security details, just from being there?" He shook his head. "I can try, but I don't think it will work — I think all I'll see is that it's a dangerous place."

That wouldn't be much of a news flash. Alex sighed. "OK, so we can't count on that. Kara, how easy will it be to break into the offices?"

"Not easy at all, but it sounds like it's our only hope." Kara's expression was arch, as if she wasn't surprised that the half angels weren't turning out to be more useful. She picked up a pencil and started sketching on a spare piece of paper.

"OK, here's the cathedral, with the tabernacle beside it. The tabernacle still has a small chapel people can use — the new office area is behind that. You reach it from inside the cathedral, from this door." She darkened a line with the pencil. "The information should be on the priest's computer or in his files. Unfortunately, digital keypads seem to be in vogue — they've added one to the main office door now. So if we're getting in there, we'll have to find the code for it somehow."

"Maybe a video camera?" suggested Wesley. As everyone turned to look at him, his cheeks darkened; he went on, his voice gruff. "I mean — hundreds of tourists take videos in there every day. So we could use the zoom lens to focus on the door whenever someone's punching in the code."

Alex nodded. "Yeah, good idea. Nice one, Wes." Kara was busy adding more details to the office area and the cathedral—hallways, the altar, the layout of the pews. He propped his hands on the table as he studied the homemade map. "How accurate is this? Can we get actual floor plans showing the office area, or is that classified now, too?"

"Extremely classified, now that the cathedral is Church of Angels central, Mexican style," said Kara gloomily, putting down the pencil. "This isn't too bad, I think. Luis showed me around the office area once."

"No, it's not too bad." Seb stood scanning the map. "You've missed some things, though."

Kara gave him a cool look. "Like what?"

He picked up the pencil. "There are cathedral doors here and here." The lines he drew were precise, unhesitating. "This one's very small, easy to miss. And I don't know if it's still there, but in the tabernacle there used to be a fire exit, here. You could get out through it, but not in."

Alex had straightened up, watching carefully. "Are you sure? How do you know all this?"

Seb shrugged and tossed the pencil aside. "The *catedral* was a good place to pick pockets. All of us on the street knew every inch of it."

It wasn't a surprise to Alex; Willow had told him a little about Seb's past when he'd asked her. He hadn't mentioned it to the others, though. Now Trish and Liz stared at Seb speechlessly; the guys all gave each other *Did you just hear what I heard?* looks.

Kara shot Alex a glance that said she held him personally responsible for this. "So you're telling us you were a pickpocket," she said.

"Oh, yes," said Seb mildly, pushing back his loose curls. "For many years. When I wasn't breaking into houses."

Alex had a sudden feeling that Seb was enjoying this—that the guy was perverse enough to delight in making everyone even more suspicious of him than they already were. From what Willow had said, he hadn't even broken into houses that often; it'd been mostly for a few months when he was thirteen. Naturally, Seb did not volunteer this information.

"A thief," summed up Sam, his broad face creased with disgust. "Now, why doesn't *that* surprise me? Alex, did you know this?"

"Shut up, Sam." Alex leaned against the table, watching Seb. "Do you think you could help us get into the offices?"

"I don't know," said Seb. "My skills weren't very . . ." He glanced down at Willow beside him; she seemed to sense the word he wanted.

"Subtle," she suggested.

"No, not very subtle. Just smash the window, grab some things, and go, you know? As much as I could carry." Alex managed not to roll his eyes at Seb's guileless tone. Yes, he was definitely enjoying this. Willow seemed to think so, too; her mouth had pursed, as if she was try-ing not to laugh.

"Well, that's not very helpful here, unfortunately," said Kara stiffly. "Alex, believe me — we're only going to get one chance at that office, and it better be a good one."

The larger map of the Torre Mayor was still spread out, sleek and professional next to Kara's hand-drawn lines. Looking at it, Alex thought he'd find some way to get the team in there if it was the last thing he ever did — but without more information, it wouldn't be much bet-ter than a suicide mission.

"OK," he said finally. "I'll keep checking out the Torre Mayor, in between training the team. Kara, I want you to start casing the cathedral. Figure out the routine there, and find a way for us to break into the offices — we'll get you a video camera like Wesley said. But we've got to know what we're going to be walking into."

"Will do," said Kara. Glancing at Seb, she hesitated, her reluctance clear. Like the others, she hadn't warmed to him; Alex doubted that his little revelation just now had helped. "Seb, if you wouldn't mind — would you go over the map with me, see if I've missed anything else?"

From the amused spark in Seb's eyes, he knew exactly how much Kara didn't want to be dealing with him. "Yes, I'd be happy to."

Everyone started dispersing, heading off to the kitchen or the TV room. Alex gave Willow a dry look as they walked across the firing range. "The guy doesn't like making things easy for himself, does he?"

Willow glanced over her shoulder as Seb and Kara bent over the map. "He just . . . is who he is, I guess."

Alex could hear the unmistakable note of fondness in her voice. Unbidden, a conversation he'd had with Kara that morning came rushing back.

She'd been standing at the kitchen counter, long legs crossed at the ankle. Blowing on her coffee, she'd said, "So . . . how are things going?"

His eyes had narrowed at her knowing tone. "What do you mean, *how are things going?*"

Kara's shrug had been elaborately casual. "Willow and Seb seem awfully close already, don't they? They're always talking whenever I see them."

They were always talking whenever Alex saw them, too. "They're friends, that's all," he'd said shortly as he took a teaspoon out from the drawer.

"You said he wants more, though. And boy, he's really good-looking, isn't he? Those eyes and that sexy stubble. Willow has to have noticed."

Alex had made a face before he could stop himself. Earlier, he'd seen Willow's cheeks go pink when Seb had come out of the shower room wearing only his jeans, his chest damp. And though her cheeks probably would have gone just as pink if it had been Sam or one of the others, Alex still couldn't help wishing that the only other half angel in the world had been short, with acne.

"I'm glad you've got the hots for Seb," he'd told Kara coldly, jamming a piece of bread in the toaster. "Do you actually have a point you're trying to make?"

341

She'd given him a level look. "Just be careful, OK? I don't want to see you get hurt."

The genuine concern in her voice had grated at Alex. It still did; he pushed the memory away. He and Willow had reached the stairwell by then, where it was relatively quiet for now. She reached for his hand. "Alex, look — I know you and Seb haven't really hit it off, but he's a good person, OK? And he's my friend."

"Yeah, but —" Alex broke off; he'd been about to say, *Yeah, but you know the guy's in love with you, right?* It was completely obvious; Seb couldn't take his eyes off her.

"What?" said Willow.

"Nothing," said Alex finally. He shook his head in annoyance at himself. "Sorry, it's just all this Council stuff — I guess it's getting to me. Yeah, I know you're friends. I'm fine with it."

She seemed to smile despite herself. "What — really?"

He smiled, too. The love in her eyes was so obvious that he felt like a jerk for caring about Seb at all. "Yeah, really," he said. "I'm glad you've got another half angel to talk to. Anyway, how's the aura training going?"

Willow's green eyes sparkled suddenly. She stood on a step so that she was taller than he was and wrapped her arms around his neck. "I'll tell you if you kiss me."

He grinned in surprise, slipping his hands around her waist. "I don't know. You drive a hard bargain. . . . All right, I give in."

She trailed her fingers over the back of his neck as they kissed; Alex shivered, pulling her closer. "Maybe we could sneak away into your room later," she whispered against his mouth.

"Maybe we could just spend the rest of our lives in there and never come out again," he murmured back. Nothing sounded better to him. His lips traveled down to her neck and pressed against her warm skin; he couldn't help smiling. "And don't get me wrong, I definitely like the idea — but you always used to be so worried about us not having enough privacy in there."

"I still am," she said faintly. "But, Alex, I just —" She pulled away to look into his eyes; he saw deep happiness in her expression. "I just really want to be close to you. I mean —" She gave a wistful smile as she touched his cheek. "Well, as close as we can be, with a dorm full of people just outside."

Which unfortunately wasn't as close as either of them wanted — but was a lot better than nothing. "Oh, man, it's a date," said Alex, drawing her back against him. Then he stopped as his responsibilities crashed over him like a freight train. They had less than three weeks now. *Three weeks*. He glanced tensely toward the firing range. "But I should probably head over to the evening service at the cathedral first and check the place out, then look over the blueprints for the Torre Mayor again, see if I've missed anything —"

Willow put a finger over his lips. "It's OK."

He reached up and gripped her hand. "No, it really isn't. You deserve —"

"I deserve to be with you, and I am. Always. Alex,

it's fine. This is so important—don't you think I realize that?" He could hear her frustration, though, and knew how much she hated it that she couldn't go to the angel-filled cathedral with him and try to pick up something psychically. From the moment they'd met, they'd been a team—having to sit at home with her half-angel aura must gnaw at her.

"Of course I know you realize it," he said softly. "God, if anyone in the world understands what's at stake, it's you." He tucked back a short strand of her hair and smiled. "So, have I earned the right yet to know how the aura work is going?"

Willow sighed. "Still not that well, actually," she confessed. "It's a lot harder than I thought."

Discouragement was clear on her face. Alex squeezed her hand, then shook his head in joking disbelief. "After all that? You got—wait a minute"—he counted on his fingers—"one, two, three, four, *five* kisses out of me? And the aura work isn't even going well?"

She grinned and pressed close to him again. "So sue me," she murmured against his lips.

My psychic skills had always come so effortlessly that I'd thought disguising my aura would be easy, too, once Seb explained it to me. It wasn't. Just *seeing* my aura took practice at first. It seemed so unnatural to even notice it, like being awakened by your own snores. After three days, I could finally bring my aura easily into view, but now trying to change it made me feel like I was in second grade attempting advanced calculus. And for Seb it was all so simple — not to just see his aura but to then sort of mentally grasp it, changing its colors with his thoughts.

"You have to be friends with it," he said for about the dozenth time. "Be *simpática*."

It was the day after the team had gone over the blueprints. Seb and I were down in the exercise room again, where he sat straddling the weight machine. Stubble covered his firm jaw — he'd apparently taken me at my word about the shaving thing. All he needed now was a leather jacket and screaming groupies, though that would be so un-Seb-like as to be completely unreal.

I nodded, determined to get it this time. "All right. Let me try again."

Perched cross-legged on the sofa cushion, I closed my eyes and took a deep breath. My aura swam into my mind's eye. I sat still, noticing the way it radiated out from my body: buoyant when I was happy, drawing in closely if I was upset. It was kind of medium-size now, with a focused sense that matched my own. I watched its lavender lights drifting through the silver . . . and then I mentally reached out, frowning as I strove to catch hold of it.

Blue, I told it. You need to be sky blue now.

The aura in my mind's eye stayed calm, intent . . . and silver. As usual. Opening my eyes, I gazed at it glumly.

There was a creak from the weight machine as Seb got up. "Maybe we should try something different," he said. The sofa cushion dipped as he settled next to me; as always, a pleasurable tingle went through me at the mingling of our auras. "Just feel what I'm doing, yes?"

As we sat there together, I could sense Seb's light concentration, so different from my own grim focus. His state of mind was almost like an afterthought, or daydreaming. Gently, he nudged his aura with his thoughts; I felt it shiver as the colors he was imagining swept through it. Green. Then a dull gray. Green again. Silver.

Neither of us moved as Seb changed his aura over and over. Almost without realizing, I began to echo his sense of relaxed detachment, so that after a while I was practically losing myself in my own aura: whispers of silver and lavender trailing over my skin, gleaming with emotion.

"I think I get it," I said. "I've been trying too hard, right?"

Seb nodded as he leaned back on one hand, his hazel eyes amused. "Perhaps just a little, *querida*."

"Don't call me *querida*," I said automatically. "OK, let me see if I can do it now."

Closing my eyes, I merged dreamily back into my aura's glow. *Don't force it*, I cautioned myself. When I felt ready, I mentally stroked its shimmering lights and imagined them turning blue.

I caught my breath as my aura wavered and gave a flicker. Close, but no cigar. My heart started beating more quickly. No, *don't get excited — stay detached*. It was easier said than done, though; when I tried again, my life energy didn't even flutter. Or the next two times that I tried. In my mind's eye, I stared at the silvery glow in frustration.

Oh, God, I *had* to get this. How was I supposed to be there for the Council attack if I didn't?

There was a ripple of emotion from Seb . . . and when I opened my eyes, he sat watching me very steadily, all trace of humor gone. With one of those undercurrents that happened more and more often between us now, I knew he'd heard my thought—and that he hated the idea of my taking part in the attack every bit as much as Alex would. Just the thought of my being hurt made him turn as fierce as those months when he was thirteen, so that he'd do whatever it took to protect me.

We each knew what the other was thinking. A little shaken by the depth of his feelings, I started to say something, then stopped. There was no point in arguing. I'd learn how to change my aura in time, and I'd be there when the team confronted the Twelve — that was all there was to it.

I could tell Seb had picked up the gist of that and was letting it go for now — though from the tension around his mouth, he wasn't happy. "Do you want to try again?" he asked finally.

And for then, that was all either of us said about it.

CHAPTER SEVENTEEN

HAVING SEB IN THE HOUSE changed everything for me.

Though Alex was, obviously, totally on my side, he was often too busy to really notice everything that went on with me and the others: the minor snubs, the sideways looks. It was all so stupid that I hated the fact it even got to me sometimes, and I didn't blame Alex in the slightest for not always noticing — God, I wouldn't even have *wanted* him to. Because, let's be honest, he had one or two more important things on his mind just then.

But Seb noticed it all. Suddenly there was someone whose gaze I could catch when Trish tensed if I came too close or if Brendan got that deer-in-the-headlights look. Seb's eyes would be smiling as we glanced at each other, the corner of his mouth lifting almost imperceptibly. If we were near enough, I might even catch what he was thinking, which was always something like, *Madre mía* —

and you look so harmless. Have you got a machete up your sleeve or something? Once or twice I gave in to the laugh tugging at my lips—which then had the others staring at me in alarm while Seb just quietly stood there, looking innocent. The difference all that made to my sanity was . . . well, not small.

Just having Seb to talk to helped. There were so many things about my life that made sense now: strange feelings that had always set me apart, but that I hadn't even known to question until I met him. Like how I've always been sensitive to the moods of places, when other people hardly seem to notice them, or the feeling of duality that I now realized I'd had all my life—the certainty that there was more to me than just the "me" I knew, even if I hadn't been sure, then, what the rest of it was. These and a hundred other things were just part of being a half angel, it turned out —because Seb had always felt exactly the same way.

"Did you know your father?" I asked.

We were in the TV room, about a week after he'd arrived. The others were out, and as usual when they were on a hunt, frustration nagged at me that I couldn't be there with them. I kept reaching psychically for Alex, needing to know he was safe. We all had cell phones now, but texts weren't the same. Every time I found his energy, the familiar feel of it was like an embrace.

Meanwhile, Seb had finally forced me to take a break, and he was right—after hours of no luck, my brain felt limp. Being gentle and offhand sounded like it should be the easiest thing in the world, but the problem was that it *mattered* so much. My pulse kept skipping the second my aura started to change, which then sent it snapping right back to silver. *Frustrating* wasn't the word. How was I supposed to convince myself that I didn't care about this?

At my question, I was aware of Seb's mind opening to mine, without him really thinking consciously about it. He shook his head. "No, I never knew my father. I always knew he was an angel, though — I'm not sure how. Maybe my mother told me."

"Did you ever see him in her thoughts, like I saw Raziel in Mom's?" I'd told Seb about Raziel and the Church of Angels.

"Not really." His mouth twisted ironically as he sprawled back against the sofa, settling himself on the cushions. "I didn't have much of a — link with my mother, I think is the word."

I got a sense of isolation; a brief image of a woman in her twenties who looked like him. I wasn't surprised Seb hadn't been close to his mother — in all the pieces of memory I'd seen, she'd either been crying while her boyfriend hit him or shouting that it was his fault. It was a relief to glance at him now, so healthy and relaxed. I felt my gaze lingering on him and looked away.

"How badly did your mother have angel burn?" I asked.

Seb propped his wrist under his head as he thought; the firm muscles of his arm flexed slightly. "Very badly," he said. "It was different from your mother, though. I think her mind was damaged, but she could still talk, still do things." He knew I'd had to hide my mother's mental illness from everyone when I was younger. Apart from Alex, he was the only person I'd ever shared that with.

"The main thing was that my mother had cancer," he went on. "That's what killed her."

I nodded. He'd told me before that when he was nine and living on the streets, he'd found out his mother was dead. She hadn't visited him even once after leaving him at the orphanage — not in all the years he was there. It made my throat tighten whenever I thought of it.

Seb stretched his white-socked foot so that it nudged at my ankle. "Willow, don't. It's all right."

This happened a lot now, so that our half-psychic, half-spoken conversations would have sounded very weird to anyone else. I shook my head. "It so isn't. I hate it that you were in that place."

"The *reformatorio* was much worse," he said with a shrug. "And it was in the orphanage that I found out about my angel. There was a room they locked me in. . . . He first came to me there. So it was worth it."

He wasn't as relaxed as he sounded. I felt his slight tension as he remembered and got a flicker of fear — a dark, cramped room where he'd been imprisoned for days. Oh, Seb.

"Besides, I would never have started to read books without the orphanage," he added. "Never. And I think reading has been to me what fixing cars is to you."

I slowly shook my head. "You're never going to

convince me that the orphanage was actually a good thing. I've seen it, remember? I know what you went through there."

"Yes, I know you do," he said softly. He gave a small smile. "You're the only person in the world who's ever known me."

Our auras were mingling where his foot rested near me on the sofa; I could hardly feel where mine ended and his began. I smiled, too. "Maybe that's because you've never told anyone the truth in your life. Your great-grandfather was a gondolier, huh? *And* you stole that trucker's cigarettes after telling him that."

Seb looked genuinely surprised. "But it's true, what I told him. My people were Italian. There was a gondolier strike in Venice, in 1840 — they came here by the thousands."

My eyes widened. I almost said, "Really? A gondolier strike?" And then felt how teasing his aura had become and burst out laughing. "Oh, you're good," I said. "Real good."

"So are you," said Seb, his voice casual. "Look at your aura."

Startled, I brought it back into view. Its lavender lights had shifted to forest green, companionably matching Seb's. "Oh!" I gasped, sitting straight up. The second I did, it flicked back to lavender. I stared at Seb. "How long has it been like that?"

"The last few minutes, maybe," he said with a grin. "So you see, you *can* change your aura."

I half laughed, groaning. "When I don't know I'm doing it — great."

But the tiny victory helped, and I started practicing with Seb every spare moment I had — even in the evenings sometimes, while Alex and the others went over whatever video footage Kara had managed to take that day, trying to get the door code. I helped with that whenever I could, but I was so aware of time ticking away and the days passing. I had to learn how to do this.

Not that the others seemed brokenhearted that I was doing something else. I kept trying to act normal around everyone, but knew that nothing I ever did would be "normal," as far as they were concerned. At least with Seb there, I didn't feel as self-conscious about it now. That prickling, too-aware feeling that I often used to get had faded away completely. It was a relief; I'd hated feeling so vulnerable and scrutinized.

Seb never said much when the others were around. If he did, it was always some mild comment that sounded innocent on the surface, but then you could see the person frowning as they thought about it, like, *Wait — what did he mean by that?*

It made me laugh, but it also exasperated me. I knew from what I'd seen in his hand that Seb usually got along with people perfectly well; there was just this spark of mischief in him that couldn't resist a situation like this — everyone being so suspicious of him when he hadn't even done anything.

"Playing with their minds doesn't actually help, you know." We were out in the courtyard, where there was a battered picnic table; the Shadow was parked near the back door. In the evenings when the rest of the team was home, we usually ended up out here or on the balcony.

"I can't help it," said Seb seriously. "I say things without thinking, all the time — the words, they just fly out of my mouth. It's very unfortunate. I think there must be a medical name for it."

"Really? Maybe we should donate you to science so they can study you."

Seb's mouth twitched. He was sitting up on the tabletop, wearing a cotton long-sleeved shirt with his Cinco de Mayo T-shirt over it. "Yes, maybe. But I'm the teacher, so you can't. Come, *querida*, try again."

I nodded, though it was getting pretty hard not to feel discouraged. I could change my aura's color for a few minutes at a time now, but only if Seb was right there, sort of bolstering it up. Whenever I tried to shift it on my own, it collapsed right back, no matter how relaxed I thought I was. My dreamy state felt like a self-imposed con now — and it was like my aura knew it. With a mental sigh, I closed my eyes and geared myself up for another bout.

"No, stop," said Seb suddenly. "You're all —" He laughed as I looked at him. "Like this," he said, hunching his shoulders tensely. "It's a gentle thing, like play. Look, forget about changing your aura tonight. Let's try this."

He jumped down off the table and went over to the back door; leaning inside, he flicked off the light that

354

hung over the doorway. The courtyard plunged into dimness, still lit by the ambient glow of nearby streetlights but much more mysterious now — shadowy.

"All right, are you ready?" said Seb as he returned. His eyes were impish.

I shook my head, smiling. "Ready for what? Is this some secret half-angel thing?"

"Yes. Well, sort of. Here, stand up." He tugged me to my feet. "OK, look at my aura."

I brought it into view. He'd shifted to his natural colors — the bright, shining silver and the deep forest green. "Now watch," said Seb. He held up his hand, wrapped in a silvery glow. Then he whipped it through the air. A silver trail followed, so quickly it seemed to glitter. He lashed his hand back again; made gleaming circles and loops.

My mouth had fallen open. "Oh, my God, let me try that." I focused on my own aura and a few seconds later was doing the same — swirling my hand and making silver trails all around me, as if I were one of those gymnasts with the long, streaming ribbons. I laughed to see Seb writing his name in the air; my own name followed, shimmering and vanishing in a heartbeat. We were like two kids with sparklers. I couldn't stop smiling. I wished I'd known about this when I was a little girl. How cool would that have been, to have had a perpetual sparkler?

"That is so . . . amazing," I said when we finally sat back on the picnic bench. I stroked my hand through the air, watching it shimmer, aware that this lighthearted feeling was exactly what I'd been struggling to find. "How did you figure that out?"

"Just messing around, when I was boy." Seb sat beside me as I played with the silver glow; he looked delighted at my delight. "We weren't allowed to talk in the orphanage at night — I'd lie in bed doing that instead." He lowered his voice confidingly. "The other boys thought I was very strange."

A flash of my elementary school playground: a group of girls standing in a cluster, whispering and giving me hard looks. I nodded. "Join the club. I freaked people out a lot when I was little. I thought everyone was psychic; I didn't understand why people got upset when I told them things." I glanced at Seb with a smile, wishing more than ever that we'd known each other as children. I wouldn't have cared about the playground at all back then if I'd had him as a friend. We could have just sat under the jungle gym and been weird together.

Seb's expression had turned warm as he looked at me. He started to say something else, then we both looked up as the back door opened and Alex poked his head out. My heart leaped — I'd hardly seen him all day; he must be finished with the security stuff for the night.

A flicker of resignation showed on Alex's face to find Seb and me out here together; then he smiled. "Hey," he said, walking over to us with his hands in his back pockets.

"How's it going with Kara?" I asked as he sat on the bench beside me. I had a feeling he wanted to put his arm around me but was restraining himself; it would seem too much like *This is my girlfriend, back off.* Meanwhile I could practically feel Seb closing off, becoming aloof and watchful.

"Not great," admitted Alex, touching his forehead. "She keeps getting video footage that shows a number or two but not the whole thing. We can't even tell how many digits there are yet; people's hands and fingers are always in the way."

I knew; I'd seen a lot of the footage. "Are you sure I can't help?" I said, touching his leg. "I could try looking through the videos again."

"Maybe," said Alex. He knew as well as I did that I didn't get anything psychically from film — it felt totally cold and flat to me. It was similar for Seb; though he could see auras on film, he didn't get much else. "But I think we're just going to have to keep trying to piece it all together," Alex went on. "Brendan's making a spread-sheet that might help. Oh, and Kara said the church map is a lot more accurate now," he added to Seb. "So thanks for that."

Seb nodded. "Any time."

A silence fell. I racked my brain for something else to say, but it felt like a lost cause. Conversation did not exactly flow when these two were together. Finally Seb rose in an easy motion. "Maybe I'll go read for a while," he said. He glanced at me. "Remember what I said. Don't practice anymore tonight, OK?"

I made a face; I'd been planning on trying again that

night in the dorm, once the others were asleep. "Seb, I feel like maybe I could really do it now —"

"No, just relax," he broke in firmly. "Tomorrow's soon enough."

It was frustrating, but I knew he was probably right — I needed to savor just being friendly with my aura for a change, before plunging back into trying again. "Yes, OK," I said with a sigh.

"See you in the morning," he said, his eyes gentle. I sensed him almost adding *querida* and stopping himself just in time; felt his flash of humor that nearly had me smiling, too, though it shouldn't have. "Good night," he added to Alex.

" 'Night," said Alex.

Once Seb had gone inside, Alex put his arm around me, kissing my head. "Hey, you," he murmured into my hair. I could feel how glad he was Seb had left. Though I was happy to be alone, too, I still wanted to say, *You know, you and Seb could get along if you just gave each other a chance.* Except I wasn't really sure it was true. They were both such strong personalities — Seb in his quiet way and Alex in his direct one — and neither liked being pushed around.

I caught myself; time alone with Alex was too precious to spend it thinking about Seb. I wrapped my arms around him, slipping a hand under his T-shirt and caressing the smoothness of his skin — relishing how my fingers glided over the warmth of him. "Remember the cabin?"

I said after a while. "What the sunrise was like there?"

There'd been a few times at our refuge in the mountains when we'd stayed up all night talking, then sat outside with the sleeping bags draped around our shoulders, watching the sun come up — pink and golden fingers that edged up the peaks like fire from within. The memory made me wistful. I'd known then how lucky we were to have that time together, but I'd had no idea how soon it would be before we hardly even got a chance to talk.

"Of course I remember." Alex kissed my neck. "We'll go back someday, Willow. I mean it. If we defeat the Council . . ."

He stopped. I felt the worry grip him again; the grim tension that was never far away. I hugged him hard, wishing desperately I could say something that would help. We had less than two weeks now — and whether we managed to get further security details or not, we were going to have to enter the Torre Mayor and make some kind of attempt against the Twelve.

We — because mentally, I was including myself in the attack. I'd learn to change my aura in time if it killed me.

"What are you thinking?" Alex had pulled away slightly, watching me with a considering smile. "You look like you've got a million thoughts whirring around in there." He tapped my brow.

I smiled. "Maybe not quite a million." I wasn't about to tell Alex. He was already worried sick about all this; there was no point adding to it until I knew how to disguise my aura at will. I was just glad he wasn't psychic — he'd have picked up on what I was planning in about two seconds, the same as Seb had. I thought of the steady look that had been in Seb's eyes, that moment in the basement. We hadn't discussed the issue out loud yet — it didn't really feel necessary; we both knew exactly how the other felt.

Without trying, I got a sudden image of him. He was sprawled on his bed reading a book — I could picture him so vividly that I could see the Spanish title on its front cover; the brown hair falling over his forehead in those loose curls that I knew drove him crazy. The image made me smile; he looked so engrossed. I closed it away as quickly as it had come. I don't know when I'd first realized I could sense Seb's whereabouts when he wasn't around — somehow it just felt natural to know where he was.

Why was I thinking about Seb again? I pushed him away, irritated, and studied Alex's face in the faint glow of the streetlights — its strong, beautiful lines. I kissed his nose. "You have a very nice nose; are you aware of this fact?"

He laughed for the first time in days, warming me like a hot drink on a winter's evening. "No, I can't say that I am. I don't think my nose has ever gotten a compliment before."

"Poor nose. It deserves lots of compliments." I kissed it again.

Alex shook his head with a grin. "My nose and I both thank you. Why do I get the feeling you're trying to distract me? You know, I did actually notice that you didn't tell me what you were thinking."

"Maybe that's because I didn't want to. Maybe I'm busy having lots of secret, private thoughts."

"Hmm, very mysterious . . ." As Alex drew me to him again, a sound came from inside the house, almost like someone shouting.

We glanced at each other, startled, and then it came again, and this time there was no doubt. Sam's voice, bellowing: "Guys! You guys, get in here! Everyone, now!"

The TV showed a reporter who stood facing the camera, speaking in rapid Spanish. Behind him was a broad conference table with twelve well-dressed people sitting around it, though you couldn't really make out their faces. Sam sat hunched on the sofa, his muscular forearms on his thighs. "They're talking about *los ángeles gobierno*," he said tersely. "That's the Council, right?"

"Oh, my God," murmured Trish.

No one else said anything. Everyone was there, including Seb, still holding his book: Sam's shouts had brought us all running. I sank onto the arm of the sofa, staring at the TV. Alex stood next to me; I was glad to feel the warmth of his arm against mine.

From the doorway, Kara began to translate. "I was brought to this secret location blindfolded, to maintain the security of the group that calls itself the Seraphic Council — the government of those heavenly beings here on Earth. I'm talking now to their spokesperson."

A woman with intense gray eyes appeared on the screen. A chill went over me. This was actually one of the Twelve: one of the ones we hoped to kill. Yet somehow the features of her face were oddly difficult to grasp hold of; it was like you kept forgetting them every second you looked. In a daze, it struck me that I didn't know what this angel looked like, even though I was staring right at her.

The angel spoke in apparently flawless Spanish — but her voice had a strange resonance, almost like several people talking at once. My mouth went dry. "We are speaking to the world today because there have been recent statements made that are false and must be corrected," Kara translated. "This will be our only public statement."

"OK, these are some seriously creepy angels," muttered Brendan. The faces of the others said he'd taken the words right out of their mouths. I reached for Alex's hand; felt his fingers squeeze around mine.

"We are the angelic ruling body. We want to let the world know that regardless of what you may have heard, things are indeed going to change. We speak for all angel-kind — and we are the only angels with the authority to do so." She paused to let that sink in.

And suddenly I got what this was about. Raziel. He'd appeared on TV and promised nothing would change — as if it were up to him.

The reporter's face was pale. "What changes can we expect?"

The angel gazed directly at the camera for the first time. Her chorus of voices turned lower, more deliberate. "Primarily, there will be imminent changes in how the Church of Angels is run."

"Do you mean—?" started the reporter.

She spoke right over him. "We'll keep on with the tradition of an angel heading the Church for the time being—and, in fact, we will soon appoint an angel to head the Church here in Mexico. However, this angel's name will not be released; from now on, we'll be keeping a much lower profile in your world. Any angel who you know by name will soon be retiring from public view. That is our promise."

The gray eyes burned as the angel echoed Raziel's words. I swallowed. I had no sympathy at all for Raziel, but I was glad I wasn't him just then. I could imagine his impotent fury so clearly that for a second it was almost like the emotion beat through me.

Beside me, Alex's expression was intent as he took it all in, trying to see if there was anything here that could help us. Seb stood frowning. His feelings about the angels were a lot more complicated than mine—he'd had a love-hate relationship with their fierce, powerful beauty for years—but I knew he was as disconcerted by the Council as I was.

The angel seemed to remember the reporter's presence. She gave something I think was meant to be a smile, though it made him visibly recoil. "This is *your* world—we angels will allow you the running of it. Our administration of the Church is only in response to your unavoidable worship of us—beyond that, we have little interest in associating with you."

Kara stopped translating for a second; she let out a short, disbelieving laugh. "Man, I never thought I'd dislike any angel *more* than Raziel." Then she continued as the reporter stammered, "Is—is that why you're in Mexico City? To appoint a head for the Church here?"

The eyes turned aloof. "Partly," said the angel. "We are currently conducting other business here, too—vital business for all angelkind. You humans here in Mexico City, and then also around the world, may notice certain effects. This interview is now at an end."

"What did *that* mean?" yelped Brendan.

"I don't know—but they're already *affecting* humanity more than enough," Wesley spat out. He was glaring at the screen, his normally closed-off face alive with anger. Remembering what Alex had told me in confidence, about his entire family having angel burn, I didn't blame him.

"Quiet, you guys," said Alex.

The final image showed the Twelve in their angel forms, their winged figures glowing brightly. Kara translated the reporter's voice: "We *chilangos* can be proud that the Seraphic Council chose Mexico City from which to address the world. But for now . . . we can only wait and wonder."

"God, we can't do away with *them* soon enough," Liz

burst out as a desk appeared with two commentators talking excitedly. "Talk about doing the world a favor!"

"At least they don't seem to like that smarmy Raziel very much." Kara stood leaning against the doorway, her nose wrinkled in distaste. "It sounds like he may not even be holding on to the Church much longer."

"Yeah, but none of this *matters* unless we can actually get into the Torre Mayor," growled Sam. "Alex, what's up with that? You've got a plan, right?"

I looked at Alex, wondering what he'd say. I knew that when he wasn't taking the team on practice hunts, he'd been hanging out around the rear of the Torre Mayor, watching the service driveway. Though I'd had the sense for days now that a plan was forming in his mind, he didn't seem to want to talk about it yet.

He obviously didn't want to talk about it now, either. "I'm working on something," he said. "Don't worry: we'll get in. But first things first, guys. We've got to get the security info, or we'll be working blind once we *are* in."

Seb spoke, his quiet voice searing through the room. "What I want to know is, what is this 'vital business for all angelkind' that they're up to?"

"No idea," said Alex. "But for now, I'm only concerned about it if it affects the attack." As he kept his gaze on the TV screen, he looked relaxed enough — but taking in the faint lines on his forehead, I knew he wasn't.

"Let's hope it won't," I said.

Alex glanced down at me, and I could almost see his tension ease; for a second we were the only two people in the room. With a small smile, he briefly touched my back, his fingers warm through my shirt. "Yeah, let's hope," he said.

Things became even tenser after that, more determined: the team had actually seen who they were going to be fighting. Alex was still taking them out on daily hunts, which made me curse my inability to disguise my aura more than ever. I hated having to just stay at home when the danger was increasing with every hunt—because the angels had to be aware by now that there were AKs in the city. I could never really relax until everyone was back again. Alex was careful to never fall into a predictable routine, though. He always took the team to different places and at different times; they even went at night sometimes. And the AKs were improving by leaps and bounds. I knew Alex thought that if we could just get the security information, we'd have a real chance against the Council now.

When asked, all he would say was that he had a plan to get us into the Torre Mayor, but he was working out the details.

"Do you have a plan?" I whispered one morning when we were alone in his bedroom. I was lying in his arms, savoring the feel of his skin against mine. I'd slipped into his room while the others were having breakfast—I knew Alex would already have had his; he was an early riser. When I timed things right, we could sometimes have almost half an hour alone together. It was incredibly precious to us both—and not just as a time to talk. Now

I stroked his bare chest. "Or are you just trying to keep morale up?"

Alex sighed. Keeping an arm around my shoulders, he stretched up a hand to bat at the dust motes that were drifting past. "Yes, I've got a plan—but I don't like it very much," he admitted. "I don't want to say anything to the team until after we get the security information. I'm hoping we'll find out something that'll improve on it."

I bit my lip. That bad. I didn't say anything; he clearly didn't want to go into it. After a pause he rolled toward me, and we lay gazing at each other without speaking. I felt myself falling into his blue-gray eyes, so vivid under their black lashes. As I caught a wave of his emotions, my throat tightened: a deep yearning, a suppressed fear that the two of us wouldn't have the long life together that we both wanted. The thought filled me with dread.

He reached out and touched a strand of my hair as if he'd never seen it before, and then lowered his lips to mine. I could feel how much he needed to lose himself in me; it was what I needed, too, with him. I held him to me tightly as we kissed and wished there were no time limits, and no other people, and that we could just do exactly what we wanted. Because even though I tried not to think about it, in my darkest moments I couldn't help wondering if we'd really survive all this. And I didn't want to die without ever truly giving myself to the boy I loved.

"Alex, maybe . . ." I whispered now. My heart was thudding; my body felt flushed and prickly.

He rose up on his elbows, scanning my face. Before

he could say anything, we heard Sam and Brendan come back into the dorm, arguing about basketball. Basketball, when we were a thousand miles away from the NBA. I closed my eyes tightly; I felt like crying. Alex let out a breath, then kissed me.

"Soon," he said, and I could tell from the determination in his voice that he was going to make it happen, no matter what.

With only one digit left on the six-number security code, it turned out that they changed the code every week, knocking us back to square one. Everyone was stressed — especially Kara, I think, whose job couldn't be hurried, though we all longed for it to be. There was just over a week left now. The rest of the team spent any spare time either grimly working out or watching TV in near silence.

That wasn't my only worry. Once or twice now, I'd gotten glimpses from Seb of the same powerful emotion I thought I'd felt in him the first day we'd met — warm, deep flashes that told me exactly how much he still hoped something more than friendship would happen between us.

He usually kept it far below the surface, though. And selfishly, I was glad of it. I didn't want to face his feelings for me. I didn't want anything to change between us, not ever — because Seb and I just clicked, on every level. He really did feel like a brother: a soul twin who'd somehow found me again, after a lifetime apart.

Blue. I imagined an airy pale blue, like the sky on a summer's day. As we sat outside in the courtyard, I focused only on my aura, lightly keeping the sense of oneness, of play. My aura shifted, its silver lights turning obediently to the color of the sky. Somehow I kept myself detached, ignoring the distant pounding of my heart. For a change, Seb's energy wasn't bolstering me up, though I could feel him sitting nearby, silently willing me on.

Then a car alarm went off and I started; my aura snapped back to silver. When I tried again, I knew I'd totally lost the sense of lightheartedness — I'd have to go into aura-sparkler mode again to get it back. I sighed as I opened my eyes. Now that I'd reached this stage, Seb kept saying I needed to lock away the aura part of my mind and keep it separate, so that nothing could distract me, but I just couldn't seem to get the hang of it.

"You really are doing much better, you know," he commented. We were outside at the picnic table again; Seb was sitting backward on the bench, with me up on the tabletop beside him.

"Yes, but —" I broke off, scraping my hands over my face. "Oh, *argh*. Why can't I get this, when you can do it so easily? This is worse than being back in algebra class!"

"I learned when I was a small child — I think this made it much easier," Seb pointed out mildly. He sat back against the table edge, propping his elbows to either side as he gave me a curious look. "You took algebra?"

I shrugged. "Not by choice. It was required." I'd told

Seb a lot about high school; like Alex, it was something he'd only seen on TV. I pulled my knees up, sitting cross-legged. "Would you have wanted to go, if you'd had the chance? To high school, I mean."

A ripple of surprise, so I knew the answer before he said it. "Yes, of course. Even if I'd felt alone there, the way you always did—I'd still like to know more than I do." He made a wry face, as if he didn't want it to matter too much to him. "I could have learned how not to get caught at stealing, maybe."

Actually, Seb read so much that he knew a lot more than I did about some things. I studied him, trying to picture him in high school. Like Alex, he'd have had every girl in the place after him if he'd gone. Though I had a feeling Alex would be out on the basketball court, while Seb would be holed up in the library somewhere.

He pushed lightly at my leg. "Anyway, I know *you* didn't like school very much, but there must have been something about it you enjoyed."

Enjoyed was pretty strong. I started to laugh and say, *Guess again*—and then I remembered my art class. I'd always loved making things with my hands. When the whole Church of Angels thing happened, I'd been working on a kinetic sculpture that used pieces of old engines. If I'd managed to do it right, the different pieces were actually going to move on their own.

I described my sculpture to Seb; he listened with interest. "Yes, I can imagine you doing that." Then he stroked his stubbled jaw, looking deep in thought. "You know, I think this means I was right," he decided. "There *is* something you enjoyed."

"Yeah, I guess," I admitted. I glanced down at him with a smile, shaking my head. "How did you even *know* that?"

He gave me a smugly arch look. "Ah, you see — I know you better than you know yourself."

And he really did sometimes; that was the funny thing. In some ways Seb knew me better than anyone in the world, even Alex. I rested my arms on my thighs; in the background there was the never-ending drone of city traffic. "Can I ask you something?" I said finally.

"You know you can."

I cleared my throat. I'd been dying to ask him this ever since we first met but had felt embarrassed for some reason. "I was just wondering . . . if I could see your angel."

I felt a leap of emotion from him. "I've been wanting to ask you that, too," he admitted. "Very much."

Both of us were shy suddenly. My cheeks heated. I tucked back a short strand of my hair. "Um — so how should we —?"

"We'll go at the same time," suggested Seb, straightening up.

I shifted down to the bench and perched cross-legged facing him. "OK, on the count of three."

He nodded. "One . . . two . . . three."

I closed my eyes briefly on *three*, bringing my angel to me in a bright burst of energy. I merged with her, then sent her flying gently from my human body to hover over me.

I opened my eyes. Seb was sitting beside me . . . and above him was his angel.

I stared with both my angel and human eyes. Seb's angel looked just like him—leanly powerful, with a beautiful, high-cheekboned face—except that he was radiant with light. His wings stretched out over the table, stirring the night air. I could hardly breathe at the wonder of truly seeing another of my own kind for the first time; I thought I could never drink him in enough. From Seb's expression, I knew he felt exactly the same. More, even— he'd been longing for this for so many years.

Seb's angel wore jeans and a T-shirt, and suddenly I realized that my angel could be clad in anything I wanted. I shifted my angelic robes to a vintage dress from the sixties that I'd always loved and saw Seb's slight smile as he noticed. Hovering in my angel form, I took in his ethereal hands, how strong and shining they looked. I longed to reach out my own hand—to see what it was like to touch another of my kind in this form, too. Something held me back, and with an effort, I kept my arm where it was. It just seemed . . . too much, for now.

On the bench, Seb's eyes were steady on mine. They caught and held me; I felt almost dazed with wonder that somehow the two of us had found each other—that he had found me. My mouth went dry as I sensed again the true depth of his feelings for me, but I couldn't have looked away from Seb just then to save my life. I was so aware of how much I wanted to send my angel self soaring with his, the two of us flying so far up that we'd find the stars beyond the city lights — but we both knew it wasn't safe here.

Finally, with a last long look at each other, our angels returned to our human bodies in a rush of gleaming wings, so that once more it appeared to be just Seb and me out in the dingy concrete courtyard together. Neither of us moved as we sat there, our gazes still locked. It felt . . . I can't describe how it felt. We'd seen this innermost part of each other, shared our true selves

I saw Seb's throat move. His eyes were bright. Without speaking, he reached for my hand; I was reaching for his in the same moment. Our fingers met and twined together, gripping each other hard. It didn't even feel like we had a choice. Seb and I had to touch just then — had to somehow try to express what we'd just experienced. Letting out a ragged breath, I leaned against the firm warmth of his arm, our fingers still tightly linked.

We sat that way for a long time, with the urban night humming gently with life around us.

CHAPTER EIGHTEEN

"SO HOW ARE WE getting into the Torre Mayor?" Sam demanded for the hundredth time. "'Cause with as long as Kara's taking, I'm starting to think we better forget the security stuff. Hell, let's just bust in there, do what we gotta do, and get out again!"

They were heading back from another hunt, at Alameda Central this time. The Metro was less crowded than usual, allowing the AKs to sit together in an almost-empty car. Alex groaned and dropped his head against the window. "Sam, we've had this conversation," he said to the ceiling. "Tell me again, why is it a good idea for us to go storming in there without any idea what we're walking into? Oh, yeah, I forgot—we're in a Rambo movie."

"Well, we can't just keep waiting for Kara to get the goddamn code," grumbled Sam. He sat sprawled back in his seat: a large, disgruntled Texan. "The Council'll be gone before she gets it at this rate."

Alex didn't answer, fully aware that if worse came to worst, they'd have to make an attempt on the Council anyway. He sighed, massaging his forehead. The angels in the city were definitely on the alert now. There weren't nearly as many of them out feeding as there'd been just a couple of weeks ago, and those that were seemed to be feeding somewhat perfunctorily, less inclined to savor their prey. Even so, the team had managed to bring down four today — and three of them had blasted straight back at him. Distantly, Alex wondered what kind of damage he was taking from all the angel fallout lately. Martin, his father, used to be riddled with it sometimes.

To Alex's side, Liz and Trish were talking in excited, low voices about the hunt; Wesley and Brendan sat across from them, joining in occasionally. Wesley in particular looked psyched, almost smiling for a change — he'd gotten two of the creatures. The team wasn't doing badly; they really weren't. But they had less than a week now.

"You still haven't told me what the plan is," observed Sam, tapping his fingers on his leg.

"No kidding," said Alex. He had no intention of telling Sam or anyone else until he had to; morale would plummet. Well, maybe not Sam's morale — but the sane members of the team's, definitely.

He'd spent days scoping out the Torre Mayor's deliveries entrance while he pretended to be fiddling with the Shadow's engine in a nearby parking lot — and by now he thought he had a pretty solid plan for how he could get the team in there and up the service elevator. Juan's white van would be perfect; half the deliveries came in white vans. The service elevator would be sure to have that top floor locked off, but they could reach the floor below, then take the stairwell, where he'd shoot out the security cameras immediately. The sudden blank screens in the security office would probably bring someone to check within minutes, but they'd be in by then — it would take no time at all to get up the stairs and shoot the door open with a silenced pistol. If they could get to the Council quickly after that, Alex thought their chances of getting in and out alive weren't terrible. It was conceivable that they could get down the main elevator and be out the front door before anyone even figured out what had happened — especially in the chaos of all the angels suddenly vanishing.

It was that word *quickly* that kept him awake at night and made him keep the plan firmly to himself. Because they just didn't know what was going on now. They couldn't get to the Council quickly when they had *no idea* if the schedule was still the right one; *no idea* what the layout was or what room the Twelve would be in. Alex had nightmare visions of the team wandering around looking in doors while security came racing toward them, having tipped off the angels that there were intruders in their midst.

The train came to Zócalo station; Alex stood up abruptly. The others looked at him in surprise — their stop was still several stations away. "Let's get off here," he said, shoving his hands into the front pockets of his sweatshirt. "I want to check something out."

As they came up the stairs, they could hear shouting on the sidewalk — there was a shoving match going on between some of the Crusaders and the Faithful. "My mother is dying!" screamed a man. His face was wild, contorted with fury. "There are no beds for her, no doctors —"

"If she had true faith, the angels would help her!" someone bellowed back. There were signs waving, elbows flying, as people scuffled. Alex and the others skirted around them; a man in a business suit lurched backward and just as quickly flung himself into the fray. Trish looked worried as they passed, glancing back over her shoulder. Alex could see that she wanted to somehow defuse the tension, just as she always wanted to smooth things over for the group.

"Alex, this looks like it could get serious —" she started.

"I know, but ignore it," he said, not breaking his stride. "We don't want to get involved." The police mostly seemed to ignore the Crusaders, unless things got violent — then, undoubtedly, whoever they arrested got dragged off to the angels.

Trish bit her lip but nodded. When they were directly across from the slightly tilting mass of the Catedral Metropolitana — no, the Catedral de los Ángeles; he kept forgetting — Alex dug his cell phone out of his jeans pocket. Tapping the buttons with his thumb, he sent Kara a text: WE'RE AT ZOCALO. WHERE R U? CAN U CHECK OUT CATHEDRAL WITH US?

A few seconds later, a reply came: I'M HERE 2. MEET U OUTSIDE CATHEDRAL IN 5.

Alex texted a quick yes and tucked his phone away again. Good — he'd thought she'd still be there. Though he'd been to the cathedral several times now to study the layout, he felt twitchy with impatience suddenly — he wanted to see the place again, see if he'd missed anything. "Come on, we're going to check out the cathedral," he said to the others.

"Well, hallelujah, we're finally doing something," said Sam with a grin.

Alex gave him a level glance. "Yes, we are. We are going to go in and look. Not start shooting. Got it?"

Sam made a face. "Yeah, I got it. Don't worry."

They headed across the broad stretch of the Zócalo, accompanied by the incessant beat of drums from Aztec dancers. Alex knew that in December the city usually erected a giant ice-skating rink in the square, but this year there was nothing — either El DF no longer had funds for it or they'd decided it would detract from the glory of the converted cathedral. There were hardly any Christmas decorations up around the city, either; he'd heard on the news that a lot of people saw the holiday as lacking in meaning now. Many were planning to start celebrating Arrival Day — October 31 — as their main holiday instead, to honor the angels. *Great*, thought Alex in distaste, picturing it.

They passed through the cathedral's wrought-iron gates; the faded red-and-black tiles that had once been underfoot were now celestial silver and light blue. Wesley looked up at the golden angel, holding its wreath to the sky.

"I still can't believe they did that," he muttered to Alex. "That angel was, like, the most famous monument in Mexico City."

"It still is," pointed out Liz, overhearing. "Even *more* famous now. But that empty column on the Paseo de la Reforma just looks weird—like it's waiting for something to happen."

Kara was standing beside the cathedral's massive wooden doors. Despite his worry, Alex held back a smile when he saw she had on a pair of pink satin angel wings. "They're really you," he said as they reached her. "Or have you got angel burn, and I should shoot you?"

Kara rolled her eyes; the long, braided wig she was wearing made her look like Cleopatra or something. "It's called camouflage, dear. You should probably all get some too, so our group doesn't attract attention. This is Church of Angels Central—where the people are whacked out and the angels are plentiful."

Sam recoiled. "What, us wear those things? No way."

"No, it's a good idea." Alex reached for his wallet; he took out a few hundred pesos and handed the bills to Sam. "Here, go get us some, OK?" As Sam opened his mouth, he added, "And no complaining, Tex, or I'll make you wear the pink ones." The others snickered; Sam gave him a dark look and headed off to one of the angel-wing vendors wandering around the square.

"Listen, I was just about to text you myself," said Kara in a low voice. "I managed to get the security code again today—the whole thing, first try. If they only change it once a week, it should be good for another three days."

Alex's heart leaped. "Really? Are you sure?"

"Yeah. And I've got an idea of when the best time might be for us to try to break in, too, but . . . meanwhile, something's come up."

"What?" Alex felt his exhilaration fade. The look on Kara's face did not herald good news.

She fell silent, her beautiful features twisted in thought. "Let's wait till we get inside," she said finally. "You can see for yourself what I mean."

Sam returned with a cluster of angel wings, and they put them on, helping one another straighten them. "Perfect—you all look like real devouts now," said Kara. "Just gaze around wonderingly, and you'll fit right in."

The white wings on his back felt ridiculous. But the team looked ready, Alex saw with approval—alert and reasonably relaxed, a big change from less than three weeks ago, when they'd had their first hunt.

"OK, I want all of you scanning and prepared, in case any of us is attacked," he said. "Stick together—don't anyone go wandering off. If we do have to defend ourselves, try to do it without being noticed; I'd sort of like to avoid starting a riot today."

"Riots, bad—got it," muttered Brendan.

A cavernous coolness fell as they entered the cathedral. When Alex had been here years ago, an altar had stood just inside the entrance. Now it was gone, as was the organ behind it, turning the cathedral into a vast, airy space. White pillars marched in a silent line to the single lavish, golden altar far away down the aisle—it stretched from floor to ceiling, ornate with detail, glinting like liquid. A gold angel took pride of place here, holding a trumpet to its lips as smaller angels cavorted around it. From some unseen source, harp music fluttered through the air.

There were hundreds of people inside, though the cathedral was so large that it didn't seem crowded. Many sat praying in the long pews; others wandered respectfully about, taking photographs and videos, or lighting candles that stood on small winged stands. Alex spotted several people being fed from, their faces alight as angels stood beside them—hands buried deep in the humans' life forces, their halos burning brighter and brighter.

Sam had seen, too; Alex could practically feel him twitching for his gun. "Steady," he whispered to him.

The AKs moved down the central aisle, their feet echoing on the marble floor. Kara gazed dreamily up at the domed ceiling, with its newly painted pink and white rococo angels. Alex knew he couldn't do the blissed-out look as well as she did—he just tried not to look like he completely hated this place.

To either side, the spaces where chapels to individual saints had once stood were now devoted to different aspects of the angels' love. Pretending to be showing them the "love for our planet" chapel, Kara led the AKs to a painting of three angels holding a globe of the world.

She pointed upward, as if indicating a detail of the artwork. "OK, don't look now, but that door behind me leads to the main administrative offices," she said to the team. Alex had seen it several times before; he took a sideways glance anyway at the dark arched door in the corner.

"You can see the keypad right beside it," went on Kara. "Like I was just saying to Alex, we've got the code now, and it shouldn't be changing again till Thursday—and from what I've seen, there are a few times during the day when we might be able to slip in without being noticed. Evening service is the main one—everyone seems pretty distracted then. There's another issue that's come up, though."

Alex had been standing with his back to the stone wall as he listened, pretending to look at the cathedral while he kept an eye out for angels. The two that had been feeding were gone now, at least in their angelic forms. Scanning, he didn't sense any of the creatures in the main space—but a tingle crawled up his spine at the number of them in the unseen office area.

He bent his head toward Kara. "Jesus, how many of them are *back* there?" he muttered.

"That . . . is the problem," said Kara. Her eyes met his. "It's a new development we have to deal with—'cause I've got a bad feeling it's here to stay. Come on, let's give the rest of these guys a quick look around at the layout, then maybe we can all go to a café or something. I've seriously had enough of this place for one day."

They exited the cathedral soon after, climbing its worn stone steps into the late afternoon. As they crossed the road and started across the square, walking alongside the long, tan stretch of the Palacio Nacional, Alex took out his phone and texted Willow: HOME IN A WHILE, WE'RE OK. I LOVE YOU. Her response came promptly, making him smile: HURRY BACK, I MISS YOU!

He'd bought cell phones for the rest of the team the day after Seb arrived, not wanting to ever again be in a position where someone was missing and he had no idea what was going on. Now he and Willow often had a few texts going back and forth during the day — tiny notes that made him feel more laid-back about Seb's presence in the house. Not that much, though, if he was honest.

Alex shook his head at himself in disgust as he walked. He'd never thought he was a jealous person — and he trusted Willow completely. But knowing that she and Seb were alone together all day, even though all they were doing was working on her aura, nagged at him like a pebble in his shoe. Not to mention that he'd lost count now of how many times he'd walked in on them having one of their long, intimate conversations. Just a few nights ago, he'd found them out on the balcony; Willow had been wearing Seb's sweater draped across her shoulders as they talked. Though they'd been sitting at least four feet apart, the sweater had irritated Alex far more than it should have; it had been an effort to even be civil to Seb. It wasn't the kind of thing you could mention, though, without sounding like a jealous jerk.

But he couldn't have held back what he *had* said to save his life — the words had finally burst out of him, after two weeks of biting them back. "So you know he's in love with you, right?" he'd asked once Seb had gone back inside, leaving his sweater on her shoulders.

Alex had been sitting beside Willow on the cool concrete floor with his arm around her. She'd gone still as she stared up at him. "I know he cares about me a lot," she said finally. "But, Alex, we're just friends. I told him that the first day."

"Willow. Come on, seriously — haven't you noticed? The way he looks at you all the time — plus you must *feel* it, can't you? With both of you being psychic?"

Her cheeks had tinged. With one hand, she'd fingered the sweater's sleeve, apparently unaware she was doing so. With an effort, Alex had managed not to yank the thing off her shoulders.

"No, not really," she said, her voice soft. "I mean, once or twice maybe, I guess I've gotten a flash of something, but —" She stopped, then seemed to notice that she was holding the sleeve and dropped it, rubbing her hand on her jeans. "We're friends," she repeated. "He knows that's all it is."

Alex had stared down at her, taking in the short spikes of hair that looked almost cherry-colored in the half-light.

Right then, they'd almost matched her cheeks. And looking down at her face as she gazed out over the courtyard, Alex had longed to be psychic himself—to be able to just reach into her head and find out what she was thinking.

Walking across the Zócalo now with the rest of the team, Alex told himself for the hundredth time that he was being ridiculous—because he *knew* how much Willow loved him. And unlike she and Seb, when they were alone together, they didn't sit four feet apart. Just that morning, they'd managed some time in his bedroom: soft words; Willow's body against his; her lips as she kissed his neck, his tattoo, his chest. He went warm, remembering . . . and tried not to dwell on the fact that if she didn't talk to Seb so much, they could be alone like that more often.

Alex's phone beeped again in his jeans pocket. Pulling it out, he saw another text from Willow: DID I TELL YOU I LOVE YOU, BY THE WAY? THIS WAS A HUGE OVERSIGHT IF I DIDN'T.

His irritation over Seb faded. Christ, he really was an idiot. OVERSIGHT CORRECTED, he texted in response. DID I TELL YOU THAT I WANT TO KISS YOU FOR A VERY LONG TIME LATER?

Her reply came in seconds. THAT'S DEFINITELY A PLAN I CAN GET BEHIND.

Alex smiled as he put his phone away but felt slightly wistful, too. God, he wanted it all with Willow, everything—and he'd never realized it more than these last few weeks, with the fate of humanity hanging in the balance. If they managed to defeat the angels, the only thing he'd ever want would be to live the rest of his life with Willow. Marry her, if that's what she wanted. Just *be* with her, forever.

But for now the present was all they had, and the only promise he could make was that he loved her. Because the reality was that no plan they put into place would be foolproof: when the AKs made their strike, there was a chance that he and the team would die. Alex didn't let his thoughts go down this path very often; the idea of any of his team being hurt was agony. He shoved his hands in his pockets, trying not to think about it now.

Anyway, maybe he didn't know what the attack on the Council would bring, but at least now that the team was trained, he could leave them on their own without worrying too much. And so for just one night, he and Willow were going to have some real privacy, like he'd promised them both. Alex's blood quickened at the thought. She didn't even know yet; he wanted to surprise her.

No Seb, no other people. Just the two of them in each other's arms, being truly together in the way they both longed for.

I nudged gently at my pale-blue aura, watching it shimmer and change to a vibrant rose. It wavered before me for a few minutes, the color of sunrise. OK, how about green now? Green would be nice . . . and though I'd thought I was totally immersed in it, somehow my thoughts drifted then to the Council attack. Alex. How important it was that I got this. And the playful mood was gone, slipped away like mist in the wind.

I opened my eyes and stared at my silver aura. The house was silent around us.

"Willow, stop — you're doing so well," said Seb, responding to the silent berating that was going on in my head.

He had on the same long-sleeved gray T-shirt he'd worn when I first met him, with the sleeves pushed up slightly. The hair on his tanned arms was lighter than on his head; almost golden — from years spent on the road in the sun maybe. Pushing the thought away, I slumped back against the sofa. "It doesn't feel like it."

Seb shrugged. "You must keep your aura separate from everything now, that's all. Like, you can walk and talk at the same time, yes? You don't think about walking. It's like that."

He was always so patient — he'd told me all this about a hundred times now. But as he stretched across to rustle another cookie out of the bag, I could sense again the conflict that had been with him since almost that first day: he wanted me to be safe around the angels, yet as far from the Torre Mayor as possible when the team attacked.

I sighed. I hadn't really meant to discuss this with him, but I heard the words come out anyway. "Seb, I've got to be there when it happens. For so many reasons. I can't just sit here at home."

His eyes met mine. He didn't ask what I was talking about. "If you learn how in time, then I'll be there, too," he said.

I bit my lip. I hated the idea of anything happening to Seb, almost as much as I did anything happening to Alex. "You're part of the team now, though," I said. "Wouldn't you go anyway? Whether I did or not?"

"No." Seb looked down, turned the cookie over in his hands and then rested it on the table uneaten. "When the attack happens, I'll be wherever you are — doing whatever I can to protect you." He gave a small smile. "I wouldn't be anywhere else."

On the one hand, I was touched — enormously. On the other, I felt a little irritated that he seemed so convinced that I couldn't take care of myself. "Seb —"

"*Querida*, no, that's not it," said Seb before I could say anything else. "You know I don't think that; you can take care of yourself very well. But if there's an attack and the team fails, the angels will find out everything. I won't leave you on your own in that kind of danger." He shrugged again; his eyes held a gleam of humor suddenly. "You can try to make me if you like. You won't have much luck, I don't think."

My chest tightened — what I felt was far too deep to put into words. Thankfully, with Seb I didn't have to try. I let out a long breath.

"You're still calling me *querida*," I pointed out finally. "Brothers don't do this."

"Sorry. I'm very forgetful sometimes." He picked up the cookie and took a bite; stretching back against the sofa, he rested one long leg out in front of him.

I smiled; if there's an opposite of *sorry*, that's how he looked. "Seb . . . you know I appreciate everything you've just said. God — so much. But when we attack the Twelve, I have to be there with Alex. I *have* to be. I've got to learn this."

Seb's eyebrows drew together in thought as he finished eating; I could sense him putting aside his own feelings. "You will — I'm just not sure how else I can explain it to you," he said. Brushing his hands off, he sat up and held them out to me. "Here, see again what it's like for me."

I wasn't sure what good it would do — we'd tried this so many times. I moved beside him on the sofa anyway; putting my hands in his, I closed my eyes. The half-angel energy felt completely familiar now, wrapping around me like a comforting blanket. And the sensation as Seb changed his aura was like second nature to me by then, too . . . but this time, as I drifted into the lights of my own aura, I realized with a twinge of surprise that I could feel something different.

In a daze, it came to me: Seb and I had been growing closer every day, so that now I was able to sense what he was doing on every possible level, almost as if I *were* him — and it let me grasp a detail I hadn't managed to catch hold of before. He'd told me this over and over, but for the first time I was experiencing it for myself — the way he kept his aura locked safely away, where it couldn't be disturbed. I could feel how protected that part of his mind was, how cradled away from everything. He'd almost built a sort of barrier around it, though I knew he wasn't even aware of it; he must have done it instinctively as a child.

Mirroring him just as I'd done over two weeks ago, when we'd only barely started, I carefully constructed the same mental shield. Immediately, I felt a calm come over me — as if on a deep level I knew, really *knew*, that whatever I did with my aura now was secure.

Blue, I thought, and felt it shift.

I could tell Seb had sensed what had happened, and why. His hands tightened in mine. "Look," he said in a whisper.

I opened my eyes. My aura was a clear sky blue with lavender hues. I swallowed, half expecting it to crash back to silver. Deliberately, I thought of the Council attack, of how much I needed to be there, of every distracting, worrying thought I could throw at myself.

My aura stayed blue.

I reached out in wonder and watched the blue lights gleaming on my fingers. Exhilaration rushed through me.

"Seb, I've got it! I've really got it!" I lunged forward, hugging him. He returned my hug with a laugh; I could sense his deep relief that I had it now, despite his reservations.

I sank back onto the sofa, staring at my still-blue aura.

I experimented with changing it a dull, stunted gray. The colors dimmed and shrank. It looked like used dishwater clinging around me. I hated it. So would an angel.

I'm not sure how much time went by as I sat playing with my aura, shifting its colors with my thoughts. Seb watched in silence. Finally we glanced at each other, and my excitement faded. The closeness between us that had let me finally learn this suddenly seemed like a double-edged sword — because when the team attacked the Council, Seb would be there now, too, risking his life. Alex and I didn't have a choice, but Seb did. I wanted him to be safe, just as much as he wanted the same thing for me.

He shook his head, responding to my unspoken thought. "*Madre mía,* Willow," he said softly. "Do you really think I'd go somewhere and be *safe* while you're taking part in that?"

My chest felt tight. "Seb . . . you could die. And it would be for a cause that isn't even yours, really."

Almost the moment I said the words, I got a flash of a small girl with big eyes — the same girl I'd seen once before. *Run, niña!* With a frightened gasp, she took to her heels, darting away through a whirling, dancing crowd.

I stared at Seb. "Who is that?"

He shrugged, his eyes distant. "I don't know. A street child." He told me what had happened; how he'd saved her from an angel. I sat without moving, picturing it all so vividly — and feeling limp with relief that he'd somehow managed to kill the angel with only a knife.

As Seb finished, he made a face at himself. "The whole time, I was thinking, *You stupid* cabrón; *what are you doing? You're finally so close to finding her — why are you risking it for this?* But I knew afterward that I'd do it again. That it was worth it."

"Because she could have been you," I said, watching him. He sat with his head down, playing with the cuff of his shirt; his strong features looked almost sculpted. "You helped her when she needed you, the way you always wished someone would have helped you."

"Yes, I guess that's it." Seb turned his head to look at me; he seemed to be studying me down to my soul. He smiled slightly. "Even when it happened, I knew you'd understand."

My face heated. We didn't talk much about how it had always been me who he was looking for — as opposed to just any half-angel girl.

He looked down again, pushed his cuffs up to his elbows. "Willow, I'll be wherever you are when it happens," he said. "Let's not bother arguing, OK?"

"OK," I whispered finally. And in a way it felt inevitable that Seb would be there, but, oh, God, I hated it — the two people I cared about most in the world would be risking their lives at the same time.

I'd stopped being aware of my aura as we talked, and now I brought it back into view. It was still as I'd last imagined: gray and unappealing. *Purple,* I thought, and watched it turn a rich plum color. "So I guess I've got the hang of this," I said at last.

Seb was gazing at my aura, too. "Yes. Maybe a few more days, to make sure."

I nodded, though I think we both knew I really had it now. But Alex would be sure to insist on the same thing. I sighed, suddenly wanting him here so badly. No, actually, wanting both of us to be somewhere else: up at the cabin, maybe, going for a walk in the mountains — knowing that we had all the time in the world together.

As if brought on by my thoughts, my cell phone beeped. I pulled it from my jeans pocket and found a text from Alex: HOME IN A WHILE. WE'RE OK. I LOVE YOU.

I smiled and texted a quick response, then put the phone away. "They'll be here later."

And then I saw the way Seb was looking at me — the depth of feeling in his eyes. The wave of emotion from him felt suddenly cut off, as if he'd quickly tried to stifle it, but it still made me catch my breath. I glanced away, pretending I hadn't noticed, even though all at once my heart was banging in my chest.

"So, um . . . we've got time for me to keep practicing for a while," I said. My throat felt too small to get words through.

"Yes, all right," said Seb. He sat up, not looking at me as he reached for another cookie. "We'll see how fast you can change it."

I swallowed, taking in the slight flush that had appeared in his cheeks. "Actually — actually, I'll be right back," I said, jumping up. "Do you want a Coke or anything?"

Without waiting for Seb to answer, I went to the kitchen, where I opened the fridge door and let its chill waft over my face for a few minutes. Finally I took out a pair of Cokes and bumped the fridge door closed with my hip. Then, for some reason, I found myself putting them on the counter and sending another text to Alex, telling him that I loved him.

When I went back into the TV room, the awkward moment had thankfully passed, and I could tell myself that Seb was just my brother again.

Chapter Nineteen

"OK," SAID KARA once the AKs were settled in a café.
The view was of Aztec ruins, with the cathedral rising up
behind. She blew on her coffee. "That gang of angels back
in the offices appeared a couple of days ago." She glanced
apologetically at Alex. "I wanted to get more information
before I said anything, with how tense everything's been
lately."

He nodded, not really able to fault her for it, though
he'd have preferred to know earlier. "And?"

Kara sighed. "From what I've managed to pick up, it's
the angel that's been chosen to run the cathedral, along
with his groupies. And I don't think they're going anywhere. I don't know if they're discussing details or what,
but they mostly seem to be hanging out in the reception
area — that means anyone who goes into the main office
has to go right past them."

"Are they still there at night?" asked Trish, fiddling worriedly with a packet of sugar.

"I don't know," said Kara. "It doesn't matter; after evening service they kick everyone out and lock up — and their security setup is a lot better than we're equipped to deal with. Here, look." She showed the team a series of photos taken surreptitiously with her phone — state-of-the-art motion detectors and steel doors installed over the ancient wooden ones that looked like they slammed shut automatically if anything went off, trapping you inside.

Alex had seen the photos before but still found himself grimacing as he scrolled through them. Despite his distrust of the CIA, he wished they had some way to get in touch with Sophie — they could seriously use some of the high-tech toys those guys had right about now. He handed the phone to Sam, who'd been craning to see over his arm. "So even with the security code, it's not looking great, is it?" he said grimly. "Not if the offices are chock-full of angels now."

They'd all taken their angel wings off and dropped them in a small, satiny pile between their table and the wall. Kara still had on the long wig, though; she absently twirled one of the braids around her finger. "They haven't been feeding as much as I'd expect, really, but . . . yeah, getting past them is definitely going to be high risk. Between them, I think they've sampled everyone in the offices by now."

Glancing around him, Alex saw that the team looked a little sick. He didn't blame them.

"But I think there's a way," Kara went on. "Because I don't get much sense of these angels interacting with humans — so they can't be that familiar with how the place is run. And during evening service, I don't feel any humans back there, just these angels. So if someone walked past them into the office then and looked sort of official — like they had an after-hours job to do — then I don't think they'd challenge them."

"No, just feed off them," said Brendan with a shudder. "This really isn't my all-time favorite plan that I've ever heard so far."

Suddenly Alex knew. He dropped back against his seat. "Seb," he said.

"Or Willow," agreed Kara. Her voice was businesslike. Whatever she thought about half angels, she was hiding it for the moment.

Alex shook his head, his mind already ticking, thinking through possibilities. "No, she still hasn't gotten the hang of the aura work. But Seb . . . God, if he'd do it . . ." The irony of having to ask Seb for assistance wasn't lost on him; he and Seb barely spoke if they didn't have to. Seb had agreed to help them, though, and he'd have to see that this was too big for their personal feelings to get in the way of.

Sam's face was screwed up with distaste. He took a slurp of his beer. "Does someone want to explain to me what's going on? Why are we talking about that half-angel guy?"

"Because he can change his aura, idiot, remember?"

397

said Liz, shoving lightly at Sam's solid arm. "That's what he's training Willow to do — remember?"

He glowered at her. "Yeah, but I thought that was just to make it look *normal*."

"No, he can make it look really unappetizing, too," said Alex. "You know — like the last aura in the world an angel would ever want to feed from. Willow said it's what he does when he sees one on the hunt."

Wesley's habitual frown was back in place, his expression intense. "What about the computers? Won't they have passwords on them?"

Kara gave a reluctant shrug. "I think, unfortunately, that's the part we're going to have to play by ear."

Alex blew out a soft breath. He'd known already that breaking into the church offices wasn't as sure a bet as he'd like when it came to getting the security plans. But it was their only real hope.

"I'll talk to Seb when we get home." He circled his beer in its ring of condensation as he considered how they could best provide Seb with backup. No immediate way sprang to mind — not with that many angels back in the office area, and in the narrow hallways that Kara had described. If any trouble broke out, it would be slaughter to have anyone posted back there; Seb was most likely going to have to be on his own.

"Jesus, this is going to be risky as hell," he muttered. He felt a short, fierce relief that Willow hadn't learned to disguise her aura yet.

"Well . . . there *is* something else we might try, but I

don't know how well it would work," said Kara slowly. "The evening service two nights from now is going to be a special one, to celebrate the appointment of the new angel head—and the priest's going to be giving blessings on behalf of the angels."

Her eyes met Alex's as he took in what this meant.

Liz blinked. "Yes? And?"

"A blessing's seen as a really serious thing to ask for, so probably not that many people will go up," explained Alex. "But the ones who do, the priest will hold their hands, maybe for as long as a minute. So Seb could try to get the information psychically first." Even though Seb had said he didn't always get specific details, it was definitely worth a shot. Not that this option was without risk, either; the angels might decide to make an appearance and sense something amiss. But at least in the main cathedral the team could provide cover to Seb.

"Will we be able to get in?" he asked Kara. "Every devout in the city's going to want to go."

She nodded. "It's a ticketed event. I got tickets for all of us the second I heard."

"Listen, are you sure we can trust that guy?" put in Sam, leaning on his forearm. "What if he gets in there and starts talking, or something?"

"He wouldn't," said Alex. He was sure of that much at least; Willow would never speak to Seb again if he betrayed them. He drained his beer. "Come on, we'd better get back so I can talk to him."

They left the café and started walking toward the

Metro station. It was coming up to rush hour, with a steady flow of people all heading in the same direction. Far across the square was a pair of circling angels. Though the AKs couldn't bring them down in daylight with such a crowd around, Alex saw several of the team glance at them speculatively. Good—they were doing scans now without being told.

He hung back a little, walking with Kara. "Can I ask you a favor?" he asked.

She glanced at him in surprise. "Sure."

Alex cleared his throat, wondering how to phrase this. "Well—you know Willow and I don't get much time alone together. So I thought I'd take her out for the night on Friday. Would you be in charge while I'm gone? We'll just be at that hotel on Alfredo Chavero; if anything comes up, I could be home in five minutes."

Though he knew Kara still had reservations about him and Willow, she smiled. "No problem—I'll babysit the troops." She gave him a thoughtful look. "Planning a romantic evening, huh?"

Alex's ears reddened; he jammed his hands in his back pockets as they started down the station stairs. He'd gotten one of the hotel's nicest rooms and arranged for flowers and chocolates to be in it, plus a special dinner to be delivered by room service. It had pretty much cleaned out his personal funds, but he wanted it all to be so completely perfect.

"Yeah, sort of," he said.

"Sounds nice," said Kara, her voice neutral. "I hope

you have a really good time." As they bought their tickets, Alex was glad she was keeping her thoughts to herself— and even more glad that the issue was settled. Because to be alone with Willow, really alone with her, for an entire night . . . God, right now there was nothing on the planet that he wanted more.

When they got home, Willow and Seb were both in the kitchen; Willow was peering into the fridge. "Hi," she said, straightening up as they came in.

Her green eyes lingered on Alex's, smiling. He smiled back. Knowing that just a few nights from now they'd be alone together made it easier to see Seb standing there against the counter. Like always, he'd gone quiet, though Alex had heard him and Willow talking as everyone came in.

Alex had the impression there was something she wanted to tell him; then she glanced at the others and seemed to decide to wait. "I was just thinking about fixing dinner," she went on. "How does chili sound?"

"Thanks, but I've already got some chicken marinating," said Liz, coming into the kitchen. Her tone was so polite, it was practically an insult.

Alex saw Willow give a small sigh as she closed the fridge door. "Well, just let me know if you want any help."

The others disappeared without saying much, heading to their dorms or the TV room. As Kara followed after them, she gave Alex a *Tell me what he says as soon as you talk to him* look, and he nodded. Meanwhile, Liz had taken

Willow's place at the fridge and was pulling out a covered dish. With a flash of irritation at Liz, Alex went to Willow and kissed her, though they didn't usually in front of the others.

He saw her look of pleased surprise as they pulled apart, and resisted the urge to kiss her again. "Hey, can you do something for me?" he said, caressing her arms. "The Shadow's been acting kind of funny — would you take a look?"

Liz glanced up, startled. "What — you fix *motorcycles?*" she blurted out.

"Yes, when I'm not fixing dinner," said Willow mildly. Liz colored and looked away. Still propped silently against the counter, Seb's mouth twitched, and Alex knew that none of this had passed by him, either.

"'Funny' how?" Willow asked. She was wearing jeans and her green camisole; the pendant he'd given her caught the light with a tiny sparkle.

Alex described how draggy the Shadow had been behaving the last time he'd driven it to the Torre Mayor. He'd forgotten to mention it afterward, and now he was glad — the look on Liz's face had been pure gold.

"The air filter might be blocked," said Willow thoughtfully. "Or it could just be the spark plugs. But I don't have a tool kit anymore, remember?"

"There's one in the hall closet — I saw it the other day." Alex went to the hallway and dug it out. "The Shadow's parked out in the courtyard."

"There's not enough light out there now, though,"

said Willow. He held back a smile; he could see she was itching to start tinkering. "Could we bring it into the firing range, maybe?" She smiled. "You can be my able assistant. And there's something I want to tell you — we can talk while I fix it, OK?"

The desire to pull her into his arms was almost overwhelming. Alex managed to restrain himself and squeezed her hand instead. "OK, I'll be in with it in a minute." He glanced at Seb. "Can you give me a hand?"

Seb's eyebrows rose, but he nodded. "Yes, sure."

Out in the dimly lit courtyard, Alex briefly explained the situation. He spoke in Spanish — Seb's English was good, but he wanted to make sure there was no misunderstanding about this. As the moths battered against the bare lightbulb overhead, he could hear the sound of a TV from one of the nearby buildings.

"What do you think — will you help us?" he finished finally.

Seb was lounging against the Shadow with his arms crossed over his chest; Alex could see a long, thin scar on his forearm. He gave an ironic smile. "Yeah, I'll help, but I hope I can get the information psychically — 'cause I really can't say I like your backup plan very much. Search the office with twenty angels hanging around outside? Amigo, you have got to be kidding me."

"No, I'm not kidding," said Alex. "But yeah, I'm not crazy about it, either. Look, what I most need to know is what time the private audiences are going to be and where exactly, so that we can head straight for the Council once we're in — if you can get that from the priest, then forget about breaking into the offices. Do you think you'll have enough time?"

"Yeah, maybe," said Seb thoughtfully. "I mean, it'll probably be on his mind anyway, so with any luck —" He broke off. A troubled look flickered in his eyes; he went silent, frowning.

"What?" asked Alex sharply.

"Oh, hell." Seb rubbed at his stubbled jaw. "Willow."

"What about her?"

"She's going to want to come, too."

Alex shook his head, picturing the ornate cathedral with its crowds of people; the cruising, feeding angels. "I don't want her anywhere near there. Her aura's way too distinctive with so many angels around."

"Believe me, I don't want her anywhere near there, either. She's told me about how those Church of Angels *cabrones* want her dead. But her aura's the whole point. She finally learned how to disguise it today."

Alex went still as he took in what this meant. So this was what Willow had been going to tell him. "She's really mastered it?"

"Once you've got it, I guess you've got it." Seb grimaced as he kicked at the concrete. "And I know she'll tell you this if I don't," he added gloomily. "She's better than me at getting details from people. If both of us went to the cathedral, you'd have a lot better chance of getting what you need — unfortunately."

Alex saw that in this one thing at least, he and Seb were

totally united — neither of them wanted Willow exposed to any danger. He pinched the bridge of his nose, wishing he could just not tell her about the plan. He couldn't even use the possibility of someone recognizing her as a reason to keep her away now; Kara had been disguising herself with wigs and makeup every day to get in there.

Somewhere in the darkness, a cricket was creaking. "Maybe I'm wrong, and she won't want to do it," ventured Seb, not even sounding like he believed it himself.

"Oh, she'll want to do it," said Alex.

Seb exhaled. "Yeah . . . I know," he admitted. "God, I should just search the office — she couldn't help much with that; she doesn't speak enough Spanish to read the documents."

Now, *that* was appealing. But he couldn't let Seb take that kind of risk unnecessarily — and it was true that if Willow helped they'd have better luck in getting what they needed. No matter how fervently he might want to, he couldn't put his girlfriend's safety over that of the entire mission; not if there was a reasonable chance she'd be all right.

Reasonable chance. Fear lurched through him; he pushed it away. "We'd better go talk to Willow," he said finally. "Come on, let's get the bike inside."

Seb detached himself from the shadow and flipped up the kickstand. "At least this isn't as dangerous for her as the Council attack," he muttered as he wheeled it over to the back door. "When *that* happens . . ."

Alex had just been moving to the step to help lift the

bike through the doorway; now he stopped in his tracks, his spine stiffening. "The Council attack?"

Seb gave him a surprised glance, then shook his head with a soft snort. "*Hombre*, how well do you actually know your girlfriend? I know you're not psychic, but come on — you *have* to realize what she's been thinking, don't you?"

Alex hadn't, but suddenly it dropped into place with icy certainty: the Council. With a human-looking aura, Willow could be there when they attacked. He swore as he slumped against the outside wall of the house. "Oh, Christ, I'm an idiot." He scraped a palm across his face. "I can't believe I didn't see this coming. . . . I am such an idiot."

"No argument from me," said Seb. He twisted at the bike's throttle. "Still, you couldn't have *not* wanted her to learn to disguise her aura," he added grudgingly. "Or even put it off, really. She had to know how; it was vital."

"How long has she been planning this?" Alex asked, massaging his temple where a distant ache had started.

Seb shrugged. "I picked it up from her a couple of days after I arrived. But knowing her, probably from the second she heard about it being possible." His gaze went over Alex, considering him. "She's determined to be there, you know," he said finally. "And not just to help the team — she loves you very much."

Coming from Seb, this should have given him a feeling of satisfaction; instead he was just worried sick. "Yeah, I love her, too," said Alex. "So much that I think I'd rather see her get together with you than come along on the Council attack."

Seb's mouth quirked into a humorless smile. "That wouldn't get an argument from me, either. Just say the word; I'll kidnap her and take us both far away from here."

"Don't tempt me." Alex dropped his hand and let out a breath. "OK, look — we still have to get the security info if we hope to even have a chance. Let's just focus on that for now."

Seb helped him get the motorcycle into the house, then they wheeled it down the hallway into the firing range. Willow was crouched on her haunches inspecting the toolbox. "I'd thought you'd both absconded," she said, looking up with a smile. Then she took them in more closely. "Hey, is everything all right?"

Alex propped the bike on its kickstand. "So I hear you've got something to tell me," he said, stalling for time.

Willow raised an eyebrow at Seb. "You already told him?"

"Yes, I'm sorry," he said. "I should have let you do it." Alex was impressed despite himself by how relaxed Seb seemed — there was no hint that anything was wrong.

But Willow's forehead had creased. Slowly, she rose to her feet. "Something's going on; I can feel it," she said to Seb. "You're really worried."

Seb's smile faded. "Willow . . ."

"Something about me and the cathedral." She moved

closer to him, her eyes searching his. "Seb, what is it?"

Alex watched, his emotions suddenly off-kilter. Why was it Seb's feelings Willow was picking up on so strongly and not his own? Meanwhile Seb stood almost motionless, looking down at her . . . and at the expression on his face, Alex's jaw tightened. Christ, couldn't Willow see that being her *friend* was the last thing on Seb's mind?

Only seconds had passed; Willow was gazing at Seb, frowning intently. Alex almost had the sense that they were still communicating. Then she shook her head and fleetingly touched his arm. "You're blocking me out. I can feel it."

Seb sighed. "We'd better tell her," he said to Alex.

Yeah, thanks for the news flash, Alex thought. All at once his skin felt like it was prickling with heat. What the hell did "You're blocking me out" mean? Was Willow really that used to wandering around in Seb's mind now, sharing everything with him?

Willow's face was tense as she turned to him. She wove her fingers through his, squeezing his hand. "Alex? What's going on?"

Her touch was warm, grounding. With an effort, he shook away his thoughts. *Stop being ridiculous,* he told himself. *Yes, they're close — they're both psychic, for God's sake. It doesn't mean anything, at least not as far as Willow's concerned.*

"Why don't you start fixing the bike, and we can talk about it?" he said. "You, too," he added tersely to Seb. As much as he wished he could drop-kick the guy into another country, he had a job to do; this concerned both Seb and Willow.

While Willow got to work on the bike, Alex explained their plan. Seb sat against the wall, his legs crossed at the ankles. Soon Willow had disconnected a pair of leads and taken off two small, grimy units which Alex assumed were the spark plugs; she inspected them briefly. Even through his distraction, he was impressed. He'd never actually seen her work on an engine before; he himself would have been clueless.

"So . . . that's what's up," he finished.

Willow rested the spark plugs to one side as she considered him. "Are you asking me to go there with Seb? And see what I can get psychically?"

"Yeah," he said after a pause. "I guess I am."

He could see she knew exactly what this was costing him. "Of course I'll help," she said. "And, Alex, it'll be OK."

"I know it will," he said. He picked up a wrench and rapped it hard against the floor. "Because I'm going to have the whole damn team in there, covering both of you." *Especially you*, he thought, and was grimly grateful she couldn't read his thoughts as easily as she seemed to read Seb's.

Willow chose a screwdriver and removed the air-cleaner cover, ducking her head down to inspect it. "Aha," she muttered as she extracted a plastic bag that had gotten caught in the filter. Then, as if to prove what Alex had just been thinking, she looked over at Seb — who hadn't even moved as far as Alex could tell. Her mouth moved in a small smile. "Hey — I won't be in any more danger than you are, you know."

Seb didn't deny whatever he'd been thinking. With a sigh, he brushed back the brown curls on his brow; Alex saw again the scar on his forearm. "Yes, that's probably true — but you see, I don't care if *I'm* in danger," he said. "When?" he asked Alex.

Sometime next decade, Alex wanted to say. "Day after tomorrow," he said instead. "That's when the special service is. We couldn't wait any longer anyway, in case we need to use the security code after all. At least it gives you a little more time to practice," he added to Willow.

She nodded. "I will, but I really think I have it now." She darted him an impish look, her green eyes dancing suddenly. "What's your favorite color?"

He couldn't help smiling. "Blue."

"OK, check it out."

He concentrated, and Willow's aura came into view — a clear sky blue with lavender lights floating through it. Alex stared. He'd been expecting it, but wasn't prepared for his own reaction. Seeing Willow's aura look so different, as if she were just an ordinary girl, not the girl he loved . . . it was as if she'd somehow moved far away from him, someplace where he couldn't get her back. As he took in her life force's gentle blue glow, he felt ridiculously close to tears.

"Alex?" She rested her hand on his thigh, then winced

and pulled away, glancing down at her smudged fingers. She wiped her hands off on a rag, giving him an anxious look. "Are you OK?"

Alex was uncomfortably aware of Seb, who sat watching with an expression that seemed to understand far too much. He cleared his throat. "It's great," he said. "Seriously . . . it's great. How about one that the angels wouldn't want to touch?" He'd barely gotten the words out before her aura turned a sickly grayish brown. It shrank in front of his eyes, hanging listlessly near her body.

Alex blinked. "Wow," he said. "That's — pretty amazing." The realization rushed through him: no matter what else this meant, he'd never have to worry about Willow's aura again. For the rest of her life, she could walk down the street and be safe from the angels.

"Thank you," he said to Seb, and he could hear the relief in his voice. "That's going to save her life someday."

"You're welcome," said Seb. "I didn't teach her how to do it because of you, though."

"Yeah, I know you didn't," said Alex. There was a beat while they regarded each other — then both seemed to remember at the same time that Willow was there. Alex saw her watching them with a faintly exasperated look. She shook her head and scrambled to her feet, grabbing up the spark plugs.

"I have to find a wire brush and clean these off; they're way too dirty," she said. "I'll just be a few minutes."

She left the room, her short red-gold hair gleaming in the light. Alex watched her, taking in her narrow shoulders, the green straps resting on her smooth skin. Then, turning, he saw that Seb's eyes were following her, too. He'd known they would be, but suddenly it felt like the last straw.

As Willow's footsteps faded away up the stairs, he said in Spanish, "You could give it a rest sometimes. I mean, you don't *have* to watch her every move, do you?"

Seb's voice was mild. "I don't know. Maybe I do." He closed his eyes and leaned back, crossing his arms over his chest.

Alex picked up a screwdriver, tapped it against his leg. "So how's that whole unrequited love thing working out for you, anyway? Hasn't she figured out you two are meant to be yet?"

Seb lifted his head and gave him a long look. "Please tell me that you don't seriously want to have this conversation. Because personally, I can't think of anything I'd rather do less."

"Yeah, I do want to have it, actually." Alex tossed the screwdriver aside. "Does Willow know you're just biding your time, pretending to be her friend?"

Seb's gaze was cold. "I'm not just biding my time. I *am* her friend."

"Oh, sorry. No, I guess it's never even occurred to you that if you hang around long enough, being the perfect *friend*, she'll come to her senses and fall for you. Right?"

Shaking his head in disgust, Seb closed his eyes again and settled back against the wall. "You are so far off base, *hombre*."

Remembering his conversation with Willow on the balcony — her pink cheeks as she tried to explain away Seb's feelings for her — Alex had an insane urge to ask Seb if Willow felt the same way about him. Just having the thought made him feel like an idiot. God, he was glad Willow wasn't listening to any of this.

"What's the scar from?" he asked after a pause, nodding at Seb's arm.

"Dios mío." Seb gave a soft, snorting laugh. "Have I told you how much I enjoy these conversations of ours? It's from a sword fight. Or a knife fight — take your pick. The other guy won, if you're interested."

"Not really. Can you use a gun?"

Genuine amusement flashed in Seb's hazel eyes as he lifted his head to look at Alex. "Are you challenging me to a duel? Pistols at dawn, best man gets the girl?"

"Dream on," said Alex. "No, I'm thinking about when you and Willow go into the cathedral — if I should give you a gun or not. I'll be right there on the other side of her when you both ask to be blessed, but if anything happens to me, you'll be the best-placed person to defend her. Because she's not bad when it comes to shooting at targets, but if she had to take a shot at another person —"

"She wouldn't," said Seb immediately. "Not unless someone was threatening you. Or maybe me. But it's so totally against her nature — I can't see her doing it to protect herself; I think she'd hesitate."

It made Alex's jaw tighten to realize how well Seb knew Willow — not to mention that he'd included himself

413

in that list. Though Alex had an uncomfortable feeling he was right. "I know; that's what I'm afraid of," he said. "So — can you?"

"I've fired a gun a few times," said Seb. "Tin cans in fields, that kind of thing. I couldn't do what you do, but I could probably peg someone who was coming at us."

Alex made a face. Why was he not feeling reassured? "Are you any better with a knife? You've got one, I'm assuming."

"Yes, and yes." Seb pulled a leg up and rested his forearm across his knee; his expression as he regarded Alex wasn't friendly, exactly, but it held understanding. "Look — you really don't have to worry about this," he said. "If Willow's with me, I'll keep her safe. No one will hurt her while I draw breath."

"Yeah, I know that," confessed Alex. And he did — it was one good thing about knowing that Seb loved Willow as much as he himself did. The only good thing, in fact.

Willow came back downstairs then. She gave them an arched-eyebrow look, as if she knew they'd been talking about her, but didn't comment. "That should do it; they were completely *black*." She started reconnecting the spark plugs. "Between them and that bag choking the flow to the carburetor, it's no wonder the poor Shadow was acting draggy — it could hardly breathe."

Alex smiled, but was uncomfortably aware of what he and Seb had just been talking about, and what Willow would think if she knew. Meanwhile, smells of dinner were starting to drift out of the kitchen — he could hear Liz moving around in there.

Seb stood up, stretching silently. His T-shirt lifted, and Alex glimpsed another scar on his flat stomach — a raised, ugly one this time, like a twisted worm on his skin.

As Seb dropped his arms again, Willow gave him a teasing look. "Aren't you glad you quit smoking?" she asked.

Seb shook his head in amusement. "You can always tell," he said.

Willow began putting the air cleaner cover back on, twirling the screwdriver deftly. "Well, it's not difficult. You are practically *oozing* with nicotine cravings, dude." There was a smudge of grime from the spark plugs on her cheek. With her short hair, it gave her an urchin look that made Alex want to pull her into his arms.

He saw the same warm look in Seb's eyes; then Seb gave a sigh, mock-resigned. "Thank you for the sympathy — it's very comforting. I'm going to go take a shower before dinner. If we're finished?" he added to Alex.

Alex nodded. And as Seb headed off, all he could think was: Willow could sense Seb's nicotine cravings, but not the fact that Seb was in love with her? When it was completely evident even to him, who wasn't psychic at all? No way, he thought, gazing at her. *She just doesn't want to face it for some reason.*

Why not? Was it to protect herself, somehow? Maybe if she let herself see the depth of Seb's feelings, she'd have to acknowledge her own. The thought came from nowhere, slithering coldly into his stomach. No way; he *knew* that wasn't true.

But Willow's pink cheeks on the fire escape. Her hand on Seb's arm. *You're blocking me out. I can feel it.*

Willow peered up at him from the bike. "So, what were you and Seb talking about just now?"

The words came out with no thought. "Couldn't you get it from him?"

She briefly closed her eyes, then gave him a level look. "I didn't try. We don't get *everything* from each other psychically, you know. It's just flashes when we're talking sometimes."

"OK," he said. It felt like there was something hard and icy inside of him. He picked up one of the screws from the floor, rolled it between his fingers. "It sort of seemed like more than a flash, though. The way you were looking into each other's eyes before."

She touched his arm. "Alex, he's just my friend — that's all. You *know* that."

In what universe does that guy only want friendship from you? Alex didn't say it. "Yeah, I know that," he said. "It's just that it's a pretty intense friendship, isn't it?"

She went still. "Is it?"

He shrugged, putting the screw down. "In each other's heads. Talking together all the time."

"We don't talk *all* the time. But yes, I guess we do talk a lot." Willow drew her hand away. "Look, it's just being with another half angel and both of us being psychic. I suppose there's a sort of bond between us, without even trying."

"You really care about him."

Her green eyes were steady. "Of course I do."

"I mean, not just because he's a half angel. Because he's him." Jesus, why was he *doing* this? Why couldn't he just shut the hell up?

"Alex, will you—?" Willow broke off, looking frustrated. "Yes, OK? I care about Seb a lot. I'd care about him a lot even if he weren't a half angel. The fact that he *is* just makes it an even stronger connection. But I don't—" She worked the screwdriver against the panel again, turning it almost angrily. "I don't want that to make you feel pushed out or ignored. I love you. My friendship with Seb has nothing to do with our relationship."

"No, except that it feels like there's three of us in it sometimes." He'd been thinking that for weeks; it was a relief to finally say it.

"Alex."

"Well, sorry, but it does. I hardly have any time with you now—do you realize that? We hardly had any time together before, and now we have even less. And even when we're alone together—"

Her eyes had gone very large. "Even when we're alone together, what?"

"You're always thinking about him."

"I—" She stopped abruptly, cheeks reddening. Flustered, she glanced down; he saw her swallow.

Alex stared at her. It was something he'd wondered

but hadn't really believed. He'd expected her to tell him he was being ridiculous. "You do, don't you?" he said slowly. "When we're alone together, you're still thinking about *him*. Do you think about him even when we're —?"

"No!" she cried. "God, of course not! How can you even say that?"

"Well, I don't know what to think! Help me out here, OK? How exactly are you thinking about Seb when we're alone together?"

"I don't! It's — there's this sort of link between us, that's all. Like, I can see what he's doing or where he is in the house . . ." She trailed off at the look on his face.

"Say that again," he said, the world ringing in his ears. "You have a *link* with him? You can psychically see whatever he's doing?"

"Not *all the time!* Just — I might get a flash sometimes."

"Like when you're thinking about him," he said acidly, and saw her cheeks turn redder. "So what about him? Does he have this link, too? He can watch everything you do?"

"Alex, you're getting totally the wrong idea about this, I promise you —"

"Answer the question!"

"I don't know!" she exclaimed. "I haven't asked him."

"So give me your best guess," he gritted out. "Yes or no — can he do this, too, with you?"

There was only one screw left to attach; Willow shoved it into place. Her hand on the screwdriver was unsteady, her jaw tense. "I don't want to talk to you about this now. You're too upset."

"Oh, man, you haven't even seen *upset*. This is a *yes*, isn't it? You're telling me that all he has to do is think about you, and he can see you, no matter what you're doing."

She looked close to tears but also angrier than he'd ever seen her. "It's not like that! You're making it sound really sleazy."

"Yeah, sorry — this is just a pure friendship thing, isn't it? So if you thought about Seb right now, in the shower —"

She jammed the tools away in the toolbox and jumped to her feet. "Stop it," she snapped. "You're acting like a lunatic. Which part of *we are just friends* do you not understand?"

He rose, too; he could feel the blood beating at his brain. "Oh, yeah, because it's really my comprehension skills that are the problem here — I just don't get it, do I? You know what? Maybe I get way more than I want to."

Her face went white. "What's *that* supposed to mean?"

Alex gripped her arms. "It means *he is in love with you*," he hissed into her face. "And now you're telling me you think about him even when you're alone with me, and the two of you share this amazing psychic bond that means he can picture whatever you're doing, whenever he wants — and I'm supposed to be *happy* with that? I'm supposed to go, 'Oh, yeah, I guess all that's just *normal* when you've got a half-angel girlfriend.'"

Willow was struggling against tears. "Alex —" She

took a breath. "Look—please, please, can we talk about this later, when we've both calmed down? I promise you, it isn't like what you're thinking."

Alex stared at her for a moment, then swore and started out of the firing range. She caught up with him, grabbed his arm. "Wait—where are you going?"

He pulled away from her. "Where the hell do you think? To throw him out of the house."

"No! Alex, *stop*."

"What? Are you saying you don't want me to?"

"Of course I don't want you to!"

He could not remember ever having been this angry; it was like a fire raging through him, sizzling his thoughts. The rarely used front door was nearby, and he grabbed her hand and pulled her along to it with him; got it open and them both outside, then slammed it shut behind him.

"Let me get this straight," he said in a low voice, with the night air suddenly cool around them. "You don't want Seb to leave. You've just told me that he can *conjure you up in his thoughts*—but that's OK with you, and you want him to stick around."

She had her arms crossed tightly over her chest. Her voice was thin but steady. "You're making way too much of this," she said. "It's just *flashes* sometimes. And I think our angels would stop it from ever being too . . . intimate, if neither of us wanted that."

Alex was too angry to even be relieved. "He *does* want that, though. Did you hear me, about him being in love with you?"

Her cheeks went pink. "Yes, I did. Look, I know he wants to be more than my friend. But he's OK with just friendship. I told him that's all it would be the very first day."

Alex stared at her. How could she actually believe that? She and Seb were each the only half angel the other knew — there was no way the guy was going to be happy with just being friends forever. And the two of them were so close already, after less than three weeks. What happened when Seb finally made his move? They'd be so entwined in each other's minds and hearts by then — how was she supposed to resist feeling the same?

He stood against the door, rubbing his forehead against a vicious headache that was starting to pound. "I'm not happy with this," he said finally. "I don't care if you have friends who are guys, OK? I really don't. But this, this is something else. You're in each other's heads. You have this intense — *need* for each other or something."

She seemed to have turned into a statue. "What exactly are you saying?"

He dropped his hand. "I'm saying I want it to stop," he said. "You know how to change your aura now, so you don't need to be alone with him all the time anymore. And once this is over with, I want him gone."

Willow started to say something and stopped. She gazed out at the shadowy street, her face tense. "Alex, this isn't fair. He's my friend."

"And I'm your boyfriend. Which is more important to you?"

She gave a short laugh, looking at him in disbelief. "You're not seriously saying, *It's him or me*, are you? This is ridiculous!" She took his hand and held it tight. "Please, please listen to me—I am in love with you. I love you more than anything in the world. I want to grow old with you. Seb is just my *friend*."

Her fingers felt warm in his. For a moment all Alex wanted to do was hold her; then he pulled away. "Yeah, and you want him around when you're old, too."

"Not in the same way!"

"Yes, but you *do*, don't you?"

He watched her let out a long breath. "If he wants to be, yes," she said finally. "I don't want him to—to hang around when nothing is going to happen between us, if that doesn't make him happy. But if he wants to be with me—" She swiped the heel of her hand harshly across her eyes. "Look, you're right; I *do* need him—he's the only other half angel I've ever met. I need to have someone in my life who understands what this is like. I felt so alone here, before. I—" She stopped, hugging herself.

Alex didn't let himself feel the tenderness that washed over him, the urge to take her in his arms. "Except it's not just that he's a half angel, is it?" he demanded. "It's that it's *him*. Look, I'm sorry you've felt alone; I do get that. But I can't handle this. It used to be enough that it was just us, but if that's not good enough for you anymore—" He broke off.

"What?" she whispered.

Part of him couldn't believe he was saying the words, but he was helpless to stop them. "Just choose. You can have your wonderful friendship, or you can have me. You can't have both."

She didn't move as she studied his face. "Is this really how much you trust me?" she said, her voice dull.

He felt like punching the door. "Oh, don't even play that card! After everything you've just told me? You can't stop thinking about him! You're attracted to him — do you think I haven't noticed?"

The anger was back in her eyes. "Maybe I am," she said. "In the same way you're attracted to Kara."

"What?" He stood staring at her. Where had *that* come from?

She gave him a level look. "Seb's attractive. So's Kara. You'd be blind not to notice Kara, and I'd be blind not to notice Seb. That doesn't mean I don't trust you around Kara — even if she wants more than friendship, too. Or did you think I hadn't noticed?"

His head felt like it might split in two at any moment. "Jesus, what is this — the best defense is a good offense? I have done nothing wrong here —"

"Neither. Have. I," she said with clenched teeth. "I'm sorry you don't trust me, Alex. I will do everything possible to make you see that you can trust me. But you are not going to tell me who my friends can be."

"Yeah, and what if you weren't with me, what then?" he said, his voice low and fierce. "Would you still only want to be his friend?"

She started to answer; stopped abruptly. "That's—not a fair question."

Deep down he knew she was right, and that if the same question was posed to him about Kara, his reaction would have to be the same. It didn't matter. "No, but you just answered it anyway," he bit out. "Like I said: Choose. I don't want that guy in my life."

Willow's chin snapped up; he saw again how furious she was. "No, I won't choose — you're being completely unfair. Seb's the only other half angel I know in the world; I'm not going to never speak to him again just because you're acting like a jealous jerk." As he stood staring at her, she let out a breath, pushing her hands through her hair. "God, look, I'm sorry — *please* can we forget all of this and talk about it tomorrow? We're both upset; we're saying things we don't mean."

There was a pause, with the sounds of the city thrumming around them like a living heartbeat. "No, I'm not," said Alex finally. "I'm saying exactly what I mean." He opened the door to go back inside and glanced at her as she stood there, with the backdrop of the street behind her. She was so beautiful that it wrung his heart, even now.

"Enjoy your friendship with Seb, Willow," he said quietly.

CHAPTER TWENTY

I DON'T REALLY KNOW how you can come back from an argument like that one.

I didn't eat any dinner that night; there was no way I could have choked food down. Instead I went into the girls' dorm and stayed there, lying on my bed and thinking, *Have Alex and I just broken up?* The words brought back with a chill my premonition from the first time I'd ever seen this house, the unhappiness I knew I'd find here.

God, I hated being psychic sometimes. I lay curled on the faded blue bedspread listening to the traffic, the distant sound of rock music playing somewhere. And I wished that I'd never even *met* Seb. Then I sighed. No, I didn't. I couldn't wish that; I could never wish that.

Had Alex and I really broken up?

I kept coming back to that, like a boring scratched record. We couldn't have, could we? Because he still loved me. I knew he did — and I loved him so completely that the thought of not being with him was like not having air to breathe. Surely he'd calm down by tomorrow, and see how unfair he was being. Wouldn't he? I'd go downstairs and his blue-gray eyes would meet mine — we'd slip off somewhere alone together, and he'd hold me and say, *I'm so sorry, babe. Of course I trust you. Forget every word I said.*

I stared at the ceiling with its uneven plaster, taking in the shadows cast by every lump and bump. It was a nice fantasy, but I had a feeling that's all it was. I'd never seen Alex so angry. It wasn't like I didn't understand *why*. I knew I wouldn't be thrilled if he'd told me that he and Kara shared a psychic bond. Understatement. The thought would probably gnaw at me day and night, and that's with me being psychic and able to tell whether anything else was going on. Alex couldn't do that — I could hardly blame him for being upset.

No . . . but I could blame him for not trusting me. For so obviously thinking I had a thing for Seb, and that it was only the fact he and I were together that was keeping me from disappearing off into the sunset with him.

Seb. I swallowed as I lay there. Somewhere in the back of my mind I was aware of how badly I wanted to psychically seek him out. He had to be aware that Alex and I had fought, and I knew how concerned he'd be; he'd want to know I was OK. Almost without realizing it, I started to reach out to him — and then stopped, my cheeks catching fire as I heard Alex say, *So if you thought about Seb right now, in the shower* . . . I cringed. There was no way now I could ever feel comfortable again about what had seemed such a natural thing—something that, for all I knew, *was* a natural thing between half angels, just an extension of our friendship. Feeling completely and miserably alone, I pressed my face against the pillow.

There was a soft knock at the door.

I sat up, my heart pounding. I knew instantly that it was Seb, and I hated the relief that rushed through me; it seemed to validate every accusation Alex had flung at me. But I couldn't help it—I really needed someone right then, and I should have known Seb would sense it and that he'd be here. That nothing would keep him away.

I'd hardly even known I was crying, but there seemed to be streaks of dampness on my cheeks. I wiped my face and swung my feet off the bed; as I started across the dorm, I scraped my hair back with both hands. It was probably standing up in wild, burning spikes like a bunch of lit matches.

When I opened the door, Seb stood in the hallway with his hands tight in his jeans pockets, his brown curls tousled. His gaze scanned me worriedly. "Can I come in?"

I am so, so glad to see you. Please, can you just hold me for a while, and let me turn into a blubbering mess on your shoulder? With an effort, I didn't say it. I nodded and opened the door wider. As he stepped inside, I hesitated, then closed the door behind him. Regardless of what the others might think, I needed privacy right now. Whatever Seb and I spoke about was nobody's business.

We sat on my bed; I leaned against the wall. For a few

minutes neither of us spoke, and it was such a relief — to be with someone who understood me so totally without words.

"So, this pretty much sucks," I said at last.

Seb grimaced. "It's because of me that you fought, isn't it? You don't have to answer," he added dryly. "Everyone heard. Half of them could hardly wait to tell me about it."

Great. I gripped my arms. "I can't really blame him for being upset," I said. "He's just found out that — " I stopped. I'd never mentioned to Seb that I could sense him even when he wasn't around. Heat swept my skin.

"Oh," said Seb softly, picking up the thought from me. "That — can't be easy for him, I guess." His tone was neutral; I knew he didn't like Alex much more than Alex liked him.

"Is it the same for you?" I asked after a pause. I felt shy, suddenly. "With me, I mean?"

Seb nodded slowly. He was sitting on the bed with one foot on the floor, the other leg bent at the knee in front of him. "Even when I'm not thinking about you, you're always in my head, somehow." He gave a small shrug. "With anyone else in the world, it would be too much. But with you, it just seems . . . natural."

It was exactly how I felt. Oh, God, I *could* see why Alex was so upset. What if he had this with Kara?

"I don't know if it's only because we're both half angel, or — " Seb shook his head. "Perhaps it's a mix," he said. Though he'd left out a thought, I knew what he meant. Some of this had to be from being half angel and psychic, but maybe it was enhanced by just—who we were. The closeness we shared.

"How were things left between you and Alex?" asked Seb finally. "What was said at the end?"

I gave a short laugh, swiping at my eyes. They seemed to be leaking again. "A lot of things that I hope weren't meant." Because Alex couldn't seriously expect me to shun Seb's company, could he? The only other half angel I knew?

Seb sat silently, studying my face. "Willow . . . would it be easier for you if I leave?"

I went very still. No—*please, please*, no. "Leave?" I echoed.

"It's me being here in the house that's making things so bad, yes?" He stroked a tear from my cheek with a finger that couldn't have been gentler. "I don't want you to cry any more, *querida*, you see?"

Even through my mental turbulence, I could sense Seb's mixed emotions: how much he hated seeing me unhappy versus what he hoped for between the two of us. Remembering Alex's words and the look that had been on Seb's face just that afternoon, my chest clenched. Oh, God, I didn't want Seb to be in love with me. I didn't want him to be unhappy because of me, ever, not in any way.

"It doesn't matter what's easiest for me," I choked out. "What matters is—I don't want to be unfair to you, Seb. I can't ask you to stay just because I want you here. Not when I don't . . ." I trailed off. It was the first time I'd told him, however indirectly, that I knew how he felt about me. It was practically the first time I'd really admitted it to myself.

He knew what I meant. He always did. "You're not being unfair," he said, his voice level. "You've been honest with me from the start. I know that you're in love with Alex. And I—" He touched my hair; I saw his throat move. "I love you in all the ways there are to love someone," he said finally. "That includes as a friend and brother. If you want me here, then I'll stay. I just don't want to make things harder for you."

"I love you, too," I whispered. "As a friend, I—" My throat closed; I couldn't finish. It all seemed so hopeless— Seb being in love with me when I only loved him as a friend, the argument with Alex that was still pounding at my skull. The things he'd said. What if we really *had* broken up?

As I started to crumple inside, Seb moved beside me on the bed and put his arm around me. I rested my head on his shoulder gratefully; it felt strong against my cheek. "I shouldn't—I shouldn't let you do this," I got out as I started to cry. "I can't expect you to comfort me when I'm in love with someone else; it's too much—"

"Be quiet and let me hold you," he said firmly.

We sat like that without talking for a long time, Seb's hand stroking my arm as I cried, his cheek against my hair. I concentrated only on externals: the comforting warmth of him as I pressed against him; the slight prickle of his stubble; his clean, woodsy smell. And I tried hard not to think of anything at all.

After a while he smoothed the hair away from my face and said, "The others will be coming upstairs soon. . . . Will you be all right?"

I nodded and sat up, wiping my eyes. "I'll be fine."

His gaze searched mine; he knew I wouldn't be. Not really. "I wish I could stay here with you tonight," he said.

"I know. I'll be OK."

Seb's mouth moved in something that tried to be a smile. His arm still around me, he leaned close and kissed my hair, his lips warm as they pressed briefly against my head. I could feel how much he cared — the depth of it embraced me, held me close. Something fluttered inside of me; I pushed it away and closed my eyes, letting Seb's kiss comfort me.

"I'll see you tomorrow," he whispered.

"OK," I said. "And, Seb — thanks."

He rolled his eyes as he stood up. "You would have had to board up the door to keep me out, querida."

I hugged my knees, watching as he started across the room — so different from Alex, with his lightly-curling chestnut hair, but his back and shoulders just as firm. As he reached for the door, it swung open.

Kara stood there.

Her eyebrows shot up as she took in Seb, me, the empty room around us. She didn't say anything, and neither did Seb — I saw him start to, and then I think he realized it was pointless; Kara was not going to be too interested in anything he had to say. Instead he glanced back at me. I knew he was saying, *I'll see you tomorrow* again with his eyes, and I nodded.

As he left, Kara came in and shut the door. She lounged against it, crossing her ankles. "Well," she said. "That looked interesting."

"Yeah, I'll bet," I said curtly. I unfolded myself from my bed and slid open my dresser drawer, taking out my pajamas.

"So . . . are you with Seb now?"

I stiffened and turned to face her. She met my gaze blandly, her exotic face impossible to read. She had on black jeans; a pink top that showed every line of her sleek body. I could see her AK tattoo peeking out from under her shirtsleeve and suddenly hated it fiercely. It was Alex's — it didn't belong to her.

"No," I said. "Seb is just my friend." *Just* my friend — when, except for Alex, he was the most important person in my life. Language is so stupid sometimes.

"OK," said Kara, glancing down at her nails. "I was just wondering. 'Cause Alex seems to think so. And, you know . . . Seb was just up here in the room with you for over an hour, the two of you alone together. Kind of easy to get the wrong impression."

I tried to ignore what she'd said about Alex, even though it made my heart fall off a cliff. "You may find this difficult to believe, but it's actually possible for friends to be in the same room and not do anything," I said.

She gave an elaborate shrug. "Look, I don't care what you do. But I'll tell you one thing — Alex doesn't need this kind of stress right now. So if you wouldn't mind figuring out which one of them you want, that would be a good thing."

"I *have* figured it out," I snapped. Angrily, I yanked off my top, childishly glad that I'd been working out for the last few weeks and was looking more toned myself now. "Look, do you think I don't know you've got a thing for Alex? I noticed it the very first day."

She nodded slowly, watching me. "And do you know he's got a thing for me?"

For a split second, ice froze my veins, and then I caught myself and laughed out loud. "That is a total lie. I'm *psychic*, remember?"

"OK. So what do your psychic powers tell you about his first crush? Or about his first kiss, actually?"

I just stood there in my bra and jeans, staring stupidly at her.

"Alex had a crush on me for years," she said, speaking slowly as if I needed it explained in small words. "I used to catch him looking at me sometimes, and he'd blush — it was cute. And now that he's older . . . well, I think there could definitely be something there." She peeled herself away from the door. Long and lithe, like a jungle cat. "You know, I would never try to make trouble in his relationship if I thought he was happy. But this? Right here, now, with you? Nuh-uh." She shook her close-cropped head. "You are not making him happy, Willow. You're playing mind games with him — you and that other half angel. God, just flap off out of here together, why don't you, and leave Alex alone? It's not like he hasn't got *enough* on his mind."

My mind was reeling, caught in a storm. "I am not playing mind games," I said in a low voice that somehow didn't shake. "I'm in love with Alex, not Seb. Is that really so hard to understand?"

Kara snorted and turned away. "Yeah, seems to be," she said coldly. "'Cause I don't think *you've* got a handle on it."

Alex was gone when I got up the next morning.

I'd been planning to get him on his own so that we could talk about all this again, calmly this time. But I could tell he wasn't there the second I went downstairs; there was an empty feel to the house, even though it was full of people. I made a mug of foul-tasting instant coffee and drank it slowly in the kitchen, trying to take in the fact that he'd actually gone somewhere without telling me. It seemed even more final than his parting shot the day before: *Enjoy your friendship with Seb.*

Trish came in, her hair damp from her morning shower; she stiffened when she saw me. "Um — where's Alex?" I asked. Heat crept over me, that I even had to ask the question.

"He went to check out the cathedral again." She moved past me to the loaf of bread that sat on the counter. Putting a couple of slices in the toaster, she gave me a tense sideways look. "So . . . have you two broken up, or what?"

434

"No," I said, and walked out of the kitchen.

I wanted to find Seb but was so aware of what everyone would think now, if they saw us together. Correction: what they'd been thinking all along, from the sound of it. Finally I went into the TV room. Everyone else was there already, apart from Seb. Then, with a sinking heart, I saw that everyone else *wasn't* there — Kara was missing. Of course; she'd gone to the cathedral with Alex. My muscles tightened at the thought of the two of them alone together, of what she must be saying to him.

The room had gone silent as I entered. Sam glared; the others didn't look much friendlier. I tried to ignore them all and perched on the footstool, still sipping my coffee. The TV was on. I couldn't tell what was being said, but it was obviously about the Crusaders and the Faithful again. There were crowds of hundreds, signs bobbing in the air, people shouting in frenzied Spanish.

"Shouldn't you be with Seb?" said Liz. I looked up. She was watching me, her sharp-featured face hard. "I thought you were supposed to be practicing your aura stuff."

"We're practicing outside today," said Seb, appearing in the doorway. He had on faded jeans, and his blue sweater with a white T-shirt peeking out from under the collar. He nodded at me. "Are you ready?"

Relief. We hadn't discussed going outside, but it sounded like heaven; the atmosphere in the house would choke me if I had to stay here all day. I put my coffee down and scrambled to my feet. "Yeah, I'll just get my sweatshirt."

He held it up, and I felt like hugging him. "When's Alex back?" he asked the others as I moved to join him.

For a change, Brendan was sitting almost without moving, staring stonily at the screen. "He said around three."

"Yeah, so that gives you two lots and lots of time to be alone together," drawled Sam. His muscular body was sprawled on the sofa; he flicked a glance over us. "Don't go runnin' off again."

I stiffened; decided not to answer. "I can see all your secrets, you know," Seb said to him mildly as we turned to leave. And nothing was funny just then, absolutely nothing . . . but even so, the look of guilty alarm on Sam's face was priceless.

Outside, it was a gorgeous sunny day, with a cool breeze. I shifted my aura to dull, lifeless gray and pulled on my hooded sweatshirt. As Seb and I started to walk, I took my phone out and sent Alex a quick text before I could think about it: I'M SORRY WE FOUGHT. WE REALLY NEED TO TALK. I LOVE YOU.

No reply came.

Seb and I walked for blocks. The shabby businesses around us turned into department stores made of sedate old stone, with bright signs and large windows. The sidewalk grew busier, bustling with people. Satin angel wings, briefcases, morning bags of shopping. I clutched the phone in my hand, glancing down at it every few seconds while my heart slowly died in my chest.

Finally Seb gently pulled the phone away from me

and tucked it into his jeans pocket. "I'll tell you if it goes off," he said. "Come on, are you hungry? Let's get some breakfast."

I had never been less hungry in my life. "No, I'm fine," I said distantly.

He ignored me and steered me toward a sidewalk vendor selling tamales. I could see steam rising from the metal cooking cart. "You didn't eat last night," he said. "And I'm hungry, even if you aren't. So you can keep me company, yes? And then I'm going to show you around El DF. You've hardly seen it at all since you've been here."

I managed a faint smile. "You hate Mexico City."

He shrugged as we waited at the tamale stand. "It has some nice places. The only rule is you can't ask if you've gotten a text, all right? I'll tell you — I promise. Just forget about it for now."

Thank God for Seb that day. If it hadn't been for him, I would have slowly gone insane while I waited to hear from Alex. Instead, he showed me things he knew would interest me, so that even though the sick worry never went away for a second, it didn't completely drown me. An art museum that was all towering ceilings and baroque gold. A plaza where Aztec ruins sat side by side with a medieval church and a modern office building. Another church; a small stone one that tilted so dramatically that I felt dizzy just walking through it. "This is what happens when you build a city on mud," said Seb, smiling at my expression.

Afterward we went to a park across the street and sat drinking Cokes on the steps of a monument. Someone was playing guitar; the smell of cornmeal and spices from food carts wafted past. The afternoon had grown warmer, so that Seb had pulled off his sweater and tied it around his waist; I'd done the same with my sweatshirt. We hadn't seen many angels feeding today, which was a relief. The city seemed to have a calmer feel to it than usual. I wished I could say the same for my thoughts.

"I think you saved my life today, you know," I said, glancing at Seb.

"I saved mine, too, then," he said easily. "So I'm being very selfish, really."

He was sitting back against the steps with his legs stretched out, his soft-looking curls ruffled by the breeze. I saw a girl about our own age eye his lean figure appreciatively, and suddenly realized again just how attractive he was.

If you weren't with me, would you still only want to be his friend?

I flushed and looked away, trailing a finger over a crack in the worn stone steps. Because just like when Alex had asked me that before, I didn't know what the answer was. All I knew was that from the moment I'd first touched Seb's hand and sensed him so strongly, I'd felt incredibly drawn to him—and each day that passed had brought us even closer. He was such a basic part of my life now; I could hardly imagine being without him. I went cold as I thought of my dream, and the flutter that had gone through me the night before.

My God, I wasn't falling in love with Seb, was I?

I shook the idea away in a daze. No. I wasn't. Because I *was* with Alex, and that's all there was to it. I loved Seb as a friend — that was all.

My stomach had gone guiltily tense anyway. "What time is it?" I asked, praying that Seb hadn't been picking up on any of that.

He pulled out my phone again. "A little after two."

Still no text. My gaze met his. Seb's eyes were concerned; beyond that, I couldn't really tell what he was thinking. I was glad, given the direction my own thoughts had been taking.

And I'd see Alex in less than an hour now. Anticipation mixed with dread. The textless screen on my cell phone seemed louder than any shouting from the night before.

"I guess we should go back," said Seb finally, putting my phone away.

I nodded, and we walked through the park and headed home, taking the Metro. I sat on the hard plastic seat in the crowded subway car, staring at the signs in Spanish. Home. It was the only word that fit for where we were going . . . yet right then, it didn't feel like a home at all.

"OK, here's the layout," said Alex.

We were all in the firing range, gathered around Kara's map of the cathedral. Alex's dark hair fell across his forehead as he tapped the cathedral's altar on the map. "About halfway through the service, the priest will ask if anyone wants to be blessed by the angels; probably only about a dozen people will go up. Willow, I don't want you

439

and Seb to be the first ones, or the last, either. Let a few other people go up first."

His voice was neutral, professional. Deep down, his blue-gray eyes held a hint of something else as he glanced at me — mostly they just looked as I if were a member of his team he was giving instructions to. I nodded, trying to focus on what was being said instead of my rigid muscles. Every word, every action of Alex's, confirmed it: his cell phone had not been turned off, and my text had not just vanished into the ether somehow.

"I'll be sitting with you and Seb; when you go up, I'll go, too," Alex went on. He'd already explained that he and Kara had managed to get another ticket for me. "Willow, I'll be on the other side of you as you're being blessed, ready to cover both of you if you need it. Seb, I'm going to give you a gun, but I want you to spend the rest of today and tomorrow practicing with it."

"Yes, all right," said Seb, his voice just as detached. Though we weren't standing right next to each other, the edges of our auras were touching; I could feel his anger at Alex, like a low, simmering fire.

"That doesn't affect you, does it, Willow?" continued Alex. "You can do the aura work on your own now, right?"

The sentence seemed laden with meaning, but again his tone was bland. I cleared my throat. "Yeah, I think I've got it now. In fact, maybe I should get in some target practice, too." I was heat-pricklingly aware of the rest of the team standing right there watching all of this — and what the topic of the day must have been once Seb and I left. Kara's brown eyes were aloof as they flicked over me.

"Fine, if you think you need it," said Alex. "But don't stop practicing the aura work; maybe do half and half." He turned back to the map, pointing. "Sam, I want you and Trish stationed here, about five rows back — in aisle seats, if you can get them. Kara, I want you in the front row like we discussed, or at least as close to it as possible. Wesley, Brendan, and Liz —"

I tuned out as I stared down at the map. Alex had already returned by the time Seb and I got back to the house. He'd been in the TV room watching the news with the others — there was a special on about the Crusaders, who were planning a rally the next day, to coincide with the cathedral's special service. No one seemed to have been paying much attention, though. There'd been this awful sense of everyone *waiting* for us . . . and an even more awful sense of Alex being unsurprised that I'd been out with Seb all day. He'd said hello to me coolly, not moving from the sofa where he sat with Kara and Sam; it had felt impossible to ask him for a few minutes alone with everyone staring at us.

Taking in the smooth line of Alex's neck as it disappeared into the collar of his T-shirt, a spike of anger pierced me. Was he really willing to throw away what we had this easily? How could two people who loved each other so much be communicating so badly? When one of them was *psychic*, even?

"OK, I think that's it for the plans," said Alex, tossing

down the pencil he'd been holding. "But there's something else I have to say." I had the sense he was steeling himself for something, though his expression didn't change as he glanced around the table. "A lot of you overheard Willow and me fighting about Seb last night."

It was the last thing I'd expected. I stiffened, my throat going dry. Around me, the team went utterly still. I could sense Seb's aura stretching out toward mine, wanting to comfort me.

"It was personal; something just between the two of us," went on Alex. "What we fought about has nothing to do with the workings of this team. Willow and Seb are getting the security information for us — that means our lives are in their hands. I wouldn't do that if I didn't trust them completely. So forget whatever you heard; it's irrelevant."

Silence from around the table. Kara had a look on her face that said it was kind of hard to forget it, but she nodded. "We understand." Looking at her starkly beautiful features, for a second all I could think of was Alex's first kiss. It *hadn't* really been her — had it? He'd never even told me that he'd had a crush on her. Meanwhile, I could feel from the slight shifting of mood in the room that Alex had defused the situation a little. But only a little. It was going to be a very long time before anyone actually forgot our argument.

"That's all," said Alex. "Target practice now, if that's what you're doing. Otherwise, just take the rest of the day off and relax. Anyone who wants to go out for a while, go for it—but go in pairs, and watch each others' backs."

As everyone began dispersing, I started around the table to Alex, but he was already striding away across the firing range. "Alex!" I called, putting on a burst of speed to catch up with him. "Alex, wait."

He stopped and looked at me. I touched his arm. "Listen, we really need to talk."

"Not now," he said shortly.

"No, we do have to talk now. Look, can we just go to your room and have this out? We can't just—"

"Not. Now," he repeated, kneading his temple with his eyes closed. I stared at him, taken aback by the low vehemence in his voice. He left the range without waiting for a response. I heard him go upstairs.

No. This wasn't going to happen, not when we hadn't spoken in almost twenty-four hours. He wasn't going to brush me off. Seb was standing at the table loading a magazine; as I glanced at him, I saw that he was looking after Alex with an odd expression on his face. He shook his head slightly, as if to clear it. Our eyes met—and though I knew Seb's mixed feelings must be gouging at him, he motioned almost imperceptibly with his head: *Go after him.*

Upstairs it was quiet, bathed in shadow; everyone was either downstairs or had gone out. As I came up onto the landing, I thought at first that Alex must have gone into the storeroom, and I started toward it — but then my neck went cold as I heard him. No, he wasn't in the storeroom; he was in the bathroom.

He was throwing up.

I stood outside the bathroom door, my heart tight with sudden worry. I started to knock and found myself resting my hand on the old wooden door instead, swallowing hard.

"Alex?" I called.

No answer. The noises went on; I had to force myself not to go in. Finally there was silence, then the sound of the toilet flushing. Water running in the sink.

The door opened and Alex stood there. His hair looked black against the unnatural pallor of his skin; his face was damp, as if he'd splashed water on it. "What do you want?" he asked, massaging his head.

"You've got another migraine," I said softly. He'd told me how they made him throw up sometimes, the way the pain slammed into him so unexpectedly. I could feel it now, stabbing at his skull like a dagger. "Are you OK?"

He snorted as he dropped his hand. "Yeah, I'm so OK. Willow, seriously, what do you want?"

Did I really have to have a reason to want to talk to him now? I hesitated, taking in his face. "You, um . . . you didn't answer my text."

Around us, the house suddenly felt hollow with silence. "I didn't know what to say," said Alex finally.

What about that you love me, and you're sorry, too? The words wouldn't come. "Look, can't we just—the girls' dorm is empty; can we go in there and talk?"

A muscle in his cheek moved. "I thought that space was reserved for Seb," he said.

I stiffened; it felt like he had slapped me. I knew Kara would tell him about that. "Well, you thought wrong," I said. "He was in there last night because I was upset, OK? You can't actually think anything happened."

"Upset," he repeated. "So it's, like, my fault he was in there. Got it."

"There was no fault—nothing happened!" I stopped and let out a breath. "Alex, please. Don't do this." I couldn't help myself—I slipped my arms around his waist, pressing close against him. "Please. I love you; I know you love me."

I longed for him to lift his arms and wrap them around me. They stayed at his sides as he stood without moving, his heart beating against mine. "Of course I love you," he said. His voice was so emotionless that it sounded like he was saying the opposite. "But I meant what I said last night, Willow. I can't do this. And you've just spent, like, every waking hour alone with Seb since I told you that. So obviously you've decided."

I drew away from him, staring. He was serious. He was actually serious about me never talking to Seb again. I gave a short, disbelieving laugh. "So, I was supposed to just do what you told me, even though I think you're

445

completely wrong? Alex, I get how you feel, I really do! But Seb is just—"

"Yeah, just your *friend*, I know," he broke in. "You keep telling me."

He rubbed his temple again, his eyes closed. I could feel how much physical pain he was in—and despite everything, all I wanted was to cradle his head on my lap and stroke the hurt away. Yearning went through me for that time in his room only a few weeks ago, when I'd done exactly that. It was funny. Things had seemed complicated then—and everything had really been so simple.

"Look, I can't do this now, and neither can you," said Alex at last. "We've got to focus on the job tomorrow. If there's still anything left to say, we'll say it after that."

The lines of his face were so beautiful, so familiar. I remembered being with him in the tent in New Mexico—the things we'd said to each other, the way we'd touched—and something inside of me was dying. But when I spoke, my voice was steady. "There won't be any point. Seb is my friend; he always will be. And with the Council attack coming up . . ." I stopped, remembering Seb's quiet insistence that he'd be there. "We could all die during it," I said finally. "And I'm not going to live what might be the last week of my life ignoring someone I care about."

Alex's eyes were cold, stormy seas. "No, just ignoring someone you're supposed to be in love with."

"That's not my choice. It's yours."

He snorted. "Yeah, if you say so." His gaze scanned

over me, his jaw tight. Then he shrugged. "I guess that's it, then," he said.

"I guess it is."

And this time, I had no doubt: Alex and I had just broken up.

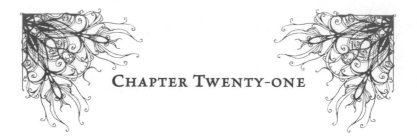

Chapter Twenty-one

"SHE'S HERE — we've made contact several times now," said Charmeine's voice.

Raziel was in the parking lot behind the cathedral; when Charmeine had called, he'd been about to drive back up to Silver Trail to go over proposed blueprints for the first Camp Angel. "Excellent," he said, resting his forearms on the roof of his black BMW. "So she believes you, then."

Charmeine sounded more tired than ever. She managed a low laugh. "Oh, yes. It was a case of 'Fish, meet barrel.' I thought you said the woman was a trained CIA agent."

The day was cold with a gunmetal sky; Raziel climbed into the car for warmth and settled against the comfortable leather seat. "Now, now, give her some credit," he chided. "Hardly anyone knows Nate worked with her.

It must have seemed quite the definitive proof that you're a rogue, too. So she's got the information now?" From what he'd gleaned from Willow, Kylar actually hadn't been doing badly on his own, though Raziel knew he still lacked several crucial pieces of information.

"Yes, everything they'll need," said Charmeine. "Plus one or two little details that'll get your Angel Killers trapped inside the building once they're finished, so that we can take care of them."

"Perfect. But she hasn't actually made contact with Kylar yet, has she?" Raziel was sure she hadn't; Willow's thoughts lately had been preoccupied with the plan to try to get the information from the church. That and her love life, which was fascinating in a sickly way.

"Not yet," said Charmeine. "I thought it would be best if she could track him down on her own, so that it doesn't seem like I know too much. Fortunately there's a mass demonstration scheduled in the Zócalo around the same time as that special service at the cathedral you said they're going to — she's already decided it's a likely place for him to be, with so many angels liable to be around. So with luck, they'll encounter each other. If not, I'll have to tell her that my rogue angel powers have figured out where they live."

Raziel frowned. "Just stay away from the team yourself," he cautioned. "My d— the half angel is extremely psychic."

Charmeine's tired voice snapped into irritation. "Raz. She's what, seventeen? I know I'm under daily psychic

attack here, but come on — you don't think I could out-
wit a complete novice?"

In the car, Raziel was still shaking his head at himself at his near slip. "There's no need to take chances,
that's all."

"Fine, I wasn't intending to go near them, anyway.
People who can shoot halos make me nervous. Which
reminds me: you really might have told them to ease off
a little. There've been over twenty angel deaths in two
weeks here — and that's with not as much feeding going
on as usual, now that the roots the Twelve have been putting down are starting to take effect."

"Oh?" said Raziel uneasily. "Is anything going to be
done about it?"

"No, I don't think so. Angels here are up in arms,
but there's not much that *can* be done, the way they're
striking — there's never any knowing where or what time."

Raziel was unsurprised; Kylar was nothing if not a
good strategist. "Well, I'll do my best to rein them in," he
said. "But they're very keen, you know."

He heard Charmeine snort. "Thanks, that's good of
you," she said. "Anyway, in a few more days it might not
even matter anymore."

"How are you holding out?" Her weary tone worried
him; she sounded like a woman struggling to hold on.

He could almost see her tired grimace. "All right, I
suppose. But I'm glad the reception's soon. I'm counting
the hours before I don't have to keep up a psychic barricade anymore."

Anxiety prickled over him. "It's getting harder for you to hold them off, isn't it?"

Her voice turned crisp. "Don't worry, I can hold out until the bitter end. Meanwhile, I suppose you've heard about Tyrel."

"Yes, I've heard," said Raziel curtly. The news in the angel community was that the Council had recently appointed Tyrel to run the Church of Angels in Mexico — an angel who'd been a hated adversary of his for eons. Doubtless, this was exactly why the Twelve had appointed him.

"Well, we're going to have the last laugh," said Charmeine. "You'll be traveling down for the fun, won't you?"

Raziel gazed out at the mountains, looming in sharp peaks against the sky. No matter what other consequences the attack might bring, the Council would soon be dead — and if their deaths killed him, too, he wanted the last sight he ever saw to be the twinkling shards of their destruction. Thinking of their recent TV appearance, with their thinly veiled death sentence to him — *That is our promise* — he gave a hard smile.

"Oh, I'll be there," he said. "I'll book a flight tonight."

"Good. Because you know, I think we actually have a chance. It's just feels *different* in this world, doesn't it? We might really survive this."

Once he and Charmeine had hung up, Raziel took his laptop out of his briefcase. With a silent click of a button, he turned it on and opened the files from Project Angel, the covert CIA department that had funded and overseen the Angel Killers. He'd managed to take it over months ago; the special agents now all had angel burn or had been killed.

Except one.

A few strokes on the mouse pad, and a photo appeared on the screen: a head-and-shoulders shot of an intense-looking young woman with shoulder-length brown hair. Sophie Kinney — a junior agent who'd been quickly elevated by the angelic invasion of her department; she and the traitor Nate had barely made it out in time to save their lives. From his exploration of Willow's thoughts, Raziel knew about Sophie's role the day the Second Wave had arrived. She and Nate had taken Willow to the cathedral by helicopter; Nate had stayed behind to help Willow with the attack on the gate — and was killed, as it turned out; the memory filled Raziel with satisfaction. Meanwhile, Sophie had escaped to a safe location. Smart woman.

But she'd been seen by the security guard at the back door. The same security guard whom she later tracked down to question in disguise, in an attempt to find out where Kylar had gone — because as far as she knew, he was the only Angel Killer left in the world. Raziel's response to the security guard's worried e-mail had praised him for his devotion to the angels and asked him to keep his encounter with Sophie confidential.

Just send me the contact details that were left with you, and the angels will take care of the matter, he'd finished. And he'd "taken care of it" to perfection. His e-mail to Sophie had been, he thought, something of a masterpiece.

> I understand you're looking for Alex Kylar. So am I. I was a friend of your former colleague Nathaniel and share Nathaniel's goals. There are several of us in Mexico City—where, as you might not be aware, there have been multiple angel killings recently. We believe Alex Kylar is here, and that he's formed a new group of Angel Killers. There are further details that I cannot disclose via e-mail, but as a matter of extreme urgency, we feel that you, our group, and his need to join forces in order to battle the threat that faces this world.

As he'd thought, Sophie had taken some time to respond — he smiled as he imagined her frantically checking out what details she could on her own, before she'd finally, cautiously written back — but eventually she'd bitten, and he'd deftly reeled her in. And now she was down in Mexico City, in touch with Charmeine the friendly rogue angel — and doubtless very, very excited that she and Kylar were about to rid the world of the angel menace. Studying Sophie's image, Raziel smirked. *No need to thank me*, he thought. *Really. I'm only too happy to help you find him.*

Because Kylar knew Sophie. He may not like her, but he knew her. He'd trust information that came from her.

And that, thought Raziel as he snapped off his laptop, was the only way to beat Kylar at his own game.

Seb really couldn't believe that Willow's boyfriend was this stupid.

As the team took the Metro to the Zócalo, Seb stood beside Willow in the crowded subway car. Dozens of angel wings surrounded them, looking bent and bedraggled in the throng. The team was scattered throughout; Alex stood with Kara and Wesley, half a car-length away. He and Willow had barely spoken since officially breaking things off the day before — when they'd had to, they'd been cool and professional with each other. Now Willow stood quietly as the train sped them all toward the cathedral, her face expressionless. The crystal pendant she'd always worn was gone from around her neck. Though she'd made it clear that she didn't want to talk about what had happened, Seb could sense her anger, the depth of her hurt.

The train lurched. Willow grabbed his arm briefly to steady herself, then offered him an apologetic smile — conversation wasn't an option with the noise. She was wearing makeup, which she never did; it made her look older, though no more beautiful. As Seb smiled back, he wished that he had the right to put his arm around her for no real reason, just to feel her pressed closely to his side. And he thought he could cheerfully throttle Alex, who *had* had the right and apparently cared so little about it that he was willing to break up with Willow simply for being friends with him. Seb mentally shook his head in disbelief. God, if Willow was his—if he could be with her the way he longed to be; if he could actually go into a room with her and shut the door and tell her how he felt with words, with his lips, hear her say the same things back while she stroked her fingers through his hair— then he wouldn't care who the hell she was friends with. Who in his right mind would? No matter how much Willow cared about him, she would never cheat on Alex, never; did the *cabrón* not know that?

By now, Seb had a lot of practice keeping thoughts like these buried. As he entertained himself with fantasies of dragging Alex to one side and telling him in great detail exactly what an idiot he was—perhaps throwing in a punch now and then to emphasize the point—the uppermost part of his mind was busy concentrating on the car around them, the advertisements, the people. Willow could have picked up on what he was feeling if she'd tried, but Seb knew she wouldn't. From the start, it was as if they'd had an agreement: he wouldn't make the fact he was in love with her too obvious, and she'd pretend not to notice it.

As the train rattled its way through the tunnels, Seb supposed he should be glad that Willow and Alex had broken up. But it was obvious how deeply they were still in love with each other. Even across the crowded car, he could sense the emotional ties that bound them; he was sure they'd manage to patch things up soon. Meanwhile, feeling how much pain Willow was in was agony to Seb, so that he found himself in the bizarre position of wanting

455

to pummel Alex until he saw reason and made things up with her. Seb smiled slightly. He wouldn't really have believed it, but he wanted Willow's happiness more than he wanted his own.

He wasn't a saint, though; sometimes it was all he could do not to just pull Willow into his arms and start kissing her. And he prayed with everything he had that she'd get Alex out of her system soon and see what was so blindingly obvious to him. Because thinking of her dream — of the whole sequence of events that had led him to her, spiraling back through his life for years — Seb couldn't believe that fate had brought them together only to be friends. It was clear to him that he and Willow were meant to be, not just because they were both half angel, but because of who they both were, their personalities. It was as if their souls had been crying out for each other their whole lives.

Seb knew if Willow never felt the same, he'd deal with it, somehow — being in her life as a brother was a lot better than not being in her life at all. It was becoming more difficult by the day, though. He'd never have dreamed he could fall *more* in love with his half-angel girl. But actually being with Willow in person, feeling the effortless depth of their connection that was like nothing he'd ever experienced — and knowing that it could still be so much more — a whole world more, if she'd only open her eyes and see it, too — Seb let out a breath as the train started to slow. He wasn't sure if it made it better or worse that he thought he'd caught glimpses of attraction from her sometimes, thoughts so fleeting, it was as if she had no control over them. On the whole, he thought it made it worse, given how much she was in love with Alex. And it definitely made it harder for him to be brotherly toward her.

That's exactly what you're going to do, though, he told himself. *Until she tells you she wants something different, you are only her brother.* He glanced down at Willow's red-gold hair, her face. She'd see it for herself someday, he thought. She had to.

She just had to.

The car reached the Zócalo station; the doors unfolded with a pneumatic hiss. "I guess this is it," murmured Willow, her forehead creased with apprehension.

"This is it," agreed Seb, pushing his thoughts away.

They jostled off the car. Everyone in the world seemed to be going to the Zócalo. Alex and the others had exited farther down; the group rejoined each other near the stairs. As they started up, they could hear a thunder of voices chanting: "El DF is dying! Funds for doctors, not angels! El DF is dying! Funds for doctors, not angels!"

The Crusaders rally, realized Seb. As they came out onto the Zócalo, they could see it — a solid, fist-waving mass of people gathered near the Palacio. Their auras were blood red; they merged together, throbbing toward the sky as they chanted, so that the crowd looked like a single angry creature. Seb stopped in his tracks for a second, neck prickling. He'd seen auras like that before—usually in street gangs before a fight. Never around thousands at once.

Nearby, hundreds of people wearing angel wings had gathered, screaming just as furiously: "The angels will provide! If you have true faith, the angels will provide!" Though mostly damaged, their auras were a furious red, too, straining toward the Crusaders. Dozens of grim-looking security guards patrolled the edges of the crowd, while several angels with glinting wings cruised overhead.

Willow glanced at Seb. Her green eyes looked larger than usual, accented with eyeliner. "This really isn't good," she whispered to him, and he knew she meant the seething auras rather than the angels on the hunt. Like him, she had to be picking up on the vibes of the rally, too—the organized fury surging all around them.

"It'll be all right," he muttered back.

"Did we know this was happening?" demanded Sam, frowning at the scene.

Seb rolled his eyes. Sam had been watching it on the news with the others when he and Willow returned to the house the previous day. "Yes, we knew," said Alex briefly, leading the way toward the cathedral. "It doesn't affect us."

Except that it did.

As they neared the Catedral de los Ángeles, they could see slow-moving lines snaking out the entrance, stretching all the way down to the tabernacle. "That doesn't look right—the doors are supposed to be open by now," said

Kara. "Alex, I'm just going to go check." Before he could respond, Kara was running off, her long braided wig bouncing down her back.

Alex glanced toward the cathedral with a frown. "Here, everyone," he said. He was carrying a large plastic bag; he dipped into it, passing out angel wings. As he handed a pair to Seb, their eyes met—Seb could see Alex's controlled dislike of him. The feeling was mutual.

Alex gave Willow a pair of lavender wings, avoiding her gaze. Willow avoided his, too, accepting the wings silently. She had on a short black skirt and black top she'd borrowed from Liz, with a jean jacket over it and a pair of unfamiliar heeled sandals that gave her a long-legged look. Seb was in a pair of gray pants and a crisp white shirt he'd borrowed from Wesley; the others were dressed similarly—Alex had wanted them to blend in with the churchgoing crowd as much as possible. While it grated to take orders from him, Seb had to admit that Alex was good at what he did. It was a job he himself would have had no desire to take on.

"Are these on straight?" Willow asked him in an undertone. She presented him with her back, where the lavender wings hung askew. Seb straightened them for her, adjusting an elastic strap where it had twisted on her shoulder and trying to ignore how the short skirt showed off her figure. Out of the corner of his vision, he saw Alex watching them and held back a snort. If Alex was jealous, it was his own stupid fault. Willow would never normally have asked for Seb's help instead of Alex's own.

"They're straight now," he told her. *You look beautiful*, he managed not to add.

He'd come so close to saying the words that Willow caught them easily; her cheeks colored. "Thanks," she said, and he knew it was for the compliment, too. "Yours are fine," she added, glancing at his white wings.

Kara came sprinting back. "Alex, it's bad," she panted. "There's been a security alert at the cathedral; they're worried about a terrorist attack with the Crusaders' rally going on. They've installed a metal detector."

"*What?*" Alex's head jerked toward the cathedral doors. He swore under his breath.

Seb went still, thinking of the switchblade in his pocket. He was carrying a gun, too — the holster felt strange under his waistband — but knew he'd have been likelier to go for his blade in case of trouble.

"So . . . what does this mean?" asked Liz finally.

"It means we'll take our guns off and go in anyway, right?" offered Brendan.

Alex's frustration was almost palpable. "What good would that do? If there's any trouble, we need to be able to shoot. *Damn* it." He shoved both hands through his hair. "We can't put it off," he muttered to himself, staring at the line of people. "The security code will change tomorrow. . . ."

"We might not need the code," Willow pointed out, her voice cool.

"Yes, but you might," he retorted tersely. "We can't take the chance; the Council will be gone in just four days." He blew out a breath. "OK," he said finally. "We're going to have to wait outside the doors for you. Both of you, give Kara your weapons. Willow, hand me your cell phone."

After covertly handing Kara her gun, Willow dug in her jean-jacket pocket for her phone, her mouth tight — Seb knew without trying that she was irritated at having orders snapped at her. Keeping his back to the crowd, he drew out his own gun and switchblade and passed them to Kara. She tucked them away wordlessly in her bag. Her opinion of him was so obvious that Seb couldn't resist smiling at her and saying, "You won't steal my blade, will you?"

Her brown eyes turned even chillier. "Don't worry. I'm not the one who steals things."

Across the square, the sound of chanting was still going strong, pounding through the air. Alex fiddled with Willow's cell, punching buttons on it. As Seb glanced at him, the moment froze.

Though he could see auras without trying, he didn't check out each one he encountered in detail; it would have been information overload. But the day before, as Alex had left the firing range to go upstairs, Seb had thought he'd seen something strange in his aura's blue-and-gold hues. He'd dismissed it as a trick of the light — yet now, in the pure, slanting sunlight of late afternoon, he was seeing it again.

Alex's aura was damaged.

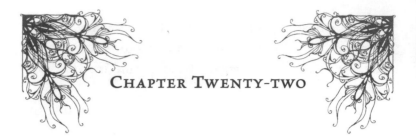

CHAPTER TWENTY-TWO

SEB STARED AT THE COLORS of Alex's life force. He'd never seen anything like this before. He'd encountered thousands of auras with angel burn in his life — was all too familiar with the gray, sickly look it caused, with the aura's natural colors trying to regain themselves through the pallor. This was similar but different: the colors themselves looked faded. The blue — which Seb was sure had been a rich ocean blue when he'd first met Alex — now looked dull and grayish, the gold almost tarnished, with faint black spots.

The damage looked as if it had been caused by angels . . . and yet not.

Willow's question barreled back to him: Do we *cause angel burn to people when we touch them?*

It wasn't something Seb had noticed; certainly none of the girls he'd ever been involved with had shown anything like this. But then his chest went cold as it hit him. He'd never been with a girl for any length of time, had he? He'd only had flings — a day or two at most. Willow had been with Alex for months.

Only seconds had passed. Alex handed the phone back to Willow. "Here — I've put my number on speed-dial. Keep it in your pocket; we'll be right outside once the service starts. If there's any trouble, just hit the send button and we'll get in there somehow."

Seb tore his gaze away, his thoughts spinning as he remembered Alex's migraines, his constant headaches, and thought of the dozens of ominous issues those things could mean. His first and main concern was for Willow. If this was what he thought, it was going to kill her to find out she'd been hurting Alex.

Willow hesitated as she took the phone, scanning Alex's face as if searching for a hint of softness. There was none. She slipped the phone back into her pocket, her expression abruptly aloof.

"Yes, all right," she said.

She glanced down, buttoning her jacket. And then Seb saw the look she'd been waiting for flicker across Alex's features, turning them young and vulnerable — and he knew Alex was in as much torment as she was but too stubborn to admit it.

Willow cleared her throat. "So I guess we'd better go get a place in line," she said. The rest of the team was standing a little apart now, talking among themselves; Seb could feel Sam's disappointment in particular that they weren't going in.

Alex appeared impassive again. "Yeah, all right. We can't wait with you; it would look suspicious if we peeled off before we hit the metal detectors. Be careful, OK? We'll be right outside." Though he sounded sincere, he also sounded like he was talking to any other member of his team, and Seb longed to take a swing at him. *Just apologize, you stupid jerk.*

Except that it was too late for that now, wasn't it? Studying Alex's aura again, Seb could see even more clearly that he hadn't been mistaken. His throat felt like sand. How exactly was he supposed to tell Willow this?

She nodded stiffly at Alex's words; he could feel the depth of her hurt that he wasn't backing down even now. "Seb, are you ready?" She turned toward him — and her face slackened in surprise as she picked up on his anxiety.

"Yes, I'm ready," he said, burying his thoughts as best he could. His gaze met Alex's. A fierce look flashed in the blue-gray eyes, and Seb knew Alex was telling him to take care of Willow, to keep her safe in case some rabid church member recognized her and raised the alarm. As if he really had to be told that.

"OK, you've both got your tickets — and you know the code if you need it, right?" said Alex out loud.

Seb nodded; he and Willow had both memorized it. "Don't worry," he replied evenly. And added in his head,

Believe me, hombre, I'm not keeping her safe for you — *but I'll keep her safe with my life.*

He and Willow started across the uneven expanse of the square; she was taller than usual in her heels as she glanced at him worriedly. "Seb, what's wrong?"

"I'll tell you later," he said.

"But . . ."

He heard the strain in his own voice. "Please, *querida.* I'll tell you later. I promise."

Willow wavered, searching his face, and finally nodded. "OK."

The line moved slowly once they joined it, but everyone seemed cheerful, chatting happily about the angels and how exciting it was to be going to such an important service. He and Willow fit right in with their satiny angel wings. After a while they could see the stairs that led down to the cathedral entrance, with the rectangular shape of the metal detector set up at the bottom of them.

"I'm relieved to finally be doing something, you know," Willow said in a low voice as they inched forward. Her gaze was fixed on the metal detector ahead and the guards flanking it as people shuffled through, showing their tickets. "I've hated having to just sit at home while all this is going on."

Her aura, like his, appeared gray and listless. Seb wasn't surprised that she hadn't noticed Alex's. Her natural psychic focus just wasn't centered on auras; she didn't tend to bring them into view unless she thought there was a reason to. And in Alex's case, why would she? Seb had told her himself that she wasn't causing him any harm.

He cleared his throat. "Yes, I know how much you've hated staying at home."

At his noncommittal tone, Willow smiled. "Let me guess: you wish I were still there. Honestly, you're as bad as—" Catching herself, she broke off with a sudden wince, her expression pained.

Seb couldn't help himself; he put his arm around her, squeezing her shoulders as he drew her against his side. *It'll be all right*, mi amorcito, he wanted to say. But he didn't really see how it could be, once he told her what he'd seen. Oh, God, this was going to destroy her. And what did it do to Seb's own hopes? True, it probably meant that Willow would never get back together with Alex, but for it to happen like this—when she was still in love with him, when she knew she'd hurt him with her touch—she'd never get over him, then. Never.

Willow was gazing up at him, her eyes full of dread. "You're thinking about . . . whatever it is again," she said softly. "It's something to do with me and Alex, isn't it?"

He was saved from answering. Just as they reached the top of the stairs, there was a squeal and a flurry of angel wings. Three pretty girls raced up to them. "Seb! *Salut!*" exclaimed the one with dark hair. Before Seb quite knew what was happening, she was kissing him on both cheeks; he reciprocated automatically. The other two girls followed suit. Willow blinked, looking taken aback by the social kisses.

"You left the hostel!" chided the dark-haired girl in

French with a laugh. Céline, that was her name. "None of us knew where you were; one day you just vanished." Her gaze went to Willow, taking her in curiously.

Seb was acutely conscious that the three girls were devouts, and had almost certainly seen Willow's photo on the news or the Church of Angels website. "Oui, I met my girlfriend," he said, his arm still around Willow's shoulders. "Maria." It was the first name that came to mind. In English, he said, "Maria, this is Céline, and — I'm sorry," he said to the blond. "Is it Nicole?"

The girl tsked and shook her sleek head; she looked pale and too thin. "Ah, you see, he forgets all about us once he has you," she teased, glancing at Willow. "Maria, *this* is Nicole" — she indicated the third girl, a tall red-head — "and I am Adèle."

"Hi," said Willow, offering her hand to them.

They started moving down the stairs; to the irritation of the people behind them, the trio showed no signs of leaving. Céline was still gazing at Willow. "You look so familiar," she said suddenly. "Are you an actress?"

Seb's muscles went tight as Willow tried to smile. "No, but everyone says that," she said. "I think I must look like someone."

"So this is where you girls ran off to — I thought you'd abandoned me," said a cheerful American voice. A guy with floppy brown hair had come up behind them. Mike. He caught sight of Seb, and his face burst into a grin as he slapped his shoulder. "Seb! God, man, where have you been?"

"He has a girlfriend now," said Céline, pouting and tucking her arm through Mike's. "I am very sad at this. You'll have to comfort me later."

"Oh, hey, that's too bad," said Mike in a soothing voice. "Yeah, we'll have to have some serious comforting time when we get back."

They'd reached the bottom of the stairs; somehow the three girls and Mike had gotten ahead of them. Smiling widely, Mike turned and gave Seb a double thumbs-up as the girls started filing through the metal detector.

Willow's expression was slightly dazed. "Friends of yours?"

Seb shrugged; he could hardly believe they'd all appeared. "I know them from the hostel I was staying in."

Something in Céline's handbag set off the machine; the guard went through it as Mike and the girls clustered around. The other guard motioned for Seb and Willow to wait.

Willow watched as Céline laughed and flipped back her chocolate-brown hair. "The girls are all very pretty, aren't they?" she said in a neutral tone. "That one, Céline, really seems to like you."

Seb stared down at her profile. Was he imagining things, or had there been a glimmer almost like jealousy from her? Then Willow seemed to shake her head at herself and the sense faded. The guard motioned her through; she groped in her pocket for her ticket and moved forward, heels clicking.

They came out into the packed main cathedral, with its unfamiliar airy, open feel. As Seb had seen before when he'd been here, the place's bones had been altered somewhat since his boyhood—its flesh was now completely different. Far away down the aisle, golden angels shone from the ornate floor-to-ceiling altar; smaller ones held candlesticks aloft from the corner of each pew. There were several real angels too, gliding through the high, domed space, wings flashing like mirrors. Reaching out with his mind, Seb found the throng of them sitting in the unseen office area—easily over a dozen.

"Look, here's a seat," said Céline, tugging at his arm. "There's room for all of us, if we squeeze."

"Thanks, but Maria and I will—"

Céline ignored him and reached across to take Willow's arm instead, laughing as she drew her into the pew. "Come, come! We haven't seen Seb in weeks—we want to meet his girlfriend!"

Behind them, people were waiting to get past; Mike shoved Seb good-naturedly into the pew ahead of him, beside Willow. "Nice wings, dude," he whispered. "You took my advice, didn't you? Told her you're a devout."

Seb's eyes met Willow's as they both realized: it was either make a scene and risk drawing attention to themselves or stay where they were. "I think it'll be all right," murmured Willow to him as they sat down. "The service will be starting soon, anyway."

"We must play a game," announced Céline once they

were settled. "What actress does Maria look like? Because she looks so familiar, it's driving me insane. Seb, who do you think?"

He shrugged. His heart was suddenly pounding. "I don't know," he said, gazing at the redone cathedral and trying to sound uninterested. "She's more beautiful than any actress."

The three French girls all cooed in delight. Mike nodded. "Definitely the right answer." He offered his hand to Willow. "I'm Mike, by the way. I'm from Sacramento, what about you? I heard an American accent, right?"

"I'm from Maine," said Willow, shaking his hand. Seb could sense her anxiety. "Bangor."

"Yeah? What brought you down here?"

Her lavender wings moved as she shrugged. "The same as everyone else, I guess."

"How did you two meet?" asked Nicole, leaning forward. Her eyes had circles under them. She looked approvingly at Willow's angel wings. "Did the angels bring you together?"

"Um . . ." Willow swallowed and glanced up at Seb, her gaze searching his. "Yes, sort of."

Her hands were tense on her lap; he took one of them, and she gripped his fingers tightly. "It's a long story," he said. "But I'll tell it if you like. It's very romantic." He was already planning how he could spin it out, make it so boring that they'd completely lose interest in Willow.

"Wait, wait, I know the actress!" burst in Céline, bouncing slightly in her seat. "It's that girl with long blond hair—what is her name? She's been in so many things!"

Seb froze. Long blond hair. *Madre mía,* in another moment she'd have it.

"No, people usually say Keira Knightley," said Willow quickly. "Or—or Katie Holmes."

"Keira Knightley?" Céline frowned in surprise. "No . . . well, maybe a tiny bit. . . ."

To Seb's immense relief, the service started then with a rippling of harp music, and conversation stopped. The three French girls faced forward, eyes shining as the priest made his way up the small spiral staircase to the angel-winged pulpit. Willow let out a breath. Seb stroked his thumb across her fingers, aware that he wasn't at all sorry to be posing as her boyfriend.

The priest looked younger than Seb had imagined, with dark hair and a wide smile. He raised his hands to the sky, smiling out at the congregation as he spoke into a microphone. "*Bienvenidos al Catedral de los Ángeles.*"

An interminable sermon about the angels' love; how lucky Mexico was to now have its own personal angel; lots of standing and singing hymns and then sitting down again. Céline and the other girls knew the hymns by heart, though the lyrics were in Spanish. Willow pressed close to Seb as they shared a hymnal, her head down—obviously trying to keep her face away from their notice now.

Finally the moment came when the priest asked if anyone wished to be blessed on behalf of the angels. He came down from the pulpit to the balustrade, his questioning tone echoing through the speakers. Thankfully, the angels they'd seen when they first entered the cathedral were gone now, apparently sated. When Seb checked, he could sense they'd joined the others in the office area for the time being.

A few people started going hesitantly toward the front, footsteps echoing on the shining marble. Willow gave Seb's fingers a meaningful squeeze before she released them. He nodded. "Excuse us," he whispered to Mike. The American's eyebrows shot up; Seb could practically hear him thinking, *What — really?* But he didn't comment as Seb and Willow edged past.

Neither spoke as they went down the long center aisle. They both knew that more angels could appear at any time and sense his and Willow's energy, if they got close enough. Willow's chin was up, her gaze steady on the balustrade where people were kneeling. The priest was already blessing the second applicant, lips moving in prayer as he held the man's hand. The woman he'd just blessed stayed on her knees, head down.

And from nowhere, the thought flashed through Seb's mind how right this would feel, if circumstances were different: to walk toward an altar like this with Willow someday. If she felt the same, he'd even do it now, despite both their ages. Because as he glanced down at her beside him, he knew that this girl — this woman — was the only one he'd ever love. She'd had his heart for almost his entire life; she was woven into the very fabric of him.

They reached the balustrade with the great golden altar gleaming before them and knelt side by side on blue velvet cushions. Willow bowed her head; Seb could sense her complete focus on the job at hand. Pushing away his thoughts he cleared his own mind, getting himself into the relaxed state that he used for his readings.

It seemed to take forever, but finally the priest reached Seb, his eyes gentle. "Do you wish to be blessed by the angels, my son?"

"Yes, Father," murmured Seb. He held out his hand; felt warm fingers close around it.

A burst of sensation, images, knowledge. Seb's heart sank. This wasn't the usual priest at all — the usual priest was sick. This man was visiting from another state, and though ecstatic at the thought of meeting the Seraphic Council in a few days, he'd arrived only hours ago — had hardly even had a chance to speak to anyone before he'd been asked to do the evening service and had to prepare. Seb probed deeply, but knew already that there was nothing here to get — this man didn't know the details of the reception yet.

The priest touched Seb's bowed head with a murmured prayer and moved on to Willow. Seb stayed where he was. He could sense her discouragement after a moment and knew she'd found out the same thing as him. At last the priest moved on again, to a man wearing a gray business suit.

Seb turned his head on his clasped hands, gazing sidelong at Willow. Their eyes met; she bit her lip and glanced at the arched door in the shadows. "Seb, we've got to go in there," she whispered.

He nodded reluctantly, eyeing the office doorway.

Maybe he could leave Willow in the corridor, while he attempted to go past the angels himself.

She was regarding him with a small smile. "Think again," she murmured.

Seb blew out a breath and looked back toward the door. As he did, he saw the first woman the priest had blessed, still kneeling with her head on her hands . . . and his eyes widened as he took in her aura. The other life energies at the balustrade were either gray and sickly or soft pastel hues of devotion; hers was an ugly, furtive mustard yellow, with angry red veins.

As he watched, one of the woman's hands left the top of the balustrade and pressed something underneath it. She rose and walked quickly away.

Seb's skin crawled with sudden apprehension. Turning, he saw at least ten people with similar auras, all of them now hurrying toward one of the side exits. The woman was running now. A man spun around as he reached the door and shouted, "El DF is dying! Funds for doctors, not angels!"

As the first explosion rocked the cathedral, Seb lunged for Willow, tackling her to the ground and shielding her with his body. He heard her cry out and closed his eyes tight as another explosion came, and then another. Things were pattering to the floor around them; something small and hard bounced off Seb's back. The smell of smoke — Willow's body trembling under his. Shrieks of fear and pain mixing with the thunder.

Finally the explosions stopped.

Screams echoed through the cathedral as the congregation started stampeding for the doors. Seb dared a look up and saw pews and bodies lying twisted and tangled, debris, the golden altar blackened. The man in the business suit sat slumped against the splintered balustrade, covered in blood — the young priest lay motionless, half his head blown away. Seb had barely taken it in when a flock of angels with furious faces streamed out through the wall from the office area. They circled once in the smoky air, then angled up and out, vanishing through the high ceiling.

Urgency pounded at him; they had to get out of here. He struggled to his feet, helping Willow up — she was pale and shaking. As he glanced back at the entrance, his gaze somehow found Mike sprawled across a pew, obviously dead. Mike. Seb stared, stunned, wondering fleetingly if Céline and the others were all right. He couldn't tell; the main entrance had turned into a seething mass of people, screaming and struggling to escape.

Suddenly a stained-glass window erupted inward, the glass angels shattering as the crowd outside rammed something through its panes. "El DF is dying! Let the angels die, too!"

Willow stood staring at the priest with tears running down her smoke-smudged face. Seb grabbed her hand and pulled her after him as he started running toward the back of the cathedral, to the exit he'd told Kara about.

Willow was still crying but stopped short, tugging at him. "Seb, no! We've got to go back into the offices; this is our only chance!"

Forget about saving the world—I just want to save you! But she was right. Seb held back a curse; still gripping her hand, he turned and headed for the shadowy corner. They both had their arms to their mouths, coughing. As they passed the mangled altar again, Willow's face was pale but resolute—he could sense that she was holding on to herself tight, determined to do what had to be done. They reached the office door, where she jabbed out the security code unhesitatingly.

A green light glowed. Seb threw open the door, and they ran down a narrow stone hallway lined with paintings of angels. As the door closed behind them, the sound of shouts and crashes cut off abruptly; an almost eerie silence descended. Around a bend were the new offices— a large reception area with sofas and chairs. The door just beyond stood open; through it Seb could hear the hum of computers.

They rushed in—there was another door to the right. Opening it, Seb saw a large mahogany desk and leather chair. This computer, too, was on; he slid into the chair and tapped the mouse. The box requesting a password came up, and he swore. He glanced at the mouse again, rested his hand on it. He wasn't usually very good with objects, but he didn't need *details*, just some kind of hint; a clue—

Only jumbled images of angels came. *Angeles*, he typed. Wrong password. *Iglesiadelosangeles*. Nothing.

Willow had gone for the filing cabinet, tugging at it fruitlessly. She ran over. "Keys, are there any keys?"

As she spoke, Seb's gaze fell on a carved wooden angel beside the monitor. A tickle of knowledge came, and he grabbed for it — small silver keys lay underneath. He snatched them up and gave them to Willow.

"Try the mouse for me — we need the password," he said tensely.

"Oh, God, I'm not great at this . . ." She touched the mouse, frowning. "Um — something about the angels' glory, maybe?" She sprinted back to the files. "What's Spanish for 'Seraphic Council'? And 'security'?"

Seb told her, furiously typing in *gloriadelosangeles*. It worked, and he heaved a sigh of relief — but no sooner had he accessed the e-mail account then the lights in the office flickered and died. The computer screen went black. No! Seb stared blankly at it. At the filing cabinet, Willow gave a surprised yelp; then her angel appeared overhead, casting light on the files.

Somewhere, a rhythmic banging noise had started.

Seb looked up, his scalp prickling. He reached for his own angel self, sent it soaring down the hallway. As he burst out into the main cathedral, he saw that most of the congregation had now escaped, but the place was full of rioters — tipping over pews, smashing windows. Several of them were battering at the locked office door with an angel statue, their auras blood red as they yelled obscenities. Wheeling on one wing, Seb saw the wooden door start to buckle. Someone else ran up—a man shouting at the others to move aside. He pulled a gun and began firing at the door.

Seb sped back to the offices; as he merged, his human self was already lunging toward the filing cabinet. "Willow, we've got to go!"

She shook her head anxiously. "Wait, this file might have something—it feels important—"

Seb heard the door crash open down the hallway, the echo of shouts. "Now!" He pulled Willow bodily from the filing cabinet; she resisted for a second, hanging back to yank the file out, and then they were both running, Willow with the file clutched to her chest.

They raced back out into the narrow hallway. Around the bend, it sounded as if the rioters were ripping the paintings down from the walls and smashing them. Then came running footsteps, heading their way. Seb and Willow were already tearing down the corridor in the opposite direction, her angel flying overhead to light their way down the dim, windowless passage.

As they turned another corner, Seb saw that the fire exit he'd remembered was still there, its sign looking blessedly ordinary as it beckoned to them. He threw himself against the door's metal bar, and they spilled out into the cool twilight, in a car-lined street behind the cathedral.

There was no time to be relieved—they'd burst out into another battle. The Crusaders and the Faithful were fighting in a seething mass, at least a hundred of them: fists swinging, the sticks from signs being used as weapons. Angels with furious faces flew overhead, occasionally ducking down to rip away the life force of a Crusader. A man screamed, clutching his chest as he fell to the ground. The fighting continued around him like churning water.

Seb and Willow ran along the side of the cathedral. Her angel had returned to her, leaving them bathed in shadow. All at once Seb stopped short, feeling both Willow's sudden, pulsing fear and a rushing sensation like a wind tunnel: a huge flock was heading right toward them.

Oh, God, their half-angel energy — Seb didn't know if the angels would stop long enough to sense them; couldn't take the chance. Too hurried to be gentle, he shoved Willow up against the rough stone wall of the cathedral, his body hiding hers as he grabbed hold of both their auras with his thoughts — struggling through sheer force of will to bring them so close to their bodies that they couldn't even be seen, so that he and Willow were only shadows in the darkness.

Their auras seemed to scream in protest; Seb's muscles shook with the effort to hold them in the unnatural position. Energy roared over his senses as more than fifty angels sped past barely a wing's-length away, soaring over the cathedral.

The rushing faded. Mental silence, with only the physical sounds of fighting still going on. Abruptly, Seb became aware of how closely he was pressed up against

Willow — the warmth of her body next to his. Letting go of their auras, he pulled away, drained and trembling.

Willow's eyes were huge. "I — I didn't know you could do that," she said faintly. Wailing sirens could be heard now, growing closer.

Seb swallowed against a dry throat. "No, me neither."

Behind them, the fighting was still going strong, though the angels had all departed, apparently joining the larger flock. The sound of breaking glass; in the distance he saw a pack of dark figures running. A car on fire.

Suddenly Willow gasped. "Oh, my God — Alex! I totally forgot —" She fumbled in her jacket pocket for the cell phone, then searched her other pocket, her expression turning frantic. "My phone's not here! It must have fallen out in the cathedral —"

Seb slapped at his pants pocket but already knew that he didn't have his phone, either; he was so unused to carrying one that he always forgot it. The thought faded as he stared at the burning car. Without answering Willow, he reached for his angel self and flew upward into the night, hovering above the cathedral as he scanned the streets around them.

The *centro* was on fire.

Or at least that's how it looked at first glance. Riots had broken out all around them — people were surging through the streets, breaking store windows, setting things alight. The sound of gunshots echoed from somewhere, and more sirens. The Zócalo appeared to be a single heaving mass of people; Seb could hardly even see

480

the Metro entrance. It was the same in almost every direction he looked. And the AKs' house lay over mile to the south, just past the thick of it all — attempting to go back there now would be madness.

Willow's angel had joined him in the air; she swooped in a circle, her lovely features distraught. On the ground, Willow's human self was staring at him. "Where are Alex and the team?" she said in a strangled whisper. "I can't see them anywhere! Do you think —?" She broke off.

Seb gripped her hand. "Can't you sense them?" He meant, *Can't you sense Alex?* He himself wasn't close enough to any of the team to bother trying. The only person he'd ever been close enough with to sense was Willow.

As their angels returned to their human bodies, Willow closed her eyes tight. Finally she gave a small nod. "They're alive," she said. "I think — I think they're all OK. I can't really tell; I'm too upset to get much." Her expression was pained. Seb knew she was thinking about Alex, and dread kicked through him as he remembered what he still had to tell her.

The shouts behind them intensified; more people were throwing themselves into the fray. Glancing back, Seb could hardly even tell if it was still the Crusaders fighting the Faithful or just herd mentality turned vicious. With a chill, he remembered the angel wings they were both wearing. "Come on, we'd better get these off," he said, yanking the elastic straps from his shoulders. A moment later, both pairs of wings lay on the ground beside the cathedral.

"What now?" asked Willow in a tiny voice. She was

still clutching the file to her chest, and Seb could sense she was barely holding on to her composure — that the deaths they'd witnessed were battering at her, threatening to take her down. She cleared her throat. "I — I don't think we're going to make it to the house anytime soon."

"No, it's not safe," agreed Seb. He felt bludgeoned by what they'd seen, too; he ached to take Willow in his arms and just hold her forever, comforting them both. But they needed a safe place to go until this was over — and given the way Céline and the others had almost recognized Willow, none of the city's devout-filled hostels or hotels would be it.

The only direction that had looked relatively clear was to the north.

As the answer came to him, Seb's jaw tightened with grim humor. He might have known that he wouldn't get out of going there — that somehow events would herd him to the place like a dog herding sheep. Only with the *centro* literally in flames would the neighborhood of his childhood ever seem like a safe haven, so that he could even consider taking the girl he loved to it.

Willow touched his arm. "Seb, what is it? Where are you thinking of going?"

"Tepito," he said. He took her hand, barely resisting the urge to kiss it. "Come on — I know someplace there we can go."

CHAPTER TWENTY-THREE

ALEX STOOD WITHOUT MOVING as Willow and Seb headed across the square toward the cathedral. Willow looked amazing in the short skirt, but he wouldn't have been able to take his eyes off her even if she'd been wearing her usual jeans and sneakers. He watched her figure grow smaller, her legs striding briskly in the heeled sandals.

She didn't look back. He hadn't really expected her to. As she and Seb disappeared into the line of waiting people, he let out a breath.

"You OK?" asked Kara.

"Yeah," said Alex briefly. For a second he longed to go running after them, to draw Willow to one side and . . . what? She'd made it clear there was nothing else to say, that she cared more about her friendship with Seb than her relationship with him. Deep down, he knew it wasn't so simple — that there were shades of gray among the stark blacks and whites that had kept him awake, staring into the darkness, these last two nights. He felt incapable of untangling them. All he could see was Willow's pink cheeks when he'd accused her of always thinking about Seb — the look on her face as she'd touched the sleeve of Seb's sweater that night. He was still so in love with her that it hurt, but he had no idea where her head was anymore.

Forget all of this — just forget it. He was sick of his own stupid thoughts.

"Come on," he said to the team finally. "Let's make a move."

Half an hour later, they were standing in front of the cathedral, listening to an angelic hymn drifting out. Behind them, someone was yelling through a megaphone about the inequity of a city that would spend money on angels but not on beds for its dying. As the crowd roared in approval, the Faithful screamed their protests, trying to get past the security guards — who looked pitiably few in number now, shouting unheeded orders at Crusaders and Faithful alike.

"Man, they're going to lose that battle any second now," murmured Kara, watching the guards struggle. "And when they do, that's going to turn nasty."

Alex nodded; just being near the scene was making him jumpy. The AKs couldn't have chosen a worse time to be here if they'd tried. He took out his cell phone again and glanced at the screen. No call from Willow.

"Wait, what's happening now?" Brendan peered down the dark steps to the entrance. "The singing's stopped."

Alex couldn't make out the priest's words, but it seemed about the right time for the blessings to be taking place. *Be careful, babe. Please be careful.* He was helpless to stop the thought. Hands jammed in his pockets, he stood against the outside wall of the cathedral, resisting the urge to look at his phone again.

He jerked upright as an explosion rumbled, the force of it trembling the ground under his feet.

"What the hell—?" Sam's eyes were wide, his voice drowned out by the thunder of several more explosions.

Oh, Jesus, there *had* been an attack, and Willow was in there—Alex bolted for the entrance while the explosions were still going, hurled himself down the steps. He met a stampede head-on—thousands of shrieking, panicked people all fighting to get out. The metal detector was trampled to the floor with a crash; people were pushing at him, shouting, forcing him back up the stairs in the swell of humanity.

"Let me through!" he yelled in Spanish. He propelled himself into the hysterical crowd. "Let me through!" Three crying girls shoved forward, shouting in French. Alex lunged past; found himself grappling a man with a frantic face. Howling obscenities, the man threw a punch that connected hard with his chin; Alex punched back without thinking and was past him in a second, battling his way against the tide. Willow was in there. Willow—

Others were fighting to get in, too—there were

485

shouts of "Kill the angels! Kill the angels!" as some of the Crusaders barreled through in a group. A dark-haired woman clutching a baby stood crying in fear, battered from both directions; he saw her start to go down. Despite his own frenzy to get inside, Alex couldn't ignore her— she and her child were seconds from being trampled.

Gritting his teeth, he got over to the woman and put his arms around her and her child, then fought his way across to the wall, shielding them. He could feel the woman shaking as he was pounded from side to side, rocked by the crowd. "It's OK. You'll be OK," he kept repeating in Spanish, and all he could think was, *Willow. Please, God, let her be alive.*

Finally the crowd thinned; an opening appeared on the stairs behind him. "You'll be all right now, *señora,*" he said quickly, stepping back. She threw herself at him, kissing his cheek.

"*Gracias, señor, gracias*—" She turned and ran, holding her child tight; she hadn't even made it to the first step before Alex was racing into the smoking cathedral. Several of the pews were crackling with flames; bodies lay scattered like abandoned toys, surrounded by hymnbooks and debris. The rioters were everywhere—pulling statues over, smashing paintings into splinters, shooting at the stone columns that marched down the center aisle. With a cheer, a gang hurled a pew through a stained-glass window; the glass crumpled into brightly colored fragments.

Alex drew his gun and made his way coughing to the front, checking out every body that he passed—terrified that one of them would be Willow, her green eyes empty and unseeing. *Oh, God, Willow, I'm sorry; I didn't mean anything I said. Please, just be alive—we'll work it out, I promise—*

In front of the altar near the charred and crumpled balustrade, he found Willow's phone lying on the floor, its screen cracked. He gripped it hard as he looked wildly around him. Had she dropped the phone while escaping? Or had she been so close to this bomb that there was barely anything left of her? He shoved the thought away. The office, maybe they'd searched the office—he ran toward it, weaving past the sprawled, lifeless bodies.

The office door had been shot open by rioters. Suddenly he was in a smoke-filled tunnel. He plunged forward, eyes streaming as he held his arm over his face.

"Willow!" he yelled hoarsely. "Willow, are you in here?" A bonfire crackled halfway down the corridor: oil paintings warping and twisting. He took a running jump and got past it somehow; half fell as he landed and kept going. When he reached the office door, more smoke was pouring out—the reception area and inner offices were all in flames, furniture lying on its side, files scattered.

"Willow!" he called again. He searched the smoke-filled den the best he could, crouching low and feeling his way around the floor. The heat was a solid wall; the smoke was in his throat, up his nose—fogging his brain, making it hard to think. A splintering crash came as a desk collapsed. Sparks flew, sizzling at his exposed hands and cheeks.

"Alex!" Kara had appeared, holding someone's jacket over her face as she tugged at his arm; her eyes looked like burning red coals. "We've got to get out of here—"

"No!" he choked out. "Willow—"

"She's *not here!* Do you want to die, you idiot?"

He resisted, but the smoke had made him weak. Kara half dragged him from the office. In the corridor, smoke lay heavy in both directions; taking the slightly better way, they found that the paintings had almost burned out. They got past the sputtering flames and burst back into the relative clarity of the cathedral. Police had arrived, struggling with the rioters—Alex saw someone go down as an officer clubbed him over the head.

"They won't like us any better," gasped Kara. "We've got to get to that side exit Seb told us about."

Alex was bent over, coughing. He shook his head, wiping his streaming eyes. "No, I've got to keep looking. She could be in here—"

Kara gripped his arms hard, her nails gouging at him. "Listen to me!" she hissed. "There is an angel *war* going on outside, and your team's on their own! If she and Seb are alive, they'll take care of each other. If they're not, it's too late, anyway—so come *on!*"

Even through his shirt, Kara was clutching him hard enough for her nails to break the skin. The pain cleared his head. She was right. He hated it, but she was right. With a last look at the bodies that lay scattered around them, Alex nodded. It felt like he was tearing his heart out and leaving it behind.

"Let's go," he said shortly.

As they escaped out the side door, he thought to do a scan, cursing himself for not doing it sooner. He lifted above his chakra points while they pounded back toward the Zócalo, searching feverishly while all around them shouting gangs were smashing windows, looting from stores, rocking cars over. He couldn't feel Willow's distinctive half-angel energy anywhere. So either she'd gotten away and was somewhere on these riot-choked streets, or she was dead. The thought was a cold fist clenching his soul. No, he refused to believe the latter. He refused.

Take care of her, Seb, he thought as they reached the Zócalo again. *Oh, man, I beg you — take care of her.*

There was no further time for thought. The riot raged through the square as Crusaders and Faithful battled it out; the police were there but not enough of them. Overhead, dozens of angels swooped like fiercely beautiful birds. In a bizarre way, the scene was reminiscent of the Love the Angels concert he and Willow had watched their first night here.

"Where's the team?" Alex couldn't see them anywhere.

Kara stood staring, her beautiful face smudged with smoke; she held a pistol half hidden under her bag. "I don't know! When I went in after you, they were still near the cathedral, but —"

She broke off as a flying angel exploded into nothing near the Palacio Nacional.

"There!" said Alex. With his own gun drawn, they

took off at a run, skirting the edges of the crowd. A ripple had passed through the angels at the death — they were now gliding in the same direction as he and Kara. Dozens of them, and he was still too far away to help the team.

Please don't all be sticking together in a group again, he prayed as they ran. Their only hope was to use guerrilla tactics and hide in the mob, picking off the angels one by one. They'd be massacred otherwise.

Almost as soon as Alex thought it, he spotted Sam's broad shoulders and blond hair. He grabbed Kara's arm, and they ducked into the throng. Reaching Sam, Alex found him gazing up at the sky, blue eyes narrowed.

"Where's the rest of the team?" he demanded, raising his voice above the shouts.

Sam leaned close, bellowing in his ear. "Don't worry! I've got 'em posted all over. We've got our phones on vibrate, too, so you can call us in when you need to. The designated meeting spot is over by the Palacio, near the main doors."

Relief made Alex's muscles weak. "Good work," he called back. "Really good work, Sam; I mean it."

Sam was squinting up at the sky again. "Yeah, it's this asshole lead I'm stuck working under — guess maybe he taught me a few things."

Alex clapped him on the shoulder. "Come on, we'll fan out, too," he said to Kara.

She nodded. Her eyes met his as she slipped away into the crowd, and he saw the same thought that was in his own mind: without the security information, their attack on the Council might now be doomed — but at least they could do something about what was happening here. Alex's jaw tightened. More than that, taking some kind of action might stop him from going insane right now.

Hidden by the battling crowd, Alex chose his moments carefully — only firing when he had a clear shot and trying not to get sucked into the fray. Soon he'd brought down three angels; as he aimed at a fourth, it burst into glittering leaves of light. *Nice one*, he thought to whoever had gotten it.

"Alex!" called a female voice.

Willow? His pulse thudded as he spun in place. But the woman struggling her way toward him was around thirty years old, with shoulder-length brown hair. For a confused second, Alex couldn't place her; then his muscles stiffened. Christ, he'd never expected to see Sophie Kinney again — would have been just as happy not to, the way she'd left Willow to die in Denver. What was she doing *here*?

With a flash of radiance, an angel dove at someone right behind her. Alex quickly took aim, and felt dark amusement as Sophie stopped short, eyes wide — she apparently thought he was about to blow her head off. He pulled the trigger; the creature vanished into fragments. Sophie gave an alarmed cry as the rush of energy from the kill swept past. It affected you like that at first. Then you got so used to it, you barely noticed anymore.

"An angel," Alex explained as he closed the distance between them.

Sophie gulped, nodded. "Yes, of course." She glanced

nervously at the boiling throng around them. "Alex, I need to talk to you."

Before he could reply, frenzied screams broke out, along with a pulsing, hissing noise. People shoved past, drenched and running. Alex grabbed Sophie's elbow, moving them hastily with the flow. More police had arrived, and they'd brought water cannons — jetting merciless blasts that were knocking people off their feet, making them scramble away on all fours. In a matter of minutes, everyone still here was going to be arrested and probably handed over to the angels. Jogging now, Alex veered toward the Palacio Nacional; through the dispersing crowd, he glimpsed Trish and Brendan, already heading that way. As he and Sophie ran, he pulled out his phone and punched a few buttons, calling the rest of the team in.

"I've rented a truck — it's parked nearby," panted Sophie.

He brought her aura into view, scanning it. No sign of angel burn. "Good," he said. "We'll need it, to get through these streets." And under everything was the constant heartbeat of Willow, *please be OK — please, please* . . .

As the team gathered, Alex frowned to see Wesley clutching his left arm. "What's wrong? Are you hurt?"

Wesley's face was an ashen gray. "Yeah, an angel was reaching for my life force. I shot it, but I think it tore away a little bit over my arm."

Alex's heart sank as he and Kara glanced at each other. He knew that doctors could do nothing — Wesley would regain the use of his arm as his aura tried to heal, or he wouldn't. It was how Cully had lost a leg. He tried to quell the immediate voice that told him this was his fault; that he shouldn't have had the team out on their own yet.

Wesley's expression had turned to a scowl, watching them. "What?" he demanded, his pointed eyebrows lifting. "It'll be better in time for the attack, right?"

"If we're lucky," said Alex. Their late-night conversation in the firing range came rushing back; hiding his doubt, he clasped Wesley's good shoulder. "Seriously, it could be totally fine—we just need to get you back so you can rest."

"Alex, I have got to take part in the attack—"

He broke off as Trish drew closer, her blue eyes concerned. "Wes, are you OK?"

Wesley nodded, his features softening a little. "I'm fine," he said. Like everyone, he got along well with Trish; Alex wouldn't be surprised if he'd even told her about his family having angel burn. Trish touched his arm, looking unconvinced.

"Man, that's gotta hurt," said Sam, wincing. Then he noticed Sophie and frowned. "Who's this?"

Alex saw that the police had arrived in full force now, sweeping through the square. "CIA," he said. "It's OK: we can trust her. Come on, we've got to get out of here."

Sophie's poise had returned, so that she was once again as cool and businesslike as he remembered. "My truck's parked nearby—let's go." She led the way, hurrying across the square.

Liz glanced around as the team followed. "Wait, where are Willow and Seb?"

"I don't know," Alex bit out, walking in long strides. "Still alive, I hope."

Liz started to say something else and stopped, looking stricken. Kara cleared her throat. "Hey, is Miss CIA who I think she is?" she asked, obviously changing the subject.

Alex had told Kara what had happened the day of the Second Wave — how Sophie had left Willow at the cathedral with no escape plan. "Yeah, that's her," he said grimly.

Sam was still glowering with suspicion. As they reached the street, he hauled Alex to one side. "That's *who*? She's not another half angel, is she?" he hissed.

And despite everything, Alex almost laughed. "No, Sam. She's not another half angel."

It took us over half an hour to walk to Tepito by back streets. The sandals pinched at my feet; I ignored them and walked even faster. When I peered over my shoulder, I could still see a reddish glow in the sky over the *centro*, hear the incessant blaring of sirens. Once there was a far-off explosion — a burning car, maybe. My breath clutched at the sound; for a second I almost went faint, seeing again the bodies in the cathedral. Seb glanced at me in concern, his fingers tightening around mine. We hadn't stopped holding hands since we'd started walking. Distantly, I supposed I should pull away, but there was no way I could have brought myself to right then. If it hadn't been for the warmth of Seb's hand, I'd have gone crazy.

Swallowing hard, I searched mentally for Alex again. At first there was nothing, and then faintly, through the chaos of my mind, came the familiar feel of his energy. It was like getting a staticky radio station, but it was there. He was alive. That was pretty much all I could tell, and in a way it was enough — though remembering the cold look that had been in his eyes before Seb and I went into the cathedral, my heart ached even more than before.

Stop it, I ordered myself harshly. *It was over between the two of you, anyway. If you doubted it, then that should have been your tip-off — because if he were still in love with you, there's no way he'd have let you go in there without telling you. None.*

The thought of it really being over between us — of Alex not being in love with me anymore — hurt far too much to dwell on it. I'd put the file that I'd stolen under my jean jacket, buttoning it into place, and now as we walked, its stiff cardboard jabbed against my rib-cage. Focus on that, I told myself, not Alex. And absolutely not on what happened in the cathedral. Focus on the file, the sandals hurting my feet, Seb's hand. Just focus on Seb's hand — the firm grip of it; how warm and caring it feels — and not bodies, sprawled helpless and bloody across the cathedral floor. Not the young priest, with half his head blown away and one eye staring up at the painted angels on the ceiling.

Definitely do not think about these things.

The sidewalk had become trash-ridden and more crowded with people now; the buildings to either side looked run-down and grimy. I could sense from Seb's sudden reluctance that we were almost there, though his body language was as laid-back as ever. He let go of my hand and put his arm around my shoulders.

"You're my girlfriend again, OK?" he said. "Don't look around you too much, no matter what you see. They don't like outsiders here. They think of them as prey."

I nodded, my throat almost too dry to speak. "No matter what I see?"

We turned a corner, and there was a marketplace ahead: a long, dingy street filled with lit stalls. I could see clothes for sale, jewelry and cell phones. Vendors were shouting at customers in Spanish, hawking their bargains. Seb's face as he took it all in was twisted with more bitterness than I'd ever seen on it before.

"This is the place where you can buy things," he said. "Drugs, weapons, the end of someone's life. Just ignore anything you see."

Entering Tepito was like ducking into a long, rustling tunnel formed by the plastic awnings of the market stalls. They seemed to close in around us just like the thudding rock music that was suddenly everywhere. There were stalls selling angel statues, angel key chains, angel T-shirts. DVDs of popular movies, lots with the titles misspelled. Racks of "designer" clothes with labels that were just as wrong. I glimpsed two men off to one side; one tucked something inside his jacket as money changed hands. White, flashing smiles.

I tore my gaze away and tried to pretend I was back in Pawtucket, scraping through the hangers of the town's single JCPenney, so bored that my eyes were glazing over. Even so, I couldn't help staring when we passed what looked like the entrance to a small chapel. There was a skeleton sitting on a throne inside, wearing a tiara and a frilly white wedding dress. Flowers and lit candles were spread in front of it. There was even a glass of wine sitting there, as if the skeleton might decide to have a drink.

"Santa Muerte," said Seb to my unspoken question. "Saint Death. Many people here worship her." He snorted slightly. "At least she's not wearing angel wings yet."

I knew how much Seb hated being back here; I kept getting flashes of memory from him that made me cringe. But as he walked, his lean body had an indifferent look — as if he belonged on these streets and still had his switch- blade in his pocket. His arm looped around my shoulders seemed just as relaxed. A few people glanced speculatively at us, took him in, and then looked away again.

And even though it was only Seb, who'd probably had his arm around me half a dozen times by now . . . something in me had gone very still at the nearness of him. Remembering the weird moment of jealousy that had come over me when Céline had kissed him — how for one second I'd actually hated her for the attraction that had shone so clearly in her eyes — I shook my head in confusion. God, what was wrong with me? I was still so conscious of the pain over Alex that it was like a boulder pressing on my heart. I couldn't deal with whatever this was now; my emotions were tattered enough already.

Seb didn't falter as he took us through a gap I hadn't even noticed between two stalls. With a rustle of plastic, we were suddenly out on another street, just as crowded and tunnel-like as the first. No wonder the locals could tell who didn't belong so easily; only someone who'd been raised in Tepito could prowl it with no hesitation. Seb stayed quiet as we wove through the stalls — and I knew that the violence and death we'd just witnessed made his memories at being back here even more raw. Scrounging food from a trash can because he hadn't eaten in days; hiding fearfully under a stall table, hoping his mother's boyfriend wouldn't find him. I swallowed. I'd seen images like this from him before, but never so loaded with emotion.

Suddenly I had that prickling feeling again, as if I was being watched, like I used to get so often back at the house — only this time when I looked, there was actually someone there. A stocky guy in his early twenties stood nearby, leering as he took in my short skirt. I held back a shudder; it felt like clammy hands pawing over me.

I realized my eyes had met his and looked hastily away, but it was too late — he came sauntering over, blocking our path. Though shorter than Seb, he was a lot broader, with beefy muscles. With a silky smile at me, he made a comment in Spanish. Seb answered tersely, trying to steer us past. The man grinned and sidestepped in front of us; my stomach turned at the smell of stale sweat and too much cologne. He looked lingeringly at my chest — and then with a smirk he reached out and stroked my cheek, saying something that sounded slimy no matter what the language.

I jerked away, but Seb was faster. He'd stiffened when the man spoke; now he grabbed his shirt and shoved him off me, low, furious Spanish spilling from his lips. With a lunge, the guy pushed him back, sending him staggering a few paces. They faced each other on the sidewalk, eyes locked.

"Seb, it's all right!" I clutched his arm. His muscles were rigid as he stared at the man; I could feel the hard swell of his bicep. "Whatever he said, it doesn't matter — please, just forget it."

The guy sneered and said something else. You didn't have to speak Spanish to get the gist: *Yeah, listen to your girlfriend. She knows I'd flatten you in a fight.*

I ignored him and took Seb's hand, squeezing it. "Come on, let's go." Trying to laugh, I added, "Look, I didn't even *understand* what he said. Really, just forget it. It's OK."

Seb's hand gripped mine as if it were a lifeline. Finally he let out a long breath. "Yes, you're right," he said softly.

Without another word, he put his arm around me again, and we walked away. The bustle of the marketplace around us continued without even a ripple; no one had paid any attention to the scene. The man called something after us, laughing.

Seb's jaw was still tense. I could feel how tightly he was holding himself together and knew it was all caving in on him: what had happened at the cathedral and now being back here. Of its own accord, my arm slipped around the lean warmth of his waist, and I pressed close against him. A shiver ran through me. Nothing made sense right then, especially whatever I was feeling — I just knew that I wanted so badly to comfort us both.

Seb looked quickly down at me. Neither of us spoke. I couldn't sense much from him — my own emotions were in too much turmoil. Everything seemed so surreal, like a dream I'd wake up from any second now: the plastic blue and yellow awnings, the bodies on the cathedral floor, the fight with Alex.

Alex. My mind flinched away as if I'd jabbed a bruise.

Don't go there, I thought as we continued through the rustling tunnels of Tepito. *Just . . . don't.*

Somehow Sophie battled her rented 4x4 truck through the *centro* — almost a full square mile of riots, cars on fire, howling gangs. Alex scanned nonstop as they drove, searching for Willow's energy. There was no sign of it anywhere. None.

Finally they reached a street where everything was quiet, apart from a single car that sat smoldering. Sophie pulled over and killed the engine. "What are you doing?" demanded Alex. "We've got to get Wesley home."

"No, I don't want to know where you live," said Sophie. "It's safest, in case I get caught."

"I'm OK," said Wesley from the back. He sat stiffly

against the seat; his voice sounded tense. "It doesn't really hurt. It's just numb."

"Come on," said Sophie, opening the truck door. "This is for your ears only, Alex."

He started to protest, but she was already striding away up the dark street. He swore under his breath and followed, banging the truck door shut after him. She stood waiting in a nearby doorway. She'd just lit a cigarette; its tip glowed red in the darkness.

"What's going on?" he demanded, joining her. "How did you find us?"

Sophie blew out a stream of smoke. "Ever since the Second Wave arrived, I've been putting out feelers, trying to locate you. A rogue angel down here heard about it and got in touch with me."

Alex leaned against the doorway, watching her. "A rogue? I haven't seen any signs at all of rogues in this city."

Sophie shook her head. "No, most of them have been assassinated by the angels — apparently there was a mass execution just after the Second Wave. But there's at least one left who they don't know about; she's working covertly with the Seraphic Council. Her suspicion was that you might be down here with a new team, because of all the recent angel deaths." She offered a tight smile. "Well done."

"Yeah, go me," said Alex shortly. "So why didn't this rogue get in touch with me herself?"

"She hasn't been able to find you yet; it's difficult

for her to get away without raising suspicion. But I had a feeling you might be in the Zócalo tonight, with that demonstration going on."

That's not why we were there, he started to say, but Sophie was still talking, her tone urgent. "Alex, listen to me — it's vital that the Seraphic Council be killed. If they are —"

"Is this seriously what you came thousands of miles to tell me?" he broke in. "Look, we know all about it — the Council, the reception, everything. That's why we're in Mexico City in the first place."

Sophie didn't miss a beat. "Good, that makes things easier." She unzipped her purse and pulled out an envelope. "Here," she said, handing it to him. "There's a memory stick in there with all the details you need. You've also got ten VIP passes to the reception; they'll get you and your team onto the top floor of the Torre Mayor."

Slowly, Alex reached out and took the envelope. He could feel wallet-size plastic cards inside. "Where did you get this?"

"From my contact. Her name is Charmeine, and she used to know Nate; she worked with him back in the U.S. until he joined the CIA. She'll help you any way she can." She nodded at the envelope. "Like I said, all the details you need are in there."

All the details they needed. Alex tapped the envelope against his palm, frowning. "So it sounds like *Charmeine* was pretty confident you'd find us in time," he said at last. "Was there a backup plan?"

"No one was confident about anything, believe me," said Sophie. "And no, there's no backup plan — she's the only rogue left; if she tried to act on her own, she'd be killed before she even put a dent in the Council. A trained team of Angel Killers is our only chance."

Alex snorted. *Our* — yeah, just as if Sophie had been down here helping them out from the start. "So what's the proof that Charmeine's definitely a rogue and this isn't a trap?" he said.

"She's legit; I'm sure of it." Sophie took another puff of her cigarette; the smoke looked ghostly in the dark. "She knows things about Project Angel that only Nate could have told her."

"Angels are psychic," he reminded her dryly.

"Not *that* psychic without touching you. Listen, I took some convincing, too, but she was definitely friends with Nate — she has all the inside information on exactly how we attacked the gate when the Second Wave arrived. Plans, details, everything. The only way she could know all of that is if Nate told her. And if she wasn't on our side, then they'd have tried to stop us at the time."

"OK," said Alex finally, sticking the envelope into his pocket. "We'll check it out — compare it with what we've already got." Which wasn't *that* much, but at least they had the classified blueprints to double-check things against.

"Yes, do that," said Sophie. "You'll find that it's all accurate."

Alex nodded without comment. But Jesus, if this was for real . . . then it was the answer to all their prayers. It also meant that if Willow hadn't survived, her death had been for nothing. He shoved the thought away before it could drown him.

"And I'll be there, too, for the attack," added Sophie. She stubbed out her cigarette against the concrete wall. "I'll meet you in the lobby of the Torre Mayor before you go up, and do whatever I can to help."

"Wow, really? You mean you're not going to get whisked off to a safe location this time?"

Sophie's expression didn't change. "No, not this time. Here." There was a jingling sound as she pulled the 4x4's keys from her purse and handed them to him. "My hotel's just a few blocks away — you can drop me off in the truck and get your team back home. Keep it until after the attack. I only rented it in case I found you all."

Alex accepted the keys; as his fingers closed over them, he thought of something else. "Where's Willow's mother? Have you got her someplace where she's protected?"

Sophie's brown eyebrows shot up. "Have I what? Alex, didn't you see on the news? Willow's mother and aunt were killed in an arson attack the night of the Second Wave."

"But I thought . . ." Alex stared at her in the dim light. "You mean that wasn't staged?"

"Not by me," she replied, zipping her bag shut. "I've hardly had any resources since the Second Wave; I've been working on my own. To pull off something of that scale would be totally beyond me." She glanced at him. "Why? Is there reason to believe it *was* staged?"

"No, I guess not," said Alex after a pause. He had no idea what this meant but wasn't about to go into the details of it with Sophie. At least Willow had been able to sense that her mother was OK, wherever she was.

They made the short drive in silence, with Alex driving this time. The team sat quietly, their faces carefully neutral in the rearview mirror, though he knew they must be dying to hear what had been said. When they pulled up in front of Sophie's hotel, she cleared her throat. "I added something else to that memory stick, too," she said. "A sort of proposal for you. I'm hoping we won't need it after the attack, but it's what I've been working on since the Second Wave. Anyway, see what you think."

"All right," said Alex, keeping his tone noncommittal. "So we'll see you in a few days, I guess."

"Yes, you will." Sophie hesitated, gripping her purse with both hands; he could tell she wished they were speaking alone again. "And, Alex, look — I know we have our differences, but you're the finest AK I've ever seen, bar none. I'll be honored to do whatever I can to help."

"Yeah, OK," he muttered, embarrassment battling with dislike. Sophie could say whatever she wanted; he was still never going to warm to her.

After Sophie had disappeared into the hotel, Alex got out, too, leaving the 4x4 idling. "Drive them home, OK?" he said through the passenger window to Kara. "And start checking this stuff out." He gave her the envelope as she emerged from the backseat of the truck.

"What's in it?" she asked, gazing down at it in her hand.

"VIP passes and all the security details we need for the attack. Don't ask me about it now," he added. "I'll tell you when I get home." Half hidden by the truck, he checked his pistol. "Can you give me some of your cartridges? I'm running low."

Kara took out her gun and ejected the magazine; her eyes were worried as she handed it over. "Where are you going?"

He clicked her cartridges into his own magazine, his thumb working with a quick, steady rhythm. "To try to find Willow," he said tersely. He tucked his gun back into its holster. "If she and Seb are at the house, call me, OK? The second you get there."

"I will, but, Alex, those riots are still going strong—"

"Here," he broke in, handing her the empty magazine. "Get Wesley home."

"It's no use arguing with you about this, is it?" Kara's face looked pained with concern. He didn't reply, and she leaned forward and kissed his cheek. "All right. Please take care of yourself."

He nodded. As Kara climbed into the truck with a flash of long legs, he turned and jogged down the shadowy street toward the *centro*, where he could still see orange blazes licking at the sky. He scanned nonstop as he went, searching for Willow's energy, praying with every second that passed that he'd suddenly feel it. Their fight seemed inconceivable now—something he'd done in another lifetime. OK, she was close to Seb; maybe she was even attracted to him. So what? He himself was the one she was in love with, and he *knew* that. How could he have been so jealous, so stupid?

The city had taken on a nightmarish feel of flames and shouting; the sound of breaking glass and sirens came from somewhere nearby. *Oh, God, babe, please be alive,* thought Alex as he raced toward the chaos and the looting. If Willow had died, his heart would have died, too. Though he knew he'd still try to save the world from the angels — for his family and Willow's family and everyone else who'd been hurt by them — for him, it would be too late.

The world would already have ended.

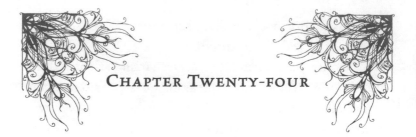

Chapter Twenty-four

FINALLY WE LEFT the plastic tunnels of the marketplace behind and came to a dark street full of warehouses and boarded-up buildings. I felt Seb scan briefly; decide it was safe. "This is it," he said, heading down the side of one of the warehouses.

Half the streetlights weren't working. I stepped carefully as I followed him, squinting to see where we were going. A rustling noise came from some nearby weeds. A cat, maybe. I hoped. To one side was a tall chain-link fence, with razor glints of barbed wire curling over the top.

Seb led me to a dim corner, where the barbed wire lay flattened for a foot or two. "Can you get over?" he asked.

I eyed the fence. "You'd better go first," I said. "Then I can land on you if I fall." I wasn't totally kidding; high heels weren't ideal for things like this.

Seb nodded and grasped the fence; it rattled as he climbed up and swung himself over. He dropped the final few feet, landing nimbly on the cracked concrete. I took out the file from beneath my jacket and slid it under the fence. Then I followed, angling my sandaled feet awkwardly in the metal diamonds. Maneuvering myself over the top, I was hotly conscious of my short skirt, and just how much leg I was showing.

Finally my feet touched the ground again. Seb was barely visible — just his white shirt and the slant of his cheekbones catching the faint light. "It's over here," he said. He went to the back of the warehouse, where I could just make out a pile of trash lying against the metal wall: an old sofa, some broken office chairs, scraps of plywood.

He glanced at me. "I'm sorry — we have to crawl. There's a loose panel behind this we can get through."

I thought of the rustling noise from the weeds, but I nodded. "That's OK. How did you ever find this place?"

Seb was already on his hands and knees, edging behind the sofa. It lay at an angle against the warehouse, forming a sort of entrance. "Just poking around, after I escaped from the orphanage," he replied, his voice muffled. "I used to have lots of hiding places, all around the city. Most of the buildings are torn down now, though."

A metallic creaking noise, then a long pause.

"Seb?" I called, hugging the file to my chest.

The sound of a match striking. "Yes, it's all right," he called back. "Come on."

I buttoned the file into my jacket again, then knelt

down and started to crawl. The old velvet sofa smelled moldy; gravel dug into my palms and knees. Ahead, a sliver of light beckoned from the warehouse wall, where a piece of corrugated metal didn't quite lie flush.

The panel lifted as I crawled toward it — Seb, holding it open for me. I squeezed through past his arm. Once inside, I got to my feet and brushed myself off, looking around in amazement. The light came from a cluster of lit candles that seemed to be growing from the concrete floor. A sleeping bag lay beside them, along with a stack of children's paperbacks with worn spines. I picked up the top one, surprised that I recognized the cover — *The Incredible Journey*. Our fourth-grade teacher had read that out loud to us. I carefully placed it back, straightening it so it lined up with the others again.

Seb stood with his hands in his pockets, looking embarrassed. "When I was a boy, I stayed here often," he said with a shrug. "I stole all the books," he added.

I cleared my throat. "It's OK, I think you get a special pass for stealing books. From what I hear, it's something book lovers would understand." It felt like we were both treading water to stay above the surface, avoiding all the topics that might drag us under. I pulled out the file and laid it on the sleeping bag. "What *is* this place?" I gazed into the shadows beyond the candlelight. "Is it just abandoned?"

"No, someone owns it." Seb bent down and snapped a candle from the floor; it came away like a small tree, with waxy roots spreading out. "Come, I'll show you."

Our footsteps echoed on the concrete. I couldn't hold back a gasp as the first face appeared from the gloom. Statue after stone statue stood scattered throughout the warehouse, like some weird silent cocktail party. Propped up against the walls were several huge stained-glass windows — the candlelight flickered at their panels, sending a rainbow of colors sparking around us.

"Is this all from a church?" I touched the cold stone face of the nearest statue: a man in robes, his expression kindly. As if he might have some answers to everything that was going on, if only he could speak.

Seb was beside me holding up the candle. He nodded. "Even before the Church of Angels really got started here, a few smaller churches were taken over by angel worshippers. I think someone must have stored these things here then, to keep them safe maybe. But it seems forgotten now." He lifted a shoulder. "Perhaps whoever stored it died or got angel burn."

As I let my hand fall from the statue, I saw a small room built against the opposite wall. "What's in there?"

"Just an office," said Seb. "There's a bathroom, too," he added. "It used to have running water; maybe it still does."

"Really?" I could hear the relief in my voice. "Can I borrow the candle?"

The black shadows of the bathroom shrank away in the candlelight as I entered. By some miracle there *was* still running water, and even a little toilet paper. A few minutes later, I stood washing my face in the tiny sink as

I tried to get the worst of the grime and the smeared eye makeup off. Gazing at my candlelit image, for a second all I could think of was that slumber-party game Bloody Mary. A chill prickled over me. I tried to push it away and dried my hands as best I could on the jacket.

When I returned to the sleeping bag, I found Seb examining the file in the glow of the candlelight. I put my candle with the others, then kicked off my sandals and sat next to him, curling my legs under me as I looked down at the Spanish words. The document he was reading seemed to be an e-mail printout.

"Is there anything there?" I asked.

Seb nodded, rubbing his jaw as he turned a page. "Yes, a lot. We've got what Alex wanted, and there's more, too — floor plans, information about the reception. Even the code for the stairwell door." He closed the file and put it to one side. "Your instincts were very good, *querida*."

I held back a shiver as I remembered the church office — the banging noise that I'd completely disregarded. "So were yours, to get us out of there in time."

Seb looked down, and I knew he didn't want to think about the cathedral any more than I did. His hand tightened to a fist, tapping against the sleeping bag. "Willow, I'm sorry," he said after a moment. "When we met that man in the marketplace —" He broke off; I could sense his turmoil. "I haven't let anyone get to me like that in so long. I should have just gotten both of us away from there —"

"Seb, no, stop," I said, touching his arm. "I know how

hard it is for you, being back here. I could feel it, every step of the way."

"It doesn't matter," he said tersely. "I should have better control than to almost get in a fight with some *cabrón* who means nothing—especially when I'm taking you through Tepito."

I shifted on the sleeping bag, watching him. "So . . . what did he say?"

Seb went silent. One of the candle flames flickered. "He asked if I'd like to share you," he said finally. "And the way he looked at you—I don't think I've ever wanted to hurt someone so much in my life."

"I'm glad you didn't," I said softly. Not that I'd care if anything had happened to that pile of sleaze, but to Seb . . . I swallowed. "Anyway, don't blame yourself—we were both upset. After what happened—"

I stopped, my chest tightening as I saw it all again, in gut-wrenching detail. I couldn't hold it back any longer, and a trembling breath that was weirdly like a laugh escaped me. "Oh, God, Seb. They're supposed to want to *help people.* . . ."

His throat moved; he took me in his arms without speaking. Burying my head against his firm shoulder, I clung to him and wished I could wipe out everything we'd seen. I knew I'd never be able to, never—even the tiniest details would be with me forever. The priest staring at the ceiling with his one eye flashed through my mind, and I wondered dully why I wasn't crying.

"Most of the Crusaders can't have known about it,"

said Seb roughly. "It had to be a—a smaller group who planned it, working on their own."

I knew he was probably right; it didn't help much. "What's the use of being psychic if we can't stop something like that?" My voice sounded distant, as if I were speaking from outside of myself.

"I know," whispered Seb against my hair. I could feel his pain; it was as helpless as my own. "But that's not how it works; you know it's not."

Inside of me, my angel was straining for his. I let her fly free, and Seb's angel was there almost immediately—radiant and powerful, his beautiful face etched with our shared sadness.

The light from our ethereal bodies cast a tender glow in the warehouse as we hovered, facing each other. Somehow just seeing Seb's angel was a balm; it soothed the very core of me in a way that I didn't even understand.

His eyes on mine, Seb's angel reached out his hand. And this time I didn't hesitate—I stretched out my own angelic hand to him.

Our fingers touched in a burst of light. I caught my breath at the sensation, watching in wonder as our hands merged in a blue-white glow. The details of the cathedral attack mercifully receded, leaving just Seb and me, and this feeling that was like nothing on earth—having no boundaries at all between us, our energy turned one.

This is way too intimate, I thought belatedly. But I couldn't have taken my hand away for anything. Seb's angel and I gazed at each other in awe; slowly, he stroked his hand up my arm, and without quite knowing how I was doing the same to him — feeling the slight resistance against my fingers as they caressed their way through his energy, the warm shiver in me as he explored my own.

In our human forms below, Seb and I had both gone very still. He pulled away a little as his gaze searched mine, the golden flecks in his hazel eyes clear in the candlelight. I was trembling. I could feel the depth of his love for me, how much he longed to hold me in a way that wasn't brotherly at all. Somewhere far away where I couldn't face it was the pain over Alex — but right now there was only Seb, my friend Seb, who I cared about so much that it almost hurt, and whose angel hands were making me feel things I'd never felt before in my life. In that moment I didn't know whether I loved him only as a friend or something more — I just knew that I never wanted him to stop touching me, never.

I'm not sure which of us moved first. I saw Seb swallow; one or maybe both of us leaned forward . . . and then somehow I was running my hands through his loose curls, and his lips were on mine, so warm and gentle that I was falling.

Time faded to nothing as our mouths teased each other — tiny, sipping kisses that sent electricity pulsing through me. Seb's curls were so soft under my fingers, just as soft as I'd always imagined, and I could feel the prickle of stubble near his mouth; the strength of his hand as he lightly cupped it around the back of my neck. He murmured my name, pulling me to him. The kiss slowed, deepening into heat as our mouths opened together, exploring each other. Seb's arms were locked around me as I pressed tight against him, stroking his firm back and feeling his heartbeat pounding with mine, and if I could have gotten even closer to him, I would have — and meanwhile our angels were still touching hands above, and there was nothing in the world but this kiss, this kiss that was the most amazing thing I'd ever felt.

The minutes passed. We sank onto the sleeping bag, our mouths still drinking hungrily at each other. Whispering something in Spanish, Seb kissed my neck, then my mouth again, his hand caressing its way up my side . . . and I wanted it to feel as wonderful as it had at first, but little by little, unease was growing in me. Seb's lips weren't the ones I was used to; his body against mine felt different. I shoved the thought away — I refused to think about Alex now; I didn't want to think about anything; I just wanted to keep losing myself in this warmth, this moment — but then slowly, slowly, the kiss ended.

Seb raised his head, looking down at me.

And it all felt so wrong suddenly that I wanted to cry.

The weight of what I had done came crashing down on me. I sat up shakily as our angels rushed back to us. "Seb, I — oh, my God, I'm so sorry —"

He sat up, too. His mouth looked bruised where I'd just been kissing it. "Why are you sorry?" But from the expression in his eyes, he knew.

I hated saying the words; they tasted like bile. "I'm

not in love with you. I shouldn't have done this — it was a mistake."

Seb hesitated. Almost in slow motion, he touched my hair, just as he'd done the first day that we'd met. "You are in love with me, a little," he said softly. "I can feel it."

I shook my head, hardly even aware I was doing it. "No. I love you as a friend. That's all." My words came out quiet and certain. Because no matter how wrong it had been, kissing Seb had done one thing at least: rid my mind of any confusion I might have had. Everything seemed so clear now, as if the world had just leaped into sharp focus.

His throat moved. The candles still burned around us, their warm golden light playing on the wall. "Maybe this was just too soon — maybe someday you'll feel different." He reached for my hand and gripped it tightly, his emotions raw on his face. "I've loved you for so long, Willow. It's always been you, my whole life."

My heart was breaking. I wished so much that I *were* in love with Seb; that it was possible for me to say that someday I might be. But it wasn't. Whatever strange alchemy it is that makes you fall in love with one person and not another just wasn't there for me with him. Maybe I'd been picking up on his feelings and mistaking them for my own a little — but now, when I was really looking at it, I could see the truth.

Gently, I disentangled my fingers from his and cleared my throat. "You know, my dream was right," I said. "I hate the thought of ever being without you, Seb. You're one of the most important people in my life. And you deserve an amazing girl who's just — so completely in love with you. But I don't feel that way. I'm sorry."

A long pause spun out around us. "You don't have to apologize," said Seb at last. "You never have to apologize."

I pushed my hands through my hair, leaving it in wild spikes. "I do! I shouldn't have kissed you, not when I wasn't sure —"

"It was very nice, though," he said, trying to smile. "I think I'll manage to forgive you."

Maybe, but I'd never forgive myself. Oh, God, why did everything have to be such a mess? Unconsciously, I touched my neck — it felt bare and wrong without the crystal pendant Alex had given me hanging from its slender chain. Remembering his coolness as Seb and I had gone into the cathedral, I wrapped my arms around my knees and rested my cheek on them, wishing so much that I'd seen a hint, just a hint, that he still felt the same way about me.

"Yes, he still feels the same," said Seb quietly.

I looked up quickly, my heart tightening with sudden hope. Seb sat gazing down at the sleeping bag; when he felt my eyes on him, he glanced up and shrugged. "I saw him, when you weren't watching. The look on his face —" His mouth twisted. "He's still in love with you, just too stubborn to back down yet."

I should have been relieved — instead, staring at Seb, dread started growing in me like a dark, tangled vine.

"There's something else, isn't there?" I said. "Whatever it was that you said you'd tell me later, back at the cathedral."

Seb let out a ragged breath. Leaning back against the corrugated metal of the warehouse wall, he scraped his hands over his face. I could feel his reluctance like a weight on my throat.

"Seb?" I whispered

"*Querida*, please believe me," he said finally. "This is the last thing in the world I want to tell you."

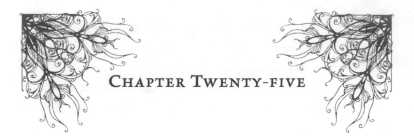

CHAPTER TWENTY-FIVE

A LONG TIME LATER, I was lying on my back on the sleeping bag, staring up into the dark shadows. Seb still sat against the wall. The flickering light had drawn in around us as the cluster of candles burned lower. One of them had sputtered out altogether, dying with little hissing noises.

I still couldn't sense Alex very clearly, no matter how much I wanted to. I kept searching for him and feeling that he was alive, but I was getting nothing about his emotions. His energy was there, though — his warm, familiar energy that I loved so much — and I ran my thoughts gently over it, wondering what he was thinking, whether he was still angry with me.

After what Seb had told me, I hoped that he was. That he never got over being angry, ever.

"I'm sorry," said Seb again, for about the tenth time. "I really didn't know. When you first asked me, I was sure that we didn't, but . . ." He trailed off.

"It's OK," I whispered. I could hardly even imagine how Alex would have reacted if I'd tried to break things off with him because Seb had told me that we cause angel burn — I think he might have tried to kill Seb.

Even though it all fit. Oh, God, it all fit — his headaches, his migraines. The worst ones always seemed to happen just a few hours after the two of us had been close together. I had a flash of lying on his bed in his arms and closed my eyes tight against the sudden pain. I wiped my cheek with the heel of my hand and tried to marshal my thoughts.

"The Council attack is the most important thing, for all of us," I said. "So when we go back to the house, I can't touch Alex, not at all — I have to stay as far away from him as I can. If he got a migraine during the attack—" I broke off; the thought was too terrible to contemplate.

Seb's gaze on me was very still. "And if he tries to make up with you? What will you tell him is the reason for not touching him?"

"I don't know," I said softly. Alex had always refused to even consider the idea that I might cause angel burn. No matter what was happening with his aura, I knew he was unlikely to start believing it now. Even if he managed to view his own aura and see the damage, I could just hear him saying that it didn't matter; that we couldn't be certain it was because of me.

"I don't know," I repeated — but really, there was only one option, wasn't there? My brain flinched away from the thought of it. "Maybe — maybe he'll still be angry at me, and then it won't even be an issue. We can just keep avoiding each other."

And after the attack — if by some miracle we managed to succeed, and there was an "after" to think about — I could never be with Alex again. I just prayed that whatever damage I'd already done to him would get better in time; that it wasn't permanent. I felt cold even in my jean jacket as I stared up into the shadows. How ironic, though. I'd just told Seb that we could never be together, but if we hurt humans with our touch, then there was no one else in the world for either of us, was there? Literally, no one else in the world. And so perhaps we *would* end up getting together someday — years from now, maybe, once this pain had faded a little — but I knew it would never be anything like what I'd had with Alex. Nothing else would ever be like that. Not in my whole life.

"No," said Seb, his voice fierce.

I glanced over at him. He sat staring at me angrily, his hand a tight fist on his thigh. "You were right: what happened was a mistake," he said. "If it happens again between us, it won't be because we're the only two half angels. It will be because you're in love with me, as much as you are now with Alex. I don't want you any other way — I'd rather be your brother forever."

"Seb . . ." I didn't know what to say. Oh, God, now I'd hurt Seb, on top of everything else.

He shook his head. "This isn't the time," he said shortly. "But I know what we could have together, Willow. And I won't take anything less."

I let out a breath. "Look, I'm sorry. It was just a stupid, random thought, that's all. You weren't supposed to hear it." I didn't blame Seb for feeling the way he did but knew it meant that nothing would ever happen between us again in that case, not even decades in the future. I covered my eyes with both arms, suddenly feeling beyond weary; battered by the past few days. "Can we just . . . not talk about this anymore?" I asked in a small voice.

I sensed rather than saw his cool shrug. "We'll never talk about it again if you don't want."

I didn't answer. If Seb was still hurt, I seriously couldn't deal with it right now.

We didn't speak for a long time. Another candle choked out, casting us into a deeper gloom that seemed hideously symbolic. I could sense my angel inside of me and had a flash of hatred for her so intense that it curled my stomach. How could I ever forgive myself for hurting Alex? How could I go through life, knowing my touch would damage anyone I got too close to?

Anyone I got too close to. The thought froze me so that I could hardly breathe, and I sat up with a gasp. No. No.

"Willow?" Seb moved quickly from the wall; the sleeping bag made a soft noise as he knelt beside me.

"Mom," I whispered. "Seb, what if—what if I was making her angel burn worse, all those years?" I covered my face with my hands as I began to shake — seeing her sitting in her chair, her dreamy smile. And all the hours I had spent sitting next to her: holding her hand, stroking her arm. Each memory was like being kicked in the stomach. Oh, God, I couldn't live with this; I just couldn't — if it was true, then I didn't even want to live anymore.

"Stop, *querida*, stop —" I felt Seb start to take me into his arms.

Somehow what had happened between us made it impossible for me to touch Seb now — even though he was the only person I *could* touch. I pulled away. "Don't! I can't — I can't let you hold me anymore —"

"Willow!" Cradling my head in his hands, he forced me to look at him. His expression was almost haggard with worry. "Listen to me. Tonight didn't happen — I'm still your brother. Please let me help."

I hugged myself, struggling with everything I had to hang on. "Nothing can help," I said finally. My voice sounded dead and buried. "Nothing, not ever again."

I could feel Seb's compassion, so tender that something inside me gave way. He put his arms around me again as I started to cry, drawing me close against his chest. I didn't have the energy to resist this time — didn't even want to anymore. I let him hold me, and I cried against his warm shoulder while the shadows danced on the wall beside us.

Eventually I must have fallen into an exhausted sleep. When I woke up later, Seb and I were both lying down. My eyes felt bruised and puffy. The crying hadn't helped — my head throbbed with thoughts that hurt too much to dwell on. Only one candle was going now, its flame sputtering weakly.

Seb was still holding me; he'd fallen asleep, too. In the dim light, I stared at his sleeping face — at the mouth that I'd kissed so passionately — and knew with a sinking heart that he was wrong. Tonight had happened. And because of it, the dearest friendship of my life had been soured. Seb could never really be my brother again.

I didn't have the boy I loved, and I didn't have my best friend, either.

The next morning as Seb and I walked back to the house from the Metro station, I could hear the tinkling, glittery sound of glass being swept up. Storekeepers were out taping sheets of cardboard over broken windows; burned-out cars sat here and there like weird sculptures. But shoppers strode by as usual on the sidewalk, and in the street, cars and taxis swept past. Already, life was returning to what passed for normal here in Mexico City in the wake of the Second Wave.

Though Seb and I tried to talk the same as we always had, awkwardness had settled between us like thick fog from the moment we'd woken up that morning. As we reached the street where the house was, Seb stopped suddenly, touching my arm. "Willow, please — can't we just forget it happened and be like we were before?" His hazel eyes were deep wells of worry. "We kissed; that's all. It doesn't have to change what we are to each other, not unless we let it."

I shivered, not looking at him. All I could think of was Alex. I hated my hands as they gripped my elbows, knowing that I'd hurt him with them. Except it wasn't just my *hands*, was it? No, it was all of me, like poisonous venom oozing through my veins. Every time I'd caressed Alex's body, kissed his lips, I'd caused him harm.

"I'll try," I said at last.

"*Querida* —"

"Don't —" I broke off and shut my eyes hard against the sudden pain; it was a fist gripping my heart. "Don't call me that," I said.

"All right," said Seb softly. And I knew that this time he meant it, and that the easy banter we'd once shared was gone. Though it made me feel ten times worse than before, in a weird way it also seemed like no more than what I deserved.

Seb sighed and jammed his hands in his pockets as we started walking again. "Don't blame yourself," he said, sounding tired. "You're the kindest person I know — you would never have touched him if you'd realized."

Even now, he could read my thoughts so easily. *So what?* I wanted to say. *I've still been causing only God knows what damage to the boy I love more than anything.* I didn't bother saying the words out loud. And when it came to Mom, I couldn't think about it at all. I just . . . couldn't.

We neared the house; it looked as vacant as always.

I hesitated outside for a moment, the cool Mexico City breeze stirring my hair. I had the file buttoned up under my jacket again, and I touched its cardboard outline against my chest. I wanted to see Alex so badly, and at the same time I dreaded it more than anything in the world.

Please still be angry at me, I thought. *Please — that'll make it so much easier for us both.* Otherwise, I could hardly stand the thought of what I was going to have to do.

"Seb, will you help, if I need you to?" I asked finally, my voice faint.

"Yes, I'll help." But he looked troubled, and I could feel that he hated this almost as much as I did.

When we went inside, Kara was sitting at the kitchen table with her head slumped on one hand, an untouched cup of coffee in front of her. Her chin jerked up as she saw us, her brown eyes going wide.

"Hi," I said. "We, um — we ran into some trouble." Remembering the blasts that had trembled through the cathedral — the screams, the bodies — my voice came out sounding thin and unreal.

Kara slowly shook her head; she hadn't stopped staring at us. "Oh, my God, you're really OK," she murmured. To my surprise, a broad smile grew across her face. "Listen, I know someone who is going to be very pleased to see you!" She leaped up, sending her chair skidding. "Alex!" she bellowed in the direction of the boys' dorm. "Alex, Willow's here!"

Apprehension and longing filled me. I swallowed and took the file out from under my jacket, setting it on the kitchen table. Though Seb was standing several feet away, I could sense his concern.

Kara turned to me with a relieved grin. "He was out all night looking for you. He just got back about an hour ago — I've never been so worried about him, not even after Jake died. He was sure you'd been killed —"

"Willow!" Alex burst into the kitchen. His gorgeous face was bruised and burnt; there were dark circles under his eyes — and his aura had exactly the damage in it that Seb had described. I had a heart-wrenching glimpse of tarnished blues and golds, and then Alex scooped me up into his arms before I could stop him. "Oh, Jesus, you're alive —" I could feel him shaking as he held me, and for a helpless moment I couldn't stop myself from hugging him back. I pressed my head tight against his warm neck, the hard strength of his shoulder. *Alex.*

"Willow, I'm sorry — oh, God, babe, I'm so sorry —" He buried his fingers in my hair as he kissed my cheeks, my eyes, my mouth. "I've been such an idiot. Please, please forgive me."

Kara had tactfully melted away somewhere. Seb still stood near the table, his face expressionless — and I knew to my absolute dismay that I was going to need him here to make this believable.

It took every molecule of strength that I had to pull myself away from Alex. "Don't, um . . . don't do that, please," I said, taking a step back.

He froze as if I'd just cracked a slap across his face. I saw his throat move. "Willow, I . . . I know I've been acting like a controlling jerk. You're right to still be angry at me—if you never forgave me, I'd deserve it. But—" He glanced at Seb with a sudden frown and gently put his hand on my shoulder. "Look, let's go someplace private, where we can talk—" He broke off as I shook away from his touch.

"No, don't. I mean . . . thanks, but there's no point."

"No point?" he echoed, staring at me.

I tried to make my voice sound normal, as if I weren't dying inside. "No, there isn't," I said. "Alex, I'm really sorry, but . . ."

He looked from me to Seb. His eyes widened. "No," he breathed. "No way."

"I'm sorry," I said again. "It just happened." And the fact that something really had happened made my cheeks flush guiltily. I used it, hurrying on before I could weaken. "Last night we were hiding out, and . . . somehow we started kissing. One thing kind of led to another, and . . ." I trailed off; I couldn't finish. The frozen look on Alex's face—the stunned hurt, the anguished disbelief—was killing me.

"One thing led to another," he repeated.

"Yeah," I got out. "I still really care about you, but . . . I just can't help what I feel for him. I'm sorry."

He slowly shook his head, like a dazed animal. "What are you saying? Are you telling me you and he—?" He moved so quickly I hardly saw it; suddenly he had Seb slammed up against the wall with a thud that echoed through the kitchen. He spat something in Spanish; the muscles in his arms were rock hard. Seb didn't move, didn't try to defend himself.

"Alex, no!" I tugged uselessly at his arm. "Please stop — it's just the way I feel; I can't help it!"

He and Seb were inches apart; Alex's jaw was rigid as he stared at him. Finally he let go of Seb with a shove.

"So let me get this straight," he said. "While I was out all night in the middle of riots looking for you, going out of my mind, thinking maybe you were lying somewhere dead — you and Seb were —" He broke off as a muscle in his jaw leaped, then he turned away and raked a hand through his hair, breathing hard. When he spoke again, his words were flat, dead. "OK, got it. That's really good to know. Thanks for coming here to tell me what a fool I've been."

"Alex . . ." I was close to tears; Seb must have sensed I was wavering. He put his arms around me from behind, drawing me close. I leaned against his chest, and wrapped my arms around his to hide my trembling.

"It's all right, *chiquita*," he said, kissing my head. "Sorry, man," he added to Alex. "These things happen, you know?"

Chiquita. It was Spanish for "babe." Alex stiffened, his nostrils flaring, so that for a second I thought he was going to punch Seb even with me in front of him.

"No," he said suddenly. "No, I am *not* just going to stand here and —"

He grabbed my shoulders and pulled me away from Seb, his hands tight on my arms. "Look me in the eyes,

Willow," he said in a low voice. "Look me in the eyes and tell me that you really don't love me as much as I love you. I don't believe it—I don't care *what* you did with him; I don't believe it—"

I loved him so totally that I knew he must see it written all over my face, must feel it even through my clothes, burning out of me like the sun. In another second I was going to blurt out the truth. Alex would argue with me; he'd tell me that his sick-looking aura had nothing to do with me at all—that his migraines were only a coincidence. I wouldn't be able to resist him a second time. I'd just curl up in his arms for the rest of my life, like I was a fraction away from doing now.

And then all of us, the whole world, might be lost.

From somewhere deep within, I found the strength to say words that would make him hate me forever. "It's true," I said. "I never told you, but the dream I had about the Council—Seb was in it, too. I dreamed about him before I even met him. It's why I wanted to come here, because I knew it's where he would be."

Slowly, Alex's hands fell from my shoulders. "What?"

"I dreamed about him," I said levelly. "That's how he found us; he saw my dream in my shirt. And in my dream, I didn't want to leave you, but I knew that I never wanted to be without Seb. That . . . he was the one I really loved." Except for the most important words of all, everything I was saying was true—and I knew Alex heard it in my voice. He stared wordlessly at me.

My throat was sand. "I do care about you," I said

again. "I'll never regret anything that happened between us. But Seb and I are both half angel, and . . . I just can't fight that."

Seb put his arm around me. "Sorry, man," he repeated to Alex with a shrug. "She didn't want to hurt you, but I guess it's just fate, you know?" And even though I could sense how much he wasn't enjoying this, I had a stab of hatred for him, that he was playing his part so well.

The expression on Alex's face made me feel like I was being battered inside. To keep myself from throwing my arms around him and taking it all back, I reached up and gripped Seb's hand as hard as I could. "We . . . found the information about the Council's visit," I said shakily. "It's in that file." I nodded at the table.

Alex didn't look at it. He put his hand over his face, rubbing his temples. "Get out, both of you," he said finally.

I licked dry lips. "But what about the Council? We still want to help; you'll need everyone you can get—"

Alex dropped his hand, and my chest clenched at the utter hatred in his eyes. "You have *got* to be kidding me," he hissed. "Do you think you're actually going to stay here in this house and still be part of the team? I've got news for you; the team doesn't trust you, neither of you. And you know what? I don't trust you now, either. Just get out—get your things and get the hell out. I never want to see you again, Willow." His gaze fell on Seb. "And if I ever see *you* again, I swear to God I'll kill you."

He turned and left the room. I stood motionless, staring

after him, taking in his dark hair, the firm line of his shoulders. The way he moved. Alex. *Alex.*

Seb gave me a quick shake. "Hold yourself together," he ordered, letting go of me. "I'll get our things."

I shook my head, stunned. Somehow I hadn't expected this. "But, Seb, we can't actually leave," I said in a small voice. "What about the attack?"

"We've seen all the information," he said. "We can go there, we can still help them. But for now—" His mouth twisted grimly as he glanced in the direction Alex had gone. "I think he means what he says."

The world was crashing in my ears. "All right," I said after a pause. "I'll get my own things."

No one was in the girls' dorm; it was a relief. I changed out of Liz's clothes and left them neatly on her bed— she'd probably burn them or something, once she heard what had happened—and pulled on a pair of jeans, a T-shirt, my hooded sweatshirt. My purple Converse sneakers. I remembered buying them with Alex, the way he'd grinned and said, *Is this another girl thing?*

No. Don't think about it.

I didn't have a bag anymore, but there was a plastic carryall in the closet that looked like it had been there forever. I shoved the rest of my things into it. The necklace with the crystal pendant Alex had given me lay at the bottom of one of my drawers. I hesitated and then took it out, slipping it into my jeans pocket. Its chain felt cool against my fingers.

When I returned to the kitchen, Seb stood waiting for me, wearing jeans and his long-sleeved gray shirt, with his knapsack over his shoulder. I was keenly aware of how silent the house was. Somehow I knew that everyone knew — I could just *feel* them all sitting back in the TV room, talking in low whispers. Alex was in his room; I could tell without even trying. And he thought Seb was the one I was in love with. That the two of us had . . . I swallowed; I could hardly even complete the thought.

Suddenly the only thing I wanted was to leave the house by myself and not have to be with anyone, not even Seb. No — especially not Seb. The thought of being alone with him now, knowing what Alex believed — and knowing the grain of truth that had been our kiss — made me cringe.

All of this came and went in a second. Seb stiffened as he picked up on it; I sensed his pain in a quick stab. Responding to my unspoken thought, he said quietly, "I'm not leaving you on your own. Even if there were no angels, El DF's a dangerous place for a white girl who doesn't speak Spanish. Once all this is over, I'll go away if that's what you want — you'll never have to see me again. But I'm not leaving you by yourself in this city."

I felt cold, locked away from myself. "OK, you're right," I said finally, my voice dull. "And I didn't mean that I never wanted to see you again. It's just . . . everything's really complicated right now."

"With you and Alex, yes. With us, it's only as complicated as you're making it," said Seb shortly. He took the carryall from me and wrestled it into his knapsack. The material bulged as he zipped it shut. His face was expressionless as he swung the bag over this shoulder again. "Ready?"

I almost asked where we were going, then realized I didn't actually care that much. Slowly, I reached into my jeans pocket and drew out the necklace. I gripped it in my hand, feeling its facets against my palm and remembering the look that had been in Alex's eyes when he gave it to me. Then I lay it on the kitchen table beside the file. The teardrop crystal rolled a little as I put it down, sparkling like a diamond.

"Ready," I said softly.

CHAPTER TWENTY-SIX

SOMEHOW THAT DAY PASSED — Alex wasn't really sure how. Once Willow and Seb had left, he went over the plans on the memory stick in detail, ran target practice with the team, ate a dinner that tasted like sawdust. From the forced conversation and concerned sideways glances, everyone knew that Willow had been busy spending the night with Seb while he, like a complete idiot, had risked his life looking for her on the riot-choked streets. He supposed Kara must have told them — he'd run into her as he'd headed to his bedroom and told her exactly what had happened. The look of shock on her face had been almost gratifying.

"Oh, Alex," she'd whispered. "I am so sorry —"

"Yeah, well don't be," he'd said. "I'm better off."

The muscles in Kara's slim arms were taut; she was as furious as he'd ever seen her. "God, I don't believe it! And I actually sat there and smiled at her! I'm going to —"

"Don't do anything — just let them go," he'd broken in coldly. "I just want them gone, OK? That's all."

And so they'd left without incident, though Willow's necklace on the kitchen table had provided an extra knife in the gut when Alex had found it later. Kara had been in the kitchen, too; her eyes had flown to his. "Alex . . ." she'd started.

"Forget it." He picked up the necklace with its shining pendant — the pendant that had reminded him so much of Willow's angel self, with her wings glinting in the sun — and shoved it roughly into his pocket, wondering why, exactly, he wasn't just pitching it into the trash.

"OK," he said. "Let's go over the plans."

And for a few hours, he'd almost been able to lose himself in them, even though some little voice inside of him was still dazed, bleating over and over, *I don't believe it; Willow wouldn't do this. She just wouldn't.* Whenever he thought it, he mentally kicked the voice to death until it shut up. Because all he could see was Willow in her short black skirt, reaching up to hold Seb's hand; hear the calmness in her tone as she told him that, by the way, she'd forgotten to mention it until now, but all along her dream had included Seb, and he himself had apparently just been the chauffeur to get her to Mexico City. God, no wonder she'd looked so thrilled when she first met Seb, her green eyes shining with wonder — probably the only thing that had been on her mind from that point on had been how quickly she could dump Alex, now that she'd found another half angel.

This thought came to him later that night in his bedroom; he only barely managed not to punch the wall. He couldn't just sit in here; he'd go insane — he pulled on a pair of sweatpants, yanked on a T-shirt, and headed out. Sam, Wesley, and Brendan were awake in the dorm, playing cards. They looked up at him as he passed through. Wesley's arm was in a homemade sling; it hadn't improved much since the day before.

"Hey, bud, you OK?" said Sam, his voice casual.

"Great," said Alex. He opened the cabinet where the towels were kept and grabbed one.

"You working out? Want me to join you?"

"No, thanks."

Down in the exercise room, he did fierce, pumping reps on the machines for almost an hour, then ran for miles on the treadmill, until the sweat was streaming and his muscles felt limp. Finally he stopped, panting. He'd pulled off his T-shirt as he ran, and now he used it to mop his face and chest. The house was quiet around him; he knew it must be after midnight.

His frenzied workout hadn't helped much. It hadn't even obliterated the fact that this was the night he'd been going to take Willow to the hotel, so that they could finally have the privacy they'd both been craving. He'd actually bought *flowers* to put in the room, and chocolates that now the maid or someone would eat. He'd wanted it to be so incredibly special for them both, but especially for Willow.

And instead she had been with Seb.

Oh, God, do *not* think about this. He wadded up his shirt and threw it across the room. Restlessly, he went upstairs to the TV room, where he sat on the sofa and opened up Brendan's laptop to study the plans again.

When he'd first looked at them, his relief had been almost indescribable. This was exactly what they'd needed: someone on the inside, getting them in as guests. The attack might actually succeed now — Charmeine the rogue angel had thought of every conceivable detail. Any doubts he might have had about the information's authenticity had vanished as he read through the notes; Charmeine clearly wanted the Council dead as much as they did. The VIP passes meant they could just walk right in through the main entryway without being stopped. There were also floor plans of the VIP area; a schedule for the afternoon's events; notes pointing out where the private audiences would take place and at what times. Best of all, the team now had an audience with the Council themselves. There was a note that said:

> The first private audience will be for "Mexico City University." This is you. To catch them off guard, keep your minds as blank as possible and wait until they're talking to open fire. Don't hesitate. The Twelve have

extremely strong psychic abilities, though we don't
know whether these extend to humans. It's essential
that they're dispatched, without ever letting them get
the upper hand — or else your team will be summarily
executed and humanity will not stand a chance.

Alex tapped his thumb against his mouth as he read, frowning slightly as he pictured the scene. If Wesley's arm wasn't healed by then, there would be six of them against the Twelve. The target practice they'd done earlier had focused on that — all of them standing in a line, each going for their own particular two targets. The team was proficient enough by now that this slight variation on their skills hadn't fazed them; they'd all been at well over ninety percent by the time he'd finally called a halt. Alex hoped that Wesley *would* be OK, though — they could really use a cleanup man standing over to the side, to shoot any angel that the others might have missed. If Wesley was still injured, then Alex would have to fill that role himself, nailing his two angels quickly and then going after any others.

Earlier, he'd brought the paper file that Willow had given him in here, too, and now he leaned forward to the coffee table and flipped it open. Neither he nor Kara could read Spanish nearly as well as they spoke it, but he could make out enough to see that most of the details were exactly the same as on the memory stick. The only discrepancy had to do with one of the hallways. The computer file said they should exit by that route to reach the elevators quickly — the paper file said there were renovations going on and the doorway at that end was blocked. But the computer file was clearly more up-to-date; the work must have been completed by now.

As he glanced at the laptop again, Alex suddenly remembered what Sophie had said about some kind of proposal for him. On the main menu screen, he found a file he hadn't noticed before: Nevada.

He clicked it open and discovered plans showing an underground camp in the desert — a huge, sprawling bunker, sleekly modern. As he read, he learned that the place had been used for some kind of military training and was now in the hands of the CIA, who apparently had been considering moving his dad's camp up there. A note from Sophie read:

> It's fully stocked with survival gear and weaponry —
> with the addition of holographs for training, it would
> be a perfect base for the AKs. There was limited
> knowledge of the facility even when Project Angel was
> running; I am reasonably certain that this information,
> along with the access codes contained here, are now
> known only by myself.

Reasonably certain — great. *I've already got a base*, thought Alex as he moved the laptop to one side. Besides, they'd only need a place to operate from if they failed to kill the Council — and if that was the case, the odds of the AKs even being around afterward seemed pretty slim.

In just a few days, he could die.

Alex sank back against the sofa, staring at the ceiling. Being raised as an Angel Killer meant that deep down, he'd always expected to die young—and he wouldn't mind, not if it rid the world of the angels. The only time he'd ever wanted more had been these last few months with Willow, when the desire to actually be around long enough to have a life with her—seeing her smile as she woke up beside him every morning, hearing her laugh—had given his fight against the angels more of a purpose than ever before. Even now, he loved her so much that uppermost in his mind was gladness that she wouldn't be there for the Council attack. That no matter what happened, she'd at least be safe.

God, what a sap he was. When she was with Seb right this second. He closed his eyes against the sharp twist of pain.

"Hey," whispered a soft voice. The sofa cushion sank down as someone sat beside him.

His eyes flew open. Kara was there, clad in the shorts and T-shirt she wore to bed. "I came down to the kitchen and saw the light on," she explained, tucking her long legs up under her. "You OK?"

"Fine." He stayed slumped where he was, not bothering to straighten up. Distantly, he was aware that the house felt cool now, prickling at his bare chest. "Couldn't be better."

Kara was silent for a long moment. Without makeup, the dramatic lines of her face looked softer, more vulnerable. "I know how you feel," she said finally. "I really do, Alex. I never told you, but do you remember David?"

At first Alex didn't. The camp in New Mexico had been home to hundreds of potential AKs over the years. A lot of them didn't have what it took and ended up being escorted out again — without ever having known exactly where the camp was, in case they later got angel burn and tried to confess everything. Then he vaguely remembered a good-looking guy with broad shoulders and red hair, like a Viking.

"Wasn't he a college football player or something?" he asked.

"That's the one," said Kara with a humorless smile. "Mr. All-American. Anyway, we sort of had a thing going for a while. And what can I say? I fell in love with him — totally, completely in love with him. I thought he felt the same way, but . . ."

Alex didn't say anything — memories were starting to come back. David had ended up leaving the camp unexpectedly with a married AK named Susie; gossip had buzzed at the camp for days afterward. "Did you know about Susie?" he asked after a pause.

Kara shook her head. "Nope. Didn't have a clue. I found out later that she hadn't even been the only one. I felt like such a . . ." Her voice faded, then she cleared her throat. "And you know what? The stupid thing is that part of me still loves him. I mean, I'd spit in his face if I saw him again, but I still love him. Almost as much as I hate him."

543

"Yeah," murmured Alex. That pretty much summed it up. He'd die for Willow even now, but he'd meant it when he said he never wanted to see her again.

Kara was sitting sideways on the sofa, her legs still curled under her. "Jake was so great, you know, after all that," she said. "He let me cry on his shoulder so many times. That was when I started to think that maybe someday . . ." She looked down. "Your brother was a really good guy," she said. "I miss him."

"I know," said Alex. "I miss him, too." He wondered what Jake would have said about Willow. After he'd finished kicking Alex's ass for being involved with a half angel in the first place, he had a feeling Jake would have taken him out to get drunk a few times — and brought lots of pretty girls over to their table, as if Willow could be replaced by anyone with two X chromosomes.

He became aware of the stillness of the house. He turned his head and looked at Kara. She was sitting very close, her brown eyes fixed on his; he could smell the gentle scent of body lotion.

She hesitated — and then in slow motion, she reached out and stroked her hand up his bare arm. When she came to his tattoo, she explored it as if she'd never seen it before, tracing its letters. The heat from her fingers was like little suns.

"Remember the Christmas party that time?" she asked.

He knew immediately the party she meant — it had been just a few months after Kara had first come to the camp. She'd worn a Santa hat and carried around a sprig of mistletoe, giving everyone quick, laughing kisses. Including him—his first kiss ever. The other AKs had thought it was hilarious; he'd just wanted to grab the mistletoe from her and do it again.

Kara still had her hand on his arm, trailing her fingers back and forth. "Yeah, I remember." His voice was rough.

"Al, listen," she said quietly. "I know you're still in love with her. But you and I really care about each other, and in a few days we could both be dead. Maybe we could just . . . keep each other warm for a little while."

Pain and longing mixed within him, so that all at once his heart was beating fast. He'd wondered ever since he was fourteen what it would be like with Kara. So why not, when the girl he loved was lying in someone else's arms right now? Why the hell not?

But for some reason the words *Yes, great idea* wouldn't come.

The room grew heavy with tension, like the air before a storm. Looking down at her hand, Kara slowly glided it across Alex's chest, inch by inch. It dipped up and down over his muscles, making him shiver. Finally her palm came to his other shoulder and stopped. For a long moment, her eyes searched his . . . and then she leaned over and kissed him.

Alex sat very still. Her lips were so soft, so gentle, and this was Kara, *Kara*, who he used to lie awake nights thinking about. He was enjoying this, he told himself—a gorgeous girl he'd had a crush on for years was kissing him; of course he was enjoying it.

The image came from nowhere: Willow, sitting at the picnic table in Chihuahua. The smoothness of her neck under his palm as he kissed her; her laughter as she complained that his lips were too spicy.

He pulled away almost harshly. Kara sat back in surprise, her eyes wide.

"Sorry," he muttered. His throat was so tight he could hardly speak. "I can't. I just can't."

Lying in bed later, Alex stared unseeingly into the darkness and wondered what the hell was wrong with him, that he couldn't even bring himself to kiss someone else. As if he thought he'd be cheating on Willow or something, when she'd dumped him as thoroughly as it was possible to be dumped. When according to her, she'd been using him for weeks just to get to Seb.

He couldn't believe it. He still just couldn't believe it.

Wake up; it happened, Alex told himself harshly. Anyway, to hell with this. He had a team to take care of. He had to be there for them these next few days; that was the only thing that mattered. Thinking of the upcoming attack, Alex was aware of the same dread Willow had sensed in him that long-ago night in New Mexico. But everyone was going to be OK, he'd make sure of it. *He could die; that was fine*—but not his team. He'd do everything in his power to keep them safe.

And if he still had a life once this was over with, then he'd get on with it and forget about Willow.

He had a sudden flash of her lying beside him that

was so vivid he could almost smell her shampoo, feel the silky warmth of her skin. The memory gouged at him.

Yeah, sure, he'd forget all about her. Nothing to it. Who was he kidding? The only way he'd ever get Willow out of his mind would be to have a brain transplant — and even then, he had a feeling she'd still be twined around his heart and soul for good.

CHAPTER TWENTY-SEVEN

RAZIEL COULD SEE the Torre Mayor from his hotel window: a curved green tower that caught the sun's rays like a promise. There was a minibar in the room; while he gazed out at the tower, he poured himself a glass of cognac, the golden liquid swirling into a cut-crystal glass. Angels couldn't get drunk, of course, but the taste of anything so vintage and expensive was pleasant. He took a slow, savoring sip, his eyes narrowing at the Torre Mayor as he remembered how the Council had threatened him in his own cathedral — the slurs they'd been casting on his leadership ever since they'd arrived.

The Zócalo, with its converted cathedral, was also visible; the building's exterior looked placid and undisturbed even after the terrorist attack earlier that week. Raziel took in its solid, ancient form, thinking of how the Twelve had appointed Tyrel as head of the Church in

Mexico just to insult him. Not to mention their televised "promise" of his demise. Oh, he was looking forward to this afternoon, all right. No matter what happened, he was looking forward to it very much indeed.

Luckily, the chaos caused by the terrorist attack hadn't kept Sophie Kinney from encountering Kylar; it was a relief to have the information safely in the Angel Killers' hands. Sophie had been surprised to find out that her role in the operation was now at an end, though — Raziel himself had done the honors the day before, just hours after arriving in Mexico City. When he'd glided into her hotel room in his angel form, she'd been sitting curled up in an armchair, tensely watching TV. He'd latched on to her mind with a smooth shimmer.

"Hello, my dear — we meet at last," he'd said as he started toward her.

She'd known who he was immediately but had been powerless to do more than gape at him. "You . . . But how . . . ?" she stammered, staring up at his radiant form.

"Yes, it's me," he said gently, reaching for her aura. "I have my ways. I'm an angel, you know."

Annoyingly, it turned out that Nate had marshaled her, making her energy so unpalatable that Raziel had only been able to feed for a second before breaking off in distaste. So instead he'd simply had to dispatch of her — crude but effective. He'd left Sophie still sitting in her chair, looking far more peaceful than when he'd found her. A heart attack. What a shame, in someone so young. Still, smokers were prone to them.

Raziel leaned against the windowsill, one hand casually in his jacket pocket as he took another sip of his drink. The AKs must be getting ready by now; the attack was only hours away. It was irritating that he couldn't know for sure, now that Willow had split off from the others. She and the other half angel had returned to his bolt hole in Tepito — the boy was as resourceful as Kylar, in his way. Raziel hadn't been checking on his daughter as much since then; he'd found her heartbreak these last few days fairly tedious.

Even so, thinking of Willow's upcoming death, Raziel felt a twinge almost like regret. After the attack, if his gamble went as hoped, he'd be on hand to tidily do away with the Angel Killers, trapped like rats in their dead-end hallway. Kylar's death, of course, would be nearly as pleasurable as the Council members' to witness, but in a strange way he knew he'd miss Willow — he'd become very used to the workings of her mind. He had little doubt that she'd be there for the attack, regardless of what had happened between her and Kylar. She was determined to take part in it, and like Raziel himself, things she was determined about tended to happen. He started to dip into her thoughts again, then restrained himself; it felt somewhat morbid, when he knew his daughter was about to die. He couldn't deny that he was curious to see her face-to-face again, though — this girl he now knew so well.

Pity. Never mind.

Gazing at the sleek lines of the Torre Mayor, Raziel

drained his drink and started to put the empty tumbler onto the windowsill. As he did, it caught the sill's edge — the crystal shattered in his hand. He hissed as a dagger of glass sliced deep into the fleshy part of his palm. Swearing, he went into the bathroom and eased the glass out, his hand throbbing as ribbons of blood streamed down. His human body could feel pleasure; the annoying correlation was that it could also feel pain. At least he knew the blood would stop quickly.

By the time he left to go to the Torre Mayor, it would be just as if nothing had occured at all.

Seb and I were on the Metro when it happened.

We'd been sitting on the rattling train car without saying very much, which wasn't unusual for us now. Sometimes over these last few days, it had been all I could do to make conversation with Seb, when before there hadn't been enough hours in the day for us to talk. As he sat beside me, I could sense the depth of his sadness over this, that he'd do anything in the world to have our friendship back the way it was. I couldn't help him. I knew it was me who had changed, but I felt too battered inside to try to figure out why, or how I might be able to fix it. All I could see was the look of stunned hurt that had been in Alex's blue-gray eyes. It made my heart feel like some small wounded creature that had curled up, whimpering, in a corner.

The attack was in less than two hours.

We'd gone shopping earlier with what was almost the

last of our money, so that we could blend in with the others at the reception. I looked down at the clothes I had on: black pants with a turquoise top. It was weirdly reminiscent of what Beth Hartley had been wearing a lifetime ago back in Pawtucket, when I'd given her a reading and seen an angel, its radiance reflected in the shimmering water of a stream. That was what had started all this, so it was sort of fitting that I was wearing almost the same thing now.

Our plan, such as it was, was to go back to the house and join the team as they left for the attack; it was where we were going now. I had no idea how Alex would react when he saw us. But regardless of how agonizing all of this was between him and me, he must know that he'd need every single person he could get to help; he was too good a leader not to. Imagining seeing him again made my veins turn to ice. If the hatred was still in his eyes, I thought it might kill me to see it.

Trying not to think about it, I stared at the grimy Metro map on the wall. Since leaving the AK house, Seb and I had been hanging out at the bridge in Chapultepec park a lot, watching the Torre Mayor. I'm not really sure what we hoped to achieve by it; mostly it was just something to do that might be vaguely useful.

But whatever was going on in there felt . . . weird. Actually, so did the whole city. As I'd noticed a few days before, the energy felt different, calmer — more so now than ever. That sense of "New York on a caffeine jag" was gone. And when I looked at the Torre Mayor, I kept getting an odd mental image of roots curling down; thick, gleaming coils of energy that twined deeply underground and then wove under the city in a dense tangle. Far away in the distance, I could just sense thinner shoots heading off here and there, in all directions.

"What do you think they are?" I'd said uneasily to Seb when we'd first noticed them. It was almost the only thing we'd said to each other in an hour. We were also standing in practically the exact same spot where Alex had caught us holding hands that first day; I'd shoved the thought away with a painful twinge.

Seb had shaken his head, staring upward. "I don't know," he said finally. "But they feel . . . alive."

Neither of us had said anything else, but my scalp had chilled; it was exactly the right word. On the Metro now, I sat tensely in the hard plastic seat, wondering again what the Twelve were doing. The roots they'd put down felt practically pulsing with purpose, their energy a part of the earth. As if the Council's energy had been part of the earth all along.

A mariachi singer strumming a guitar was wandering through the train. His warbling voice pounded at my skull like a bad dream. Beside me, Seb had his knapsack with all our stuff in it — neither of us had really wanted to leave it behind; it would be too much like admitting we might not survive this. His switchblade was back in his pocket, too; Kara had left it lying on his bed at the AK house, where he'd found it when he went to pack his things. I could feel how aware of it he was — his knowledge that soon he'd probably have to use it.

Glancing at Seb's profile, I was heavily conscious of the silence between us. I hated it, when we could both be dead so soon — but somehow I could still hardly think of anything to say to him. It was like there was a wall separating us now, and I was unable to break through, even though I'd put it up myself.

I started to rouse myself to say something anyway; I don't even remember what. Before I could, I gasped and clutched my hand.

Pain — I'd cut myself. A shard of glass, a windowsill. I stared down in confusion, expecting to see blood streaming down my palm.

"Willow?" said Seb, watching me with a frown.

I shook my head as I ran my fingers over my undamaged skin, half sure I was going to encounter glass sticking out. I could *feel* it in there — no, it was being pulled out. I gritted my teeth at the sliding sensation, the warm rush of blood. A sink that was a stylish white slab. Pink water swirling down the drain. *Good thing it'll stop soon — wouldn't do to look less than perfect when the Council dies, now, would it? After all, it might be my first moment as the new Seraphic Head.*

The images and the internal voice faded, leaving me reeling.

Raziel.

"Willow, what's wrong? What are you seeing?" Seb's

voice had turned urgent over the noise of the train; he started to reach for my arm and then pulled back.

"Wait," I murmured. "I just have to . . ." Jumbled thoughts were sweeping over me: the energy stream my first night in Mexico City, so strong and pulsing that I'd been afraid it might drown me — how it had trickled to nothing seconds later. That sense of being watched sometimes. My angel's distress, and the way whatever had been bothering her had just vanished the moment both Seb and I went looking.

The train, the people, had all taken on a surreal edge. I closed my eyes and searched fervently once more, feeling my frustration mount with every second. There was *nothing there*. But I'd felt Raziel — what he was doing, what he was thinking. He was *in* there somehow; he had to be.

And then it came to me. If I couldn't find him inside of me . . . then maybe I was inside of him.

I flicked my consciousness from within to without and tried to sense my own energy, the same way I looked for Alex's — drifting, searching, letting it come. After a moment, a silver and lavender flutter appeared. I swallowed as I took in its gentle light, wondering if my hunch was true. Instinctively, I knew that I had to be very, very careful.

With only the tiniest nudge of my thoughts, I touched the grain of energy . . . and found myself in Raziel's mind. A world with tall towers and robed beings, an amphitheater where lectures were given psychically, and it was all so boring, boring; the wall between worlds where he'd slipped through thousands of times to indulge himself on humanity.

Knowledge flowed into me like water pouring into a glass. I caught my breath, cold with shock. Oh, my God, it wasn't just that there was a spark of me in Raziel; there was a spark of him in *me*, too. Nausea rose in my throat as I realized he'd been spying on me all along — taking in all my private thoughts, my feelings. Knowing all our plans. And now I could see his. Sophie, a memory stick. False directions for escape.

I felt dizzy as the details washed relentlessly over me. It was a trap. Destroying the Council might not kill all the angels after all; that was only one possibility. And as the other scenarios came to me, my blood turned to ice.

One of them showed the earth trembling — major cities all around the world collapsing into dust.

I sat stunned, hardly able to believe what I was getting. This couldn't be true; it just couldn't be. So many people might die. Raziel didn't even *care*. If it happened, he thought any surviving angels would still have plenty to feed on, especially with the way "the creatures" bred. And no matter what, Mexico City was certain to go if the Council was killed — those roots of their own energy that they'd woven deep below the city's surface would ensure it.

My stomach lurched. The second I had everything, I rushed out of Raziel's mind and back to my own. I had to get rid of it, get it out of me *now*.

He'd hidden it so, so well, nestled deep in my consciousness. I'd never have guessed in a million years that the tiny flame of his energy was there. Vibrant silver, with a purple tinge. I eased it from its hiding place, loathing its familial feel. With an urgent flutter, my angel appeared and took it from me; cupped in her shining hands, the spark glowed brighter, and then vanished. Raziel couldn't spy on me anymore — but it was a little late for that now.

My eyes flew open. Panic was crashing through me, I stared blindly at the crowded Metro train, the mariachi singer who was still strolling through. Seb sat half twisted in his seat, his hands gripping mine. I didn't know how long he'd been holding them, but from the expression on his face, long enough. He looked just as sick and pale as I felt.

I could hardly get the words out. "Seb — did you see ?"

"Yes, I saw," he said grimly just as the train reached our station. He snatched up his knapsack from the floor by his feet. "El DF for certain, and maybe even more."

"We've got to get to the house in time! We've got to stop them —" I jumped from my seat and pushed through the crowded train car with Seb right behind me; we hit the platform running and pounded up the concrete stairs onto the street. Everything we passed, every car, every person, suddenly seemed as vulnerable as an eggshell. My lungs were burning as we raced toward the house, and in a weird way it was almost like that first day, when we'd run after the angels through the park.

Except that if we didn't manage to stop the attack, then Alex and the others were all going to die . . . and so might millions more.

"OK, I think that's everything," said Alex.

He'd just finished putting Kara's bag in the back of Juan's white van along with the rest of their luggage. As he emerged, he glanced up at the house, trying to think if they'd forgotten anything. That morning it had suddenly occurred to him that after the attack there'd be no reason for them to remain in Mexico City. Either they'd have succeeded, in which case they could all head home to the United States, or else they'd be on the run for their lives and need to get the hell out of the city anyway.

There was a third option, of course. He set his jaw and ignored it.

Kara was standing in the drive. "Good, we're almost ready, then," she said. Her nails were red again today, with little flecks like diamonds; they matched her bright-red top. Thankfully, things hadn't been too awkward between them since the other night, though Alex had the impression that Kara thought he was kind of an idiot not to just take what she'd been offering and enjoy it. He couldn't really argue.

Sam appeared, carrying a cardboard box on his shoulder. "Have we got room for this?"

"What is it?" asked Alex.

"Just some of the food supplies. Munchies for the road."

The decision that they should pack up had been met

with obvious relief by the rest of the team. Though Alex hadn't expected it to act as a morale boost, it obviously had — it gave the attack this afternoon a sense of *when* we succeed, instead of *if*.

"Yeah, I think there's room." Kara moved past him to delve into the van, shifting Alex's tent and sleeping bags to one side. Alex looked away, remembering lying in that tent with Willow. If he was still alive after the job today, he'd soon be putting hundreds of miles between them, with no idea where she even was anymore. Frankly, it was part of the appeal of taking off. He wanted to get as far away from memories of Willow as possible.

"I still think we should just steal the 4x4," said Sam, passing the box in to Kara. "Man, I have *traveled* in this van. It's like rolling around in a box of marbles."

"We'll be all right," said Alex. He had the 4x4's keys in his pocket; he was going to follow the others over to the Torre Mayor to return it to Sophie.

The others had drifted out and were standing in the driveway. Now that the time was almost here, the mood was a pulsing mix of anticipation, fear, excitement. Everyone looked unusually polished, like a group about to go on job interviews. The girls all had on pants this time instead of dresses; the need to draw their weapons with a complete lack of fumbling had trumped fashion. Alex himself was wearing gray pants and a dark-blue shirt. He'd considered a tie but decided against it — he'd never worn one in his life and wasn't really going to start now, on what might be his last day ever.

Wesley stood flexing his arm. "Are you sure you're OK?" asked Alex in an undertone. Though Wesley claimed his injury was healed now, Alex wasn't convinced.

"I'm fine," said Wesley. He looked more like a young Will Smith than ever as he glanced sideways at Alex; raised an arched eyebrow with a slight smile. "So don't go hassling me 'bout it, all right?"

Alex was painfully aware that Wesley was one of the best shots he had — but if he wasn't fully functioning yet, no way did he want to send him in there. "Wes, if you're not sure, you've got to tell me now."

Wesley's brown eyes flashed. "Listen to me. I *am sure*. Don't do this to me, man. You know why I've got to be there today. *You* understand better than anyone."

"Yeah, I understand," said Alex quietly. He felt the same way; what had happened to his own family was half the reason he was doing this. "But if your aim's off—"

"Then maybe I die," broke in Wesley. His voice was low, fierce. "And maybe I don't care much if I do, and maybe I'd rather be there *trying* than anything else in my whole sorry life — OK?"

Alex let out a breath. The harsh truth was, he wasn't in a position to say no to someone who was willing; even injured, Wesley could be a tremendous asset. And more than that . . . he didn't think he really had the right to tell the guy he couldn't come, when it meant so much to him and he was aware of the risks.

"Yeah, OK," he said finally. Relief swept Wesley's face; he nodded wordlessly.

Trish cleared her throat. She was standing to one side; from her pained expression, Alex could tell she'd heard some of their conversation. "So . . . are we almost ready?"

Alex glanced at his phone, checking the time. They were leaving a little earlier than planned — no one wanted to hang around now that they were packed. "Almost," he said. "I'll just look through the house again, make sure we haven't forgotten anything."

"I'm sure we haven't," said Kara, clambering out from the van.

He headed back inside anyway. As he wandered through the vacant rooms, the place felt like a ghost of itself; as if everything that had happened here had happened long ago, to other people. The kitchen table, where they'd talked and squabbled and even laughed occasionally. The firing range, where he'd made his first announcements as the lead and then spent hours training the team — saw them slowly come together, learning how to be actual AKs instead of just angel spotters with guns. *I can be proud of that*, he thought, gazing at the targets hanging motionless on their chains. *No matter what, I can really be proud of that.*

His bedroom.

Alex stood motionless against the doorway as he took it in. The room was full of Willow. He had a flash of her stealing in one morning: the look in her eyes as she'd slipped into bed with him, the smell of her as he'd brushed his lips against her neck. With a grimace, he shook the memory away. OK, this had been a bad idea.

He pushed himself off the doorjamb—and then stopped, looking up at his shelf.

Willow's necklace was still there, where he'd tossed it after finding it on the kitchen table. He deliberately hadn't packed it today. Now he realized with grim certainty that this was what he'd come back for. Somehow he couldn't just leave it behind. Feeling more idiotic than ever, he shoved it in his pocket, cursing the memories attached to the thing. The way he felt about Willow seemed like a sickness now. He never wanted to be this in love again—it wasn't worth it. But the necklace remained in his pocket.

He went back outside. "We're ready," he said.

Kara nodded and reached for her keys; she was going to drive the van. As everyone started to climb in, Alex cleared his throat. "No, wait a second. Guys, listen . . . No matter what happens, I'm proud of you, OK? The way you've trained these last couple of months has just been amazing. You're all good AKs now—really good. We can do this thing; every one of you has got what it takes."

The group had gone very still as he spoke, with varying expressions of shy pride on their faces. From the driver's seat, Kara's brown eyes met his. He had the sudden feeling that she was thinking of his father, and the back of his neck warmed.

"Yeah, yeah, enough of the mushy shit," said Sam finally. "We love you, too, you jerk. Now, come on, let's get the hell out of here and kill some angels."

"Kill *all* angels," corrected Liz firmly.

"Yep—kill 'em all. Yee-haw!" bellowed Sam to the van's ceiling.

Suddenly the mood was exuberant. Alex knew it wouldn't last, but it was good for now, exactly what they all needed. With a grin, he started back toward the 4x4. "OK, I'll see you there," he said over his shoulder. "You've all got your passes, right? Meet me in the lobby if—" He broke off, shock stiffening his muscles.

Willow and Seb were running up the street.

"Oh, what the hell is this?" muttered Kara, swinging herself quickly out of the van. Sam got out, too, scowling. The rest of the team stayed put, watching warily as the two jogged to a stop in the driveway, both breathing hard. Willow's eyes went straight to Alex's as if the others weren't even present.

"Alex, the attack can't go ahead," she gasped. "It's a trap—a trap."

"What?" He stared at her in distrust, hating the way his heart had leaped when he saw her.

"It's Raziel: he's using you! He was using all of us—he wants the Council dead, but—" She gulped, struggling to catch her breath.

"It's true," put in Seb. He stood near Willow, though not touching her. "You must listen to her."

"Raziel? The angel in charge of the Church in the U.S.?" Kara's eyes narrowed. "And why would he want the Council dead, pray tell, when it means that all angels will die, including him?"

Willow's bright hair moved as she shook her head impatiently. "Because it *doesn't* mean that! It might, but it might not! The Council's going to take his leadership away, and he's willing to take the chance—"

"How do you know this?" Alex broke in.

"Yeah, I'd sorta like to hear that, too," said Sam in his low drawl. He was leaning against the van, one foot propped up behind him.

"I—" Looking at the other AKs, Willow seemed to really notice them for the first time. She swallowed. "Because I was able to read Raziel's thoughts," she said at last. "He's my father," she added before Kara could ask.

Seb moved closer but still didn't touch her. A stunned silence; every face was gaping at her. "You have got to be kidding me," breathed Kara. "Alex, did you—?" She cut off as she saw his face. "Oh, my God, you did! You knew this!"

"It didn't seem important," said Alex tersely.

Kara's voice rose. "Not *important?* Your girlfriend's father is like, Mr. Head Evil Angel, and that wasn't *important* enough to ever mention it to us?"

"She's not my girlfriend anymore," snapped Alex. He turned to Willow. "Look, what do you mean you were able to read his thoughts? What's going on?"

Willow glanced at the others again; her expression was tense but determined. "Could you and I go inside, maybe, and I'll explain?"

Alex blew out a breath. Part of him wanted to tell her

that if she had something to say, she could say it right here — but her eyes were pleading with him. "Fine," he bit out.

"Alex —" protested Kara, straightening in alarm.

"I'll just be a minute." He turned and strode back to the house, heading for the front door; Willow and Seb followed. *You and I* had apparently meant Seb, too.

"This seriously *cannot* take long," Alex said from between gritted teeth as they went inside. "We've got to go."

"I know — we were coming to help you," said Willow. They were in the firing range; she stood against the wall near the basement door. "But then on the Metro . . ." She hesitated, visibly shaken. Alex ignored the concern he felt; Willow wasn't any of his business anymore.

She collected herself and went on: "On the Metro, I found out that I have a sort of . . . link with Raziel."

Just the word made Alex's hackles rise. "Really? Is this like your link with Seb?"

Seb gave him a narrow look. The tips of Willow's ears turned red, but her voice was level. "No, not really," she said. "When Raziel and I fought in Denver, it's like we exchanged particles of energy or something. He's had a spark of his energy in me, and I've had one in him. I didn't know anything about it until now, but he's been using it to spy on us. Alex, he's been manipulating everything all along."

"Manipulating how?" he demanded.

"Everything! It's why Luis suddenly trusted Kara; it's why Sophie suddenly appeared to give you security details and VIP passes—"

A chill went over Alex. "How did you know about that?"

"I just told you! I've been in Raziel's head!" Willow's voice rose in frustration. "Things are different in this world from the angels' world. It's not definite that all angels will die if you take the Council out; that's just *one* option. What Raziel's hoping is that only the Twelve will die, and that he'll still be alive to take everything over, but—but there are other possibilities, too. . . ." She faltered to a stop, her face pale.

"El DF will be destroyed; that's almost certain," put in Seb. "The Council has put down roots of energy here—if they die, they take the city with them."

"But not just Mexico City!" said Willow, sounding anguished. "Alex, they've done the same thing all over the world, in every place that they think feels out of control. There are so many major cities that could be affected now, *everywhere*—there could be earthquakes, cities falling— millions dead—"

The hair on the back of Alex's neck rose as he stared at her. "This doesn't even make sense," he said in a low voice. "If the angels destroy so much of humanity, how will *they* live?"

"It's not the angels; it's just Raziel!" cried Willow. "He knows the Twelve will kill him anyway, so he's willing to take the gamble! And if it pays off for him, the AKs will all be executed — the information Sophie gave you is flawed. There's a — a hallway or something on the map that's not right. You can't get out that way."

Remembering the plans, Alex suddenly felt cold with dread; his stomach clenched so tightly that he felt physically sick. Oh, Jesus. Was this really true?

"Please believe me," said Willow softly, her gaze fixed on his. She made a motion as if to take his hand and then pulled back, her eyes pained but imploring. "No matter what's happened between you and me, you know I wouldn't lie about this. Alex, the attack can't go ahead. It just can't."

"OK, that is *enough*," hissed Kara's voice. "I don't know what she's been saying to you, but I hope you're not believing it."

Alex spun and saw that she'd come in through the kitchen; Sam was behind her. Seb had straightened too, his eyes watchful as Kara strode over to them, her boots rapping against the floor.

"Let me deal with this, Kara," said Alex curtly.

"Alex, please," whispered Willow, ignoring everyone but him. Her hands were tight fists at her sides. "Please."

"She's Raziel's daughter!" exclaimed Kara. "Of *course* she's trying to get you to stop the attack — she's trying to save the angels!"

Alex slowly shook his head, staring at Willow as he remembered her sobbing with relief in his arms, to know that her mother was still alive. "She hates Raziel; she always has," he said. All he could think was *millions dead*.

Even if there was a chance that it wouldn't happen, if it was a possibility at all, they couldn't take the risk.

Watching him, Sam's expression had turned dumbstruck. "Alex, you can't really be listening to her, right? This is *saving the world*, man! We gotta do it — we don't have a choice!"

"Yes, tell me you're not listening to her," said Kara, her eyes hard. "She *lied* to you, remember?"

"I remember." Alex's gaze was still locked with Willow's; on some distant level, his heart felt shredded just from being next to her. Yeah, she'd lied to him — but he couldn't doubt her, not about this. He let out a breath. "Look, guys, I think —"

Kara moved so quickly that he hardly saw it. Suddenly she'd jumped at Willow and grabbed her from behind — one arm tight around Willow's throat, the other holding a gun to her head. Willow gave a choked cry.

Alex's pulse jumped, and he started forward; in a blur he was aware of Seb lunging, too — of Sam throwing himself at Seb in a flying tackle. The two of them crashed to the floor with a heavy thud, struggling.

Kara flicked the safety off her gun, stopping Alex in his tracks.

"Think again," she said. The muscles of her forearm were rigid against Willow's neck. "I am *not* letting you compromise this mission, Alex. Drop your gun. Now."

"Alex, don't," gasped Willow, clutching Kara's arm. "I'm only one person; it doesn't matter about me —"

"You don't even know what she said!" burst out Alex

at the same time. "Kara, listen to me! It's true; the attack can't go ahead—"

"Did you hear me?" she snapped. "Because I'll blow her brains out right now if you don't drop your gun."

Out of the corner of his vision, Alex saw that Seb was making a decent showing for himself as he and Sam scuffled, but the Texan outweighed him by at least fifty pounds. There was the sharp crack of fist against skin— and then the next second Sam had him down, as Seb let spew with a string of Spanish that it was lucky Sam didn't understand.

Alex kept his eyes locked on Kara's, not letting his glance flicker to the weapons cabinet on the wall behind her. They'd packed most of the guns away into the truck, but a couple of small pistols were still in there—cheap .25s that none of them liked using. If he played along with Kara for now, he might be able to get to one.

Slowly, he reached for his gun and tossed it onto the floor.

Kara didn't stop watching him for a second. Her forearm still mercilessly tight around Willow's neck, she transferred her gun to the other hand, shoving the muzzle up under Willow's jaw. In a single motion, she bent and scooped up Alex's gun, tucking it away into her waistband.

"Good," she said as she rose again; Willow was gasping for breath. "Now your VIP pass and the keys for the truck."

Alex's muscles were clenched, watching. The cabinet was about ten feet away. If Kara's attention left him for even a heartbeat, he'd go for it. He dug into his pocket. His fingers hesitated as he touched what was in there; then keys and card followed with a clatter.

"You're making a mistake, Kara," he said. "Raziel *wants* the Council dead — and if they're killed, millions of people could die."

"Is that what she told you?" Kara's lip curled. "God, you're still so in love with this little liar that you can't even think straight." With no warning, she bundled Willow away through the basement door; he heard Willow cry out.

Alex dove for the weapons cabinet. Locked. Oh, *Jesus*, since when did they ever lock it? He raced for the basement, dimly aware of Seb's shouts and the intensified struggle between him and Sam. As he reached the open doorway, Kara burst out and shoved him hard at the stairway. He spun toward her, trying for her gun — but the next second, Seb had slammed into him, and they'd both gone tumbling down the stairs.

Chapter Twenty-eight

ALEX SCRAMBLED TO HIS FEET and barreled back up the stairs just as the door slammed shut; he heard the latch bolt and threw himself against the unyielding wood anyway. "You're making a mistake!" he yelled. He slammed the door with his fist. "Kara! Don't go ahead with the attack! Don't!"

"I'm sorry, Al," she called, her voice already fading. "But believe me, you'll thank me for this someday." At the sound of the front door closing, Alex gave a wordless bellow of fury and frustration and shouldered himself against the basement door again; it shuddered but stayed firm.

"Somehow, I don't think we're going to break the door down," said a dry voice. Seb was there, his cheek already looking bruised and swollen. Reaching into his pants pocket, he pulled out his switchblade.

"What, you had a *knife* the whole time?" demanded Alex.

Seb flicked the knife open and angled the blade through the gap between the door and the wall, probing at the bolt and trying to slide it back across. "You had a gun—and you weren't even getting your face smashed," he pointed out. "At least I managed to hold on to my blade."

As the knife scratched and scraped, Alex glanced down the stairs at Willow. She stood at the bottom, holding on to the railing, grimacing slightly as she rolled her ankle. Their eyes met. "Are you all right?" asked Alex after a pause.

She nodded and put her foot to the ground, testing it. "Fine. She just—pushed me really hard."

Even now, Alex's impulse was to go to her and hold her. It wasn't his place anymore—it was Seb's. He looked away.

The minutes dragged by. Seb swore softly as the blade skittered across the bolt. Finally he shook his head and started on the hinges instead, twirling the knife's tip deftly in each screw head. "Oh, man, that's going to take forever," muttered Alex, shoving his hair back. The party would be starting soon; their private audience was the first one scheduled. They had maybe an hour, tops.

"I look forward to hearing your much better idea," said Seb without looking at him. One of the screws came out; he tossed it aside with a tiny clatter. After what seemed a hundred agonizing lifetimes, all the screws had been removed. Alex helped Seb lift the door off, and they burst out into the firing range.

Alex raced to the weapons cabinet. A heavy wooden chair sat against the wall nearby; he picked it up and swung it at the cabinet in almost the same motion. There was a splintering crack as the door gave way. The two .25s were there, just as he'd remembered. Alex shoved one into his holster and glanced at Seb and Willow, who had joined him.

Seb nodded at Willow. "Give it to her; I've got my blade."

Alex handed it over wordlessly. "Thanks," said Willow; her voice was a ghost of itself. She reached past and took a spare holster from the cabinet, turning away from both of them as she strapped it on under her pants. *Why bother?* thought Alex bitterly. Both he and Seb had seen her undressed.

As they passed by the TV room, Alex ducked into it. The paper file was still on the coffee table; quickly, he found the sheet with the code for the door on the angels' stairwell. "OK, come on," he said, tearing the code off and shoving it in his pocket. Though none of them had discussed where they were going, they all knew. Alex thought how ironic it was — he was now allied with Willow and Seb against the team he'd been ready to keep safe with his own life if necessary.

Willow swallowed. "How are we getting there? The Metro will take —"

"The truck," said Alex. He led the way out the front door.

She blinked. "But you gave Kara the keys."

"No, I gave her the keys for the Shadow." Out on the driveway, Alex saw that someone had thrown all his stuff out of the van before they'd taken off. *Thanks, guys*, he thought wryly. He grabbed up his things and dug into his pocket; his fingers briefly brushed against Willow's necklace as he pulled out the keys to the truck.

Seb got into the back of the 4x4, tossing his knapsack on top of the sleeping bags; Willow sat up front with Alex, her face taut. They had less than half an hour now.

Spinning the wheel, Alex screeched them out of the driveway, and soon they were speeding through the *centro*. The streets were relatively clear; he still found himself driving like a maniac, swerving in and out of traffic with horns blaring in his wake. What had Kara told the team? The last-minute mutiny must have stunned them. The thought made him inch the speedometer still higher. Their performance might be thrown now; if he didn't get there in time to stop this, they could all die when they faced the Council.

His hands tightened on the wheel. No. They would not die.

"Tell me everything," he ordered.

Willow did so, gripping the dashboard with white-knuckled fingers. As Alex listened, he became more certain than ever that this was true. Christ, of *course* Raziel had been spying on them; it was how Charmeine had known the details about their previous attack against the angels. His jaw tensed at the news that both Luis and Sophie were dead, though it wasn't a massive surprise. One devout to the angels, the other dedicated to stopping them. It didn't matter; they'd both gotten in the way, and so they'd been discarded like used toys.

"OK, do we know that killing the Twelve will cause damage to our world?" he asked as he steered them onto the Paseo de la Reforma. Up ahead, the empty column where the Mexico City angel had stood for decades was like a solitary sentinel with traffic streaming past on both sides.

"It'll definitely cause damage to Mexico City," said Willow. "Apart from that — no, we don't know. It might be that killing the Council really will destroy all the angels. That's what most angels think will happen. Or it might be that it kills only some angels and not others, and the rest of the world will be fine. But — " She broke off, screwing her eyes shut. "I just don't think so," she whispered. "They've put down roots like that under dozens of other major cities, too. There's a chance those may not have had time to take effect yet, but their energy feels so entwined with our world now — I can't imagine that there aren't going to be major consequences all over."

With just over ten minutes to go, they were nearing the Torre Mayor. It rose up above the other buildings in a graceful curve of green glass, its half-moon slice gleaming. As he turned onto the Río Atoyac, Alex swore suddenly.

"What?" demanded Seb from the back.

Alex explained, his voice terse. His plan for getting the team into the loading dock area had depended on their having the white van, which actually looked like a delivery van — he'd then announce a delivery for a company that always took forever before sending someone down to let the guy onto the elevator.

"Plus I was going to piggyback along with the afternoon FedEx delivery," he finished grimly. "So that we could get onto the service elevator when someone let the FedEx guy on." He rapped the steering wheel, trying to think. They were going to have to force their way past the guard, except how could they? Somewhere overhead, security had its beady eyes on the video screens — they'd bring the service elevators to a screeching halt the second they saw guns being waved around.

Willow shot him a concerned glance; for a second it was as if things were the same as always between them. "Go to the gate and tell the guard you've got a delivery," she said suddenly. "I think I might have an idea."

Seb seemed to sense whatever it was; in the rearview mirror, Alex saw his face slacken in surprise. "Willow, I'm not sure this is even *possible* — and besides, you've never tried it!"

"Well, no time like the present," she muttered, shoving a hand through her red-gold spikes. "And since it happened to you once, it shouldn't be impossible for us to do it at will, right? In theory, anyway."

The conversation with half its words missing did nothing to reassure Alex. But they didn't have much to lose. They were almost at the service entrance by then, with the building looming up over them; he turned into the barricaded driveway and stopped by the guard booth.

Putting on a relaxed smile, he said, "*Buenos días, señor.* I've got a delivery for Ortega Graphics."

The guard frowned, his gaze scanning over the blue 4x4. Just beyond the security barrier, a blocker rose out of the driveway: a huge metal wedge that faced them like a solid wall. It would stay there until the guard lowered it into the ground.

"Oh?" said the guard. "What company are you with?"

Alex named a company that often made deliveries to Ortega. In a white van, which this so totally wasn't. Not to mention that he looked like he was dressed to go to church or something

Beside him, he was aware of Willow concentrating hard; shifting his consciousness, he saw her angel self soar out of the truck and hover unseen near the guard booth. Meanwhile, the man's expression had turned even more suspicious. "*Un momento,* I'll have to confirm this." He rarely confirmed deliveries for Ortega—just let the drivers through and then buzzed someone to come down.

Alex could feel Willow's human self straining with effort. And then slowly, her angel became more . tangible. There was no other way to describe it. Instead of an ethereal being of light, she shifted until she looked almost solid, as if Alex could reach his hand out the window and stroke one of her gleaming wings. It was what the angels of the Second Wave had done, he thought in a daze: slowed down their frequency so they could be seen.

Instead of reaching for the phone, the guard stood gaping, taking in the radiant creature that had suddenly appeared before him, emanating peace and kindness. The psychic blast that Willow's angel sent toward him was so strong that Alex caught it, too: *Let them in. It's all right. Let them in.*

Alex had seen hundreds of people encountering angels; the expression on the guard's face now was as awe-struck as any of them. Staring at the angel with a wonder-ing smile, he slowly pressed a button. The security barrier swung open; beyond it the blocker sank into the drive.

"*Gracias*," said Alex hurriedly, and gunned them through before the guy came back to his senses.

The loading dock was a dimly lit cave. Willow's angel merged with her again as they parked with a shriek of wheels. They scrambled out of the truck, then ran up the concrete ramp to the service elevator. Someone was just wheeling an empty cart off it, and they plunged through the open doors.

They stayed tensely silent as the elevator hummed its way to the fifty-fourth floor. With an effort, Alex kept his eyes off the security camera. Glancing sideways, he could tell how drained Willow was from the effort with her angel — and felt a stab of anger toward Seb, who gave her a concerned glance but then just stood there without even putting his arm around her.

Though Willow looked nervous, her chin was lifted firmly. *She's determined to be there, you know. She loves you very much.*

As the words came back to him, Alex went still, taking

in Willow's face. He realized he was staring and looked away. *Get a grip*, he thought, irritated with himself. He had nothing to do with why Willow was here anymore; she was in love with Seb.

"Is there a plan?" asked Seb as the elevator neared the top. He looked almost relaxed, his eyes coolly determined; suddenly Alex could see clearly the street kid he'd once been.

Alex shook his head. Glancing at his phone, he was agonizingly conscious that their private audience was due to start in less than a minute. "I wish. Just follow me, as fast as you can — I know where the team will be heading. We've got to get to them before they go in."

The elevator stopped; the doors glided open. A few seconds later, they were in the stairwell, rushing up the concrete stairs. Time slowed; Alex was hyper-aware of everything: Willow ahead of him, her short spikes bouncing as she ran; the thin scar on Seb's arm peeking out from his shirt cuff; the adrenaline pumping through his own veins.

They reached the door at the top. Alex punched in the code; the light turned green, and he threw the door open. High glass ceilings, a glimpse of blue sky and clouds — and then they were hurtling their way down a carpeted corridor toward the lavish reception ahead.

At promptly five past three, Raziel shifted to his angel form with a smooth ripple; wings spread, he glided out into the Mexico City afternoon. The metropolis of over twenty million people stretched out to the horizon in every direction, ringed by low purple mountains in the far distance. Raziel could feel the unnatural calmness here since the Council had been interfering, as if a soothing blanket had been draped over everything. It irked him, so that he was almost glad that the place was about to be leveled.

A shame about the cathedral, though. He circled it once on his way to the Torre Mayor, taking in its ornate, ancient lines and the golden angel newly gleaming at its peak. Once the interior damage caused by the rioters was repaired, it would have been a fitting place of worship indeed. Still, it was satisfying to know that Tyrel was about to have such a prize snatched away from him.

Why, Raziel, that's rather dog-in-the-mangerish of you, he thought, and chuckled as he flew on to the Torre Mayor. It rose up over the city, its green glass curves reflecting the clouds.

At exactly three fifteen, Raziel landed on the building's helipad, touching down at its precise center. The view from here was no better than when flying, but it was still pleasant to change to his human form and survey the city with his hands behind his back, feeling the wind lick at his hair and suit jacket. He'd pondered for some time before deciding what to wear. Even a gate-crasher wanted to look his best — especially if the clothes he put on might be either the last thing he ever wore or the outfit in which he'd finally take leadership. At last he'd decided on a dark-gray, almost black suit, with a rich purple shirt, open at the neck.

When Raziel finally received the psychic call from Charmeine, he'd long since become bored with the view and started to pace about the helipad. He stopped in his tracks, pulse quickening as he felt the unmistakable pull of her energy. "About time," he murmured.

He shifted to his angel form and flew into the glass portion of the building. The plan was for him and Charmeine to be in an adjacent room when the shootings took place, so that they could properly savor it. Feeling the Twelve's deaths would no doubt be painful if he survived, but Raziel was looking forward to it, anyway, with a dark anticipation. Every death pain would mean that another of the Twelve was gone.

He cruised over the VIP floor, taking in the lavish reception: waiters gliding along with silver trays; a high, slanted glass ceiling overhead; a crowd of excited-looking humans. Some of the Twelve's angelic entourage were there, too, feeding from starry-eyed victims, and Raziel smiled to himself. *Don't look like you're having too much fun; you'll get into trouble.*

Letting the tug guide him, he soared through a tall white wall.

A slam of energy, a binding, as if several invisible nets had been thrown on him at once. Instantly, he felt like a cartoon cat, frantically trying to backpedal in midair. Because Charmeine wasn't alone in the room: the Council was there, all seated at a long conference table.

"Raziel," said Isda mildly. "How good of you to join us. We were looking forward to seeing you in your cathedral again, but this is even better."

He struggled to free himself, but his psychic bindings drew tighter with every wing stroke. Down below, a broken-looking Charmeine stood slumped against the wall in a short black dress, her face wet with tears. The Twelve sat in a row down one side of the long table, male and female angels alternating, with Isda at the center. They all stared up at him dispassionately, as if he were of no more interest than a trapped moth.

As their energy slowly reeled him in, Baglis, another of the Twelve, spoke, his resonate voice echoing through the high room. "We were most surprised to hear of your plans for us, Raziel. However, your friend Charmeine doesn't seem quite certain of all the details. Perhaps you can help."

They kept him a foot or so off the floor, making him hover, even though every movement of his wings was agony now. Raziel's eyes met Charmeine's; she gave an almost imperceptible shake of her head. So the Council knew there was a plot — but *what* exactly might still be hidden.

"I don't know what you mean," he said aloud, then cried out as a dozen mental whips scorched across his mind.

"Oh, we think you do," said Isda. "Charmeine, as it turns out, is very good at hiding things — but I rather imagine you'll be easier to delve."

There was a knock at the door. It opened a cautious crack, and a human attendant stuck her head in. "Excuse me, Señora Isda — but it's time for the private audiences. Shall I send the first group in? It's the one from Mexico City University." She didn't even glance at Raziel; in his angel form, he was as invisible to her as air. Remembering that this first group was the AKs, Raziel shoved the knowledge away as hard as he could.

"Just give us a few minutes, and then send them in," directed Isda.

Once the attendant had withdrawn, Isda sat back in her seat, her gaze fixed on Raziel as he hung suspended before them. The faces of the Twelve were bland. *You don't seem to have taken our warnings to heart, Raziel,* she said on the psychic level. *Such a shame.*

He cried out again as he felt himself shifted by force into his human body. The sensation was exceedingly unpleasant. *Conspiring to assassinate us is treason,* continued Isda as a chorus of psychic voices joined hers. *And we will get all the details out of you before your execution. For now, you may watch and learn while we show you that it's possible to feed without getting carried away with gluttony.*

Trapped in his human form, Raziel felt just as ensnared as before, as if he'd been bound from head to toe. He stood weakly against the wall, keeping the surface of his mind as impassive as possible. Underneath, he was fuming. At least he had a ringside seat for what was about to occur — and oh, was he going to enjoy it. He watched the door, thankful he was out of direct view. He only prayed that neither Kylar nor Willow would see him until it was too late.

The Twelve shifted to their angel forms and lifted up in a fiercely burning row, glowing even brighter as they lowered their frequency so they could be seen by humans. And like a tiny, apologetic tendril, Charmeine's thought came creeping into his mind: *I'm sorry, Raz. They delved me when I wasn't expecting it. I just couldn't hold them off anymore.*

Raziel shrugged mentally; it was too late to do anything about it now. Then the door opened, and a group of six young adults filed in — three males and three females.

Where is Kylar? Raziel only just managed to restrain the leaping thought. Were these the assassins or not? He reached quickly for his connection to Willow. It was gone.

She knew. His pulse rate doubled, and Isda gave him a sharp look. He writhed under the sudden pain of her psychic probe — and knew that this time, he hadn't managed to hide the group's identity. The awareness of the humans' intentions rippled ominously through the Twelve, their expressions never changing.

Looking nervous, the team faced them, blinking from the glow. A tall black woman with exquisite features and masses of long braids nodded to the Twelve. In Spanish, she said, "Good afternoon; we're from Mexico City University. It's an honor to —"

She broke off, startled, as the Twelve swooped forward in a rush. "Now!" she cried, ducking back.

A few AKs fumbled; others grabbed their weapons

smoothly and started firing. As the first bullets found their targets, the room erupted into flapping wings and exploding light. Raziel could feel the Council's shocked fury that their move hadn't caught the AKs more off guard; that they were actually being destroyed by *humans*, of all creatures. Standing so close meant that the pain juddered at Raziel like machine-gun fire, yet it was his mind that was under assault more than his body. He'd always assumed it was the physical connection with the First Formed that was the vital one — but as one after another Council member erupted into nothingness, Raziel knew it was the mental connection that would destroy him. He could feel his mind starting to buckle. The Twelve were leaving the world. It couldn't be. The angels would be adrift without them, forever adrift.

Only seconds had passed. Seven of them were gone now. The guns' muffled thuds kept on. Awash with numb despair, Raziel slid down the wall to the floor, watching the shards of radiance floating all around him. What had he done? He could sense the other angels in the building, still in their divine forms — dazed and in pain, some of them dying already from the shock.

Fight this! he screamed at himself. *It's a delusion, a momentary weakness. Once the Twelve are gone, I'll have exactly what I've always wanted!*

He gritted his teeth, focusing on that, only on that. Somehow he managed to wrest his mind back, though his body was still held captive. Overhead, the remaining five rallied as one and flew at their assailants. And as they reached out psychically toward the AKs, Raziel knew with a dark twist of joy that their power was already greatly depleted — because the bonds on him had just weakened.

Alex pounded down the corridor with Willow and Seb right behind him. Up ahead was the soaring room where the party was taking place. Music from a string quartet floated through the air, competing with the noisy buzz of conversation. Alex glimpsed a few angels in there, too, feeding but weirdly motionless; their victims stood gazing with adoring awe.

The AKs were nowhere in sight — their audience with the Council must have already started. Alex drew his gun as they reached the meeting room door and flung it open.

Five angels, brighter than any he'd ever seen, were in combat with his team — blurs of burning-white light that dove snarling at the human attackers. Only four AKs were shooting. Alex stopped in his tracks, blood chilling as he saw that Trish's face was damp with tears; she was pulling frantically at Wesley's arm as he struggled with her. "Don't shoot!" she sobbed. "We can't do this; we can't hurt the angels!"

Oh, God, no. Trish.

Kara and the others looked dazed but were still battling. Somehow Alex shoved aside his feelings — and having drawn his gun, he saw suddenly that there was nothing to fire on, unless he was going to start shooting at his team. He wouldn't, not even to save the world.

With every instinct screaming to aim his gun at the angels, he instead hurled himself at Kara and wrested the pistol from her hands. "Stop the attack!" he yelled. "Everyone, stop firing *now!*"

"No!" Kara's face contorted with desperate fury as she fought him. Meanwhile Willow's and Seb's angels had appeared and were darting around the room — blocking shots from the AKs at the same time they were protecting the team from the Council. Alex saw Willow's angel swoop between a Council angel and Liz, spreading her wings over Liz for a second time.

Across the room, another Council angel vanished in a spray of light; Alex couldn't tell who'd gotten it. The human Willow stood pressed against the wall beside Seb; she'd drawn her gun but obviously realized, like him, that there was nothing she could do with it. Wesley was still trying to fend off the crying Trish. As Wes shot again, Seb's angel flinched in the air; the human Seb staggered.

Fleetingly, Alex noticed a woman with pale blond hair struggle to her feet. She surveyed the room with a small, satisfied smile and slipped out; then one of Kara's punches almost connected, and he forgot about the blond woman. He got Kara's arms pinned behind her. She was almost crying. "Alex, she's got you under a spell! Don't do this!"

He ignored her. "Stop the attack!" he shouted again. "This is what Raziel *wants* — it could destroy our world!"

Most of the team members were panicked now; no one even seemed to have heard. Another Council angel dove straight at Sam, who froze, wide-eyed — then shook himself with a roar as he aimed and shot. Willow's angel darted in front; the bullet went through her as the Council member twisted away.

Alex heard the human Willow gasp in pain and had to force himself not to go running to see if she was all right. Instead he shoved Kara hard to one side and threw himself at Sam as the Texan fired again. They crashed to the carpeted floor. Sam squirmed out from under Alex and kept firing; another Council member, a male, went down in a spray of radiance.

Only three angels remained. They grew brighter, glowing with a painful light that throbbed at the air. Brendan was running back and forth as he dodged Willow's angel; in a blur Alex saw Willow herself sitting on the floor with her eyes closed. Seb had his switchblade out but hardly looked capable of using it. Another bullet hit his angel and he stumbled, catching himself against the wall.

"Stop! We can't do this!" Trish was pulling frantically on Wesley's injured arm. Alex saw him cry out and clutch at it, dropping his gun.

"Wes, look out!" he shouted. But a Council angel had already taken the chance to fly right at him; Wesley froze as he stared into its eyes. The next moment he was theirs.

"No — we can't hurt the angels — what are we *doing*?" he gasped. He lunged at Brendan, sending them both sprawling. "Stop! Don't hurt them!"

Sam was taking aim at another angel; Alex grabbed at his arm, and the shot went wild. Suddenly Alex noticed the man in the dark suit who sat slumped against the far wall, and his breath froze. Oh, Christ, it couldn't be. Raziel.

Willow's father shook his head briefly, as if shackles were falling from him. Taking in the scene, his handsome jaw hardened. Wesley's dropped gun lay nearby, and he reached for it, fingers closing around the weapon.

Still on top of the struggling Sam, Alex aimed his own gun and started firing, even though he knew it would do no good; angels couldn't be killed in their human forms. Raziel gave a hiss, recoiling as the bullets rained into him — but still he lifted the gun, aiming at a Council member who was attacking Liz.

Sam saw him, too. Abruptly, the fight went out of him; his shocked gaze met Alex's. "Stop!" he bellowed. "Y'all, *stop!* He's right!"

It all happened in seconds: Brendan shoved Wesley off and fired at the same time as Raziel; the Council member went down in a fountain of light. Another angel swooped at Brendan, tearing at his life energy; he staggered with a cry and went down, clutching his leg. At the same time, Kara had grabbed a fallen gun and was struggling with the hysterical Trish — she battled away Trish's flailing hands and nailed the angel who'd given Wesley angel burn, sending it flying into fragments.

Then Kara saw Raziel. Her eyes went wide; she gave Alex a startled look. Flying unsteadily, Willow's and Seb's angels both started toward Willow's father — who stood aiming the pistol at the last of the Twelve.

No! The hyper-awareness came back to Alex. In slow motion, he and Sam scrambled to their feet, lunging across the room in unison; dimly, he was aware of Wesley still on the floor and Trish grappling with Kara again. A muscle in Raziel's jaw tightened as he took aim. His wounds were bleeding, staining his expensive-looking suit.

Alex had the blurred impression that the last Council angel was trying to do something—wield some kind of power over Raziel. Though she was now burning so brightly that he could barely look at her, whatever it was wasn't successful. Raziel's lip lifted in a sneer.

"My world, my rules, Isda," he said softly.

Willow's angel was a little ahead of Seb's; she darted in front of the final Council member just as Raziel shot. In the same moment, Alex and Sam tackled Raziel, bringing him down with a crash. It was too late. Alex looked over his arm and saw that the bullet had passed through Willow's angel and hit its mark: the final Council member was shuddering in the air, her scorching wings flapping helplessly. Willow's angel was now nowhere in sight.

The explosion as the last of the First Formed died was silent, but Alex felt it through every inch of him, and ducked his head against the blast. It roared past, a vortex of gut-wrenching sensation that tore at his skin and hair. A shudder seemed to pass through the world—and then, gradually, calmness fell. When he looked up, only twinkling lights remained, glinting like fireflies on a summer night.

Alex lay breathing hard, aware that the others had been thrown to the floor, too. Bizarrely, only minutes had passed since they'd entered the room. In the sudden silence, he could still hear the string quartet playing Mozart.

Willow. Was Willow OK? He scrambled to his feet. Against the wall he could see Seb, clearly still weak but sitting up now, gripping Willow's hands and talking softly to her. Alex's shoulders sagged as he saw her eyelids move. His relief was matched only by the longing to go to her himself.

Sam had risen also, his broad face bruised and swollen. "Alex . . . look," he whispered, staring at the floor.

Raziel had gone still.

Alex's heart started beating painfully fast as he gazed down at Raziel's body — the moist blooms of darkness on his purple shirt; the crisp black hair with its widow's peak. He heard Willow's voice again: It might be that killing the Council really will destroy all the angels. That's what most angels think will happen.

"I — I think maybe we've done it," said Sam in a choked voice. "Oh, God, I think maybe we've really done it."

Kara was just getting up, looking shaken. Suddenly Alex did a double take around the room, his skin prickling with alarm. Wait a minute. Where were Trish and Wesley? No, he wasn't imagining things — they were both gone.

The moment he registered it, their shouts drifted in from the party: "They've just killed the Council! They've killed all the angels!"

Oh, *Christ*. He and Kara moved at the same time, leaping for the door and banging it shut. There was another exit from the room; he hoped they'd get a chance to use it. Sam joined them. "Grab the table!" ordered Alex. Gripping the heavy wooden table, they dragged it in front of the door as the sound of shouts started heading their way. He and Sam threw a few of the chairs on top for good measure; it would hold them for a few minutes at least.

A faint rumble shook the building.

It came and went in a second. Kara breathed in between her teeth, and Alex knew she'd felt it, too: the sense of something having come loose in the world. "Oh, my God," she whispered, staring at him. He saw the fear in her eyes. "You were right, weren't you?"

There was no time. Brendan was struggling to his feet, wincing on his injured leg; Liz stood still, apparently dazed. Seb staggered as he rose, his arms around Willow, who slumped against him.

"OK, you guys, *move*," barked Alex as a pounding started up on the door. "Go out the other door, but don't turn left; it's a dead end. We're taking the stairwell. Kara, you help Brendan; Sam, help Liz, but make sure she doesn't have angel burn first. If anyone gets separated, don't hang around — just *get out of here*. Now!"

As the others leaped into action, Alex rushed over to Seb and Willow. "Is she OK?" Seb had lifted her into his arms; she lay limply against his shoulder with her arms around his neck, her cheeks white.

Seb nodded. "She's just passed out, I think." He still looked pale himself. As he shifted his grip on Willow, Alex could see how unsteady he was.

"Give her to me; you can hardly stand," he said brusquely. The table shuddered as people banged on the door, shouting. The others were all gone now—Liz must be OK.

"I'm fine," said Seb with obvious effort. He stumbled slightly as he started for the other door.

Alex took Willow from him just as Seb's knees buckled. She clung to Alex with a small moan, not seeming to notice it was him. Alex held her tight against him and put his other arm around Seb's shoulders; he seemed about to pass out now, too. "Come on, *hurry*—"

"Must you really go so soon?" inquired a low, silky voice.

Alex whirled. Raziel was on his feet, wan but very much alive as he pointed a pistol toward them. "You know, I'm rather going to enjoy this," he confided. "Isn't it nice when the tables are turned?"

Alex stared at him dumbly as the shouting outside the door intensified. *Or maybe only the Council will die. No. No.*

The sense of déjà vu from the cathedral in Denver was almost overwhelming. Though he knew it wouldn't do any good with Raziel in his human form, Alex took his arm from around Seb and shot anyway. It didn't even slow Raziel down this time. With a sneer, he leveled the gun at Alex's head and pulled the trigger. There was an empty click.

The angel stared down at the gun in furious disbelief . . . and then shifted to his ethereal form and soared from the room.

Alex cursed but couldn't get him now. Clutching Willow, he grabbed hold of the drooping Seb again, and hauled him into the back corridor. The shouts were louder out here—part of the mob must be coming around from the other direction. "Come *on*," he gritted out to Seb, half carrying him down the hallway. "I am not going to die because of you. You don't get to die, either—I promised to kill you, remember? *Move*."

Seb seemed to rouse himself by sheer force of will. "Yes, I remember," he murmured. He pulled from Alex's grip, managing to break into an exhausted run.

Willow had her arms weakly around Alex's neck; her hair smelled just like it always had. *I'm getting you out of here, babe; I won't let anything else hurt you,* thought Alex as they ran down the corridor. Frenzied shouts sounded behind them; doors banging open as people searched for them.

Sam and Liz came rushing back from the other direction. "They've cut us off; the stairwell's blocked," gasped Liz. "There's a whole crowd there, waiting for us."

"Where are Kara and Brendan?" demanded Alex.

"I don't know; they were ahead of us! They must have gotten through." Sam ran his hand nervously over his blond spikes. "The elevators are blocked, too. Oh, man, what now? Do we try to shoot our way through?"

There was a door directly to his left; Alex cast frantically through his mind but couldn't remember where it led. Just then there was another rumble — overhead, the light fixtures swayed. It made him decide.

"In here," he said, throwing the door open. Stairs leading up. *Up?* thought Alex as they raced up them. *We're already on the highest floor.*

A locked door waited at the top of the stairs. "Stand back," said Sam, taking aim. He shot; there was the whine of bullets on metal as the bolt gave way. He flung the door open, and they poured through.

Open sky; wind whipping at their clothes. "Oh, shit," breathed Alex, still clutching Willow to his chest.

"Yeah, that about sums it up," said Sam tightly. Liz stared around them helplessly; her mouth opened and then closed again. Seb let out a curse in Spanish, glancing back at the stairs — where Alex could now hear the sound of shouts coming up. The crowd had found them.

And they were up on the helipad.

CHAPTER TWENTY-NINE

ALEX AND I HAD ALWAYS wondered what would happen if my angel self was injured. As it turned out, it felt like being smashed over the head with a hammer. With every bullet my angel took, the force of it slammed through my skull until I thought it was going to splinter. During the attack I sat slumped against the wall, fists tight as I somehow clung to consciousness, focusing all my attention on my angel as she flew. The Council saw who I was, of course, but they were too distracted to react to either me or Seb. I could sense their utter shock over what had happened, their impotent rage. In over three millennia, no one had ever dared to attack them.

Raziel was there, too. Naturally—where else would he be? This was his glorious hour.

He didn't hesitate for an instant when my angel self swooped in front of the final Council member. I saw his face gazing coolly upward as he aimed. The force of the bullet slammed through me, and I felt myself drifting, barely able to make it back to my human form. Against the wall, my fists slowly unclenched as a dark tide washed me away.

Then there was Seb, picking me up in his arms. *Seb, I'm sorry. I want things to be the same between us again,* I thought, but I couldn't get the words out. I clung to him as the world swam and slipped away from me once more. Vaguely, I had a dream that it was Alex holding me instead; the feel of his embrace was so real that I wanted to stay wrapped up in it forever.

When I came to, I was looking up at the sky. Distant shouts; a scraping noise. I sat up, my head still groggy — and saw the view from my dream. All of Mexico City was spread out below, stretching into infinity. There was a weird hush in the air, as if the very world were holding its breath. My scalp prickled. The roots that the Council had put down felt loose now, dangerous — like the bodies of headless snakes moving restlessly about, causing ripples in the earth.

I struggled to my feet — I was on a helipad. There was a door nearby; Alex, Seb, Sam, and Liz had just dragged some sort of spare metal unit in front of it. The door jolted rhythmically as the sound of shouts came through.

"Hold on, everyone!" called Alex. Even through his shirt, I could see his muscles flexing as they all strained to hold the barricade in place.

Still feeling dizzy, I ran to add my weight to theirs.

The metal unit looked like part of a giant air conditioner. I shoved myself against it and pushed. Seb was beside me — head down, hands propped on the metal edge as he groped for purchase with his feet. "Are you OK?" he gasped, glancing at me.

"I think so," I said with an effort. Alex's eyes met mine, and I could see the deep flicker of thankfulness in them; then he turned away without speaking as the metal unit scraped across the cement. The door burst open a few inches, then banged shut again as we all heaved. Incoherent shouts, a glimpse of angry faces.

"Oh, God, they're going to get through!" Liz's cheeks were red with exertion. "Alex, what are we going to do? There's no place to hide up here!"

"Start pickin' 'em off one by one as they come through," grunted Sam on the other side of me. His broad shoulders looked like they had softballs in them as he pushed.

"Yes, that will work for about two minutes, maybe," said Seb, raising his voice over the shouts. The door was shuddering, shaking. "How many cartridges do you have?"

"Enough to make them sorry they ever followed us up here," said Sam grimly. "I'm going down fighting — that's all I know."

"But we'll still go down," said Liz, sounding agonized. "There are just too many of them! And Trish and Wesley —" She broke off with a sob. I felt like crying myself. Trish, who everyone had loved so much; Wesley, who'd wanted only to avenge his family. Were we supposed to open fire on them now?

The screams intensified as the door shoved open by almost a foot; we struggled to close it again.

"OK, don't panic," said Alex. "We'll have the advantage as they come through the door. We're going to have to let go of the unit and position ourselves over to the side. When the crowd bursts through, start firing. Try a couple of warning shots first, but don't waste too many cartridges if it doesn't work."

Though his tone stayed matter-of-fact, I knew how much he must hate this; he loathed the thought of using a gun against another human being. He wasn't the only one. I imagined pulling the trigger, seeing someone crumple in front of me. My lips went dry. I didn't think I could do it.

"When we go, give me your gun and get behind me," Seb said to me.

I swallowed. "Seb, no — I can't let you shield me —"

His voice was strained. "Please, just do it. You don't think you can shoot, and I can."

"Seb's right," put in Alex. "Stay behind both of us."

And as our eyes met again, I saw what I already knew in his: Liz was right, too. There were too many of them for us to fight — and from the sound of their shouts, they weren't going to be slowed down much by warning shots. Unless we could think of something else, fast, we were going to die.

"OK, on the count of three," said Alex, loudly to make

himself heard. The shouts were almost deafening now, the door thudding open and shut like a heartbeat. "*One.*"

I looked wildly around us, frantic to find something that maybe the others had missed. Like an elevator — that would be a good thing to find. My gaze came to the edge of the building and stopped. I stared at it, my thoughts tumbling.

The unit almost hopped as it scraped forward six inches. "Two," said Alex, his jaw tight.

My dream. The tower that I'd flown from, the way my wings had felt so heavy. Seb turned his head and stared at me as he picked up what I was thinking — and it was so completely insane that I knew it was our only chance.

"*Th*—"

"No, wait!" I cried. "I've got an idea!"

It took an agonizing minute or so for Seb and me to prepare ourselves, while I tried desperately not to focus on the metal unit sliding steadily backward, or the door inching open. Beside me, Seb was straining as both our angels hovered. He obviously found this just as hard as I did. Finally I reached up . . . and touched my angel's foot as she looked down at me. Her face was my own, white as a statue; her wings gently fanned the air. The foot felt cool and firm. It was a very weird sensation, to literally touch another you.

Seb's angel looked just as solid. I glanced at him and he nodded. "We're ready," I said, lifting my voice. I managed to keep the fear out of it. If I was wrong, then we were about to plummet to our deaths.

Alex's brow was damp as he struggled against the unit. "On the count of three, then — a good shove, and then run. One — two — *three*."

We heaved hard; howls came from the door as people were shoved back. Then we raced for the edge of the building with the two angels gliding overhead. There was a loud scraping noise as the air-conditioning unit was shoved aside; I could hear people stampeding through, screaming.

We'd already decided how we would manage it. Seb was stronger than me, so his angel was going to have to hang on to two of them, plus Seb himself. But his angel couldn't support both Alex *and* Sam — and I definitely couldn't support the burly Sam.

So it was only common sense that I took Alex. Even so, my heart thudded as we reached the edge, and I knew that what we were about to do was only part of it. For a second, Alex's blue-gray eyes were unguarded as we glanced at each other; my pulse skipped at the expression in them. Oh, God, if I knew for certain we were about to die, I'd tell him everything.

The crowd of almost a hundred people had seen our angels now and stopped uncertainly. Some carried makeshift weapons — jagged pieces of wood that looked like they'd been torn from picture frames. Raziel appeared from their midst in his human form, his face contorted as he yelled at them. You didn't have to speak Spanish to get what he was saying: *See, they have no halos! They're not real angels; it's a trick! They killed the Council — don't let them get away!*

Trish and Wesley burst up from the stairwell. "They're Angel Killers! Stop them!" Feeling sick, I tore my gaze from their familiar faces. This was *not* the time to think about it.

"OK, let's do it," said Alex grimly. He wrapped his arms around me, and I held on to him, feeling his heart beating against mine. Beside me, Sam was lifting Liz up into his arms as Seb stood behind him, supporting him across the chest. My eyes met Seb's as both of us silently urged the other on. Our angels hovered overhead, centering themselves, getting ready.

The crowd charged. Trish and Wesley were gaining on the others, still shouting. At the head of them all, Raziel ran with his suit jacket flapping — and as I looked back at him, for a dizzying second I was catapulted into his head again. I caught my breath in shock at what I found there, my arms tightening around Alex.

Half the angels in the world were dead.

Raziel knew it instinctively, just like he knew his own heartbeat. Half the angels were really gone. *Gone.* I felt a rush of dazed relief . . . then stiffened as other knowledge came. Raziel was intrigued by me, sorry that I had to die. He'd enjoyed wandering around in my thoughts.

Suddenly it was like a gate had been slammed shut,

severing the connection. "You don't actually think you'll get away, do you?" called my father, the wind whipping at his words as he ran toward us.

I shivered as I stared at him. I hated it that he'd been in my mind; if I could dip my brain in bleach, I'd do it.

"One way to find out," I said softly. And as my angel put her arms around us, Alex and I stepped over the edge.

Wind whistling past — a glimpse of angry, screaming faces. The street below spiraled, rushing up at us; I could see our falling reflections in the curved green glass. In my angel form, my wings beat frantically as I struggled with the unfamiliar weight. A little away from me, Seb was having the same trouble, only worse — his angel was carrying three people.

I was not going to let us crash. I strained harder; somehow managed to get the fall under control. It was as if a parachute had opened, snapping us into buoyancy. Below us, I saw to my relief that Seb's powerful wings were in charge now, too.

"Are you OK?" said Alex over the wind. It was lashing at us, ruffling our hair.

"Fine," I got out, my arms still tight around him. I could smell his warm Alex smell. We were so close, just like we'd been a thousand times before; all I wanted was to lift my face to his and kiss him. I looked away, but not before I saw his throat move.

"Willow . . ." he started — and then broke off as a sound like thunder rumbled. I went cold at that ominous sense of the Council's roots, moving on their own now. The Twelve's absence had unbalanced everything, like a boulder teetering on the edge of a cliff.

"It's not good, is it?" said Alex, watching my face.

Before I could answer, my angel self stiffened in alarm — and in a bright blur, Raziel swooped down out of the sky at us.

"You know, I think this whole scenario would go better if there was more *falling* involved," he said, and he beat at my angel with wings of light that jolted through her and threw her off-kilter. My human hands went clammy as our fall accelerated again — we were still about thirty stories above the ground.

"Hang on," shouted Alex in my ear. He let go of me with one arm to reach for his gun. Raziel saw the motion; with a snarl, he whipped around in the air, reaching for Alex's life energy.

No! In my angel form, I let my wings go completely still, plummeting us downward like a rock. My human self clung to Alex as we started to tumble, earth and sky and wings flashing past. I almost lost my grip; his arms tightened. "I won't let you fall; I'll never let you fall," he murmured, and I knew he wasn't even aware he'd said it out loud. The wind was tearing at me; my angel self could barely move her wings. No, we were *not* going to die this way. Panting, I beat frantically.

I righted us just as Raziel appeared again. With the concrete city behind him, his wings flashed through the blue sky as he dove at Alex from behind.

"Alex!" I shouted. He turned sharply, but my angel's wings were in his way; she was too exhausted now to maneuver. He swore as Raziel drew closer. My pulse was racing. No. This was not going to happen. Steeling myself, I drew my gun and aimed at his halo.

"Oh, I don't think you'll do that," sneered Raziel as he craned toward us. "I know you very well now, my daughter."

Without answering, I pulled the trigger.

I missed, but it was enough to startle him; he jerked backward, flapping. I could see Seb above us with Sam and Liz; sense his distress that he was unable to help. Sam was firing on Raziel, though, and the angel hissed as he realized it, darting away. Alex finally got a clear shot and aimed, holding on to me tight with his other arm. "Oh, man, he is so going to die this time," he muttered.

The world met us with a crash as we landed on a stretch of grass beside a parking lot. My angel self had slowed us down as much as she could, but it still felt like we'd slammed into a brick wall. I cried out as Alex and I rolled together; there was a shout of pain from someone as Seb and the others landed nearby. My angel merged with me again, limp and exhausted—I could feel her relief that she'd gotten us down safely.

For a moment I just lay on the grass, muscles quivering, Alex and I still holding each other tight. "Are you OK?" he whispered.

My face was against his neck. I closed my eyes, savoring the warmth of his skin against my lips. "Fine."

Somehow my voice sounded steady. I pulled away and sat up, my heart beating hard.

And then I stared at the sky above us.

Raziel was high overhead now, out of reach of our bullets — but he wasn't alone. Charmeine, the female angel I'd seen in his thoughts, was speeding toward him, her long hair whipping in the wind. Several dozen angels were following her. "There's the traitor who assassinated the Twelve!" she called. "Don't let him get away!"

Of *course*, I thought dazedly, remembering what I'd glimpsed of the power-hungry Charmeine from Raziel's mind. He only thought he'd totally delved her; she'd fooled him and the Council both. Her gamble had paid off — and now that he'd helped her do away with the Twelve, she didn't need him anymore.

The angels' wings glinted like knife points as they descended; somehow I knew this was all that remained of the Council's hundred-strong entourage. With a snarl of fury, Raziel shot straight up in the air, twisting away from the small army. I watched, sickly fascinated; I knew that I was about to see my father's death.

I cried out as the ground bucked like a living thing. I could feel the roots flailing about below, dangerous and unfettered. The sound of breaking glass came from somewhere. Car alarms going off.

The ground shook again . . . and all at once a thick strand of energy burst out of it.

It snapped through the air, whipping wildly — almost invisible, an *intensity* more than something you could see.

606

It mowed through the battling angels overhead, sending them scattering; lashed back again, so that some of them erupted into bursts of light. My arms went cold. I couldn't tell who was who anymore — what was happening?

Alex had been watching, too. "Come on, let's get the hell out of here," he said, scrambling to his feet. He offered his hand to me. I started to take it and then remembered, drawing back just in time. I couldn't touch him again, not for any reason — already, I might have damaged him even more.

"Sorry," I muttered, standing up.

Hurt flashed across Alex's face; his jaw hardened. He glanced over to where Seb and the others were. It looked like Sam had twisted his ankle — he was scowling as Seb helped him to his feet, leaning heavily on him.

"Here," said Alex curtly, handing me the keys. "Go get the truck; we'll be there as fast as we can."

I nodded, longing to be able to explain. Instead I turned and ran. The Torre Mayor was right beside us; overhead, the remaining angels were just a few bright, struggling blurs. Running footsteps drew up alongside me as Liz appeared.

"This is so not good," she panted as another rumble shook the ground. Trash cans clattered nearby. I couldn't answer; suddenly urgency was hammering through me, making me run faster than I'd ever run before.

We rounded the corner onto the Río Atoyac. The guard had abandoned his booth; we ducked under the barrier and scrambled over the metal blocker, skidding our way down the other side. In the loading dock, the 4x4 was just where we'd left it, looking weirdly ordinary as it sat there.

Liz got into the front next to me as I started the engine. I spun the wheel, screeching us into reverse — and then stared at the blocker at the top of the driveway. From this angle, it was a steep ramp jutting off into space. As another tremor hit, I sent my angel speeding to check the guard booth. The buttons on the display panel needed a key to operate them — there was no key in sight.

"What — what are you going to do?" asked Liz as my angel returned in a flurry.

The Dukes of Hazzard flashed grimly into my mind. "Um — I think seat belts might be an idea," I said, buckling mine on. My mouth felt dry; the ramp was looking steeper by the second. I gripped the steering wheel and took a deep breath, keeping my gaze fixed on it.

Liz clicked on her own seat belt, her pale cheeks growing paler as she glanced at me. "Willow, you're not really going to —"

"Hang on," I said — and floored it.

We hit the ramp going almost forty miles an hour and for a heart-stopping second catapulted through the air, clearing the barrier. We slammed to the ground front wheels first; the truck rocked like a bucking bronco, wrenching us forward and then back. Somehow I kept control; I pumped the accelerator and threw the wheel hard, lurching us out onto the road and then back toward where we'd landed.

"Oh, my God, we actually made it!" gasped Liz. I let out a shaky breath. I was kind of surprised myself.

Alex and the others were half a block away. When I pulled up beside them, Alex threw the car door open, and he and Seb helped Sam in.

"Christ, I swear I've broken it," muttered Sam, dropping his head back on the seat. His face was white.

Alex slammed the door shut once they were all inside. "I think it's just a sprain — but you got off lucky, OK? We all did."

I could feel Seb's anxiety prickling at my skin and knew that he could sense the same thing I could: the giant roots were completely out of control now, surging through the earth. We had to get out of this city now.

As I roared away from the curb, I saw that there were only two angels fighting up above now. Two. Did that mean Raziel was still alive? The road shivered, and I accelerated, trying to keep ahead of the tremor as another whip of energy slashed through the air. As it swiped past the two angels, there was a burst of radiance, like sun sparkling on water.

And then nothing at all.

My heart felt ready to burst in my chest. Was Raziel really gone now? Briefly, my eyes met Alex's in the rearview mirror. I could tell he didn't know, either — but I knew the answer he was hoping for. Then I swerved the truck onto the Paseo de la Reforma, and we couldn't see the place where they'd been anymore.

I swerved us in and out of traffic, completely ignoring

the honking horns. The road got clearer as I went on — as the tremors continued, people were pulling over to the side. Mexico City got a lot of earthquakes. In an ordinary one, not driving was probably the sensible option. I had no intention of taking it, not with the way the energy of this place suddenly felt. A truck was in my way; Sam howled in pain as I hurtled us up onto the grassy divide and then back onto the road again. And as we continued north down the Paseo de la Reforma, I saw with a chill how right I was to want to get us out of here as quickly as possible.

Up ahead was the empty column where the Mexico City angel had once stood, holding her golden garland up to the sky. It was swaying back and forth like a too-tall Jenga tower.

"Dios mío," whispered Seb from the back.

There was no way around; I gritted my teeth and sped toward it. As it started to fall across the road, Liz screamed, scrabbling backward in her seat — then we'd shot underneath it and were out the other side.

Sam laughed weakly. "Oh, man — where can I nominate you for driver of the year?"

My hands were so clenched, it felt like they'd been glued to the steering wheel. "Don't push our luck," I said, keeping my eyes on the lurching road. "Maybe you should hold off until I actually get us out of the city."

"You will," said Alex, his voice firm. "You will."

✦ ✦ ✦

And somehow I did.

By sunset, we were wending our way up a mountain road. The quake didn't seem to have been so bad here, though we still had to maneuver around fallen trees sometimes. It felt peaceful, though: the way the mountains reached toward the sky as if they'd always been there and always would be.

Peaceful was good. Peaceful was very good.

Alex had taken over driving; I was in the back beside Seb. He sat without talking, his gaze distant, and I could feel his pain over what had happened to the city of his birth. Because as I'd finally reached the outskirts of Mexico City, I'd seen something in the rearview mirror that had stolen the breath from my lungs: the earth had reared up from the *centro* and was literally rolling. Buildings shuddered and fell as the concrete tidal wave passed; cars slipped into crevices. I'd pulled over to the side of the road, shaking too hard to drive as we all stared.

Finally the wave had juddered out into nothing. And then there'd been the most complete silence I'd ever heard, with dust rising up in a great plume.

That's when Alex had taken over, getting out from the back and opening the driver's door. "Get in the back; you've had enough," he said, his face like stone from what we'd just seen. I didn't argue.

Hardly any of us had spoken after that. Hardly any of us were speaking now, several hours later. The expression on Seb's face wrung my heart. He'd always hated Mexico

City because of all he'd been through there, but for him to see it flattened that way . . . I swallowed, my temples throbbing. Though I ached to hold him and be held, somehow I still couldn't break through the awkwardness between us, no matter how much I wanted to.

From the front, Liz cleared her throat. "I wonder if Kara and Brendan are OK," she said in a small voice. She didn't mention Wesley and Trish. I didn't blame her. Just thinking about them hurt too much.

"Hope so," said Alex tersely, shifting gears. We'd tried to call them, but nobody's cell phones were working. And what we all knew hung in the air, unspoken: they could easily have been attacked by a mob on their way down the stairwell, especially if they were slowed down by Brendan's injured leg.

I pressed my forehead against the cool window as I stared out at the passing trees. I'd told the others what I'd sensed from Raziel, about half the angels in the world being dead. It should have felt like a victory, I guess . . . but right now it didn't seem like much of one.

As we drove around a bend, a view of the city was spread out below us in the dying rays of the sunset. Alex stopped and we all got out, even Sam, supporting himself with a hand on Alex's shoulder. We went over to a ledge and stood gazing down at the ruined city in silence. True to its status as the most earthquake-resistant building in the world, the Torre Mayor was still standing, its green glass walls curved against the sky.

It was almost the only thing that was. All around it

in a rough circle that must have spanned several miles, the city had been virtually wiped out: a few other buildings were half-standing; most had collapsed into rubble. Though I could make out the flat rectangle of the Zócalo, I couldn't see the cathedral at all.

Liz shivered, hugging herself. "Do you think this really happened all around the world?" she whispered. "Or just here?"

None of us had an answer for her.

Finally, Alex let out a breath. "OK, come on. Let's find a place to stop for the night."

Seb stood motionless, still staring at the city as everyone started back to the truck. Glancing up at him, I saw the dampness on his cheeks. It unlocked something inside of me, and I wrapped my arms around him with a sob. He hugged me hard, clutching me to him; we stood trembling, holding each other tightly. And oh, God, I'd been so stupid, so completely wrapped up in my heartbreak over Alex. Seb was right. We'd kissed; that was all. It didn't have to change things between us unless we let it.

"I'm sorry," I whispered against his collarbone. "Seb, I'm so sorry. I want things to be like they were between us again."

"I want that, too," he said raggedly. "I want that more than anything."

Closing my eyes, I let out a shaky breath as I pressed against him. I could feel the prickle of his stubble against my hair, the strong warmth of his arms around me. Nothing had changed; everything had changed. I had my friend back. I knew Seb was still in love with me, and he knew that I wasn't in love with him; but somehow it didn't matter, not to either of us — we needed to be in each other's lives anyway. A deep thankfulness washed over me. After everything we'd just been through, to know that Seb and I still had this together — that our friendship was still intact — felt more wonderful than words can express.

Finally I pulled away and kissed his cheek. "Come on," I said, wiping my eyes. "Would my brother walk me to the truck?"

"Anytime, *querida,*" he said with a small smile. And he put his arm around my shoulders and we headed back.

CHAPTER THIRTY

THE MOON WAS JUST RISING by the time they stopped, high in the southern Sierra Madre. Up here with the stars and trees, it was as if nothing had happened at all. It was a relief, thought Alex. Never, not for as long as he lived, would he forget the sight of that concrete wave as it took down the city.

And his team was now tattered into shreds.

Somehow he shoved it all aside and did what he had to do in order to hold what was left of his team together. Seb produced a lighter from his knapsack, and they built a campfire. Alex put up the tent for Willow and Liz to sleep in; he and the other guys could crash in the back of the truck. He tore one of his shirts into long strips and bandaged Sam's ankle; the minute he got it snugly bound, Sam's broad face relaxed. Which in turn relieved Alex—it probably wasn't broken, in that case. And that was good, since God knew when they'd manage to find a doctor if other places in the world had been affected the same way as Mexico City. The idea was too catastrophic to take in, like trying to imagine what lay beyond the edges of space — so he didn't think about it and thought about food instead.

He found a few energy bars in his bag. That was dinner for them all. There were also a couple of bottles of water in the truck, plus a stream nearby. Sam took a swig of water and grimaced as they sat around the campfire. "I sure wish this was something stronger," he said glumly. "A couple of shots of Jack would go down good right about now."

No one responded. From everyone's faces, they were all thinking, *Join the club.* Liz stared bleakly into the fire; Willow and Seb sat close together, though not touching. Alex tossed a stick onto the snapping flames. Remaining in charge was the last thing on the planet he wanted to do after today — but he knew that he had even less choice now than before.

"OK, guys, here's the deal," he said finally. "We're not going to let this destroy us. We all did what we thought was right — and if we had it to do over, we'd all act the same way. So there's no point in wallowing. The important thing is that half the angels in the world have been killed. We wouldn't have chosen to do it this way, but it's a victory, so we'll take it."

Everyone was watching him; Sam nodded slightly. Willow's gaze was gentle on his, then she glanced down, playing with the hem of her turquoise shirt. He saw her throat move.

"What now?" Liz asked finally.

Alex shrugged. "Personally, I plan to keep fighting." He told them about the base in Nevada that Sophie had been offering; the memory stick with the details was safe in his bag. "So we've got a place to go," he finished. "It's fully stocked, and I have the access code."

"We?" echoed Willow. Her face in the firelight was very still.

Alex nodded. "Yeah. You're all welcome to join me if you want." He kept his voice neutral. For a while there, in the aftermath of the attack, things had actually felt the same as always between him and Willow: a delusion that had been forcibly dispelled when she wouldn't even take his hand to help her up. Having her around all the time, when she was with Seb, would be more painful than he really wanted to imagine. But he needed every person he could get now — and besides, they were part of his team. Even Seb. Bizarrely, something had shifted between the two of them today; Alex thought he could actually work with the guy without killing him now.

Willow looked worried as she and Seb glanced at each other; he seemed to be trying to read an answer from her eyes.

"Don't give me an answer now, any of you," said Alex. "And don't feel obligated to come." He scraped a hand over his face, trying not to see the city falling again.

Or Wesley and Trish as they'd run after them with the mob, shouting. He felt weary down to his bones. "Today was . . . the worst," he said finally. "But it still may not be as bad as it ever gets. So think about it. Think about what it means, to keep on with this. I wouldn't blame any of you if you wanted to just hide out in the mountains somewhere and try to build a life for yourself."

Sam snorted. "Who the hell would do that? Yeah, I'm in; I can tell you right now." He was sitting against a fallen log; he shifted, keeping his injured leg straight out in front of him. "No way am I gonna hide away and do nothing after today."

"Me, too," said Liz softly.

Willow cleared her throat, not meeting his gaze. "We'll think about it, OK? And tell you tomorrow."

We. Alex tried not to feel the sting. "Yeah, sure," he said, tossing another stick onto the fire. "It'll take us a few days to get back to the U.S., anyway — if that's where you're going," he added.

Seb looked at Willow again, searching her face with a slight frown. "I don't think we know yet," he said.

No one said much for a while after that. Though the fire burned down some, it still kept the coolness of the night away; Sam crossed his arms over his chest and closed his eyes, looking half asleep where he sat. Eventually Liz got up to go get the other bottle of water from the truck. When she didn't come back, Alex went after her and found her curled up asleep in the front seat, looking beyond exhausted. He started to wake her up so she could have

618

the tent but decided against disturbing her. She'd be OK out here; he and Sam would sleep in the back. Thinking of Willow and Seb in the same tent that he'd shared with her was a further kick in the guts, but he supposed he'd survive it. After today, he could survive anything.

When he got back to the campfire, Sam's snores were filling the air. Willow and Seb were obviously deep in conversation. They broke off when he reappeared; the tension on Willow's face made Alex feel like an intruder. It also made him want to put his arms around her and hold her forever — a longing he seriously didn't need right now.

"I'll get some more firewood," he said, and walked off without waiting for a response.

There was a clearing not far away, awash with moonlight. Alex sat down against a rock and stared up at the sky. All the familiar constellations were still there — the same as they'd been after his father's death, and then his brother's. The night sky's patterns always remained predictable, no matter how much your world had just been rocked. At times in his life, he'd found this soothing, and at other times, infuriating. Now he just felt numb, cold as starlight.

Wesley and Trish, rabid with angel burn. God, he'd known Wesley's arm wasn't better yet; he should never have let him take part. OK, so maybe neither of them had actually died, but angel burn had always seemed almost worse than death to Alex; it took away a person's choices. If he'd just managed to do things better — get there faster, stop the attack after all — then maybe it wouldn't have happened. And he didn't even know if Kara and Brendan were still alive or not. Even if they'd somehow managed to make it out of the Torre Mayor, what were the odds that they'd actually left the city in time? Or that Juan's old van had made it through those lurching streets?

Alex pinched the bridge of his nose as the thoughts pummeled him. He didn't have any answers. None. And now the world would never be the same again, and he had to keep on being a leader somehow — just because there was no one else around to do it.

"Hi," said a soft voice.

He looked up. Willow stood in the moonlight. "Hi," he said after a pause.

She swallowed. "Can I, um — sit with you for a while? I think we should probably talk."

Standing there in the silvery light, she was so beautiful that it made him hurt inside. He shrugged wearily. "If you want."

Willow sat near him, keeping a careful distance. Tracing at the ground with her finger, she cleared her throat. "Alex, I just wanted to say that . . . I'm really sorry I hurt you."

He sighed. Yeah, this was exactly what he felt like talking about right now. "Can we skip this conversation?" he asked, rubbing his forehead. "Seriously, I'd rather not have it. I don't need to hear how sorry you are."

She sat watching the motion of his fingers anxiously; then seemed to catch herself doing it and glanced away.

"All right." Her voice was thin, strained. "But, Alex, I don't think Seb and I will be going with you to Nevada. I just don't think it's a good idea for — for me to be so close to you. So I don't know if I'll see you again after tomorrow, and I wanted to tell you" — her voice broke; Alex froze, his heart aching as he saw she was close to tears — "to tell you that I still love you," she got out. "I really do, Alex, and — and I'm sorry for everything."

Wiping her eyes, she jumped to her feet. Alex leaped up, too, pained bewilderment clutching at his throat. "Willow, wait! What —?" He touched her arm; she pulled away, hugging herself.

"Please don't," she said in a small voice.

She looked miserable, almost frightened. Alex stared at her. "Don't what? Don't touch your arm?"

Willow almost said something and stopped. "I — I'd better get back." She started to walk away.

"No, wait." He dodged in front of her; a sudden suspicion had taken root and was growing by the second. "Willow, why can't I touch your arm? Why wouldn't you take my hand when we fell on the grass?"

She gripped her elbows, not meeting his eyes. "I just didn't want to — that's all. I'm sorry. I didn't mean to hurt your feelings or anything." She was a terrible liar. And now Alex recalled that same flat tone had been in her voice when she'd stood there with Seb in the kitchen, and even earlier, back in the storeroom before their first hunt, when he'd asked her what was wrong. She'd had that same look on her face then, too—complete agony as she started to tell him something but didn't.

Oh, God.

The truth slammed into him. He reached for her arms again without thinking; she jerked away. "Don't! Don't touch me!"

"You think you're giving me angel burn," he said urgently. "That's it, isn't it? That's why you broke up with me." She didn't answer; she didn't need to. She covered her face with one hand, her shoulders shaking.

He could barely hear his own words over the pounding of his pulse. "Are you really in love with Seb? Did you two really—?"

"No," she cut in. "We kissed. That's all. And it was totally wrong, and it just made me realize how—how much I—" She broke down then; Alex wrapped his arms around her and held her tight, his heart racing with sudden hope.

"Tell me again that you're not in love with Seb," he whispered into her hair. "Please, please tell me again."

She shook her head against his chest; her voice was muffled. "I'm not in love with Seb; I never was. I do love him but not like that. Alex, I shouldn't be touching you—"

He ignored her. "What about your dream?"

"It was true—all except the part about being in love with him." She looked up, her eyes wet. "I didn't mention it to you at the time because I didn't even believe it; I didn't see how I could ever feel so strongly about a boy who isn't you. But now I see that I can, only it's just friendship; it's like he's my brother. Alex, I *can't* touch you! Let me go; I'm hurting you——"

"You're not hurting me! Willow——" He pulled away, gripping both her hands. "I'm still in love with you," he said fervently. "I love you more than anything. Do you still feel the same about me?"

She stood without moving, the moonlight glinting on her face. For a moment the look in her eyes was salvation——and then her expression went dull. "Of course I do," she whispered. She pulled her hands away from his. "And that's why I can't be with you. I knew you'd do this; it's why I didn't tell you before. You think I'm not hurting you, but I *am*. I can see it in your aura right this second."

"My aura?"

"Yes! It looks——" Her face crumpled slightly; she regained herself with visible effort. "It looks sick," she said. "And it's because of me. It's something about my energy, being half angel——the effect must be cumulative, but it's *there*. It happens."

"What effect? Willow, what are you talking about?"

Her spiked hair looked darker than usual in the moonlight; her elfin face lined with sadness. "Your migraines and your headaches are because of me," she said. "I know they haven't always been, but the ones you're having now are. Alex, your aura looks"——her gaze went to the outline of his body, scanning it——"faded. Not healthy. And there are these dark spots. . . ." She trailed off.

"But——" He stared at her as images came and went in a flash: his father, back at the camp; Cully, after an extended hunt. Himself, sitting on the Metro wondering how much damage he'd been taking lately. "Willow, did you think that was because of you? Oh, babe . . ." He tried to put his arms around her again; she sidestepped out of his reach.

"Of course I think it's because of me! What else am I supposed to think?"

"It's because I'm an AK! It's something that happens if you're exposed to a lot of angel fallout; the aura takes damage. Willow, my dad used to get the same thing!"

She went very still. On her face he saw doubt battling with a longing to believe. "So how come you didn't have this when we first met?"

"Because the aura usually renews itself! I only killed about an angel a week back then. But I've been going on hunts every day for weeks now — go check out Sam's aura; it'll be just the same!" His words spilled out quickly; he felt desperate to make her see the truth.

She gave a short, humorless laugh, wiping her eyes. "Sam's aura is *not* just the same. Sam's aura looks fine, actually."

He pushed his hair back in frustration. "OK, well, I don't know — maybe it is cumulative, then; I've been doing this for years. But, Willow, it is *not you*. I swear to you, when I looked at my dad's aura once, it was just the same. And there were no half angels at the camp, all right?"

The moment stood poised on a knife blade. Slowly, Willow shook her head. "I could still have something to do with it. You don't know for a fact that I'm not hurting you, and neither do I. Haven't you noticed that every migraine you got was less than a day after — after we got really physical together?"

"Fine, and what about all the times we got really physical, and *nothing happened* — except we both enjoyed it a whole lot? Willow, it's just a coincidence!"

Her expression was the same as when she'd told him she was going to try to stop the Second Wave — sad but determined, unaffected by any argument he might make. "You can't know that, and I won't take the chance," she said. "I won't hurt you, Alex. I refuse."

He stared at her in disbelief; the statement was so ludicrous that he barked out a short, bitter laugh. "You think breaking up with me *didn't hurt* me? I've been in hell these last few days. Complete hell."

Pain creased her features. "Me, too," she whispered. "But —"

"And even if you *are* causing it, even if you're making me sick in some terrible way we don't know about — Jesus, Willow, I could be killed tomorrow anyway! I don't expect a *long life* doing what I do, OK? And however long I've got left . . . I want to spend it with you." He took her hands; held them between his and kissed them. "Please," he said. "I want to spend it with you."

Her eyes were damp, her face filled with longing. For a moment he thought she was going to relent — then she gently pulled away. "And what if being with me makes your life even shorter than it would have been?" she asked. "What if you die a year sooner than you would have anyway, and that year would have made all the difference in fighting the angels?"

"Yeah, and what if being with you makes me so happy that I get a few *more* years, because I've actually got something to live for?" he said hotly. "We can't know! You don't get to just decide this for both of us!"

"But it's not only about *us*. Don't you see?" Her eyes were agonized. "I already have to live with knowing that — that I played a part in what happened today. A whole city — all those people . . ." She trailed off helplessly and shook her head. "Do you think I'd do anything, anything at all, that might hurt the world even more?"

"None of it was your fault," he said in a low voice. "It was Raziel — he used you; he used all of us. Don't you think I'm scared? Two of my team members have got angel burn now; two are missing — I couldn't stop any of it! But I've got to keep on, and so do you. Don't let him tear us apart, on top of everything else."

She let out a breath that was almost a sob. Hugging herself, she stared at a nearby tree, as if she was taking in its every detail in the moonlight. "Alex . . . I just can't. I'd be terrified every day that I was hurting you; I'd be worried sick every time we touched."

The thought that this was the only thing keeping them apart was torture. "Willow, you're *not hurting me.*

And if you really break us up over this, when you love me as much as I love you — it'll be the biggest mistake ever." He took her hands again, gripping them hard. "How do I convince you that you're wrong? Christ, what do I say, what do I do? Please, help me out here."

For a long moment Willow didn't answer. She gazed down at her hands in his . . . and then squeezed his fingers and softly drew away "There's nothing you can say, and there's nothing you can do. Because neither of us can know for sure. And I won't take the chance." Her voice was thick with unshed tears "I'm sorry. Please don't touch me again."

No. No. He couldn't let her do this to them; he had to get her to see the truth. The ridiculous thing was how psychic she was — with anyone else, she could just touch their hand and see the truth for herself. But her emotions were so entangled when it came to him that Alex knew she'd get nothing.

The answer came to him all at once, along with a rush of hope so intense it was almost painful. "Wait!" he said as she started to turn away. "Willow, what if Seb reads me? What if he sees in my hand that I'm right — what then?"

Her face went blank with surprise as she stared at him, statue-still in the silvery light. Then her throat moved as she swallowed. "That . . . would be the most wonderful thing in the world," she said in a tiny voice.

When they got back to the campfire, they found Seb still there; he'd built the fire up again and was gazing into its flames. Sam lay snoring softly against the log, out to the world. They sat beside Seb as Alex quickly explained.

"So do you think you can help?" he finished. His muscles were tense; he was suddenly all too aware of what a gift on a silver platter he was offering Seb — all the guy had to do was tell Willow that, yes, she was causing him angel burn, and that would be the end of their relationship forever.

Seb hadn't commented while Alex spoke; now he shook his head, his stubble glinting in the firelight. "Willow can't read you because her feelings are too involved — but you don't think mine are, too?" he pointed out dryly.

"Not as much as mine, not when it comes to reading Alex," said Willow. She touched his arm. "Please, Seb, just try. I've got to know the truth."

Seb glanced back at Alex. Finally he gave a shrug. "Yes, all right. I'll try." He closed his eyes for a moment, seeming to center himself with a few slow breaths. Then he opened his eyes and held out his hand; his gaze met Alex's impassively.

Alex put his hand in Seb's. It felt warm and dry, slightly rough; fleetingly, he thought how weird it was to be sitting here holding another guy's hand. No one spoke as Seb concentrated; the only sound was the low crackle of the fire, and Sam's steady snores. Alex watched Seb's face, hoping for some hint of what he was picking up — what he was going to say.

At last Seb let go of his hand. He gave Alex a considering look, as if he was thinking how to choose his words, and Alex felt his heart drop. "So . . . what did you get?"

Seb rested his forearm over his knee. "Your father had migraines, too," he said. "So did his father. The men in your family, they've all been leaders and they all care very much — it makes them too tense."

Alex remembered now his father telling him that his grandfather had had migraines, though he'd forgotten this. "Yeah, OK, but—"

"I tried to look at your future, and see what might happen to you," went on Seb. "I didn't get very much, because I think I'm there, too." Alex's pulse went faster: surely Seb wouldn't be there if Willow wasn't. He glanced at Willow; she sat watching Seb, her face taut. Seb went on: "But I saw your aura looking healthy again, then looking sick after a hunt. And you keep getting migraines. You should take care of yourself better," he added mildly. "Look for ways to not be so tense — long walks, meditation; these things would help."

Alex suddenly felt like Seb was his therapist; he had to resist the urge to shake him. Before he could say anything, Willow cleared her throat. "What does all that mean, exactly?"

Seb's expression was gentle. "I don't think his migraines are anything to do with you, *querida*. And his aura looks bad, but his father's often looked worse. It got better — his will, too. I don't think you're causing him angel burn."

I don't think. Alex winced; he knew Willow wouldn't be convinced by this. Sure enough, she bit her lip as she stared at Seb. "You don't know for sure, though?"

Seb reached for her hand and squeezed it. "I am maybe ninety-nine percent certain," he said. "If I could have gotten more, then I think I'd be a hundred percent certain. For only one percent, you should take the chance and be happy with him." He lifted a shoulder with a small smile. "If you were one of my customers, this is what I'd say to you."

As the fire crackled gently, Willow sat staring at Seb as if she hadn't understood the words—then all at once she lunged forward, throwing her arms around his neck. "Thank you," she whispered. "Oh, thank you."

"I'm glad I was wrong," Seb murmured back.

The relief was indescribable. Alex let out a breath, his shoulders sagging.

Willow detached herself from Seb and looked at him. Her expression was wondering, almost shy. In slow motion, she reached out and stroked back a strand of his hair; the feel of her touch shivered through him. "So, um . . . I guess—"

Alex stopped her with his mouth, cradling her head in his hands and kissing her almost fiercely, and then they were in each other's arms, holding on as hard as they could. *Willow. Willow.* He felt her shaking and realized she was crying; he kissed her hair as he clutched her to him, then buried his head against her neck and simply savored having her in his arms again. Dimly, he was aware that Seb had slipped away.

"Come be with me in the tent," he whispered against her smooth skin. "I want to hold you all night—I want to feel you next to me."

Willow nodded vehemently; she pulled away to wipe her face and then just gazed at him for a moment. She swallowed. "You really, really can't imagine how good that sounds."

She went to the truck to get her things. Alex's own bag was on the ground nearby, where he'd left it after rummaging for the energy bars. As he started toward it, he caught sight of Seb—he was standing in the clearing with his hands in his pockets, looking upward.

Alex hesitated, and then went over to him. For a few seconds, neither of them spoke as they took in the night sky with its piercing stars.

"So why did you do it?" asked Alex in Spanish. He glanced over at Seb, studying his profile. "You didn't have to tell her the truth. Maybe she thinks she only loves you as a brother now, but that could have changed if you'd told her something different."

Seb gave him a dry look. "We're both psychic, amigo. I can't lie to her."

"When she was already so worried about it anyway?" Alex shook his head. "No, I bet you could have managed to lie if you'd wanted to."

Seb didn't respond at first, and then he shrugged. "I

want her to be happy," he said. The moonlight played on his high cheekbones as he looked up at the stars again. "You make her happy. It wasn't exactly a complicated decision."

Alex's throat clenched, and he thought how ridiculous it was that after everything that had happened today — the mental ruin of friends and teammates, the uncertainty over Kara's and Brendan's fates, the sight of the destroyed city — it was this unexpected decency from Seb that was making him choke up.

"Thank you," he said finally.

"You're welcome." Seb's mouth lifted slightly. "I didn't do it for you, though."

"Yeah, I know you didn't." They regarded each other; Alex was almost painfully aware of how much he'd misjudged the guy. "So, you're coming to Nevada, right?" he said.

Seb went quiet, rubbing his jaw with the back of a finger. "I'd like to," he said finally. "I never had a way before to fight what the angels are doing here — I guess I never even really knew I wanted to. But now, after what's happened to my city . . ." His face tightened. "Yeah, I'd like to come. Even if it wasn't for Willow, I'd like to come."

"Good," said Alex.

Then Seb raised an eyebrow. "But are you sure you really want me to? I'm still in love with her, *hombre*. If I can take her away from you, I will."

Alex tilted his head up. The stars were so incredibly clear up here; even clearer than in New Mexico. "If I'm not keeping her happy enough to hold on to her, then

I'll deserve it," he said. "Yeah, I want you to come. You're part of my team."

The tent was lit with a soft glow from the campfire. For a long time, Alex and I just lay in the sleeping bags with our arms around each other, listening to the sound of our heartbeats, the crackle of the fire. I closed my eyes as I ran my hand over the familiar warmth of Alex's chest; felt him stroke my bare back; gently kiss my neck. I knew the vision of the leveled city would never leave either of us — that it would visit us in nightmares for years to come — but for now, just having this together again felt like sanity. Blessed, healing sanity.

Neither of us spoke just then. Neither of us needed to. Later, of course, we would. In the days that followed, we talked about everything — how Alex's deepest fear, right from the start, had been that something would happen to his team, how I'd been so scared of my angel's actions but somehow couldn't talk to him about it. How Sophie hadn't been the one to protect my mother after all — which panicked me when I heard, so that I had to check Mom again and again to reassure myself that she really was all right, even if we had no idea where she was or who she was with. Alex's old crush on Kara, and the way she'd kissed him in the AK house; my own kiss with Seb. My friendship with Seb, which was never going to go away, ever — and which Alex really was fine with now. It turned out that he had been ever since the night of the terrorist attack, when he thought I'd died and had spent

633

hours searching for me — it "kind of put things in perspective" for him, he said.

We'd talk about all of these things later; we'd hash them out and look at them from every angle and make them all OK . . . but for now, the only thing that mattered was the two of us in the tent together. The softness of the sleeping bags, and the warmth of our bodies.

At last the glow from the campfire was almost gone, leaving the tent cast in shadow. We'd heard Seb and Sam go to bed in the truck a long time ago; the world was quiet. Alex rolled over onto his side and lay looking down at me in the dim light, propped up on his elbow. The expression in his eyes was as serious as the first time he'd told me he loved me. He took my hand and kissed its palm, his lips pressing against my skin . . . and my heart quickened. I knew before he said it.

"Willow, listen . . ." He stroked a strand of my hair back. "I know we said we wanted to wait until it could be perfect, but —"

"This is perfect," I interrupted. I touched his face. "We're here together. It couldn't possibly be more perfect."

Alex didn't say anything, but I caught a wave of his emotions as he bent down and kissed me, and my breath caught with their intensity. Then he pulled away, stretching down to the bottom of the tent. I raised myself up, admiring the beautiful lines of his body as he reached into his bag and pulled something out.

He came back up and put the small box he was holding to one side — and the expression in his eyes as he turned to me made my heart twist. Alex. Oh, Alex. I wrapped my arms around his neck, pulling him down to me; his heart was beating as hard as mine was.

"No, wait," he murmured suddenly. Straightening up, he reached across me for our pile of clothes, fumbled in the pocket of the gray pants he'd been wearing.

"Here, sit up," he said softly. I did, the sleeping bag slipping off me with a rustle. I saw a flash of silver in his hand, and my eyes widened.

"You kept it," I whispered. I reached up to touch the cool facets of my pendant as he fastened the chain around my neck. My fingers clasped around it tight. "I thought you'd — throw it away, or —"

"I tried to. I couldn't leave it behind." He kept his hands on my neck for a moment, his forehead resting against mine. "Willow, things feel more uncertain than ever now," he said finally. "But I love you. For as long I live — if that's fifty years from now or just next week — I'll love you."

I could hardly get the words out. "I love you, too," I said. I kissed him, our lips lingering together. Then I swallowed, my hand on the back of his neck and my crystal gleaming between us. "And . . . let's stop talking for a while, OK?"

When I woke up, it felt like early morning; the blue nylon sides of the tent had a faint glow to them. I was lying in Alex's arms, our bare limbs entwined. I lay without moving for a few minutes, gazing at the rise and fall of his chest, the curve of his dark eyebrows. I kissed his tattoo gently, loving the feel of his warm skin. The pain of the ruined city was still there, like a heavy weight inside of me — but now there was this new joy, too. The night before had been . . . well, let's just say it was worth waiting for. Very, very worth waiting for. And it showed every sign of being something that would get even better.

I stretched across Alex and found my clothes, squirming in the sleeping bag as I put them on. Drowsily, he opened his eyes and stroked my arm. "Where are you going?"

"Just outside for a minute." I kissed his cheek. "I'll be right back."

The morning air hit me coolly as I crawled out of the tent, zipping it shut behind me. The truck sat a little way off; no one else was awake yet. I started down to the stream . . . and then I saw a break in the trees and stopped. Though I hadn't noticed it the night before, you could see Mexico City from here, too.

I walked over, drawn helplessly by the shattered view, and stood staring down at the remains of the city for a long time. And as I did, a chill went over me. There were no helicopters flying over it, no sign of relief aid. What did that mean? Even if no one else in Mexico could help, what were things like in the United States, if they hadn't sent aid after such a major catastrophe? The only answers that came to mind weren't really ones that I wanted to dwell on.

I thought I saw a few angels circling over the ruins,

though — bright moving glimmers that somehow I knew weren't just a trick of the light. A shiver went over me as I watched them.

Footsteps on the grass, and then Alex was there; he had on jeans and a T-shirt, his dark hair still rumpled from sleep. Without speaking, he put his arms around me from behind and drew me back against him as we both stared down at what used to be one of the largest cities in the world. I knew from the tightening of his muscles that he'd noticed the lack of helicopters, too, but he didn't comment. My chest felt empty as I watched the tiny angels glinting over the devastation. The sorrow I felt was too great for tears now — too deep for anything that could be verbalized.

"OK, enough," said Alex finally. He turned us both around so that we were facing the mountains to the north. "Look that way instead," he said, his voice firm. "That's the way we're going."

The view was clear, uncluttered, and something in me eased. Somehow, looking at the soaring mountains with the sunrise on them made me able to breathe again. Alex was right. We couldn't live our lives looking back — no matter what, we had to move forward to whatever waited for us. Alex and me, Seb, Sam, Liz, and whoever else we managed to recruit — we all had to keep moving forward, or else we were lost.

After a long time, I cleared my throat. "So, anyway, when we get to Nevada . . . I think we should rethink your dad's rule."

Alex glanced down at me and smiled—the first real smile I'd seen on his face in a long time. "You know what? It's already been rethought and completely ditched," he said. And he wrapped his arms around me as we stood looking up at the mountains, with the rising rays of the sun lighting them from the east.

ACKNOWLEDGMENTS

Angel Fire was a book that, at times, I really didn't think was going to get written.

While writing the first book in the trilogy, *Angel Burn*, the fictional world I'd envisaged grew and changed, and so did my perceptions of the characters. This meant that although books two and three had been planned out in some detail, I realized when I reached the end of *Angel Burn* that a lot of my ideas about the sequels weren't really valid anymore. So, even though he's fictional, my first and most heartfelt thanks must go to Seb. When he suddenly appeared out of nowhere — this former street kid and thief who's so in love with Willow, and who, not incidentally, is another half angel — I knew I'd found the spark that would propel not only this story, but the next one, too. The sheer relief of that day is something any writer will understand. Thank you, *querido*.

Thanks are also due to:

Linda Chapman and Julie Sykes, for e-mails, coffee, shared spa days, and being the first people on the planet to read and offer comments on *Angel Fire* — not to mention their patience in listening to me talk about it nonstop for almost a year now! Love and thanks to you both. My agent, Caroline Sheldon, as always, for being such a stalwart, constant support. My editor Deborah Wayshak, whose enthusiasm for the story and her perceptive comments for improving it were everything an author could have wished for. My U.K. editors, Rebecca Hill and Stephanie King, for all of their insightful suggestions — between them and Deborah, I really do have a dream team of editors! Copy editors Hannah Mahoney and Erin DeWitt, for giving the text such a thorough review, leaving it clean and sparkling. Publicity and marketing teams on both sides of the Atlantic, for doing such a fabulous job in promoting the series. My brother and sister, Chuck Benson and Susan Lawrence, for being so thrilled over their little sister's career. Love you both! All of the friendly and helpful people my husband and I met in Mexico City when we went there for research, particularly our driver Fernando (I wish I'd gotten your last name!), who cheerfully answered all my nosy questions about life in the amazing Mexican capital. Neil Chowney, for his much-appreciated advice on motorcycle repair — if I got something wrong, it's not Neil's fault! Helen Corner, who told me one night in a London pub that Willow absolutely could NOT have shoulder-length brown hair, and that I had to give her a short, funky cut with startling color instead. You were totally right, hon. My fab friend Julie Cohen, for her spot-on story instincts and all the lame carbonite jokes. Composer Bear McCreary, whose music has played in the background almost every day that I've written this story. All of the wonderful bloggers who've taken the time to review *Angel Burn* — thank you. It's enthusiastic readers like you who make it all worthwhile! Everyone who contributes to the *Angel* trilogy Facebook pages on both sides of the Atlantic (www.facebook.com/angel.trilogy and www.facebook.com/AngelBookTrilogy)—I love reading your comments and seeing your picks for the stars in a fantasy movie version of the series. (Some of the picks for Alex have been SO hot; I can hardly wait to see who you suggest to play Seb!) A huge thank-you as well to my followers on Twitter, for having such a passion for the series and being so eager for *Angel Fire* to come out. I can't tell you how many times a tweet from one of you has made me smile. Particular thanks goes to @MarDixon, @DarkReaders, and @EmpireofBooks. And, to all of my readers who've loved the story and wanted more—thank you, more than I can say.

Last but absolutely not least, my husband, Peter, who really could not be blamed if he wished he hadn't married a writer, but is in fact an endless source of support, encouragement, and love. Thank you, Pete. I love you. x